Wild Hunt

The Complete Series

Lola Glass

Cover by JoY

The Savage Fae's Mate

Wild Hunt 1

To the books and people that don't break your heart.

One

The sound of Christmas music playing from speakers above my head melded with the unfortunate melody produced by the wheels of my rolling trash cans. Cleaning the strip-style outlet mall was never a blast, but it was much worse at this time of year.

A cold gust of wind blew past, making me shiver and tug the hem of my beanie further down my face. It cut off my vision a bit and awkwardly smooshed my long, dirty blonde hair against my neck, but it was better than being cold.

The lights on the carousel a ways ahead of me had been left on, and the ride was still spinning slowly. The stragglers at the movie theater to my left were finally leaving, but my crew had at least another three hours of cleaning to do.

Yay.

I picked up trash as I walked past the wishing fountain that everyone and their dog tossed coins into. I wasn't one of them—didn't have a penny to spare, anyway. Living in my car didn't exactly leave me with much spending money.

"Hey, Ari," my closest work-friend called out.

I didn't bother to turn around, waving at her over my shoulder.

We couldn't have been less alike if we tried. Linsey was a rich girl, whose daddy was forcing her to work this job for a few months so she could learn how the "lower class" lived. She'd only be there one more day; it was December 21st, and she would be done on the 22nd.

And me?

This was the only job I could get.

Turns out a few years in juvie for killing the foster dad who assaulted you doesn't exactly make you look like a golden candidate for a job. Or an apartment. Or anything else, really.

"Ooh, the fountain." Linsey sighed happily as she caught up to me, not even bothering to reach out for the trash can she was supposed to be pushing. That was why we were friends—because I didn't give a shit whether she helped or not.

And she never did.

"My wish came true yesterday," she announced, brushing a strand of her thick, dark hair behind her ear. Her skin was light brown, her eyes a stunning blue, and her clothes clearly expensive.

I bit my lip to stop myself from rolling my eyes.

"Jake called me back, and we totally hooked up. It was awesome." She dug into the pocket of her fancy red coat and came up with a couple of pennies. "Come on, you need to make a wish too."

She grabbed one of my trash cans and used it to drag me toward the fountain.

"It's a waste of money," I said with a sigh, accepting the penny she handed me.

I knew from experience that she wouldn't take no for an answer. Usually, I just tossed the coin in without a second glance. The only thing wishes would do was give me false hope, which was the last thing I needed.

"It's a penny. You'll survive. Actually *try* to wish for something, and maybe it will even work." She tossed me a dirty look that said she knew exactly what I had been doing every time she handed me a penny.

Then she stepped up to the fountain and lifted the coin to her lips, murmuring her wish to the damn thing. Sometimes she really seemed her age, and sometimes, I wondered why the hell I'd been forced to grow up so fast. We were both twenty, but experience-wise, we might as well have been from different planets.

She delicately tossed her penny in, then turned and watched me expectantly.

I sighed again.

"Come on, it's not going to kill you," she teased.

Damn, I hated her positive attitude sometimes.

I dragged my thumb over the head of the penny, my gaze lingering on the fountain. It was nothing fancy, but then again, neither was I.

I didn't want to make a wish—to let myself hope.

But Linsey wasn't going to let me walk away without making at least a fraction of an effort.

So, as I tossed the penny, I murmured almost silently, "I wish for a way out."

Out of my shit-show of a life, out of living in my car, out of my dead-end job...

Out of everything.

The penny landed in the water with the tiniest plop, and I watched it sink.

A long, silent moment passed.

My heart clenched.

I shouldn't have let myself wish. Wishing could be detrimental to my—

In the blink of an eye, the water fountain exploded.

Water shot in every direction, spraying from the damn thing like it was an erupting volcano. And along with the water, came the men.

Five gigantic guys, each of them massive and scarred. They had different skin colors, different hair colors, different tattoos, and different clothing—but they all towered over me, with the kind of muscles that people didn't just *have*. Their ears were long and pointed. That, coupled with the size of them, and the way they'd burst out of the fountain, told me one thing:

They weren't human.

Or from Earth, if I had to guess.

Their chests heaved, water dripping off of them as their gazes scanned the outside hallway of the strip mall. And one by one, their attention landed on *me*.

Shit.

"Shit," Linsey squeaked.

I took one step backward, and it was like I'd broken a silent wall.

"Her," one of the men growled.

Growled, like an animal.

As one, they lunged for me.

I wasn't fast enough.

No one would've been fast enough.

In a heartbeat, one of them had me in his arms and was hauling me back into the fountain, which was still spraying water like a damned fire hydrant.

I didn't have the time—or the energy—to scream. Water sprayed me and then engulfed me.

The strong arm around my abdomen was a metal bar, dragging me under the water. The world turned, my stomach flipped, and my lungs burned.

I wondered if the inhuman men had captured me only to drown me.

But finally, when I started seeing stars, we burst back through the water.

I was set on my feet on some kind of brown sand as I sucked in air, desperate relief flooding my veins. My clothes were soaked and glued to my body, but wherever I was, it was hot enough that I was sweating rather than shivering.

I was alive, so it was fine. I'd keep telling myself that, at least.

Sure, I'd been taken into a fountain, which had apparently transported me into some other place. Maybe even another world.

And sure, I was surrounded by gigantic men who looked like they could kill me with a flick of their pinkies, but—

Okay, what the hell was I doing, trying to be positive about the situation?

I was screwed.

The men were all staring at me, so I stared back, asking, "Why did you grab me?"

There was a moment of silence.

My gaze scanned the three in front of me. The two behind me, I'd check out later.

One had bleach-blond hair that was shaved on the sides, pale skin, and was covered in black, orange, and red tattoos from neck to toe, all that inked-up skin evidenced by the colorful shorts he had on.

Another had buzzed, black hair and dark brown skin, with a few shimmering tattoos on his gigantic biceps. He wore a pair of shorts similar to the blond guy's, but in navy fabric.

A third had brown hair that was cut like most of the choir boys who'd been such dicks to me back at my high school. His skin was light with a bit of a sun-tan, and he had on a pair of tight black pants with cuts in the knees.

They all looked so... different.

I mean, massive, sure. But I'd survived a co-ed juvie long enough to know that size didn't mean a damn thing—and that meant bastards came in every shape, color, and gender.

These guys hadn't hurt me yet, so I was giving them the benefit of the doubt.

"Welcome to Vevol. We are the strongest of the seelie fae. To your people, we are the Wild Hunt," one of the men behind me said.

I turned around to see him. Giving any of them my back was dangerous, but they encircled me, so there wasn't a way around that.

Since I wasn't sure which of the men had spoken, I eyed them both.

The one on the right had tan skin, a few tattoos, and a mass of curly light brown hair tied up in a man-bun. He wore a pair of small shorts that showed a hell of a lot more than I wanted to see.

The one on the left had black hair, curly on the top and cropped close on the sides. His skin was light, and he wore a pair of black pants along with a shirt that looked like a gray muscle-tee.

"Our lake has begun the process of changing you. When it's done, you will run, and we will hunt," the dark-haired man said.

His voice was low and smooth, way sexier than it should've been considering he had kidnapped me with the rest of his seelie fae bastards.

"I will *what*?"

"Run." The man's gaze was intense, and I nearly shuddered.

"Why run?"

"Because it's Winter Solstice, and your people promised ours one of your females every year. Whichever of us catches you first will mate with you," one of the guys behind me said.

I spun back to the guys back there, my eyes narrowed and scanning the group. Once again, I didn't know which one had been talking. "Mate, meaning what?"

"Eternal companion," the choir boy dude said.

Shit.

"Like a wife?" I checked. "As in, person you spend your life with?"

"Yes." The blond guy flashed me a feral grin.

There was no way I'd be able to outrun any of these guys.

"I don't feel like I'm changing," I told him. "Can you take me back to Earth?"

"No. Even if we wanted to, the portal only opens for two minutes during the solstice every year. You're stuck with us." His eyes gleamed.

That was what I got for wishing on a damned penny that I should've kept. Hadn't pop culture taught me to be careful what I wished for? Wishing for *a way out* was practically setting myself up to be abducted when a person had luck as shitty as mine was.

"The change will be completed shortly," one of the guys told me. "Brace yourself."

Brace my—

Oh, shit.

Two

Sharp, hot pain cut through my chest, and I stumbled. All of the men stepped back—none of them reaching out to catch me before I crashed to my knees, hard.

At least it was sand beneath me instead of concrete.

I sucked in air like a drowning person while heat coursed through my body. I thought I was burning—that I was dying.

But then the heat faded.

A few minutes later, I managed to open my eyes.

“A phoenix,” the guy with the bicep tattoos and buzzed hair said, folding his arms over his chest. “Mine.”

“Careful, brother. You know she could belong to any of us,” one of the men behind me drawled. “Type means nothing.”

Type of what?

There wasn’t time to ask the question aloud.

“You have until sundown, little phoenix. *Run.*” The buzzed-head guy’s eyes bore into my soul.

I didn’t wait for another invitation. Something about his words felt like a kick to the ass, anyway.

Without turning to check out the ocean I could hear violently crashing against the shore behind me, or the tall, skinny trees that reminded me of freakishly overgrown palm trees, I took off at a sprint into the weird forest in front of me.

My heart pounded like a freight train as I crashed through bushes, barely dodging rocks and tree trunks as I went. The trees only vaguely reminded me of the ones on Earth, the coloring of their leaves a much more vibrant green and blue than anything I knew. Their trunks were much thicker around, and they didn't have the same roughness as the ones I'd seen—they looked shiny-smooth, and were all either black, white, or the same bright colors as their leaves.

The whole place smelled really good; I was attentive enough to notice that as I ran for my damned life. It was like rain and the beach, and something fresh and light that I couldn't put my finger on.

The sun was still shining overhead, but those guys hadn't seemed like the patient type. If this was some kind of wife-hunt, they would probably be coming for me as soon as it was even *close* to sunset. I needed to make as much progress as possible, even though my whole damn mind was spinning.

To go from standing in that strip mall, tossing a penny in a fountain, to here? In a different world, on the beach and then running through the jungle?

I was reeling.

Factor in the whole wife thing, and the big old bastards who would be hunting me...

The Wild Hunt.

Hadn't I heard of that in a TV show or something? I was pretty sure it had something to do with mythology of some kind, but I wasn't sure. Maybe that was something they taught the teenagers who got to graduate high school; not the ones stuck in juvie for defending themselves from would-be rapists.

A sharp stick or rock cut up into my foot, through the massive hole in the bottom of my shoe, and I muttered a curse as I kept running.

Damn old shoes

Damn shitty job.

Damn juvie.

Damn lawyer foster dad who thought he was such a 'good person' for 'helping those in need' that he 'deserved' the 'pleasure' of raping me.

Fury coursed through my veins, urging me onward.

The Wild Hunt and seelie fae bastards could go to hell right alongside my foster dad.

I was no one's prize.

I wasn't someone they could hunt down and mate with.

They might have dragged me in from Earth, but I sure as hell wasn't about to go down without fighting. If one of them tried to do what my foster dad had, they'd sleep with the worms just like he had.

No one got to *use me*, human, or fae, or any other creature.

My anger propelled me on, and on, and on, pumping through me so hotly that I didn't notice the thick scratch marks on the trees or the glimmering bits of scale mixed in with the dirt.

WHEN THE SUN started to go down, I knew I had to find a place to rest.

I was exhausted, I was dripping in sweat, I was starving... I could've kept running anyway, but with the sun going down, I had no idea what kind of animals might come out, and no way to see when the darkness of night descended fully.

So I slowed to a fast walk, eyeing the trees around me. They had changed a little, growing thicker and sturdier-looking, but the colors were the same and the trunks still looked more like stone than wood.

When I saw a massive tree with a hole carved in its trunk that looked wide enough for me to fit inside, I slowed further before stopping and eyeing the thing.

I didn't know what I was waiting for; for a damned fairy to come flying out of the center of it?

My fists clenched, ready for a fight.

A minute passed, and then another.

No fairy.

No sign of anything, actually.

I took two steps closer, my body still tensed and waiting.

When nothing happened for another two minutes, I bent down and grabbed a rock off the dirt ground beneath me. My fingers wrapped around a hunk of some kind of smooth obsidian-looking stone, but my eyes caught on something...

Glittery?

It was a dark red color, and looked smooth, like some kind of gemstone on a ring, but bigger.

One hand tightened around the obsidian, and the other reached for the dark red thing.

It had to be a rock, didn't it?

I picked it up carefully, pinching the thin red thing between my fingers and lifting it out of the dirt like the damn thing might come to life and bite me.

It didn't come to life.

I eyed it anyway.

It was just as smooth as I had thought, formed into a diamond-like shape with three rounded corners and one flat edge where the fourth corner would've been. Unlike a rock or gemstone, it was mostly flat, only curved the tiniest bit.

Staring at the thing, I tried to come up with what it might be, but couldn't think of a damn thing.

And I needed to be running, still. Or hiding, at least.

The bastards would be coming after me soon.

I tucked the strange red thing into the pocket of my faded, ripped jeans—I'd tossed my coat and sweater into the forest shortly after I started running—and tugged the hem of my old t-shirt down.

It occurred to me as I stepped closer to the hole in the tree, that the seelie fae might be able to see in the dark. I knew nothing about them except that they looked massive and were hunting me in hopes of *mating* with me, so there was every possibility that they had some kind of supernatural abilities.

Hell, they had said that I was one of them. If they were right, maybe I would have magic of some kind too. I hadn't noticed anything while I was running, but that didn't mean the magic didn't exist. They *had* called me a phoenix.

I sure as hell wouldn't complain if I found myself getting taller and stronger, like those bastards, though. Being able to defend myself? Hell yeah.

Looking around the random bit of forest I'd stopped in, I debated my options.

Stay there, and hope they couldn't find me...

Or keep moving.

Running would be more dangerous in the dark, but it was better than being a sitting duck. So, running it was.

I tossed my obsidian rock back into the dirt and took off into the forest.

Screw waiting for one of those big bastards to show up and make me his damn wife.

My blistered feet resumed pounding the ground again, and again, and again.

I'd run for as long as I had to if it meant staying alive—and staying single.

As the sun went down, the forest seemed to come alive around me. I started hearing strange noises, from animals I undoubtedly didn't have names for.

Birds flew overhead, many of them much, much bigger than anything I'd seen back on Earth. I was thankful for the weird, vibrant trees hiding me from those bastards.

After a bit of time passed, a blast of wind hit me hard.

My head jerked back and forth as I looked around for whatever had caused it.

When I tilted my head back and peered up into the trees, my breath caught in my throat. I stumbled, then stopped altogether.

My hair whipped around my face as I gawked up at the sky.

Because above me, not all that far away, there was a *dragon*.

It was massive, its scales a glittering dark gray color that reminded me of some of the expensive cars that would fly past my Honda Civic and its faded silver paint on the freeway back at home.

I watched it soar overhead, and when it had gone far enough that I couldn't see it through the blue leaves above me, I relaxed slightly.

And tried to run faster.

It was getting darker, but my eyes seemed to be adjusting to the darkness, so I barely noticed the change in light. The colors were growing less neon and vibrant to my eyes, and I wondered if that had something to do with the way I had apparently *changed*.

I was too tired to think any more about it, though.

So, I kept running.

And didn't look back.

ONLY A FEW MINUTES after the dragon flew overhead, everything in the forest seemed to quiet down.

I eyed the trees suspiciously, as if those weird bastards could tell me what all the silence was about.

They couldn't, though.

At least, not that I knew of.

I kept running, avoiding the trees a bit more now that I'd realized there was a chance the damn things might be able to talk or even just think.

The forest grew quieter and quieter, until all I could hear were the sounds of my feet crunching the leaves.

There wasn't even any damned wind.

I pushed myself harder, ignoring the pain and stress and fear—and then skidded to a stop when one of the massive bastards from earlier stepped out from behind a tree in front of me.

Three

"What the hell?" I snarled at the man, my heart pounding wildly as every ounce of terror I'd ignored for the past few hours surged to the surface. "Don't touch me."

The man studied me, his gaze sort of... thoughtful.

It wasn't the tatted, blond guy with the scary grin, luckily. Or the buzzed-head bicep-tat guy, who had given me that intense stare.

The guy in front of me was the one with black hair and light skin, and the muscle tee and pants.

At least it wasn't one of the half-naked ones.

"What do you want?" I demanded, when he didn't say a damned word. "I *won't* be your mate."

He kept studying me.

It was way worse than if he'd just said something slimy.

When he finally spoke, he said, "You've almost made it. If you hadn't picked up that scale, you would've."

"Almost made it *where*?" I ripped the red thing out of my pocket and eyed it for a moment.

Scale.

Dragon scale.

I chucked the damn thing into the forest, earning a hint of a smirk from the black-haired man. Fae. Fae-man. Thing.

Whatever the hell he was.

"The Stronghold. When a woman isn't claimed during the hunt, she goes there." He nodded his head in the direction I'd been running. There was nothing visibly *there*, but it was in the direction of a mountain range that had seemed like the easiest target to run toward. "Your beast's instincts have been taking you there, I'm sure."

My *what*?

Screw this conversation.

"What will it take for you to leave me here, without touching me, so I can go to the damn Stronghold by myself?" I practically growled at the man. "A kiss? A blowjob? A punch to the nuts?"

The question earned me an amused chuckle. "Who said I was going to ask for something in exchange?"

His response caught me off guard for a moment, but I scowled at him anyway. "You're a man. Men are predictable."

His amusement died, and then his eyes darkened. I hadn't realized they were light until he took two steps and somehow closed the gap between us with just those motions.

Our bodies were only an inch apart.

My head tipped back and his tilted down as he said in a deadly voice, "I'm a *dragon*, female. You may know men, but you know nothing of me."

His fingers brushed the side of my throat, and an electric pulse rushed through me. I inhaled sharply, taking an instant step backward. "Don't touch me," I snarled at him, my voice a hell of a lot shakier than I wanted to admit.

"The Stronghold is this way." He tilted his head in the direction of the mountains. "If you'd like to avoid being claimed, we'll need to hurry."

He wasn't claiming me, then.

At least there was that.

That was a hell of a lot better than being grabbed and raped, like I'd assumed was going to happen.

My heart still pounded like crazy, though.

The man started jogging. I didn't ask how he could do so with bare feet—I doubted I wanted to know the answer. Even if I did, I didn't want to hear it from him.

I jogged with him, and ignored the fact that he was moving slowly enough for me to keep up.

As we ran, I noticed that my exhaustion seemed to have faded a little. My feet hurt less than they had earlier, too.

That must've been the adrenaline kicking in. Maybe this bastard should've found me earlier.

We jogged in silence, and I noticed that the forest around us remained just as quiet as it had gotten earlier, right after the dragon had passed.

After a few minutes, I started to accept that he wasn't going to attack me. Some men were snakes—I'd definitely seen that in juvie. You had to hold your breath around most of them.

But some of them weren't awful. He seemed like he might be one of the not-awful ones, at least for the time being. And we were running in the same direction I'd already been going, so if he was lying about where he was taking me, it wasn't like he was doing any real damage to the distance I'd put between myself and the others.

My stress and curiosity got the best of me, and after a few minutes, I asked, "Why is the forest so quiet right now?"

"The creatures around us know an apex predator when they see one," he said, as if that answered all of my questions.

"What the hell does that mean?"

His lips quirked upward, in that hint of a smirk he'd shown me earlier. "I told you, I'm a dragon. You're a phoenix, but until you've shifted, the land won't recognize you."

What the hell?

Did he mean…

"You can actually turn into a dragon? I demanded. "What color are you?"

He had to be the gray dragon I'd seen flying over my head, right?

"Quite an offensive question, but you don't mean offense," he mused.

Shit.

Time to change the subject.

"What kind of animal is a phoenix?" I checked, since I was pretty sure it was more than just the little bird I'd seen in that one Harry Potter movie years ago.

"A massive bird made of fire, earth, and liquid gold."

Damn.

"And you think I can turn into one of those?"

"I don't *think*, female. You *can* shift into the form of a phoenix, and you're just as indestructible as they are."

"Don't call me female. I'm not my damn gender," I finally shot back, after far too long of a pause.

"You haven't told me your name," he countered.

Bastard.

Clever bastard.

He had a point, though.

"Ari. Short for January." I didn't know why I tagged on that last part. He didn't need to know my full name. There was a reason I didn't go by it.

"January," he murmured, as if trying to get himself used to the name, which was a word they probably didn't have in whatever his language was. I had been able to understand them since they first appeared on Earth, which I was chalking up to whatever magic they had that could connect our two worlds, even if it only worked on Winter Solstice like they claimed.

"Do you have a name?" I asked. Maybe the question was rude, but they were a different kind of creature than I was.

"All living things have names in Vevol." He sounded amused by my question, rather than insulted, which was good. "Names have power here."

Names had some kind of power, and I'd just given him mine without a damn thought about it.

Fantastic.

"You'd better give me your name then," I huffed at him.

He chuckled. "Calian."

"Cal-ee-in," I sounded it out, testing the unfamiliar word.

"Mmhm." His murmur sounded a bit different, but I couldn't pinpoint how or what about it seemed that way. "Don't give anyone else your full name, whether male or female. Should they learn it from someone other than you, it won't harm you. But if you give it to them yourself, you give them power to call on you. Your full name should only leave your lips the first time you give it to your mate."

Power to *what*?

"That's absolutely insane," I told him, panting a little thanks to the pace I was pushing myself to keep.

There was no way Calian was his whole name. He clearly didn't want me to be his mate, so he wouldn't have given me a way to call on him, whatever that really meant.

Asshole.

"We're here. Slow down, before you—"

I slammed into something really hard, and really invisible, before I could slow down.

Curses flew from my lips as I crashed to the ground, my face aching from collision. My nose was throbbing, but my eyes weren't watering and I didn't feel any blood dripping from it at least.

"Damn you," I groaned at Calian, peeling myself off the dirt. He was kneeling beside me, a hint of a smirk on his lips as he offered me a hand.

I took it, swearing and jumping back when he shocked me again, like he had the first time we touched. "What the hell was that?" I grumbled at him, shaking my hand out and taking a couple of steps away from the guy.

He was doing his stupidly-attractive half-smirk thing again as he turned toward the invisible wall, and I didn't realize he had ignored my question until he knocked on the invisible thing I'd attacked with my face.

The sound that echoed from the rap of his fist reminded me a hell of a lot of a front door.

He stepped back after knocking, and I followed suit, rubbing at my nose. Strangely enough, it had stopped hurting already. Probably because I was a damn phoenix now.

The place he had knocked on swung open a moment later, and a woman holding a gigantic sword and wearing a fierce scowl stood in what was definitely a doorway. The door had way too many locks, though—and the thing was at least six times as thick as any other one I'd seen. Looked like it was made of solid stone, too.

Her gaze landed on me, but she didn't lower her sword. Her eyes were an unnatural bright gold, and her hair was a normal, human deep brown. Like me, she had pale skin and thin lips. "Name?"

Suddenly, I understood Calian's warning.

If a simple name could give me power over someone, or give someone power over me, that was a loaded question.

And he had set me up to protect myself.

A wave of gratitude hit me hard, though I knew better than to thank him for what he'd done. Thanking someone implied that they'd done you a favor, and that you owed them… and I didn't want to owe him.

"Ari," I said to the sword chick.

Her eyes narrowed and flashed suspiciously at Calian before looking back at me. "*Full* name."

"Ariana Faust."

The admission relaxed her slightly, though she didn't know it was a lie.

"Welcome to Vevol, Ari. I'm Ana." She reached a hand out and grabbed my arm, then unceremoniously yanked me inside the Stronghold.

The door slammed behind me, and she released my arm before quickly getting to work on the locks. "Did he touch you?" she demanded as her fingers moved deftly over the mechanisms.

The woman had clearly done this more than a few times.

"Um, not really, no."

"Good." She was halfway through all thirteen of the locks—I counted. "Lian isn't one of the worsts, but being touched by any of the seelie bastards is a good way to get yourself locked into a mating you don't want."

Did she mean being touched at all?

Because he had touched me, just barely—and twice.

And she had called him Lian, pronounced Lee-in, which was clearly a shortened version of his name.

Which meant he had given me his whole name.

Which meant...

Oh, shit.

"Bastard," I hissed between my teeth.

"What?" She shot me a demanding look. The woman didn't seem to have any other settings besides suspicious and demanding.

"He did touch me—twice. It felt like getting electrocuted. And he said his name was Calian."

Her expression twisted into a grimace. "You're screwed."

After turning, she spun and started walking down the hallway a hell of a lot faster than I expected.

I had to jog to keep up with her. "Does it mean what I think it means?"

"That he's decided you're his mate? Yes." She didn't bother glancing at me. "We'll throw you a funeral when you're gone."

My eyebrows shot upward as she led me into a large room full of couches, books, and strange-looking screens that sort of reminded me of TVs. "He's going to *kill* me? I thought it was like marriage."

"We call them funerals because they're the end of your humanity," another woman chirped.

My attention jerked toward her, and I found her curled up on a couch off to the side of the room. She held a book in her hands, and a soft-looking blanket was draped over her legs. She wore a sweatshirt and a pair of fuzzy socks, along with what looked like leggings from what I could see. Her curly black hair was up in a puff on top of her head, and her expression was a hell of a lot more relaxed than Ana's. Her skin was dark brown, and her eyes soft hazel.

At least she looked comfortable. That meant the Stronghold wasn't a prison.

"What? I thought we all change when we get here," I argued. "They said I'm a phoenix."

"Yep, we can all shift into a legendary beast form like they can. You won't transform until you've bonded with your mate or been taken to the unseelie half of the world, though, and you have to last five years here to make it to the unseelies. If Lian has decided you're his mate, I doubt you'll make it one."

Shit, this was a lot to take in.

"What's your name?" the laid-back woman checked.

Lie again, my instincts practically screamed.

I'd never really played well with others.

I didn't need to lie, though. My nickname—which I did actually go by, ninety-nine percent of the time—was enough.

"Ari. What about you?"

Considering the power of names, I felt like I needed to ask, not just assume she would give it to me.

"Mare, if we're only swapping nicknames." She gave me a quick wink. "I don't blame you for wanting to keep your full name quiet. The only person I told mine to was Ana, but she's been running this place for five years now."

Five years?

I glanced back at her. "I thought you said the unseelie take you after five years."

"They do. I'll be leaving tonight," Ana admitted, her expression a bit stiff.

Damn, no wonder she was so angry.

Or maybe that was just her personality. I wouldn't blame her either way.

"How are the unseelies different?" I asked.

"We don't really know." Mare shrugged on the couch. "We try not to talk to the fae guys very often, so we don't give them the wrong idea, but we haven't met the unseelies."

"How many of you are there?" I checked, looking around the room. No one else was hiding, as far as I could see.

"Five, right now. The fae are getting anxious about it, too. Usually one of them finds a mate every two or three years—we made it five. Looks like you're going to break the streak." Ana didn't sound thrilled about that, either.

"Where are the others?"

"Dots and Sunny are setting up for my funeral. North is asleep, probably. She keeps weird hours, and avoids us." Ana shrugged. "Things are pretty chill here. Or they were, until you showed up."

So this would've been a helluva place to be, if Calian hadn't touched me and told me his full name.

Great.

Just my damn luck.

"You won't have a room until Ana leaves, but you can borrow mine to shower in," Mare offered. "You don't want to miss it when the unseelie show up, but you have an hour or two, I'd guess."

I glanced down at myself.

Shit, I had forgotten what bad shape I was in. I was a damned wreck.

I looked back up and jerked my head in a nod.

"That would be great, thanks."

"I'm at the end of the hallway, on the left. Door has my name on it, can't miss it." She winked at me.

I nodded again, stepping up and slipping down the hall.

Damn, my brain was spinning.

Four

I SPENT LONGER in the shower than I probably should've, but it was the first time since I'd been out of juvie that I didn't need to rush through a shower at the cheap gym I'd joined for that purpose. I hadn't realized how much anxiety had revolved around showering until I was behind a locked door, my shoulders relaxing under the hot stream.

My feet weren't blistered, despite the terrible pain I'd had for part of the time while I was running, and my muscles weren't sore. I wasn't even hungry anymore. And though I was tired, it wasn't the shaky-legged exhaustion I would've been feeling if I was still human.

Damn, it was cool to be fae.

Despite my initial horror of being transported to a new world and told to run for my life before some bastard caught me and turned me into his mate somehow, I was feeling sort of... positive about my experience thus far.

I was alive.

I was safe.

I wasn't living in my car anymore.

There was no more record of juvenile detention or murder on my shoulders.

No one to refuse me an apartment or a job because of what I'd done to my bastard of a foster dad.

No more Earth to remind me of the shitty hand life had dealt me.

In Vevol, I was just Ari.

Sure, I had given a fae dude my full name, which was probably a terrible decision, but it hadn't come back to bite me in the ass yet. It probably would, but for now, everything was actually kind of great.

I needed to watch myself, though, because I had a terrible tendency to get all hopeful right before everything turned to shit and then burned me to a crisp right afterward.

My mind wandered back to the strange forest, with Calian.

He had said that a person's full name was a way to call on them, whatever the hell that meant.

I was sure it wasn't something magical—at least, I was pretty sure.

I considered trying it out by saying his name while focusing on trying to call him to me, but decided against it until I could ask one of the other girls about it. Although, they might not actually know. It sounded like none of them had ever hooked up with the seelie fae dudes in the time they'd been there, so they might not know nitty gritty details like that.

Hmm.

Now I was getting curious.

Curiosity was a shitty quality, though. It only ever led to disappointment or horror.

I shampooed my hair vigorously, trying to tamp down that stupid curiosity. I didn't understand a damn thing about the power of names; trying it out would be absolutely stupid as hell.

But that didn't mean I didn't want to try it.

I conditioned my hair quickly. The shower, shampoo, and razor all looked like our normal earth-style shit, which made me feel a little more comfortable. Not that I required comfort to shower, or function, or do anything else important. I excelled at doing uncomfortable things while living in discomfort.

It was a shitty fact, but a fact nonetheless.

Knowing I needed to get out before I did something really, terribly stupid, I rinsed my hair and then turned off the water.

After I dried off, I wrapped the thick, white towel around myself and stepped out of the room, holding onto the thing tightly.

Wearing a towel was one of the prime times a person could get attacked. Any vulnerability was a weakness that a girl like me just couldn't afford.

My gaze swept the room.

Empty, still.

And the door was shut.

My shoulders relaxed slightly.

What if I really was safe there?

What if I could just... live?

If that was the case, I was really damn grateful for the penny Linsey had practically forced me to take.

A knock sounded on the door, and I tensed.

"I left clothes for you on the bed," Mare called from outside the room. "Feel free to use my brush, bandages, and anything else you might need. It's in the bathroom, and the fae supply all of it."

"Thank you," I called back, ignoring the panic that had swollen in my chest.

I was still fine.

The door to the bedroom hadn't been locked when I went in to take a shower —I hadn't wanted to piss Mare off when she was being kind to me. So, it wasn't surprising that she'd been able to come into the room. That was fine.

I was fine.

Shit, I hated being vulnerable though.

I crossed the room and quickly locked the door.

Getting dressed in the soft, sturdy leggings and oversized sweatshirt calmed me down a bit. I was built thicker than Mare was, so everything was a bit tight, but I was used to that after a childhood full of thrift-store clothing.

Back in the bathroom, I tugged a brush through my hair. Unlike the clothing, it didn't look like it was from Earth. The bristles were strange, and the handle was made out of the white, stone-looking wood I'd seen so much of in the forest. It felt odd against my fingertips, but not uncomfortably so.

I looked through the rest of the cupboards, checking for anything that might possibly be suspicious. When I didn't find anything, it didn't make me more comfortable. If anything, it just reminded me to wait for the next pin to drop.

Fully dressed, with my hair combed and my feet bare, I padded out of the room a couple of minutes later. Mare shot me a quick smile from her seat on the couch. Ana was eating something that looked suspiciously like cake, sitting beside three girls I didn't recognize. I waved at them, and they waved back.

Not feeling like I was in the mood to socialize, even for the possibility of cake, I headed over to the couch where Mare was sitting. I wouldn't sit next to her—didn't want to annoy her—but she felt safer than the other girls, so I'd stick with her.

Though I didn't want to read, I pretended to scan the books on the shelf. I had a shitty case of dyslexia that made it difficult to read at all, and while I could push through it when I wanted to, I had no desire to do so at the moment.

What I really wanted was a nap, but I wasn't going to get that. Not until I had a room of my own, with a lockable door. A place to feel safe.

I would've given anything for that back on Earth. I'd just have to embrace it for as long as I had it now that I was in Vevol.

I grabbed a book and sat down. Opening to the first page, I stared at the words. I was skilled at pretending to read—people reading books seemed laid-back and unconfrontational, which were two very good traits to possess in juvie.

So I *read*.

And silently watched everyone interact.

I only had two minutes to study them before there was a knock on the gigantic door.

All four of the other girls went silent.

"It's time," one of the ones I didn't know murmured.

"Dammit." Ana sighed, tucking her hands into the pockets of her jeans. I noticed that she had cleaned up and changed. My gaze followed her as she grabbed a backpack that I hadn't noticed sitting on the floor by her feet.

"It's going to be great," one of the girls promised.

"It's going to be hell," another one grumbled.

"I'm going to survive, which is what counts," Ana shot back at both of them. "And so are you. Don't touch the guys, don't let them touch you. I'll see you when your time is up here, okay?" She looked around the room, and her gaze made it back to Mare, and then stopped on me. "Good luck, newbie."

I shrugged back.

No point in thanking her for wishing me luck. Luck had never been what kept me alive.

If she was going to wish me something, I'd rather she wish me good food and a safe place to rest my head.

The person at the door knocked again, louder.

"The seelie won't wait—but the unseelie will," Ana murmured, as she started across the room."Remember that. The seelie are the wild ones—there's no control here."

Shit, I liked the sound of that.

No control.

No power-obsessed bastards who thought they could own you.

No one to figuratively hold you by the tits or the throat.

I'd take a fist fight over a verbal battle any day of the week.

Everyone followed Ana to the door, myself included, though I trailed behind at the back of the group. Mare walked beside me, not leaving me behind.

"Who's next?" I murmured to her.

"Me," she admitted, her gaze a bit wistful. "I've been hoping for a seelie fae to come knocking at the door for me, but it hasn't happened. Something about the unseelies just seems... cold. You'll see, when one of them shows up for Ana. The other girls prefer that, but... not me."

I nodded, my damned curiosity flaring a bit.

The safer I felt, the more the ridiculous character trait seemed to grate on me.

"REMEMBER, always answer with a weapon pointed at the fae," Ana warned us, as she began undoing the locks. "Don't accept invitations from fae who haven't been camped outside for more than three months. Trust each other—and no one else."

Damn, that sounded like a shitty way to live.

Then again, I lived by most of those rules myself. So I couldn't exactly argue.

"Don't worry about me," she added. "I'll screw up any fae who tries to touch me, seelie or unseelie. I'll see you ladies soon."

With that, she pulled the door the rest of the way open.

There was a knife in her hand, though—keeping the fae away from her.

"Ana," a familiar voice drawled.

My body tensed.

Calian.

"Lovely to see you again. Let me introduce my friend, Druze." Calian gestured toward a man beside him. He was just as tall as Calian and the other gigantic fae I'd met, but had short, wavy blond hair, pale skin, and was wearing something that resembled office clothing back on Earth—a button-down shirt, and pants that resembled slacks.

"Basilisk," Ana hissed at the man.

His lips curved upward wickedly. "Pretty little human." He said the last word like it disgusted him.

Ana muttered something that sounded suspiciously like, "I wish," but the man's gaze had already lifted to the rest of us, and was slowly dragging over our group. Something about the intensity of his gaze as it landed on me made me shudder slightly.

"Brother." Calian's voice was clipped as he smacked the basilisk dude on the back. "Eyes off that one. January is mine."

The basilisk's gaze skidded to Calian, flooded with interest.

I didn't hear whatever he said to Calian—the words *January is mine* were thundering too loudly in my mind.

The other girls' gazes jerked to me, and I felt my face reddening.

They couldn't use my full name against me since I hadn't given it to them myself, if Calian was to be believed. But still, having it spoken aloud made me feel sort of... naked.

Vulnerable.

My defenses rose, and I stared at the basilisk man because suddenly, he was the safest target for my eyes.

Screw Calian.

Screw everyone.

I could do it; I could ignore him for five damn years for the sake of getting away from the bastard.

He had lied to me and claimed me like I was a damn loaf of bread, and touched me.

The bastard deserved to be ignored for five years, and then abandoned. He could try his luck with some other poor human chick.

I was not his *anything*.

"Shall we?" the basilisk drawled to Ana, holding out his elbow.

"I'm not touching you," she growled back, shoving her knife at him. He took a smooth step backward and she filled the space he left, using it to slide past him.

Damn, I kind of wanted to be Ana.

Angry, kick-ass, and confident?

Sign me up.

"Ladies." The basilisk guy nodded at us. "I'll see you soon."

His gaze lingered on me before he turned around.

Shit, I hated how his eyes felt on me.

I definitely did not want to see him soon.

But if I wanted to get away from the seelie, I would have to.

Dammit, why couldn't there be an easy, good alternative? Maybe a magical castle where I could be single and alone, with my own space, food, and clothing, for the rest of my life?

Despite Ana's warning, the girl who replaced her in the doorway didn't have a weapon in her hand.

"I request entrance," Calian said smoothly, after Ana and the basilisk guy were gone.

"Fuck off." The girl in the doorway shut the thick stone slab in his face, hard.

I almost felt bad for the guy.

Almost.

FIVE

ALL OF THE girls were looking at me when they turned away from the door.

"January, huh?" one of them asked.

My cheeks flushed a bit. "Didn't give myself that name, if that's what you're asking."

"I like it," Mare remarked. "I wish I could get my actual name out in the open, honestly. Lian did you a favor, even if you don't realize it now."

My face heated further. "His name is Calian."

"Even hotter than Lian, somehow," one of the girls muttered.

"Lucky bitch," another one of them sighed dramatically. My gaze flicked to her, and lingered. She was the one who had been in the doorway, and my eyes widened slightly when I saw her, only because she looked so much less human than the rest of us. "I'm Sunny," she offered. Her hair was black at the roots but faded to gray, and then white by the time it reached the ends. She'd pulled it up into two puffs on top of her head, reminding me of the space buns that had been in style when I was in high school, which I'd never been brave enough to try. Her skin was dark brown, and her lips were painted black. One of her eyes was silver while the other was the same shade as her lips.

My face was burning when I realized I'd been staring.

Staring could get a girl shanked.

"It's okay, I'm used to it." She shrugged. "I'd stare at you if you were as stunning as I am." She gave a little half-twirl that made me snort.

"Some of our appearances seem to be more affected by the magic than others," another girl said. "I've got this massive tattoo over my back and arm. It appeared a few weeks after I got here." Her skin was the same pale shade as mine, but she had more freckles than I knew was possible. Her hair was a bright golden color that mine sure as hell didn't resemble, even though the colors probably belonged to the same family. Mine was a solid dirty-looking blonde.

"I'm Dots, by the way."

"I've always wanted a tattoo," I admitted. "Never had the money."

"Maybe you'll get lucky with the magic, then," she suggested.

"Unlikely." The last girl whose name I didn't know pushed past me. "Good luck with the king, dead girl." I didn't get a great look at her, but from what I could see, she was pale and thin. She was wearing a high-necked long-sleeve shirt, as well as leggings and socks. With her long, thick black hair swaying around her face, I barely saw an inch of her skin.

"That's North. Don't let her offend you; she just hates being here. She hated Earth too, though. She's a hellhound and has patches of burnt-looking skin everywhere her scars used to be. She had a *lot* of scars," Dots explained in a hushed voice.

Damn, I hoped they didn't always gossip like this. I shuddered to think what they'd say about me.

I'd be on board with burn marks, though. At least then, my appearance would tell people to back off without me saying any actual words.

"None of us had good lives, back on Earth," Mare murmured. "I'm sure you were in a shitty boat too. For some of us, this is the second chance we always hoped for. For others, it's another hell. You get to choose how you see it."

She looped her arm through mine, and the sudden touch made me jerk a bit.

It wasn't terrible, though.

It was actually kind of... nice.

How long had it been since anyone touched me?

Other than Calian, who I hadn't wanted to touch me?

How long had it been since I actually sort of trusted someone?

I didn't want to think about that.

"Come on, let's get you settled in your new room. Ana went crazy with the cleaning spray while you were gone. As suspicious as that girl is about everything, she never hesitated to do her part around here," Mare said cheerfully, tugging me down the hallway by my arm.

"I'm going to miss that crazy bitch," Sunny remarked, as she and Dots walked alongside me.

The fact that they were going to miss her told me plenty about her. She might have been a little insane, but she had to have been a decent friend—because there were very, very few people that had ever treated me well enough for me to actually miss them after they were out of my life.

Then again, I'd grown up the grumpy, sad girl in the foster system. I wasn't one of the cute little ones who bounced back from the shit they went through and found forever homes—I was one of the temperamental ones who moved around and never found her place.

Maybe now that I was out, and free, that would change.

As long as I could stay away from Calian, that was.

"Here we are," Dots announced with a flourish of her hand. "Home sweet home. It's nothing fancy, but definitely a hell of a lot more comfortable than the forest outside."

"Amen to that," Sunny muttered.

"The fae will bring clothes, food, and other supplies for you over the next few weeks. They usually drag it out so they have an excuse for us to let them in, so more of the men can meet us. Although none of us have ever been claimed by one of them, so I'm not sure how that will affect it..." Dots trailed off, her expression contemplative.

"How do they convince you to let them in?" I asked, curiosity getting the better of me again.

"The bastards aren't stupid. They know we're suckers for good foods, new movies, new books, new clothes... anything we don't have access to in here already. We're well-stocked with the basics, this world's version of beans, rice, and enough spices to make it taste good. But I'll be damned if their chocolate cake doesn't make my mouth water just thinking about it," Sunny said with a grin. "It's been a few weeks since the last fae bribed us for a meeting. Ana made them wait outside for a month before she'd let any of us talk to them. Now that she's gone, and you've got a fae on your ass, hopefully we'll have more of their desserts."

I could definitely see where she was coming from with that. Hell, maybe I agreed.

For a whole damn chocolate cake, I could put up with a hell of a lot.

Then again, accepting a chocolate cake from Calian would probably give him an idea I didn't want him to have. So, I'd have to think hard before I accepted anything from him.

"So how did all of you make it here without one of them catching you?" I wondered as I walked around the room. None of them seemed like they were in a hurry to leave, or like they were judging me for checking for anything that might resemble a weapon or a hidden camera.

"Oh, the hunt is just a big theatrical thing. They need you to move fast for it to work the way it should. Assuming you jog for most of the time before the sun sets, you'll reach the Stronghold before any of them can make your scent out. The ocean washes it away well enough that only a fae who's a compatible mate will be able to smell you well enough to track you."

What the hell?

Calian has said it was because I picked up the scale—not because he could smell me.

Which was another damned lie.

That bastard could take a hike.

No way in hell was I going to let him make me his mate.

"Well, I'm going to start on dinner. Go ahead and make yourself at home, even though you don't have much yet. I'm sure Lian will be back with some stuff for you soon enough," Mare said cheerfully.

She and the others left me to my room.

It was pretty much bare—no clothes in the square, walk-in closet. No blankets on the mattress, though it still looked a hell of a lot more comfortable than the back seat of my car, which was where I had been sleeping for nearly a year. No toiletries in the bathroom, no shampoo in the shower, no comb in the drawers, which seemed to be styled to look like the ones we'd had back on earth.

It was still the best place I'd lived in almost a decade.

For a couple of minutes, I sat on the bed—which was ridiculously comfortable—mentally going over everything that had happened.

Then my stomach growled, and with a sigh, I stood.

It was time to eat, and then face the fae who thought I was his, whenever he showed up with more stuff for me.

Dinner was fun, to be honest. The girls were chatty, but not annoyingly so. North didn't make an appearance, but Sunny got her to open the door long enough to take her portion of the food—and there was plenty of food.

It wasn't awkward.

I even found myself looking forward to the next meal when it was over.

Mare turned on a movie while we all cleaned up, and we were done in time to get cozy on the couch when it started. The action was so foreign to me, but a happy warmth spread in my chest that I hoped would never leave.

And there I was, hoping again even though I knew I shouldn't.

Oh well.

I could enjoy the fun while it lasted.

Partway into the movie—an action film I had never seen—there was a loud knock on our massive door.

Four grins turned my way.

"If he has chocolate cake, give him whatever he wants," Sunny told me.

I rolled my eyes at her, but...

Chocolate cake sounded really damn good.

"Do I really need to open the door with a weapon?" I asked them as I slipped off the couch. They paused the movie for me, which was really damn nice. I couldn't say I'd ever had friends who would pause a movie for me before.

"Nah. The fae don't have any women of their own, so hurting one of us is worse than a death sentence. Bastards might try to touch your arms or face or something, but never go further than that," Sunny said.

Her words comforted me, to be honest.

Though I was kind of shocked they didn't have any women of their own, I guessed it kind of made sense according to what I did know.

Why would they bother taking women from Earth if they could find mates among their own people?

I felt slightly more comfortable than I expected to as I walked to the door.

Six

It took me a lot longer to open all those damn locks than it had taken Ana. The fae on the other side of the door waited patiently, probably hearing me working on the stupid things.

When I finally wrenched the door open, I found myself face-to-face with Calian. I hated the way my breath caught in my throat at the size of him, and the power I could sort of feel swirling around him.

"Hello." His lips curved up in a half-smirk.

The same one from the jungle that made me want to punch him.

I ignored the urge though, because there was a duffel bag hanging off his shoulder, and he was holding a cake in his hands. It didn't look like chocolate, but cake was cake.

"I'm not your possession," I told him flatly. "And you already lied to me multiple times, so I'm not interested."

"I never lied to you," he corrected me. "And I'm very much aware that you don't belong to me yet."

Yet.

That bastard.

I started to shut the door in his face, but he caught it easily with a foot planted in the door's way.

"You need these." He tugged the duffel bag's strap off his shoulder with the hand that wasn't holding the cake, and carefully maneuvered it past me, setting it on the ground. "And this." He smoothly placed the edge of the cake's platter against my abdomen. None of the frosting got on my sweatshirt, and my hand automatically lifted to cradle the mouthwatering dessert.

"How can you possibly think you didn't lie to me?" I finally recovered and snapped at him when he lowered his hand off the door. And dammit, I didn't shut the thing. "You bluntly told me that I needed to get to the stronghold or I would find myself mated."

He dipped his head in a nod, still wearing that damned smirk. "Mated to *me*. I only have so much control, woman."

I blinked at him.

Who the hell was this guy?

His smirk morphed into a full-out grin when my eyes narrowed. "And the scale?"

"I would've watched you make it here from afar if you hadn't picked it up. Seeing another man's scale in your hand forced the beast in me to react." He shrugged slightly.

"Are scales special?" I demanded.

"No. We shed them the same way we shed hair."

Then why the hell did he care that I was holding someone else's?

"You asked me for my name," I argued, though my anger was sort of... losing steam.

"I'll need it at some point."

"And you seriously gave me your real name?" My voice was raising, flooded with frustration.

"It's yours to use any moment you wish to see me," he agreed, that damn smirk back in place. "Preferably while you're naked."

Bastard.

I resisted the urge to smash the cake in his gorgeous face.

That would be a sad, sad waste of cake.

"I'm not going to do that," I shot back.

He was still smirking.

Damn him.

Damn him straight to whatever this world's version of hell was.

"I'll collect more of the items you need and bring them by in the morning. Different groups produce different things, so it'll take some legwork. Luckily for you, I have great legs."

"You have wings," I shot back.

His smirk curved into a wicked grin. "Glad you noticed."

With that, he turned and strode away.

I slammed the door to stop myself from staring at his incredible ass.

My fingers struggled with the locks one-handed, but Dots walked up and took over.

"What did you have to do for the cake?" she checked.

"I'm surprised you guys didn't listen in," I grumbled.

She flashed me an amused smile. "Ana would've, but we're not into that. If you want to hook up with the sexy fae, that's totally your call."

I heaved a sigh. "He didn't ask me to do anything; just handed the damn thing over. Said I needed it. Maybe he thinks I'm too skinny or something."

"Answering the door was enough this time," Dots mused as she finished the last of the locks. "Next time, it won't be so easy."

Great.

"We'd better enjoy this cake then, because it's the last one we're going to have for a while."

She laughed. "That's the spirit. Welcome to Vevol, and all that." She winked at me, grabbing the duffel bag and tossing it over her shoulder.

My stomach clenched at the way she picked my things up without so much as asking permission. I had to force myself to follow her without starting a fight in an attempt to get it back.

Not everyone was so panicky when it came to holding on to their possessions.

I stood in the doorway while Dots set it just inside the doorway of my room, then shut the door behind her.

"I'm surprised you guys don't split everything," I said, relaxing slightly now that my things were in my room, as safe as they could be for the time being.

"Whatever you get from the fae is rightfully yours. If you don't want to share, you don't share. Even when it comes to cake." She shrugged a bit and walked beside me as I headed toward the kitchen. "I kissed one of them for a tub of their version of ice cream. So damn worth it. Because I shared, the other girls also shared their food whenever they got it from one of the fae who came to meet them. That's usually how it works around here."

Damn.

I kind of loved that.

"Whatever you do, don't touch North's shit. She's not into sharing," Dots warned.

I could understand that, too.

Maybe I'd bring her a slice of cake as a peace offering.

Or maybe not. It would probably depend on how good the cake was.

When we got to the kitchen, though, the curiosity in me won out. I wanted to see what would happen with North if I brought her something without expecting her to reciprocate. I had been the prickly bitch enough times to know that there was always a reason—and that it was just a defense mechanism.

So, I halved the cake and cut it into five pieces, saving some for tomorrow. I'd probably need the sugar to cheer myself up after I turned down whatever the hell Calian asked for in exchange for the next treat he brought me. Especially if it was the fae version of ice cream; I was a damned sucker when it came to ice cream.

After giving three pieces to Dots so she could distribute them, I carried my cake and North's over to her door, then knocked on it.

"Fuck off," she yelled in response.

I fought a grin.

How many times had that been my answer to people trying to talk to me?

Pretty much every damn time when I was a teenager.

"I brought you cake. Not sure what flavor it is, but it's sort of a cream color. Smells incredible," I called out. "No expectations come with it. It's just cake."

There was a moment of silence, and then the door was ripped open. Gorgeous, reddish-gold eyes glared back at me. "Everything has a price," she growled at me.

The other girls said you couldn't shift until you found a mate or went to live with the unseelies, but smoke was definitely curling off of North, as if she was on fire or was about to catch on fire.

"I know. I grew up in foster care. Went to juvie at fifteen after killing one of my temporary parents. Nothing on Earth is free, and I'm sure Vevol is the same. But I paid the price for the damned cake, and all it cost you was a little chat in your doorway." I put the plate against her abdomen, like Calian had done to me, and hid my tendril of amusement when her arm lifted to cradle it the same way mine had. "I'm Ari, and I'm not dead just because some fae bastard thinks I'm going to be his wife."

With that, I turned and walked away.

I felt her gaze on my back, but it wasn't anywhere near the first time that had happened.

People always stared.

When it bothered me, I'd stare right back.

None of the other girls commented on me giving cake to North when I sat back down on the couch. We started the movie again, and my body slowly relaxed.

Watching the movie with them felt... nice.

Hell, maybe it even felt happy.

I wasn't going to let myself think too much about that though, because happiness was always ripped away after I acknowledged it.

After the movie was over, Dots volunteered to do the dishes as a thank-you to me for sharing my cake, and I didn't disagree. I was the one who had to deal with the fae bastard who might be a little obsessed with me, even if he hadn't actually lied to me.

I was still pretty pissed about his reasoning behind what he'd said, though. That he couldn't have controlled himself forever, and I was in danger of getting mated if I'd stayed in the forest with him.

Especially the part where scales were basically strands of hair, and he got possessive when I picked up someone else's.

He had to be the gray dragon, I decided, as I walked back to my room to see what I had in my new duffel bag. I would give Mare back her clothes, too, because I didn't know who she'd needed to talk to in order to get them. I didn't want to disrupt the balance of sharing that the women in the Stronghold had, and I sure as hell didn't want to owe Mare anything.

Back in my room, I grabbed the duffel bag by the strap and carried it to the mattress, setting it down kind of carefully since I didn't know what was in it or if anything was breakable.

The zipper looked a bit different than the ones I was used to, but it was easy to work, so I had the bag open a moment later.

On top, there was a pile of fabric, so I pulled it out of the bag. When I quickly realized that it was a thick and ridiculously-soft blanket, I hugged it to my chest, inhaling the fabric deeply. It smelled fresh and light, like the forest had when I'd run through it, and I loved it.

I was never letting that thing go if I could help it.

The blanket was placed carefully on the bed, and I pulled out the next thing—a thin, smooth bundle of fabric that reminded me of a sheet. The texture was slightly different than what I was used to, and it was shaped like a big pillowcase instead of elastic-lined, but I didn't hesitate to wrestle it onto my mattress. When it was on securely, I draped my blanket over it, and then let my gaze sweep up and down the bed.

It was already more welcoming than any other one I'd ever used.

I loved it.

Returning to the duffel bag, I pulled out a pillow. It was squishier than any I'd used before, the texture softer but also thicker somehow. I put that at the head of my bed and fought to ignore the happiness swelling in my chest again.

No acknowledging happiness.

Happiness only ever led to shit falling apart.

Back at the duffel bag, I found bottles of shampoo and conditioner. They smelled more manly than Mare's, but not in a way I disliked. The scent actually kind of reminded me of the way the blanket and pillow smelled.

There were a few other simple toiletries in the duffel, and when I had them all put away in the bathroom, I returned to the bag.

And then stared down inside it.

I blinked once at the final thing inside, and then again.

When I reached inside, I had to bite my lip hard.

My fingers slid over the large, glittering, dark gray scale.

I should've left it in the bag, but something within me wouldn't allow it. Honestly, I was fascinated by it. By the magic of this world I'd been dragged into, by the fact that a man—even if he was technically a fae man—could transform into an actual dragon.

I had seen him flying over me; I knew he was real.

And that meant the world was real too, as insane as everything was.

Despite its insanity, I wanted it all to be real so badly that it hurt.

I tucked the scale into the fabric case that my pillow had come wrapped in, then stripped off my borrowed clothing and tucked myself under the insanely-soft blanket. I wasn't going to sleep in Mare's clothes—they were hers, and I didn't want to wreck them in any way since I'd be returning them as soon as I had some of my own.

Theoretically, I would have some of my own in the very near future. Calian had said he'd be back in the morning.

So, I tugged the blanket up to my chin, not expecting to fall asleep quickly. But with the delicious scent in my nose and the gentle pressure of the heavy, soft blanket on my bare skin, I was out almost instantly.

Seven

A SOFT KNOCK at my new bedroom door woke me up the next morning. A semi-familiar voice called out, "January, there's a fae here for you."

It took me a minute to stumble out of bed, remember where I was, and why there was a fae there for me. I threw on the clothes I'd borrowed from Mare the day before while I struggled through my exhausted thoughts.

When I opened the door, a cheerful-looking Mare stood outside my room, fully dressed. Her curls were down and gorgeous, and I blinked at her a couple of times until she pointed me toward the front door.

I quickly made it to the door and struggled through all of the locks before tugging the door open.

Calian's expression was hard as I opened it, but it softened as his gaze trailed up and down my figure.

That was weird, but whatever.

"What?" I asked him, eyeing the bag over his shoulder. It was at least twice as big as the one from the day before, and for the life of me, I couldn't guess what he could've possibly put in there. No way in hell did I need that many clothes, and clothes were pretty much all I was missing.

"You look calm," he told me.

I blinked at him.

His lips curved upward just the tiniest bit.

I noticed circles under his eyes.

"I thought you said you'd have to go to multiple places to get everything else you thought I'd need," I told him.

"I did." He easily lifted the bag off his shoulder and pretty much tossed it into the room behind me.

"So you lied?" I checked.

His eyes narrowed. "Why do you keep assuming I'd lie to you?"

"I assume everyone will lie to me," I shot back. "And you definitely didn't answer my question."

His eyes narrowed further. "I said I'd need to go to multiple places. During the night, I flew to those places, collecting your things. Now, I'm here." He gestured to the huge bag. "And so are your things."

I blinked. "You didn't sleep?"

"I can sleep while I'm waiting out here to convince you to consider me as your mate." He gestured to a place along the stronghold's invisible wall. I noticed what looked like a tent built up against it.

Damn.

Ana must've really made the fae men camp out for a month before letting anyone talk to them.

Not gonna lie, I respected her for that. It would've been nice to have someone protect me like that, at any point in my life.

"Unless you don't plan on making me wait," Calian said, studying me.

"I don't plan anything. Personal rule. Plans lead to heartache." I grabbed the door. "Thanks for the stuff, but I've gotta go." I swung it shut, and to my surprise and relief, he didn't try to stop me.

With the door closed between us, I let out a breath I hadn't realized I was holding.

I didn't feel as relieved as I would've hoped, though.

I actually kind of missed the big, smirky dude.

Which had to be the fault of whatever ridiculous magic was thundering through my veins now that I'd come to Vevol, because I refused to miss anyone. That was the kind of shit that led to depression, and anxiety, and other mental crap that I most definitely couldn't afford to have. That kind of thing killed women who'd been through the hell I'd survived.

So I grabbed my new bag and dragged the massive thing over to my door. Mare was the only one awake, so I thought it was probably at least sort of early, though I hadn't seen a clock. The sun was up when I answered the door, though, so maybe most people just preferred to sleep in at the Stronghold. I definitely wasn't against that idea, though I wasn't sure I'd be able to get my mind on the same page. Good sleep was a luxury I hadn't had in a long time.

With the door to my room locked, I felt safe as I started unpacking my bag. That was a huge thing for me, feeling safe, but I didn't want to acknowledge it because acknowledgment always led to shittery.

The first thing in the bag was a set of clothes, which I expected.

What I didn't expect was the style of them.

The other girls had clothing that was either from Earth or styled after what we had on Earth. They even had their own styles. Mare had oversized sweatshirts and leggings, North had tight black clothes that covered almost every inch of her, Sunny had old band t-shirts...

Earth clothes.

The things in my bag were definitely not from Earth.

There were multiple pairs of short, thick shorts that reminded me of the shit the preppy volleyball chicks at my high school used to wear, and tank tops made of the same material. The damn thing would leave at least an inch or two of my abdomen on display, and I wasn't even tall. Only average height.

"You have got to be kidding me," I muttered, tossing the clothes onto the bed and grabbing the next pair.

Another pair of booty shorts and another tank top.

Beneath it was more of the same shit.

"Asshole," I snarled, tossing them to the bed.

There was no underwear to go with the clothing, and no bras either.

"You okay in there?" Mare called from the hallway.

My first instinct was to pull back, to keep quiet, but... I actually liked her.

So I crossed the room and opened the door, tossing a hand toward the bed. "That asshole gave me a bag full of lingerie instead of clothes.

Her eyes widened. "Are you serious?"

"Look." I stalked back across the room and plucked one of the sets off the bed, lifting it for her to look at.

Mare relaxed slightly. "I totally get what you're coming from, and it's shitty, but the fae don't consider that lingerie. They gave Dots a set of those too, and the fae who brought it explained that most phoenixes wear those. She's a phoenix, like you. The constant shifting means that they're constantly catching on fire, and those clothes are both fireproof and stretchy enough to survive shifting. May I?" She held a hand out toward me, and I tossed her the pair.

She pulled on them a bit, showing me how they stretched. "Supposedly, these outfits are extremely expensive, which is why Dots only got one. If Lian brought you a couple of pairs, he must've spent his own money on them. The phoenix and hellhound guys are always wearing them, either the shorter or longer version, but most of them only have one or two pairs."

I glanced back down at the pile.

One, two, three, four...

Shit, there were fifteen.

I didn't even have fifteen pairs of clothes back on Earth. I had eight, so I could wash all my shit in one trip to the laundromat, one day a week.

Why the hell would I need fifteen sets of their fancy lingerie?

Maybe lingerie wasn't the right word, if the clothes were only made small because the fabric was expensive...

"How often do they shift, though? I thought you guys never shift?" I asked.

Her expression grew sheepish. "The fae have offered to teach us, but Ana was worried if we spent that much time with any of them, we'd start to like them."

I snorted. "Good old Ana."

"Right?" She laughed, a bit self-consciously. "Supposedly, there's a school that fae created for humans to go to in order to learn how to shift without getting stuck in one form or another. Blood Academy. But it's in the unseelie land, and we belong to the seelies until the five years have passed. Ana will be at Blood Academy right now; that's where the unseelies take us. They're the rule-followers, from what we know, so even Ana wasn't nervous about that part."

Nope, I did not like that. Belonging to unseelies? Hard pass.

I must've made a face that said how much I didn't like that idea.

"It's more like they've got first dibs," Dots said, stepping into the doorway and leaning heavily against the wall. Her golden hair was wrecked, and there were a few spots of what had to be drool on the collar of the gigantic t-shirt she had on, with no pants beneath it or anything. "One of the guys told me that the seelies are the ones who figured out how to break into Earth on the Winter Solstice about twenty years ago, so they made the five-year rule to buy themselves time to convince us to fall in love with them. It's been an epic failure though; only two seelie guys have ever found their mates. And both women convinced the men to join the unseelie, afterward. So there are fifteen previously-human chicks in the unseelie court, and only five of us here."

Shit.

That was probably why the unseelie guy had been so interested in Calian's new obsession with me.

"Have any of you guys shifted before?" I asked.

"Nah. We can all feel the discomfort of the wild magic beneath our skin, trying to break out, but we're professionals at ignoring it at this point." Mare winked at me. "I don't think Calian sees that in your future, though."

My gaze lowered back to the pile of expensive clothes.

"Those are actually way more comfortable than they look. I wear mine as underwear. Haven't worn actual panties or bras in the two years I've been here." She lifted the hem off her huge t-shirt, and my eyebrows shot up when I saw the short-shorts and tank top she had on. There was no way she could've known we were talking about those outfits, which meant she genuinely liked to wear them.

"Seriously, she washes them every day. It's kind of disgusting," Mare teased.

Despite their jokes, I was looking at the clothing items with a lot less anger now.

"So, he was being thoughtful," I finally, reluctantly said.

"Mmhm," Mare agreed.

"And from what I understand, now that you've found your mate, your magic will grow more uncontrollable, so you'll probably start shifting soon," Dots added.

Damn, I wasn't looking forward to that.

Although, phoenixes were massive birds... so could they fly?

It was probably my luck to be a damned flaming flamingo, with wings that didn't even work, so I wasn't going let myself get hopeful about that.

"Ladies!" Sunny yelled from the living area. "You're going to want to see this!"

I exchanged confused glances with Dots and Mare before we all headed out of my room—but I did stop long enough to close the door behind me. Just in case.

One of the bookshelves against the wall had been stripped and dragged to the side, and the couches next to it were loaded with books. A large window was built into the wall, but had been completely hidden by the bookshelf the day before.

Through the window, I could see that a fight was going on. I couldn't see who was fighting, but I saw flying fists, heaving bare chests, thick arms, and insanely-large thighs. There were a few people—well, a few fae—beating the shit out of each other.

"I didn't know there were windows," I said, my eyes glued to the fight.

"Ana hid them all behind bookshelves," Mare murmured, her eyes just as glued to the fight as mine were.

"I'm out." Dots beelined it for her room.

I looked in her direction, frowning as her door shut hard.

"Abusive dad growing up. Abusive boyfriend from sixteen to twenty-two. Life's been a lot better for her since she accidentally got transported here," Sunny told me. "And she wouldn't mind me telling you. We're a family, for better or worse."

Damn.

That made my throat close up, just a little.

One of the guys slammed his fist into another's face, knocking him out.

I winced at the sight—and then froze when Calian grabbed the next guy.

He was the one who had knocked the other one out.

Oh, shit.

"Is this my fault?" I asked aloud.

"I'm thinking yes..." Mare trailed off.

Another two gigantic guys went down.

Calian was a damn *beast*.

Sunny whistled. "Guess we know why he's sort of their king."

My gaze jerked toward her. "He's *what*?"

"The unseelie don't have packs, or families, or organization at all. The Wild Hunt keeps everyone safe… and Lian runs it, even if the others won't admit it. One of his buddies told me that," Sunny said, her gaze glued to the fight. "The running joke is that he's the Savage King. The unseelie king, who is actually a king, they call the Tamed King. He's a really boring guy but apparently already mated to a previously-human chick."

"Damn."

I continued staring out the window.

The more I saw, the more I understood the word used to describe him.

Savage.

I had seen more fights than most people could imagine, but I'd never seen anyone move like that. So easily, like fighting came as naturally to him as breathing.

The fae guys went down, one, by one, by one.

All of us watched, both in awe and horror.

"These guys believe in soulmates," Mare whispered to me.

"Not the same way we do, though. They think you have multiple possible soulmates, but the bond doesn't grow until you've picked one. Your magic will grow wilder and more uncontrollable until you're bonded, though, after you've met a potential mate. If word spreads that the king started bonding to you…" She trailed off. "Usually, they have five years to meet us for themselves, so they can decide whether or not they want us."

"How long until the magic gets too wild?" I checked.

"A couple of weeks, I think. Maybe a couple of months. We've never seen it, so all we know is what the other seelie guys told us." Sunny shrugged. "And none of them wanted us."

"Not for lack of trying," Mare muttered.

I felt bad, but didn't know what else to say.

The fighting finally ended as the last fae crashed to the ground, leaving Calian standing on his own. He wiped a bit of blood from beneath his nose—it looked like it had been broken—and smeared it on the blood-spattered tank top he had on.

Then he stepped back and leaned up against the window.

The whole stronghold was invisible, somehow, so he probably didn't know it was a window.

I stared at his biceps, though.

So.

Damn.

Huge.

The other fae began to get up. I couldn't hear what they were saying, but they looked angry.

Some of them clenched their fists.

"They're going to start fighting again," Sunny said, surprise flooding her voice.

"I'm not sure whether to sit down and enjoy the show with some kind of sick satisfaction or try to intervene," Mare admitted.

Sunny stepped around the couch closest to us and dropped onto the cushions. "What do you think they're fighting over?"

"The guys probably want to meet January, to see if she's their potential mate too. If I had to guess, I'd say Lian's answer is no, and they don't like it."

My face paled.

Shit, what if that really *was* what they were fighting over?

The fighting had made Dots uncomfortable in her own home, and I knew how shitty that was.

"If they don't stop soon, I'll go out there and break it up," I said, biting my lip and hoping the fight would come to an end.

Another fae went down, and another, and another.

How long would Calian really last with all of those guys coming at him?

EIGHT

THERE WASN'T a clock to let me know how much time passed, but I waited as long as I could stomach it before going out there. I'd seen too many fights, but that didn't mean I enjoyed watching them. And eventually, I got too damn tired of watching Calian pummel people.

Plus, they were tiring him out. He was taking more hits—and his nose was bleeding more—the longer he stayed out there.

Something about that made me feel more nauseous than the way he knocked them out so easily. The fae healed so fast that it wasn't even a big deal to get knocked out, but his blood...

No, I was *not* going to sit around and think about why I hated seeing him bleeding so damn much.

"Good luck," Mare murmured, looking more ill than my twisted abdomen felt.

"May the force be with you," Sunny called, her fingers lifted toward me with the middle and ring finger separated. I was pretty sure the hand thing was something from *Star Trek*, and the *force* thing from *Star Wars*, and bit back a snort at the pop culture references.

I was getting slightly faster at undoing all the locks, but still struggled with some of the heavier ones. A couple minutes had gone by when I finally tugged the heavy-ass door open, and I reeled backward when I found the men fighting right outside the door. There were a lot more of them than I thought there had been when I'd been looking out the window, and—

"Get back inside and lock the damn door," Calian snarled at me, interrupting my thoughts.

His cursing—and his anger—surprised me.

He'd been so *tame* the last few times we talked.

It caught me off guard, but I recovered quickly.

"Why the *hell* are you fighting right outside my house?"

Technically, the Stronghold wasn't mine, or really a house, but I was rolling with it.

"Get back inside."

His voice was rougher, and sharper. If I had been someone softer, maybe the change would've scared me. But I understood anger, and could tell his wasn't directed at me.

"Stop fighting," I snarled back.

Someone's fist collided with his temple, and he staggered backward a bit.

Shit, that was a hard hit. Hard enough to kill a human man, at least.

Enough was enough.

I shoved past a few men, who seemed to be waiting their turns for a fight or something, and threw myself between Calian and the guy hauling ass toward him.

My self-preservation wasn't really shining in that moment, but I had healed really fast the day before.

And I was a phoenix, so according to my knowledge, I may as well have been unkillable.

Multiple men roared as two of the fae barreled toward me.

Time seemed to slow down.

The men's eyes went huge; they couldn't stop.

Adrenaline pounded in my chest, loud enough to flood my ears with the sound of my heartbeat.

Calian ripped me backward, his back crashing to the dirt loud enough to rattle both of our bones. He rolled us both, twice, before we stopped. In an instant, he was crouched over me, shifting and roaring.

I gawked upward as the gorgeous man morphed into a massive gray dragon.

Some of the fae scattered.

Others shifted too.

And in a few moments, I was flat on my back, staring out at a group of mystical creatures in shock.

There were dragons.

There were phoenixes.

There were basilisks.

There were sabertooth *creatures*.

There were even fiery hellhounds.

Most of them were snarling.

All of them looked furious.

But none looked quite as pissed as the dragon above me, who had literal fire licking off his scales, curling into the air.

Maybe dragons didn't only *breathe* fire in this world.

Something thrummed within me.

Something foreign, and big, and deadly, and...

Alive.

"Oh, shit," I rasped.

And then, I caught fire too.

It was like the thrumming thing inside me had gotten too big to stay contained.

I felt my body change.

It didn't hurt—it actually felt good. Like stretching, but more dramatic.

My muscles and bones settled into their new positions, and I looked down at myself.

My gigantic legs—or claws, or talons, or whatever you called bird legs—looked as if they were made of gold. But the gold didn't look solid, it looked *molten*, like it was moving or flowing, even though I couldn't feel it in motion.

The feathers that met the golden legs were all the colors of a fire, with reds and oranges and golds and blues and whites melding together. Physical flames danced over them, rustling them as the fire swirled.

Damn...

I was gorgeous.

And strong.

Though I wasn't small, and was definitely solid, I could just barely feel the dragon's chest resting against the top of my head. He was breathing hard—and still roaring at the other fae.

I wanted to duck out from underneath him and spread the large wings I could feel tucked against my sides, but we were already in a shitty situation.

Ducking out?

Bad move.

What I needed to do was shift back so I could talk some sense into the bastard who had been fighting so damn many other fae, but I had no idea how to do that.

As if that one simple thought—that I wanted to shift back—was enough, my body began to change again.

The shift back was just as smooth as the first one had been, my body morphing as if it was something I'd been doing my whole life.

I landed on steady legs, staring in shock at my arms, hands, and the rest of my body.

I had shifted.

Into a damn bird.

There were even a couple of golden feathers on the ground, as physical evidence.

The dragon above me shifted in the blink of an eye, and then was a gigantic fae dude roaring at the other men while blocking me from their sight with his massive body.

I was slightly disoriented, but glanced down at myself and realized quickly why he was blocking me.

Oh, wow.

Yep.

Naked.

No wonder he brought me the fireproof lingerie.

"We have a right to meet her," one of the other men snarled back, speaking above the other growling and snapping creatures. "You can't *claim her.*"

"I can and *did.* Touch her and your life will end. Go ahead; test me."

Something told me this was what the whole savage thing was about. Dude had a murderous streak.

That was my cue to get right the hell out of there.

I took one big step backward—only to have Calian spin around, putting his back to all the men who seemed to want him dead, and plaster his bare chest to mine.

Did I have to wonder if he was naked?

No, I did not. There was definitely an overly-large dick pressed up against my abdomen.

And I *really* didn't hate it as much as I should've.

Like, not at all.

Which was a problem of its own, but one that my future self was going to have to deal with.

"What are you doing?" he growled at me.

"You threatened to kill all of them," I whispered back. "Violently."

His eyes flashed to a steely gray that matched his dragon scales. "You are *mine.*"

"That's exactly why I'm leaving. Out of here. Now. Should've been ten minutes ago. Why aren't they attacking you?" I was still whispering, and my words and brain were jumping around like popcorn in the microwave.

"You risked your life already. They won't dare put you in danger again."

"I think I should go. Now." I said curtly, though I didn't move.

"On that, we agree." His words were low and growly.

Before I could try to take a few steps, to walk away on my own, his arms were around my back. He pinned me tighter to his chest, then lifted my feet unceremoniously off the ground and hauled me back to the doorway.

Where he proceeded to set me down on my feet.

And then he stepped back, and shut the door.

I stared at the back of the thing like it could answer the many concerning questions running through my mind.

But it couldn't.

"Wow," Sunny remarked.

She was sitting on the floor, having apparently pulled a couch up close enough to see out the door. Mare sat next to her, and I swear they would've been eating popcorn if any was available.

"That was better than a movie theater," she added.

"Are you as confused as I am?" I asked her, looking between both of them. "Did you see everything?"

"Yes to both questions," Mare said.

A loud crashing noise had all three of us jerking our gazes back to the window, where we saw that the men had resumed fighting. Only now, they were fighting in their beast forms. Things looked... more intense.

And bloodier.

"I've got to stop this before someone dies," I told the girls. "How?"

"You've got to put some clothes on," Sunny corrected me. "Going out there naked isn't going to do a damn thing."

She was right.

I needed to stop them, though.

Calian had seemed mostly sane before he was surrounded by guys trying to... what, talk to me? Meet me? Sniff me? He'd already threatened the hell out of them to the point where I didn't think any of them would dare try to touch me.

If it would stop them from killing each other, I'd meet every damned fae and each of their dogs. There was nothing that stuck with a person the way a death did.

Nothing.

Despite all of the insanity, I still shuddered as the face of my foster dad crossed my mind.

"I need to get him away from them," I said aloud. "And alone. Using his name is supposed to call on him. Do either of you know what that means exactly?"

Both girls shook their heads.

"Guess I'm going to find out." I paused. "After I get dressed."

I jogged over to my room, which thankfully wasn't far, and slammed the door shut behind me.

After grabbing the first pair of fireproof clothes I could reach, I tugged the charcoal-colored tank over my head. The straps were spaghetti-style, but felt plenty sturdy as it settled into place. And Dots was right; it did somehow hold my boobs in the way a bra should—only far more comfortably.

The shorts were just as comfortable, and for once, I was glad I had ignored my first instinct.

"I'm not sure how this is supposed to work," I mumbled to myself, feeling incredibly stupid as I looked around the room. "Calian?" I spoke his name, and felt a sort of magical tug in my chest that I couldn't explain. "Calian, I'm... calling on you? Come here, I guess?"

My words weren't very magical, but following them, there was a sort of shimmer in the room. Then there was a gigantic, bloody man surging toward me.

He stopped before we collided, blinking in surprise as he looked at me, and then around the room. His pupils were dilated, and he looked even more wild than he had earlier.

I hated that I found it kind of sexy, and ignored the hell out of *that* feeling.

"I can't believe that worked," I said aloud.

His eyes softened slightly. "You used my full name; of course it worked."

"That's not a thing where I'm from," I reminded him.

"Of course." He ran a hand over his head, making his wild, sweaty hair stick up with blood. It was black, so at least the color hid the dark red fairly well.

"You went crazy," I told him, matter-of-factly.

"Not crazy. I knew exactly what I was doing. When your mind is shifted, things just look different." His eyes closed for a moment.

I waited for him to thank me for stopping him from murdering more people, but he didn't.

"I'm pretty sure you owe me a thank-you," I drawled, putting a hand on my hip.

His eyes opened and narrowed at me. "I'm still going to kill any of them who refuse to back down. You're *mine.*"

"I don't think you realize how annoying it is to hear that," I shot back. "I'm not a possession. What if I kept calling you mine and started attacking everything that looked at you?"

His eyes flashed, and he took a step toward me, stopping with his chest only a breath away from mine. He leaned his head down, and I tilted mine back. If I'd gone up on my tiptoes, my forehead would've kissed his chin. His voice was low and smooth when he murmured, "Then I'd be a *very* lucky man."

I scowled. "You are so full of it."

"And you are so damn beautiful."

There was a tense moment of silence before I finally stepped back and shook my head, hard.

Maybe if I kept shaking the damn thing, I'd lose the interest in this damned fae that just kept getting bigger and bigger. He was an enigma, and I hated how much I liked that.

"What do those guys want, exactly?" I asked him curtly.

His eyes narrowed. "To spend enough time with you to establish that you are in fact not theirs. Which I already know."

I scowled back at him. "What if you were them?"

"I knew the moment I caught the scents of the other women that they weren't mine, just as I knew the moment I smelled you that you were. The fact that they're too weak or too oblivious to do the same is not my problem."

What a *bastard*.

I had to admit that I could see his point of view, though. My world was every man for himself, same as this one.

"What would we have to do to prove that to them?" I asked.

"Seal the mating bond."

That sounded like going through with a marriage, which was a hard pass from me.

"Or?" I pressed.

His expression darkened. "Meet them. Which is not an option."

I lifted a hand to my hip. "One of us is going to have to give up here, and it's not me." I gestured between us. "I don't know how you seal a mating bond, and that's not even an option at all. So I need to meet all those bastards."

His eyes went glittery gray again. "Like *hell* you do. All it takes to seal a mating bond is a few promises."

A few promises?

Nope, I was not marrying him. Not a chance in hell.

"What's the worst that could happen if I meet them? One of them might think I smell good?" I demanded.

His fists and jaw clenched.

Shit, the dude was really serious about this possession thing.

Why was that hot?

"No." His voice was hard and flat.

"Seriously, Calian. There's got to be a way for you to accept me going out and talking to those guys." I tossed a hand toward the door out. "The other girls said that it's been *years* since any of the seelies have been attracted to a human. There's no way they're all going to want me when all these other gorgeous chicks are being ignored."

He scoffed. "It has nothing to do with *attraction*. Looking for a mate is about *connection*. It's far better to be alone than to be with the wrong person."

"Exactly, and I'm positive I'm the wrong person for everyone. You included, probably, but it seems a little late to convince you of that."

His scowl deepened. "You're one of us. Seelie. When we look at you, we see fire. Freedom. Refusal to fall in line. For most of us, that will be far more than enough connection."

I tossed a hand in the air. "I don't know what to do with you."

"As I don't know what to do with you," he growled back.

"So what, then? What's the solution? There must be something that would make you willing to walk out there with me. I already have too much death on my conscience; I can *not* take another one."

His eyes darkened. "Fly with me."

I blinked.

Okay, that was not what I was expecting.

"Trusting another with your life is the first step in a mate bond. Fly with me, and I'll let you meet them." He paused, then added in a growl, "Assuming you let me touch you while you meet them. I'll need the contact to stop myself from ripping their throats out."

Well...

That honestly wasn't anywhere near as bad as I thought it was going to be.

I could do that, sure.

But I had to be careful about how I told him that. I already knew Calian well enough to know that he was going to take every inch I gave him.

"I don't know," I grumbled. "You're asking too much, Lian."

I'd never called him by his nickname before, but I thought it was kind of hot, so I was going with it.

And I was a shit liar, but I'd known that for years.

His eyes narrowed further. "Should I add that you'll wear my clothing over yours while you meet them?"

Dammit.

This man was a total bastard, and I hated myself for being *here for it*.

"Fine. I'll fly with you after I meet everyone who's gathered, and you can touch me while I meet them. Not intimately, though." I didn't think that last part was necessary, but I added it just in case.

He grunted an agreement.

I figured that answer was as good as it was going to get.

"All right, let's get this shit over with."

Nine

My gaze was glued to his perfect damned ass as he strode over to my newest bag of clothes. He pulled out a few things I hadn't yet gotten through before tugging out a pair of pants that were clearly his.

I looked at the ceiling, pretending I hadn't been staring at his butt as I drawled, "Putting your own clothing in my bag? Pretty big assumption, buddy."

"I'm a big man," he drawled back.

My eyes tried to drop back to his figure, but I forced them to stay trained on the ceiling.

"And it wasn't an assumption. I knew you'd eventually get curious enough or desperate enough to use my name."

"What the hell does that mean?"

"Your magic will grow wilder the longer we go without sealing the mate bond that's begun growing between us. Mine will, too, but I've had longer to learn it than you have. I can shift and fly out the tension that would grow if you refused to see me; you cannot. The longer we're separated, the more at risk you are of wrestling with your magic until it takes control and forces you to spontaneously shift."

Damn.

"Flying will help. Physical contact of any kind, too."

I couldn't hear him getting dressed, but putting pants on wasn't exactly a loud event.

His hand touched my elbow, and my gaze jerked toward him as that weird electric shock feeling cut through me.

"Why does it feel like that?" I asked him, tugging my elbow away.

"It's the concept of mates. Our magic is meant to complete each other. When yours has to nudge mine, or vice versa, we feel the shock."

"What does that mean, though? Nudge?"

He leaned back against one of the walls, and damn, something about having him in front of me, shirtless and massive and gorgeous… it messed with me. "Your feet were wounded in the forest, after you'd been running; my magic met yours, encouraging it to heal you faster and more effectively. It also helps with hunger, exhaustion, pain, and a few other things."

Shit. "Then how can we be compatible with multiple people?"

"That's only a small possibility. And a connection requires compatible magic, nothing else."

My eyebrows shot upward. "So love doesn't matter."

"*Doesn't matter* is subjective." The man studied me carefully. "My people only started finding mates when we discovered your world, and only a fraction of the women we've brought from your world have proven to be potential mates with any of our people. There are no proven rules for mating; all any of us can do is learn as we go."

He continued, "Among the unseelies, the few mated pairs are not together for love, at least as far as I'm aware. As far as the majority of our people know, a mate bond either happens or doesn't the moment you meet, but those of us functioning as leaders of a sort theorize that it can happen slowly, too. We haven't announced that, though, as the women would likely be bombarded."

Damn, that was *not* what I was expecting him to say.

"So when you call me mate and declare that I'm yours, you're not proposing a romantic relationship? No sex, no kissing, nothing except… touchy, claimy friendship?" I checked.

He remained silent for a moment.

I stared back.

"Shall we get going, as you said?" The bastard gestured toward the door.

"Tell me the truth." I put a hand on my hip.

"The truth?" He lifted an eyebrow.

Bastard was totally avoiding the question, and trying to delay his answer.

"Yes, the truth. If you want to be friends, say that straight-out. If you want to be more, say that. I want to know exactly what I'm getting myself into here." I gestured between us.

"Truthfully, I don't know. I assumed when I first caught your scent that I would be looking for the strength that comes with the bond between us. And then I met you."

"And?" I demanded.

"I find myself feeling urges and desires I didn't know were possible." He continued studying me. "I've never heard of this before. This sex you spoke of. How does it work?"

Oh, no.

Hell no.

I was out.

"Let's go." I grabbed him by the stupidly-attractive arm and dragged him toward the door.

"Your reluctance to speak of it tells me it's something I'll be interested in knowing about," he said, his voice low and sexy.

"Fuck off," I growled back.

"That word translates strangely in my language, you know," he countered. "I've wondered for centuries why the word *connect* is such a popular curse among my people. *Fuck* is only a stronger type of connection, or so the translation magic tells me."

I dragged him through the building, ignoring the stares from Mare and Sunny, as well as the words the man was saying.

None of the women had told me that fae dudes didn't know what sex was.

Did they not know?

I guess none of them had mentioned getting propositioned by fae guys, so...

Shit.

Was I supposed to *tell* him?

What if he attacked me if I did?

A shudder tore through my spine at the thought, at the *memories*.

No, I wasn't going to tell him.

No way in hell could I take that risk.

They had to already know about jerking off, but...

No, I was not thinking about that.

We reached the door, and Calian stopped me with a palm to the stone. "Holding your hand won't be enough," he warned me, his voice low. "The level of possessiveness I feel is..." He seemed to search for a word.

"It's fine, I've seen it. This is my part of the bargain, so I'll uphold it. Don't worry." My voice came out softer than I expected it to, but I didn't want to think about that.

He dipped his head in a nod and worked on the top locks while I started from the bottom. He did a couple more than me, but didn't seem to mind that as he stepped back to let me tug the door open.

Of course, when I pulled the thing open, his hand wrapped around my bicep.

He was trying not to just *grab* me, I could tell. But if he was new to boobs, vaginas, and all other things womanly, then he probably wasn't even sure *how* to grab me.

I found myself pulling his hand off my bicep and dragging it down to my hip. He stilled behind me as I turned my back to his chest, and froze in place when I stepped back far enough that my ass met his crotch.

His erection pressed against my butt, thicker and harder than I knew was possible.

I tried to ignore it, and my screaming conscience as I grabbed his other hand and put it on my other hip.

"If your hands are on me, they're not ripping anyone apart," I told him in a low voice.

He didn't respond.

If that was his first time touching a woman, and he'd really been alive for centuries, I didn't blame the guy for being speechless. First times were a weird, unique thing for everyone.

Even ancient fae bastards.

Our bodies remained practically glued together as we stepped through the doorway.

My heart pounded a hell of a lot faster than it should've, and not because we were stepping out into a lion's den—because of the gigantic rock digging into my ass, and the massive hands on my hips. Those damned palms were so big, and my shorts were so short, that he could've dragged his fingers over my bare thighs if he'd tried.

Luckily, he didn't try.

Or unluckily. I guess it probably depended on your perspective.

But that thick strip of his six-pack pressing against my back made me consider another perspective.

A newer, riskier one.

I wouldn't let myself think about it, though.

"This female is mine," Calian told the group, his voice low and certain. "She wishes to let you smell our combined scent, so you can realize she's not yours. Form a line."

The other men didn't move smoothly, or follow any sort of rhythm, but they made their way into a haphazard line that stretched toward us.

Calian held me securely in place against his chest as the first man stepped up to us. His grip on me tightened as the other man leaned in. The man's nostrils flared as he inhaled.

A moment passed, and then he stepped back, turned, and strode back into the forest I'd hiked through.

Calian's grip tightened when the next man stepped forward and repeated the movements of the first. It tightened again with the third man, and again with the fourth.

He was holding me like I was his anchor as the line of fae dudes kept moving. His grip on me was so tight it borderlined on painful, but I loved it.

I *really* loved it.

I'd never had anyone hold me like that before. Like I mattered to them. Like if anyone made a wrong move toward me, they'd find the end of their lives in the hands that held me so fiercely.

It unnerved the hell out of me too, though.

When the crowd finally dispersed, I eased myself away from Calian. He was reluctant, but let me go without a complaint.

The distance I put between us when I took a couple of steps away helped me breathe a lot easier.

"Now, we fly," Calian told me, his gaze intense as he stared at me.

I jerked my head in a nod, looking at the forest and focusing my attention out there.

I just wanted...

Well, I didn't know what I wanted.

But I had promised a flight, so that's what I was going to do.

My gaze followed Calian's hands to the waistband of his pants, and tracked them as he stripped the clothing off.

Holy hell.

The man was ginormous.

I tried not to stare at his monstrous dick, but totally failed.

When he started changing forms, his intense gaze burning into my damn soul, my gaze followed him.

Something about the way his body morphed and grew and changed was sort of beautiful.

The curve of his huge, smooth head.

The glittering expanse of his wings.

The stretch of his neck as he raised it, his chin lifting.

He was preening for me, I realized, and barely bit back a grin.

This whole damned world was something else altogether.

"I haven't really seen any other dragons," I remarked, stepping up closer to him. His body tensed as I reached a hand toward his body, and I looked up at him, frowning.

His head turned and lowered toward me, giving me permission to touch him, so I carefully lifted it and pressed it to his scales.

They were insanely smooth, and much warmer than I expected.

"You're amazing," I admitted to him, slowly moving my hand over his head. His eyes closed, and he blew a puff of hot air toward me.

A laugh escaped me, and I pulled my hand away.

He stepped back just a little, and then lowered himself to the ground. His head dropped to the dirt, and he gave me an expectant look.

Another laugh almost escaped me.

He was kind of adorable.

Not that I was into adorable—or him.

I wasn't sure how to climb onto a dragon, so I eyed him.

He puffed a little smoke toward me and then wiggled closer.

Fighting another grin, I reached an arm up to his gigantic neck and tried to throw a leg upward. When I moved, he rolled sideways to meet me.

A slightly-terrifying moment later, I was settled on his back with my face snuggled up against his warm, smooth neck.

The thrill of it had my chest clenching, my heartbeat thudding loudly. That magic inside me seemed to be thrumming faster, like it had been earlier when I shifted.

Calian tilted his head back, stretching his neck out and letting loose a thick jet of fire.

Gray flames danced down his neck, reaching toward me.

Despite my instinct to move away from them, to slide off of him or find a way down, I reached toward him.

I had erupted into flames myself earlier, so no matter what my instincts said, his fire wasn't going to kill me.

Calian took off from the ground as his flames circled my wrists, flooding me with a strange, magical heat. The wind whipped against my face, my hair, and my arms, but I didn't pay it a shred of mind; the magic had me completely and utterly enthralled.

Lian's fire snaked its way to my shoulder and then over my torso, growing thicker and brighter as it continued to climb over my body.

The world around me flickered whitish blue, and a heady electric charge cut through my body.

My eyes closed, and everything seemed to spin for a moment.

The heat and flames began to die down, then.

The spinning around me seemed to slow, and I found myself relaxing. My hand on Calian's scales still felt hot, but it also felt right. There was a calmness that accompanied the physical contact, one that I didn't have a name for.

It almost felt like safety.

Whatever it was, a girl could get addicted to a feeling like that.

I found myself leaning down against his neck, my cheek pressed to his scales as my eyes traced the world below us. The forest was so vibrant and alive, the clouds puffy and swirling in the thick wind blowing past us. It didn't seem to mind that Calian was creating his own wind; it just kept moving.

The dragon glanced back at me, as if to reassure himself that I was still there and alive, before he soared higher. My heart and magic thrummed within me, and I felt the power growing wilder, the way he'd told me it would if we didn't seal our bond. It twisted within me, swelling and arching, until I was struggling to breathe.

His voice pierced my mind, a soft but firm stab toward some invisible, undefinable part of me. *"Fly with me, mate."*

As if that was the only encouragement it needed, my magic burst into life.

I felt myself slide off Calian's back as the shift happened. For one heart-wrenching moment, I was free-falling.

Then my wings were spread in the wind, and I was no longer falling.

I was flying.

My heart still pounded, and my head still spun, but now the feelings crowding my mind were ones I'd never known.

Freedom.

Joy.

Peace.

Bliss.

Hope.

The emotions were so strong and thick that my throat was swollen, even in its strange new form.

I had thrown that coin into the fountain and asked the world for a way out, and it had given me something even better.

A second chance at life.

Not just any life, either—a happy life.

If I would've been human in that moment, the eyes that I'd spent so many years training not to cry would've been watering.

I didn't have to fight just to survive anymore.

If I wanted to, now, I could live.

Love.

Enjoy.

My instincts screamed at me that it was just a dream. That the first moment I let myself feel this hope, I would lose everything once again and find myself even worse off than I'd been before.

But for once, I ignored those instincts.

And as fire licked the feathers on my new, powerful body, I let myself love my life so much it hurt.

Ten

Time flew past as Calian and I soared over the forest. I knew which direction I would need to fly to get back to the Stronghold, even though I wasn't sure I could find the clearing easily, and that made me feel better.

When we finally landed, the sun was setting behind the forest. I was grinning like a crazy person, my heartbeat even and happy just like the rest of me.

I had never felt that good before. Not for one minute of my life on Earth.

Calian shifted faster than I did. His nudity didn't faze me as I lunged toward him, throwing myself at him. My arms wrapped around his neck as I hugged his body fiercely to mine, gratitude thick enough to drown a dolphin making my throat swell again.

"That was amazing," I told Calian, squeezing him tightly.

"It was," he murmured, his arms wrapping around my back until his grip on me was as tight as mine on him.

"Thank you," I whispered, my damned eyes stinging. "Thank you so much."

"You shouldn't thank me for something that brought me pleasure, January."

"Just Ari. But shut up and let me thank you."

He chuckled, the sound low and sexy.

I was too exhausted and exhilarated to care. There was a bit of an electric current running between us, too, but I barely noticed it as it slowly worked to drain my exhaustion away.

"Fly with me again tomorrow?" he murmured, his hands sliding up my back until one of them cradled my neck.

I jerked my head in a nod. "Definitely."

"There will be more men outside come morning. I can feel their energy now as they watch us."

The back of my neck prickled, and I fought the urge to turn and look around. "Don't kill them while I sleep," I whispered.

He gave me another low chuckle. "I make no promises."

I bit my lip. "Seriously?"

"If any of them have decided your scent calls to them, they'll try to kill me for the chance to pursue you. So yes, seriously."

Damn him.

"Can you just... sleep on the floor of my room or something? That wouldn't be breaking any rules, right?" I checked.

"There are no rules," he said, his voice flooded with humor and something else I didn't have a name for. "And yes, if you wish, I can sleep in your room."

Good.

No one would die, then.

And since he didn't know about sex, I wouldn't have to worry about him pulling any sketchy shit.

"Okay, then... come on." I stepped back, slipping my hand into his. I tried not to let our fingers slide between each other, but failed, and the damn things knitted together like they had minds of their own.

I kept walking, towing him with me.

We knocked on the door and waited for one of the other girls to open it. Sunny finally answered wearing a big ole' smirk.

"Don't," I warned her, stepping past and tugging Calian in behind me.

"Mmhmm," she said, so damn much sass in that one sound.

I tried to pull my hand out of his, but he picked that moment to tighten his grip, like he'd been expecting me to pull that shit.

I led Calian into my room behind me, and shut the door hard.

He stopped a short way into the room, studying me again as I stood with my back to the door. "You like them."

I knew he was talking about the other women, and I didn't want to acknowledge it. "I don't like much of anything."

His gaze grew a bit curious. "There must be things you liked about Earth."

"If there were, I wouldn't have wished to get away from it."

Suddenly questioning my decision to bring the man into my bedroom, I stepped past him and padded across the room. "I'm going to shower. Stay out here." I'd lock the door, but the warning would help.

After grabbing another pair of the clothes I'd left strewn all over my bed like a damned slob, I ducked into the room and shut the door.

Having the slab of stone between me and Calian made me feel slightly better, even if I knew he could probably break through it if he wanted.

I rested my back against it, my eyes closing.

There was a quick knock on the door a moment later. "January?" Lian murmured.

It didn't seem to matter how many times I told him to call me Ari.

"What?"

"Would you mind if I stepped out to make you something to eat? Or would you rather I wait until you're finished in the shower?"

My mind blanked for a long moment.

Had he just... asked me what I wanted?

What the hell?

Who did that?

"Uh..." I paused after saying the word, not sure what I would prefer.

I definitely wouldn't say no to food, but something about the idea of him being out there chatting with the other human girls while I was in the shower made my jaw clench.

"Just wait for me," I finally said.

"Of course." His voice was soft, but I could picture that damned gorgeous smirk of his.

I stepped further into the bathroom, and my gaze caught on my reflection in the mirror.

Damn, I looked... different.

My hair was still its usual dark blonde, but the color seemed richer. Shinier.

When I turned my head, I noticed that my ears were pointed at the edges and lifted my fingers up to them, to trace the new shape.

"Damn," I murmured to myself.

Physically, my body shape was the same—curvy, but not super curvy—only my skin looked sort of... glowy.

When I got closer to the mirror to see my eyes better, I was startled to see that their usual muddy brown had morphed into a vibrant green color that reminded me of the leaves on so many of those crazy-looking trees in the forest.

My gaze traced my arms and legs, looking for some kind of magical tattoo. Disappointment flooded me when all I found was more glowy skin.

Oh well, I'd survive.

Glancing over at the shower, I hesitated. I'd been on fire for most of the day—literally—and didn't feel dirty in the slightest. I actually felt really, really good.

And food sounded great, even though I wasn't very hungry.

Would it be gross to forgo a shower in favor of watching the fae dude who claimed I was his cook for me?

I guessed I could help him, too, if I wanted to be nice.

My teeth caught on my bottom lip while I debated my options.

Ultimately, the smartest choice would've been to take a long shower and then feign exhaustion and go to sleep. That would buy me time away from Calian and the other girls, and prevent me from bonding with them further in any way that might make me sad when they inevitably ended up treating me shitty, betraying me, or being taken away.

My self-preservation instincts had my thoughts spiraling into defense mode, preparing for the worst.

But the hope and happiness that had begun to sprout in my chest while I was flying whispered that I should make another choice.

One that I would *enjoy.*

I didn't want to accept that I was choosing hope, but I found myself yanking the door open anyway. My eyes widened when I found Calian putting the clothes I'd left on the bed away in the closet.

He glanced over his shoulder at me, and my chest squeezed when he gave me a slow, sexy smile.

Panic had me shutting the door again, harder.

Nope.

Screw off, hope.

Shower it was.

Eleven

Half an hour later, I padded out of the bathroom, wrapped in a towel. My body was so relaxed from all the warm water that I couldn't even bring myself to worry about the man I knew would be somewhere in the room, waiting for me.

And yep, there he was: sprawled across my bed like he owned the damn thing.

He was the one who had picked up the blankets and sheet and everything else from wherever it had been before he gave it to me, so I couldn't exactly hold it against him. Plus, he looked really damn delicious draped over the bed like that, which did a number on whatever anger I should've felt.

My hair hung tangled down my back, water dripping from the ends as I headed to the closet. The bags and everything that had been inside them were put away, and as expected, I found them tucked neatly into the closet along with the rest of my clothes. My gaze dragged over all the pairs of comfortable, fireproof clothing, but lingered the longest on the section that I hadn't seen yet.

A few pairs of pants (way too long to be my own) and a couple of muscle-tees like the one Calian had been wearing the day we met.

So I could wear my clothes... or his.

So many options.

I didn't mind that fact as much as I expected to.

The shorts and tank top felt like another layer of skin as I pulled them on. Most of them were in shades of black and gray, which I liked, but I picked out a set that was made of deep crimson fabric. Something about the color reminded me of flying, and I loved flying.

I didn't want to go out and hang with the girls in shorts that only covered a little more than underwear, so I grabbed a pair of Calian's pants and tugged them up my legs. The fabric was thin and ridiculously soft, and I found myself petting it like it was a damn dog.

That was weird, I knew, so I stopped before I stepped out of the closet.

His eyes devoured me the moment he could see me again, the orbs hooded as he just *stared*.

How was he so damned gorgeous?

And how did he make me feel so much, especially when I was trying so hard not to be affected by him?

"Ready?" he asked.

"Yep." I tried not to let him see how much he was affecting me. "Let's go."

The man eased himself up off the mattress, and I almost drooled at the way his abs looked while he moved.

He grabbed one of his tees off the dresser and tugged it on before he pulled the door open. When he gestured for me to go first, I slid through, ignoring the way his eyes made me feel like my damned skin was burning.

"You're beautiful," he murmured to me.

I ignored the compliment, but felt my face flushing anyway.

"The kitchen's over here," I told him, feeling a couple of stares on us as we walked. Sunny, Mare, and Dots were on the couch, watching a movie, as far as I could tell without looking back at him.

"She'd better be tapping that," Sunny muttered.

"I'd give up a boob," Dots agreed.

My face flushed hotter.

This was a terrible idea.

"Maybe we should—" I began, but Calian cut me off by grabbing me by the waist. He set me on the countertop in one fluid motion, not at all winded by having just dead-lifted my heavy ass.

"You don't know our spices, I assume," he said, brushing a chunk of wet hair off my face with the back of his fingers. I acted like the touch hadn't made goosebumps erupt over my arms and legs.

"I don't know any of your foods," I agreed. "The main thing we eat here seems like your version of our rice and beans, but tastes better."

He made a noncommittal noise. "No one taught you how to make it."

I looked at the other girls. They were the ones who had cooked.

Mare shook her head, though she was fighting a smile.

"They figured it out," I told Calian, looking back at him.

He flashed me a smirk. "I'm sure they did."

The man turned back to the stove. He didn't move flawlessly through the human-style kitchen, but also didn't have a problem going through cupboards to find everything he needed. I found myself studying every movement he made, tracking his body and following every move of his muscles.

He didn't touch my hair again as he cooked, but explained to me the names of each of the foods, as well as what kind of plant they came from. It turned out that the "beans" we'd been eating were meant to be boiled, mashed, and then whipped, and the "rice" was supposed to be fried in a pan with a bit of some strange kind of oil.

When he started seasoning things, he filled a tiny bowl with the oil and dipped a finger into it, before shaking a tiny bit of the seasoning onto his finger and holding it out to me. "Taste."

I stared at him for a long moment before finally shaking my head and forcing myself to snap out of it. "What?"

"Taste, so you know the flavor." His lips were curved up in a wicked smirk. "Unless you're scared."

Bastard.

He must've already realized that I typically refused to admit to being or feeling scared. Fear was good for nothing other than realizing that shit was about to hit the damned fan.

"So much better than a movie," Dots whispered from the living room.

I flipped her the bird without looking over, and earned a round of snorts and quiet laughs.

Bitches.

I hated that I liked them.

With a sigh, I parted my lips.

He slipped his finger into my mouth, and left it there as I licked the seasoning off the huge digit.

The flavors that hit my tongue were nothing I had words to describe—but tasted really good.

"Wow," I managed, as he pulled his finger away and put it in his own mouth.

Nope, I was not acknowledging that he'd licked my saliva off his skin.

He washed his hands with the bar of rough soap beside the sink, then returned to cooking.

I thought I was in the clear, but after a couple of minutes passed, he repeated the process with another spice.

His smirk was back, his gaze hot as he lifted his finger to my lips.

Oohs and snorts came from the peanut gallery again, and I ignored them this time.

"I can do it myself," I countered, pushing his hand away.

His eyes turned the gray of his dragon form, and he reached forward, dragging his finger over my bottom lip. The touch surprised me, and the warmth that slowly blossomed on my skin was weird.

My tongue slid out to drag over the seasoning, surprising me with its light, sweet flavor.

"This one is rubbed into the skin when someone is sore or in pain," he told me, lifting his finger back to his lips and cleaning it quickly. "It warms and relaxes you. Makes injuries bearable."

"What would happen if someone put it on their genitals?" one of the girls asked from the other room.

Dammit, Dots.

"Theoretically," she added hastily.

Calian didn't so much as glance at her, his intense gaze focused solely on me. "Hours of fierce pleasure." His eyes lowered to my lips. The bottom one was still warm and tingly, and starting to feeling a bit swollen too, but not in an uncomfortable way.

"Get back to cooking," I grumbled at the man.

A smirk teased his lips again, his body relaxing as he turned back to the stove.

My mind spun a bit.

He didn't know about sex... but of course, he knew about masturbating. There was no way that, in a world full of men, no one had figured out how to jack off.

Dammit. Now I had that oh-so-pleasant thought keeping me company.

He repeated the tasting thing a few more times as he made our meal. Despite the intensity of the last thing he made me taste, I parted my lips when he brought his finger to them.

I was weak...

And he was gorgeous.

And the fact that he was giving me his complete attention while also cooking for me did not pass my notice.

CALIAN'S VERSION of beans and rice was a hell of a lot better than ours. The rest of the girls and I downed it like we were starving, all of us seated randomly around the couch, and North in her room of course. Mare had been writing notes while Lian was cooking, and she questioned him further while we ate. He was relaxed, sitting a little too close to me and working on his own bowl of food.

When we were done, the girls turned the movie they had been watching back on. It was a chick flick, which I wasn't sure I really wanted Calian to see, but I didn't want to take him back to my room either.

We watched for about an hour before things got steamy—and my face got really damn red.

Calian was watching the screen with way too much interest, so I grabbed his hand and towed him to my bedroom, muttering a goodnight.

The bastard was going to have way too many questions for me.

He didn't ask a thing though, as I locked the door and made my way over to the bed. When I plopped down on it, I sprawled out over the middle so the bastard would know I wasn't inviting him to sleep with me.

The room was dead silent after he settled on the ground, a couple feet away from my bed.

I felt like a total bitch for not giving him a blanket or pillow, but I only had one of each.

A few long, long minutes passed before I got too stressed to leave the silence between us. "Well?" I demanded.

"Well what?" He sounded amused.

"You must have questions."

"You don't seem interested in answering them, so I planned to keep them to myself." His voice was soft and playful, and I hated the way it calmed my anxiety so immediately.

A heavy sigh escaped me.

I couldn't believe I was going to do it, but...

I was going to do it.

"You've gathered that women's bodies are built differently than men's. You have dicks."

"And you do not," he agreed, his voice still playful.

I grimaced up at the ceiling. "We have breasts and vaginas, instead. Which you've seen. Or at least felt, when we were naked together. Vaginas are... weird."

He was quiet, giving me more time to explain.

"They're sort of the opposite of dicks. Dicks stick out, and vag's... go in. It's kind of like a body-cave. Which sounds disgusting, and is, but dudes like them. Sex is when a dick goes inside a vagina. It's a tight fit, but it works. Theoretically, it's supposed to be pleasurable for both people, but most of the time it's only good for the guy."

The moment was long, tense, and awkward, but there was no way around it. He had to know. And at least he could tell his fae buddies himself, so no other human chicks would have to have the same weird conversation with other dudes.

"That's not a secret," I added. "'You should tell the other guys, so it's not so awkward."

More silence ensued.

Too much silence.

"Are you good?" I asked him.

"If extremely hard and vivaciously curious translates to *good* in your language, then yes," he murmured.

A snort escaped me, and a low laugh came from his side of the room.

A few moments passed before Calian spoke again. "I can understand how sex would be pleasurable for a man, but how does a woman's pleasure work?"

Oh.

Awkward.

Might as well get it over with.

"It's weird. Women have a thing on the outside of their vagina called a clit. It's kind of like a pleasure button, if you use it right. There's another pleasure point inside of a vagina called a g-spot, too, but they're pretty much impossible for guys to find. There are a ton of jokes about them back on Earth because of how shitty men are at making them work.

"Mmm." Calian's voice was low, but flooded with interest. "I assume you've never had a man find yours."

"You assume correctly." I stared at the ceiling, my humor fading. "There's another thing back on Earth, we call it sexual assault. Or rape. It's when a guy forces himself on a woman. You don't have anything like that here, right? Between men or women?"

He growled, "Of course we don't. We like killing far too much. If anyone so much as considered something like that, their death would be horrible."

That made me feel slightly better, even though liking killing didn't exactly seem like a logical reason to not have sexual assault.

"Did that happen to you on Earth?" Calian asked me a few minutes later, his voice lower and deadlier.

I bit my lip, but didn't answer.

"Should any man give you any unwanted touch in my world, you tell me immediately. I will relish his dismemberment," the fae told me.

My throat swelled, but I said nothing.

"Should I ever do anything to hurt you, there's a chink in every dragon's scales. A soft, vulnerable spot, where a knife will end his life instantly. It's in a different place on every dragon, and mine is on the inside of my left thigh, regardless of my form."

Regardless of his form?

"I don't know what that means," I whispered back, though I did know.

He was giving me a way to kill him, in case he ever hurt me.

"Come here," he told me, his voice quiet.

I didn't get up at first, but then curiosity and trust engulfed me so thickly that I could no longer ignore them.

My feet landed on the cold stone, and I shivered a little as I crossed the room. When I kneeled beside Calian, he was already sprawled out on the floor, no pillow or blanket in sight just like I expected.

"Can I take your fingers to the spot?" he asked me, his voice low and steady. His eyes were so gorgeous, the damn things practically held me captive.

I jerked my head in a nod, putting my hand to his.

He dragged my hand over his thigh, and neither of us acknowledged the erection bulging so obviously in the soft material of his pants.

"It's a depression in my skin," he murmured, his fingers wrapping around mine until he had my pointer finger out. When he pressed it lightly into a spot inside his thigh, I felt a small indentation. It was smaller than my pinky, but when I pressed carefully against it, I felt that the skin in that spot was much, much softer than the area around it.

"Can I feel without clothes?" I asked him.

Maybe it was stupid, or ridiculous, but I wanted to know exactly where his weak spot was. Not because I expected I'd need to kill him, but... because I just wanted to know, I supposed.

"You don't need permission, mate. I'm yours to touch," he said, releasing my hand.

I guessed he wasn't going to guide my hand if I put it in his pants, but I didn't mind that.

The fingers touching the spot through his clothes remained where they were, and my other hand slid under the waistband of his pants.

His whole body tensed as my palm dragged over his bare pelvis, past the erection that bobbed for me as I moved past it. His eyes closed, and his jaw clenched as he leaned his head back.

"Are you okay?" I whispered to him, as my fingers found the spot.

He made an agreement-like noise, his jaw still clenched.

My thumb dragged over the *chink in his scales*, and my bare arm brushed against the side of his erection.

We both froze for a moment.

His cock bobbed against the side of my arm, the hot, hard silk dragging against me.

"Shit," I finally whispered. "Sorry."

I carefully withdrew my arm from his pants, trying not to drag it over his erection.

"Do human women often apologize for giving a man the most pleasure he's experienced in his entire life?" Calian asked me, his voice gravelly.

My face flushed. "No."

"Then withdraw yours, January."

I bit my lip. "How does one withdraw an apology?"

"Usually a simple, 'never mind, I'm not sorry,' suffices," Calian drawled back.

His cock was still bobbing in those damn soft pants, though, and the thing was practically hypnotizing me.

I bit my lip harder.

Was I sorry for feeling him?

No, I was not.

And I wasn't about to give him a damned handjob, but *withdrawing an apology* seemed so pointless.

"On Earth, we don't withdraw apologies. We just do things to cancel them out. Like..." I slid my hand into his pants again and wrapped my fingers around the top of his cock, squeezing him. He was so freaking huge, and I could feel a bit of his hot desire leaking on my hand from the head of him. "See? Not sorry."

"Not sorry indeed." His voice was strained.

I couldn't help it; I pumped my hand down his length once, and then dragged it back up.

A snarl escaped him, and he grabbed his erection around my fist as it throbbed with his pleasure, soaking both my fist and his pants.

Shocked pride cut through me, and my body flushed something fierce.

"I am so sorry," he growled at me. "I—"

"No, don't be. I feel... sexy." An awkward laugh escaped me. "And powerful. That's kind of a rush, huh?"

His eyes pierced me to the damn soul, and he said nothing.

I slowly slipped my hand out of his pants, then stood and went into the bathroom.

His eyes tracked me the whole way.

Soap lathered over my fingers as I scrubbed them clean, my mind spinning.

I'd never been completely relaxed with a man since I was attacked. I'd had sex a few times, just to prove to myself that I could, but I'd always felt like he had the power. Like if he wanted to, he could hurt me. And that had scared the hell out of me.

But back there, with Calian, I had felt strong. Powerful.

All I'd done was touch him, and he'd erupted all over my hand.

I had done that; made him feel good.

And shit, that made me feel like I was in charge.

What if *sex* could feel like that?

What if he could get me off, too, and I could feel like that while he did?

What if I could actually enjoy myself while he was touching me, and lose it the way he had?

Did I want that?

My heart clenched.

I did.

I really, really did.

The connection, the relaxation, the pleasure...

It was thrilling.

I couldn't just go out and ask him to touch me though, could I? He hadn't even known what a vagina was, and he wasn't expecting us to fall in love despite our mate-connection thing.

But if he wasn't expecting love...

Well, then maybe the bond between us was perfect.

I could call the shots.

We could make each other feel good.

And the connection between us was so strong and permanent that even if we didn't fall in love, it wouldn't matter. We could just be friends who had awesome sex.

Shit, that sounded amazing.

My mind was made up, as I slipped back out of the bathroom.

We were going to be friends with benefits.

Twelve

Calian had changed into a pair of clean pants and was sitting on the edge of the mattress, shirtless, when I walked back into the room. His arms were positioned on the bed behind him, his body sprawled out, somehow both relaxed and tensed at the same time.

Damn, what a masterpiece.

His eyes tracked my movement like I was his prey.

I'd left my pants in the bathroom, so my legs were mostly bare.

His gaze stroked my skin. Though the room was dark, I felt like he could see every inch of me.

"Thank you," he said to me, his voice low and sensual.

"On Earth, we *show* our thanks." I sat down on his lap, and noticed his fingers dig into the blanket.

"I didn't know if that would be welcome." His eyes dragged over my face and then down to the swell of my breasts, where they lingered. "Nor do I have the experience you deserve from a man who would touch you."

"Not all women want man-whores," I countered.

He gave a low chuckle. "Do I want to know what that means?"

"Probably not." I eased myself further up his thighs, so his erection pressed exactly where I wanted it, but didn't rock against him. The pressure was light, making my body throb. "You don't know what you're doing—but I know exactly how I want you to touch me, and I'm pretty damn sure you're willing to figure it out."

"More than you know." He leaned upward, changing the angle he pressed into me, and my body tensed.

"Put your hands on my hips," I told him, rocking against him lightly. "Touch me however you want."

His hands lifted to my waist, skipping my hips because they were covered. His fingers dragged slowly and reverently over the bare skin there, stroking and tracing it while I continued moving against him, just enough to make myself even more horny.

His hands slid under the hem of my tank, the thick digits dragging over my ribcage.

"Tell me what you're thinking," I told to him, trying not to arch too much as he moved toward my breasts.

"I want to bury my face between your thighs and inhale your scent." His voice was low, his hands sliding further up my ribs until his fingertips found the undersides of my breasts.

I hadn't realized the undersides were sensitive, but when he touched them like that, they sure as hell were.

He took his sweet time, stroking them slowly, taking in every inch of my skin as his hands moved upward. When they finally found my nipples, my head dropped backward and I pressed closer to him, fighting a moan.

"I want to feel these hard tips on my tongue," he said, his voice lower and more gravelly. "I want you to lose yourself to pleasure while I devour your breasts with my hands, with my tongue, with my teeth."

When I started to open my mouth, to tell him that orgasming from tit play alone wasn't really a thing, he gripped my breasts hard enough to make me cry out.

One of his hands let go, just for a moment, and then my skin was bare, my top lost to the bed or the floor.

Wherever it was, it could have it.

His lips were on my nipple a heartbeat later, his palms full of my tits. The way he massaged them was intense, but the way he devoured my nipple was something else altogether. He may not have known what he was doing, but he had heard my command to do whatever the hell he wanted to me—and he was definitely doing it.

He sucked, licked, and lathed until I was snarling at him for more. His teeth finally came out, dragging over my nipple, and I cried out, so damn close to the edge. My hips rocked frantically, using his erection to try to push myself over the edge.

Just before I reached it, his hand left my other breast, grabbing my crotch and squeezing it hard in his hand.

I cried out again, so freaking close.

"Let me use you," I snarled.

"You said I could do whatever I want to you." His eyes were silver, his pupils dilated, and his erection was throbbing against my thigh since his hand was blocking me. "I want you to lose it without my cock or fingers. You're close; I can feel it and smell it."

He could *smell* how close I was to shattering?

How—

His lips wrapped around the nipple they hadn't touched yet. Another cry escaped me as I arched into his hand, and my body clenched around nothing.

That bastard didn't know anything about sex, and still took control when I—

His teeth scraped my nipple, and I was gone.

A scream escaped me, my body arching, and arching, and arching as I shuddered through the orgasm.

It was so much more intense than I'd ever realized it could be.

I was panting when my vision finally cleared and found myself still rocking against his palm.

"I want you on your back," the bastard growled at me, his eyes so bright they were glowing as he continued doing exactly what I'd told him to. "I want to see, touch, and taste every inch of you. I want to bring you pleasure with every body part I have. I want to make you so damn insane that my name is the only word you can think anymore."

Holy hell, what had I done?

I opened my mouth to tell him that wasn't what sex was usually like, but before I could say a thing, he had me on my back on the bed, and was stripping my shorts off me.

My gaze caught on his face and followed it down to those massive muscles, to his otherworldly-perfect body.

His huge hands easily parted my thighs, and then he dragged me toward him until my ass was hanging off the edge of the bed. I pulled the pillow with me, so my head was raised enough that I could see—so I could watch him touch me—watch him taste me—watch him work me with his fingers

My core was open wide to the world, every inch of me exposed to the man staring at me so intensely it was a wonder he didn't burst.

A long moment passed before my core clenched at the weight of his attention, and then he moved.

His nose was at the center of me, inhaling deeply, and a savage snarl flooded the room.

When he lifted his gaze, it was silver again, and glowing. "Mine," he said, his chest heaving.

My eyes were practically dinner plates as I stared back at him. He'd done the possessive thing before, but something about claiming me with his eyes full of my core, with his hands holding me open so he could see every inch of me, was so much bigger.

My lips parted, and I intended to tell him to stop. To tell him that I wasn't as invested as he was, that he didn't own me, that I wasn't his.

But then his thumb dragged over my clit, and my brain short-circuited.

And then his tongue dragged up my center, from the top to the very bottom.

In that moment, I probably would've agreed that I belonged to him if it would get me a few more minutes with the man.

But he didn't ask me to agree.

He just devoured me.

His hands parted my center, releasing my thighs, which immediately clamped around his head. He used his tongue, his lips, his teeth, his nose, his fingers... every damn part of him worked my body, feeling my core and rubbing my clit. The scruff on his face burned, but in a way that drove me insane.

I shattered in less than two minutes, my body completely new to being touched and loved the way Calian was doing it. The scream he got out of me was small and hoarse, and the only acknowledgment he gave it was a bite to my clit that made me jerk in his arms.

The pressure was so intense, and he never let up—not when I shattered a third time, or fourth.

I was gasping, sucking in massive breaths of air after the fourth orgasm, and he was still going so hard.

"I want your cock," I snarled at him, my heart pounding and my desperation growing as my breathing started to go ragged again.

"Give me one more." He lifted his glowing gaze from my core for the shortest second.

The way he was looking at me, his face wet with my body's desire, paired with the brutal way he continued to work me, had me screaming again a moment later. This one was different, though—I felt my body gush as the pleasure hit a level I'd never experienced.

Did I just squir—

Calian interrupted my thoughts when he rose to his feet, his grip on my thighs still tight in the best way. His pants were gone, his cock dripping as it bobbed, and his eyes still glowing.

"You are mine," he told me, his voice low as he lined himself up against my entrance.

I was too far gone to listen to his words.

My legs hooked around his ass as he plunged into me, my body arching at the thick, heady pleasure of being filled so completely.

He was huge, and hot, and—

He thrust in and out once, and then again.

I felt like I was being broken and remade again, into something fiercer, hotter, needier, and—

He roared.

The room flooded with fire, and I screamed with him as we lost it together. The pleasure was so much that I saw stars.

Everything smelled burnt when he grabbed me off the bed and pulled me to his chest, his eyes still silver. He was looking at me like a dragon, not just a man—and it was hot.

Or it would've been, if I wasn't so thoroughly spent.

My body felt heavy as he stood, holding me against him.

Electricity danced between us, the magic of our bond probably working in overdrive as it attempted to recharge us after *that.*

"I'm taking you to my mountain," he told me.

I nodded against his chest, pretty damn sure that one or both of us had burned everything in my room, if the smell was any indication.

There was a moment's pause, and then we shot up into the air. Lian shifted as we soared, my body glued to and protected by his as a massive cracking noise sounded.

Had he broken the damn Stronghold?

A moment later, I felt the breeze on my bare skin. I could hear the flap of wings even though I didn't open my eyes to see what was flapping. It had to be Calian—there weren't really any other options.

When I paid attention to the place our skin met, I realized that I felt scales where his skin had been, and I relaxed slightly. He must've been holding me against his lower belly, in his gigantic talons. Enough of my body was covered that I knew I wasn't flashing the world below us.

The rhythmic flapping of his wings lulled me into a thick, heavy sleep.

Thirteen

I woke up with my entire bare, sweaty body plastered to Calian's. His erection dug into my leg, my nose was resting against his neck, and his arms were holding me securely.

It probably should've made me feel trapped.

Instead, I just felt comfortable.

My hair was glued to both of us, the long strands stuck to our skin in random chunks, bits, and pieces. When I tried to move my head, a bunch of different strands tugged right back.

Yep, definitely trapped.

"January?" the big lug mumbled, his voice thick and gravelly.

At least I wasn't the only wrecked one. "What the hell happened?"

"We had sex."

I scowled into his neck. "I remember that part, thanks."

His hands gripped my ass. "Had to make sure."

"What happened afterward?"

"A mating bond, I think. It's a hell of a lot stronger than the ones between the other humans and fae, though."

"Shit," I mumbled.

"I have more power running through my veins than I ever knew was possible. Whatever the connection did, it's far from a bad thing," the man said, his voice low.

It was time to change the subject. "How long have we been out?"

"Sun's rising, so a few hours. My brothers are probably on the way." That last part, he said with a grumble.

"Your brothers?"

"The rest of the Wild Hunt. We're the strongest seelies, so we work together to keep the unseelie bastards on their side of the world. Usually, it's not a big deal. Sometimes it is."

Dammit, there was so much more to this world than I knew. If I was aware of all the right questions to ask, maybe I could start figuring shit out. But I was so damned clueless about so many things.

"Do you have clothes for me?" I checked.

"No. I picked them up after I grabbed your blanket and pillow from here." His hands slid up my bare back, following the curve of it as well as sliding down to my waist.

I wanted to hate the contact, but couldn't.

"Look, about the sex," I began.

Somehow, I had to make sure the bastard and I were on the same page. It was incredible sex, but I was not his wife. I wasn't going to follow his damned orders, live in his house, or do anything else wifely.

He was still mostly a stranger to me.

"Hmm?" His hands slid down my back, dragging over my ass and wrapping around it.

Shit, he was going to make me horny again.

"We had sex, and it was great, and I know we have no control over the mating bond thing you've mentioned so many times, but I'm still not your possession. You can call me whatever you want, but as far as I'm concerned, nothing has really changed."

Except that I was looking forward to having sex with him every day, assuming he was on board. And no way was he stupid enough not to be on board.

He didn't respond, so I went on, "I'm still going to live in the Stronghold. If you broke it, you're going to have to fix it. I'm not moving in with you. We're not a couple. We're just... friends with benefits."

"You say that like it's a term I should know."

"It's a human idea. Friends who have sex. *With benefits* just sounds more polite, I guess."

"Then *with benefits* would be the unseelie way of saying things." His hands squeezed my ass. "I hear what you're saying and respect your opinions."

"My *opinions*?" The annoyance in my voice was thick.

"Yes, *opinions*."

"Screw you," I hissed, rolling off of his body. "I wasn't giving you my opinions, I was telling you what's going to happen between us. You can't force me to be your wife."

The sound of flapping wings cut off our argument.

"We *will* talk about this later," I practically snarled to him, my head jerking around as I tried to establish where I was and where I could find clothes.

There were only three walls around me, and none of them were actual walls. They were slabs of stone, curved and oddly shaped, as if they were part of an overhang that created an almost-cave.

Considering I could see trees out in front of me where the fourth wall should've been, I decided I really was inside some kind of shallow cave.

Calian crossed the room in two strides and grabbed a set of clothes off a rack of sorts that I noticed as soon as he was close to it. He was back at my side in a heartbeat, tugging the gigantic muscle-tee over my head.

"Better keep those breasts hidden," he said playfully, helping me as I shoved my arms through the holes while also glaring at him. "They're mine."

I scoffed as he calmly bent down and held the pants out toward me. Despite my frustration, I shoved my feet into the leg holes. "Better get some pants on that ass," I shot back. "It's *mine*."

The gaze he gave me from where he kneeled in front of me was a hot one, but kind of smirky too. "Yes, it is."

He slid the pants up my thighs. The way he looked at me while he did so made me feel like the fabric was his hands on my skin.

Bastard can't even let me get the upper hand when I sass him.

He was pulling his own pants on when a massive phoenix fell out of the sky, shifting dizzyingly-fast as he spiraled downward. The man landed on his feet without so much as a wince, despite the ridiculous fall he'd just survived. Or performed, I supposed.

It was the jacked guy with the buzzed hair and bicep tattoos, the one who had claimed I was one of his on that first day when they stole me from Earth. His gaze wasn't nearly as intense as it had been when we met, but was now flooded with interest as it swept up and down my figure.

I resisted the urge to wrap my arms around my probably-pointy nipples and instead put my hands on my hips. "What do you want?"

A group of three animals came running and slithering over the ledge the phoenix guy had landed on. My eyes widened as they all shifted back to their male forms. They were all bigger than the creature-forms of any of the fae Lian had introduced me to outside the Stronghold the day before, and if I looked closely at one of them, I could sort of *feel* his magic.

From what I could feel, their magic was really damn strong.

But what could the fae even do with their magic, other than shifting forms?

The fiery bear-dog, which I knew was a hellhound, shifted into the blond, inked-up guy with the feral grin from that first day. The sabertooth-monster shifted into the tight pants guy with the shortish hair. The gigantic snake thing changed into man-bun guy and his short-shorts.

Damn, that was a lot of huge, manly dudes in a small space.

Calian stepped up behind me and wrapped his arm around my waist, pulling my ass back to his erection.

How was he always hard?

"What happened?" the phoenix guy asked, his head tilting sideways a little.

I wondered if I did bird-like shit when I was in my human form.

Part of me expected Calian to give them a savage grin and declare that *sex* had happened, but of course, he didn't.

"My female and I have become one," he said instead. "The bond has settled between us."

"Damn." The sabertooth guy grimaced. "Anyone who didn't have the chance to catch her scent will want you dead."

"I look forward to the fight," Calian said, his voice filling with that savagery I'd been waiting for.

At least it wasn't geared toward sex, though. For now.

"I can't believe you convinced the poor little beast to mate with you so quickly," the hellhound guy drawled. "She seemed so *fiery*."

"*She* is," I growled back. "We had sex. If I had known it was going to mate us, I would've thought twice about it."

That last part was a lie.

It had been so damn good I still would've done it.

But at least then I would've known what I was getting myself into.

"Sex?" The basilisk guy looked at Calian.

"A connection of bodies and souls," Lian replied.

Cryptic bastard.

There was no point in dancing around it. Guess I was explaining it to the other fae after all.

"Men have dicks. Women have vaginas. Dicks fit inside vaginas. When it happens, it's called sex." I gave a shitty explanation but saw the gears in their minds turning.

Had they done something to the other human women to make them stay quiet about it? Or had the women just kept their mouths shut because they didn't know that the fae were so unaware, like the girls back in the Stronghold?

I was going to need to tell them about the whole sex thing when I got back there. No way around that, no matter how much I wanted there to be one.

"Shit," the hellhound guy growled, glancing behind him, as if looking toward the Stronghold.

"If any of those women were meant for you, their scent would have infected every thought that goes through your mind," Lian warned him, his voice low and dangerous.

The hellhound guy growled back, *"Probably,"* but made no move to turn around. I remembered what Calian had said, about the leaders thinking that mate connections could possibly happen over time too, even though they hadn't proven it.

"None of my people had a chance," the sabertooth guy said, his voice lowering. "When they hear about sex, they will come for you."

"I'll await it eagerly," Lian drawled.

A snort escaped the phoenix guy, and I jerked my head toward him as he said, "Your power feels like mine now, brother."

Calian's chuckle made my shoulders relax slightly. "It feels different. Both phoenix and dragon." He held out an arm, and I watched fire dance along it. The flames looked different than they had the day before—less like his and more like mine. "What do the borders look like?"

"No sign of unseelies yet, but they'll be sending a party to check after the disturbance of your mating. You should meet them there."

Lian dipped his head in a nod. "We'll head there after we pick up clothes from the Stronghold."

I was going to be meeting unseelies at the border between their lands?

That sounded kind of awesome.

"I saw the hole you left in its roof, brother," the phoenix remarked with a bit of a grin. "Do you have someone to fix it yet?"

"Not yet. I'm sure there's a line of volunteers outside, though."

"I'll do it," the sabertooth guy said.

"I'll help," the basilisk added.

Now that they'd heard about sex, I figured the bastards wanted another chance to sniff around the ladies inside the Stronghold. I'd warn the other girls before we left them alone with the Wild Hunt bastards, if I had the chance.

"Thank you." Calian nodded toward them, and both men nodded back.

They both turned and headed back into the forest, shifting smoothly as they went. I couldn't imagine what it would be like to feel so in tune with my animal side that I'd shift as easily and quickly as they did, but something about the idea sounded really damn appealing to me.

"Get out of here. I need a minute with my female before we fly for the border," Lian growled at them, his voice taking on a bit of teasing.

"We'll hold it for you. Enjoy, brother." The hellhound guy smirked before he too turned and shifted.

The phoenix fae studied us for a few long moments before he shifted and took off into the air, fire licking the space he had been a moment earlier as he vanished into the sky.

"Do powerful bastards always get together and team up?" I asked Lian. I couldn't decide whether the group of them reminded me of prison, my foster homes, or my high school.

"Like attracts like." The man shrugged. "If you don't have family, it's because you haven't found the right people yet.

He had no idea how hard his words hit me, but my throat swelled anyway.

I didn't say a damn thing as I stepped away from him.

"Leave the clothes here so you don't burn them in your shift," he instructed me, watching me closely. Maybe he could tell that my mood had changed.

"Yes sir," I muttered, tugging my top off first.

The way his damned gaze trailed over my skin made my cheeks flush, but I ignored the heat.

My pants joined the shirt, and then I jogged out the cave's opening, seeking the power I felt thrumming lightly in my veins. When I found the sensation, I focused on it, and the beat picked up faster.

The change took over my body, and warmth flooded me as I shifted forms. A grin stretched my cheeks before they shifted, my shape morphing as the fire and liquid gold of the creature I'd become took hold of me.

My wings spread, and I lifted my chin at the powerful stretch of them.

Damn, I was something incredible.

"My gorgeous mate," a male voice murmured. The sentence wasn't spoken aloud, but was somehow in my mind, or within me.

My heartbeat picked up.

"Tell me I did not just hear you in my head," I shot back.

Lian's low, gravelly chuckle was the only response I got back.

My wings pumped hard, carrying me into the sky, and my eyes closed as the thick, powerful wind rushed against my face, my burning feathers, and the thick legs hanging below me.

There was *nothing* as amazing as flying.

"You're perfect, January." Lian's voice touched my mind again.

The words made me shudder, even in my phoenix form.

"Don't," I whispered back. *"You have no idea who I am or what I've done. My life has been very, very different than yours."*

"And yet you fly before me, strong, certain, and powerful. Your past has little to do with your present perfection."

The pure certainty in his voice was enough to make my chest hurt. *"Just stop."*

He didn't speak again, but through whatever magic connected us, I could somehow *feel* his curiosity about why I was so against his compliments.

We flew the rest of the way in silence. Eventually, I relaxed again, despite the reminders of my past that his words had dredged up.

When he knew the hell I'd survived and the damage I'd done, he would never call me perfect.

Fourteen

My eyes squinted as we approached the Stronghold. The longer I stared at the small gap in the trees, the more I thought I could actually make out the hidden building within.

That was insane—it was invisible.

"You only need to be in tune with the building's magic to see it, Love," Calian murmured to me.

My chest clenched. *"Don't call me that."*

His chuckle brushed my mind, and he otherwise didn't acknowledge my words.

We landed in front of it. While Lian shifted in the air before he landed on two feet, I had to hit the ground and focus on getting myself back into my human form before I managed to shift back.

By the time I was back in my skin, the man's front was pressed up against my back, his arms around my chest and waist to keep my lady bits out of the sight of the other men around us.

A few of them yelled as Calian ushered me into the building—the door of which opened just in time to let us in.

Sunny slammed the door behind us with an unceremonious *oof* and leaned her back against it. She flashed me a wild grin. "This place got so much more exciting when you got here."

A snort escaped me. "You're welcome, I guess."

Her grin widened. "Next time you're going to have screaming-hot sex with a gigantic fae, mind warning us so we can get out of here? Or taking it back to wherever that bastard lives? I'm all for the sex, but would rather not hear about all the excitement I'm missing."

My face flushed, and an awkward laugh escaped me. "Sorry. Will do."

"Don't apologize for getting some. I wouldn't say no to hot fae sex myself." She glanced over her shoulder at the door behind her.

Lian's arms tightened around me.

She hadn't clarified which gigantic fae she expected me to be having sex with, which his mind told me he didn't like one bit.

"Be careful, they're clingy," I called to Sunny, as the gigantic fae hauled me to my bedroom. Her laughter made my lips curve upward a bit, even as Lian slammed the door.

He set me down and stared at me with narrowed eyes. "Your humans aren't monogamists?"

"Most are. Some aren't. It's complicated." I shrugged.

"Should you touch another man, I will destroy him." Lian's eyes went silver and got all glowy. "You are *mine*."

"Stop. I'm not planning on having sex with another fae, alright?" I tossed a hand in the direction the other fae were gathered. "I don't consider us married, like you do, but I do understand your clinginess and the permanence of our connection. Besides that, I have no desire to touch any of your buddies. So just... stop."

The glow in his eyes faded slightly.

I finally turned away from him and looked around the room.

Shit.

The blanket and sheets I'd loved were totally roasted. The walls had taken on a blackish hue. The floor was covered in bits of dust that I imagined was something that had been charcoaled. The ceiling had a wide hole in it, and leaves and dirt had already started falling in through the thing.

"Damn," I mumbled.

The only things that didn't look at all singed were the fireproof outfits lined up in the closet.

Sadness and irritation engulfed me, and I tried to ignore them as I slid into the closet and tugged one of the sets of black fireproof lingerie over my skin, covering my tits and ass, but not solving my new attitude problem.

I'd loved that room.

It was mine.

And...

Well, it was wrecked.

I pushed hair out of my eyes and shoved my sadness away.

I should've expected to lose the place; I always lost everything. Hoping for a different outcome was an utter waste.

My stomach was clenched when I stepped out of the closet and found Calian studying me with narrowed eyes.

If he said something judgy, I was going to go off on him.

"Let's go," I growled at him.

There was no point in looking for the door when we had a gigantic hole.

I shifted forms and then launched myself up into the air, tucking my wings in tight before I shot up through the hole. The stone scraped my body hard enough that I smelled a little blood, but I welcomed the pain.

I'd started letting myself get way too comfortable.

Nothing in Vevol was guaranteed any more than it had been on Earth.

Nothing was safe.

Nothing was certain.

Dropping my guard was so stupid. I should never have let Lian touch me, or considered a friendship with benefits for us.

If I was going to survive, the only person I could trust was myself.

"You're upset," the dragon said to me, as we flew. He'd taken the lead, and since I didn't know where we were going, I didn't try to argue with him about it.

"Back off," I snarled back.

He said nothing, though I could feel the bastard's curiosity seeping through our stupid connection once again as we continued to fly.

I'd cooled off a little by the time we reached the place he said was the border between the two fae lands. It was a valley within the massive range of vibrantly-colored mountains, and he told to me that the curve of the valley stretched along the entirety of their world. I had no idea how big said world was compared to Earth, and when I asked him, Calian didn't have an answer. He just said that it took about a day to fly the circumference of Vevol.

We landed off to the side of a thick stone building that was shaped like a gigantic triangle, and was surrounded by melted snow. My claws sliced through the snow without feeling any of the chill, but when they shifted back to feet, my toes curled at the iciness engulfing them.

Then my feet burst into flames—I could feel the fire coming from within me and my thrumming magic—and the ice melted into a steaming puddle. My body relaxed, and for a minute, I felt like I was in a sauna.

Calian's hand captured mine. When I looked at him, I realized he had put on a pair of shorts that reminded me of the hellhound and phoenixes. I'd only seen two pairs of them in his cave, so I didn't think he was a huge fan of the things, but I had told him to cover up.

The fact that he respected my wishes felt important, so I shoved it away and tried to pull my hand out of his.

"You're free to be angry with me, but while we're on neutral territory, you must act like you've accepted that you're mine," the dragon said into my mind. I stopped trying to tug my hand out of his, but didn't grip him as securely as he did me.

I didn't know he could do so while we were in our person forms, and grimaced now that I knew.

"Why?" I asked, my voice snappier than I intended.

"The unseelie have many rules. If they believe I'm trying to force you to be my mate, they will attempt to take you from me, and our people will go to war. They believe in control, in all of its uncomfortable forms. Our wildness is savagery in their eyes, rather than the freedom it feels like to us."

My throat constricted a little.

As much as I hated to admit it, I understood what he was saying. I too had been around people who tried to enforce stupid, pointless rules that only served to make those who had created them feel more powerful.

And I too had found freedom in the seelies' wildness.

So I tightened my grip on his hand.

"This doesn't mean I've decided to be your wife," I growled at the man whose hand I gripped like a lifeline.

"Of course not," he said, his low chuckle making me warmer than I wanted to admit.

Despite our disagreements, we walked into the triangle-shaped building like we were united.

My gaze skimmed over the group of men waiting inside, all of them with their arms folded as they glared at each other. Among them, there were two that I knew and four that I didn't.

The two I knew were the hellhound guy and the phoenix dude—the four that I didn't know were all unseelies, but I recognized them for what they were because they all had on matching button-up shirts and slacks, none of which looked comfortable to me. The basilisk guy who had come to pick Ana up on that first day wasn't among them, but he had been wearing the same thing when he showed up to get her.

"Brothers," Calian said, his voice a lot less warm as he spread an arm toward them—the arm that wasn't wrapping around my waist and pulling my body closer to his with every step we took.

I didn't turn to eye him, hiding my surprise at the sudden change in his personality.

Was he putting on some kind of a mask for them?

Hadn't I done that dozens of times as a kid, when shit would change and I would need to change with it to survive?

The men seemed to call each other "brothers" a lot, but only with the other members of the Wild Hunt had I seen Calian actually seem to mean the word.

"Lian." One of the men watched me, his eyes piercing.

"You must not be too concerned, since you haven't brought the full council," Calian drawled back.

I was officially as nestled against him as was possible, his entire front glued to my whole back. The man seemed partial to holding me that way, and honestly, I liked it.

Not that I'd admit it to him.

“Druze and Ashvyn are dealing with the little female *problem* you handed us,” one man countered. Something about the plethora of tattoos on his dark skin and the way he held himself reminded me of the hellhound guy a few feet to my right.

“You made the five-year rule, not us,” Calian replied.

“And you know we couldn’t have taken them any sooner,” the growly guy countered.

The blond hellhound dude grinned. “Careful, Rien. Your hound is showing.”

“Wouldn’t want to let anyone see the beast you hide away so carefully,” Lian agreed, that infuriating smirk so evident in his voice.

“Enough playing, *Calian.*” The man who spoke emphasized my dragon’s full name, something the other men must not have known until Calian gave it to me, if I understood the name-secrecy properly. If he had known it, I assumed Lian would’ve been snarling at him or trying to kill him or something. “Aren’t you going to introduce us to your little phoenix?”

Being called his little phoenix was insulting, but I held my tongue and settled on glaring back at the man.

“My mate, you mean?” Lian squeezed my hip playfully. “Don’t tell me you’re jealous, brother. It’s been far too long since any of our people found a compatible human—and it’s pretty apparent none have been as lucky as I am.”

Dammit.

The bastard was going to flaunt the fact that we’d had sex, wasn’t he?

The man’s eyes burned into him. “I felt the shift in Vevol when your bond solidified. That didn’t happen with the rest of us, so what did you do?”

“He fucked his mate.” The blond hellhound guy smirked. “Apparently, our bodies are meant to intertwine with a female’s.”

I was going to kill all of them.

The Wild Hunt was going to die.

End of the damn discussion.

“She’s glaring at you like you’ve spilled her gender’s most closely-kept secret,” one of the unseelie bastards remarked. His gaze flicked to me. “The other females will hate you, I’m sure.”

The question was a taunt, but it was utter bullshit.

"Sex isn't a secret. If you've got twenty women here and none of them have ever tried to screw one of you, it's because you're ugly bastards. Your fault, not mine." I flashed him one of his awful smirks.

The man was just as gorgeous as the rest of them, but they didn't need to know that.

"Looks like Vevol made a wise match. A fire-tongued she-devil to go with the Savage King." The hellhound who I was pretty sure had been called Rien glared at us.

"And nothing but loneliness for the cold, unseelie council," our hellhound replied.

I wasn't sure when I'd started thinking of myself as one of the seelie, but it was too late to change my mind. I was one of them—whether I liked it or not.

"You can smell that our scents have merged. Whether or not the female could've been anyone else's, she belongs to me. Take that news back to your king and his icy mate." Lian's fingers pressed lightly into my skin, and I understood the silent push.

We were moving, right then.

I turned as he guided me, walking in front of him and not saying a damn thing when he blocked my ass from their sight with his ginormous body.

"You know this could be the start of a war between us," one of the men called from behind me and Calian. "Your people can't support this. You're too wild—and too reckless."

"Bring us the war, and you'll see just how wild and reckless we can be," Calian's phoenix friend said.

I felt more than heard the seelie hound and phoenix following us out of the building.

"Are they really going to start a war over us getting accidentally mated?" I whispered to Calian, when we were far enough from them that I knew they wouldn't hear me.

"Probably not. But if they do, our people will fight, and we will win. The one thing we all agree on is the freedom we deserve," the dragon told me. "Shift, Precious."

I about gagged at the nickname, and heard him snort at my reaction even as his form shifted.

Mine followed soon after his, and faster than I would've thought possible a few days earlier, we were in the air.

Fifteen

We flew all the way back to the Stronghold, and Calian left me to my thoughts. I wasn't sure where my mind was at—mostly, it was just a mess.

Everything had happened too quickly, and I was past overwhelmed. If Lian could read my emotions the way I had started to be able to read his, he would realize that and back the hell off.

When we got to the Stronghold, the phoenix guy circled overhead, and the hellhound one followed us to the door, snarling and snapping at the other men waiting outside. He stood behind us while we waited for one of the other ladies to get the door. When Dots pulled it open, eyeing the guys behind us, the hellhound guy dipped his head and gave us a feral grin before he took off into the trees.

The door closed behind us, and Calian made quick work of the locks. Not as quickly as Ana had that first day, but he didn't have the same experience.

"So?" Sunny demanded as we walked into the living room. She, Mare, and Dots occupied a couch, and were clutching their pillows and blankets with excitement.

I guessed things usually got pretty boring in the Stronghold.

"Tell us everything," Dots ordered.

My instincts were to clam up and hide out, but that wasn't how shit worked in the Stronghold. And the girls there... well, I wanted to be close with them, like they were with each other.

I liked them, even if it might have been a shitty call on my part.

So, I ignored my instincts, collapsing onto a couch. When Calian dropped next to me and pulled half of me up onto his lap, I let him.

I had to pick my battles with that bastard, after all.

I told the other girls everything that had happened and everything that I'd learned. About the fae not knowing what sex was—that one shocked the hell out of them and led to way too much laughter—about the Wild Hunt guys, about the seelie versus the unseelie... everything I'd heard, which turned out to be a hell of a lot more than they'd learned in their time in Vevol.

Then again, I'd had a front-row seat, while they'd been safely tucked away in the Stronghold.

When I finally finished explaining and headed to the kitchen for something to eat, I noticed North leaning up against the doorway of her room, her eyes narrowed but not angry as she stared at me.

She must've come out when she realized what we were talking about.

When she realized that I'd noticed her standing there, she spun around and stormed back into her room, slamming the door hard behind her.

I shrugged it off.

Calian cooked for all of us—I was pretty sure I was going to have to fight Mare, Dots, and Sunny for the bastard if he kept doing that—and then he and I retired to our room. I tossed my middle finger over my head when Sunny hollered to keep the sex quiet this time, and ignored my burning cheeks.

I was exhausted, and having a full stomach only made me want to sleep even more.

When the door was closed behind us and we were alone in my room, it took me a minute to look around and see what had happened. Someone had fixed the hole in the roof—Lian's friends, I assumed—and left a new sheet and blanket tossed haphazardly over a fresh mattress. The ashes or whatever had been on the ground had been swept up and removed. Even though the scorch marks remained on the walls and floors, the space smelled clean.

"Damn," I murmured, taking everything in.

Lian was already putting the sheet on the bed, the thick blanket draped over his shoulder.

"You have good friends," I admitted to him. "Or brothers, I guess. What are their names?"

Calian dropped the mattress and tossed the blanket over the bed. "The hellhound is Priel. He's a bastard, but the most loyal fae you can find. Ervo is the phoenix. He's the most intelligent of us, notices every detail that the rest of us miss, but he's private. I know less about him than the others, despite the centuries we've known each other." He waved me over, and I slowly, reluctantly, shuffled toward him. "Nev is the basilisk. He's a sneaky asshole, but could make a damned forest mouse laugh."

"A forest mouse?" My voice was dubious.

"This big. Fuzzy." He moved his hands in about the same size as a loaf of bread.

Shit, I did *not* want to meet one of those mice.

"Mean bastards. Sharp teeth, hard to kill, foul meat." He shrugged. "Teris is the sabertooth. He'd sooner start a fight than have a logical conversation, which is both his best and worst quality."

I snorted, and Calian's lips tilted up slightly. I finally reached him, and his hands wrapped around my hips, drawing me closer until I was nestled between his thighs. I felt tiny in his arms, and didn't hate that feeling at all. "And what about you?" I asked him.

"What about me?"

"If I was asking them the same question about you, what would they tell me?"

He grimaced. "That I'm the obnoxious one, I suppose. In everyone's business. Won't leave the bastards alone. Showing up with food, forcing them to get up and do shit when they want to be alone."

Well, that didn't sound obnoxious to me.

Not at all.

"What kind of food?" I checked.

"Cake, usually. Who do you think told the bastards outside that they should bring treats when they wanted to convince the human women to talk to them?"

I snorted. "That was actually a great idea."

"Thank you." His lips curved up further. "What would your friends say about you, January?"

My humor died. "I don't have friends. Friends are just people who pretend to like you until they're ready to screw you over."

"I'm sorry." Something about his gaze felt far too much like the pity I'd never wanted from any of the many people who had pitied me throughout my life. "Are you ready for bed?"

I stepped out of his grip, and he released me, though I felt the reluctance in the way his touch lingered. "I want to be alone tonight. I need space to think. Time, too. Everything's happened too fast since I got here."

His jaw clenched and his eyes narrowed. "Space?"

"Yes, space." I stared back at him, my eyes just as narrow as his. "I still haven't agreed to be your wife, remember? You were probably hoping for sex, but you're going to have to deal with space instead."

His eyes flashed silver. "Should I walk out the Stronghold's doors, I'm going to have to fight the fae who believe you could've been theirs had they met you first."

"Then you probably have a few friends out there, waiting to fight with you," I shot back.

His silent glare was all the answer I needed.

"We just met, Lian. I don't know you. You don't know me. There's more to a relationship than sex, and we don't even have a relationship. If I need to go out there and let them all sniff me so you don't have to kill anyone, that's fine, I'll do it. But you don't just get to *assume* that we're going to be together constantly now."

His jaw clenched further. "Alright. I'll spend the night making sure none of the bastards outside get in here, so you can have your *space*."

I knew for a fact that the Stronghold had been built to keep the fae out—and I was fairly confident none of them would harm us. If they intended to do that, there would've been at least some sign.

But I didn't say that.

I only jerked my head in a nod. "Fine."

Calian stood stiffly, and my eyes followed him as he crossed the room.

His muscles were tense as he tugged the door open, and my teeth cut into my lip.

The door slammed behind him, and I released a heavy rush of air.

My chest hurt, and I didn't want to think about why.

I considered going out to the living room, to watch a movie with the other girls, but I didn't want them to cheer me up. Something told me they would.

So instead, I locked the door and collapsed on the bed.

It smelled wrong.

I hated that.

But I'd slept in dozens of beds that smelled wrong, so I ignored my emotions for the umpteenth time, and shoved my body under the blankets.

Sleep.

Sleep would be good.

It took way longer than I wanted it to, but I finally managed to drift off.

When I woke up, I felt physically fine but mentally and emotionally exhausted.

I stumbled out of bed and into the kitchen, even though I wasn't really hungry.

Dots and Mare were sitting at our dinner table, playing a game that looked like Scrabble. I was shitty at Scrabble, and grumpy enough that seeing them play it made me scowl.

"Don't go outside. Looks like a crime scene out there," Dots murmured to me. "I didn't see any bodies, at least."

My chest tightened painfully, and I muttered a thanks as I grabbed some kind of weird-ass fruit. I'd seen the other girls eat it like an apple, even though the shape was like a pear and a star had a love-child and the skin looked like a lizard's.

I bit into it, and glared at the damn thing when it tasted incredible.

My back rested against one of the cabinets, and I stared daggers at the fridge while I ate. The girls behind me finished their game and then cleaned up and headed to their rooms, saying something about showering.

After a few minutes, North stalked out of her room. Almost all of her skin was still covered, and she glared at me like always.

This time, I glared back.

Neither of us said a word to each other as she grabbed a pear-star thing for herself.

She headed back toward her room, but stopped halfway. I didn't glance over when she returned, her fist wrapped around her alien pear.

"You're not the only one who's had a hard life," she snarled at me. Fire danced in the orbs of her eyes, and I fought to keep my shock off my face. "If you're going to be a bitch, stay in your room."

With that, she stormed back across the living area. Her bedroom door slammed behind her.

There was a long moment of silence before I finally sighed to myself.

I *was* being a bitch.

Being in a shitty mood and questioning everything I knew and felt didn't mean I had to act like a damn storm cloud.

Was that why North stayed in *her* room?

Because she'd had a hard life and didn't want to make everyone else as miserable as she was?

I didn't know if we'd ever be friends, but that short interaction already made me see her differently.

I shuffled over to one of the couches and took a seat, tucking my legs up onto the couch next to me and then tugging a blanket over them. My anger chilled a little as I worked on my lizard-fruit, staring at one of the bookshelves like it held the answers to everything.

Though I knew it didn't have a damn thing for me, it felt good to hope.

Mare came back out of her room a bit later, wearing a clean pair of clothes and smelling kind of like the fruit I was eating. She flashed me a quick, small smile as she pulled a book off the shelf. It looked well-loved, and I wondered how many times she had read it. Or, had it been one of the previous women's favorites?

"You okay?" she asked me, distracting me from my thoughts.

"I don't know," I admitted.

Mare took a seat on the couch that I'd noticed she frequented—the thing was practically her own. "Want to talk about it?"

"I..." I bit my lip.

Talking about things only ever made them worse for me, but I did know that for some people, talking shit out was how they worked through it. Therapists wouldn't have jobs if it didn't, right? And I'd never met a therapist I actually liked, but plenty of people had, so they couldn't *all* be bad.

Theoretically.

"Calian thinks we're married," I admitted. "I've never even had a boyfriend. He was smothering me, and I liked it, but I was afraid of how much I liked it. That probably sounds stupid, but..." I sighed. "I don't know."

"It's not stupid. Not many people would be able to go from a life they hated in a world they didn't want to be in, to a new world where a man considered her the love of his life without a little stress. Or a lot of stress."

I groaned. "You make it sound even worse."

She laughed. "Knowing it's a weird situation just makes you more capable of dealing with it, January."

January.

"Why do you guys all call me that? I've never gone by my full name in my entire life. My first foster parents thought it was too weird."

She gave me a small smile. "It just fits you. Back on Earth, January is a fresh start. A new year. We've all experienced January so many times, but every time it comes around, people still walk into it with new goals they want to accomplish and ideas about the new person they want to become. January is just... hope, I guess. You might not be a super hopeful person, but you're a survivor. Anyone can see that, Calian included, I can imagine. And there's something innately hopeful about looking at someone and seeing that they survived shit that would break most people."

I grimaced. "Survival *definitely* broke me."

She shook her head, biting her lip and looking out a window. "I..." she trailed off, and her gaze lingered on the window the girls had uncovered a few days earlier. "When things were bad, I read books. I hid in worlds that never existed. I always have, and I probably always will. I didn't survive things, I just... ignored them. Pretended they weren't real. I'm not proud of that, either. The only thing I've done that I'm actually, genuinely proud of was wishing on the star that opened the portal for the Wild Hunt to bring me here, and I almost didn't do that. So yeah, I respect you, and I don't think you're broken. You look your demons in the eyes, and I don't. That's something I've always wished I could change about myself."

"Keeping your head down isn't hiding from your problems. It's another survival tactic, one I've always wished I was better at," I argued, leaning toward her. My lizard-fruit was still in one hand, two-thirds eaten and yet forgotten at the same time. "There's nothing shameful about choosing not to pick a fight."

"*Those who stand for nothing fall for everything*," Mare said quietly. "No one really knows who said that quote, but it feels like it was written about my fucking life."

I didn't know that I'd ever heard her swear before, and I kind of loved it.

"*Live to fight another day*," I countered. "I have no idea who said that one, but I think it's a much better summary of your life, and I don't even know what kind of life you've lived."

A snort escaped her. "I wish you were wrong."

"Well, I usually am. So don't get used to this." I leaned back against the couch, fighting a soft smile I never usually showed.

We were both quiet for a few minutes.

Mare broke the silence, though her voice was soft. "Have you told Lian that you want to take things slow and get to know each other? In the years I've been here, he's checked up on us more than all of the other fae put together. He takes care of people. If you explain to him that you're not ready for the kind of relationship he wants, but that you might be in a few weeks, or months, or years, I can't imagine he would walk away."

I bit my lip, considering it.

She was right; I didn't have a damned doubt about that.

Lian would take whatever I gave him, even if he was pissed about doing so.

"He deserves more, you know? Like... he's not innocent; he's probably killed a hundred fae."

"At least," Mare agreed.

I sighed heavily. "Not innocent, but not experienced in the ways I am. I don't think this world has the kind of darkness that I've seen back on Earth, honestly. And I don't want it to, but that makes it hard for me to consider a relationship with someone who can't understand me."

"Can't, or hasn't been given the chance?" Mare countered.

I shot her a glare. "Why do you have to make me think about these things?"

A laugh escaped her. "You're the one trying to force me to reconsider my whole outlook on life. Live to fight another day, my ass."

A smile teased my lips. "Fine, so we both need to shape up. That's not new for me."

"Me either, unfortunately." She flashed me a small grin. "I'll give it a try if you will."

"I'm going to hold it against you if it doesn't work," I warned her.

She laughed again. "Is that a promise?"

I offered her a hand, and she reached out and shook it.

It felt like more than a promise to try to get out of our comfort zones, honestly.

It felt like... friendship.

Sixteen

Despite my conversation with Mare, I put off a real talk with Calian for a few days. He brought cake every day, and we both ignored the bits of dried blood on his various body parts every time. The bastard even came in to cook for me twice a day, something the other ladies definitely didn't complain about.

I didn't ask any serious questions other than making sure the unseelie weren't starting a war yet (they weren't), and he didn't push me for more. It was... honestly, pretty nice, even though we both knew we were avoiding the elephant in the room.

The other ladies and I spent our days playing games of poker with rocks for chips—all of us losing horribly to a grinning Sunny—as well Scrabble, which Dots and Mare alternated winning, and long games of Monopoly. I never won any of them, but to my surprise, I didn't mind. Having people to play games with was something new for me, and honestly, I was kind of falling in love with it.

A week had gone by before I shuffled to the bathroom one morning and blearily blinked at my reflection.

It took me a minute to really look at myself, but when I did, my jaw fell open.

Thin, elegant golden markings had appeared all over both of my arms. I spun quickly, looking at my back in the mirror, and ripped my tank top off so I could see the magical tattoos better.

They climbed over my shoulders and up my neck, then stretched down my back and wrapped around my ass and thighs.

When I gaped down at my legs, I found more of the golden ink stretching across my skin.

"Holy shit," I whispered to myself, my gaze glued to my arms and legs, following the gorgeous markings. "Holy shit!" I suddenly understood why people did victory dances after they won things.

It was *awesome*. The markings were unique, and gorgeous, and fun—it was like the world's magic had heard my desire for tattoos and answered it!

My heart beat quickly in my chest, excitement thrumming with the fire magic in my veins.

I didn't know it could take that long—was my body still changing?

It didn't matter.

I was excited—and there was one person I wanted to tell above the others.

I rushed toward the door out of my room, but halted abruptly before I could open it.

Shit.

Why was Calian the first person I wanted to tell?

That felt like a bad sign, that I wanted to tell him more than I wanted to tell the other girls. I had been spending plenty of time with all of them except North, but my mind always seemed to go back to the time Lian and I spent flying—and screwing—and just... talking.

Yeah, I was really thinking it was a bad sign.

Was I starting to like the big bastard as more than a friend? Or more than a friend-with-benefits that I'd only *benefited* from once?

"Friends like to tell each other things," I told myself aloud. "It's normal. Natural. Not something to stress about."

Now I was being insane, talking to myself, but whatever.

Wanting to tell Calian about my new tattoos was fine. It was just because we were friends.

Yep, I was going with that.

As I stepped outside my room, I forced myself to slow down, since we were just friends and all.

None of the other girls were up yet, but I was confident that Lian would be awake and outside. As far as I could tell, he hadn't gone back to his cave to change once since I told him I needed space.

I opened the last few locks on the doors—we'd been leaving most of them undone to save time—and tugged it open before slipping outside. The air was slightly chilly in the mornings, but it felt good against my always-warm skin now that I was a phoenix.

Calian was in his massive dragon form, his body stretched out in front of the door, preventing anyone from leaving or entering.

So much for needing the locks.

The dragon turned and lifted his head, looking slightly surprised that I was outside that early. Because I had been avoiding serious conversations, I'd been forced to avoid flying and spending any time alone with the man as well, so I'd sort of been hiding out in the Stronghold.

"Look," I whispered, excitement probably showing through my voice even though I was trying not to act like a damned puppy.

His body shifted as his gaze dragged over my skin. "The magic has finally set in completely." His voice was a rough murmur, and I was fairly certain I'd pulled him out of sleep. "It suits you beautifully."

My face flushed.

Yeah, that was what I'd been hoping he'd say. I wasn't about to admit that out loud, but it was the truth.

"Thanks."

"You'll have nature magic within you now, too. When you're ready to learn how to use it, let me know."

Nature magic?

Was that the power I could feel coming off of the fae so often? Was it how the Wild Hunt guys had managed to fix my roof so quickly and so perfectly, or why Calian lived in a cave?

There were so many questions I wanted to ask, but asking them would mean accepting the bond between us in a way that I wasn't sure I could handle.

So I didn't ask.

Instead, I bit down on my lip.

This was...

Not what I'd hoped.

His comments were everything, but when I'd come out of the room, I'd just...

I don't know.

Wanted more, I guess.

Maybe I didn't want as much space as I thought I did.

A bird cawed loudly overhead, and my chin lifted as I tried to peer up into the sky, through the thick tree branches above our heads.

"It's Ervo," Lian told me, stepping closer but not putting his hands on my skin.

I suddenly missed them violently, those days when he'd touched me every chance he got.

"What does he want?" I asked.

"I don't know."

A brief moment of silence passed, and then a massive phoenix dropped out of the sky.

My stomach clenched at the sight of him, and the thrumming power in my chest went a bit wild.

It had been too long since I'd been in my own phoenix form—since I'd had the chance to fly.

"The unseelie council is in the valley. They've come to negotiate in hopes of avoiding a war," the phoenix said, not bothering with a hello or any other pleasantries.

"The rest of our brothers?" Lian asked.

"On their way as we speak. We've warned our men to be ready for a battle, as well."

Calian dipped his head in a nod. "I'll let mine know and meet you there."

"May the winds favor you." Ervo nodded toward me, a silent, polite greeting, before he launched himself back into the air, shifting and taking to the skies.

"What will they ask for?" I looked at Calian.

"No way to predict with the unseelies." His gaze lingered on me. "I'll return and let you know as soon as I can."

Whoa, what?

I grabbed his arm before he threw himself up into the sky like Ervo had.

"You're not seriously going to leave me here." My voice was somewhere between surprised and offended.

"You wished for space. I won't take you in front of the unseelies while you're uncomfortable touching me; any sign of weakness will only encourage them."

Shit.

"You think I'm uncomfortable touching you?" My voice had a weird lilt that I didn't know what to think about.

"That seems clear, yes."

My throat swelled a bit.

This was an important moment between us—I could feel it.

I hadn't realized he thought I was uncomfortable around him. If I didn't do something to prove that I wasn't, that feeling would stick around for him.

If I did... then I would be removing the space I'd forced him to put between us.

My conversation with Mare came to mind, and in that instant, my choice was made.

I covered the distance between us in a heartbeat, burying my hands in the back of his hair and pressing my lips to his.

Lian gave me a moment to take it back, a moment to step away, before his massive hands swallowed my hips and his tongue was in my mouth, his lips devouring mine.

Our bodies were plastered together, interlocked as much as they could be without any privacy.

And damn, I'd missed kissing him.

He kissed me like I was his everything, and held me like he was afraid he might lose me.

And the fact he felt that way, that he cared about me as much as he did, was staggering.

Damn, I loved it.

Calian walked me backward as he kissed me, until my shoulders met the firm, somewhat-invisible barrier of the Stronghold. His hands slid down my thighs, caressing my skin in a way that made me want him so much I could hardly stand it. Then he grabbed them, hauling me up and pinning my pelvis against his. His erection ground against my core, and I groaned into his mouth.

Maybe I'd spoken too soon about the whole *without privacy* thing.

His fingers slid inside my shorts, wrapping possessively around my ass cheeks and spreading me wider.

I ripped my face away from his, the back of my head knocking into the wall as I panted, "Wait."

His fingers clenched my ass, his silver eyes burning into me.

"We have an audience, probably." I jerked my head toward the forest.

His head whipped around, his eyes narrowing.

His fingers tightened on my ass again, the grip so tight it hurt a little, but in the best way.

"And the unseelies want a war. We have to talk to them. Afterward..." I bit my lip. "We can go back to your cave for a day or two."

His eyes darkened, and he dipped his head in a nod.

Lian's lips captured mine again, and he gave me one last scorching kiss before he tossed me over his back, shifting before I collided with his warm skin, and took off into the air.

My magic pulsed in my chest as we picked up speed and altitude. Flying had come naturally to me when I shifted, but there was no doubt that Lian was faster. He had done it a hell of a lot more than I had, and he was just plain old massive.

Maybe I'd eventually be able to keep pace with him, but at the moment, I was content with the fact that he could outfly me.

Despite the magic and my own yearning to shift, I felt through our bond that Calian wanted me where I was. I'd been avoiding paying attention to the connection ever since I told him I wanted space, but his emotions had still brushed against my mind every now and then. They did so enough to let me know how difficult it had been for him to give me the space I needed.

And now that we were touching again, they let me know that he needed me to remain in physical contact with him.

It was a strange thought, that he needed me.

I'd never been needed before.

As much as I hated to admit it, I liked it.

We flew for a few hours, and the more time I spent snuggled up on Calian's back, the more I started to wonder if space was what I had ever wanted from the man at all.

Seventeen

Eventually, we landed in the valley. I slid off Calian's back before he could grab me, managing to crash to my feet instead of the ground. When he landed beside me in his man form, his arm wrapped securely around my waist. I leaned in closer to him without thinking about it, and when I did think about it, accepted that I just wanted to be close to him.

"They don't know what to think of you," he murmured to me as we walked. "That's an advantage for us. If you feel it can help at any point, speak up. No need to hide your opinions or hold yourself back."

My eyebrows shot upward.

No one had ever told me not to hide what I was. That was the name of the game in foster care; they wanted us to become someone entirely different so we'd appeal to the *bleeding hearts* who might eventually want to adopt us. I had hated that so much—the insistence to be on our best behavior and show respect even if the potential families treated us like garbage. Sure, maybe some of them actually might have been good people, but I'd lived with more than a few who were just in it to make money off of us.

"You don't want me to stay quiet?" I asked, as we reached the entrance to the pyramid-shaped building.

"Not unless you prefer to." He squeezed my hip lightly, and our eyes met.

The contact made me bite my lip to suppress a wave of emotions I couldn't control or understand.

We stepped into the building, and I let my gaze trail over the room.

It was the same as it had been before, but there were a few more people inside. Three unseelie men I didn't recognize—one of which was wearing a crown that was just as big as his gigantic head. It gleamed like some kind of black metal, but my attention didn't linger on it.

It lingered on the woman next to him.

She was tall and willowy, with piercing blue eyes and thick, dark hair. Her skin was a dark tan color, and one of her arms was coated in spiraling letters that weren't English, but looked like some other language's version of cursive. Though she stood next to the guy wearing the crown, there were at least two feet of distance between them, and her posture was stiff.

Guess she didn't want to be there.

Her eyes fixated on me though, and there was curiosity within them.

"The Tamed King emerges," Calian drawled. "Suppose you couldn't wait any longer to meet my female, could you?"

The man said nothing, only staring at us with narrowed eyes.

"I'm sure you've come with the desire to take Lian's new mate," the phoenix guy, Ervo, said calmly. "As you know, we'll refuse. What's the compromise you came to offer?"

My gaze skimmed all of the men on the other side of the room. There was only one I didn't recognize, so I figured he was the one who had been with Druze and Ana, trying to deal with their *human problem*.

One man spoke for their king. "Give us the rest of the females, and we'll allow your connection."

My eyebrows shot upward.

Was he serious?

There was a moment of silence.

"If your people were going to be drawn to their scents, it would've happened by now," another unseelie said coolly. "We deserve the chance to see if they're ours, same as your people."

None of the seelies said anything, and I felt multiple sets of eyes on me.

"We have yet to prove whether or not a mate bond can occur in time," Teris, the sabertooth guy in our group, said. "You've been with your human for nearly two decades, yet yours still hasn't settled the way Lian and January's has, so who can say that the connection doesn't take time?"

The king's nostrils flared, but he remained silent.

My mind was frozen on the part where the seelies weren't sure if a mating bond could develop over time. If they could... then Mare and the other girls might want to stay in the seelie part of the kingdom.

Lian had told me to listen and go with my gut, so...

It was time to lie.

"One of the other human girls confided in me already that she's felt drawn to one of the seelie fae for a few months now. We're pretty sure that a bond can come on slowly." I rattled off that bullshit like I was the best liar ever, even though I wasn't fantastic at it. "If you take them, you might break the beginning of a bond, as well as make the women furious enough to refuse to consider the rest of you at all."

Now, I had every eye in the room on me.

"She has a fair point," the other human girl admitted. "And we've all seen the bond growing between Druze and Ana on our side of the world, even if they both refuse to admit it exists."

My gaze jerked to the blond unseelie who had come to pick up the fireball of a woman when I first arrived in Vevol.

A tense moment of silence followed her admission.

"The balance of power is unsteady," the unseelie king finally said, his voice low and growly. "The seelie must give us something to steady the scales."

"Your land has far more mated couples than ours," Priel, our hellhound guy, growled back. "As you well know. If your females don't like you enough to screw you, even for the security of a bond, then you don't deserve the power anyway."

All of the unseelies' eyes narrowed at him.

"Your opinions mean nothing to us," the king finally said. "The imbalance remains. Give us the rest of the women, or we go to war."

Bastards.

The woman beside the king looked pissed. "No." Her voice was clipped, and one look at her proved she was trying her damndest to keep from losing her temper. "We do *not* want war. I'll talk to the other mated women, and one of us will have sex with our mate so that both sides have a couple with a complete bond. No one needs to die."

I looked at the girl with new eyes after she'd said that.

She was… sacrificing herself? Or one of the other mated human chicks?

Classy, if she was the one making the sacrifice.

Shitty, if she wasn't.

"Make sure only one of you does it or we'll be the ones calling a war," Priel, our hellhound, growled.

The woman dipped her head in a nod. "That's not going to be a problem." Her voice was clipped, and from what I had heard, she had a damn good reason for it.

"Is that all?" Lian asked, looking around the room and pulling me closer.

"For now." The unseelie king still studied us with a heavy, dark gaze.

"January?" The woman spoke up as Lian started to turn me away from everyone, to lead me out in front of him.

I glanced over my shoulder at her, and met her slightly-troubled gaze.

"Are you okay?" she asked, her voice low. "No one's forced you to do anything?"

My judgment of her was officially leaning toward classy. I'd put money on her being the one to seal the deal with her mate, even if she didn't want to. A shitty sacrifice, but one I could definitely respect her for making.

"I'm fine. If anyone tried to force me, I'd cut their dick off," I tossed back.

Her lips curved upward slightly. "We need to get all of the ladies together one of these days."

"Good luck getting past all these assholes." I gestured with my head toward the group of male fae flooding the room.

Her lips lifted further as she dipped her head in a nod.

I nodded back before slipping outside, with Lian's hand still gripping my waist in a comfortingly-possessive way.

"You did better than I could've hoped for," Calian murmured into my head. It had been so long since he spoke to me through the bond that I shuddered a bit at the feel of it.

"Do you guys have meetings like this a lot?" I wondered. *"Mostly pointless?"*

His chuckle was silent, but his fingers stroked the skin beneath my hip bone. *"The unseelie would never admit it, but they have a dramatic streak wider than the damned sky. They attempt to use it to force us to follow them a few times a year."*

Damn.

"So this is just a normal day in Vevol?" He must've been able to hear my question, and his lips curved up in response.

"It is. Though usually, one of the unseelies will be bleeding when we leave. They love pissing off Priel."

My lips formed a small grin. *"He seems like he might be just as dramatic as they are."*

"Oh, he is." Lian shot me a grin that mirrored my own, before he pulled me close and shifted forms.

My magic thrummed too excitedly to protest his hold on me, so when I started to shift, I did so on Calian's back. He flashed me a sharp-toothed smirk when I almost fell off, unused to balancing my huge-ass bird-self.

"You're stunning," he told me, his voice soft and sexy.

"Or are you just stunned?" I countered.

His scaly forehead sort of wrinkled.

"It was a rhetorical question, so I didn't expect you to answer."

The wrinkle on his forehead didn't budge, so I tried to explain.

"It's like the saying, 'beauty is in the eye of the beholder.' Everyone's definition of attractive is different, so calling someone or something beautiful is a waste of time. It doesn't matter if the girl in the cell next to yours is even filthier than you are; what matters is that they were stunned by her. They found her beautiful, and it worked to her advantage. You told me I was stunning, and I replied that in actuality, you were stunned by me."

A low chuckle traveled through our bond. *"To me, you are the most beautiful thing in both of our worlds. Is that a better compliment?"*

The fire on my feathers and wings grew a little hotter. For some reason, it felt nice. *"It is."*

"Do you still wish to go to my mountain?" His voice was firm enough that I knew he wanted me to say yes, but soft enough that I knew he wouldn't be upset if I said no.

There was no pressure either way, which left me with the chance to give him the truth.

"I do," I admitted.

He flashed me a slow grin over his shoulder, his ginormous teeth glinting a bright white. *"I'll race you there."*

A laugh burst out of me as the dragon rolled sideways, knocking me off his back. My wings spread through the sky, the wind forcing them open as the massive appendages kept me upright.

I glided below Calian for a moment. *"Ready?"* he asked, his voice a bit wicked.

"Yup." It was silly—I knew he was going to win, and he did too. But the adrenaline was still there, and the idea still made me ridiculously happy.

As we took off toward his mountain, flying harder than I ever had before, I admitted to myself that for the first time in the entirety of the life I could remember, I was happy.

Eighteen

The thrill had cooled off by the time we made it back to his cave, and then I was just sort of uncertain.

All of this was new for me. The world, the magic, the mating thing...

He hadn't known what he wanted from me or with me the last time we'd talked about it, but I was pretty damn sure that had changed.

And now, we were going to be alone in his cave. On his mountain.

I landed beside him, still shifting slower than he did. It would be a long-ass time before I could change as fast as he could, but I didn't mind.

In fact, I kind of looked forward to it.

When we were both in our skin again, his gaze slowly moved up and down my body. Whether he was checking me out or just checking me for injuries was debatable, but I didn't want to wonder about it.

"I never had the chance to show you around," he remarked, lifting his gaze from my chest. "May I?" He held an elbow out to me, and my heart squeezed.

I was totally screwed.

And not just in a fun way, either. Because I wanted to be near him as much as he wanted to be near me, which was kind of terrifying.

I took his elbow anyway, fighting off the wild emotions rummaging in my abdomen.

"You mentioned a cell, before we took to the air," he said as we walked.

My stomach squeezed further.

This was getting stressful.

I needed to kiss him, or screw him, or... bail.

The urge was overwhelming, but I ignored it.

"I was in juvie. There was... someone tried to hurt me. I killed them. It wasn't an accident. It landed me in jail for a few years." The words tumbled from my lips in short, choppy sentences.

"Your people imprisoned you for protecting yourself?" His voice was low, and I heard anger lining it.

"They thought I could've protected myself less violently. I probably could've. Really, I only went to jail because the man I killed had been friends with the people who decided whether or not I'd be punished." My voice was quieter. "I don't like to think about it. Or talk about it."

"I understand." His words were gravelly, though, and I could feel his fury seeping through the bond.

Something about the anger he felt toward them made me feel more justified in my own. It made me feel kind of loved.

"In our world, you never would have suffered for choosing to protect yourself. In the unseelie packs, perhaps, but not here. Here, we are free."

I bit my lip and nodded, those wild emotions in my chest only swelling higher.

The pressure of the serious conversation was starting to overwhelm me, though, and I began to feel a little trapped.

"Here we are." Lian's words had my gaze lifting off the dirt beneath my feet. Surprise raised my eyebrows as I took in the beauty in front of me.

Nestled between the rocks and trees was a lake with a thick, slow-flowing waterfall leading down into it. It was twice the size of Calian in his dragon form—so pretty damn big—but something about it looked cozy and comfortable. The water was a vibrant blue color that reminded me of a more muted version of some of the trees.

"Shit," I murmured.

It was the kind of place that normal girls would pin pictures of on Pinterest for, of their dream vacations, and the kind of place that rich people would create those pins about.

It was incredible.

"This is yours?" I looked at Calian.

"The land belongs to all of us." He lifted a shoulder lightly, his lips curving up. "But no other fae walk onto this mountain without my permission. To do so would be a death sentence."

"So yes, it's yours." I stared back at the lake. "Is the water warm?"

"Not on its own. But I think between our magic, the two of us can heat it fairly quickly."

My lips curved up at that.

He was right; we couldn't get cold without our fire turning itself on and warming us up. If we were in the water, it would do the same to the lake.

"It's safe to swim in?" I checked.

To answer my question, Calian swept me up off my feet and threw me in. A scream escaped me as I fell into the water—and then I gasped and kicked upward as the icy lake engulfed me.

The fae grinned massively when I surfaced, as he strode into the water himself. He'd dropped his pants, which didn't surprise me for a second, considering how much I knew he didn't like the fireproof clothing.

I tried not to stare at his erection.

Despite his nudity, I knew he wasn't coming into the water to have sex with me. If steamy shit happened, neither of us would protest, but that didn't seem like the reason he'd brought me there.

He'd brought me there because it was beautiful, and because he wanted to share it with me.

"Bastard," I yelled at him, even though the water was warming up around me already, and I was fighting a grin. My soaked hair stuck to my neck until the place it met the water, and from there, it flowed around me. It was its typical color, not having changed when my magical tattoos appeared.

And said tattoos glowed lightly under the water, catching my attention and widening my grin.

"You were thinking too seriously. The land insisted I take care of it," Lian tossed back. He dove under the water, surfacing again only a few feet in front of me, grinning broadly. "I've missed having you to myself, Ari."

Something about the way he used my old nickname made my grin widen. "You've missed having me naked in your arms, you mean."

He chuckled. "That too."

My eyes closed as the water around me warmed further. It was blissful. "You never taught me to connect with my land magic," I told him, opening my eyes a few moments later. The man was staring at me without an ounce of shame, his attention never wavering.

"Come over here and I will."

Touché.

I bit back the urge to distance myself from him, to put space between us and protect myself from whatever future pain could come of it, and swam toward the man.

He caught me in his arms, pulling me to his chest. My legs wrapped around his waist, and he didn't have a problem keeping us both above the surface of the water.

"Connecting with Vevol is easy," he murmured to me, his arms wrapping around my lower back. His grip was steady, and that calmed me despite my racing heart. "Just close your eyes and feel."

That didn't make a drop of sense, but I closed my eyes anyway.

"Everything in my world has come naturally to you, as if this place was created for you and you for it." Lian's voice was a soft stroke to my spine, moving along with his hands.

I pushed away the emotions that responded to both his words and his touch, and tried to *feel* it.

Water was engulfing most of my skin, and I could feel both of our magic thrumming within it. Beside the magic, there was something else.

Something... more.

Something *alive.*

"That's it," the man holding me murmured. "Embrace it, and whisper to it. Should you ask it to do something it's willing to do, it'll follow your will."

I focused on the magic around me, not my magic or Lian's, but Vevol's. As I focused on it, I felt it focus on me in return.

"Dance," I whispered silently to the magic. It wasn't all of Vevol—it was only the part making up the water around us.

As if someone had flipped a switch, the calm water surrounding me began to move.

A laugh escaped me when it tugged us around in a small whirlpool, and I opened my eyes to watch the water come to life.

Waves built and crashed on one side of the lake, currents coming to life and whisking away portions of the water. More whirlpools formed, small, soft ones, only to turn into new currents as the old ones morphed themselves into waves and whirlpools.

"It's beautiful," I admitted to Lian, my attention fixed on the lake even though my legs were wrapped around his back and our chests were plastered together.

"Or do *you* just find it beautiful?" the fae teased.

A laugh escaped me as I turned to face him. My lips were parted, ready to tease him back for using my ideas against me, but the words died in my throat.

He was grinning at me, staring at me like I was the only thing in his world that mattered.

I couldn't help it anymore; I grabbed his face and kissed him.

His arms tightened around me as our lips moved together, our mouths parting so our tongues could find each other.

Calian's fingers tightened on my thighs as he dragged me down, nestling his erection against my core exactly the way he knew I wanted it. I inhaled sharply as his hardness pressed into me. I'd been ignoring and avoiding intimacy with him for too long; I was too needy.

We kept kissing, my core rocking against his erection. The need built hard and fast in my lower belly, but I didn't want to lose it by myself.

If I was going over the edge, I wanted to take him with me.

"I want you inside me," I ordered him mentally, so I didn't have to untangle my mouth from his.

"I want your pleasure first," he growled back.

"That can come later. Right now, I want you."

He growled at me again, aloud this time, but his fingers moved down my ass.

He didn't bother removing my shorts, just pulled the damn things to the side. The water was warm on my bare skin, and I gasped into his mouth when the tip of his cock met my entrance.

Shit, I'd forgotten how big he was.

My body throbbed with need.

"*Now, Calian,*" I snarled at him.

His sexy chuckle only heated my body further as he guided his tip into me, just an inch, while his fingers teased my clit lightly.

I groaned into his mouth when he pulled out afterward, his hands on my core, parting me and playing with me. *"Bastard,"* I moaned silently.

He slid into me again, this time a little further, holding my hips firmly as I arched so that he remained in control. The man had a dominant side, and I hated how much I loved it.

My core clenched around nothing when he pulled out again.

He slid inside me again, pulling out one more time and squeezing my ass in punishment when I tried to shove myself further onto him. Our lips separated as I cried out, my head tilting to the sky when he pulled out again. "You're mine," he growled at me, his voice a mix between possessive beast and playful tease.

"Don't torture me," I panted, my eyes closing as the desperation clutched me.

"It's preparation, not torture." He slid into me one more time, and this time, he dragged me down, and down, and down.

My words stalled in my throat, my body ceasing to function as he sheathed himself fully inside me.

He was...

And I was...

Shit, the pressure was so insanely intense.

The man was touching, *stretching*, every part of me in a way that made me dizzy with need.

He throbbed inside me once, and then again.

A low snarl built in his chest, and then he was moving us.

The pressure and fullness were so intense. I cried out as the orgasm hit me hard and fast, desperation and pleasure raising my voice as he made love to me, bottoming out and pulling back so hard and fast I couldn't take it.

One orgasm turned into another as he finally roared, shattering inside me. His throbbing took me over the edge a third time, and when I dropped my face to his shoulder, both of us were breathing raggedly.

"Dammit," I groaned into his skin. "Why are you so good at that?"

"You taught me properly, I suppose," he tossed back, breathing just as hard as I was.

It definitely wasn't just me, though. "I did *not* teach you all of that."

"You taught me how to bring you pleasure; I figured out how to do it the way I wanted to." There was both satisfaction and humor in his voice, and the emotions teased me, too.

"Well, you're good at it." My grip on him tightened.

The foster kid in me wanted to take possession of him, to tell him that if he ever so much as looked at another woman, we would be done. Or to kick in and let him know that sex was just sex—and that it wasn't anything serious.

But I didn't do or say any of that. The instincts were there, but the desire was absent.

I wanted Calian more than I wanted that emotional safety, I guessed.

"You asked me what I wanted from you, from our mating, once," Lian murmured to me. My face was still planted against his shoulder, his cock still buried inside me. "I admitted I didn't know. Now, I have no doubts."

I bit my lip, tasting the salt from both of our sweat when I did.

"I want you to be mine, in every way there is. Heart, body, soul, and mind. You have all of me; I want to have all of you as well. I know you'll need time because human relationships don't work as quickly as my people apparently prefer them to happen, and I accept that. I'll wait for as long as you wish. But as far as I'm concerned, we belong to each other, fully."

My heart swelled. "This is insane," I whispered back. "But I think I want that too. I'm not ready to proclaim my love or promise you my soul or anything, but eventually... I want that. All of it."

His lips brushed my shoulder, and then the back of my neck. I was still dressed—and my shorts were probably tugging against his erection, but he didn't seem to care.

In fact, he throbbed inside me.

"You're ready for round two?" I asked, humor in my voice.

"You say that like it's surprising." He rocked inside me just a little, and my entire body throbbed. "I'm buried inside the most beautiful woman in two worlds. Why would I not be ready for round two?"

"It's..." My mouth dried, and my whole damn body clenched when his fingers slid up my inner thigh and found my clit. He pinched me lightly, and I rocked against him.

What the hell had he done to me? I was insatiable.

"Turn me around," I rasped, my chest already rising and falling quickly.

A moment later, his hands were hot on my thighs, and he lifted me off of his cock just long enough to turn me around.

When I sank back down onto his erection, I was panting. "Shit, Lian."

"On your lips, it's Calian," he growled back at me, his fingers hot on my clit and hip as he lifted me and sank me back down, again, and again, and again.

"Calian," I repeated, my eyes closing as I focused on the sensations. Him inside me, while he played with my clit, was just too much.

I cried out as I lost it, my eyes squeezing shut as the hot pleasure coursed through me.

He snarled and went over the edge with me, throbbing inside me.

"You're incredible," I panted, dropping my head back to rest on his shoulder.

He leaned forward and captured my lips with his in response.

Nineteen

After a long, slow, lazy kiss, we finally parted.

He slid his erection—yup, he was already hard again—out of me and fixed my shorts before he stepped around me, tugging me up onto his back. I wrapped my arms around his neck, and my chest pressed up against his ridiculously-muscular shoulders.

"What are we doing?" I checked.

"I'm going to show you something." His voice was playful again, and I loved the happiness I felt radiating off the man. It was such a simple emotion—but one I didn't think I'd ever get enough of.

He swam toward the waterfall, and I eyed it curiously. The water had gone back to its natural state at some point, so everything was quiet and calm again.

"Is it under the waterfall?" I studied the stream of water, looking for a clue that whatever he wanted to show me was hidden behind it.

"It is. Hold your breath."

I did as he instructed, and we dove beneath the falling water.

When we surfaced, I looked around in awe. There was no cave full of treasure, like I'd kind of expected given the whole dragon-and-treasure thing I'd heard fairytales about, but the cave was gorgeous. Glowing vines stretched across the walls of the space, which was twice as large as any bedroom I'd ever stayed in. A makeshift mattress of what looked like dozens of thick blankets piled on top of each other stood off to one side, with more flowers and vines growing around it, weaving the blankets together and making the bed glow.

Glittering formations of shining stone stretched down from and grew up toward the ceiling, while other bits of the stuff seemed to have dripped down the walls, creating what looked like a melted ice cream effect that made everything sparkle gorgeously.

"Damn," I murmured.

"Welcome to my mountain." The dragon gestured toward the cave. "This is the home no one but me has ever seen."

Shit, so the other cave was just to trick his brothers?

Clever.

I liked it.

"It's fireproof, I might add. The glowing flowers are called *hilsolev*, and they drop undetectable pollen that is Vevol's way of preventing fire from destroying anything beautiful."

"Nature's fire extinguisher," I murmured, looking around.

Knowing that Calian and I couldn't destroy the room, no matter how kinky things got, was definitely a relief. My room had been wrecked after the last time we were together, and I was still trying to get over that.

"How did you find this place?" I wondered, still looking around. "Or did you make it?"

"It's a long story." Calian flashed me a small grin.

"I have plenty of time."

He grabbed my hand. With a quick tug, he towed me to the bed. "Snuggle with me, and I'll tell you."

It had been a long time since we'd been in bed together.

Too long.

And even if I wanted to, I couldn't have resisted the damn snuggling.

I nodded, and he pulled me down onto the makeshift mattress with him. My clothes were already dry, thanks to their strange nature and my own heat.

We got comfortable in the bed together, with me lying on my back while Calian was propped up on his side beside me. I rested my head on one of his biceps, and his free hand sprawled over the part of my abdomen that my clothing left exposed.

"A long, long time ago, our world was almost destroyed. No one knows precisely how it happened, or how close we were to destruction. I assume that's when we lost our female fae, but no one truly knows." His fingers stroked my abdomen as he spoke. "The unseelie and seelie were already divided then, but we worked together to create the valley separating our lands to prevent more fighting after a particularly gruesome war. I was injured and set out to find a place to call my own for a time, as did the rest of the seelie. I stumbled across the cave you slept in the last time you were here, and stayed there while I healed."

His hand continued stroking my abdomen as he continued talking. "Many of our people were lost. Some, I was very close to. Life felt very bleak. When I no longer wanted to be alone in my cave, I wandered around the mountain. As I wandered, I found the lake and took a swim. While I was swimming, I felt drawn to the waterfall, and beneath it, I found this cave. It felt like the land's whisper to me that all was going to be well in the end—and that Vevol heard me, so I wasn't alone. Things were still lonely at times, as I suppose they are for everyone, but this place was a constant reminder that our land watches out for its people to the best of its ability."

Surprise and wonder mingled in my mind at his story. "That's kind of amazing."

He made a noise of agreement, continuing to stroke my abdomen. His fingers had nudged my top up a little, exposing more skin, and I sure as hell didn't mind.

"What was life like for you after that?" I asked, curious. "Things here seem so... simple."

"They are simple," he admitted. "We create fights just to prevent ourselves from going insane at times. We have books to read, and some of our people found ways to take movies and other entertainment from your world, but we lack purpose. The moment I caught your scent on Earth, I knew everything was going to change—and I couldn't wait."

My throat swelled a bit.

"What was life like for you on Earth? From what you've said, it doesn't sound pleasant."

Well, he was right about that.

And I didn't want to tell him the truth, at first. Didn't want to acknowledge the shitty life I'd survived.

But... he was holding me.

I was in his cave, his sacred, secret place.

And as crazy as it was, I trusted him.

So, I forced my instincts to leave me the hell alone, and I told him.

"It was hard. I told you about juvie. Before that, I had no parents. No one to raise me. No one wanted me or loved me. I was just... in the way. I guess that's probably why I push you away; I'm always afraid I'll lose everything and everyone again, or that it will all end up being a lie. I didn't have a real home or a job I enjoyed. It took everything I had just to survive on Earth. Here, things are simpler. Softer. Nicer, I guess, as crazy as that sounds when you consider that the people in this world turn into monsters."

Calian's hand caressed my abdomen and ribcage. At some point, my top had slid up to rest just below my tits. "I'm sorry," he said, his voice low. "I wish I could've retrieved you from your world earlier, saved you from some of that heartache sooner."

"Thank you." My words were barely above a whisper.

The air in the room felt heavy and tense, and I wanted to fix that. To distract myself from my painful thoughts, to... go back to the ease we had shared before.

So, I slid my hand up Calian's thigh.

The man stilled as I carefully ran my fingers over his balls.

His hand moved further up my shirt, and I bit my lip when he found one of my nipples.

"Tell me of your happiest Earth memory," the man growled at me, gripping my breast before sliding his hand down and pinching my nipple between his fingers. I rocked a little, my body responding naturally to his touch as I dragged my fingers upward and wrapped them around his cock.

"You don't want to know."

He pinched my nipple, hard. "Tell me, January."

The use of my name kicked its accompanying magic into gear, and the words came out before I could stop them. "The first time I had sex with a human guy.

It wasn't good sex—he was shitty. But no one could stop me, or force me to do something else. It felt like taking control of my life for the first time."

A low growl escaped him. "Tell me how he touched you."

"No." His words surprised me, and mine surprised me just as much. "I like what we have, Lian. I don't want my past to taint it."

He growled at me again, his hand sliding out of my shirt and then down my abdomen. My whole body clenched when his hand slipped into my pants. His fingers slowly dipped into the wet heat of my core.

I inhaled sharply when he dragged his finger over my clit. My fist clenched around his cock, but he didn't even flinch. Two orgasms in a row could do that to a man, I supposed.

"I want to know exactly how every man has touched you," he said, his voice low as he continued fingering me. "So I can erase your memory of their hands on your skin and replace it with my own."

"Possessive, huh?" I managed to ask, my body clenching and rocking as he rolled my clit between his fingers. A hiss escaped me when he pinched it hard.

"Extremely."

I closed my eyes. "I don't remember everything."

"Don't lie to me, January." His voice was lower, his snarl fiercer. "Tell me how they touched you."

A groan escaped me. "The first time, we were under bleachers. People were around, above us. It made it more thrilling. He was grabby. Too needy. He—" A sharp inhale cut me off. "Shit, Calian. Easy." He'd pinched my clit again, and it hurt in a way that made me dripping wet.

"Continue." His command had my back arching.

"He barely touched me before he pulled my pants down, and only licked me for a second. When I moaned, he thought I'd orgasmed, and pulled his cock out. Wore a condom." I panted, gasping between every word as Calian buried his face between my thighs and devoured me. "It was over fast. Not pleasant. I wished I'd waited for someone I loved."

Calian spread my legs wider, and his fingers slid inside me. I cried out a moment later, tightening on his fingers as I lost control.

We were both panting when he lifted his face from between my thighs, his mouth trailing over my hip and up my body.

When his erection was between my thighs, he stopped and lowered his face so his nose rested against mine. "You belong to me." His voice was low and dangerous. "Right, January?"

I was so turned on that I couldn't even think straight. "Right," I breathed.

He pushed inside me, and I cried out at the intensity of feeling all of him inside me again.

Shit, I would never get used to the insane thrill of it.

"Forget your bleachers. No one has ever, or will ever, touch you like I have," he told me, his chest rising and falling as our eyes remained locked together. "It's you and me now, January."

"You and me." I panted the words out as I moved with him.

We lost ourselves to the pleasure, then, growing silent as we worked each other until I was screaming and he was erupting inside me.

When we were both satiated, we collapsed into the position we'd been in a few minutes earlier.

"I want to hear the rest of your stories," he told me, his voice low. "I don't want any secrets between us."

"Fine," I breathed, my heart still beating rapidly. "But I told you, none of them were good. You're incredible."

"And possessive." His voice was growly. "I will make you mine in every way any other man has done it, and a million more."

Damn, that was a turn-on.

"Your funeral," I whispered back.

He chuckled, and his hand landed on my abdomen. "Tell me more about your childhood."

My throat swelled.

I didn't want to talk about it, but I could understand why he asked. And honestly, it had felt good to get some of that shit off my back with him earlier.

So I opened my mouth, and I told him everything he wanted to know.

TWENTY

SOMETHING about that cave felt magical. It felt... safe. When I told Calian about my life, it didn't feel like I was breaking my walls down; it felt like opening myself up to the possibility of love.

We could've been in there for days or weeks, talking, screwing, and laughing together. I loved every moment of it—especially the ones where he pulled out that damn pleasure-spice and rubbed it over way too many of our body parts. But eventually, we slipped out of the cave and into the water. After swimming around for a while, cleaning ourselves off, we got out and took to the skies.

Lian and I spent the better part of a day flying, trading stories, and teasing each other through our mental connection. It was, honestly, blissful.

When we grew tired, we flew back to the Stronghold. The forest around it was loud, and packed full of fae, but I knew that all of them had accepted that Calian and I were together.

I stumbled into Calian after shifting—mostly because he'd tugged me into his arms. My front was plastered to his, and I flashed him an annoyed look while he smirked at me. "Too many male eyes around here."

I went on my tiptoes to peek over his shoulder, and saw the forest legitimately *full* of fae dudes. "Holy shit."

There were four messy lines of men waiting, and it didn't take me long to figure out what the lines were for.

Each of the unmated chicks.

A snort escaped me when I saw that each of the men was holding a cake or something similar.

"I'd say news spread about the fact that mate bonds can form slowly," Calian drawled.

I couldn't even see the front of the lines, where the entrance to the Stronghold was.

"And the news that sex is a thing," I countered.

His lips lifted in a feral grin. "That too."

I smacked him on the arm, though I was grinning too. I'd never in my life smiled as often as I had during my time with Calian.

We made our way through the crowd, Calian's hand on my ass to keep me somewhat covered as he carried me. Whoever didn't move out of our way, my fae shoved with his shoulder or a wayward hand.

By the time we made it there, Calian was swearing under his breath.

"Move or lose your damn head," he growled at the last few fae in the doorway. Luckily for them, they stepped aside.

He threw the door open. To my surprise, the damn thing wasn't even locked.

We found the other members of the Wild Hunt in the living room. My eyebrows lifted as Calian carried me past all of them without so much as a greeting.

Sunny gave a wolf-whistle as she got an eyeful of my man's ass, and I caught a glimpse of Dots reaching over to cover her eyes, even though she was also grinning and checking Calian out.

My bedroom door closed hard, and I heard a couple of growls and snorted laughs from the other room.

"I can get my own clothes," I told Lian as he set me on the bed and strode into the closet.

"Of course you can." He returned with the clothing and a grin. "But it's much more enjoyable when I get them."

He tugged my shirt over my head, taking plenty of time to play with my tits in the process. When he pulled the shorts up my legs, I rolled my eyes as he did the same with my ass.

"So damn gorgeous," he growled into my mind. *"And all mine."*

"Your possessiveness seems to be getting worse, not better," I drawled back.

"It's definitely getting worse. And I expect it will continue to do so as I continue to realize how lucky I am." He leaned in and captured my mouth with his. It had been too long since we'd been together, and after that long flight, I wanted him.

But there were people in the other room, and I still didn't know whether or not the girls needed anything from us. There had to be a reason they'd let all the wild hunt guys in, right?

"After we've figured out what's going on, we'll head back to the mountain," Lian growled to me, out loud that time, as he ended the kiss. "And then I'll hold you captive for a few more days. Maybe a few more weeks."

A snort escaped me. "I don't think it counts as holding me captive when I'm there willingly."

"You can play along." His grin grew wicked.

I couldn't help but return it.

"Put your pants on before I get too horny," I complained, reaching out to grab his erection.

"Too late." He dragged my mouth toward him with a hand on my cheek, and I parted my lips to take his cock. Teasing him with my tongue a few times, I sucked a little just to make him harder.

When I pulled away, I tilted my head back. "Hurry up. The sooner we get this shit figured out, the sooner we can get back to our love cave."

He snorted. "Love cave?"

"It's the perfect name. I'll break your nose if you argue."

A laugh escaped him. "Love cave it is."

He stepped into his pants, and when I handed him one of his muscle-tees with a threatening stare, he tugged that on over his head. Once he was dressed, his hand caught mine and towed me back to my feet.

We made it out of the room and found everyone right where we'd left them.

Mare was pacing the kitchen, her hands tucked into the pocket of her massive sweatshirt. Sunny and Dots were sitting on the couch together, and Dots kept eyeing Sunny like she was afraid she was going to have to grab her or something. North was nowhere to be seen—so in her room, I assumed.

Priel, the hellhound guy, was sprawled across one of the couches, wearing an amused smirk. Ervo, the phoenix, sat on the armrest of a couch, his expression as serious as the damned grave. Teris, the sabertooth, was leaned up against the wall beside the window, his eyes scanning the lines of men as if he was waiting for someone to do something wrong. And Nev, the basilisk, was sitting on a couch of his own, staring at Sunny and Dots. I couldn't tell which of the women he was really staring at, but I supposed it didn't really matter if there was no mate-like attraction between them.

"What happened?" Calian asked everyone in the room.

"You decided that mate bonds can occur over time," Sunny said, lifting an eyebrow at Calian. "Didn't think that news would get around? You fae bastards have nothing to do but run around and gossip."

I bit back a snort.

It was kind of true.

"Best we could do to get the seelies under control was make them line up." Priel shrugged lazily, still grinning. "The unseelies have taken to sending letters."

"Letters?" My eyebrows shot to my forehead.

Mare grabbed a thick stack of them off the counter and held them up for me. "Look. Now that they know about sex, and that bonds can form over time, every one of these bastards wants us."

"Almost every one," Sunny corrected, tossing a hand toward Priel. "I already hit on that one. He's not interested."

Priel snorted. "Don't need pity sex, thanks. Pretty sure it would mate us, anyway, and I'm not interested."

Mare scowled at him. "This is serious. These people aren't looking for sex, they're looking for permanent attachments. Relationships. Love. We need to figure out a way to get them to calm down and just... leave us alone."

"Our people have been alone for a long time." Calian's voice was steady. "The only way you'll get them off your back is by mating with someone else. Even if sex wasn't on the table, they would still be here. We have no purpose right now; a mate gives us purpose."

"Lian's right. The other fae aren't leaving unless they know you're mated or you agree to see them," Nev said, still staring at Dots or Sunny. "There is an alternative, though."

"What is it?" Dots asked. "I like cake, but I don't need a couple *hundred* of them."

"The same thing we've all realized, I'm sure," Ervo spoke for Nev. "You all start bonds with us."

There was a moment of thick, stunned silence.

"We *what*?" Mare practically yelled.

"I already *tried* propositioning one of you." Sunny shot Priel a dirty look, and he lifted his hands in surrender.

"How would we even start bonds?" Dots protested. "We've gone on little dates with most of the guys out there; if we were interested or potential mates, we would've realized it by now."

"You've talked to them, but you've never touched them," I said. It was the first thing I had to offer to the conversation, but I did know more about having a mate than any of the other ladies in the room. "Kissing would probably be enough to start it. Snuggling, maybe."

All of the girls stared at me.

Mare looked like she thought I was crazy.

Sunny was grinning.

Dots seemed to be considering it.

"Absolutely not," North snarled from the doorway of her room. She turned her glare to the man beside me. "They call you their king. Send them away, and they'll listen."

"That's not how the seelie work," I answered for Calian. "The unseelie call him their king because they're trying to fit us in a box, but we don't fit. We're free. If he goes out there and tells them to leave, they'll fight him for the chance to stay. And there are enough of them that they'll eventually overpower him."

"This is on us," Dots agreed, though her voice was slightly reluctant. "We've got to build bonds if we want them to stop bringing us cake."

"I'm on board." Sunny shrugged. "Ever since I heard how much January enjoys screwing her fae, I've been on board."

A snort escaped me. "Classy."

"Just like you." Sunny winked at me.

She had a point, and we exchanged grins.

"Fine, I'll do it." Mare's face was looking a bit ashy, but her eyes were steely. "I don't want to go to the unseelies next year anyway."

All of us looked at North.

She still stood in her doorway, her fists clenched as she glowered at us.

"You don't have to do this," I told her. "But they're not going to stop coming for you if you don't, so it's a chance to take your life into your own hands."

Her jaw clenched; I saw the slight shift through her hair.

Another tense moment passed before she finally ground out, "Fine. I'm not getting with him though." She pointed a finger at Priel, who lifted his hands in surrender, still grinning.

"We'll draw names. I'm not doing a schoolyard pick," Sunny said, folding her arms over her chest. "Been there, hated that."

"We should get a veto, at least," North snarled.

Mare cut in. "No. Whichever name you draw, you get. If there's no choice involved for some of us, there's no choice involved for any of us. Otherwise, it's not fair for us or the men."

It took a moment, but finally, nods went around the room.

I didn't say a word, because I wasn't really involved in it. I'd already found my mate; neither of us was about to get roped into a fake mating.

"Fine." North gritted the word out. "January sets it up, so there's no bias."

I was actually kind of flattered that she trusted me enough not to be biased in favor of the other women.

Another round of nods circled the room.

"Here." Mare went over to one of the bookshelves and pulled out a few sheets of paper and a marker. I tugged Calian to the kitchen with me, taking the stuff too.

"Are the guys drawing the girls' names, or girls drawing guys?" I checked, as I tore the paper into four pieces.

"Girls are drawing." Sunny didn't hesitate.

The others agreed, so that was that.

Calian retrieved a bowl for me, and when North growled at him that he wasn't allowed to be involved, he stepped around to the other side of the counter and waited with the other guys. He didn't seem offended by her growl—only amused.

The whole thing seemed to amuse him though, and I had to admit I felt a little of the same. If I were in the other ladies' position, I wouldn't have found it funny though, so I kept my humor on the down-low.

I wasn't sure how to spell their names and didn't want to piss my dyslexia off, so I had the guys all write their names out a piece of paper, and then I folded each of the papers twice and put them in a bowl.

"Who's first?" I checked, shaking it up and stirring the papers around with my hand.

"This is a really messed-up Secret Santa game," Sunny muttered.

"Me." North held her hand out.

"No one opens them until we all have one," Mare warned, as I carried the bowl over to North.

She glared into the bowl, studying the papers before finally grabbing one and stepping back.

The other girls didn't care about the order, so I went to Mare, Sunny, and then Dots.

The air in the room was so thick it was hard to breathe.

Without a vocal instruction, they all opened them at once, staring down at the papers.

Not gonna lie, my heart was beating pretty damn hard. Mostly out of excitement. Also, because I was nervous for all of them.

North crumpled her paper and dropped it on the ground before turning and storming back into her room.

The door slammed so hard the damn thing rocked.

"Ervo," Mare said, biting her lip as she lifted her paper so we could see the names.

"Nev," Dots said, lifting hers too.

"Teris." Sunny followed suit.

Which left North with Priel.

...Who was currently grinning like a demon, of course.

"Let's get this over with." Sunny strode across the room and stepped in front of Teris, who was still facing the window. Then she placed her hands on his shoulders, leaned in, and kissed him.

"Can we talk in my room for a minute?" Dots asked Nev.

He dipped his head in a nod, standing smoothly when she did and then following her across the space.

Mare was biting her lip hard.

When I glanced back at Sunny, I found her and Teris still kissing—though they seemed to have graduated into an intense makeout session.

"We're gonna go..." I grabbed Calian's hand, tugging him toward my bedroom, towing him behind me. I shot Mare a thumbs-up as I went, and she gave me a panicked look in response.

There wasn't a damn thing I could do to make kissing Ervo any easier for her, though, so I shut my bedroom door behind us.

Calian grinned at me as I collapsed against the door, my shoulders shaking as I fought back laughter.

"Shh." He lifted his finger to his lips, stepping up to me so his pelvis met mine. His hands cradled my face, tipping it back and kissing me slowly and lightly. "They'll need time to talk to each other and get bonds started. When they're done, we'll address all the fae outside together. They're going to be pissed."

"Are the other guys going to have to fight?" I asked.

"I'm sure they will. They'll be thrilled about it, though. It's been too long since most of them had a real fight." His finger dragged over my lips before he leaned in and captured them.

He kissed me slowly, like he wanted to savor me.

His hands skimmed my sides, sliding down to wrap around my ass.

Our magic thrummed together, as if we were in tune with each other's power.

"You'll need to be quiet," he murmured against my lips. "Up for the challenge?"

"So damn up. Won't make a peep," I mumbled, slipping my hands under the hem of his shirt. It took a minute to work it out from under my thighs, where I'd trapped it. When it was free, I tugged it over his head, then tossed it to the ground.

He had my tank top off a moment later, and then smoothly turned me around. My tits met the door, and neither of us bothered to remove our pants.

His hand slipped into my shorts, and I clamped my jaw shut to stop myself from moaning when he stroked me, rocking his erection against my ass while he played with me. My breathing picked up, my body already hot and wet for him.

"You ready?" he growled into my mind.

"Hell yes," I panted back.

He tugged my shorts to the side. A heartbeat later, he slammed his cock into me in one hard, fluid motion. Our bodies rocked as they slapped together, and we froze for a moment, making panicked eye contact about the unintentional noise.

A snort escaped me, and he flashed me a wicked grin before he resumed. The man set a brutal pace, knowing exactly which angle was the best for me, and working my clit with his fingers at the same time.

The door shook as we made love, but neither of us cared—we were lost to the moment, to the pleasure.

I cried out into Calian's mind as I lost control, and his teeth clenched down on my shoulder as he held back his snarl. We shattered together, and as we lost it, a thought flittered across my mind.

If this wasn't love, I wasn't fucking interested.

Twenty-One

Calian—6 Months Later

The sound of flapping wings and paws on the ground met my ears as my palm slid over the smooth skin on January's back. She was asleep on the mattress in our less-friendly cave, the one she called our Home Cave. The other one, with the glowing flowers, was still the Love Cave. I didn't give a damn what she called them, so long as she slept in them with me.

And I was a lucky bastard, because she *always* slept in them with me.

Her snores were soft, her body more relaxed in sleep than it ever was during waking hours. I loved her when she was sleeping—then again, I loved her when she was awake, too.

I didn't bother with pants before striding out of the cave. My brothers were outside; I could hear them, and none of us cared if we were clothed. When you've seen one cock, you've seen them all.

They were arguing about something, but had stopped far enough from the Home Cave that they hadn't woken January, which was wise of them. If they'd woken her, I'd be pissed. When my female was tired, I wanted her sleeping. Especially considering I was the bastard who usually tired her out.

Recently, her scent had started to change. I didn't understand what the newest additions to it meant, and she said she wasn't ready to talk about it yet, but she'd started to tire easily and sleep more.

Even before approaching, I already knew what my brothers were arguing about.

It was always about the same thing, after all.

The women in the Stronghold, and the other fae who still insisted on fighting over them.

We enjoyed fighting, but six months of it nonstop was enough to wear anyone out.

"I'm not doing it anymore," Priel snarled. "I'm tired of the blood."

"What's the alternative?" Teris's weary voice countered. "Lock her in a room with you until you convince her to screw you?"

"Might as well ask one of us to kill you," Nev replied, his voice smooth and even.

Priel growled, "I'm going to throw her over my shoulder and haul her back to my cave. At least there, I have people who will keep the other bastards away long enough to get some real sleep."

"We don't need to kill him, then," Ervo mused. "North will do it for him."

They all turned to me when I reached them. "What's this I hear about abducting a female?"

"Technically, she's mine. I convinced her to kiss me, after all," Priel countered.

"You can't abduct her," Teris growled.

"Why not? Would any of you stop me?" His gaze scanned the group of us. "You know I wouldn't do anything messed up. Just take her somewhere safe so I can get a few nights' rest."

No one said anything.

His lips stretched in a wicked grin.

Damn, he was really going to do it.

"See you assholes in a few days." He didn't bother with any other pleasantries, turning and running into the forest without so much as a backward glance.

The bastard was faster than most of us; he would probably beat us there by a long shot.

But none of us made an effort to run after him.

"The bastard's idea isn't terrible," Ervo admitted, running a hand over his buzzed hair. "Maybe I'll get desperate enough eventually."

Teris shook his head. "Not worth it. Piss off one of those girls, and they'll all castrate you together."

"I can confirm that," January agreed.

My head jerked to the side, surprised to hear her voice. She was walking toward us, her arms wrapped around her abdomen. The woman was a damn goddess, having embraced the wildness of being both fae and seelie. The markings on her skin glowed, her eyes were bright, and her expression was calm. "What happened?"

"Priel's going to abduct North. Says he needs a few days of sleep," I explained as she stepped up to my side and snuggled in.

She snorted. "Bastard doesn't know what's about to hit him. That girl's going to kill him all on her own; she won't need the rest of us."

"Probably true," Teris grunted.

There was a moment of silence before January spoke up again. She was biting her lip, like she did when she was nervous, and I studied her closely.

"So, I have news," she said. "I didn't tell you guys everything about sex."

I narrowed my eyes at her.

What else could there be? We couldn't keep our hands off of each other most of the time, and she sure as hell enjoyed it at least as much as I did. I made sure of that every time, and prided myself in doing so.

"I didn't think it mattered, because none of us are human, but on Earth, if you have sex, it can lead to pregnancy."

There was a long pause.

She had me with that one.

"Women can grow babies, on Earth. Small people. They grow into bigger ones. I'm sure you've seen baby animals, on Vevol?" She looked at me, her face pinker than usual.

Was she embarrassed, or nervous?

I pulled her closer.

The other men nodded, and I realized she was waiting for confirmation, so I nodded too.

"I haven't had cycles since I've been here, so I didn't think it was possible, but..." She bit her lip again.

"Out with it," I growled at her.

She sighed. "I'm pretty sure I'm pregnant."

There was a long, heavy pause.

"Growing a baby?" I finally asked.

She dipped her head in a nod. "I won't know for sure for a few months, if I start showing, but other than not having a period, I have all the other symptoms. Exhaustion, bloating, excessive hunger… You're staring at me weird. Why are you staring at me weird?"

"This baby… it's Lian's?" Ervo asked.

She snorted. "Yes, definitely."

"And it's growing in your…" I trailed off.

"Uterus. Down here, below my stomach." She tapped her lower belly.

I sank to my knees in front of her, shock coursing through my veins.

My hands found her hips, and I leaned in toward her belly.

"Congratulations," one of the men said. "It's time we take our leave."

The other men agreed, and the forest grew silent as they left.

I was still staring at her lower belly, inhaling her changed scent. When I lifted my gaze, I found her eyes watering as she looked down at me. "You're excited?" she whispered.

"There are no words to describe my emotions." I leaned in, pressing my forehead to her abdomen. Her hands tangled in my hair.

"I was worried you'd hate me," she admitted.

My gaze lifted to hers, and then I stood smoothly, taking her in my arms and capturing her lips in mine for a long, thorough kiss. When I pulled away, I growled softly, "There's nothing in this world or the next that could make me hate you, and you know it."

Her cheeks reddened again. "Yeah." She bit her lip again, and after a long moment, admitted, "I love you, Calian. At first, I was terrified about the baby, but now… now, I'm so damn excited I can't even explain it."

I dragged her back into my arms, recapturing her lips with mine. The kiss was hot, fierce, brutal, and…

I pulled away. "You're having a *baby*?"

"*We* are having a baby," she corrected me.

My lips stretched in a grin. "And it'll resemble us both?"

"Hopefully, it'll just resemble you. But yeah, it should theoretically be a mixture of both of us."

I dragged her into my arms and took her lips again, pulling away when I couldn't stand it anymore. After tugging her shirt over her head, I tossed it to the ground near our feet. "You are everything I never dared dream for myself, and so much more."

Her shorts followed, and I kneeled in front of her, staring up at her.

Her knees shook a bit. "Right back at you, big guy."

I snorted, and her lips stretched into a wide grin.

My chest was so warm I thought it might burst.

I grabbed her by the ass, parting her legs and taking her weight as I dragged her core to my lips, kissing her until she fell apart in my arms.

When she was dripping wet, with dilated eyes, and was panting like she'd flown around the whole damn world, I laid her down on her back and lowered myself over her.

"You are my everything," I told her again, my voice rough and gravelly as I positioned myself against her slit. "And so much more."

Her eyes watered as I slid inside her.

The whole world could've been staring at us as we made love on our mountain, but neither of us cared.

We were together.

We were *one*.

And that was all that mattered.

The Feral Fae's Human

Wild Hunt 2

To the books and people who make dark days a little brighter.

One

My music played loudly enough to drown out the sounds of the men fighting outside. The northern wall of my bedroom was covered in wet paint; its newest mural was a gruesome picture of fire, hellhounds, and death.

That was all I saw when I closed my eyes, after all.

Myself, burning.

Priel, my fake fae mate, dying.

All the hounds in this damn world, turning to ash.

And me, at the center of them.

It wasn't any kind of future-sight, as far as I knew. My brain was just really damn twisted.

There was a knock at my door.

"I'm not hungry," I snarled at whoever was there.

I felt bad for snarling, but not bad enough to chill. If they came in, they'd see the evidence of my dreams and nightmares all over the walls. Some of them knew that I painted, but most of them didn't. I didn't really care whether they knew or not, as long as they didn't see how messed up my brain was. They'd probably kick me out of the Stronghold, and I was not interested in trying to deal with this messed up world of single fae dudes alone.

The fae had no women, so they wanted us—ex-humans that they'd dragged through a portal from Earth because we were stupid enough to make a wish to escape our world on the one night of the year that the fae dudes could break through.

There was a loud crack, and then my locked door swung open.

I was on my feet in an instant, my eyes burning as I snarled at the person in the doorway.

But it wasn't someone who would fear my fire.

It was the hellhound who haunted my dreams—and not just the nightmares. If I had one more sex dream about the bastard, I was going to burn my bed. On *purpose* this time.

"*Get out,*" I roared at him.

"No can do, little flame." Priel (pronounced 'preel') crossed the room, stalking toward me like a damn predator.

I didn't step back. I knew better than to run from someone who could take me down. "Don't fucking touch me."

"Sorry, love. Got to get some rest." With that, he grabbed me by the waist, threw me over his shoulder, and took off out the door.

Fucking hell, I was screwed.

He shifted into his bear-like hellhound form as he made his way out of the Stronghold, moving too fast for any of the other women to stop me, even if they'd wanted to.

I doubted that they wanted to, though. We weren't on great terms. Or good terms. Or even... terms.

Yeah, no.

Those chicks weren't going to rescue my grumpy, hostile ass.

My fingers dug into Priel's thick, fiery fur. It looked like it was made entirely out of flames, but the fire didn't burn me. Honestly it felt kind of nice on my skin.

Not that I'd ever admit it.

"Put me down!" I yelled at the fae guy, as he sprinted into the forest a hell of a lot faster than I'd realized he could move. My clothes—a long-sleeved shirt with a high neckline and long, loose pants, all made out of black fabric—didn't burn away somehow, so maybe he could control whether his fire was hot or not.

We barreled past about a million other fae guys as we went—many of which turned and started sprinting after us.

The Wild Hunt guys were keeping the other men away from me and the other ex-human ladies by pretending to be somewhere along the mating process with us. Unfortunately, that didn't stop the other fae from challenging them to fights. And more fights. And more damn fights.

If we'd actually been deep in the mating process, our scents would've started intertwining, so me and the other girls had to stay inside for the most part.

That wasn't abnormal for us, though.

And considering that now, the other fae could see me and smell me—and probably reach me—I knew everything was about to blow up in our faces.

"Hurry!" I yelled at Priel, gripping his fur tighter.

He didn't speed up, but a few more minutes passed, and I realized none of the fae chasing us were gaining on us. If anything, they were getting a little further behind us.

Priel kept running, and the distance between us and them started to widen.

And eventually, I couldn't see any other fae on the horizon.

It was just me, and him.

He slowed as we approached some jagged-looking rocks. I expected him to stop and let me off before we reached wherever we were going, but all of the sudden, he dove downward, and the ground seemed to drop out from underneath us.

A yelp escaped me as we plummeted into some kind of hole.

He landed smoothly, and I slowly lifted my face off of his back so I could look around the area. It seemed to be some kind of cave, and thanks to the magic coursing through my veins, I could see in the darkness of the room without a problem.

Before I got a good look at anything, Priel started to shift, and I flung myself off his back. I collided with the hard, smooth stone floor and instinctively made a pained noise even though it didn't really hurt.

A pair of gigantic hands grabbed me around the waist, plucking me off the ground and setting me on my feet.

"What are you doing?" The bastard sounded amused.

I stepped further away from him. "I'd rather not end up plastered to your human body, considering you *abducted* me."

"There's nothing *human* about me, female." His eyes reminded me of my own transformed orbs. The reddish-gold scared me every damn time I looked in the mirror.

I couldn't stop my gaze from sliding quickly down his body.

The man was a fucking work of art. He was massive, thick everywhere and much bigger than any human man could possibly be. Red, black, and gold tattoos covered almost every inch of his skin, and since all he had on were a pair of colorful shorts, there was plenty of skin showing.

I hadn't actually been calling him human; I wasn't that moronic. Priel couldn't have passed for a human if he tried, and he definitely didn't.

But it had annoyed him, so I just shrugged a shoulder and stepped to the side, intending to check out the cave he was holding me in.

He had made it very clear that he wasn't interested in being anything other than fake mates, so I knew he wouldn't try to feel me up or anything. That removed pretty much all of the fear that should've been involved in the abduction.

His voice followed me as I walked away from him. "I haven't slept more than an hour or two in months. My pack will keep the other fae away while we're here, so I can rest. When I've recovered, I'll take you back to the Stronghold."

I didn't respond, my eyebrows lifting as I took in the walls of the cave.

They looked like the walls of my room.

Minus all of the death, of course.

And the hidden bits and pieces of my sex dreams featuring the hellhound who wanted to keep things very, very platonic between us.

I'd been dreaming about him long before I drew his name and ended up fake-mated to him. I had tried to convince the other women to consider letting us choose our fake mates, too—or at least let us each have a veto to make sure we didn't end up with, oh, the fae we'd been sex-dreaming about for a year.

It hadn't worked, and of course, I drew the flaming bastard's name.

My gaze moved slowly over the images on the walls. Most of them were gorgeous landscapes—renditions of Vevol's beach, of its trees, of its mountains. Many of them featured the flaming bear-wolf creatures that the fae called hellhounds.

I was one of said hellhounds, though I had managed to stop myself from shifting thus far.

"You haven't said anything," Priel growled at me.

I silently flipped him my middle finger.

A low chuckle rumbled his chest. I wished I was pressed up against him, so I could feel that rumble, and then cursed myself silently for wishing that.

"Wake me up when you get hungry."

He stalked away, and I heard the rustle of blankets somewhere off to my right.

I'd never dreamed about us being together in this cave before, obviously. But based on the home I had imagined us together in, I wasn't at all surprised by how sparsely-furnished Priel's place was.

All of the walls were covered in paintings, but otherwise all he had was a huge bed, a shelf and table that were loaded with their world's version of art supplies, a bathroom, and a small kitchen.

I heard Priel's breathing even out a minute later.

My stomach clenched unpleasantly.

Clearly, he was nowhere near as attracted to me as I was to him. I didn't think there was a chance in hell that I'd be able to fall asleep in the same room as him.

Since I had nothing else to do, I slowly walked the perimeter of the room, checking out the paintings. I noticed a smallish hellhound in every one, and figured Priel had just painted himself a little smaller than he really was to make the landscape shine.

I wandered over to the art table after I'd studied all of the paintings.

There was an assload of paint, and something within me was settled by that. None of the tubes of paint seemed to have been opened recently, and they were all extremely clean and well-taken-care-of. The first fact was probably my fault, considering the bastard had been fighting off other fae to keep them from trying to hook up with me. But the second one made me curious.

Priel definitely wasn't a slob, if his living space was any kind of evidence. I... sort of was. It wasn't that I tried to make messes, or enjoyed having a messy living space. When it started to feel cluttered, I would move things.

I just wasn't a fan of the typical organization method that involved throwing everything into bins or lining it up on shelves. Leaving things exactly where I would use them next was far more logical to me.

My eyes moved over a massive stack of what sort of resembled sketch pads. The papers were all connected by some type of vine, which I found kind of fascinating. I'd never been great at sketching, preferring to figure shit out while I was painting it and just throw a little black or white on there if I needed a reset button.

Paint worked with my hands and mind; pens and paper usually did not.

That was the real factor, I supposed.

My eyes landed on a set of strange equipment next, and my forehead wrinkled.

It looked just like the strange, magical tattoo gun I had dreamed about Priel using on both of us at different times. Not *all* of my dreams of us together were sex dreams; just most of them.

There was a sharp bit at the end, and a bunch of small jars of paint around it. I picked it up carefully, studying it.

Though I'd seen Priel hold it to my skin in my dreams, I had no idea how it was supposed to work, or even how my subconscious had invented something that actually existed.

The needle would need to go up and down, wouldn't it? To break the skin?

Hmm.

I unscrewed the lid on a jar of silver paint and then rolled one of my sleeves up just enough to expose one of the bruise-like burns that covered much of my skin. When I came to Vevol, I'd had an assload of scars. And when my magic settled a few weeks after I'd arrived, I'd woken up on fire one day.

The flames hadn't hurt, but my clothes had been roasted, and all of my many scars had morphed into terrible-looking purplish-black patches that looked like a mix between bruises and burns.

I kept them covered so I wouldn't scare any of the other women... and maybe just in case a fae guy came to the door for me.

Preferably a blond, inked-up fae guy.

It hadn't happened since the beginning of my time in Vevol, which was my fault. I knew it was my fault.

But I still kind of wished the men would come.

That *he* would come.

Or at least, I *had* wished that, until the fae men realized that the mating bond could form over time. Then they'd started flooding the Stronghold. And I didn't know how to talk to them, or how to consider them, so I just... didn't.

But I'd always seen the way my parents loved each other. They were shitty people, honestly. Good to me and my older sister, but shitty people.

None of my scars had been their fault. At least, not directly or intentionally.

And damn, I missed them.

My chest was tight at the thought of it.

There was no way back to Earth, though. And if I had found a way back, I eventually would've regretted going. My parents' business would've been unavoidable, and I would've ended up doing shitty things myself.

At least I had escaped before that happened.

I NEEDED to force my thoughts back to the present, so I dunked the tip of the magical tattoo gun into the ink and then lowered it to my skin. I didn't know what I'd create, but then again, I rarely did.

Biting my lip in preparation, I carefully stuck the tip into my skin.

A sharp flash of pain followed—and blood gushed over the small cut as I lifted it back out, muttering curses under my breath.

My eyes stung a bit.

Whew, that hurt.

"What the hell?" Priel's tired, grumpy ass growled from the bed. "Why do I smell blood?"

"I'm fine," I shot back, setting the tattoo gun back down and easing my sleeve over the discolored patch of skin again. When I pressed the black fabric to the wound, it soaked up the blood quickly.

Maybe I was bleeding more than I'd realized.

Heavy footsteps sounded on the ground, and my stomach clenched.

Fuck, I was terrible at talking to Priel. I didn't know what to say, or how to say it, or how not to sound like a complete bitch. Or if I even *wanted* to not sound like a complete bitch.

He was gorgeous.

And I was... not.

I mean, my face was fine. I'd never really been allowed to talk to guys, so I didn't have many interactions to base that idea off of, but I hadn't been told I was hideous or anything. My parents had homeschooled me and my sister, because going to school would've been too dangerous for us given my parents' questionable life and business decisions.

They were sort of... mafia.

Okay, not sort of.

They *were* mafia.

They'd even arranged my sister and I into those damn mafia-family marriages you read about in romance books. My sister was happy with her man, but I didn't know what those authors were smoking, because my experience sure as hell didn't resemble a romance book.

I'd ended up jumping out of a moving car to save my own life before the supposed marriage. That led to being alone and injured in the damn forest for multiple days, before my parents found out what happened and sent someone to find me. After that, I'd spent a month in the hospital recovering from said jump.

The PTSD was a nightmare. Therapy had helped a little, but that and my parents' overprotectiveness had been the reason behind my wish on a bunch of birthday candles for a fresh start.

That wish—and having a birthday on what was apparently Winter Solstice—got me dragged to Vevol.

I hadn't wanted to leave my family, or even my life. I just...

Well, I didn't know what I wanted.

I'd been in Vevol for well over a year and a half, yet I still hadn't figured that shit out.

Maybe I never would.

At least I had paint.

But anyway, my body wasn't art. Not the way Priel's was. I wasn't nice to look at; I could imagine his potential cringe vividly assuming he saw the patch of bleeding, bruised-looking skin, and tugged my sleeve down further.

He walked up to me and plucked the tattoo gun from my hand. The tip of it caught on fire, and my blood burned off of it quickly before he set the tool back down on the table, exactly where I had picked it up from. "What are you doing?

"I was trying to give myself a tattoo. Couldn't figure out how that thing worked." I tossed a hand toward the tool. "On Earth, they have motors."

At least, I thought they did. I didn't know anything about them, honestly.

"Giving a tattoo requires altering a person's magic. You don't break the skin with that," he grumbled at me, grabbing my hand.

His sudden grip surprised me. It took me a minute to process the warm, comforting feel of his skin on mine.

Before I recovered enough to tug my hand away, he peeled my sleeve up my arm.

And then stared down at my patch of skin—and the already-healing cut—for way too long.

I tried to tug my hand from his grip again, but it tightened around my wrist.

"What is this?" He finally looked up at me.

"Don't worry about it," I snarled.

He still wouldn't let go, so I shoved my knee up toward his crotch. The bastard caught it deftly, and I swore when he held me by the arm and knee both.

"Where and when did you get this?" Priel's eyes were fiery, as always. The color wasn't always so bright and intense, but fire blossomed within the orbs whenever he got all riled up, and I seemed to rile him up almost constantly.

"Let go of me," I shot back.

He released my knee, but stepped closer to me, his eyes dipping back to my forearm. "I need an answer, North. This kind of marking is something we call Vevol's Brand. She only brands those who can tap into her magic on a deep, dangerous level." He *finally* let go of my arm and stepped back.

My eyes flew open wide when he stripped his shorts off, turning his back to me and flashing a gorgeous, tight, tattooed ass in my direction.

Shit.

Holy shit.

His finger pointed to the back of one of his thighs, and my eyes finally unglued from his butt long enough to see what he was pointing to.

A large, purplish-black bruise-burn that he hadn't touched with any ink. It had become a part of his body's artwork, blending in with everything else, but I had seen enough of them to know it was the same as mine.

A *Vevol's Brand.*

"I caught fire shortly after I figured out how to break through the veil between our worlds to bring women through to Vevol, and this appeared," he said, his voice low as he looked at me intensely over his shoulder, studying me. "When did yours appear?"

Oh, shit.

He thought I only had the one brand.

Honesty would probably be best, but if those things were supposed to be rare, then I couldn't just tell him I had dozens.

"A few weeks after I was brought here." I tugged my sleeve back down my arm, ignoring the awful feeling of the damp, bloody fabric dragging over my skin.

His eyes narrowed. "Before or after the last time I brought you supplies?"

Did he actually remember doing that?

I had been pretty damn sure he thought I was the most uninteresting person ever. He hadn't even bothered flirting with me, like he did the other women.

That didn't stop me from having sex dreams about him.

"Before."

If he questioned how perfectly I remembered those times and our interactions in particular, I'd make another attempt at kneeing him in the balls.

"You should've told me." His words were nearly a snarl.

My snapped response came out before I could think it through. "Why the hell would I do that? The other girls got pretty magical tattoos; I got awful-looking burns. And you were *far* from interested in me or my life."

His eyes narrowed. "Burn*s*?"

The emphasis he put on the "s" made me curse silently.

I glared back at him, literally biting my tongue to stop myself from saying things I would regret.

"Where's your other one?" he demanded.

"None of your damn business. And if you try to strip me to find it, I will scream until one of the other fae shows up and kills you for *hurting* me."

His eyes burned with fury, and he grabbed his shorts off the ground, turning as he yanked them up his body. "I would never fucking do that."

"Then back off." I spun around, stalking to the bathroom and shutting myself inside. The door locked behind me, and I collapsed against it. My eyes were stinging, and my body was shaking.

My burn-bruises were *brands*?

Special markings that somehow represented Vevol?

What the hell did that mean?

Two

When I eventually calmed myself down enough to step back out into the room, I found Priel sitting on the edge of the bed, tapping his foot harshly on the floor. I'd come up with a plan that would get me away from the bastard. It wasn't an ideal plan, but it was a hell of a lot better than spending the next few days alone with him in his home.

His gaze jerked up to me as I stepped out, and darkened when he saw me.

"I've decided to face the rest of the fae and look for an actual mate to end the fighting," I told him bluntly. "Thanks for trying to protect me, but I'm done with this whole fake-mate shitshow."

Forcing myself to remain calm, I crossed the room until I was standing right below the hole we'd fallen into to get into the place.

When I eyed the wall, I realized there were handholds and footholds of sort.

Of course the fiery bastard had to climb a literal rock wall to get out of his house.

"You can't do that." Priel's fingers wrapped around my wrist as I reached toward the wall.

I flashed him a glare. "Why the hell not?"

"Because if anyone sees a glimpse of either of those brands, you'll become worth a lot more than any of the other women."

I blinked.

Women were the most valuable thing in Vevol. There were only twenty of us, to *hundreds* of men. And while we weren't treated like objects, or property, or money, we could get almost anything we wanted just by batting our eyes at the men.

"Why would that make me *worth more*?"

"Vevol branded you. She *chose* you. Your power will be far more intense than any of the other women. There are only two of us male fae with brands, North. I discovered and opened the portal to the human world. The unseelie king turns his half of the world into an icy mess to enforce the borders between our territories."

Shit.

So the markings were even worse than I thought.

That sounded like just my luck.

Priel's gaze was steady as he stared at me. "You need to learn how to access whatever power Vevol gave you when she branded you, so you can protect yourself, before you even consider choosing a mate."

I scoffed and pulled my wrist from his grip.

He let me go, that time.

I argued, "It sounds like what I *need* to do is choose a mate before word gets out about my magic."

His eyes burned hotter. "Our supposed connection will protect you. None of the other fae will take you from me; they know that doing so could convince me not to open the portal between our worlds, and they're desperate to find their other halves."

I tossed a hand toward him. "They don't even believe that we're together. If they did, we would've had sex by now, and they wouldn't be challenging you. Right?"

His jaw clenched.

Yeah, I had thought so.

The only thing we had done to create the beginning of our "mate bond" was a quick peck on the lips. It had been awkward as hell, and I'd shut myself away in my room for a month afterward so I wouldn't have to see him again.

Seeing him, kissing him...

Well, my unconscious self already had a crush on the guy. The sex in my dreams was unreal, and there wasn't a chance in hell that it could ever happen like that in real life, even if Priel was interested in me.

Which he was not, nor had he ever been.

I went on. "Right now, they're all chasing me because they don't think I've made a real connection. If I can make that happen with someone and my scent actually changes, would most of the fae back off?"

The fierce clench of his jaw told me that my hunch was right.

"If these brands are as important as you claim, and I'm really in danger because of them, then I need to act. Right?"

"Right. But there are many ways to *act*." Priel ground the words out.

"Well, I've already made up my mind." I spun around, stalking toward the rock wall. My toes found the first hold, and I pulled myself up a few inches before his hands latched onto my waist.

He plucked me off the wall and set me on my feet, before stepping up close. Our chests pressed together, and I inhaled sharply at the contact.

"The fae already believe I'm pursuing you, at least somewhat. They know that our connection has begun to form, even if they don't truly believe we have a relationship. If safety is what you seek, *I* am the answer. Not another male." His voice was a low, harsh growl.

Maybe if he'd been asking because he wanted me, I would've agreed.

Maybe if he'd told me he was attracted to me, or called me his, I would've kissed the hell out of him.

Because he didn't, I ignored the flashes from my dreams that rolled through my mind with his ideas.

I opened my mouth to tell him to back off, but then his hips trapped me to the wall.

My mind went blank when I felt his erection against my belly.

"My pack doesn't believe I've claimed you because my scent isn't on your body. We change that, and we'll earn the pack's belief. They'll spread the word faster than I ever could."

"How would we do that?" I argued. "I'm not having sex with you."

"Of course not," he scoffed.

My defenses rose, and I tried to shove him away from me.

He didn't budge. "Sunny and Teris merged their scents slightly by kissing more intensely. We'll do the same."

"Like hell we will. Step away from me, now," I bit out.

He took the tiniest step back.

His erection was still trapped against me, but I forced myself to remember that he wasn't attracted to me; he was attracted to the fact that I was a woman.

"I'm not doing this," I told him, forcing my voice to remain steady.

His nostrils flared, and hot anger burned in his eyes.

He did step back, though.

Finally, I could breathe.

"My pack lives close by. I spoke with them; they're keeping other fae away while I rest. They're trustworthy. I can introduce you." His words were ground out.

Was he offering other men for me to make out with, to combine my scent with?

Hurt bloomed in my chest.

The bastard *really* didn't want me.

"Let's do it now. You can sleep while I talk to them," I agreed, hiding the hurt behind my angry façade.

I *was* angry, but mostly...

Overwhelmed.

Worried.

Sad.

Fuck, I hated having emotions.

"Fine." He stepped past me, and my eyes were glued to his backside as he made quick work of the rock wall that really *was* the exit of his home. My body was stronger since I'd become a fae, but I still moved slowly as I began climbing up. It was at least fifteen or twenty feet, so... scary as hell.

Priel's hand stretched out as I neared the top.

I wanted to take it, but then again, I also wanted to be naked with him.

In his bed.

While his face was between my thighs.

Yeah, I needed to chill.

To focus, too.

My mind was a mess. Guess that came with the territory of the fae you were crushing on introducing you to his friends so you could hook up with them.

Maybe I'd get lucky and it would end up like one of those reverse harem books. A handful of hot, powerful fae would declare me theirs and be more than happy to dote on me and share me, and I'd never have to look at or dream about Priel again.

Although, I was a virgin. So, not really sure I'd know what to do with one dick, let alone five.

Maybe I should just hope one of them would catch my fancy and fill my dreams from here on out.

I ignored Priel's outstretched hand, hauling myself out of the cave and collapsing on my ass before I took a quick look around. The space was rocky, and there were massive, harsh cliffs surrounding us.

When I looked overhead, I saw a bunch of flying creatures. They had to be fae, but the jagged rocks far above us jutted out in spiked angles, protecting us from the winged beasts.

"Why is she bleeding?" A low male voice jerked my attention to the group of men around us.

I tried not to take a step back when I saw them.

There were so many massive male fae surrounding me, it made my head spin. They were all wickedly strong, but with a variety of skin colors and face shapes. Every one of them was totally inked-up, just like Priel.

I counted them silently.

Nine.

Nine damn men.

Please let this not be a reverse harem situation.

Nine dicks was way, way too many for this chick.

Nope, I could not do it.

Not my thing.

Send help.

"Stuck herself with my tattoo pen," Priel grumbled. "North wants to get to know you while I sleep. Don't overwhelm her, and don't even fucking think about touching her."

With that, the bastard shifted and jumped smoothly back into his cave.

Asshole.

I tried not to let my body fold inward at the thick weight of the fierce attention of eight massive, gorgeous men.

"We'll take turns. Alphabetically," one of the men finally growled.

The others grunted their agreement, and quickly made themselves sparse, leaving me with one of the guys. He had dark skin, and I tried not to stare at the colorful tattoos stretching across his body. They weren't as gorgeous as Priel's, but they were still gorgeous.

"Who does all of your ink?" I asked him, peeling my eyes off him and focusing out on the forest in front of us. "Most of it is in the same style."

I was ninety-nine-percent sure I already knew the answer, but wanted to be certain.

"Priel. Manipulating magic thoroughly enough to mark the skin permanently requires more power than most of us could imagine," the man admitted.

Dammit.

"What's your name?" I checked.

Hopefully someone had set a timer or something. If I was going to speed-date a bunch of fae, I needed that damn timer to keep it from getting awkward.

"Bovay."

"Nice to meet you, Bovay." My words were polite, even though I didn't feel them.

A stretch of silence had me cringing inwardly.

"So, how does the pack work? Priel is the leader?" I asked, trying to keep things from getting worse.

"We have no leader. Priel was branded by Vevol, so he's the strongest of us. We respect him because of that, but we're a family, not a kingdom."

So they didn't do the Alpha shit that werewolves supposedly did according to the many romance books I'd read on Earth.

"What does that mean? That he was *branded by Vevol*?" I asked carefully, making sure not to come across as too eager or curious. Suspicion was not something I wanted to attract.

"Vevol chooses the strongest fae and blesses them with an extra gift of power."

So Priel had told me the truth.

Dammit again.

I searched my mind for another question. There was so much shit I didn't know, and hadn't had a way of finding out. I just had a hard time remembering all of the questions when I was in the moment.

"Why did some of the fae follow me here when they could all just wait back at the Stronghold to meet the other women?" I asked. "Wouldn't that be easier?"

"It's all about scent." Bovay tapped the side of his nose. "The fae are in line to meet the females that smell the best to them. Those are probably their best chance for a compatible mate."

Oh.

I wasn't sure whether that was interesting or insulting.

"So when a guy isn't interested in me, it's because I smell wrong?" I asked.

"Or just don't smell right," Bovay agreed.

Damn.

Maybe that was why Priel had never wanted me.

I *just didn't smell right* to him.

That made me want to punch something, though.

"Why don't you guys smell different to me, then?" I asked.

"You haven't shifted."

Huh.

"Does shifting hurt?" I had always wondered that, but never been brave enough to ask.

"Of course not. You're a hound as much as you're a fae."

I'd never thought about it like that.

"Can you teach me how?" I asked him, suddenly sort of eager. I'd fought so hard not to shift back in the Stronghold, but now...

Well, I wanted to try it. To see what happened.

"After you've met the rest of the pack," Bovay agreed. "You don't smell right to me."

Of course I didn't.

With him, I was kind of glad about that though.

He stood and nodded toward me before strolling off into the trees. Another man came out immediately, jogging over to me and sitting down.

He flashed me a grin, and I fought one of my own. I couldn't help it; the guy was gorgeous, and looking at me like he thought I was too.

"I'm North," I offered.

"I know. I'm Clevv." He offered me a hand, in a very human gesture that he must've learned just for a situation like this one.

Not wanting to be rude, I shook his hand. Most of the time, I didn't mind the rudeness. Rudeness was good for creating space between you and the people you wanted space from.

But it also hurt people, and I felt bad about that often.

"You have beautiful hands," he offered me, as he shook my hand longer than was necessary."

My face heated. "Thanks."

"Are you an artist?"

"How did you know?"

He chuckled. "There's paint beneath your fingernails. I'm surprised Priel's flames didn't burn it away."

Oh.

"His flames didn't feel hot when he was running here."

The man lifted an eyebrow. "That takes a lot of control. I should thank him for taking care of my future mate so well."

A snort escaped me, and he flashed me a grin as I slipped my hand out of his. "So how bad do I smell to you?"

"You smell like smoke curling off a cooking klomre. Fucking delicious."

I bit back another snort. "I'm not looking for a permanent mate. I just need someone to bond with so my scent changes enough that the other guys stay away."

"You can use me in any way you'd like." He winked at me.

A laugh escaped me. "I'll keep that in mind."

"So what kind of things do you paint?" His expression was so full of interest that I couldn't stop myself from answering.

"My dreams, mostly. I have strange, vivid dreams."

He looked intrigued. "Some say Vevol herself communicates through dreams."

"Do they?" I didn't buy into that shit, so I feigned interest. "I've never heard that before. None of the other fae ever referred to your world as a goddess before, either."

"Different types of fae have different beliefs. All of us feel that Vevol is female, and alive. Some believe she has a physical form and can appear to people. Hellhounds, for the most part, believe she is the consciousness of our world as a whole, without a fae-shaped body."

Interesting.

January had never said anything about that, and she knew the fae much better than any of the other girls who had been in the Stronghold.

"What about the dragons?"

"Dragons are solitary fae. They don't run in packs, other than Lian. And he only works with the rest of the Wild Hunt because there has to be one of each type. Though dragons typically believe that Vevol is alive, they have no reason to think she has thoughts or a will of her own."

Huh.

He continued explaining the beliefs of the fae as I went through the different types, and I tried hard to store all of the information for later. I didn't ever have anything to contribute to the other girls in the Stronghold, but maybe if I did...

Well, maybe things could change.

It wasn't likely.

I had pushed them away for a long time. At first, because I was scarred by the way I'd been ripped away from my family. And then, because of my awful dreams.

But there was a chance that I could maybe become friends with them, and honestly, I wanted that. Even though it sounded really out of my reach.

The next fae replaced Clevv after a bit more time had passed, and then a new fae was sitting down next to me.

Time moved quickly. The fae were mostly friendly, though three of them were painfully awkward. I did my best to keep the conversation moving with all of them (despite my own awkwardness), and learned a hell of a lot more about the fae than I had ever known.

THE SUN HAD SET when I finally made it through the last man, and then they all made their way back over and reformed the group they had been in earlier. I chatted with a few of them, appreciating the new, relaxed feel that the group had taken on after I got to know them all a little.

I wasn't ready to choose one of them to be my mate permanently—that much, I was positive about—but I did need to connect myself to another man to free myself from Priel.

And I was really hoping the end of our connection would be the end of my damned sex dreams about him.

When my stomach growled, all of us made our way to a cave nearby where we could eat. It was shaped the same way Priel's place was, with a big drop into it and a climbing-wall leading out. The inside held a large kitchen, though, with a pantry of sorts built into the stone walls and filled to the brim with food.

Across from the kitchen, there were a few massive cushion-things that reminded me of large bean bags. Those of the men who didn't start cooking settled onto them, still talking and laughing. They were discussing a hunt they had done together, so I mostly ignored them.

My mind went back to the hot moment with Priel earlier.

The way he'd had me pinned against the wall, and his body's clear desire for me.

My heart clenched as I remembered his disgust with the idea of having sex with me.

Fuck, I needed to get away from him.

Not just distance-wise, but emotionally.

My gaze slid over the men before it settled on the flirty Clevv, who had joked about me being his future mate.

He felt me staring, and flashed me a grin.

The man had offered to let me use him. He didn't care whether or not I wanted permanence—which I didn't, yet.

He was the perfect choice.

I let the decision to form a temporary bond with him settle in my mind as we all ate together. The food was incredible, and *so* different than what I'd eaten back in the Stronghold. It was nice to try something new, honestly.

And after we were done, I was ready to try something *else* new.

Making out with a fae.

It was go time.

Three

THE OTHER MEN TRICKLED OUT, some of them headed for their homes to sleep for the night. Others went out to guard the land we were in, though they reassured me that no one was stupid enough to waltz in without assuming they'd lose their head.

But Clevv stayed, and I did too, until we were the only ones left.

Swallowing my nerves, I walked over to the bean bag he was pretending to doze on.

His eyes opened, and he gave me a slow, animalistic grin. "Decided to take me up on my offer?"

I forced myself to bite back a smile. "I did."

He sat up, maneuvering so he was sitting on the edge of the bean bag with his feet pressed against the floor.

I stepped closer, and his hands remained on his knees.

"Here." I grabbed his hands and awkwardly set them on my hips.

A rumble of approval escaped him as his fingers slowly squeezed, feeling my body through my clothes.

No way in hell were those things coming off.

The brands needed to stay hidden, after all.

And honestly, I wasn't super attracted to Clevv. He was gorgeous and had a great smile, and I hoped he could make me forget about my eighteen months of attraction to Priel. But he didn't make my blood hot or turn me on the way the blond hellhound did.

Then again, if *hot blood* was the only reasoning behind why I was with a guy, I'd probably end up regretting that decision at some point.

Maybe not at the beginning, but eventually.

I'd never kissed a guy before my awkward peck with Priel, but after so many insanely-realistic, hot dreams, I didn't hesitate when I pressed my mouth to Clevv's.

He let me take the lead, his hands gentle on my hips while I slid my tongue into his mouth.

He groaned, parting his lips and swiping his tongue against mine. He didn't taste bad, but didn't taste good, either. And his tongue didn't feel wrong... it just didn't feel *right*.

The kissing was still enjoyable though, so I put my hands on his shoulders and stepped a little closer.

He took that as permission to pull me where he wanted me, and dragged my pelvis to his. His erection was near my core, and it felt okay. Not horrible, but not great, just like everything else with him.

I was new to all of it though, so maybe it would get better with time. And none of it felt bad or wrong, so I didn't protest.

His hands dragged up my back, pulling my shirt higher before his fingers dug into my hair.

We kept kissing, and he seemed to be getting hotter and heavier. I wasn't getting horny, but the way his hands moved over my back and in my hair told me he was.

Which meant I probably needed to think about ending the kiss, but I was still mostly enjoying it.

A roar in the distance had me jerking my mouth away from Clevv's, my head turning in the direction of it. We were underground, so I didn't see anything, obviously.

"Someone's always roaring here," he murmured to me. He looked down at my tits, and I noticed that my shirt had ridden up, revealing a strip of skin and two or three of my *brands*. I yanked it down into place as his hands wrapped around my face and dragged my mouth back to his.

I was pretty done with kissing after accidentally flashing him my brands on top of not really feeling it, but let him slide his tongue into my mouth again.

There was a thud off to my left, followed by a furious snarl, and then massive hands were ripping me away from Clevv.

I landed on a squishy beanbag-thing just in time to watch Priel throw the other man against the wall. Priel's fist flew into Clevv's face, and an awful crunch had my eyes widening in horror.

"What the hell?" I sputtered.

Priel's fist slammed into Clevv's face again, and I let out a shocked sound that I didn't want to admit resembled a whimper.

Priel's head jerked toward me, and I saw his eyes flooded with fire. His face was twisted in a furious snarl, and for the first time outside of my insane dreams, there wasn't a shred of humanity in his expression.

The only time he ever looked like that in my dreams was when he was losing himself inside me at the end of a particularly kinky round of sex.

And of course, my body responded to the mental images that flickered in my mind next.

Images of Priel.

Making out with Clevv hadn't done a damn thing to turn me on, but apparently just thinking about the Priel of my dreams was enough to get me going.

Great.

A furious roar escaped Priel, and he slammed another fist into Clevv's face. If Clevv was fighting, I didn't know. I couldn't look at him. Not while I could smell his blood.

My arms wrapped around my stomach, and I hunched in on myself. I wanted to be the kind of chick who ran into a fight and broke it up, but I just... wasn't.

Five more thuds sounded, one after another.

"What happened?" another male hound growled.

"Help me get Priel off of him," another one ordered.

All of them launched into the fight.

My arms squeezed my abdomen painfully tight, and I watched in awful, tense fear as they wrestled Priel away from Clevv. Clevv collapsed to the ground immediately after Priel was removed from him, and I hoped like hell that he wasn't dead.

"North," one of the men wrestling Priel snarled. "Come over here, now."

His command had me freezing in place even more completely.

What if Priel hurt me?

What if—

"He's going to kill us if you don't get over here," another man snarled.

That was enough to get even my terrified ass off the beanbag.

I hurried over to them.

One of them grabbed my arm, rolling away as he yanked me downward. He shoved me right on top of the fighting Priel, his gigantic hands pressing me into the furious hellhound now bucking beneath me.

My long, dark hair hit him in the face, and he froze.

A slow, feral snarl escaped him, and my whole body tensed.

His hands landed roughly on my hips.

They were in exactly the same place Clevv's had been, but the feeling was vastly different. He didn't just touch me because he liked the way I felt—he gripped me possessively, like I belonged to him.

Like he would kill anyone who tried to take me from him.

That had to be in my head. I knew it had to be in my head.

But I still couldn't stop the warmth in my chest because of it.

"We have to get out of here," one of the other men said in a low voice. "Someone grab Clevv."

"North," one of the men said.

Priel snarled furiously, and his needy grip on my hips tightened painfully. I didn't hate the pain, though. It made me feel more alive than I'd felt in the entirety of the eighteen months I'd been in Vevol.

There was a moment of silence, and then the same man said, "He won't hurt you. His beast side has taken over, and reason won't work. But he won't hurt you."

I hadn't thought he would hurt me, but the words still made me feel better.

Still, I tried not to react to them. Priel didn't seem to like the other men talking to me in his current *state*.

I remained where I was as I heard sounds that had to be the other hellhounds climbing out of the cave. My face was on Priel's chest, and I could hear his heart pounding furiously.

Despite his stillness, the man wasn't calm. Not even close.

A few minutes passed, and then he roughly rolled us both. I was pinned below him, his flaming eyes staring down at me while almost every hard inch of him pressed against me.

A long, tense moment passed.

His lips curled up in a snarl, his body heating before he growled fiercely, *"Mine."*

I stared at him with wide eyes.

Fuck.

Maybe Priel-the-man didn't want me, but Priel-the-hound seemed to feel the same way I did.

But since I wasn't sure how much of the moment man-Priel would remember, I didn't reply with the breathy, "yes" that my horny, dream-obsessed self wanted me to.

Instead, I just stared.

And waited.

A few minutes passed, and then the hellhound's nostrils flared as he inhaled deeply.

Another pissed snarl escaped him, and then suddenly he was on his feet, and I was hanging over his shoulder. A yelp escaped me as he flew up the climbing-wall, and I wrapped my arms around his abdomen from behind when he started sprinting toward his cave. I bounced a little, but held onto him for dear life as he ran.

His hands held my hips again as he launched us into the hole that was his cave's entrance, and his hold prevented me from feeling the impact of the landing.

A moment later, we were in the bathroom, and his hands were ripping my shirt over my head.

My mind spun, trying to keep up with the furious man as my long-sleeve top hit the floor. My hair fell to my belly button, wild and tangled, and my chest rose and fell quickly

"What are you doing?" I breathed to the man, when his hands found the bottom hem of the fireproof tank top I wore as a bra.

"*Mine*," he snarled at me.

I tried to stop myself from gawking at the words, but probably failed.

His hand caught a fistful of my hair, and lifted it to his nose. When he inhaled, the fire in his eyes turned bluish white, and he roared.

My stomach clenched.

Shit.

Priel's beast side seemed to have decided that I belonged to him, at least for the moment. Probably because of that little peck that started the mating process for us. If kissing another guy had ended said mating process, there was a decent chance that Priel's illogical mind wanted him to reform the bond or restart the process.

I didn't really want to be bonded to Clevv after the less-than-pleasurable makeout session—especially if Priel had decided he was interested in me after all—so I wasn't against that. My first priority just needed to be calming down Priel, before he actually *did* kill someone.

I was fairly certain he was stripping me because he wanted me in the shower, so I could wash off Clevv's smell. But I was also pretty sure that the mating process came with a smell of its own, which meant I couldn't scrub the other man's scent off entirely.

I could at least clean my hair and body, though.

Priel ripped my fireproof tank over my head without pausing to check out my tits.

Clearly, he wasn't stripping me because he wanted me naked. He just wanted to change my scent. Which was both a relief and an offense at the same time.

His hands were tugging down my pants and the fireproof shorts I wore as underwear a moment later, and I bit my lip when he kneeled in front of me, his face right in front of my core.

How many of my dreams had started that way?

Too many.

Too damn many.

He freed my feet from the clothes, apparently unaffected by my nudity or the many brands on my skin.

My pants were tossed across the bathroom, and then he was hauling me off the ground. I shrieked when he threw my bare body over his shoulder, his massive hands hot on the back of my thighs as he turned on the water.

Another shriek escaped me when the icy stream hit my ass, and I writhed against him, trying to get away from it.

His hands slid up and gripped my ass firmly.

I froze when the warmth of his palms blossomed, heating my skin as the water slowly began to warm too.

My eyes closed, and as much as I tried not to, I enjoyed the hell out of that touch.

When the water was finally hot, and I was enjoying his palms on my backside far too much, he ripped me off his shoulder and set me down on my feet.

Steam filled the air as hot water rolled over my skin. My eyes locked with Priel's burning orbs for a moment until he grabbed another long chunk of my hair and lifted it to his nose.

Another ferocious snarl escaped him.

He spun me around, pushing my chest to the wall of his shower. My tits kissed the stone, my palms lifting to brace myself against it. The scent of something fresh flooded my nose, and then hot hands were scrubbing my scalp and hair.

Those long fingers tilted my head back as he began to rinse the soap from my strands, and my eyes closed.

The man was insane, but honestly, my own feelings and emotions were such a source of whiplash that his demanding tendencies didn't bother me. And truthfully, I thought the moment was blissful. I liked his growliness, and the way he was pulling me around made me feel sort of... desired.

He washed my hair two more times, sniffing the strands between each new round of soap, before he was satisfied that it was free from Clevv's smell.

My whole damn body tensed, my palms pressing hard against the shower wall as his large hands dragged over my back, soaping me up.

Though he didn't linger on any particular part of me (even the sensitive ones), my eyes nearly rolled into the back of my head as his hands slid over my arms, down the curves of my sides, and over my nipples. I inhaled sharply as he palmed my breasts unintentionally, and my body clenched as his hands dragged down to my core.

He cleaned everything.

Everything, everything.

Literally, every fold in my lady parts, every squishy curve of my body, every crack between my toes.

He even grabbed a tube of the fae's strange verson of toothpaste, then slid his fingers into my mouth and scrubbed my tongue.

And it felt incredible.

All of it.

When he inhaled against my back and growled, determining that I still smelled like Clevv, I sent up a prayer of gratitude to Vevol, in case she existed the way Clevv seemed to think she did.

Because then Priel washed me again.

And again.

I was a puddle of horny Jello when he was finally satisfied with the way I smelled. The water shut off, and he palmed my face before he caught me on fire, as if trying to burn away whatever nonexistent pieces of Clevv's touch were still attached to me.

After a few moments, his fire died, and then a thick towel wrapped around me.

When Priel turned me around and lifted me up, the fire still burning in his eyes, my legs wrapped around his hips as he carried me toward his bed.

He lowered me carefully to the mattress before positioning himself over the top of me.

Fuck, he was huge.

I practically drooled at the expanse of bare, art-covered skin and muscle above me.

His flaming eyes devoured my face for a long moment, before he leaned down and kissed me.

I'd already been kissed that day, but the moments with Clevv were downgraded to swapping spit the first moment Priel's mouth took mine.

His hands were hot and rough on my thighs, the length of his cock pressing against my center while his lips, teeth, and tongue devoured mine. He kissed me like I was the air he needed to breathe, and fuck, it was *everything*.

His hands pried my legs open wider, and I cried into his mouth as his massive erection rubbed against me exactly the way I needed it to.

I was coming undone seconds later, keening into his mouth as pleasure rolled through my body, hotter and fiercer than I'd imagined it would feel even in the steamiest of my dreams.

When I came down from the high, I looked around the bed in dazed shock.

I frowned slightly when I didn't see him on the bed.

Slowly, and with a groan, I rolled to my side to see if he'd walked back to the bathroom.

But the door stood wide open, and it was definitely empty.

My stomach clenched as I eased myself to my feet, looking around the entirety of the small home.

Nothing.

He was gone.

The bastard had left me alone in his bed after getting me off without even touching me.

Had he really hated it that much?

Or had he really been that disgusted by me?

Hurt bloomed within my chest, and tears stung my eyes.

Of course this had happened.

When had things ever actually worked in my favor?

I was exhausted, but too furious with the fiery blond bastard to sleep.

So I stormed back to the bathroom to grab my clothes—silently thrilled that they smelled like another man.

I halted in the doorway when I found the floor bare.

After I blinked a few times, dragging my mind back to those minutes when he'd undressed me, I looked behind the door. And behind the toilet. And in the cabinets, for good measure.

They were gone.

The bastard had not only ditched me, but took my clothes with him when he did so.

Fury had me literally shaking as I stomped to the box near his bed, where I'd seen his clothes organized neatly. I dug through the shit in there, unfolding everything in an effort to piss him off when he bothered to return.

I found shorts.

Pants.

More shorts.

And more pants.

That was it.

No tops.

I snarled as I yanked the pants up my legs.

The magic in my belly clenched and pulsed with my fury. It was the fire within me, trying to break free. Attempting to make me shift.

And I wasn't having it.

The only way to stave off the bitchy magic rolling around within me was to drown it out with paint, so I stormed over to Priel's art shelves and grabbed the brushes and paint off of them.

Anger coursed through me as I filled one of his clean, perfect-looking palettes with the colors that spoke to my raging soul.

I was too furious to even bother with covering a wall in black or white to give myself a blank slate.

No one needed a blank slate when they were this pissed.

My fingers and brush moved together as I slapped my emotions onto the wall of Priel's home, immortalizing every shred of anger I could manage.

And when I couldn't keep my eyes open any longer, I collapsed onto his perfectly clean sheets and blankets without rinsing the paint off my skin.

Four

Priel

I stormed into the forest, one fist clenched around North's clothes and the other wrapped around my erection. The clothing caught fire at my will as it fell to the dirt, my spare palm bracing itself against the tree as I pumped my cock. It didn't even take a whole damn stroke before I came undone with a savage roar, the image of my female's naked body painted across my mind in every shade of red there was.

She wasn't mine.

I shouldn't think of her as mine, even when I was half-shifted and operating on instinct.

But...

Fuck, she was mine.

I couldn't handle any alternative.

I'd kept my distance when she'd shown no interest eighteen months earlier. Her scent hadn't demanded every ounce of my attention the way the other males' explained it did when a female was their mate, so I gave the other men time to see if she was theirs. That was my damn obligation.

I had kept my distance until the fact that slow-developing mate bonds were possible was revealed.

And then I'd made sure she'd drawn my name, so I'd be the one fighting for her.

Then she'd kissed me, and clearly been uncomfortable. So when she slammed her door in my face, I let her.

And when she didn't emerge from her room, I took the hint.

But when she'd kissed Clevv, I couldn't fucking take it.

I had warned my pack not to touch her. I had tried to make sure that none of them tested me. They should've known not to risk my fury.

Yet he'd kissed her.

My female.

My *mate.*

And I had fucking lost it.

I'd stripped her.

Cleaned her.

Touched her.

Kissed her, the way I'd wanted to since the moment I caught her scent.

Unraveled her on my cock, without taking her completely.

Now she was going to hate me even more than she already did, and yet I couldn't bring myself to regret it.

Not when she was in my home, her scent intertwined with mine the way it was supposed to be.

Not when her soft, bare skin was wrapped in my sheets, sprawled across my bed.

An image of her naked body filled my mind, and I clenched my cock in my fist again, still infuriatingly hard.

She was absolutely covered in Vevol's brands. There were three on one of her arms, five on the other. A large one stretched across one of her breasts. So many of them dotted her abdomen, one of them stretching in a harsh line that spoke to me in ways I couldn't find words to describe.

They spread down her back in various sizes, over that sexy little ass, down the thighs I wanted to lick every inch of.

I was stroking my cock again, I realized, my chest heaving harshly.

She had taken possession of my mind.

I would make her a part of my soul if it killed me.

To do so, I would need to win her heart. Considering her hatred for me, that wouldn't be an easy task.

The memory of the way her body had arched against mine, her flame-flooded eyes dilating as she'd teetered on the edge of her pleasure, made me roar as I came undone once more.

I'd have her again, completely. I'd mark her in every fucking way there was, before anyone else had the chance to realize how powerful or special she was.

Vevol's connection to her didn't matter. What mattered was that she would smell of me, the way January smelled of Calian.

...As soon as I figured out how to convince her that she was mine.

Five

North

I woke up to the smell of cooking food, and the sound of running water.

My stomach growled, and I groaned as I struggled to work my sluggish mind through everything that had happened before I crashed.

The kissing—lots of kissing.

The abandonment—shit, I *hated* Priel. Or at least *wanted* to hate him.

The painting—so much painting.

Why was it all so damn overwhelming?

It took me a few minutes to talk myself out of bed.

My feet met the warm stone floor when I finally managed to get myself up.

I looked down at my bare chest at the same time Priel glanced over his shoulder. He was standing in front of the sink, washing something, while food sizzled in a pan a few feet to his right.

Yeah, I didn't have a shirt.

And why the hell was he so gorgeous?

It was stupidly unfair.

I threw an arm over my tits, growling, "Where the hell did you put my clothes?"

"In the box." His eyes lingered on my skin for a long moment before he turned back to whatever he was washing. The food he had cooking smelled incredible, not that I wanted to admit it.

I stomped over to the box, pulling out my fireproof underwear and quickly tugging them on. Priel's admittedly-comfortable pants remained on the ground as I bent over, digging through the smallish box.

Where was my shirt? My pants? I needed those, badly.

"Where did you put my *actual clothes*?" I snapped at the hellhound in the kitchen.

"The shirt and pants? They're ash."

I waited for the apology.

For the promise that he'd get me new shit.

The nonchalant mention that he had a change of clothes for me ready right that minute.

None of those things came.

The bastard even started whistling as he continued washing whatever the hell had his complete attention.

"I can't leave like this," I finally snarled at the man.

"No," he agreed. "You'll have to shift so we can run back to the Stronghold without letting anyone see your brands. The way our scents have intertwined should buy us a few weeks, at least."

"So I have to learn how to shift—something I don't want to do—because *you* couldn't stop yourself from burning *my* clothes?"

"You have to learn how to shift so that you're not consumed by your inner fire," he said bluntly, without turning around. "And I wouldn't have needed to burn your clothes if you hadn't decided to kiss one of my packmates."

"Why would you care? You've never wanted me." I stood up, my fists clenching at my sides as fire throbbed in my abdomen, my magic still desperate to make an appearance.

He finally turned around, and I saw what he'd been scrubbing.

A paintbrush I'd left in a cup of water.

They worked the same after being left in paint-water for ages, but they did stain a bit thanks to the nature of Vevol's version of paint. And the bastard clearly had a problem with stains.

His eyes narrowed at me. "Not *wanting* you and not *claiming* you are two entirely different things. I've wanted you since the first moment I caught your scent."

I scoffed, the magic in my abdomen pulsing so hotly it physically hurt to keep it under control. "Don't lie to me."

His eyes burned for a moment, before the fire faded.

The paintbrush met the counter, and he stalked across the room. I stood my ground, not sure I could control my magic and move at the same time. It was pulsating more intensely than it ever had before, and I was starting to think I might not be able to get it back under control.

His hand pressed to the bare skin on my abdomen, left exposed by my tank top, and my fire pulsed in response. My fists were clenched so tight they hurt.

His voice was low and gentle when he spoke, surprising me with his lack of anger. "Don't do this; don't fight your magic. Holding back your anger or your flames disrupts your energy. Should it break through, it'll force a shift and you'll be trapped in your other form for days, if not weeks."

"January never said that," I told him through gritted teeth.

"January isn't a hound. Dragons and phoenixes have fire; you and I *are* fire."

"Then what do I do?" My voice bordered on desperate.

I'd never felt my magic this close to taking over before.

"Let out a slow breath and unclench." He removed his hand from my abdomen, showing me a fist and then slowly opening it. "Let yourself burn."

"It might force me to shift," I said, panicking a little.

"It might," Priel agreed.

"I don't want to," I hissed.

"Eventually, the fire won't give you a choice." His eyes were serious, and I hated to admit it, but I believed him.

"Can you stop it?"

His eyes darkened. "If you give me your whole name, yes."

Shit.

Whole names had power. If I gave him my whole name—or my actual name, in my case—he could force me to come to him, wherever he was. That was the only thing I really knew about full names, but they had to have more power than that, didn't they?

"No," I shot back.

"Then embrace the shift. I'll diffuse the fire, so it's comfortable for you." His palm landed on my skin again, his fingers stretching over my belly. His flames moved across his hand, and I felt the magic that had tensed in my abdomen begin to slowly unclench.

His fire trailed over me, and my breathing slowed.

My eyes closed.

More relief than I'd realized I needed seeped through me as his magic intertwined with mine and both lazily slid through my veins.

My back arched slightly, and then I felt myself falling.

I caught myself with a thud, and when I forced my eyes open, found myself on all fours.

When I looked down and saw burning paws, my head spun.

Priel's fingers stroked my head slowly, his touch and his flames calming me.

Why did that feel so good?

I looked at him, and his lips curved upward slightly. "Like the others probably told you, hounds are pack animals. Our fire craves fuel, and we fuel each other. My flames showed yours that they were safe."

Oh.

I supposed that made sense. It was probably a better answer than the one I'd assumed, anyway.

But I'd assumed it had something to do with the mate bond we'd started, and Priel didn't even want the bond, so that wouldn't have made sense anyway.

"You might be stuck in this form for a while," he told me, his hand still stroking my head. It felt really good, even if I didn't want to admit that. "Let me finish cooking and cleaning up, and then you can decide whether you want to stay here or head back to the Stronghold. I still need to rest, but I can sleep on the floor of your room if you'd prefer."

Fuck.

I wasn't looking forward to making any of those choices.

He returned back to the kitchen though, making things easier for me for the time being.

I WATCHED him cook and clean.

Not only did he have an incredible ass, but he was good at everything.

He didn't mind the work of scrubbing paint off the brushes. He didn't seem bothered as he studied (for the tenth time) the mural of flames and burning flesh that I'd left on his wall. He even whistled while he cooked.

And when I ate off a plate with my tongue like a damned animal, he grinned proudly and told me that I was one of them now.

A hellhound.

It was surreal.

WHEN THE TIME TO make a decision came, I reluctantly agreed to stay with him for a few days while he caught up on rest. He seemed relieved by the idea, and thanked me before he finished cleaning up my messes, and then went to sleep.

Since there was only the one bed, I reluctantly curled up next to him on it. When I fell asleep in my hellhound form, for the first time in over a year and a half, I slept peacefully.

A WEEK PASSED SIMILARLY.

Priel cooked and cleaned. He fed me, and rubbed my head.

I was starting to feel like his dog—or his mate.

I wasn't sure which option appealed to me more, so I refused to consider either of them.

But I couldn't shift back, which left me with zero alternative options.

Most of the time, honestly, we both slept. I hadn't realized how behind on sleep I was after so many months of nightmares and sex dreams, and the peacefulness that accompanied sleeping in my hound form was addictive.

Almost as addictive as Priel's near-constant grins, jokes, and the feel of his arm draped over my body while we slept.

And his scent?

Now that I'd shifted, I knew exactly what Priel's packmates had been talking about when they said that someone smelled attractive, or right for them.

With nearly every inhale, I was reminded how good the man had tasted. He was like a can of damn Febreeze made just for me, and it was intoxicating.

AFTER THAT WEEK had gone by, Priel looked significantly more relaxed, and I followed him out of the cave. I didn't even have to climb in my hound form; just jumped right the hell out. It was epic.

And the run was incredible.

Priel's pack ran with us. They seemed to have gotten over everything that happened with Clevv, which was a relief.

Priel ran at my side, and the rest of them circled us like they were protecting me. Clevv was kept as far from me as possible—which Priel made sure of every time he shot a glare over his shoulder.

It was a long, long run, but I honestly had the time of my life.

WHEN WE REACHED the Stronghold and the masses of fighting fae around it, I howled a sad goodbye to the rest of the pack, and they howled back to me. I noticed Priel still eyeing Clevv, but ignored him.

The hot blond wasn't really into me, after all.

The group of gathered fae only came close until they caught a whiff of my changing scent. Then, a whole bunch of them started breaking off, leaving.

Maybe those were the ones who had thought my smell was the most appealing.

Priel shifted and knocked on the Stronghold's door when we were in the clear, none of the fighting fae charging toward us and none of his pack within sight. Mare pulled it open a few minutes later, and frowned when she looked between me and Priel.

"Is that…" she began.

"It's North." His fingers stroked the fur on my head, and I tried to force myself not to nuzzle up against his side. It was more difficult than I would've liked.

"Come in, hurry." She gestured us inside, then hastily closed the door without looking at any of the fighting fae. "What happened? Why didn't they attack you?"

He smirked. "North decided to spend a little more time with me so our scents would merge."

Her eyes widened, and she looked down at me.

I scowled, and Mare took a quick step back.

"She won't hurt you. She's just tired and hungry. I'll be out to make her something to eat soon." He eased me toward the door to my bedroom while my mind reeled.

When he'd shut and locked the door behind us, trapping me in my room with him, his eyes fixated on the nearest wall. I growled at him as he studied one of the more gruesome paintings, wearing a wicked grin.

"Has Vevol been speaking to you, Gorgeous?" he mused.

I snapped my teeth at him for his use of the awful nickname he'd taken to calling me, earning a chuckle.

Damn him.

I snapped my teeth again and he held his arm out for me, his grin widening. "Go ahead. All yours."

I withdrew quickly, and he snorted.

His attention moved back to my paintings, and I growled at him again even though it hadn't done a damn thing thus far.

"I like your style," he told me, his hand sliding into the fur on top of my head. "It's much more fluid than mine, and it suits you."

If I'd been in human form, I would've blushed.

It was probably the best compliment I'd ever received.

No one ever really saw my art on Earth, and that hadn't changed since I came to Vevol. Priel's experience was the opposite; his entire pack wore his art proudly, and the man himself was a walking advertisement.

He stepped up closer to the wall with the most gruesome painting, studying it more carefully. Not wanting to see his reactions, I huffed and walked over to my bed, collapsing on the mattress. When it suddenly caught fire, I yelped, jumping off of it and lunging away.

Priel put out the flames with a simple hand motion, and then gestured for me to go over to him. Ignoring the smell of burnt bedding, I reluctantly padded to his side.

"Vevol has been sending you warnings," he told me, his voice no longer playful. "I recognize all of the fae in this painting. That's no coincidence. And given the many brands she left on your skin, Vevol has clearly chosen you as a vehicle for her warnings."

I scoffed.

He stroked my fur, and my body unconsciously moved closer to his.

The man hadn't noticed the small details from my dreams of the two of us that had embedded themselves in my paintings yet, thankfully. Mostly, they were just small, hidden images of his tattoos. I hoped he *wouldn't* notice them. My mind tried to push me to illustrate the scenes in detail, but I'd managed to prevent myself from doing so. If I painted a large image of Priel making love to me, there wasn't a damn chance I would ever move past my obsession with him.

"You see fae burning," he murmured, walking over to another wall. "Hounds, even."

I didn't bother nodding.

The walls were proof enough of what I'd seen.

"Do the other women know?" He looked down at me.

I shook my head in a "no".

"Hmm." He moved to the next wall, which my bed rested against. It was a simple mattress with a large headboard. I'd pushed it forward enough to paint behind it ages ago, and never pushed it back, but it hid the shit I'd painted there anyway.

I *much* preferred that he didn't see that painting, but fought the urge to cover it with my body.

He studied the image silently before moving to the fourth. Relief coursed through me. He hadn't noticed the brief bits and pieces of his tattoos embedded in the other paintings, which was a huge relief.

As long as he didn't look behind the bed, I was in the clear.

He finally walked me into the bathroom, quiet and contemplative. When he stepped into the shower, I growled at him.

His lips curved upward in amusement. "I'm not going to make you shower, Gorgeous. I was going to catch myself on fire to clean my skin. It's more effective than water, even if you don't *feel* quite as refreshed as if you took a real shower."

Oh.

I took a step back, giving him permission. He had a point about the flames; after being constantly on fire over the last week and a day or two, I felt clean, despite running through the forest for so long.

His body was engulfed in flames for a long moment, before the fire died. Then, the man crossed the bathroom again. He looked clean and fresh, and his white-blond hair was even spiked up all pretty-like.

He was hot as hell.

Why he was the one calling me *Gorgeous*, I didn't know. It didn't feel like he was mocking me, though. At least not completely. Maybe that was why it pissed me off so much though; because I didn't believe he meant it completely when he called me that.

"I'm going to make you something to eat," he told me, stroking my head again. "Do you want to stay in here or cook with me?"

I scowled at him, pointing toward the bed with my nose. It was still smoking slightly.

"We'll bring some jilui petals back next time we leave; they're the easiest to find of the plants that make our homes fireproof." He scratched me behind my ears lightly.

I shook off his hand, earning a chuckle as I stalked into the middle of the room, where I wouldn't put anything in danger.

He left the space without a backward glance at me, and I collapsed on the tile with a huff.

Why did I have to be so damn attracted to him? Why couldn't I just let it go? The more time I spent with him, the more I was going to want the bastard, and the last thing I needed was to want him more. My dreams were bad enough already.

Though I considered grabbing some paint and covering the bits and pieces of the paintings that could clue Priel in to my dreams about him, I shot the idea down.

All that would do was make him curious, and something told me I wasn't going to be able to hide the truth from him if he really decided he was going to figure it out.

I shut my tired eyes, and after a while, managed to fall asleep. Shortly afterward, I woke up to eat, and then went back to bed.

Thankfully, since I was still in my hound form, I didn't dream.

WHEN I WOKE UP, my slightly-disoriented gaze caught on Priel. He was sprawled out on the floor beside me, his massive form looking way too at-ease in my space. I stared at him for much longer than I probably should've, struck by the image before me.

He was gorgeous.

So ridiculously gorgeous.

I really needed to move past this obsession.

But how was I supposed to move past something I had dreamed about so many times?

Especially now that he'd kissed me the way he had, and touched me, and...

Shit.

I was screwed.

The urge to paint hit me hard, but I needed hands. My body would need to change. The desire to do so was strong enough to take my breath away, and then suddenly, my body sort of stretched.

I felt myself shifting forms, and relief rolled through me when my bare face met the warm tile I'd been sleeping against. My fireproof tank and shorts were still on, so I wasn't naked.

Easing myself to a seated position, I studied the man on the floor beside me for a few more minutes.

Having him in there with me was seriously messing with my sanity. The whole room would smell like him when he left, and I'd have to figure out a way to clean it, and—

Shit, I needed to get out of there.

I stood up swiftly and crossed the room, carefully opening the door and slipping out.

Mare was sitting on the couch, and she flashed me a quick smile.

My body clenched.

Shit, I couldn't do this.

I couldn't be obsessed with a guy who wasn't really interested in me, who kept calling me Gorgeous, who had snuggled up with me on the floor even though there was a bed just a few feet away.

I was overthinking everything, like I always did.

I didn't know how to talk to him, or be me around him.

I didn't even know what I really wanted from him. Or with him. Or... anything?

Fuck.

I needed fresh air.

Yeah; maybe fresh air could fix things. Or at least help me process somewhat normally.

Turning, I practically ran for the door out of the Stronghold.

My heart pounded rapidly, my body screaming for me to get out.

To move.

To escape.

To *run*.

The only time I'd felt that much stress pointed solely at getting away was when I'd been in that car with my arranged fiancé, and had found out that I was heading toward my death.

The memories melded with my thoughts, tangling in my mind and making me feel like the world was closing in on me. My fingers struggled with the only two locks on the heavy door that someone had bothered doing up, and then I flung the thing open and rushed outside.

Vevol's humidity met my cheeks, but it wasn't uncomfortable. I hadn't minded the warmth since the fae world had made me one of them.

There were still men fighting outside, but all of the ones who had been looking for me had left when I showed up half-mated to Priel the day before.

We hadn't exchanged vows or had sex, both of which I was fairly certain were the next possible steps in the relationship, but had gotten close enough to doing so to scare the others away or at least discourage them.

I shut my eyes, breathing the fresh air in deeply. It relaxed my shoulders more than I actually expected it to.

There wasn't any fire pulsing in my abdomen anymore, threatening to burn me alive, I realized. Now, the power was just calm and warm and quiet.

That was nice.

A soft breeze caught in my hair. It was smooth and soft, surprisingly enough, and the dark strands blew against my cheek.

Despite the sounds of the fighting, Vevol was a peaceful place. The magic there was—

A hand slid over my cheek.

My eyes flew open, my lips twisting in a snarl as I prepared to rip Priel a new asshole for touching me so suddenly.

The words died in my throat when I found a complete stranger in front of me.

I stepped backward, and collided with a hard chest.

Something screamed within me that it didn't belong to my hellhound either.

Fire erupted on my skin, and I tried to keep my breathing even as I looked around me.

They were everywhere.

Men, encircling me.

Fae with intense eyes, touching me. Not intimately, but still touching me.

"Back off," I finally breathed, struggling the panic that had swelled in my chest.

Confrontation—I was not good with it. Not at all. Sure, I could snarl and growl with the best of them when I felt safe or even safeish, but when I was clearly outgunned?

Panic.

Lots of panic.

I pushed the guy's palm away from my face with a shaky hand, but his lips only curved upward with interest as he withdrew it.

Fucking hell.

What was I supposed to do?

"Vevol has chosen a female," the man who had touched my face mused. "Clevv was right."

Clevv?

Had that bastard noticed my brands while we were kissing?

Had he told someone about—

One of my markings caught my eye, and I froze.

Fuck.

My body stilled when I realized what had just happened.

I had gone outside, into the middle of the fighting.

With my many brands exposed.

Priel had told me they would put me in danger, but that hadn't crossed my mind when I woke up and started panicking.

And now?

Well, I was fucked.

Hopefully not literally.

Unless the blond hellhound bastard was involved, because—

Shit, I needed to stop thinking about him.

What the hell was wrong with me?

I forced my terrified, scattered mind to focus.

There had to be a way to get all of the men to back off long enough for me to get away.

But if the brands really marked me as more powerful than the other women, or something along those lines, then I didn't know if that was even possible.

The sound of flapping wings distracted me, and then a massive phoenix was spiraling down toward me.

SIX

I BIT BACK a shriek and tried to move away, but only ended up pressed even harder against the random fae dude still at my back. The one who'd touched my face hadn't come any closer, at least.

The phoenix shifted as he landed, and a small amount of relief cut through me when I realized that I recognized him. He was gigantic of course, with buzzed dark hair and deep brown skin. Thick tattoos wrapped around his biceps, and I recognized the style as Priel's immediately.

This was Ervo.

The Wild Hunt guy who had formed a temporary mating bond with Mare.

He was really damn intense, but quiet. From what I'd seen, he seemed more reasonable to me than some of the other men did.

Especially Priel.

Unhappy murmurs and growls rolled through the group surrounding me.

I tried to step away from the guy who my back was pressed against, but his hands grabbed my arms, and I froze again.

Smooth as a damn snake, Ervo had the man by the throat. My arms were released, and no one else grabbed me.

I watched in horrified fascination as the phoenix's fingers shifted to talons and removed the fae's head from his body before anyone had time to blink.

My eyes widened and my stomach rolled when the head hit the ground with an awful thud.

The phoenix dropped the man's body too, and then his brutal gaze swept the group around me.

Many of the men took a step back.

They were all dangerous, all of the fae, but there was something stronger and deadlier about the Wild Hunt guys.

My eyes were glued to Ervo's hand, my knees knocking together as I watched the blood drip slowly off of his fingertips.

The phoenix's voice was low and deadly as he said, "Fighting over females is understandable. Touching one without her permission is a death sentence."

His gaze dipped to me, but it took me a minute to peel my eyes off of his dripping fingertips.

"Did any others touch you?" Ervo's voice was so calm it was terrifying.

My magic bloomed over my skin, soft flames sliding up my arms as the magic attempted to calm me.

Instinct told me to say no and protect the men who had touched me earlier, just so I didn't have to watch Ervo kill anyone else.

But if I lied about that, what else would the massive group of men expect me to say? Would they think they could grab me, or kiss me, and I'd protect them?

Though nausea settled into my damn bones at the idea of what I was doing, I lifted a finger and pointed across the group, to the man who had touched my face, and then moved my finger to two other men I had seen touch me.

"There were others, too. I couldn't see all of them," I said, fighting to stop my voice from shaking.

All attention settled on the men I'd pointed to, and guilt had my magic weaving and bobbing over my skin.

The three fae sank to their knees, bowing their heads toward Ervo.

Or maybe toward me.

"I was taken by her magic," one of the men said quickly, his voice low and gravelly.

He was so full of it, but I didn't say that aloud.

"Any others who touched her, on your knees." Ervo's voice was still so damn calm.

More fae kneeled around me.

I refused to make eye contact with them, my gaze remaining fixed on Ervo.

"Should any of the females see your faces in the next year, your lives will be forfeit." Ervo's threat wasn't growled or snarled; his calm voice was plenty terrifying. "Should you ever touch a female without her permission again, you will suffer at the hands of your brothers for months before death claims you."

The men shifted forms smoothly. The one nearest to me turned into a massive snake, and out of the corner of my eye, I watched as he slithered away.

I fought a shudder, glad for once that I was a hellhound.

Basilisks were freaky as hell.

"Priel has been hiding her away," a male voice called from somewhere in the crowd. "All of us deserve a chance to show our strength to the female Vevol's chosen. Her power is too great for him to claim her so easily."

Ervo's expression was neutral, but his jaw was clenched slightly. "I don't disagree, but North will decide what she will allow. My female and I will speak with her and determine the best way to approach the situation for all of us. Until then, the fighting ceases."

His gaze swept the group.

Growls and grunts of complaint followed, but grudging nods did as well.

"The hound stays out here with us, though," another one of the men argued.

Ervo dipped his head in agreement, then gestured me toward the Stronghold. I didn't wait for an invitation to go, and the crowd made a path for me as I walked.

When the door was shut behind us, a relieved breath escaped me.

"Where is Priel?" The phoenix asked me calmly.

I pointed toward my bedroom, and he walked in without a pause.

Grunts and growls followed. After Ervo's calm voice spoke—I couldn't make out exactly what he had said—there was a furious snarl.

A disheveled Priel stormed out of the bedroom, and my body tensed as he reached me.

"Where did they touch you?" He stalked around me, lifting my shirt and leaning in to check out my neck.

Oh.

That's what he was looking for? Some kind of evidence that I'd been hurt?

"I'm fine." I pushed his hands away, trying not to let him see how frustrated I was that his reaction was only protective.

Where was the possessive, demanding beast I'd had back in his cave? That was the version of him I wanted; the one that called me *"mine"* and didn't hesitate to claim me in every way.

Or *almost* every way.

"They'll break the door down if you don't join them outside." Ervo's voice was still infuriatingly calm.

Priel snarled at him.

"She's not going to be safe if they break in here. They've all seen the brands; there's no turning back now," the phoenix added.

"Fuck." Priel stepped away from me, starting to pace the short hallway before the door.

"What do they want?" Mare's voice was quiet.

"Me," I said flatly.

"North is covered in Vevol's brands. One brand is evidence that a fae has been given an extra portion of magic; this many are a sure sign that Vevol has chosen her for something great," Ervo explained.

"Damn." Mare's voice was surprised.

"So why can't she just bang Priel to make the bond permanent?" Sunny checked.

My attention jerked to the other woman. She and Dots were off behind Mare, watching the interactions but not joining the argument. I hadn't even noticed them there.

"An hour ago, she could have. Now that they know the truth, to seal a bond could start a civil war. The best route would be to come up with a way to establish Priel as the strongest of the fae who want her," Ervo said.

"How?" Dots asked.

Ervo's and Priel's eyes met before the hellhound growled, "Not a fucking chance."

"It's the simplest way, and our best chance at keeping the peace."

"Do you intend on competing?" Priel snarled back. "Does Nev? Or Teris? Or any of the other bastards who claim to be loyal to us?"

"Are we supposed to know what they're talking about?" Dots whispered to Sunny.

"I don't think so," Sunny grumbled back.

"Slow down and explain," Mare told the men.

A loud, rattling knock shook the whole damn Stronghold. My fire tingled over my skin as the lingering panic from earlier ignited within me.

"You have to leave. This is the only way to keep the peace." Ervo's gaze met Priel's again.

Priel's rough, furious gaze moved to me and lingered. A moment later, he was storming toward the door.

He snarled at the men outside as he opened it, and the damn thing shook our home again when he slammed it shut.

"I am so confused," Dots whispered.

"Join the gang," Sunny muttered back.

"Just start over," Mare told Ervo.

He looked at her, his neutral gaze lingering a bit longer than I would've expected before he looked at me. "When Priel discovered how to work the portal, our fae were restless. The fighting over who would go to your Earth to find the female who called us during the Winter Solstice was fierce, and no decisions were made. Priel finally devised a way to determine who would make up the group who went through; a competition of strength."

He went on, "Each fae competed amongst his own kind, and one of each species was declared the strongest and chosen to participate in the Wild Hunt. The five of us you know were the winners. If you run the same competition and agree to mate with one of the winners, it will focus the other fae and end the fighting temporarily."

Was he serious?

I stared at him for longer than was probably appropriate.

Shit, he really was.

That was their answer for this problem?

A competition?

What the hell were they smoking?

"What happens during the contest?" Mare asked, as I opened my mouth to shoot the idea down.

"It tests the aspects of strength. There's a physical fighting competition, followed by a speed test. The mental dexterity test follows speed, and then the magic test is the final challenge, unless there's a tie. In that case, another physical fight follows."

"That sounds way too complicated," Mare protested.

"It separates the men who are truly interested and worth your time from the ones who aren't," Ervo corrected.

"Not being powerful doesn't make someone not worth our time," Mare argued.

"We could make up our own version of the contest," Dots offered. "One that isn't violent. We could have a bake-off, and a poetry contest..."

I snorted.

The other girls grinned wickedly.

"If you want to put a bunch of men in their places, you'll need to add some kind of sewing competition to that," Sunny added viciously.

Oh hell, it was awful.

But also... kind of awesome.

"Maybe a cleaning contest, too?" Mare teased.

"And a painting one, if we want to touch on North's favorite things," Sunny added. "And give the hellhound bastard a better shot at winning."

"So why are all the fae after you, anyway?" Dots wondered. "I feel like me and Sunny missed something."

I sighed, and gestured to one of the marks on my abdomen. "My burn-bruise things are apparently not considered burns or bruises. The fae call them Vevol's Brands. Only two of the fae guys have them; Priel, and the unseelie king. I guess they're a sign that the person holds unique magic of some sort. Priel's lets him open the portal between our worlds."

The girls' eyebrows were all raised by the time I finished speaking.

"Damn. So you have special magic?" Sunny checked.

"According to them."

"What is it, though?" Dots asked.

I shrugged. "Not a damn clue."

"Well, hopefully a cheesy competition keeps them off our asses for a bit so we can all get outside for a while. I'm tired of being cooped up," Sunny said.

Everyone else murmured agreements.

"I don't know." I grimaced. "I don't want to give them any kind of hope, and then take it away. The way they touched me..." I shook my head. "What if I just tell them that they could write letters or something? That I'll read their letters, and decide if I want to meet any of them?"

"I don't think that will delay them for long," Ervo warned.

"Well, I'm not about to walk out there and tell them that I'm looking to hook up with one of them," I said defensively.

"What if you try to make them stop wanting you, then?" Sunny suggested.

I frowned at her.

She explained her idea. "What if you go out there and tell them that you're in love with Priel? Make up some BS about how you've wanted him since you guys met but you didn't think he was interested? Admit that our matings with the Wild Hunt guys are fake, but you finally admitted your feelings to Priel and he wants you too?"

She continued, "You could tell them that you came back here to grab your stuff so you can retreat back to his love shack and hook up with him in private. The guys are possessive assholes, but it doesn't seem like they want an unwilling woman. If you can make them think that's what you'd be, it might fix this shit."

Her idea was way, way too close to reality for my taste, but what other options were there? As far as ideas went, it was better than my letter one.

I looked at Ervo.

All of us women did, actually.

He grimaced. "It might work... but it also might backfire for the rest of you."

My stomach clenched.

I still didn't know what Priel wanted, and I didn't want to ruin things for the other women.

"We can deal with it for North's sake," Sunny said with a shrug.

Mare and Dots nodded their agreement.

Emotions I didn't want to deal with swelled within me.

They felt a hell of a lot like love. I'd tried hard not to get attached to the girls, and not to let them get attached to me, but maybe it had started happening anyway.

But Priel...

He'd called me his when he was all beastly, and he had acted possessive, but that didn't really mean anything. The fae liked fighting, and he'd never given me a reason to believe that he was really that into me.

I supposed I could always make up some shit about things not working out between us after all of this was over if he wasn't interested in me.

"Well, it's worth a try," I finally, reluctantly said.

Ervo dipped his head in a nod, then strode out of the Stronghold without so much as a glance at Mare.

When I looked over at her, her lips were pressed together in a grimace.

She hid the emotions quickly, looping her arm through Sunny's.

Dots looped hers through mine, and then we started for the door.

"Do you seriously think this is going to work?" I asked them, my voice lowering as we opened the door.

"Depends on your goal. If you want a way to hook up with Priel, definitely." Dots said cheerfully.

I tried not to grimace.

What *did* I want?

That, I didn't know.

"It's show time, ladies. Try not to look interesting," Sunny muttered to all of us as we stepped outside.

The men were all waiting in a massive group, with Priel and Ervo at the front. My eyes went immediately to the massive hellhound, and wow, he looked pissed.

Everyone was silent when myself and the other three girls stepped into a line. Our arms were still linked, I realized.

"The other women and I have been talking," I announced to the men.

My voice carried more than it should've, but I didn't let myself overthink that when there was so much other shit to worry about.

The world was deathly silent around us as the fae waited for me to continue.

"Though it may not be fair to the rest of you, I'm in love with Priel. I have been, since the first day I stepped foot in Vevol. I thought he wasn't interested in me, so I stayed quiet about it, until the other women and I came up with the idea to establish fake mate bonds with the Wild Hunt guys, to protect us from all of you."

The silence seemed to swell around me, so I hurried onward. I wasn't exactly eloquent, but I was pretty sure brutal honesty would get the point across.

"Considering I was attacked when I stepped outside earlier, it's pretty apparent that the protection was necessary," I added.

Priel started to take a step toward me, but Ervo set a hand on his shoulder, holding him firmly in place.

I went on. "Our relationship used to be fake, but when I was in Priel's cave with him, it became real for both of us. We only came back here so I can grab the rest of my things and then go back to his home to be together in peace. I understand that my brands make it seem like I have more power than some of you, and I can assure you that if anyone tries to stop me from mating with the man that I love, I will figure out how to use every drop of that power to end them. This is my life."

I continued, "The person I mate with will be my choice. End of the discussion. You can all talk amongst yourselves and fight about that if you want, but you don't get to mess with us women, regardless of how much power we do or don't possess. Bring your cake or write your letters; we're not just potential mates. We're people, too."

With that, we shuffled back into the Stronghold. I was at the back of the group, and just before I stepped inside, a shadow loomed over me.

Goosebumps went up my arms at the heat rippling off the figure behind me, and I halted.

Priel leaned in until his body was only a breath away from mine. His low growl in my ear was soft enough that no one else could've heard a damn word. "I'm going to be fighting these bastards for a while. My full name is Lopriel. When you're ready, use it."

A shiver rolled down my spine as he stepped away, and I realized the other men were already growling, snarling, and snapping.

My monologue had apparently not done much good. But it had to be better than a competition, I hoped.

As Priel strode toward the other guys, his fists caught fire.

I always tried not to watch him fight, but I'd seen it a few times. And that was exactly how he always started; with the flaming fists.

Fear clenched my stomach.

There were so many other fae. If enough of them got together, they would take him down. He was strong, and he didn't think they would kill him because of the portal he could create, but I didn't trust them.

Not for a second.

I took two steps toward the group, and their attention lifted back to me. I raised my voice louder than I had earlier.

"No more blood. If any more of you bleed today, all four of us will go to the unseelie and mate with the first bastards we find."

My gaze met Priel's, and his eyes were so furious. I could see the fire of his anger burning within them, and knew he was going to be pissed with me.

He *wanted* to fight. And I wasn't on board with it.

He didn't have to love me, or want me, or even like me.

But I wasn't going to let him get himself killed because of me.

Spinning around, I stalked back into the Stronghold. The door slammed behind me, and my fingers shook a little as I did up the top two locks. After a short moment of hesitation, I did the next two too, just to be safe.

"Damn, that was badass," Sunny exclaimed, high-fiving Dots and then Mare. When she held her palm out toward me, it took me a minute, but I finally high-fived her too.

"January is going to be so pissed she didn't see any of that," Mare said, fighting a smile. "Especially that last part. Whew." She fanned herself, and I bit back a grin.

My face ended up forming a terrible grimace, but it was what it was.

"Are you and Priel actually a thing? There was some seriously-steamy eye-banging going on between you two," Sunny said. "If I were you, I'd totally hit that."

I flushed a little. "No. He's never been into me like that. When his eyes shift, he gets sort of possessive, but otherwise he's not interested."

All three girls gave me incredulous expressions.

I bit my lip, taking a step back toward my room.

"Wait a second." Sunny held up a finger. "You seriously think that man—that gorgeous, inked up blond sex god—isn't interested in you romantically?"

"He never acted like it. Things were a little different, back at his house, but only when his mind was shifted. Then he got all caveman, but... no, I don't think he's into me. He just gets possessive because of the bond when someone pushes him." I was rambling, and I knew it. But the alternative was actually letting myself consider the impossible, so... rambling it was.

"North, every man in this world wants a mate. Priel turned Sunny down ages ago, and looked absolutely thrilled when he ended up paired with you after we drew names." Dots gestured to the couches, where he'd been sitting all those months ago.

Shit, I did not need the reminder of that day.

My mind jerked back to the moment he'd stopped me just outside the door, as I was walking in.

I blurted out a question about it without letting myself think it through. "He told me his name when I walked in here. His whole name. What does that mean?"

All three of them stared at me with wide eyes.

"I think Ana would say you're dead," Mare murmured.

"Or start planning your funeral," Sunny tossed out.

Snorts escaped me, and Dots grinned.

Good old Ana.

Honestly, it was nice to remember her, but I was glad she had joined the unseelie. Things had been much happier since then, even for me, and I typically stayed away from everyone else to keep them free from my foul mood.

"Realistically, if I had to guess, I'd say it means he thinks of himself as yours," Mare admitted. "Giving someone your full name is handing them power over you—and that's not something any of the fae would give lightly, even when trying to convince one of us to be his mate. Why did he give it to you?"

"He told me to use it."

Sunny whistled. "He wants you to call him into your room so he can have his dirty, dirty way with you."

My cheeks flushed. "Seriously, Sunny?"

Dots smiled. "Seriously, he probably wants to make sure you're okay. When Ervo woke him up, he was kind of hit with everything at once. And Ervo had some bastard's blood on his hand, so obviously someone did something to you that he shouldn't have. Priel clearly cares a lot about you."

"Clearly to you, but not to me," I muttered.

Her smile morphed into a grin. "That's what friends are for, girly."

My fire rippled over my skin, and I nodded. "Thanks. I'll think about everything you said."

"We're watching a chick flick after dinner, feel free to join us," Sunny called after me. "Also, January will probably break into your room to hear the story when she gets here, so prepare yourself."

I bit back a grin as I shut the door to my room behind me. January wouldn't break in; she valued her own privacy too much to violate mine. But she *would* be pissed that she'd missed the drama.

Seven

I WANTED to clear my mind, so I headed into the shower. Before I turned the water on, though, I remembered what Priel had done the last time he was in there. He'd just caught himself on fire, and when the flames died down, he'd been clean.

That sounded pretty nice, so I shut my eyes and reached for the hot magic in my abdomen.

It slid through my body and over my skin, and a warm peace settled some invisible part of me.

I was going to be alright.

When the flames slid back inside me, I let out a long breath.

Honestly, I felt really refreshed.

My fireproof tank and shorts were clean too, so that was nice. Not having to wash them all the damn time would be awesome.

But with that taken care of, I no longer had an excuse not to use Priel's name the way he'd asked me to. If Mare was right, and he really *was* worried about me, I wanted to know.

Plus, I was kind of paranoid that in his anger, he would start a fight, and I would really have to enforce the ridiculous threat I'd made about that.

Which would screw me, basically, because I still wanted the blond bastard.

I made it to the center of my room and wrapped my arms around my abdomen so they didn't fidget awkwardly.

My lips formed the syllables of his name slowly.

Lo—preel

What would happen if I used it? Would he just… appear?

Only one way to find out, I guessed.

Closing my eyes, I let out a slow breath and mentally urged him to come to me with a soft whisper of, "Lopriel."

The air around me burned for a moment, and then there was a massive man in front of me. His eyes were dark, his fire burning in them.

Goosebumps broke out on my arms when his flaming eyes collided with mine.

He usually did my favorite things when his eyes burned like that.

The touching, the kissing…

He stalked toward me, and I took a step backward for every one he took forward until my shoulders met the wall.

His eyes burned me to the damned soul, and I couldn't have looked away if I tried as he continued covering the distance between us.

His voice was low and feral when he asked, "Why did you walk out of the Stronghold without me?"

"I needed air," I whispered.

It wasn't a lie.

"From what?" His low voice gave me more goosebumps.

"You."

He growled furiously in response. "You've exposed your magic to every bastard in my world. Even now, the word is being spread throughout all of the seelies. Soon, the unseelies will learn too, and any number of them could try to take you from me."

"Take me from you? I don't belong to you. We're not mates. You don't even want me."

He snarled at me, his hands pressing into the wall on either side of my head, trapping me in. "You are *mine*, Gorgeous."

I growled back, "You only say things like that when your eyes are glowing. I don't understand why you get possessive and touchy when your eyes glow, and then don't give a damn when they don't. You're giving me whiplash."

The fire vanished from his eyes, but he was still just as furious as he had been a moment earlier.

I froze, not knowing he could change them just like that.

"The world looks slightly different when my mind has shifted, but I can assure you I am just as possessive when my eyes aren't glowing. I told you, I've wanted you since the first time I caught your scent."

I scoffed. "You only stopped by with supplies twice. Don't lie to me."

"A bond didn't snap between us immediately the way it did for January and Lian. I had to give the others time to catch your scent, as was our people's agreement. When I came to see you a third time, after the others had a chance to see if a bond formed, you refused to see me. You weren't interested."

"I refused to see pretty much anyone," I shot back. "Just get out." I tossed a hand toward the door.

"No." He stepped closer to me, and the fronts of our bodies pressed together. The fire in his eyes relit with the contact. "I need to see your skin. To make sure no one hurt you."

"I'm a fae, Priel. Even if someone did hurt me, the evidence would already be gone."

"*Lopriel.*" He all but snarled the word at me. "To you, I am *Lopriel.*"

"You can't have everything you want," I snapped back. "And you *don't* get to choose what I call you."

I was enjoying our argument too much—it was making me all hot and bothered. But he didn't know that, and I couldn't let him walk all over me, or he would think he could just growl and snarl and get his way every time.

"Fine. Call me what you want, but take your damn clothes off. I need to know you're okay." His harsh voice—and choice out of those two options—surprised me.

When his hands tugged my shorts down a heartbeat later, my body flushed.

His hands dragged over my thighs and ass, checking for wounds that didn't exist. When he was satisfied that I hadn't been hurt there, he slid my shorts back up, settling the hem near my waist again. His palms moved over my abdomen, and then tugged the tank top over my head before tossing it to the ground.

"Damn." His eyes burned as they slid over my bare chest, lingering on my tits.

I wasn't injured. His response was solely to the way I looked—which made me feel plenty of dirty things that I couldn't say aloud.

His hands landed on my waist, and he turned me around so my back was to him.

A strangled noise escaped him as they slid down the curves of my hips, stopping there.

I fought a groan.

Would the bastard just grab me already?

Why wouldn't he just touch me the way I wanted him to?

It seemed like he wanted it too, now, so why was he holding back?

"See?" I told him, stepping away from him after a long moment proved he wasn't going to act on whatever he was feeling.

Bending over, I grabbed my shirt off the floor.

"You can go now." I gestured toward the door as I straightened, and tried not to notice that his hot eyes were back on my tits.

"No." His gaze lifted back to mine.

I yanked my shirt over my head, shoving it into place. "What's your excuse this time?"

"We need to figure out what your magic is and how you can use it to protect yourself. The unseelie *will* come when they hear about your brands; you need to be ready for that."

My stomach twisted. "I'm not a fighter. If they come for me, I won't kill them. I don't want those memories hanging over me for the rest of my life."

"I don't expect you to. But I'm hoping your power will give them enough pause to let *me* kill them. We have to be mated by then so that your scent and appearance don't cause a damn war."

I bristled and flushed. Every time I started to think the bastard might be into me, he said shit like that. "I'm not that unattractive. My brands are weird, but they're not *ugly*."

His expression morphed into one of incredulousness. "The way you look and smell will lead them to want you as their *mate*, North. I sure as hell never said you weren't attractive."

Oh.

If he thought I was attractive...

It was time to test him. And his possibly-nonexistent feelings for me.

"Well, maybe I should've done the stupid competition Ervo wanted, then. I'd have the chance to choose some guy, to get out of your hair."

Fury crossed his face.

He started stepping toward me again—doing that thing where he drove me to the wall, and nearly pinned me to the damn thing.

His chest was heaving when my back met said wall. I was breathing fast too.

"You will not be choosing *some guy*. You belong to *me*. And as I said, *we* will have to mate completely before the unseelie come. Not you; *us*."

My anger swelled.

"You can't just skip every step in a relationship and expect me to happily jump in the sack with you," I snapped back, even though my chastisement was almost the literal definition of what I wanted to do. "You haven't even made it clear whether or not you *want me*. I may be trapped in this world, but that doesn't mean I'm going to permanently marry myself to some bastard who's offering to be my pity mate. I—"

His hands wrapped around my face, cupping my cheeks and cutting off my tirade.

"Wha—what are you doing?" My lips stumbled over the words.

His pelvis pressed against me, and the thick hardness of his erection dug into my abdomen.

He didn't say a damn thing as he tilted my head back with those hands on my cheeks.

My breathing picked up as his lips slowly lowered to mine.

Just before our mouths met, he growled, "I want you so damn badly I can't even *think*, Gorgeous."

Fire burned in his eyes a heartbeat before his lips captured mine. One of his hands dug into my hair, tightening in a handful of the dark silk. The other slid down to my ass, grabbing me and lifting me upward. When his erection met my center, I moaned.

Our kiss grew hotter, and more desperate.

My hands moved frantically over his chest and arms, feeling everything I could before the moment ended.

One of his remained in my hair, holding my face to his. The other slid beneath the fabric of my shorts, gripping a handful of my bare ass before sliding up toward the place I wanted it.

Just as his fingers brushed the slick wetness at my center, electricity raced through my skin. My back arched, and a gasp escaped me as my head crashed against the wall. Not a gasp of pleasure—one of shock, as I was yanked into one of my horrible dreams.

I STOOD in the middle of the forest, with ice on one side of me and fire on the other. The trees to my right were engulfed in the white-hot flames, and the sky was full of smoke.

Awful roars, growls, and screams pierced the air, and my arms wrapped around my stomach.

Not this again.

Not more blood.

I saw glimpses of the bodies around me before I could squeeze my eyes shut.

Priel's body.

His packs'.

The corpses of so many fae.

And off in the distance, there was still fighting.

The death wasn't enough.

It had never been enough.

These dreams had never felt completely like dreams, but they'd also never hit me in the middle of the day like this.

Was Priel right?

Was Vevol trying to communicate with me somehow?

"If you have something to say, just say it," I hissed at whoever or whatever had triggered the dream.

The air around me rippled, and when I peeked my eyes open, I realized that everything had changed.

I was now in the same location—a small clearing between the trees that was iced over on one side and not the other. But now the trees were looming over me, and the air both smelled and felt pure somehow.

"Polaris," a strange voice murmured behind me.

I spun around, and my eyes opened widely when I found myself face to face with a fae woman. She was almost as tall as the men, with the same pointed ears. Her hair was golden, her eyes a sparkling blue, and all she wore was the same fireproof tank top and shorts I had on. Glittering magical tattoos seemed to dance across every inch of her skin, constantly changing shape and color.

"Vevol?" I asked, stunned.

"Indeed."

In front of my eyes, her appearance shifted. She grew taller, her hair lightening and her eyes darkening.

I tried really hard not to gawk, but probably failed.

As soon as her appearance was settled, she began changing again. It was a total mind-warp to watch, but I supposed that as a goddess—or a whole world—she didn't really have to follow any rules.

"Have you been sending me the dreams? Was Priel right about that?" I asked, forcing my voice not to wobble.

"Your magic has the ability to tap into the futures of those around you. Most of your dreams have been triggered by your own wandering," she murmured.

Even her voice seemed to be changing as she added, "I cannot hold a form for long. Already, this drains me."

"Then why am I here? What have you been telling me?" I pleaded. I had seen so much fire and death, and I couldn't take much more of it.

"War is coming. The last time a fury like this one bloomed, it decimated the numbers of my women and forced the females into hiding." Her voice was soft and musical, and heart-wrenching as well somehow.

My lips parted. "There are female fae that were born here?"

"Not many, but yes. They remain beyond the lake your hound's portal opens and closes near. Only female fae can get past the boundary that protects them."

Fuck.

"Peace must be established. Until the future you see is free of the blood and flames your visions have shown you, the females must stay hidden." Her voice began to fade quickly, as did her form.

"Wait, how do I establish peace? How do we stop a war before it starts?" I rushed toward her, reaching for her hand.

"The Tame Queen," Vevol's voice whispered.

As if those last three words were a trigger, the dream ended suddenly.

Eight

I SAT UP QUICKLY, sucking in air frantically. My mind spun, my heart pounding wickedly-fast.

"Breathe," Mare said, her voice soft. Her hand was wrapped around my arm, her grip firm but not hard. She hadn't been in there when the dream—or vision—dragged me in, but I assumed some time had passed. A short vision could equate to an entire night's rest. Sometimes, even longer.

"Holy shit," I panted, my eyes slamming shut again.

"What happened?" Priel's snarl almost had me opening my eyes, but my head was still spinning so much that I thought I might vomit.

"Pretty sure I can see the future," I managed.

Okay, it was a lie.

I was confident that I could see the future.

Vevol *herself* had just told me I could see the damn future.

"I already knew that." His growl was fierce. "But you were out for hours, North. That can't be normal."

"Usually, I see things when I'm sleeping." I massaged my temple, feeling a harsh headache coming on as the dizziness started to calm down a little.

"Back off," Sunny snapped at Priel. "Give the girl some space."

His furious snarl told me it was time to intervene.

I finally opened my eyes, grabbing his wrist in one smooth motion and then yanking him toward me in a harsh one. My tug didn't really affect him, but he understood what I was trying to do and let me pull him over to me.

When he dropped down on the bed beside me, I set a hand on his knee to calm him down. His arm wrapped around my side, and he promptly dragged me over to him until we were practically glued together.

Well, then.

Sunny gave me a knowing smirk.

Mare fought a smile.

Dots wasn't in there. I knew she got triggered whenever someone grew angry or violent, so I wasn't surprised by her absence. Priel wasn't exactly the calm-angry kind of guy, which I appreciated, but not everyone was into that.

"What did you see?" Mare asked me.

"Vevol," I admitted. "The goddess, Vevol. She said..." I bit my lip, not sure what exactly I could and couldn't share.

Or what I *wanted* to share.

If I admitted to Priel that there were other women, there was a chance that he would stop wanting me. Fae chicks as tall and gorgeous as Vevol's constantly changing appearance was? No way could I compete with them.

On top of my selfish reasoning, there was also common sense. The less people who knew about the actual fae women before we figured out how to remove the war from our future, the better.

I needed to keep that shit quiet until things were settled.

And... maybe until I figured out whether or not Priel and I were really a thing. He had made some big claims, but I still wasn't completely sure that I believed him.

That was my selfishness talking again, but I didn't shut it up immediately. It was a part of me, as much as I refused to admit it aloud.

"She's been showing me these images because there's a war coming," I finally told them, gesturing to the walls. "Apparently I'm not as crazy as I thought."

Mare scowled. "We never thought you were crazy."

"Just pissed at the world, which is valid," Sunny offered.

I really appreciated hearing that, and shot her a grateful look.

"So how do we stop it?" Mare checked.

"She didn't really explain. Just said '*the Tame Queen*'." I formed air quotes around the title with the hand that Priel hadn't captured.

"We'll need to cross the border, then," Sunny mused.

"No." Priel's voice was hard. "Not a fucking chance."

"There's no way the unseelies will allow their ladies to cross our borders either," a voice added from the doorway.

All of our attention jerked toward it, and I saw a grinning January standing there, with Lian behind her. His arm was wrapped possessively around her torso, which I thought was weird. Then again, the two of them were usually weird together.

January looked like a damned nature goddess, wearing a pair of dark green fireproof-underwear with all those gorgeous, golden tattoos shimmering over her strong, curvy body and her long, golden-brown hair falling to her ribs all cute-messy-like. I probably looked like a scarecrow that went rolling down a rocky hill in comparison, but refused to let myself consider that depressing fact.

My self-esteem could only take so much, after all.

"What did I miss?" January asked. "Why do we want to talk to the Tame Queen?"

Sunny and Mare looked at me.

I grimaced. "Apparently, I can see the future. Vevol—the goddess—told me that there's a war coming. When I asked her how to stop it, all she said was '*the Tame Queen*'."

"Damn." January grimaced. "How are we going to get her away from her grump of a mate?"

"I can use her name," Lian said, like it was simple.

All of us ladies frowned.

January shot him an accusatory look and voiced all of our thoughts. "You know her name?"

He flashed her a small grin. "Everyone knows her name. She was the first female to come to our lands, and wasn't aware that she shouldn't share it."

"Damn." Her eyebrows lifted. "That sucks for her."

"Aev, the king, took to murdering anyone who used it, so no one dares anymore. But considering the alternative is attempting to cross their borders or calling a meeting, we'll have to take the risk," Lian mused.

"Maybe it won't be a risk at all." January's eyes gleamed as she looked at us. "I actually came back to tell you ladies something. I'm pregnant."

I blinked.

Suddenly the arm he had around her abdomen made a lot more sense.

Mare's eyes widened.

Sunny nearly choked on her own spit.

"Are we happy about this?" Dots called from outside the room.

January and Calian stepped in, letting her join the rest of us.

"We are," January confirmed.

"Then yay!" Dots threw her arms around the other woman, squeezing tightly. "Congrats."

"Thanks. I'm scared, but excited too," she confessed. "I realized we need to tell the other mated ladies, in case any of them are thinking about boning their mates. And one of them already did to stop the last potential war—so yeah, they need to know. If all of us ladies go alone, we could use the pregnancy as an excuse for taking advantage of her real name."

"Not a chance," Lian said smoothly.

"Fine, you can come," January grumbled.

"We can't bring any of the unmated females," Priel said from beside me, his voice clipped. "When Aev shows up, he'll try to drag all of them back with him. You know the bastard's still pissed that they're not all on his lands."

"Well, North has to come. She's the one who had the vision," January pointed out.

"North won't be unmated for long," Priel growled back.

There was a moment of silence.

"Why won't North be unmated for long?" January checked.

"Priel has decided that I'm his. We haven't agreed on that yet," I said, flashing him a look of warning.

He glared back at me, as if daring me to try to get away from him.

That was... an issue.

I wasn't sure how, exactly.

Or why.

Or what I'd do about it.

Because I wanted to be with him, but only if he wanted to be with me, and only if we actually started getting to know each other.

So, an issue.

An issue for tomorrow, though. Or next week. Or if I was lucky, next month.

"North's scars are actually something called brands. They mark her as ultra-powerful," Dots added helpfully. "So there are an assload of male fae who want her right now. She lied about being in love with Priel for the past year and a half to shut that down."

January's eyebrows shot up way into her forehead, and she looked at me. "Seriously?"

"Unfortunately." I grimaced.

Much of my grimacing was because my lie about Priel hadn't actually been a lie, and I felt kind of shitty for lying about lying, as ridiculous as that sounded.

"Damn."

"Yeah. I'll figure something out. I'm sure I'll come up with some way to fix the situation somehow," I said.

"Or we can just mate now and make things simple," Priel growled at me.

"Sure, if we want to start a war with the seelies before the unseelies take a stab at us," I shot back.

"Sounds worth it to me." He flashed me a feral grin.

I scowled. "You're dead in every violent vision I've seen, so you should probably change your tune."

"All of these bastards are too happy to go to war. They need something to focus on that isn't four single chicks and fighting," January said with a sigh.

"*Three* single chicks," Priel corrected, tugging me closer.

"We still haven't agreed on that," I grumbled back.

"Not shoving a fae dude away from you is usually enough agreement for them." January grinned at me. "You'll get used to it."

Shit, I hoped so.

Because I still had the most ridiculous fluttering in my stomach every time Priel touched me. Or looked at me. Or... pretty much did anything, honestly.

"You *do* have to come with us to talk to the Tame Queen, regardless of whatever you two figure out," January said, waving a hand toward me.

"There's no way around that," I agreed.

Priel growled again, releasing me and standing smoothly. His fists clenched, flames engulfing the tensed skin, ink, and muscles as he began pacing the room.

"I think we'll give you guys a minute to talk," January said, eyeing the pissed-off hound.

She and Calian stepped away, and the other girls followed them out. Dots gave me a thumbs-up and Sunny, a saucy grin.

The door closed behind them, and it was just me and Priel.

I bit my lip, not sure what to say. I definitely wasn't getting up off of my bed unless I figured that one out. The bed was safe, since Priel currently wasn't on it.

The hound continued to pace, his body tense and his expression furious.

My stomach clenched when I realized that one of the paintings featuring a strip of his abdomen and tattoos would be directly within his line of sight if he looked up from the tile he was glaring down at. It blended in with the colors of the gory picture I'd hidden it on the edge of, but it was undeniably Priel.

Don't look up.

Don't look up.

Don't look u—

His eyes lifted.

He halted.

Shit.

I could practically see the gears turning in his mind, even though I could only see the back of his head.

I'd done my best to hide the evidence of my scandalous dreams within the paintings, but that one was one of the clearest images. If you looked closely, there was absolutely no denying it.

His gaze slowly moved off of that painting, and across the walls.

I squeezed my eyes shut, knowing exactly what he would see.

An image of our intertwined hands, pressing against a mattress together.

A small painting of his large, inked hand stretched over my brand-dotted abdomen, which had a few tattoos of its own.

Bits and pieces of the art on his body, embedded in every shadow I'd painted.

In my room, Priel was *everywhere*.

The bed groaned, and my eyes flew open just in time to see Priel step behind my headboard, crouching down so he could see the paintings I'd hidden there.

I opened my mouth to give him an explanation, to figure out a way to lie to him, but failed.

Nothing came out.

I knew exactly what he was seeing; how many times had I done exactly what he just had?

Hundreds.

I did it every day.

I'd slide behind the bed frame, into the gap that I'd left there, and lower myself to the floor. And, crouched in that little space, I'd stare at the glimpse of the life of my literal dreams.

Most of them, I could ignore. I didn't paint everything I saw; I would never be able to. The dreams were too full, too dynamic.

But the image I'd painted behind my bed was one I had never been able to get out of my mind.

It wasn't anything epic or important.

It was a view from the side of me sitting on a chair, with a wall covered in gorgeous, painted landscapes visible behind me. Not the wall in Priel's cave that I'd visited—I'd never dreamed of that place before—but a different one.

My hair was at least six inches shorter, and all I had on was a fireproof tank and shorts. Instead of black, they were made of the same colorful fabric on Priel's practically-trademarked shorts.

Priel was kneeling on the floor between my parted legs, one of his hands holding the magical tattoo gun near my abdomen, and the other draped over my thigh.

At the moment of the painting, he wasn't actually inking me. Instead, he was grinning up at me, having just told me a joke. I was laughing, one of my palms resting on his shoulder and the other on top of the hand he had on my thigh.

I wasn't sure what about the image meant so much to me. Maybe the simplicity, or the mundaneness. Or maybe it was just the look of pure happiness on my face, and the devoted humor on Priel's.

Whatever it was, I had yearned for that moment so damn much that words couldn't even describe the ache.

I hadn't known it was the future I was seeing.

I hadn't even known that my dreams were possible.

I'd chalked it up to an overactive imagination and hero worship for the gorgeous man who had brought me supplies when I'd first woken up in Vevol.

And now...

Shit.

Was that moment actually possible?

What if Priel and I could really get to that moment I'd painted?

Fear clutched my abdomen.

I didn't even really know the man. Sure, I'd been crushing on him hard core, the sex dreams were unreal, and things had gotten intense between us on one occasion.

But none of those things meant I was ready to throw myself into the kind of serious relationship he would want. Or even the kind that I'd painted. I could be on board with some hot sex, but everything else? I had no idea how to be in a relationship.

I'd barely survived the arranged one my parents set up.

I jerked to my feet.

Priel was still behind the headboard, so this was probably my last chance for escape.

I couldn't leave the Stronghold, and I didn't want to.

But... I needed space.

Air.

I hurried to the bathroom, shutting the door behind myself and locking it quickly before I collapsed to the ground. My ass didn't appreciate the hard tile beneath me, but I ignored the discomfort.

My eyes squeezed shut when I heard Priel's footsteps in my room.

Maybe I needed space, but he'd made it pretty clear a little earlier that *he* did *not*.

There was a bit of pressure against the door, and when he spoke, I heard his low voice not far above my head.

He must've been sitting on the other side.

"How long have you been seeing us together?" the words were soft, and so much gentler than I expected.

I bit my lip, not sure how to answer without pissing him off or making him think I was ready for more than I actually was.

I debated it silently for a while before I settled on, "I thought they were just dreams."

"North." He knew exactly what I was doing.

There wasn't much of a point to beating around the bush, so I stopped.

"Since we met."

"Fuck." His hiss didn't bode well for me.

My stomach clenched. "Nothing is set in stone. The future probably changes all the time. It's not like you have no choice; you can still pick someone else. We're not—"

He quickly growled, "I'm furious that I didn't pursue you sooner, not angry with you. There is no one else for me; there never has been, and there never will be. As far as I'm concerned, those things you saw are our future. Period."

Oh.

Wow.

A long, charged silence followed.

I finally whispered, "We don't even know each other."

"That's easily remedied."

He wasn't wrong.

"I'm not ready to promise anything," I added.

"I don't need a promise; I've seen your future. And it belongs to *me*."

A shiver rolled down my spine. "You're so possessive."

"Incredibly." His growled agreement made me bite my lip. "Now, I need you to come out here and let me hold you in my arms while you tell me every single thing I missed while I was outside. I'm fucking losing it, if you haven't noticed."

I laughed softly. "I noticed."

"So come out here and fix that for me."

I bit my lip to stop myself from smiling, but didn't move to get up. My humor faded into a wall of serious hesitancy. "You didn't tell me how you felt about seeing us together like that in my painting."

There was a long pause.

He finally admitted, "I felt like I wished there was a way to skip right to that moment and get lost in it, with you. You still don't believe that I want you, do you?"

"I don't know," I whispered. "I know that you think I'm yours, and that I want you to be mine. But I didn't really live much, on Earth. My parents didn't let me leave our house very often, and I was barely nineteen when I was brought here. They thought they were protecting me, and I love them for that, but I always felt isolated. I'm not good with people, because of it. And I have a hard time with trust."

"Well, I'll do whatever it takes to make my desire for you constantly and annoyingly clear until you're certain about it, then."

My lips curved upward a bit. "What would that entail?"

"Kissing. Touching. Talking. Complimenting. Snuggling. Licking. Stroking. Petting. Sniffing. And fucking, in every way there is."

My face heated.

"Of course, that's only when you're willing, Gorgeous."

Taking the opportunity to change the subject, I scoffed at the nickname. "You have got to come up with something better to call me than that."

He chuckled. "Give me your full name, and maybe I will."

I bit my lip, considering it.

If I gave him my name, he'd be able to call me to him, wherever he was. It would be dangerous, but in some ways, safer too. If I were ever captured, or taken, or attacked...

Alright, maybe it wasn't such a terrible idea.

I still hesitated, though.

Honestly, I trusted him. He had fought outside the Stronghold for months, keeping me safe from the other fae who wanted me as their mate. Even if his reasons were selfish—because he'd claimed that he wanted me as his, even then—that wasn't something I could just forget or pretend hadn't happened.

He fought for me.

And I trusted him.

And damn, I liked kissing him.

"Everyone on Earth always called me North," I admitted, my voice barely above a whisper. "My parents gave me a unique name, but it was *too* unique, hence the nickname."

He waited.

I sighed softly. "My real name is Polaris. It's another name for a star we can pretty much always see on Earth, called the North Star. Hence my nickname."

"Polaris," Priel mused.

There was a slight tingle at the base of my spine when the word left his lips.

I changed the subject again, not wanting to get emotional if the topic began to revolve around my parents. "Let's make something to eat. I'm hungry."

Priel was standing when I opened the door between us. He offered me a hand, but I didn't take it, stepping past him.

A low chuckle escaped him, and he caught my arm with a smooth palm that wrapped around my wimpy bicep.

"Like it or not, female, you're mine now," he murmured to me. "And I'm going to make you so damn happy about that, you won't even know what to do with yourself."

I shot him a raised eyebrow. "I'll believe that when I see it."

His response was a scorching grin that had me fighting a wave of said happiness.

Nine

January and Lian were already cooking when we stepped out of my room, so when they invited us to wait and eat with everyone else, we headed to the couch on the far side of the room. Mare was reading close by, and Sunny and Dots were watching a chick flick I knew they had seen a hundred times already. Priel's intrigued gaze followed the screen as we passed it.

It occurred to me that the man probably had no idea how human relationships worked. It was probably going to be a long shot, trying to help him understand that I wanted to get to know him a little first instead of just jumping into the gloriously-hot sex I'd seen us having. But sex would mate us permanently, and despite what I'd seen and felt thus far, I wanted us to be on the same page about most things before we took that step.

"Hey," Mare murmured, as I sat down near her. Priel sat on my other side, his arm wrapping around my waist. His fingers dug into my hip, and my face heated when I realized I hadn't put my long-sleeved shirt and pants on.

"Hey," I mirrored her greeting, though I focused on the movie for a few minutes.

When I saw her start moving a little, I glanced over and saw her wiping her eyes a bit. They looked like they'd been watering—but why was she crying?

"What's wrong?" I whispered.

"Oh, nothing." She flashed me a small, watery smile. "I'm just reading poetry. From what I've gathered, this book came from another world that's connected to Earth, and some of the poems are really emotional. I've never read anything like them before. This is my seventh or eighth read-through, but they still get me."

It didn't surprise me that there were other worlds connected to Earth, given where we currently were.

"I'll have to read them sometime," I said, and the smile she flashed me grew wider.

Maybe talking about books was the key to Mare's heart.

SOON AFTER THE conversation about the poems, the food was ready, and we all gathered and ate together. It was strange, having a family dinner of sorts, but in a way that made my heart happier than I knew how to deal with at that point.

After we'd eaten, cleaned up, and chatted for a bit, Priel scooped me up into his arms as he stood smoothly. I yelped as my feet left the ground, and scowled at him when he grinned at me and started moving. He stopped at the bookshelf to grab the poetry book Mare and I had been talking about—which she'd finished reading through again during the movie—then carried me back to my room.

"What are you doing?" I grumbled at him.

"Reading poems from another world while spending time holding my woman." He shut the door behind him. "My portals have never taken me anywhere other than Earth, as far as I've been able to tell. I'm curious about their poetry."

That was an understandable sort of curiosity, I supposed.

Priel set me down in the middle of my mattress. There was a burned spot on one of the blankets, thanks to me, but he had flipped it around so the burn was near our feet. The book hit the mattress beside me, and then the fae was sliding into the bed, pulling my blankets over us.

"I need some of those fireproof plants in here," I mumbled, as he rolled me up onto my side and tucked his front up against my back.

"I'll get some as soon as I can," he agreed.

I tried not to let him notice the way I sucked in a breath when his thick arm wrapped around my abdomen.

He was propped up a little awkwardly on one arm—and opened the book with the hand connected to that arm—but when he buried his nose in my neck, he growled in approval.

He also gave me way too many damned goosebumps.

I forced my eyes to follow the words on the page. They were either in English, or Vevol's magic had translated them for me.

I'd never really been a poem girl, but I tried to enjoy the writing. Some of it didn't make sense, but most of it did.

After we made it through a dozen or so, I closed my eyes and just enjoyed the peace of the moment.

I'd never been held like this before. I'd never had a man's arms around me so possessively. I'd never felt so... important to him.

My father's protectiveness was mostly to blame for that.

Wistfulness engulfed me as I thought about the family I'd left behind. They weren't good for me, or for my future, but they were mine, and I had loved them. I hoped like hell that my sister was okay, that she was coping with losing me. We hadn't ever been super close, and she'd moved out a few years before I was brought to Vevol, but still, I worried for her.

Priel's nose remained buried in my hair, his chest rising and falling steadily against my back. His fingers were curled beneath my hip, getting trapped underneath me, but his thumb traced a slow circle just above the place his fingers had disappeared to.

Priel read through many more poems before he lingered on one much longer than the others.

I peeked my eyes open to see what had captured his attention, and found a poem titled *I Burn for You* by someone named Orthrus.

My gaze followed the words, and my throat swelled a bit as I read them.

Sitting beneath the shining moon, I burn; I burn for you.

Leaning against this wall of stone, I blaze, waiting for you.

Standing under this sky of stars, I watch while my flames dance for you.

Walking up a road of ash, I smoke, searching for you.

Drowning in the pain of flesh, I'm blazing, flaming, smoking, and burning... for you.

THERE WAS SO much emotion in the words that it choked me up a little. I didn't know what had inspired them, or why, but I wanted to.

Priel held the book open for a few more long moments before he set it down on the mattress.

The arm he had beneath me wrapped around my chest, dragging me as close as I could possibly get to him.

"I want to know you," he murmured to me. "Tell me everything."

"How am I supposed to tell you *everything*?" I asked, my eyes shutting as I leaned back against Priel's chest.

"I suppose you'll just have to spend the next few months lying in this bed with me until you've spoken all of it."

I snorted, and felt his lips stretch in a grin against my neck.

"Why don't *you* tell *me* everything?" I countered.

"Sure. It won't take long." His hand slid out from beneath my hip, his fingertips dragging over my abdomen slowly. My body warmed in response to his touch, but I didn't acknowledge it.

He began softly. "There's not much to do in Vevol, other than fighting, cooking, and creating art. I know men on Earth often fulfill different roles than the women there, but here, we do everything. Cleaning. Sewing. Cooking. Gardening. That was my life. I painted. Inked my brothers. Grew plants, in a patch hidden away from the other hellhounds. Life was simple, but dull. When the itch got too bad, I started fights, or joined the ones already happening. Life had no purpose, then, and a life without purpose isn't much of a life. Since I started fighting for you, you became that purpose. And now, everything has changed."

"Is that a good thing, though?" I asked.

"It's an *incredible* thing." His hand still stroked my abdomen lightly. My body throbbed with his touch, but I did my best to ignore the feelings. Nothing had ever felt so intimate... or so safe.

It was my turn to tell him about my life, I supposed.

My voice was at least as soft as his. “My parents were good to me, but they were terrible people. They killed in cold blood, hurt other people for the sake of money, and manipulated with every breath they took. They matched me to some guy in an arranged marriage the day I turned eighteen,” I admitted.

His body stilled. “Marriage?”

“Yes, the human version of mating.”

His fingers wrapped tightly around my hip.

“I didn’t marry him. The whole thing was a long, drawn-out attempt to make a statement to my parents. The other family was going to kill me. When I heard them talking about what they were going to do with me, I waited until they were near a forest, and then threw myself out of the car. It was like... jumping off a running hellhound, I guess. But humans are a lot more fragile than fae. I got horribly injured in the process, and ended up spending a few days hiding out in the forest. Almost died a few different times. When my family finally found me, I was taken to a hospital, and ended up spending about a month healing there,” I admitted.

Priel was stiff behind me. Really damn stiff.

“Anyway, I survived, but I realized I needed to find a way out of my parents’ world. The problem was, there wasn’t one. They had the money, the property, and everything I would need to get away from them. When I asked them to let me leave, they said no, and warned me that they’d have to hunt me down if I ran, for my own safety. They didn’t give me the scars on my body, but as much as I hate to admit it, their choices were sort of the reason for the physical and mental reminders. And yet they still weren’t willing to let me go.”

“The day I wished on those candles...” I swallowed roughly. “I didn’t want to leave them. I loved them; I still do. They’re brutal, harsh, and terrible in some ways, but they were mine, and for that, they had my complete loyalty. I still feel guilty for making that wish, for leaving them.”

“They didn’t deserve you,” Priel said, his voice low in my ear.

“Maybe not, but they had me anyway.”

His hands stroked my hip, and we both grew quiet for a few minutes, lost in our own minds.

When I finally spoke up again, I was nervous. A little nauseous, too.

“If I let myself fall in love with you, it won’t be soft and gentle, Priel. I don’t love that way. When I care about something, or someone, I dig my claws into their skin and I hold on like the alternative would be my end. I don’t love lightly, or sweetly. You would get all of me. The shitty, angry parts. The scared, furious parts. The intense, obsessive parts. I don't love many people, but when I love, it can be brutal, like the bastards who raised me."

"Then I look forward to feeling your claws in my skin, Polaris." His teeth brushed my throat, and I shivered. "And I can assure you that you will be loved just as fiercely as you love, should you let me in."

My throat swelled.

"Tell me about painting. When did you begin?" His hand stroked my hip.

"When I was little, I used to draw on everything..."

PRIEL and I stayed in my bed for hours, talking. We didn't touch intimately, or even kiss. But the conversations we shared, the stories we traded, were worth more than orgasms to me.

And as much as I'd fought it in the beginning, I was pretty sure that I was going to fall in love with that bastard.

The silences between stories were thick and comfortable, like a massive blanket. After one pause, I murmured, "Priel?"

He was silent.

When I paid attention to the rise and fall of his chest, I realized he was breathing evenly.

Happiness slid through me with that realization. The first day I was in his cave, I had thought it was an insult that he fell asleep so easily in my presence. Now, I knew it was a privilege that I relaxed him so completely.

I needed to pee, though, so I carefully eased myself away from him. It took a little time, but I finally made it out from underneath his thick, heavy limbs.

After I used the bathroom, I studied the man in my bed. He looked so peaceful.

My mind went back to the words of the poem we'd found.

I burn for you.

I was feeling a bit overwhelmed by the intensity of my emotions, so I slipped out of my room for just a few minutes, leaving Priel asleep on my bed with one last long, backward glance.

My eyes scanned the living room. Everyone seemed to have gone to bed, except Mare.

I padded over to her, taking a seat on the other side of the couch. My legs slid up onto the cushions, and I wrapped my arms around them.

"You okay?" she murmured to me.

The question caught me off guard.

Was I okay?

For the first time in a long time, I actually *did* feel okay, despite everything.

"I think I am," I admitted.

Her lips curved upward, just slightly. "You seem happy."

Honestly?

I thought maybe I was that, too.

"Can I ask you something?" I wondered.

She shrugged one shoulder. "Is it about sex with the fae?"

I snorted. "Definitely not."

She closed her book, leaving a finger between a few of the pages. "Then go ahead."

"You read a lot. If this world were one of your books, how would we prevent the war that I've seen coming? Vevol said the Tame Queen is the answer, but I don't know how she could prevent the hell I've seen from breaking loose."

Mare grimaced. "If there were more women, it would knock the tension of the situation down a lot, and probably kill the potential of a war. Even one woman to every five or six fae could improve things tremendously. But with four of us to a couple hundred unseelie fae, the odds aren't in anyone's favor. If we could combine forces with the rest of the humans, there would be twenty of us women. According to Ana, there are around six hundred fae in this world. I don't know where she got the information, but it seems accurate from what I've seen."

I grimaced.

The situation just kept getting worse.

Vevol's words came to my mind.

There were fae women, hidden away on an island.

"Can you keep a secret?" I asked her.

She flashed me a smile. "Of course."

I lowered my voice, leaning closer to her. She leaned in too.

"There are fae women hidden away," I whispered.

Her eyes widened. "What?"

"Vevol told me that the fighting got so bad between the fae that the women had to separate from them. I think she must've wiped their memories about it or something."

"Holy shit," she breathed.

"Yeah. The women have to stay hidden until we can de-escalate things between the fae, though. The seelies and unseelies have had issues for so long that she says we can't risk the fae ladies."

"Wow." Mare sat back, running a hand over the top of her head. Her hair was up in a poof, like it often was. "So we just need to talk to the Tame Queen and figure out how to stop the fae from fighting."

"And how to introduce a group of who-knows-how-many female fae into a group of emotionally-scarred ex-human women and horny single men," I agreed.

"Shit." She bit her lip, excitement in her eyes. "You have to go talk to the Queen, and the sooner, the better. If you leave before the sun comes up, I think you can get away from the other men before they decide how they really feel about you declaring your love for Priel."

I nodded.

She had a point.

"I'll wake him up, and he'll figure out a way to break me out of here."

She smiled. "I'll let Lian and January know where you're headed so they can meet up with you too."

"Thanks." I gave her a quick, if hesitant smile of my own. "I know I've been a nightmare to live with, and I'm sorry."

She brushed a hand through the air. "We all understand. Always have. For some of us, this place is a miracle. For others, it's a prison." Her words were simple, but they made my throat swell up.

I jerked my head in a nod.

It had felt like a prison for too long. With the terrible dreams, and the lust for someone I'd never even really talked to, and...

Shit.

That was a lot to think about.

I pushed the thoughts away.

Things in Vevol were going to change for the better. I was going to make sure of it.

The door to my room crashed open, and I lifted my eyes to a wild-eyed Priel. His shoulders were tense, one of his fists burning as he looked around the room.

Our gazes collided, and his body relaxed instantly.

The fire on his hand went out, and he dragged it through his already-wild blond hair. "You scared the shit out of me."

"Sorry." I stood up as I apologized, mouthing a 'thank-you' to Mare. She only grinned in response.

Ten

When I reached him, he dragged me into his arms, closing the door behind me and then pinning me to it. His gigantic arms landed on the door above my head, his forehead tilting toward me. Mine leaned back, and he stopped when our lips were a breath away from each other.

"What were you doing, Polaris?"

Whew, my full name sounded a hell of a lot sexier coming from his lips than it ever had from anyone else's.

"Mare and I came up with a plan," I admitted, lifting my hands and placing them on his bare chest.

"What kind of plan?"

"The kind where I admit that I know I'm eventually going to agree to be your mate and convince you to run away with me in the middle of the night."

His lips curved upward wickedly. "I like this plan already."

"I figured." I closed my eyes.

He surprised me by brushing his lips against mine, lightly, and then murmuring, "Continue."

My eyes remained closed. I was enjoying the moment too much to open them. "You and I are going to sneak out tonight to find the unseelie queen. January and Lian will catch up and join us."

Priel's lips brushed against mine again. "I'd like this plan better if it didn't include another couple."

"The goal is to avoid a war so you don't end up dead, remember? You can sacrifice a little alone time for the sake of your survival."

He chuckled quietly. "I suppose."

His lips brushed mine yet again.

I was enjoying the contact too much, and opened my eyes. "I'm not ready for us to become full-on mates yet, okay?"

"There's lots of fun to be had even without completing the bond though, isn't there?" The gleam in his eyes was wicked.

"Yes. But..." I trailed off when his lips lowered to my throat.

My fingers dug into his chest as he sucked lightly on the skin beneath my ear.

"What else have you seen of our future, Polaris?" he murmured between sucks on my skin.

The words died in my throat as he moved down the sensitive column.

Had I not told him that my dreams were pretty much full of sex?

"North?" he murmured, dragging his teeth over my collarbone and making me shudder.

"Ask me again after we're far enough away from all of the horny bastards outside," I whispered, buying myself some time.

Something told me that if he found out I'd been dreaming about him naked, he would probably *get* naked a lot more often.

And I wasn't so sure I was ready for a naked Priel who actually wanted me.

Yeah, it had been awesome when he was bare and insane in his shower and in his bed, but that was back before I knew he wanted to make things permanent between us. With the possibility of that permanence looming over my head, I was more uncertain.

It was one thing to lust after a guy for months on end.

It was a totally *different* thing to pledge your forever to said guy.

"You're ready to get out of here?" he murmured to me, still exploring my collarbone with his lips, teeth, and tongue. "I'd be more than happy to spread you out on that bed and taste every inch of you first."

Heat flared within me.

Hot damn, that sounded good.

Restrain, North.

"That's probably not a good i—" I breathed in sharply when his lips dragged further down my chest, closer to my boobs. "Priel." I shoved his face away, and he let me push him a couple of inches. "We're not doing this here. No one likes being woken up by the sound of someone else having sex."

He flashed me a wicked grin. "Is that what we would be doing?"

"I'm serious," I said, though I fought a grin of my own.

"Alright, I'll sneak us out of here. You'll have to ride on my back though, in case anyone hears us."

"Fine." I huffed out a breath.

Honestly, I'd kind of been looking forward to another run in my hellhound form.

"When we're sure we've gotten away from them, you can shift too."

Well, that was a deal.

"Alright. How do we get out?"

"Back door." He gestured over his shoulder.

I blinked.

There was a back door?

He flashed me another grin. "Nev and Teris installed it while they were here fixing the hole in January's ceiling a few months back. Figured one of us might need a secret entrance or escape one of these days."

I sighed. "I should question that, but I really don't want to."

"Good." He brushed his lips against my forehead before bending down and tugging me onto his back. I bit back a shriek as he stood smoothly, my arms wrapping around his neck.

"I am way too old for a piggy-back ride," I whisper-complained to him as he strode out of the room.

"When you get to be as ancient as me, you realize you're never too old for anything that you find fun," he whispered back.

I grimaced. "Don't remind me how old you are."

He snorted. "Alright."

He padded down the hallway—I waved at Mare as we passed the living room —and then stopped at a wall at the hallway's end that I was certain was just a wall. Reaching up to the place it met the ceiling, he paused for a moment.

Suddenly and silently, the wall slid down, opening up to the forest.

I gawked.

Secret entrance.

The younger version of me who was obsessed with Harry Potter would've squealed.

The older, jaded version of me only squealed on the inside.

Priel stepped outside, then placed his hand back on the wall. His magic kicked in, and it slid shut once again.

I watched in awe until he spun us around and began to jog silently into the forest. The way he could run without making a sound was incredibly impressive.

When I opened my mouth to ask him how the secret door's magic worked, he reached back and put a hand to my mouth, covering it.

Shit.

Right.

There were probably fae on the other side of the Stronghold, camped out and waiting to see what happened next. Or possibly fighting, even after my threat.

We needed to be quiet.

Good thing Priel was there, because I was absolutely not stealthy on my own.

Priel picked up the pace as we got further from the other fae.

When he'd been running for half an hour or so, he finally shifted. A shiver ran down my spine and an electric shock sizzled over my skin as his form stretched and changed. My whole body seemed to relax as I draped over his extremely-solid back, my arms still looped around his neck but no longer connecting at the middle.

The forest seemed to fly around us, and my eyelids grew heavy as it did. Falling asleep on the back of a hellhound probably wasn't the smartest thing I'd ever do, but I hadn't gotten around to sleeping that night, so I was exhausted.

Priel's fire curled over my skin as if whispering to me that he had me, and slowly, my eyes shut and I drifted off.

Delicious heat engulfed me.

A gasp escaped me, and my fingers dug into the sheets on the bed.

Priel's bed, in a cave I hadn't been to; I recognized the feel and smell of it from my past dreams.

His hands were wrapped around my ass and thighs, spreading me wide for him as I sat on his face, rocking and panting and making noises I'd only ever made in my dreams of us.

His teeth caught my clit, and an orgasm cut through me so sharply I almost screamed. My body trembled, pleasure burning me whole.

Fire blazed around us without burning the sheets or bed. I couldn't tell whether it was mine or Priel's—and it didn't matter.

Not when he was unraveling me, his face buried in my core and his fingers teasing my entrance.

"Fuck," I panted down to him.

Though I was living the moment, it wasn't mine. The words hadn't come from my own conscious decision to speak; they were a part of the future I was seeing.

The dream version of me breathed, "I want you inside me."

"You're not begging yet," Priel growled into my core, slowly rubbing his prickly chin over my sensitive skin.

I fought a cry that threatened to escape at the overwhelming feel of it.

"Or giving me orders." He nuzzled my clit with his nose, and I bucked a little. A gravelly chuckle escaped him as he slid a thick finger inside me slowly, blowing lightly on my sensitive bits. "I haven't even finished warming you up yet."

"Then get to work," I shot back, burying my fingers in his hair and tugging on the strands.

His grin stretched against my center, his teeth nipping lightly at my clit again. "Yes ma'am."

A second finger slid inside me as he slowly began stroking me with his tongue, taking his sweet time. He knew it was better for me that way—with the buildup.

His fingers moved lazily within me, dragging over my g-spot now and again like they were oblivious to the way I needed the touches.

They weren't oblivious. He just wanted me needy and wrecked when we were done, like he always did. It would be incredible, like it always was. He would make sure of that.

"Stop teasing," I panted, desperation beginning to clutch me.

"Or what?" my hellhound growled wickedly.

"I'll kill you," I hissed.

"You can do better than that, Gorgeous."

"I'll ink one of my brands," I shot back.

A possessive snarl escaped him, and shit, he ravaged me.

Pleasure swelled within me.

My expression contorted.

MY HEAD JERKED UPWARD, and I found Priel crouched over me, worry lining his forehead. His fingers pressed to my throat, checking my pulse and finding my heart beating wildly.

Molten-hot need burned in my veins.

I was so close—so damn close.

I would combust if I didn't lose it.

My hand slipped into my shorts.

Priel's eyes dilated as he realized what was going on.

He ripped my shorts down my thighs, watching me drag my fingers over my clit. A moment later, he'd ripped my hand away and replaced it with his tongue.

The feeling was like nothing I'd ever experienced. It was incredible in my dreams, but the dreams weren't happening to me in that moment. Nothing in my visions felt real, or nearly as intense as it was supposed to.

This—his tongue on my clit, while his hands opened my thighs—was real.

And *shit*, it was intense.

I cried out as I lost control, rocking against his mouth while I gripped handfuls of his hair like a lifeline. He snarled at me, feasting on me while I shattered.

Heavy panting shook my whole body as I started coming down from the high. My fingers still clutched his hair, but he didn't even slow down.

Damn.

This version of Priel didn't know my body. He didn't understand what I needed, or wanted.

"Slow, first," I panted to him.

His flaming eyes lifted from my body long enough to meet mine.

"Start slow, then build up," I explained quickly, still struggling for air.

When he lowered his lips back to my core, the drag of his tongue was so excruciatingly slow that my body literally quaked.

"Holy shit," I moaned, as he continued the slow, hot assault.

His flames wrapped around my body, heating me in every way there was.

When he started picking up the pace, I was a goner. I arched and cried out, the way I had in my dreams, and the pleasure was so incredible it almost hurt.

The man looked really damn proud of himself when I looked up at him, my head still spinning and his tongue still moving in those slow, toe-curling strokes.

His movements were slow for a few blissfully-hot minutes, his eyes studying me closely as he began to pick up the pace again. This time, when my breathing grew shallow, he slid a thick finger inside me.

He didn't know exactly where to touch me, unlike in my dreams. But in our reality, I was just as much of a beginner as he was. I didn't know where he should rub his fingertip or knuckle any more than he did.

But it still felt incredible.

My parents had been super controlling in more ways than I cared to admit. I'd never had a vibrator or anything similar; they would've found it and taken it away in a heartbeat. The closest I'd ever gotten to this moment was with my own fingers, and they were skinny little bitches. The way Priel's monstrous one felt inside me... it was unreal.

"Shit," I moaned, when he added another finger, still working my clit with his tongue.

It made me feel so insanely *full*, in ways I'd never even imagined.

Probably a good call, to start with the fingers. I was so tight I would've cut his damn—

All thoughts ceased when he nipped at my clit for the first time.

The arching and cries repeated, but feeling myself squeeze around his fingers as I lost it was a whole new level of incredible.

I came down from the high panting again.

"Need to stop," I groaned at Priel, when he still didn't pull away from me.

He finally dragged his tongue away from my clit, but left his fingers buried inside my throbbing heat.

"Here, let me touch you." I reached for the erection I could most definitely see raging against the seam of his shorts.

I didn't know exactly what I was doing when it came to his cock, but I'd seen myself touch him so many times that I was pretty sure I could replicate what he liked.

"You don't have to," he growled at me, catching my outstretched hand with his free one and lacing his fingers through mine. His other hand was still buried inside me, and I was enjoying it so much that I hoped he wouldn't try to take them out yet. "This was more than enough."

"I want to, though."

It was the honest truth.

I didn't want to feel like I'd received more than I'd given. I wanted to return the favor, to make sure he knew that the feelings were mutual.

"Polaris," he warned me, as I untangled my fingers from his and reached for the waistband of his shorts. He undid the strange, hidden button for me, but made no move to take them off.

"Stop trying to talk me out of it," I shot back.

His lips curved upward slightly.

The bastard always liked my sass in my dreams, too.

"Help me out here," I told him, tugging on his shorts. He grunted at me, but dragged them down a few inches right afterward.

His erection popped free, and I just stared at it for a moment. It was even bigger than I remembered, and it was slick.

I realized he'd already lost control once.

Shit, that made me feel sexy.

My hand wrapped around him, and he let out a low growl.

I watched myself stroke him slowly, using his release to slide smoothly over his length. His whole damn body tensed, the fingers he had inside me curling a bit.

His thumb found my clit even as his eyes shut and his jaw clenched, the fire around us growing hotter and more desperate.

The pleasure within me rose to new heights as I watched the sexy hellhound struggle with control before he finally snarled and pumped into my fist, losing it completely. I shattered with him, crying out as the orgasm cut through me. The flames on his skin blazed over both of us as he throbbed in my grip, the evidence of his pleasure coating my thigh as he dropped down beside me. Our chests both heaved, mine still covered by my tank top. His fire flared over my leg and his cock, and I felt the wetness disappear from my skin.

Satisfaction had me sagging against him, even though he didn't remove his fingers from my body.

"Ever planning on letting go?" I murmured to him.

"Not until you make me."

His mumble made me smile.

"Who were you dreaming about?" His growl a few moments later was a little feral, and I loved that.

"You. I always dream about you." The words slipped out too easily, and I bit my lip, worried how he would react.

"You'd fucking better." His fingers stroked my inner walls, and I sucked in a breath when I realized he'd found my g-spot without any help from me. "Was that your first sex dream about us?"

I snorted. "*Hell* no."

His gravelly chuckle made me grin out at the forest around us. "You'd better start sharing the details so I know how to compete with my future self."

I bit my lip to stop my grin from widening. "I guess I could do that."

Maybe I should've told him about my dreams earlier.

Eleven

After a few more minutes, Priel reluctantly told me that we needed to get moving again. We both shifted, then, and hit the road. Er, dirt.

Partway through the morning, a phoenix and a massive gray dragon caught up to us. They stayed above us in the air until we slowed down, and I realized we were approaching a thick stone building. It was shaped strangely, but I couldn't tell what exactly it was supposed to resemble from the ground.

"Welcome to the borders between our land and the unseelies'," Priel told me, his arm sliding around my waist. His hand landed on my abdomen possessively, and I found myself wrapping my arm around his bicep.

January and Lian landed on their feet a short distance away from us, and she flashed me a wicked grin. "Ready to wreak some havoc?"

I couldn't stop myself from mirroring her expression. "Why the hell not?"

"You guys need to stay behind us," she told Lian and Priel, as she looped her arm through my free one. "No one will try to kill us, but you're probably free game."

"Our lives are connected," Lian reminded her. "They won't kill me."

All three of us looked at Priel.

"I'm not hiding behind you," he growled back.

I sighed.

Of course he wouldn't.

It wasn't even worth the debate.

"Let's get this over with. We need to change the future." I tightened my grip on Priel's arm, and January let go of me so we could walk to the building. The snow melted beneath all of our feet as we went, exposing dirt and rocks that didn't affect my fae toes at all.

There was no furniture inside; just a large, open room that I could now see was shaped like a triangle. The walls and floors were the same cold, gray stone, and there were no windows to allow us a peek out at either the seelie or unseelie portions of the land.

"So what's the plan?" January asked me.

I grimaced. "We use the queen's name to get her here, tell her what Vevol told me, and hope for the best."

January's eyebrows shot upward. "Damn."

"Yep."

I looked at Priel, who looked at Lian.

"Naomi," he said aloud. "We need to speak with you."

I felt a wave of magic roll through the room.

The air shimmered wildly, and then a woman stepped through the glittering strip. She was slim, with perfect-looking wavy dark hair, and pale skin. There were magical tattoos all over her hands, and she wore a bell-shaped, long-sleeve sweater dress with tights beneath it. Compared to her, the rest of us probably looked homeless.

Her eyes were narrowed as she took in the building around us, but they softened slightly when she saw January.

"Aeven is going to be furious," she warned, as she straightened her dress and brushed invisible dirt off of the fabric. She pronounced the name ay-vin, and I was fairly certain she was referring to the Tame King, who the men had called "Aev," pronounced ayv.

"We're sorry, but it couldn't wait," January said, looking at me.

I didn't bother waiting to launch into an explanation. "I found out yesterday that I can see the future. And communicate with Vevol, the goddess. She's been sending me visions of a war that's coming, unless we can figure out a way to stop it. If it comes, it'll be the end of all of us—men and women, seelie and unseelie."

The queen's eyes widened slightly. "Because of us?"

"Because there are twenty of us to hundreds of men, I'd imagine," January said.

Naomi nodded. "The unseelies don't want romantic relationships, but they do want the power boost that comes with having a mate. The girls on my side are unhappy. Most of us would prefer a way back to Earth, or at least the Seelie side of the world. Myself included."

"Ours don't want to leave," January admitted.

She was right; Mare, Dots, and Sunny hadn't ever said anything positive about the unseelies, who would be taking them across the border when their five years were up.

"Women leaving the unseelies could cause a war just as easily as anything else. The men are a ticking time bomb right now," I told the other ladies. "We need a way to give all of them an equal opportunity, without favoring either side."

"They're the ones who came up with the five-year rule," Naomi said, shaking her head. "We've been trying to come up with a way out, but there isn't one. They watch us like hawks. And even if they didn't, we have nowhere else to go."

"What about here?" I asked her, looking around the building again. It was empty, but decently large. "What if we all tell them that the women are tired of their games? The unseelie have a king, and the seelie have the Wild Hunt. Why can't we have our own leadership, and make our own decisions?"

"We have no way to build, and there's not enough space here right now," Naomi pointed out. "Having our own leadership may prove useful, but what would be the purpose? Ultimately, it's still us against the men, and there are hardly any of us. We have no bargaining power, other than our bodies. And I already gave mine to Aeven, to satisfy the last deal."

I considered sharing what Vevol had told me, but hesitated.

"I'm pregnant," January said bluntly.

Naomi's face lost all color. "What?"

January added, "Babies have a lot of bargaining power. It could be a girl. There may not be many of us, but women can create life. We're fucking powerful."

My mind returned to the women hidden away. "We might have more power than we realize," I finally said.

January frowned, and Naomi didn't look convinced.

I looked over at Priel, and then Lian. "We need you to give us a few minutes."

Lian growled. "No."

Priel glared at me.

I glowered back for a long moment before turning to the women. "Vevol gave me the location for a group of female fae. They've been hiding since some huge war a long time ago. I don't know how many of them there are, or anything else about them, but I know where to find them. If we use that as a bargaining chip, we could probably get anything we want from the men. A place to live, food, lessons about how to do necessary shit to stay alive on Vevol without being attached to men..."

Both women were stunned to silence.

The men were, too, though they'd mostly been letting us figure our shit out anyway.

Priel's grip on my waist tightened.

"There could be enough of them to even the odds," Naomi finally said, her eyes bright and hopeful. "Pair that with the possibility of couples who are actually mated being able to have children... we'll have them by the balls."

"I like the way you think," January murmured to her, her own eyes still full of shock.

She hadn't been in Vevol as long as the rest of us. She hadn't seen the fae men truly desperate, and she hadn't seen the way some of the girls despised them or the land.

While she understood the male fae, she was still too new to really understand the ex-human women.

The tears in Naomi's eyes told me that maybe I was too new for that too.

"I'm going to have to call Aeven here," she told us, wiping carefully at her slightly-watery eyes. "I'll give him our offer. I already know what the other girls will say; they'll want to know how soon we can leave. If you don't want to be here when he is, I understand."

"We've got your back," January said easily. She didn't let go of Lian's hand, but I didn't really think he'd let her. The guy seemed pretty damn paranoid, and he had a right to be, considering his lady was pregnant with the first fae baby in who-knows-how-long.

"We can't be here when you talk to him," Priel told the other girls, his voice low and growly. "If the unseelie have a chance to take North before she and I are fully mated, they'll act on it in a heartbeat. Her magic is too powerful for them not to."

The other girls looked at him in surprise.

They didn't understand brands, I assumed, or the importance the fae seemed to place on them.

"He speaks the truth," Lian added. "Branded fae are known to be the most connected to Vevol, and North is undeniably one of them."

I bit back a snort.

Yeah, there definitely wasn't any denying to be had.

"You should hide out in the forest, then," January suggested. "We can come and find you after we talk to Aeven."

"No, they'll need to be farther away. If the unseelie have a chance at getting out of this agreement, they'll do whatever they have to in order to take advantage of it," Naomi said quickly. "Is there a place you can go that only your most trusted friends know about?" She spoke to Priel, and something within me sort of clenched.

If that was jealousy, it could take a hike. This chick was clearly married to an absolute asshole, with no way out of the relationship. There wasn't a chance in hell that she'd be interested in my hound; the girl was probably done with men altogether.

"There is." Priel looked at Lian.

Lian dipped his head. "We'll come find you when the deal has been made and the unseelies have fulfilled their side of whatever bargain we strike."

"Thank you." Priel's fingers pressed lightly against my hip as he began turning me around.

"Even if you decide to mate early, wait until you hear from us," Naomi added. "You're the only one who has the information they'll need, so our control over them extends only as far as your silence. We'll need to get this place built and everyone moved in before we give them what they want."

"We will." I promised her.

She flashed me a small, hopeful smile. "This means more to us than I can say."

I wasn't doing it for her, I thought, but didn't vocalize it.

Instead I just nodded lightly, and let Priel lead me out of the building.

The snow melted beneath our feet as we walked into the heavy silence of the snow-crusted forest around us. I knew that as soon as we made it out of neutral territory, the snow would end. Aeven was the only reason the snow existed there, according to Priel. It was the Tame King's way of separating unseelie land from seelie.

"So, where are we going?" I asked him, my voice soft but my body tense.

I was still worried that he would change his mind about wanting to be with me now that he knew there were actual female fae out there somewhere. What if he found the person whose scent made him positive she belonged to him, like January's had with Lian?

"It's a surprise." He flashed me one of his grins, and my shoulders relaxed slightly.

He still seemed like his normal self, so that was good.

"You're not worried after that conversation?" I asked him, as his hand slid around my hip.

"Why would I be? By the time they get all of that shit figured out, I'll have convinced you to be mine permanently, and probably claimed your skin with my ink as well," he teased.

I raised an eyebrow toward him. "That confident in your ability to win me over, huh?"

"Extremely," he confirmed, squeezing my hip lightly. "I saw it on the walls of your bedroom, Polaris. You'll be mine."

My face heated, but I didn't deny his claim.

He was right; Vevol had showed me that, hadn't she?

"What should we do if I still dream about war after they move the women?" I asked him, still holding his arm as we walked. The snow disappeared, leaving our toes crunching and our flames sizzling over dirt.

"We'll worry about that if we get there. No point in fearing a future that may never greet us."

"I wish my brain would get on board with that," I mumbled.

And I was fairly confident that everyone on Earth or Vevol with any amount of anxiety would feel the same way.

"You'll settle into life here," he promised me. "It'll be easier when most of the world isn't chasing you, trying to convince you to be theirs."

I hoped he was right.

WE SHIFTED, and then ran for the rest of the day. When we finally stumbled into the cave Priel had led me to, which was deep in the mountains, I was ready to drop.

"Why do you like caves so much?" I asked him as I shifted back, my body trembling a little after so many hours of exertion. His arms wrapped around me, and he steadied me as we ducked under a low-hanging rock, pivoting through a crevice I didn't like the looks of.

"I can feel the flames running beneath Vevol while underground. Other fae feel the same way though; the only ones who don't prefer caves are the phoenixes and basilisks, all of which live in the trees. Though, I doubt January will ever make her home in a tree."

"Probably not," I mumbled, pressing my forehead to his neck as he pulled me in close and lifted me off my feet to maneuver me through another crack in the stone.

"This is a cave that only myself and the rest of the Wild Hunt know the location of," he told me, lowering his voice slightly. "We have a few locations like this, hidden away from the others. My pack is probably furious with me after everything that's happened, especially considering that they were already acting strange before we ran back to the Stronghold together. We can't go near them again until things have calmed down a bit."

"That won't be hard. I'm pretty sure Clevv hates me now, and maybe you too. One of the guys who grabbed me outside the stronghold mentioned his name. I think he might've been working with them."

Priel growled at me. "If he's the reason they came after you, I'll kill him."

"I walked out with my brands on display, and he's practically your brother," I reminded him. "You don't need to—ohhh." A happy sigh escaped me as he set me down on a thick, cushy mattress. "Damn."

"The room is fireproof, as is the bed. I'll find you something to eat; you get comfortable." His lips brushed my forehead, but I wrapped my arms around his neck before he could abandon me.

"Wait. If we're going to complete the mate bond, I'll need some kind of plant that interferes with fertility. I'm not ready to have a kid any time soon."

He nodded. "I'll teach you how to tap into your magic and find it yourself."

My eyes widened. "Thank you."

His lips brushed my forehead. "You are very welcome, Gorgeous."

My cheeks were warm with the genuine-feeling compliment, but I fell asleep as he slipped back out of the cave.

A FEW DAYS passed by quickly, filled with both terrible dreams and fun, steamy moments with Priel. We played around a bit, and talked a lot, getting pretty damn hot and heavy both physically and emotionally, but never taking the plunge into actual matehood.

Priel always waited until I was going to sleep to slip out of the cave to find food. He did so again on the fourth night, but the moment I closed my eyes, I was pulled into a new dream.

Or, I supposed, a vision.

MARE'S SCREAM cut me to the soul.

My eyes opened, and my arms flew out at my sides as I stumbled. I caught my balance on a wall—one inside the Stronghold.

The door was off its hinges, the massive thing stuck diagonally in the hallway just in front of the doorway. Beyond it, I saw flashes of fae fighting. A massive basilisk and sabertooth seemed to be battling alongside a group of others, holding a wave of men and creatures at bay.

Inside the Stronghold, two thick fae that I recognized held a bleeding, furious Ervo, who was cuffed at the wrists and ankles in some kind of thick, stone restraints.

Another one held Mare, his sharp claws shifted and pressed to the center of her chest. Two more had Sunny and Dots, though both of the other women were draped over their shoulders, unconscious.

Horror clutched my stomach.

They wouldn't hurt us, right?

That was the whole damn deal. They brought us to Vevol, and they didn't hurt us. They couldn't.

Could they?

"Give us the location of the oracle or your chosen female will bleed," the man with the claws snarled at Ervo.

When I recognized him as Clevv, nausea made me sway and clutch the wall.

I had kissed that man.

He had touched my skin.

And now, he was threatening the closest thing I'd ever had to friends.

My eyes jerked back to the other men.

All of them were other members of Priel's pack.

They looked almost as horrified by Clevv's threats as I felt, but said and did nothing to stop him.

My heart dropped into my stomach.

I wasn't built to witness horrors. I wasn't strong enough to see terrible things happen, or watch people hurt. That was a huge part of the reason I knew I couldn't live like my parents did, and—

Clevv slashed his fingers over Mare's chest, and her next scream made my eyes water.

Ervo fought his restraints, roaring and wrestling with the men who held him back, but it was no use.

He was trapped.

Clevv lifted his hands to Mare's face, and my whole damn body quivered in shock as he threatened my friend's eyes.

I wanted to scream at him to tell them. To shout that I'd survive whatever they did to me—that I would rather have them hunting me down then hurting anyone.

But the words didn't come out.

I wasn't good under pressure—not like other people were.

And even if they had, it wouldn't have done any good.

I wasn't actually there, no matter what it felt like in the moment.

"Let the women go and I'll give you what you want," Ervo finally snarled. "I'll take you there myself."

Relief coursed through me as the claws lowered away from Mare's eyes.

"We'll bring this one with us," Clevv growled at the other men, as he shoved Mare toward Ervo.

She crashed into him, her arms wrapping around him and holding on fiercely. His furious gaze remained fixed on Clevv as his head pressed lightly against the side of Mare's, his hands and feet still bound.

"Run the other two to opposite sides of the land until you've convinced them to mate with you. The basilisk and sabertooth will chase you until you've claimed the females," he growled at the men who were holding Sunny and Dots.

They jerked their heads in nods before turning and jogging out of the secret exit.

The same secret exit Priel and I had used.

Had we alerted them to it somehow? Had I triggered it by kissing Clevv?

It didn't sound like the men planned on hurting Sunny and Dots, thankfully, but how long would that last?

"Pick them up," Clevv snarled at the other men, tossing a hand toward Ervo and Mare. The hellhounds beside the phoenix exchanged uncertain expressions, but did as he'd ordered. One of them threw Ervo over his shoulder, despite the massive size and weight of the phoenix. The other carefully picked up Mare.

"Are you okay?" he asked her in a low voice.

"No," she hissed back.

"There aren't words for a proper apology," the hound began.

Bovay; I recognized him as Bovay.

"Don't even try," Mare snarled, though her voice shook.

Sorrow filled the hellhound's eyes as he followed Clevv and the man holding Ervo out through the back door.

"Where are we going?" Clevv demanded.

"There's a cave in the mountains," Ervo growled back. "It's the first place Priel would've taken her to hide away."

I started to jog after them, to figure out what was going to happen next, but then I felt hands on my waist.

My gaze jerked down to my abdomen, but I didn't see anything.

The world tilted around me suddenly, and then I was ripped back into my body.

Twelve

I gasped as I jerked upright, finding myself face to face with Clevv.

My body froze.

Just completely froze.

A shudder rolled down my spine.

"I'm here, pretty one." The hellhound dragged a sharp fingernail down the side of my face.

My mind struggled to put the pieces together.

I hadn't been seeing the future, that time.

It had to have been the past, didn't it?

How was that possible?

"Where's Priel?" My voice wobbled slightly.

Anger flared in the man's eyes. "We have him restrained. I want him dead, but the rest of the pack wants mates."

Mates.

Right.

Priel was the only one who could get the portal open—so they needed him.

Relief nearly had me sagging into the mattress, but I was smart enough to realize that things were still really damn serious.

They still had Mare.

And Ervo.

And Sunny and Dots.

And me.

Things were *not* stacked in our favor.

"He won't force you to do anything, ever again," Clevv practically purred at me. His fingers slid into my hair, his hand cupping the back of my neck.

Instinct told me to argue. To point out that Priel had never forced me to do anything I didn't silently want to do, that he was my future, and that I wanted him.

But the possessiveness in Clevv's gaze kept me quiet.

I wasn't going to encourage him. Not even a little. But arguing would only enrage him, if he really thought I belonged to him. He had already proven he was willing to hurt Mare to find me; there wasn't a chance in hell that I'd be safe with him.

So I kept my mouth shut.

He leaned toward me, as if to kiss me, and I leaned back.

It was time to lie.

"I'm not ready," I said, letting my voice shake like it wanted to.

He stilled.

His eyes softened.

"Of course. You can have all the time you need."

When he stretched a hand out toward me, I slipped mine inside it. There was no way I was getting around that shit, and I was much more willing to hold his hand than let him kiss me.

"What are we doing?" I asked him, hoping he would believe that I considered us a team.

"Going home, of course." He slid his fingers between mine, and I fought the nausea that followed.

We were going to be fine.

I hoped so, at least.

"What about Priel and Ervo?" My voice stayed even.

"We'll have to keep them chained until you and I are mated and Mare has chosen one of my brothers, of course," he said easily.

Of course.

If my stomach wasn't empty, I would've retched.

"There's plenty of space to do so back at home," he promised, like that was supposed to reassure me.

It obviously didn't.

I stayed quiet as he led me the rest of the way out of the cave. He moved through it much more slowly than Priel had, but I would've gone at a snail's pace if it meant he didn't put his hands on me.

We finally made it out of the cave twenty minutes later.

My eyes stung when I surveyed the scene outside the entrance.

Ervo and Priel were on their knees, both men bruised and actively bleeding. Priel was slouched over, clearly unconscious, and Ervo was staring at the man in front of me with so much fury that I wondered if Clevv would combust.

Then again, it wouldn't hurt him even if he did.

We were all creatures of fire, after all.

Mare was wrapped in the arms of one of the other hellhounds. She looked somewhere between furious and terrified, but relief filled her eyes when she saw me.

Neither of us spoke, though.

What was there to say?

We had both been *captured* by an insane asshole who had decided I was going to be his, and that Mare was going to mate with one of the other hounds.

"Get the phoenix in the sky again, with your claws to his throat and to the dragon girl's too," Clevv commanded the hound holding Mare, and the four behind Priel and Ervo.

The man holding Mare bristled, just slightly. I side-eyed Clevv, trying to decide whether or not he had noticed. He hadn't.

Clevv seemed to think he had some sort of power over the rest of them. I wasn't sure where said power was coming from, but there was one thing I was sure about.

The seelie fae *hated* being controlled.

And if I could play along long enough, and maybe nudge the idea that he was acting like he was in charge, then I could probably get the other fae working with him to realize they didn't like him any more than I did.

If I could do *that*, there was a good chance I could get Mare and myself away from them.

And if Mare and I got away, Priel and Ervo would have no reason to play nice.

Then, hell would break loose.

And all of us would be free.

Deciding that was the best possible plan, I averted my eyes and remained silent as Clevv put his arm over my shoulders, watching the men as they wrestled Ervo off the ground. Mare was hauled up onto his back after he shifted to his massive flaming bird form, her body pinned between two other fae men. One of them had his claws to Ervo's throat, and the other gripped Mare tightly.

When they soared into the sky, Clevv barked commands about carrying Priel to the other hounds, then pulled me up onto his back as he shifted.

I despised the feel of his muscles beneath me when he took off running, so I grabbed fistfuls of his fur, hopefully causing him a little pain as he sprinted away with me.

As we left the cave behind, I peered over my shoulder. The man who carried a bound, unconscious Priel, followed behind us.

At least my hound was safe for the time being.

Everything else, we would figure out a way to deal with.

PRIEL WOKE up less than an hour into the long, long run. Clevv stopped running, and Ervo circled above us.

The fae wrestled him, until they all shifted and began tearing into each other.

I couldn't watch that.

"Don't fight them, Priel," I called out.

One of the men's bodies went flying, and then a bleeding, growling Priel in his hound form was glowering at me, but had stopped fighting. The other hound stood a few feet to his side, watching the stronger fae warily. Priel's front paws were still bound together, and his back ones were too, yet he didn't bother looking down.

I could tell he was checking to make sure I was okay, trying to figure out what had happened.

"We're fine. You have to stop fighting," I urged.

He snarled at me, gesturing with his head.

I could imagine what he was furious about.

Me, riding on Clevv's back.

There were bigger issues, but the fae's possessiveness was undeniable and didn't seem to be something they could control.

"If you want Priel to follow you peacefully, I need to shift and run on my own feet," I told Clevv.

Ultimately, the traitorous pack outnumbered me and Priel, so I couldn't just make an executive decision and jump off Clevv's back. Priel and Ervo were among the strongest of the seelies, but it was Priel's shitty family who had us. If anyone could keep up with the Wild Hunt, it was their own damn families.

And besides that, they had already proven they were willing to hurt Mare to get what they wanted.

Clevv growled and snapped his teeth at Priel.

Priel snarled back, and I saw the way my hound's body tensed.

He was going to attack Clevv.

Honestly, I thought Clevv and the other men would be willing to kill Priel if things got too out of hand. And considering that he was still bound, the chance of him surviving if they wanted him dead was minimal.

So I shoved away the paralyzing fear in my chest and lunged between the men.

My feet hit the ground just in time for both of them to halt and snarl at me as I stood between them.

"No one needs to die," I said firmly.

Priel's snapping teeth told me he disagreed.

I didn't know if there was a way out of this situation that didn't include at least one death, so I didn't necessarily think he was wrong.

I just wanted to make sure that death wasn't Priel's.

"I'll run on my own," I told both of them.

Clevv shifted, and I forced my gaze to remain steady despite the rapid pounding of my heart.

"Priel will take koveko or we'll knock him unconscious ourselves, then," Clevv growled at me.

Priel shifted back too, and I fought the urge to step behind him and let him protect me.

He couldn't defend me in this moment; I needed to protect both of us.

"As long as no one touches my female, I'll take the damn poison," Priel said.

My eyes widened. "What?"

Clevv glared at Priel while answering my question. "Koveko is a bulbous plant with a liquid within it that renders its drinker unconscious for half of a day." There was a tense pause. "And this female belongs to me, not you."

Shit.

There was going to be carnage.

"Get the plant. Priel will drink it," I said quickly

The man growled behind me, and I spun to face him. Our eyes locked.

I couldn't say what I wanted to say.

That I needed him to play along until we could figure out a safe way to get ourselves, Mare, and Ervo out of the situation.

So instead I narrowed my eyes at him.

He liked it when I got sassy with him; it proved to him that I was still myself, that I wasn't scared or confused.

He glared back at me, but I saw his eyes soften slightly.

His head jerked in a nod, and I looked back at Clevv.

Clevv barked an order at one of the other hellhounds—who looked irked with the command, but followed it. He disappeared into the forest for a few tense moments.

None of the rest of us moved until he came back, peeled the top off of a fruit that looked like something between an onion and a tulip, and held it to Priel's lips.

My hellhound stared at me as he drank the liquid, not closing his eyes until they rolled back into his head and he collapsed.

His pack members caught him before he hit the ground, and Clevv growled at me that I needed to shift and stay next to him.

My pounding, panicked heart and I shifted anyway, and when Clevv started to run, I followed.

WE MADE it back to the land I recognized as the pack's space before Priel woke up.

Mare, Ervo, and the hounds with them landed.

The men shifted back, and I did too. I should've stayed in my hound form though; I felt safer when I was a badass flaming-bear-wolf-thing than my wimpy human self.

Yeah, technically I was a fae, but I still *felt* human most of the time.

"North will come home with me," Clevv announced. "Chain Priel and Ervo, and compete to determine who will claim Mare."

Fury had me clenching my fists.

What a bastard.

"We haven't heard the female agree to be yours," one of the men remarked, folding his arms over his chest. His eyes blazed, and excitement coursed through me.

I knew they weren't happy with him acting as their leader.

Clevv scoffed. "She already kissed me. The oracle is mine."

"She did a lot more than just *kiss* Priel, yet he doesn't get to claim her without her permission," Mare pointed out.

Clevv growled, but murmurs of agreement rolled through the rest of the group.

"You hurt the dragon female. That wasn't part of the agreement," Bovay pointed out.

Clevv grabbed me by the biceps. I froze in place, trying not to show the bastard that I was terrified as his nails dug into my arms, shifting into claws. "I did what I had to do to claim the woman who was meant to be mine."

"You said Priel was forcing her," one of the men argued.

"He *was*. You all saw him," Clevv snarled. "She wanted *me*."

The hellhounds who had been following his orders exchanged uncertain looks.

Clevv's gaze jerked around the group.

He seemed to realize that shit was about to stop working in his favor—and he acted.

My face crashed into his back as he threw me over his shoulder and spun around, sprinting across the land. We passed half a dozen holes in the ground in what felt like the blink of an eye, and then we were plummeting.

His feet met the floor, and then my *ass* met it too. My palms smacked the stone as I held on, trying to keep myself upright.

He was shutting something over the entrance to his cave a moment later, closing us in. I watched in horror as he welded the metal door shut with his palms, and then quickly covered it with two more layers of something that had already been propped against the wall, apparently prepared to block the door.

His eyes were wild and desperate when he looked at me.

I fought the urge to curl up in a ball and hide.

"Are you going to attack me?" I asked him instead, forcing myself to feign confidence that I absolutely did not feel.

He seemed to deflate a little. "Of course not."

The fact that he still thought that was a given after injuring my friend spoke volumes about the mental stability he *didn't* possess.

He added, "We all saw how Priel forced you away from me. He didn't accept that you'd chosen me."

"I chose you as a *temporary mate*," I said, my voice harsher than it should've been given the perilous situation. "I told you I wasn't looking for anything serious, and you said you were fine with that."

His eyes darkened. "I said you would be my future mate. When I saw your brands, I knew for sure that we'd be far more than temporary. Vevol made you for me."

I choked on a horrified laugh.

Vevol hadn't *made me*. She had changed me, sure, but I was born on Earth.

And the fact that he hadn't decided he wanted things to be permanent with me until he realized how many brands I had was another strike against him.

"I never agreed to that," I said, looking away from the man and letting my gaze linger on the wall in front of me.

"Fate decided." His voice was low.

Apparently he now thought of himself as fate. Whatever the hell that meant in the scheme of things where Vevol was both the world and the goddess, I didn't know.

So I said nothing.

"I need to feed you," he mumbled to himself, raking a hand through his hair as he strode toward the small, fae-style kitchen on the other side of the room.

There wasn't anywhere to sit other than his bed, since his home was shaped the same as Priel's. I wasn't going anywhere near the damned bed, so I scooted the two feet between myself and the wall, then turned my back to the stone. Sitting up like that, I could see the entirety of the cave and was ready for an attack.

He started cooking, and I carefully watched the spices he put into the food. I knew there was at least one questionable spice in Vevol, but where there was one, there were usually more. The one I knew about, the men had said made your parts swell and tingle a bit, and would lead to hours of pleasure.

With the right partner, that sounded crazy hot. I'd seen the future version of Priel use it on the future version of me enough times to be hella turned-on when I thought about it outside of Clevv's cave.

But as far as food went, I didn't know what that spice would look like or taste like if it was put inside something. So, knowing that it existed made me extremely reluctant to touch any food that Clevv was making.

He hadn't had a problem hurting Mare, so why would he have a problem with drugging me to get his way?

My eyes flicked to the divider over the entrance to the cave, and I let myself hope that Priel was waking up and would be breaking in and rescuing my ass in the near future.

Because if he didn't, something told me I might end up with another set of scars to match the ones I earned the last time I had to escape from some bastard who thought he could do whatever the hell he wanted to me.

Thirteen

Priel

A wave of ice-cold water jerked me out of sleep.

"What the hell?" I growled, rubbing at my eyes with the back of my arm as my fire burned away the chill immediately.

"Your female has been taken, brother," Ervo's low voice had my body going still.

My mind returned to the forest.

The betrayal of the pack I had considered my family.

Clevv's hands on North's skin.

His insistence that she was his.

Her, asking me to drink the poison.

I was on my feet a heartbeat later, snarling and looking around the area.

We had returned to the pack's land, apparently.

Mare and Ervo stood near me, with a large bucket that I assumed had held ice-water a minute earlier sitting on the ground between them.

My packmates were in a small group off to the side.

I wanted their heads removed from their bodies.

But I had bigger shit to worry about, and I didn't know if any of them had actually done anything that deserved dying over.

I glowered at Bovay, knowing he would answer even if I was a risk to his life. "Where the fuck is Clevv?"

"He took North into his cave, and blocked off the entrance."

Curses spewed from me.

I started to pace.

We all wanted the privacy that came with being able to close ourselves into our homes. We'd designed our caves to be impenetrable when we wanted them to be.

With enough time and effort, I could get through the metal and stone door of sorts. I was confident in that.

But how long did I have before he touched her again?

Hurt her?

Tried to force her to mate with him?

A roar escaped me, and I fought hard to think through the fear pounding in my head.

"If he hears us trying to get in, he'll do something drastic," Ervo said in a low voice. "I think we're going to have to wait him out."

"She dreams of the future every night," I snarled back. "Of us, together. Or of the war. She can't sleep in there with him."

Mare's voice was gentle when she replied, "I don't think she has a choice."

Bovay walked up to me, Ervo, and Mare, his expression hesitant.

That hesitance was a good call, because as soon as my female was in my arms, we'd be fighting to his death.

"Clevv eats with us every night. He won't have enough food with him to last them more than two or three days," Bovay said in a low voice. "Eventually, she'll get hungry, and the instincts to feed and care for his mate will force him to emerge. When he—"

"She's not his fucking mate," I roared back, white-hot anger pumping through my veins as I grabbed the bastard by the throat. "North belongs to me, of her own free will. I gave everyone the chance I was obligated to give, and the whole damn time, she dreamed of our future together. If Clevv so much as pulls one hair from her head, I'll make your death so long and painful that you'll beg Vevol to end your life with every excruciating thought that crosses your mind."

He didn't flinch or shrink away.

Just stared at me as I glowered at him.

Finally, I dropped my hold on his throat and stepped back.

I started pacing again.

Bovay walked back to the group of traitors.

If they were wise, they would've taken the opportunity to put as much distance between us as was possible.

"You need to eat something," Mare said to Ervo. "We were flying for a long time." She looked at me. "You do too, Priel."

"My mate is locked in a cave with a man who thinks she belongs to him. I'm not *hungry*," I snarled back.

"Brother." Ervo's cold gaze was furious. Not many people knew him well enough to read his emotions, but I was one of them. "Don't speak to her that way."

I glowered back at him, but jerked my head in a nod.

He wouldn't get an apology.

Mare wouldn't, either.

They were the ones who had shown Clevv the location of the cave. They were at least a part of the reason she was down there. And though there was likely a reasonable explanation for that, I wasn't interested in hearing it.

"I'll show you which plants are edible," Ervo told Mare, his hand touching her lower back lightly as he led her into the forest, in the opposite direction of my packmates.

I halted when the answer to my problem hit me in the fucking chest.

Her name.

I had her name.

Pride and relief swelled within me.

"Polaris, I need you in my arms," I growled into the air, body tensing and preparing for a fight.

The space in front of me shimmered, and then North was on her ass in that space, falling backward as if whatever she'd been leaning against had up and vanished.

I was on my knees, holding her upright, in a heartbeat.

She stared at me in shock for a few moments.

And then, she threw her arms around me.

Her grip was hard and desperate.

Her body was soft, and shaking.

But she was there.

And she was safe.

"You're okay?" she demanded, leaning away from me and looking me up and down.

"No. But you're here, and that's what matters." I cupped her face, pressing my forehead to hers. She clung to me, the shaking in her body only seeming to grow more pronounced.

"We need to seal the mating bond. This can't happen again," North whispered, her voice quivering as much as she was.

"After I've ended Clevv's life," I agreed, standing up. I hauled her into my arms as I did so, and she buried her face against my neck.

"I can't believe I forgot about using your name," she whispered.

"It's been a long few days." I stroked her back lightly, cradling her like the precious, fragile thing she was. "And I prefer you not having to see me tear the head off of a man you kissed at one point."

She shuddered, and I held her tighter.

"Mare and Ervo went to get food; they'll be back soon. You'll feel a little better with something in your belly."

She made a noise of agreement that didn't sound anywhere near certain, but I continued rubbing her back and holding her to me.

I had no plans to let go of her until Clevv came out of that hole.

The deaths of the traitors could wait.

All of the fighting could wait.

Because my female was safe in my arms, and no one else would ever touch her again.

Fourteen

North

Priel had been growly and possessive before the abduction, but after? I wasn't sure he was completely sane. He carried my exhausted butt around until he had to put me down so I could eat. Even then, he really didn't want to let go of me, but I didn't think he could physically sit still for long enough to hold me while I ate.

So I sat down and went to town on the delicious fresh fruit and vegetables Mare and Ervo had found—which Priel refused to do—and my hound paced.

There were flames blazing in his eyes, and while I knew that didn't mean he was crazy or anything, it did mean that his emotions were sort of feral.

For the most part, I seemed to be into feral. But now, it had crossed into unhealthy territory.

Yes, I knew that Priel needed to confront Clevv.

They would fight.

Clevv was willing to hurt women, so he would most-likely die.

I was okay with that.

Hence my patience as I sat down next to Mare, eating.

She looked just as exhausted as I felt.

"You should get some sleep," I murmured to her.

"I can't," she admitted, then bit her lip.

I waited.

She remained silent, but her expression grew sort of haunted. Eventually, she whispered, "He attacked me. Clevv. I thought we were safe here, but we're not. Ana was right."

Though I was out of practice when it came to talking to people—and relating with them especially—my mom had always taken my hand or pulled me in for a hug when I was struggling with something.

I wrapped my arm around Mare's back, pulling her closer. Her arm wrapped around mine too, and we scooted closer together until we were sort of snuggling.

"This was my fault," I admitted softly. "He thought I was his because I kissed him. The rest of the pack thought Priel was forcing me to be with him because he got possessive after I kissed Clevv, so they thought they were doing the right thing. There are no excuses for Clevv; he lost his mind. But he didn't lose it without cause. I should've made sure he knew that I didn't like it when he touched me, and that I was choosing to stay with Priel."

"But shit like this wouldn't happen with the unseelie." Mare's eyes were unfocused. "The rules and the coldness... it's a protection."

"I'm sure it can be. But distancing yourself from everyone the way that they do only causes pain. I think I know that better than anyone," I said quietly.

She looked over at me, her eyes a little watery. "No one ever physically hurt me on Earth."

"Then you should count yourself lucky." I gave her a tiny smile, turning to look out in front of me.

Priel was still pacing, but when I caught a glimpse of the side of his face, I realized he was listening to our conversation.

Ervo probably was too, I thought, as I glanced over at him. He sat sprawled across the ground, his gaze focused intensely on Mare.

The way he looked at her was almost enough to give *me* the tingles.

There was shuffling and growling off to our left, and when Mare and I looked over, we found Priel and Ervo standing between us and the group of hellhounds that Priel used to consider his pack.

"Any closer to her and you forfeit your lives." Ervo's calm threat didn't scare me, but I also didn't doubt for a second that he would follow through with it.

"She deserves an apology," one of the fae growled back. "And a knife in her hand."

A knife?

In her hand?

I looked at Mare, but she looked just as lost as me.

"We should've stopped Clevv," another of the hellhounds said to Ervo gravely. "We were taken by surprise when he acted the way he did, and didn't respond correctly. Your female deserves to end us herself."

Mare's eyes flooded with horror.

I knew her well enough to be sure that she wasn't going to kill anyone.

"She does," Ervo agreed.

All of the men looked at us.

Mare's face went ashy, and she gripped my arm tightly.

I spoke up for her. "Mare hasn't decided what consequences she wants to enforce yet. When she does, she'll let you know."

The men waited a long moment before they split up. The traitors went back to the place they'd been gathered a few minutes earlier, while Priel and Ervo returned to their previous positions even more intense-like than they had before.

"You're good at that," Mare murmured to me. "Not letting people walk all over you."

I laughed humorlessly. "For this ten minutes. As soon as shit goes down, I freeze up. Probably because of my past."

"What happened to you?" she asked. "You had so many scars.

My throat swelled, but I admitted, "My parents were very overprotective, so I didn't get out much. They arranged a marriage for me, but we were betrayed. I was in the car, and the bastard I was supposed to marry told me he was going to kill me and make a statement out of it. He was so proud."

I shook my head a little. "There were two options. Accept my fate, or jump out of the vehicle. They thought I was a scared little mouse, so they hadn't bothered barring the doors or anything. I jumped. And then I survived in the forest, until my dad's people finally found me. Spent a long time in the hospital, afterward. Nothing they could do about the scars."

The horror had returned to Mare's eyes. "I'm so sorry."

"You don't need to apologize for something you had nothing to do with." I looked away from her, staring out at the scenery again. Vevol was so beautiful, with its strange trees and rocky, rough mountains.

"Still. That's just... damn. We knew you were strong, but that's next level."

"If you were in the situation, you would've done the same thing."

"I don't know if I would've," she admitted.

"Then you need to believe in yourself more. You're stronger than you realize. If you can't sleep now, focus on getting even stronger so that if something like this ever happens again, you can protect yourself. You're a damn *dragon*, Mare."

She was silent for a few minutes before she finally said, "I need to learn how to shift."

"You do," I agreed. "Calian probably knows a dragon or two who could teach you."

She sighed heavily. "I hope so."

It was time to change the subject.

"Did I tell you about the meeting with Naomi?" I asked her.

When she said I had not, we spent the next hour discussing how things would change when we created our own neutral land, never bringing up the fae women we would need to retrieve to make that happen.

By the time that hour wound down, Mare looked so exhausted that I didn't think she'd remain upright for much longer.

When Ervo asked, Priel pointed him toward one of the community caves, so Mare could sleep while he watched over and protected her.

She didn't argue, following him to the cave after giving me a quick hug.

TIME PASSED and Priel continued pacing, shooting glares at the group of hellhounds every few minutes even though they had yet to try pushing the boundaries again.

I started to wonder if Clevv was ever going to come out.

The man was at least a little insane, but that didn't tell me what would happen when he emerged. If anything, it made me less certain about whatever he was going to do next.

My yawns began, and over time, grew longer and larger.

When I curled up on the ground, Priel snapped his teeth and scooped me up.

He hauled me over to the cave where Ervo was watching out for Mare, and called into the opening, "I need you to take a turn on watch."

There was a long pause, and then Ervo came climbing out with a snoring Mare draped over his shoulder and one of the massive beanbag things clenched tightly in his fist. It dragged behind him a bit because of its size, but his gigantic muscles didn't seem to have a problem with that.

"Kill any of them you want," Priel told the phoenix, adjusting his grip on me. My head pressed to his chest, and he rubbed my back lightly. "I'll listen for Clevv."

I shouldn't have felt safe while he was telling his buddy to murder people and talking about the person he was going to kill, but I did.

Maybe I belonged in the mafia more than I'd thought.

Priel held me carefully as he jogged to his home, and jumped inside so smoothly that I barely felt the motion at all.

Those had to be some massive thighs.

I should probably study them, to see just how massive.

With my hands, if I wanted to be more thorough.

My lips curved upward slightly at the thought.

He lowered me to the bed and brushed hair out of my eyes. His lips brushed my forehead, and cheek, and throat, before he straightened and stepped away.

Something within me said he was going to start pacing again if I didn't convince him to get under the blankets with me.

"Will you hold me while I sleep?" I asked him, scooting over to make space.

"No." His voice was gruff.

I frowned. "Why not?"

His expression hardened. "You smell like Clevv."

Oh.

I hadn't considered that.

"Then why did you put me in your bed? It's going to smell like Clevv too, now." I slid out from beneath the blankets, putting a hand on the wall to help me stand on my wobbly, exhausted feet.

"We're not coming back here, so it doesn't matter." His gaze dared me to argue.

I glared back at him. "Stop talking to me like I'm the enemy. I didn't know he was coming after us until right before I woke up with him hovering over me. And obviously, I didn't know that he was going to get this attached when I kissed him, or I wouldn't have even considered it. He said he was okay with me using him just so I wouldn't get hit on by the other guys. The relationship was supposed to be fake."

"Fae don't do fake relationships, North. Look at us." He tossed a hand toward me.

"We're different. I've seen Nev and Dots together, and Sunny and Teris. They're just friends. I heard last month that Ervo even told Mare he sees her as a sister."

"They're all full of shit," Priel said, stepping toward me. There were only a few inches between our chests, and the only fabric separating our skin was that of my fireproof tank top. Both of our chests rose and fell rapidly, the anger and exhaustion functioning as one to get us both worked up over this silly argument. "Every one of them. We're selfish bastards, Gorgeous."

He studied me for a long moment.

My mouth was dry as I struggled with my thoughts.

What was he saying?

Was he suggesting that the arrangement between us and the Wild Hunt had been a setup?

His voice was low and rough. "You can't really think we offered ourselves up out of the goodness of our hearts. If becoming mates over time was possible, and there were only five female candidates, you'd better believe that we manipulated those cards perfectly. You see us as innocent because we're virgins, but that doesn't make us stupid."

My throat swelled. "Did you rig the name-drawing?"

He scoffed. "Of course we rigged the damn drawing. I wasn't going to end up mated to Dots. Have you seen how much she smiles?"

I couldn't suppress the snort that escaped me.

"Sunny was into you," I threw out.

"Sunny was attracted to my body. I wanted a woman whose soul would speak to me."

I crossed my arms over my chest. "And you think that's me?"

"I think the way you hide your sadness with anger touches my fucking heart."

His blunt words made me inhale sharply.

"And I think the way you keep your thoughts private until you're ready to share them has wrapped itself around my filthy, ink-stained soul." He covered the distance between us and wrapped his hands around my face, tilting my head back until our eyes met. "I didn't want one of the playful females. I wanted the intense one who snarls at other bastards when they get too close. I wanted the woman with paint beneath her fingernails and crusted in her hair. The one who studied me when she thought I wasn't looking, and hid paintings of my ink within her own art."

"You didn't know all of those things when we did the name drawing," I countered.

"I didn't need to."

He lowered his face and slowly brushed his lips over mine. Mine responded, but he pulled away before I could intensify the kiss. "Having Clevv's scent on your skin is making it extremely difficult to suppress the urge to throw you against the wall and fuck you, Polaris. I need you to get in the shower, now. Just burning away his touch isn't enough; I want to scrub it from your skin."

I extracted my hands from his. "I never said I wasn't in favor of having sex against a wall."

He caught my arm, his eyes narrowing. "How many times have you had sex that way?"

A snort escaped me.

Easy answer.

"None."

His eyes heated. "How many times have you had sex, period?"

Well, now we were moving into dangerous territory.

I wasn't sure how he'd react when he found out I was a virgin too.

Proud?

Worried?

Excited?

Even more possessive?

Really damn ready to have sex?

I didn't know.

But I did know that I wouldn't have his full attention until Clevv wasn't a threat anymore, so I wasn't about to proposition him. No way in hell was our first time going to be while he was listening for sounds that might mean my abductor was coming out of his hidey-hole.

"We're not having this conversation right now," I told him, stepping out of his grip and striding toward the bathroom.

"It's that bad?" he growled, fury lining his voice.

I scoffed, turning on the shower.

Even if I had been with a bunch of guys, it shouldn't matter to him. That was then, and this was now. My past was in my past, regardless of what I'd done back on Earth.

Then again, when the fae got possessive about that shit, they got *really* possessive about it.

"I need the number, North."

I stripped my tank over my head, ignoring his warning.

"Polaris," he growled at me.

I pushed my shorts down and stepped out of them, and then into the shower.

He followed me, though his shorts remained on.

I reached for the soap.

His hand caught my wrist, pinning it and the rest of my back to the shower's wall.

His flames burned over both of us, and he slid his hand between my thighs.

I sucked in a breath as he grabbed my core, the base of his gigantic hand pressing into my clit while his fingers found both of my entrances.

If I wasn't into all that rough shit, I probably would've been shocked or uncomfortable.

As it was, I was dripping wet. And not just where the water had hit me.

I lifted my hand that wasn't pinned to the wall up to his shoulder, needing something to hold on to.

"You belong to me," he said, his voice low and feral. "Give me the number."

"Tell me why you want to know," I countered breathlessly.

"So I can learn exactly how many times I need to fuck you to erase their memories from your mind."

Yeah, his snarl only made me hotter.

"You aren't very good at bartering," I told him. "You're desperate; I could ask you for anything I want right now, and I bet you would give it to me."

"You can be damn sure I would."

His thick fingers teased my entrances, and I breathed in sharply.

"You want to make this a trade? Fine. Give me the number, and I'll get you off. Don't give it to me, and I'll make you so wet that you beg me, before walking away."

"That's just mean."

"I never claimed to be nice." He slid the tip of his fingers into me, rocking the base of his palm against my clit slowly.

My heart pounded so loudly it was difficult to think.

The pressure of his touches made me pant.

He slid his fingers further inside me, and I clenched around him as I neared the edge.

The bastard wouldn't really stop me, would he? He—

Ohh, shit.

I cried out, so damn close to the edge.

But his hand stilled, right then.

I groaned, but he pinned me in place with his hips when I tried to rock them.

"The number, Polaris?" His growl only made me more needy.

The bastard had played me like a damn fiddle, and I wasn't even mad about it.

"None," I growled back.

Silence surrounded us as our eyes remained locked together. I could see the shock in his, and my toes curled as I watched it transform to hot, possessive need.

And slowly, he resumed the motions of his hand.

My knees knocked together as the pleasure swelled within me.

My nails dug into his shoulder and back as I lost control with a cry, and he growled his approval when the scent of his blood met my nose.

"I made you bleed," I panted, still rocking my hips lightly.

"If you knew how hard that makes me, you'd keep those sexy little claws to yourself," he grumbled back, not removing his fingers from inside me.

"Why? You heal fast."

"That's fucking right. I like the pain."

"I know you do. Oracle, remember?" I flashed him a smirk, and his eyes heated.

His grip on my core and hip tightened. "What are you going to do to me in our future, Gorgeous?"

I lifted a shoulder. "You'll just have to wait and see."

When I eased his hand out from between my thighs, he let me step away and grab the oddly-shaped soap. Before I could drag it over my body, he plucked it from my fingers and spun me around so my back was to him.

His hands moved slowly and thoroughly over my skin as he cleaned me. My eyes shut, and I let myself enjoy the moment.

His breath was in my ear a moment later. "As soon as I've dealt with Clevv, I'm taking you home and stripping you naked. You won't be leaving our place again until I've claimed every inch of this gorgeous, delicious body. Understand?"

"You are so damn bossy," I mumbled back.

"Always." He growled the agreement. "Get used to it. You won't be complaining when I'm ordering you to shatter on my cock. Any other time, we can argue all you want."

The bastard had me with that one.

"I thought this was your house," I told him, changing the subject before things got too sexually charged again. "I've never dreamed about it before, though."

"This was my home with the pack. They lost my trust—and will probably lose their lives too. Now, you're my pack. Along with the rest of the Wild Hunt, I suppose. I have another place hidden away, closer to my brothers' mountains. There are lakes all over the place, and many different kinds of plants. It's beautiful; you'll like it."

His soapy hands dragged down my thighs, ignoring my core for the time being. I was pretty damn confident he'd clean that too, though.

"I hope so," I admitted.

His lips brushed my forehead. "I'm sorry I didn't protect you from Clevv. The bastards snuck up on me, but even if I'd known they were coming, I wouldn't have expected them to do what they did."

"No one suspects betrayal from the people they love. I don't blame you for their choices." My eyes closed as his lips brushed my temple too.

"I still feel shitty about it, though," he admitted.

"Get over it."

He chuckled, and my lips curved upward.

My smile faded as I remembered the way Ervo had looked at Mare, though. And all of the shit that had gone down in my dream. "I know you're furious with Clevv and the rest of the pack, and you have every right to be. But I don't think anything the pack did to either of us is bad enough that they should die, Priel. Death is permanent. They could turn their shit around and become better after this."

The man's hands returned to my abdomen and breasts, slowly scrubbing my skin. "What are you asking me, Gorgeous?" There was an edge to his voice that I didn't particularly like, but this was a sensitive subject, so it didn't surprise me.

"I'm asking you to leave them alive."

There was a long, long pause.

Trying to voice things in a violent fae's perspective, I added, "Clevv abducted me, but that was partially my fault for leading him on. He didn't physically hurt me. I saw what he did to Mare, though, and Ervo was forced to watch every second of it. They held him down while Clevv hurt her. If he's really as devoted to her as you think he is, then doesn't he deserve to kill Clevv, and the traitors too if that's what he wants? Isn't what they did to Ervo's mate worse than what he did to me?"

Priel's fingers dug lightly into my belly, and my abdomen tightened at the ticklish feel of it. "You're trying to talk sense into me now, female?" he growled at me, his voice sounding tired.

The man had to be at least as exhausted as I was.

"I'm just being a good mate," I said innocently.

He gave me a gruff chuckle, and buried his face against my neck. Even with the water dulling his senses, I was certain he could still smell me, because I could still smell him. And as always, he smelled incredible.

"I'll think about it," he mumbled against my neck. "For now, just be with me."

My heart swelled.

Turning in his arms so our chests met, I went up on my tiptoes and pressed my lips to his.

He lifted me up off the ground and into his arms easily, positioning the length of his erection against my clit as he parted my lips with his tongue.

Our mouths made love as I rocked my hips, dragging him against me in a way that made me shudder. When I stopped moving, his hands on my thighs did the work for me.

I arched against him as I cried into his mouth, the orgasm tearing through me.

The motion lined the head of his cock up with my entrance, his tip pressing into me slightly, and we both inhaled sharply.

My wild eyes met his. "I want you."

His jaw clenched, but he said nothing.

"Clevv could be out any minute, and I need to find the plants that stop fertility before we go further," I said, even though what I wanted to do was slide down his erection. My breathing was already so damn fast I might as well have been jogging.

Veins in his neck and forehead bulged so much they threatened to pop through the skin.

"We can't yet," I told him, even though it hurt to do so.

He finally jerked his head in the sharpest, tiniest nod, and set me down on my feet slowly.

I felt the loss as soon as he pulled out of me.

My body clenched at the idea of having him filling me soon.

What would it be like?

He peeled a chunk of wet hair off my cheek, and it felt like he electrocuted me when his skin brushed mine.

I jumped back a little, and his eyes widened before the biggest grin stretched his cheeks.

"What was that?" I asked.

"The mate bond." His eyes were bright and excited. "Do you feel your body relaxing, and your energy returning?"

Now that he'd mentioned it, I did. Even the slight hunger I'd felt was fading.

"The magic will keep us both healthier and stronger." He tilted my head back and kissed me, then growled against my mouth, "Fuck, I can't wait for this thing to settle. For you to be mine, permanently."

"Me too," I whispered, reaching between us and wrapping my fingers around his cock.

His whole body flexed, and he groaned as I started to stroke him slowly.

"Let me take care of you now, and then we can get some sleep or go back to waiting for Clevv."

He growled fiercely. "Don't talk about that bastard while you're touching me."

I grinned. "What are you going to do to me if I refuse?"

"Maybe I'll put you on your knees and feed my cock between those sexy little lips." His grip on my face tightened.

"Don't tempt me." I dragged my tongue over his nipple, and his whole body shuddered as he roared, losing control with that sexy, tight grip on my cheeks.

Fifteen

Though the electricity between us had wiped away my exhaustion, Priel still made me get some sleep in his arms before we climbed back out of the cave and rejoined the others. Mare was still sleeping on the bean bag thing, so I climbed up next to her.

She woke up a few hours later, and we chatted as the day went on. Priel and Ervo both sat in front of us, taking up a ton of space on the ground with their gigantic bodies.

After the sexy time we'd spent together in the shower, my hound had finally stopped pacing. That made me feel sort of pleased with myself.

That night and the next day passed similarly, though without any moments of escape, despite the awful war dreams I had every time I slept. I would've tried to hit on Priel, to get him to take me back to his cave, but the man was growing more on-guard with every hour that passed. He held me when I had a shitty dream, murmuring soft, sweet words to me until the dream was nothing more than an uncomfortable memory, but I could tell his mind was on the things I'd asked him not to do.

His ex-pack had asked Mare two more times if she had determined a punishment, and both times, she answered that she was still deciding.

When the sun set on the third day, we finally heard the cave's makeshift doors move.

Priel spared enough time to growl at me that I needed to *stay right there*, before he and Ervo were jogging toward the opening.

Both men were on fire.

Mare and I exchanged nervous expressions as we stood.

Out of the corner of my eye, I noticed the pack of hounds begin moving toward us.

I nudged her arm, tilting my head toward them, and her attention spun to them.

"What are you doing?" she demanded, her voice sharp.

She was always the nicest of us in the Stronghold, so I liked hearing her get angry. It made me feel more normal.

"Protecting you," one of the hounds said, his voice low as the line of them wrapped around us.

"If you won't end us, we'll serve you until we've paid off our debt," another of the men said, his fists clenching at his sides as he stared out at the pair of Wild Hunt guys waiting in front of Clevv's cave.

"How long do you have to serve to pay off a debt that you want me to kill you for?" Mare protested.

"Eternally." The hounds' solemn response would've made me laugh if it was anything but serious.

Unfortunately, it was honest.

Mare and I exchanged wide-eye glances, and then she grabbed my arm, holding on tightly.

We peered around the hounds as Clevv yelled, "I wish to make amends."

Amends?

Was he serious?

We were definitely past that, given the fact that he'd hurt Mare and abducted me.

Just in case it came to a fight, I shifted forms. Fire and smoke trailed off of my body, and I stepped in front of Mare.

"Fine. Come out and talk," Priel called down into the cave.

If he'd already removed the final door enough, I was pretty sure they would've just jumped down and murdered the guy.

"I need something as a sign of good will," Clevv added.

"Get out now or I'll kill you where you stand," my hound snarled.

A moment passed, and then Ervo and Priel were stepping back so Clevv could get out.

If they actually let him live after hurting Mare, I was honestly going to question everything I'd learned about the fae. I wasn't passionate about death sentences, but they had made it very clear that any mistreatment of women was an offense that would result in death.

As far as I knew, it had never happened before.

But as Priel had so helpfully pointed out, they weren't innocent. Clevv had known exactly what he was doing, and still decided to do it.

Clevv stood straight and confident, even as he looked at Priel and said simply, "I made a mistake."

I scoffed.

Like hell he had.

That bastard *chose* to hurt Mare.

There was a tense pause before Priel growled to Ervo, "Your female was the injured one. This is your call, Brother."

I knew what was coming, then, with a chill that slid down my spine.

In a smooth motion, too fast for my eyes to even really track, Ervo's massive body spun and swung. His claws sliced through the hound's throat faster than Clevv could so much as flinch.

And I was really damn glad that guy was on our side.

My eyes closed before I could see Clevv's head plummeting toward the ground.

I still heard the awful thunk, though.

Mare's stomach made an awful sound.

I spun to face her, shifting back to my human form as I did, and grabbed her tangled curls to hold them away from her face as she bent over and vomited. When her stomach was empty, she murmured a thank you to me, and I released her hair.

"And the other hounds?" Ervo asked Priel in a steady voice.

Priel growled again, "Still your call. My female wasn't injured because of their decisions; yours was. If you find any of these bastards responsible for the pain Mare suffered, they deserve to die as well."

Ervo studied the hellhounds forming a divider between him and us.

And then he began stalking toward us.

Mare scrambled back to her feet and shoved her way between the men, placing herself directly in front of Ervo.

He stopped a few inches from her.

"Please don't hurt them," she said.

His eyes narrowed.

"They made a mistake; that's all. If they were okay with what Clevv did, they would've kept working with him. Instead, they helped us."

Fury bloomed in his eyes.

Fuck.

Mare must've seen it too, because she sank to her knees. "*Please*, Ervo."

He grabbed her by the waist, lifting her up and setting her back on her feet. When she was steady, he released her, still glaring at her with all that damn fury.

"You are far too important to ever *kneel* for a man." His voice was barely-controlled chaos. "If you wish the hounds to live, I'll allow it. Should they ever so much as look at you wrong, I will relish their deaths. Understand?"

Mare jerked her head in a quick, rough nod.

Ervo stepped back, his gaze lifting to the row of hellhounds. I saw her shoulders sag, like she was letting out a breath of air that she'd thought she needed to hold.

But the warning glare he turned on the hounds was enough to scare me into submission, that was for sure.

"We need to meet up with the others, to make sure their females are alright," Ervo said to Priel, when he finally stepped back and removed his gaze from the hounds.

"I won't risk taking North near them until we've solidified the bond," Priel said, his eyes sweeping quickly over the group of hellhounds too.

Whether or not he was changing his mind about letting Mare decide if any of them needed to die, I didn't know.

"I understand. You'll head to your mountain?"

"We will. Don't bring any assholes to us this time, or you'll have a *real* fight on your hands," he grumbled to the phoenix. "And my head isn't so easily removed." My hound pushed two of his ex-packmates apart so he could get through their barrier and to my side. His arms went around me, and he hauled me up against his chest like I was a damn toddler.

I didn't mind it, though.

"I'll be prepared to end anyone who so much as looks at my female now," Ervo said calmly.

"As you should. If you see Lian, tell him where to find us."

"I will."

The men nodded at each other.

I flashed Mare a quick eye-roll, and she gave me a smile that didn't reach her eyes.

And in the blink of an eye, Priel tossed me onto his back as he shifted. My fingers tangled in his fur and I buried my face against the back of his neck just as he took off running.

The speed he moved at would've been more than enough to make me dizzy if I'd been human, but I wasn't human.

I was fae.

A hellhound.

A damned oracle, too.

Pride and hope swelled in my chest as Priel continued to run.

Everything was going to be okay.

I felt that *and* trusted it, for the first time since I'd been dragged into Vevol.

WE REACHED Priel's mountain a few hours later. He ran up a well-traveled path that wove halfway up the massive mountain, and when we reached the end of the trail, he shifted forms.

His arm wrapped around my waist as he set me on my feet.

"It's easier to get through in your skin," he explained to me, his lips brushing my forehead before he set my hands on his waist and then began leading me inside.

I followed closely, holding on from behind as we slid through a tight crack in the stone, and then walked along a skinny hallway that slanted downward as we walked. A few minutes later, we turned the corner, and stepped into a large cavern that made my lips part.

The ceiling was tall and wide, with stalactites shaped like water droplets seemingly dripping toward the living space. They shimmered in many different neutral colors, and made the whole damn room feel fancy.

Stalagmites bordered the expansive room as well, shaped similarly to the ones coming off of the ceiling, but stretching upward.

As far as the space's contents, it was incredible. One side of the room held a large, bubbling pool of steaming water. Another side held a huge kitchen, with a walk-in pantry missing a door so I could see right into it. Against the third wall was a gigantic shower with just one thick, clear-glass wall, and a door leading into what I assumed was the rest of the bathroom. To the side of that, a gigantic mattress was set up.

The center of the space possessed couches, fae bean bags, and chairs, clearly designed for comfort.

The final wall, which we were standing right up against, was a massive stretch of paintings. Mural, after mural, after mural, coated the wall with Priel's gorgeous landscapes, all of them featuring a small-looking hellhound.

I noticed a slight discoloration on its back leg, and then noticed a few other similar ones.

My eyes widened when I realized what they were.

Brands.

The small hellhound was me.

My gaze jerked toward Priel.

He gave me a heart-stopping grin. "You're not the only one who dreams, Gorgeous. I thought you just had unique fur. Unlike yours, mine weren't visions. Just my imagination tangling with Vevol's magic to show me the female I knew deep down was supposed to be mine."

I opened my mouth, but then closed it when I realized I didn't know what to say to that.

It was overwhelming, but in an absolutely incredible way.

He brushed a kiss against my forehead. He'd taken to doing that often, and I loved it more than I could've even imagined.

My gaze caught on another doorless closet off to the side, and happiness swelled within me when I saw the assload of both paint and books within. Priel hadn't brought them there for me, but I knew they would be mine, too.

"Well?" He squeezed my hip, and I realized he'd wrapped his arm around my waist again while I was checking out his house.

"It's perfect," I admitted.

And as I looked closer, I realized it was the same place I'd seen bits and pieces of in my dreams.

That realization made everything feel much, much more settled.

And right.

Really, really right.

"Good." He scooped me up off the ground and hauled me toward the bed.

"What are we doing?" I asked him.

"Sleeping," he grumbled.

"You sound really excited about that," I drawled back.

"I'd rather we get naked together, but I don't trust myself to stay in control while I'm this tired," he admitted.

Control?

That was what he was worried about?

I bit back a snort.

He set me on the bed.

I didn't waste any time; just grabbed the hem of my tank top and stripped it over my head.

Priel halted where he was, his gaze dropping to my tits as I tossed the fabric to the ground.

I stood up just long enough to remove my shorts, then collapsed to the mattress with a groan.

Shit, it was really comfortable.

"Everything's fireproof in here, right?" I asked, as I climbed deeper into the bed.

He was still staring at me.

His jaw was clenched now, though, and there was indecision on his face.

"Priel?" I checked.

He blinked a couple times. "Yeah?"

"You didn't answer my question."

His eyes met mine.

There wasn't a chance he had even heard the question, and I was immensely satisfied by that.

At some point over the last few days, I had stopped doubting him when he called me Gorgeous. And I *loved* that feeling.

"Everything's fireproof in here, right?" I repeated.

"Of course."

His hands slid into his pockets.

I didn't let myself stare at the bulge in his shorts, even though I wanted to.

"We don't have to do anything tonight if you're not ready, but it would be nice to have you in this bed, with all that bare skin pressing against mine." I patted the bed beside me. "Naked cuddling. That's not illegal here, is it?"

He unbuttoned his shorts and pushed them down as an answer.

My gaze dipped to his erection, and remained as heat curled in my lower belly.

Without commenting on the way I'd stared at him, he climbed into the bed and slid under the blankets with me. His arms wrapped around my bare torso, dragging my back to his chest as he got settled on his side. His erection tucked itself between my thighs, and I bit back a groan at the thick heat of it so close to my most sensitive bits.

"You're so damn perfect," he said into my ear, as he held me close.

"Right back at ya." My eyes closed as one of his gigantic hands wrapped around one of my tits. He didn't squeeze or play with it, but just held it.

I wiggled a bit, earning a few quiet growls, but he made no move to heat things up between us.

And after a few minutes passed, I realized that I was actually pretty exhausted.

My eyes eventually closed, and I fell asleep wrapped in Priel's gloriously-warm, bare skin.

MY BACK ARCHED as his tongue stroked my clit, and a desperate cry escaped me. My hands were tied above my head, my ass hanging off the edge of the bed as Priel devoured me. His fingers dug into my skin, his hands holding my thighs almost too far apart.

I needed more.

I wanted him inside me.

Two of his fingers filled me, and I clenched around them, the pleasure growing hotter and stronger.

A third finger slowly pierced my back entrance, and I lost it.

The orgasm wasn't the end, though.

One was never enough for my hellhound; my mate.

He slowed down for a minute, his tongue sliding down, and down, and—

My thoughts pierced the vision, making the moment hazy.

This wasn't what I wanted.

I didn't want to see Priel making love to me before I lived the moment; I wanted to be *in* the moment.

I wanted to feel him inside me, to watch him touch me.

Not to dream about it, but to live it.

AS IF THAT one thought was enough, I slid out of the vision and woke up sucking in air, blinking sleep from my eyes.

I STARED out at the dark cave around me. With the way my sight worked, I wouldn't have seen any better even if there had been lights to turn on.

My body was hot, and I could feel slickness between my thighs.

Priel's breathing was even behind me, though, his grip on my breast just as relaxed as the rest of him.

He needed sleep. That was the whole reason he'd taken me away from the Stronghold in the first place, after all. He'd had time to recover since then, but more shit had gone down.

And...

I didn't think there was a chance in hell that I'd be able to fall back asleep while this horny.

Maneuvering my hand out from where he'd trapped it against my abdomen took a minute, but I let out a relieved breath when I'd freed it.

Parting my legs as much as possible, I slid my hand between my thighs.

A soft groan escaped me when I started to work out the pressure, my hips rocking just slightly. I didn't let myself move too much, not wanting to wake up Priel, but there was no way to stay completely still.

My breathing picked up as I neared the edge.

A gigantic hand tightened around my breast, squeezing it, and a cry escaped me as I shattered. I'd never been able to give myself a big orgasm, like Priel had given me, but it was a hell of a lot better than nothing.

"What the *hell* are you doing?" My hound's groggy voice was in my ear, and he sounded pissed.

"Couldn't sleep," I managed, between deep breaths.

His hand left my breast and slid between my thighs. I inhaled sharply as his long, thick fingers delved between my folds, feeling how soaked I was.

His low growl vibrated against my back. "You'd better not have gotten yourself off while I was sleeping."

My toes curled at the fury in his voice. "Why?"

"Every damn ounce of your pleasure belongs to me, Gorgeous. You steal that from me, and there are going to be consequences."

Okay, I was dripping.

"What kind of consequences?"

His fingers began stroking my clit, the movements slow but the pressure hard enough to make me see stars.

I'd seen the bastard punish me in my dreams. His hands, smacking my ass. His cock, in my throat.

And shit, he could punish me any time he wanted.

"The kind where I tie you to our bed and refuse to let you shatter until you're *begging.*" His snarl and the brutal strokes of his fingers made it hard to think straight. "The kind where I fuck you hard, without giving you time to adjust. The kind where I make you *scream* while my cock is between those hot little lips."

Yeah, now the bastard was speaking my language.

And I was *really damn grateful* that Lian had shared how sex worked with my hellhound, so I didn't have to.

"Well I already got myself off while you were sleeping," I breathed. "What are you going to do about it?"

A growl escaped him, and I heard the sexy playfulness behind it.

This was a game for both of us.

"Get on your hands and knees."

I was only too eager to obey.

My ass was up in the air a heartbeat later, my body spread wide for the man I wanted so badly it hurt.

"You don't get my tongue since you decided to warm yourself up," he growled, spreading my ass wide so he could see every inch of me.

"That's fair." My body throbbed at the snarl of approval I earned, and I sucked in a breath when the head of his cock met my entrance.

"You ready, Gorgeous?" Despite the growly playfulness, I knew he'd never do anything to me that I didn't want. And ultimately, he knew this was going to be my first time.

"Fuck, yes," I breathed.

One of his hands was on my ass, the other on my thigh, as he slid his cock inside me.

My lips parted in a silent cry, my eyes closing as I took him deeper and deeper and deeper.

There was a moment of sharp pain, and then he was driving home, bottoming out within me.

His fingers dragged over my clit, and I cried out as my body struggled to adjust to his thickness. He panted and swore, remaining still as he stroked me, bringing me pleasure even as I tried to breathe and adapt.

The pressure of him inside me slowly went from uncomfortable to really damn incredible as my tension faded.

"Not going to last long," he said to me, through gritted teeth.

"We'll go again after," I panted back, earning a pinch to my clit.

He pulled out just a little, then drove home again, earning a cry.

Everything inside me swelled—and then unraveled. I felt something click between us, something thick, heady, and magical.

I cried out as I rocked my hips, making Priel roar as he followed me over the edge. The pleasure was brutal and sweet at the same time, and when I collapsed, he dragged me into his arms and held me.

"Fuck, Gorgeous," he panted alongside me, our slightly-sweaty bodies plastered together.

Mental pictures of my bare ass in the air while my body swallowed his massive cock blasted through my mind.

I remembered what January had said about the bond—that they could communicate mentally.

Shit.

If Priel was going to hit me with pictures like that, I didn't know if I'd ever be able to leave his cave.

"Wow." I held my eyes closed, hoping everything would stop spinning and his steamy thoughts would slow down. Thinking of January had reminded me about her pregnancy—and the consequences that could follow what we'd just done. "We need to find that plant. I should've thought things through more."

"It took her half a year to get pregnant, even while having sex every day," Priel said, stroking one of my nipples. "Once wouldn't be enough to do it."

"Everyone's body works differently. We have no way of knowing," I murmured back.

"Then I'll find us that damn plant before I take you again." His growl was somewhere between amused and horny.

More of those images flashed in my mind.

My ass, in his palms.

His cock, driving into my entrance.

“You’re going to kill me if you keep thinking like that,” I groaned.

The images cut off, though he did give me a growly chuckle. “It’s going to be a long time before I can think about anything else, Gorgeous. Get used to it.”

I heaved a sigh at the idea of getting out of bed when I was this horny again already. “Let’s go get the plant, then.”

Sixteen

We put our clothes back on, and then Priel showed me how to get back outside of the cave. His lesson on tapping into Vevol's magic to discover things about plants was sketchy at best, but it was actually pretty simple. I had to rely on following my feelings, which was difficult at first, but I figured it out.

The plant to suppress fertility was a small red ball-shaped fruit with odd protrusions on the thick, fuzzy skin. They grew on trees in mass quantities, which seemed like a good thing to me. Priel taught me how to eat it as we walked back to the cave, and as he did, the fruit reminded me of an orange. The fuzzy skin needed to be peeled off—he warned me it would make me sick if I tried to eat it. Inside, the fruit was soft but creamy, with thin membranes that made it easy to take apart like an orange was.

I groaned at the flavor when I tasted it; the sweetness and texture reminded me of ice cream, even though it wasn't cold.

I'd definitely need to stick them in the fridge, or maybe talk Priel into figuring out a way to build a freezer so I could have them like actual ice cream.

If we were going to be having a lot of sex, I would have the perfect excuse to eat a lot of them.

"Why didn't anyone ever bring these to us?" I asked Priel.

He gave me a sheepish grin. "One of the fae noticed many years ago that eating the fruit changes the thickness of our release. Word spread, and no one has touched them since." He gestured to his dick, and I realized he was talking about jizz.

Right.

Interesting.

If it changed *that*, it probably affected male fertility too, which was awesome.

"So it would stop me from getting pregnant, *and* you from getting me pregnant. Double protection. Good; we are *not* having a kid soon." I handed him one of the fruits I was cradling in the crook of my arm. "Eat it, or I'm not participating in the fantasy you keep mentally-flashing me."

He snorted, but accepted the fruit and began peeling it. "So you don't want kids?"

I glanced at him sideways. "I don't know what I want; I'm not even used to living in Vevol yet. If that was going to be a deal-breaker, you probably should've asked before we did the deed."

He flashed me an amused smirk. "You think I could only want you because you can make me a baby, Gorgeous?"

I shrugged. "I don't think so, but we've never talked about it."

"Our world is still a mess right now. Bringing a small life into it would be terrifying. What if it was a girl, like January said? Can you even imagine how many men I'd have to protect her from?" He shuddered. "There's been so damn much fighting. And I enjoy the fighting, usually. But at this point, I'd like to spend at least the next decade at home with you.

"Doing what?" I asked.

"Painting. Fucking. Inking that gorgeous skin. Teaching you about our world. You've seen so little of it, and it's an incredible place. You deserve to understand who and what you are now, Polaris, and to have as much time as you need to figure out how your magic works, to prevent it from having so much power over you."

My lips curved upward. "That sounds perfect. We'll reevaluate the kid thing in a decade."

"Or two," he agreed.

My smile widened further.

We ate as we walked back, our hips bumping against each other. Soft, comfortable electric zaps zipped between us with each small brush of our skin.

Honestly, I felt so much more relaxed with him that it was almost ridiculous. Finally working through that tension and settling the connection between us made things feel so much more comfortable, even though I was totally horny.

And the electricity connecting us only served to calm me further, as if his body was telling mine that I was safe and he would take care of me.

I'd like to say that I didn't *need* him to take care of me, but honestly, I did. I was a hurricane on my best days, and I needed an anchor. Priel was uniquely qualified to fill that position, because he got it. He understood my drive to create art when my emotions grew too strong. He wasn't offended when I got angry with him, and didn't let me walk all over him—nor did I let him walk all over me.

And he understood how difficult my magic was for me. Rather than hating it the way I did for so long, he talked about my dreams as if they were something incredible.

All of those things worked together to create a man who made my future seem bright in a way it never had on Earth.

And I loved that.

When we reached the cave again, we stored the fruits in Priel's fae-style fridge. I grabbed a glass from the cupboard and filled it with water, leaning up against the cabinets and sipping at it while Priel stepped into the pantry and surveyed the contents.

"How long could we survive here without leaving?" I checked, when he stepped back out.

"A couple of years." He shrugged a shoulder. "Longer, if the connection truly nourishes us when it staves off our hunger."

Damn.

Maybe that shouldn't have made me feel safer, but it did.

"Thank you," I said, setting my cup down on the counter.

"For what?" He lifted an eyebrow, walking up to me and stopping when his pelvis met my abdomen.

"Getting all this ready. I know you didn't do it for me, but being able to come here, and see all of this paint, and know that I'm safe..." I bit my lip. "It means a lot to me. Things haven't been easy since I was brought here, but I feel like that's changing. And I'm really, really excited about that change."

"Good." He captured my face between his palms and lowered his lips to mine. The kiss was soft, and slow, and blissfully sweet.

"I have a request," he murmured against my mouth a few minutes later.

"What is it?" I grumbled, wanting the kiss to resume.

"I want to give you a tattoo."

My eyebrows lifted and I leaned away, the kissing suddenly forgotten. "I've always wanted one. Or fifty. Is this a claiming thing, though? Like you want to mark me as yours?"

"It is." He recaptured my lips.

I was pretty sure he was trying to soften me up, but honestly didn't mind. His kisses weren't going to make me any more likely to agree than I already was.

"What kind of tattoo?" I asked when I pulled away.

"I figured we could choose together."

He brushed his lips over my nose, and my face wrinkled at the playful kiss.

His soft chuckle made me smile a little, though.

"So you'd get the same tattoo? Or I could choose one for you too?"

"Yes." His hands slid down my arms, then the curve of my waist, before stopping to rest on my hips.

"Okay. Humans usually wear rings, on this finger." I flashed him the fourth finger on my left hand. "Some people do the middle finger, or the other hand, but I almost always saw the fourth on the left. I've seen pictures of people using tattoos instead. In my favorite ones, they just use the first letter of their significant other's name in cursive, sweeping across the finger." I traced an L over my ring finger to demonstrate.

"I like it." He nodded his approval.

"You have ink here already," I pointed out, picking up his hand and showing him the black shape on his finger. The larger tattoo had been designed to look like multiple vines snaking over his fingers, so the color was solid on the bottom chunk of that finger.

"I'll do it in silver. It'll stand out, and remind me of the first time you were in my home, when you accidentally stabbed yourself."

I rolled my eyes at him, but couldn't hide my grin.

He lifted my hand to his lips, pressing a kiss to my fourth finger. "Yours, I'll do in black ink."

I figured he would; the man clearly had a thing for black ink, and I was definitely on board with it.

"Alright. What was the tattoo you were imagining?" I checked. "What would be your ideal way to mark me as yours?"

"Fire, here." His knuckle brushed over my chest, directly over my heart.

I liked the idea. Flames were a huge part of my life now that I was in Vevol. Putting them over my heart would represent me, the way I was changing, and my relationship with Priel, too.

"Deal." Let's do it.

Fire burned in his eyes as he hauled me up onto the counter. "Wait here."

He disappeared into his art closet, coming back a minute later with a small box of ink and another one of the tattoo gun things I'd stabbed myself with before.

We were both quiet as he burned the gun's end, cleaning it easily.

The sex had been fun, and we were used to talking, teasing, and sassing each other. The mating bond had been building between us for so long that sealing it just felt like the next level for our relationship.

But tattoos... they were visible, and permanent.

And the moment we were about to share felt sort of sacred because of that.

"I'll show you how it works on myself, first," Priel explained to me, lifting his eyes to mine.

He was giving me an out. Making sure I knew he didn't expect me to go through with it if I didn't want to.

"Alright." I'd let him do things his way, so he knew I wasn't going to change his mind.

We were both silent as magic swelled within the room. It was so thick I could see it a little; a transparent flame-like cloud swirling around Priel.

He placed his hand on my thigh, using me as a table, then lowered the needle to his finger.

I watched in shocked interest as he used the needle to slowly cut through the air above his hand. The ink sizzled against his skin as his fire and magic worked together to slowly and permanently draw a cursive P over his finger.

I'd known he'd use a P for Polaris before he even started.

Full names were where the magic was at, after all.

It took a while, but eventually he put the gun down, and the magic in the room faded. He tensed and relaxed his fingers a few times, before putting his hand back on my thigh.

My throat swelled when I saw the long, looping silver letter on his ring finger.

"Do mine." I handed him my palm.

He chuckled softly, tilting me and the appendage a little as he set it down on the counter. A few minutes later, he began.

I watched every second of his work, transfixed by the miracle of it. He was incredible. I had no idea how he even tapped into a person's magic like that.

"Tapping into magic is easier than you think," he murmured to me, as he finished the letter and lifted his machine away from my hand.

"I doubt it."

"You've been tapping into mine since you arrived, remember? Vevol said that's how you determine whose future you see."

Oh, damn.

Right.

"I need to practice," I admitted.

"We can start with the other women. I'm sure they won't care." He lifted the gun to my chest, and then his eyes met mine. "Are you sure about this, Gorgeous?"

"Completely."

His lips curved upward just the tiniest bit, and then he was focused on my skin.

My eyes closed while he worked, and the silence was a comfortable one as he continued. He had to move my tank top down a bit, but it wasn't like I was bothered by having his hands on my skin.

The feeling was odd, since he was altering the way my magic affected my appearance a little, but it didn't bother me.

"Alright, keep your eyes closed," he warned me, as the magic faded around us.

He must've been finished with it.

I heard him put his things down, and then felt his arms as he scooped me up off the counter.

My forehead rested against his neck as he carried me to the bathroom, and his hands stroked my ass. He was hard, which made me a little warmer.

"Feet down," he warned, as he lowered me to the ground.

I obeyed, and left my eyes closed as he adjusted my hair and tank top.

"Alright, open them."

I peeked my eyes open, and they widened as I took in my reflection.

My hair was tucked behind my shoulders, between my back and Priel's front, exposing the tattoo.

It was a paintbrush, inked at a slant, with colored paint dripping off the tip. Fire blazed off of it wildly, but didn't appear to be actually burning it.

My throat swelled.

It was perfect.

A representation of me, and of Priel—and a gorgeous one.

I turned in his arms, digging my fingers into his neck as I pulled him down.

He hauled me up off the ground, wrapping my legs around his waist as he carried me back to the bed. Our mouths were pressed together as our tongues tangled and danced, our hands and bodies urging us to continue as Priel lowered me to the mattress without pausing our kiss.

His hands left my ass long enough to drag my shorts down my thighs and toss them to the side, and then do the same to his.

The thick heat of his erection pressed against my opening. I arched my hips, taking him inside me, and we groaned together as he slowly filled me.

"Fuck," he growled against my lips.

"Yeah," I breathed.

He worked my tank over my head, then threw that wherever the rest of our clothes had gone.

Lowering his tongue to my chest as our bodies slowly became one, he dragged it over the ink before focusing on one of my nipples. The attention and the feel of him inside me was so foreign, yet incredible. I was already so close to the edge that it was stupid—but I guessed the mate bond was responsible for it, at least partly.

Priel's fingers, cock, and every other damn part were responsible for the rest.

"After this, I'm going to taste you again," he told me, dragging his teeth over my nipple.

"Good plan," I panted, moving my hips as he pulled out slightly. "First, let's just—*ohh, shit.*" The last words were a hiss as he bit down on my nipple while he bottomed out inside me.

It was too much.

I shattered with a cry, and he snarled as he pumped into me faster, and harder.

I was still riding out the intense orgasm when he lost it. Fire danced off both of our skin as he stared down at me, chest heaving and eyes hot.

"You're so much better than I imagined," he growled at me.

"I'm not sure if that's a compliment or an insult," I mumbled back, my eyes half-closing.

"The biggest compliment." He eased himself up off of my body. "Do you trust me?"

I opened my eyes fully, staring at him a bit suspiciously. "Mostly."

He smirked. "Good enough."

I watched that gorgeous backside as he crossed the room, and continued watching as he opened a kitchen cupboard. When he returned to me, he was holding a small tub.

"Is that the pleasure spice?" I checked.

"Yup." He sat on the edge of the bed, his gaze wicked. "I want to take my time with you, watch you unravel a dozen times before I'm inside you again."

Who would be crazy enough to say no when they had a sexy fae offering that? One who looked like Priel and actually cared about them?

"Hell yes."

His lips curved up in a grin, and he unscrewed the lid of the tub as he climbed back onto the bed, positioning himself so his head was between my thighs.

Licking a finger, he dipped it in the spice before pressing it to my clit.

I groaned at the pressure as he slowly dragged his finger down the center of me, before dipping it back in the spice.

"Don't know if that's sanitary," I managed, as he slid the finger inside me.

My body clenched around him, my insides still drenched with both of our pleasure.

"You're a fae, Polaris. Couldn't get a disease if you tried."

He reached up to my breasts and dragged his damp, spiced finger over my nipples just as the shit began to work on my clit.

I felt the sensitive skin warm and swell slightly, and a moan slid from my lips as he blew lightly against the flesh.

He put the lid back on the spice before dropping the container on the floor and wiping his finger down the creases between my thighs.

"Not using it on yourself?" I asked him, though with the heat coursing through me, it came out sounding like a whimper.

"Hell no. I want to watch every second of your bliss. Now, wrap those little hands around the headboard, or I'll tie them there." He blew against my clit again, and I bucked my hips desperately as the first orgasm rolled through me, making me cry out.

"Shit," I moaned, my breathing staggered as I recovered. "I don't know if I can do this."

"We're just getting started, Gorgeous, and you're already perfect. Just relax and let yourself enjoy it."

I started to nod, but then his tongue found my swollen clit.

And the pleasure became all-consuming.

For a few blissful hours, the only thing on my mind was the incredible way Priel touched me and licked me.

When the spice finally began to wear off, I grabbed the man by the hair and tugged him up toward me.

His eyes were hot, his gaze so damn proud. Whether he was proud of himself or me, I didn't know or care.

I felt too incredible for that.

When I pushed him to his back, the fire in his eyes was searing.

And when I wrapped my lips around his cock, getting him off with my mouth before taking him inside me and making him lose control again, every shred of doubt had been wiped from my mind.

Priel was mine.

I was his.

And we were one.

No matter what else happened, that was always going to remain true.

The past wasn't going anywhere, but the future?

It was ours.

Seventeen

Lian finally showed up outside our cave a few weeks later, roaring to get us to come out.

Priel's face was between my thighs when the roar shook our mountain, my hands and tits plastered to the wall of our living room while he knelt below me, pinning my core to his face and spreading me open wide with his hands.

He growled at me that the bastard could wait outside, then dragged his teeth over my clit until I screamed.

His cock filled me in time to catch the end of my orgasm, and his fingers tortured my clit as he pumped into me until we both lost control together.

His arm wrapped around my waist, holding me up and blazing his fire over both of us to clean our skin as I panted and wheezed. He set me down on the bed, grabbing my clothes from wherever I'd lost them a few days earlier. When I tried to take them from him, he batted my hands away and dressed me himself.

I scowled at him, and earned a wicked grin in response.

He pulled a few of the red fruits out of the fridge, tucking them into his pockets before he strode back over to me and whisked me up off my feet. My head crashed into his chest, making me laugh.

He grinned down at me. "Ready to see if January and Naomi saved the world?"

"You know they didn't. My dreams are still shitty," I said with a sigh, as I relaxed into his arms. It wasn't a shock to him; he had comforted me after my nightmares too many times for that, and reassured me that he was okay with the horrific murals I'd painted over his wall as a result of said nightmares.

He understood my need to paint, and had no problem holding my brush or mixing my colors when I was overtaken by that need.

We had even discussed (at length) our silent obsessions with each other from the time before he abducted me, so there were no more secrets between us. Only friendship, and playfulness, and a hell of a lot of attraction.

"It'll take time for things to change." He brushed my hair out of my face as he carried me to the cave's exit. "Vevol won't give you permission to go after the women until she's certain that the war isn't in our future."

"What if that never happens, though?"

"Then we'll figure something out." His voice was light and playful. "I don't think it's going to come to that, though."

Shit, I hoped not.

We emerged from the cave shortly after, and found January and Calian waiting outside. January was grinning like a fool, and I couldn't help but mirror the expression.

"Look how cozy the two of you got," she teased me.

"Extremely cozy," I admitted, trying to worm my way out of Priel's arms.

He only held me tighter, shooting me a teasing grin.

"What happened with the unseelie?"

Her smile faded a bit. "It was rough. Really rough. I thought Naomi was going to murder Aeven for a bit, but he pulled through. All the other girls are moved in, and both types of fae have started building houses and shit around the new Stronghold. It's weird, but I think it's going to turn out okay. Only a few little fights have broken out, now that the Wild Hunt guys and the unseelie council have started banishing anyone who fights."

Huh.

That wasn't a bad idea at all.

"It's like juvie in there with all the unseelie chicks running around. They're kind of bad-ass, but really guarded, and bitchy too. I saved a room for you, though." She winked at me.

I made a face. "Thanks, but I think I'm gonna keep living here. I like being out of the way, far from the big groups of fae."

"I figured. The way they talk about you is kind of crazy. Like you're the chosen one." She shrugged. "No offense, but even with all that extra magic, you're still one of us human ladies."

She winked at me. Honestly, her words and playfulness made me feel good.

Hearing that I was one of them and I always would be, made me feel like I could belong with them if I wanted to, the same way I now belonged with Priel.

She added, "We're ready for you, though. The unseelies have vowed not to try to steal you away, and apparently their vows are unbreakable or something. It's time to go after the fae women."

Shit.

I hesitated.

"You're not convinced?" she asked.

"She's still dreaming about war," Priel said simply.

January's grin faded, and Lian's expression grew serious.

"Seeing the changes for yourselves and testing the unseelies' vows could help," he suggested. "They understand your connection to Vevol, and no one will force you to go before you're ready. No one is willing to risk the fae women."

I nodded. "We'll at least go and see what it's like."

"It's weird," January warned. "The unseelie chicks are a lot less sunshiney than our seelie girls."

I grimaced. "Thanks for the warning."

"Sure." She and Lian smoothly shifted while launching themselves airborne.

I watched the phoenix and dragon fly away before looking at Priel. "Do you think it'll be safe for me there?"

"I think I'll kill anyone who tries to touch you, so regardless of how safe it is, you're going to be fine."

I rolled my eyes at him, and he flashed me a grin.

"Seriously?"

"In all honestly, Gorgeous, you're the only one who knows where the women are. Other than Mare, but no one knows that but the two of us. No one will dare risk pissing you off until the other fae women have been found, and something tells me that after we've brought them back, everyone will be too distracted to notice you and I slipping out and heading back home."

I loved that our cave was home.

And honestly, I believed him.

We shifted together, taking off toward the neutral territory.

Or the *female* territory, I supposed.

HOURS PASSED before we finally made it there, but as we approached, I realized how much more chaotic it was then I had expected.

January wasn't kidding about the houses. The damn things were going up *everywhere*. Between trees, up in the branches, within the *trunks* of the largest trees...

The fae were moving in, the way humans usually did.

And as I passed them, I started to see more than just the half-naked seelies. There were unseelie fae with their icy expressions, slacks, and button-down shirts, mixed in with the seelies. All of them were building homes and staking their claim in the neutral territory.

When they saw me and Priel coming through, the seelies stared.

The unseelies bowed.

My grip on Priel's hand tightened.

He peeled my fingers out of his, placing them on his bicep so he could wrap his arm around my waist and pull me closer as we walked.

"You okay?" he murmured into my mind.

The ability had come with the mating connection, of course, we just usually didn't bother with it. It took more focus than normal speaking, so we'd never had a reason to.

Now, we did.

Not sure I had the focus to respond mentally, I just nodded.

His grip on me tightened anyway, his fingers curving possessively around the bare strip of my abdomen.

"These bastards need to stop staring at your ass," he growled at me.

Given how relaxed he'd been over the last few weeks—and how incredible said relaxation had made my life—I took it upon myself to at least try to preserve his calm attitude.

"Staring at my butt might result in death," I called out to the men around us. "Don't test my mate."

I felt Priel's thick, hot pride at the title, and fought the curve of my lips that tried to make itself seen.

Ervo swooped out of the sky, shifting and landing smoothly on my other side as we continued walking. Obviously, he kept up with my pace easily.

"It's safe?" Priel asked the other man.

Lian had already told him it was, but I knew Priel would feel more confident if more of his friends confirmed that.

"It's not safe, but your female isn't at risk." The phoenix didn't bother with a lie, which was both a good and bad thing.

"Who is, then?" I asked him.

"Any male who tries to speak with one of the unmated females." I saw the fury burn through his eyes. "The unseelie women have been told about our arrangement, and decided that it's over."

"That's not their call," Priel growled.

"No, but to challenge them is to start a fight, and fighting leads to expulsion from the females' territory. A way for men and women to interact peacefully must be created, or the fragile peace will end." Ervo's simple statement of the words made me shiver.

Was he threatening to do something drastic?

"He may not admit it aloud, but he considers Mare his. Anyone who gets between them right now will be seen as a target," Priel said into my mind. *"She needs to mate with him, tell him she isn't interested, or choose another male."*

"I'm sure she'll be thrilled about that set of options," I grumbled back.

His low chuckle made me smile.

"Fuck, is North smiling? What happened?" I heard Ana call from somewhere in the distance. When I turned my head, I saw her standing next to another girl I didn't recognize, talking to a group of other women. They were building something, or at least trying to, and a bunch of fae men watched them warily from nearby.

My smile morphed into a grimace, but I waved anyway.

Though I understood her overprotectiveness, and had sort of appreciated it at one point, she had encouraged us to be afraid of the fae. And that fear hadn't benefited any of us, in any way. Things had been so much happier at the Stronghold after the Wild Hunt started coming around, protecting us and whatnot.

The new Stronghold came into view, and I looked it up and down.

It was still made of the bland stone, and stuck out like a sore thumb compared to the natural-looking homes the fae were building in the forest around it.

A second floor had been added to the triangular building, and it had been drastically expanded. Now it was a typical square shape, and much, much larger.

Then again, there were twenty ex-human women, and only a few of us were mated. The mated unseelie ladies didn't live with their men, as far as I knew, which left eighteen grown-ass women in need of their own space and privacy.

When I considered that there was an unnumbered group of fae women hiding out there, I realized just how much more space we would need.

"Damn," Priel whistled.

"There are many more women, now," Ervo agreed, though his gaze was on one of the second-floor windows and wasn't moving.

I would've put money on that being Mare's window, if money was really a thing in Vevol. They seemed to have some version of it, but considering all the free time they all had, it didn't seem to matter much in the scheme of things.

We walked up to the door, and Ervo knocked.

"Walking in without permission is supposed to result in castration for male fae," he told us, his voice low. "It has yet to happen, though."

I rolled my eyes.

No way in hell was anyone actually cutting anyone else's balls off. Even Ana wasn't that crazy.

A girl I didn't recognize opened the door, her eyes narrowed and suspicious as she looked at me. "North?" she checked.

"Yup."

"Men stay outside. House rule." She pointed to a couple chairs someone had set up outside.

Priel scoffed. "Not a fucking chance."

I narrowed my eyes back at the woman, muttering silently for Priel to let me handle this.

If men had dick-measuring contests, women had tit-measuring ones. And I might not have had the biggest physical tits, but I'd make it work.

"My mate poses no threat to anyone here. We both come in, or I walk right the hell away with information that could make your life here *much* easier."

The more women we had, the more the male fae's attention would be divided, so I knew without a doubt that I was right.

Everyone's life would be easier with more ladies for the fae to bother.

She scowled at me but jerked the door open, her glare turning to Ervo. "Unmated men stay out."

He glowered back at her, but I shot him what I hoped was a promising expression.

I'd talk to Mare for him.

The door slammed behind us, and the girl glared at me for a long moment. "Where the hell have you been?"

"Relieving stress with my mate; thanks for asking. You look like you could use a little *stress relief* yourself," I drawled back.

She spun around and stormed away, her brown curls bouncing behind her as she moved.

I glanced up at Priel to make sure he wasn't checking out her ass or anything, but he was already grinning down at me. *"You're sexy when you're mean."*

"Keep it in your pants until we're out of the shark tank," I murmured back, squeezing his bicep tightly.

Ervo had been staring at the second floor, so it was safe to assume that was where I would find Mare, and hopefully Sunny and Dots too.

His chuckle made me grin as we headed toward the staircase off to my left. The place honestly still looked almost as cold and unwelcoming as it had been before they expanded it and added furniture. The living room and kitchen were set up almost exactly the same way they had been back in the old

Stronghold, but the space lacked life. No one was down there, watching a movie, reading a book, or even cooking.

We climbed the stairs while still holding on to each other. At the top, I looked around.

All I could see was another long, cold hallway, and two rows of doors.

"Damn," I whispered.

"Hmm?" Priel looked at me.

"It just feels empty and angry in here. Back at the Stronghold, it was a family. I was the pissed-off black sheep, but I still knew I was welcome," I explained quietly.

Looking around, I debated knocking on doors but just decided to go with the seelie way of locating people.

"Mare?" I called out. "Sunny? Dots?"

"In here!" Sunny yelled from the door furthest from the staircase.

Dots opened it a few seconds later, as we headed their way.

"Hey!" She threw her arms around me for a quick hug. "Come on in." When she grabbed my hand and tugged, Priel and I let her pull us inside.

My eyebrows shot upward when I saw three mattresses staggered around the room. It wasn't a big room, so there wasn't a whole lot of space. Between each of them, there was only four or five inches.

Mare was curled up on the bed in the corner nearest to the window, her thighs to her chest and a book resting against her knees. She gave us a faint smile before returning her eyes to the pages.

Sunny was sprawled out on the mattress in the opposite corner of Mare's, but she was sitting up and grinning at us. "Look at the two of you, all matey and cozy."

I snorted, and Dots laughed.

"What are you all doing in here?" I asked, letting go of Priel's arm. He leaned up against the wall, releasing his grip on me so I could go over to them and plop down on the end of Sunny's mattress.

"Hiding from the unseelie chicks," Sunny admitted.

I frowned.

"Not hiding," Dots corrected. "We're just... avoiding them."

"AKA hiding," Sunny agreed.

"They're not very friendly," Dots admitted. "When you do talk to them, they just go on and on about how much they hate the fae. They're hoping you can find enough fae chicks to distract all of the men. Even the mated ones."

My eyebrows shot upward.

I'd seen and heard enough of Priel's thoughts to know that wasn't even almost a possibility. Mated fae were completely devoted to their mate, even if they didn't show that. Ervo and Mare weren't even fully mated yet, but I'd seen him out there. Someone was going to die if he didn't see her soon.

Priel snorted. "Pipe dream."

"We think so too," Dots agreed.

"What happened to the Wild Hunt guys?" I checked.

Dots' and Sunny's expressions both soured. "The other girls scared them off. That's why Sunny's moping. Teris wouldn't ever agree to bang her, and now she can't even make out with him."

"I'm going to kill you," Sunny muttered, smacking Dots on the arm lightly.

"Then you won't have anyone to snuggle with," she pointed out.

Sunny groaned. "We need to get back to the old Stronghold. Things were better there."

"Until we were attacked and abducted," Mare muttered.

"Right. Until that." Sunny pointed a finger gun in her direction. "Any ideas how we can avoid that happening again?" She looked at me.

I shrugged. "Stay here?"

Priel spoke up from the side of the room. "Now that we know it's a possibility, my brothers will be going through our people, ensuring that none of you are in danger. Both Nev and Ervo are watching the house right now, and I saw Teris run out to meet January and Lian when they landed a few minutes ago." He gestured toward the window. "You're safe."

"But trapped," Sunny pointed out. "And lonely."

"We'll figure out a way to meet up with the guys," Dots protested. "The girls won't let us do movie nights or anything with them, but we can always go out there."

"About that..." I tucked some hair behind my ear. "Have the other girls come up with a way for everyone to interact safely with the men?"

Sunny snorted. "These chicks, interacting politely with fae dudes? That's never going to happen."

Dots' grimace confirmed that.

I admitted, "I have it on good authority that if we can't amend that, the war is going to break out one way or another."

No need to tell them that Ervo was the said good authority, right?

"Also, Mare, Ervo seems a little unhinged. Can you just open a window to smile and wave at him or something so he knows you're alive and well?"

"The windows are sealed shut," Mare murmured, not looking up from her book.

"Seriously?" I looked at Sunny and Dots.

Dots nodded.

"Who's in charge?" I asked them.

"There's a gang of them. Five chicks. They're the loudest." Dots made a face.

"No wonder January said it's like juvie." I glanced toward the door.

I was suddenly understanding why I was still having dreams about war.

There was a moment of tense silence as I considered our options.

What was there, really?

The men weren't a danger to each other anymore, but the damn place was going to implode if the women didn't change their ways.

Or... if the number of women didn't increase.

Vevol had given me the information. Technically, it should be my call as to when we went after them.

I didn't feel great about it, but didn't see another option, either.

"I think getting the other women will be our best way to delay the fighting," I admitted. "This place is a mess, but it's going to take longer to get it sorted out than I think we have to do so."

"Agreed," Sunny muttered.

"So, are you guys coming on that trip?" I checked. "I don't trust any of the unseelie chicks, and women are the only ones who can cross into the fae ladies' hiding place, so I need you. No way in hell will Lian let January run into the unknown while growing a baby."

Sunny sat up, excitement in her eyes. "I'm so down. The Wild Hunt dudes taught us how to shift while we waited to hear back about this place, so we're golden."

Dots grimaced, but nodded.

Mare finally put her book away. "I want to see them, too."

"Alright, let's get out of here." I stood up.

Maybe it would've been smarter to wait a few days before taking off, but I didn't want to risk any of the unseelie ladies trying to talk their way into the group.

Honestly, there was a decent chance the lot of them would want to go there just to hide out from the men.

Priel and I waited in the hallway while the other girls all put on their seelie tanks and shorts, or stripped down to them.

"I'm surprised the other ladies are so bitter," I murmured to Priel, as he pulled me closer and played with a few strands of my hair.

"I'm not."

I rolled my eyes at him.

He flashed me a grin. "Things were rough at first, Gorgeous. We'll figure out a way to make this work, but it'll take time."

"If only we had more of that." My mind went back to my dreams.

"Soon enough, it'll be just the two of us, relaxing in the hot spring back at home," he murmured to me. "Enjoy the wild times while they last."

The doors opened, and all three of the girls stepped out.

Emotions I couldn't identify swelled in my chest when I saw all of them wearing the same simple tanks and shorts I had on.

Modest, we were not.

But united?

Hell yes.

Eighteen

The girl from earlier tried to prevent us from leaving, the same way she'd tried to prevent me from coming inside. I threatened to punch her in the face, and she moved.

January's juvy theory was only getting more and more accurate.

It felt like a million eyes were on us as we stepped out of the new Stronghold together.

As if we'd summoned them, Nev and Ervo came strolling out of the forest and joined the group.

"We're going after the female fae," Priel announced, his voice booming into the forest. "Follow us, and you die. Seelie or unseelie, we don't care."

With that, he tossed me over his shoulder and shifted.

I grinned at the rush of the familiar motion. It was stupid, but I loved the way he threw me around like that.

I loved a lot of things about Priel, actually.

The others shifted too, and as a group, we took off. Calian and January met Ervo, Mare, and Dots in the sky while the rest of us moved on the ground. Teris caught up to us, running too.

I'd never seen the basilisks or how they moved while up close and personal, but they were fascinating. And strangely, not as creepy as I'd thought. Thicker around than me or Priel, they were absolutely massive, their bodies built out of pure muscle. Despite their size, they moved just as quickly as the rest of us, their bodies zigging and zagging smoothly.

A BIT of time passed before Priel growled at me. *"Do you hear that?"*

I frowned. *"Hear what?"*

"Someone's followed us. I need you to shift and run while I take care of it."

I growled back, *"By yourself? No way."*

"I'll be fine. Teris or Nev will break away to help, too."

I stared out at the forest as we ran, moving insanely fast. Though memories of the awful way I'd hit the ground when I jumped out of that car assaulted me, I pushed them away.

I wasn't the same weak human girl.

I was strong, now.

I could do this.

Starting the shift, I threw myself off of Priel's back.

All four of my paws hit the ground, and victory coursed through my veins.

"That's right," Priel growled back at me, his voice somewhere between satisfied and proud. *"You're incredible, Gorgeous. Now stay with the rest of the pack, so I don't have to spank that sexy little ass when we stop."*

I huffed out a snort, shaking my head at my mate and his steamy playfulness as he darted in the wrong direction.

Sure enough, Nev broke away from the group too.

Teris remained on the opposite side from me, protecting Sunny's scaly side. I noticed Lian fly lower, as if also responding to the threat, getting ready to protect the rest of us if we needed him to.

My heart swelled at the sight.

We were a damn family.

Snarls erupted behind me, and I tried to look over my shoulder, but didn't see anything.

A few minutes later, a whole group of hellhounds caught up with us.

My surprised gaze flickered over each of them as recognition kicked in.

They were Priel's ex-pack.

"They still owe Mare their lives," Priel growled to me, as he caught back up to us. *"The bastards aren't leaving unless we kill them, and considering Mare ended up on her knees to stop Ervo from ripping their throats out, that's not an option."*

"Damn," I murmured, glancing up at the sky.

Mare didn't seem like herself, but at least she had protection.

"Well, this has been quite an interesting day," I finally said.

Priel's chuckle made me grin. *"One of many, I imagine."*

My heart warmed. *"I'm in love with you,"* I told him, not wanting to keep it quiet.

He loved me too; I didn't doubt that.

"If you're trying to seduce me, it's working," he rumbled back.

A barked laugh escaped me.

"I love you too, Polaris. So damn much." His voice was warm, and I moved closer to his side. Our fur brushed as we ran, and as the sun set over our heads, I admitted to myself that I was happy.

Stupidly, ridiculously happy.

And no matter what we were going to face next, I refused to let that change.

Nineteen

Priel

We stopped for the night when we reached the lake. None of us men were willing to watch our women fly into the darkness to go after the female fae; they could wait until the sun was up so we could at least see where they disappeared at and figure out a way to go after them if we needed to.

I trusted North's magic enough not to think that would be necessary, but some of the others weren't as certain.

And I wanted to spend the night with her first, in case the trip took a few days. I despised the thought of having my female away from me for any amount of time, but there might not be a way around it.

For the sake of peace, I would survive it. Not happily, but survival was survival.

Sunny, Dots, and Mare all made their beds together, with their men nearby, watching them. Sunny invited Teris to share her blankets, but the moron turned her down.

Why he would turn down the female he'd claimed when she clearly wanted him was beyond me, but I sure as hell wasn't getting involved.

Lian and January went off together, and North grabbed my hand, drawing me away from everyone else too.

She was exhausted, so when she collapsed into my arms, I simply stroked her back, enjoying her presence.

There would be time for sex later.

Plenty of time.

An eternity.

That thought made my lips curve upward.

I drifted off to sleep quickly too, and didn't wake up until North was shaking my shoulders, positioned over me with bright, excited eyes.

"I saw the future," she told me, a bit breathless. "A *happy* future, Priel. There were kids, running around. Unseelies were *smiling*. I was right; we made the right choice."

"Of course you were right." I pulled her face down to mine, kissing her gently.

"I know you didn't doubt me, but I doubted me. And there were so many nightmares..." she shivered. "I don't think I can sleep right now. I'm too excited."

"Need me to relax you?" I murmured, sliding my hands down to her perfect little ass and squeezing lightly.

Her eyes dilated a bit, and she looked at the trees around us. "Here?"

"Why not?" My fingers slid beneath the hem of her shorts. "Make sure you're loud enough that the other men know how good I am at pleasuring you."

She laughed, until I dragged a finger over her clit.

Then, she shuddered.

And as I made love to her on the floor of the forest, I knew without a shadow of doubt that I was the luckiest male in our world.

Hell, the luckiest male in *all* the worlds.

The Brutal Fae's Life

Wild Hunt 3

To the books and people that don't make you cry.

One

I STARED out at the lake, watching Vevol's sun rise slowly over the water. It stretched as far as I could see in every direction, large enough that I had assumed it was an ocean the first time I saw it.

A man stepped into place beside me.

I didn't have to turn my head to know who. The group of hellhounds that thought they were my protectors never came this close to me.

The only unmated man who did was a certain possessive, confusing-as-hell phoenix.

And on top of that, he smelled way too good for me to mistake him for anyone else.

"You should remain here while the others go," he said to me, his voice even.

His voice was always so neutral, unless he was cutting someone's head off.

I fought the horrified shiver that threatened to roll down my spine with the memories that accompanied that thought.

The way the head had fallen...

The cold, unfeeling look in Ervo's eyes as he removed it from the hellhound's body...

My stomach's contents threatened to make a reappearance.

It wouldn't be the first time I vomited at the memory. Nor would it likely be the last.

"Why would I stay here?" I tried to keep my voice as level as his.

Maybe if I refused to let him see what I was feeling, his possessiveness would fade, and my confusing emotions would too.

He had made it very clear that despite his constant reminders about me belonging to him, he thought I belonged to him as nothing more than a family member.

A *female brother*, he had said.

My lips twisted at the unpleasantness of the memory.

That conversation had left me so confused.

"You'll be safer here," he said.

I stared out at the water for a few minutes before replying, "I stopped caring about my safety a long time ago."

How many years had I spent hoping for a second chance to be someone bigger, and stronger, and better?

My whole life.

I wanted to *matter*, dammit.

And this was my chance. Hopefully, the first of many.

Ervo said, "Precisely why you should remain here. The group doesn't need someone who won't watch their own back."

I scowled at him. "My back doesn't need watching. North's does; she's the important one."

His eyes pierced mine. "Every female is important."

"Which is exactly why I'm going with the group, to retrieve the ones in hiding." I turned back to the lake, trying to calm my furiously-beating heart.

There was a long, tense moment of silence between us before Ervo spoke again.

This time, his voice was so low I barely heard it at all. "Should something happen, my full name is Viervo."

My eyes widened.

Giving someone your full name, in Vevol, gave them power over you.

No one gave out their full name.

"Vee-air-vo?" I quietly pronounced the name, trying to embed it in my memory. Admittedly, I was terrible at remembering the fae's strange names, and the pronunciations were even more difficult.

"Yes."

I swallowed roughly, still staring out at the lake. "Thanks. I'm not going to need help, though."

There was another brief moment of silence.

I felt more than saw Ervo's body slowly tensing.

"Should something happen to you, I would burn this whole fucking world down to get you back," he finally said.

The unevenness in his voice surprised me, but I tried not to show him that.

"Like a brother, right?" I asked.

He blinked. "Of course."

I shook my head, turning and striding away before I could overthink our relationship even more than I already had.

It was time for me to move on. Life in Vevol might not have been short, but it definitely wasn't long enough to continue mooning over a man who loved me like a sister.

"Ready?" North called from across the beach.

"You have no idea," I called back.

She grinned, and I shifted forms. My body grew and elongated until I was in my slim, sapphire dragon form. I was much smaller than any of the other dragons I'd seen, which Ervo had said was because I was female. When I compared the size of him in his phoenix form to the size of January in hers, it made sense.

And I didn't hate that he was larger than me, regardless of our form.

But I wasn't allowed to think that about him.

Or to feel that about him.

It was time to focus.

Time to change the damn world... even if said world was small, and full of people I didn't particularly like.

North and Sunny climbed up onto my back, both of them still in their human forms. North was a hellhound and Sunny was a basilisk, so they needed a ride across the lake, to the supposed hiding place of a group of fae women. Dots and January were both phoenixes, so they could fly themselves, but they were constantly on fire given the nature of their forms.

I knew phoenixes could put out their flames because Ervo had done so for me when we'd been abducted by a bunch of hellhounds. But it took constant focus, which Dots and January hadn't quite mastered, so I'd been elected to carry the other girls.

I didn't mind. Honestly, it felt good to be needed, even just in the way a boat or car was.

Ervo's hand landed on the side of my neck, and my head jerked toward him. I knew it was him before I looked, because of his stupidly-incredible smell.

"Be careful," Ervo told me, his voice low. "I'll fly with you for as long as I can."

Not knowing what to say to him, I just nodded.

"Is there a force field or something that will prevent them from going in with us?" Sunny asked North.

"Not that I know of." North shrugged.

"There isn't. If there was, we would've found it by now," Priel said.

"I wish I was going," January grumbled from a few feet away. Her arms were crossed over her chest, and Lian's were wrapped around her abdomen.

From what I'd gathered, they weren't going anywhere near the female fae's hiding place. That was probably the best call, even if it wasn't what she wanted. Bringing a pregnant woman into an unknown situation that could potentially be dangerous wouldn't exactly have been smart.

Off to the other side, I noticed Nev and Dots talking, and she was smiling, of course.

That girl typically always smiled when she was talking to him. I wasn't sure exactly why they hadn't gotten together yet, but she always told me that they were just friends, and she wasn't interested in more.

"Let's get moving!" Sunny called out from behind me. "The sooner we drag more women into this shit, the better."

A snort escaped me, and a puff of smoke with it.

I felt Ervo's gaze—and the palm he still had on my neck—but ignored both of them.

The other gazes I felt belonged to a group of hellhounds who thought they owed me their lives, but that shit could wait a few days.

Or a few years, if I was lucky.

"Alright, I'm ready," Dots agreed, though she sounded reluctant. "What are the odds that the women like fighting as much as the men do?"

"Pretty high, I'd guess," North said with a shrug. "Only one way to find out. If it's triggering, you can fly back here and wait with the guys and January."

Ervo went unnaturally still beside me.

That wasn't a good sign.

"Wait," Priel growled. "You think they're going to *attack you*? And you want me to watch you fly away on the back of a dragon who just barely learned to shift? Not a damn—"

"Go, Mare," Sunny yelled.

The old me from a few weeks ago would've stopped to overthink it. To consider all the options. To debate that shit.

But the old me had been ripped out of the comfortable home she considered a sanctuary, wounded by a random fae man, and dragged across a magical world—only to watch the man I trusted most literally sever a head from a body.

My life had flashed before my eyes, and when it did, it occurred to me that I hadn't ever really felt alive.

Now, I was going to live.

Even if it killed me.

So I pushed off the ground, flapped hard, and carried us into the sky.

We wouldn't really have a head start, but hopefully we wouldn't need it.

Furious roars followed us into the sky.

"Hurry!" North yelled.

I was already going as fast as I could. Dots was right behind us, too.

"Do you really think they're going to attack us?" Sunny yelled to North.

"I have no idea," North called back.

Sunny muttered something I couldn't hear, in response.

Ervo caught up to me faster than I expected. He was carrying Nev, Teris, and Priel, but didn't even seem to be straining under their stupidly-massive weight.

He roared at me again, and then swerved in front of me in an attempt to cut me off.

Diving downward, I flapped more forcefully, pushing myself harder.

The water in front of me shimmered, and I squinted my eyes a bit.

It almost looked like... land.

"There," North yelled. "I see an island! It's hidden, like the Stronghold was!"

She must've noticed the shimmering too.

I wasn't fantastic at landings—especially fast ones—but launched toward it.

Multiple roars followed us as I crashed on the island, digging my talons into the dirt and trying like hell to stay upright.

My head shot upward, and I watched the men dive toward us.

My scaly jaw dropped open as they cut *through* the tall, tropical trees surrounding us, going straight through branches and trunks like the trees were nothing but an illusion.

"Well, this is a bigger disguise than the Stronghold's was," North muttered.

I looked back at her, Sunny, and Dots.

Dots was on her knees on the soft white sand with her head clutched between her hands. Sunny climbed off my back and hurried over to her.

North remained where she was on my back, staring up at the sky.

"Guess we're on our own," she murmured to me.

Above us, the men were absolutely furious.

Well... Ervo and Priel were, at least.

Nev and Teris seemed to be just along for the ride.

We could hear their roars as they barreled through more trees, over our heads.

I tensed as Ervo dove toward the ground, and let out a breath of relief when he simply went *through* the island's floor a few yards in front of us, as if it too didn't exist to the men.

We were completely hidden from them.

North slid off my back, rubbing at her head as I shifted to my human form. Or fae form, I supposed.

"You okay?" I murmured to her, watching the men lose their shit above us.

"Yeah. I can still hear Priel, though. Through the mate bond. He's pissed, to say the least." Her grimace was deep. "Wants us to get back in the sky. But if we leave this place, I know there's not a chance he'll let me come back here."

I felt eyes on us, and spun around.

Ervo was the usual source of that feeling—or the hellhound pack that had decided they were my protectors.

But when my eyes landed on the fae women standing between the trees, my lips parted.

"Holy shit," North gasped, apparently seeing what I did.

Or *who* I did.

The women stared at us.

We stared back.

They... didn't really look like us.

Their skin seemed to run in the same varying shades of brown, black, tan, olive, and white as ours, and they had magical tattoos the same way some of us did, but that was where the similarities ended.

Their eyes were larger. Wider. Rounder. The colors of said eyes were brighter and more vibrant, too.

Their magical tattoos were bigger, covered more of their skin, and *glowed*.

Their fingers were tipped with long nails, shaped into claws.

Where we had different degrees of curves, they were flat-chested.

Every inch of them was roped in muscle, just like the fae men. And considering that the fae valued strength, I had a feeling that was going to be an extremely attractive quality to the men we interacted with.

Looking at them, I understood why Vevol, the world's goddess, had hidden them away. And why she allowed us to be brought to her world.

Because we had still been humans once—we were still from Earth.

But the female fae belonged to the goddess.

"I definitely think they like fighting," Dots whispered, and I realized she and Sunny had come up behind North and I. "Is it too late to change my mind?"

"Yup," Sunny muttered. "We come in peace!" she called out, stepping up next to North, and dragging Dots with her.

One of the fae women stepped forward, emerging from the trees as if she had been a part of the forest.

My eyes widened at the sight of her markings. They weren't glowing, like the other women's; they were brands, like North's.

I looked at the others, checking for other brands, but found nothing. All I did was get a better look at the women.

Unlike us, they had on flowing dresses. The dresses looked like they were made of a similar fabric to the stretchy, fireproof clothing the seelie fae wore, but had sweetheart necklines, no straps, and a massive slit up to the belly button, revealing what looked like a thin band of underwear.

So basically, they were the sexier, more magical version of us.

For the most part, that was a relief. They would take a lot of the male attention.

But... at the same time, what would it mean for me?

I knew it was a selfish question, but I'd never found a fae man who wanted to be with me, and honestly, that was something I wanted tremendously.

A sexy male fae to rub my feet while I read? Or to talk about books with me? Or to cook with me, asking me about my day?

Or just to look at me the way Lian looked at January, and the way Priel looked at North?

Shit, I ached for that. For all of it.

But the one man I had ever been interested in saw me as a sister, and was cock-blocking every other guy who might be attracted to me. At first, I had wanted the cock-blocking, because a hundred suitors was way too many.

I had regretted that decision for months, though.

"What are you?" the fae woman with all the brands asked. She had dark brown skin about the same shade as mine, and her bright-white hair was done in gorgeous box braids that draped over her shoulders and fell below her ass. Given the wild genetics the fae seemed to have, I would've put money on the hair being natural.

And hell, the woman even had a sexy accent to go with all the rest of her hotness.

I noticed some kind of vines wrapped around her head like a crown, and realized she had to be a leader of some sort.

Sunny answered for us. "We're from another world, as crazy as it sounds. The men pulled us through portals, and we became fae. Not as fae as you, apparently, but still. Fae."

"Vevol sent us here," North finally said. "She spoke to me in a vision. I have her brands, like you do."

The fae women were silent for a moment.

I tried to count them, but honestly, they were unfairly skilled at hiding behind trees and bushes and things. There were at least three dozen; probably more, since those were just the ones that stuck out to me.

"Please don't kill us," Dots finally said.

The leader-woman scowled. "We do not kill without reason."

"We led a bunch of pissed-off men to your doorstep," Sunny pointed out. "That seems like a reason."

North elbowed her in the side, and she grunted.

"Vevol herself hides us. We will not be found unless she wishes us to," the leader-woman said.

Another moment of tense silence followed.

"Has Vevol spoken to you about this?" North finally asked her. "About leaving your island, and rejoining the men?"

"She has," the woman said in response.

We waited.

Finally, she added with great reluctance, "We were instructed to wait for a sign. I suppose *you* are the sign."

"I guess so," North agreed, glancing up at the sky as Ervo dove toward us again.

The bastards wouldn't give up. It just wasn't something the fae could do.

"How many of you are there?" the leader asked. "And how many of the men still live?"

"About six hundred men," North said. "And twenty ex-human women."

The leader raised her eyebrows. "More than we expected."

"Yeah, they're pretty evenly divided between seelie and unseelie, too," North added.

The leader's forehead wrinkled. "Wild and controlled? What does this mean?"

Huh?

Had the fae not been divided into factions before the women were hidden away?

North's grimace told me she was wondering the same thing.

"You will tell us of the world as it is now while we gather our things," the leader decided. "If we are to leave our home, we won't do so empty-handed."

"Okay," North agreed, though she glanced up at the sky again. I noticed her gaze lingering on her mate, and that she looked kind of worried.

He had definitely been pissed about the abandonment.

"Do you need to go back to Priel?" I asked her softly.

She shook her head quickly. "He's fine. Angry, but since he can talk to me, he knows I'm okay. It's the other men that are losing their shit."

"Which of them?" Sunny's whisper was kind of hopeful.

"Ervo," she admitted.

I scowled.

He needed to make up his mind. Did he want me to be his mate, or didn't he?

"One of us needs to head out to show them that we're okay," she said, looking at me.

"Mare is our ride out of here, so not her," Sunny said. "Dots is the only real choice, since she's the only other one with wings."

We all looked at Dots.

She smiled. "I volunteer as tribute."

Sunny snorted, and Dots winked at all of us before she took to the sky, shifting quickly and soaring up toward the larger phoenix.

The larger phoenix who did, admittedly, look like he was losing his shit.

"You care for them," the leader said, and our attention jerked back to her. "The men in the sky."

My face warmed, and I answered for us, pointing to North. "She's mated to one of them. The rest are just... like family, I guess."

Sunny made a gagging noise at my explanation.

She definitely had feelings for Teris, even if he didn't respond well to said feelings.

The lead-woman's forehead wrinkled, but she gestured for us to follow her without asking another question.

After we exchanged uncertain glances, we went.

Two

The men in the sky calmed down when Dots joined them. Ervo continued flying wide circles above the general area we had disappeared in, and honestly, seemed to have figured out the exact space that the island filled.

I kept an eye on them as we jogged into the island's tropical version of a forest behind the women, struggling to keep up. The trees were different there, taller and slimmer, but still with the same shiny-smooth bark. Unlike the other forest, where most of the trunks were either black or white, with the occasional one matching the vibrant color of its leaves, every one of the trees had a bright greenish-blue trunk.

It made the land feel much more alien to me, but not in a way I disliked.

When we finally reached the center of the island, we found groups of women already packing their things into massive bags that looked like they were designed to be carried in massive talons or claws—probably for flying, I assumed. The fae women took down their colorful fabric tents with ease, quickly packing them along with everything else.

"You really were waiting for us," Sunny remarked to the leader, who seemed to be supervising the clean-up party.

"Of course. When Vevol speaks, we listen."

Wise words, I supposed.

"Tell me of your humans, and the state of the men. Particularly their leadership, and division," the leader-woman commanded us.

All of us remained silent, glancing at each other.

"You rule, do you not?" the leader growled at North. "The most branded one is always the ruler."

"Oh, no. Definitely not," North said quickly. "I've only been here for a year and a half or so. Well, almost two years now, I guess."

The woman's narrowed eyes told me she didn't think that was a good reason for North not to be the ruler.

"We're the wrong people to ask about the world's history," I admitted. "North and Priel only just mated. We have a friend waiting on that side of the lake who would know a lot more than we do; she's pregnant, so she couldn't come with us."

The woman's eyes widened. "A life-bringer?"

I blinked.

Life-bringer?

"I guess so?" I said.

"Are all of you life-bringers?" Her gaze swiveled around to each of us. "Can all of your humans grow children?"

"Most human women can, yes," I confirmed. "We assumed it was the same on Vevol. Is it not?"

"We have only ten life-bringers remaining," the woman said. "The rest of us are merely their protectors. We will proceed with locating the strongest, most fertile males to pair with our life-bringers when we've settled. Our world must be replenished."

I blinked again.

And again.

Apparently fertility wasn't a given here.

That was... something.

"If you are also life-bringers, we will arrange males for you too," she said, as if reassuring me.

I fought the urge to take a step back.

Sunny *did* take a step back, and positioned herself behind me and North.

North cleared her throat. "Looks like you guys are almost done packing up. Should we go? My mate's probably worried about me..."

Yeah, I was on board with getting off this island.

At least with the men at our sides, we were safer. I didn't like the idea of being thrown into an arranged mating as a *life-bringer* one bit.

"No. There is more to be done. Tell me what you know of these factions," she commanded.

North looked at me.

Her expression told me she did *not* want to be the one spilling seelie and unseelie secrets.

Sunny would've already spoken up if she intended to, I knew.

"I'll tell you what we know, if you tell us what *you* know. None of the male fae remember that you exist, so we know nothing about you or your way of life," I said.

Honestly, I felt kind of proud of myself for taking charge. It had been a long time coming.

"Very well." She dipped her head in a nod, looking out at the group. "There are two classes of fae. Among the males, there are the soft—who were made to care for the life-bringers—and the brutal—who were made to sire new, strong children with the life-bringers. Among the women, there are the harsh—who defend the life-bringers—and the light, who *are* the life-bringers."

Daaaaamn.

Well, I didn't see that coming.

Not even a little.

It was strange, but also fascinating.

Granted, it would've been more fascinating had I known I wasn't about to be dragged into this society.

The leader had paused long enough to make it clear that it was my turn to share information.

"When we were brought into this world, we were told that there are two types of fae: seelie, and unseelie. The seelie are wild, and refuse to follow any leadership. They prize freedom above all else, but the strongest of them are called the Wild Hunt, and speak for them as a whole when there's a problem. The unseelies value control over themselves, and they have a king. His name is Aev. They call him the Tame King, because he's mated, I guess."

She frowned. "Mated? You said this word before, but I don't understand."

Well, can't say I saw that coming.

How could they not know about mating?

"When a male and female fae make vows, or kiss, it starts a connection between them," I explained. "They start to smell like each other. When they have sex, it seals the bond between them, and they become mates. They can communicate mentally, and their lives are tied together."

Her eyes widened in horror. "This is done by those who are not life-bringers?"

I blinked. "It's done by some of us, yes."

She shook her head, hard. "This is a disgrace."

"So your life-bringers are the only ones who have sex? Or take mates?" I asked.

"There are no *mates*. Creating life establishes a mental bond between the life-bringer and the brutal she is with. That bond is only used to arrange when the next meeting will be. The brutal is not involved in any other aspect of the female's life; that would be an atrocity."

I admitted. "On Earth, we marry for life. A man and woman become a partner, permanently." I didn't need to bring up divorce, I decided. "I guess the male fae took part of our culture and part of yours, and combined them."

She scowled. "The Great War came because the head brutal passed, and the men couldn't determine their next leader. The brutal males slaughtered the soft as they destroyed each other. We harsh joined the fight to defend the brutal connected to our life-bringers, but the damage had already been done. By the time Vevol hid us away, it was too late."

My throat swelled. "I guess it makes sense that the men divided themselves the way they did, if a power struggle was the cause of their war. How many harsh do you have?"

"Nearly two hundred." She spat the words, which surprised me. "And only the smallest fraction of our life-bringers, who once outnumbered us greatly."

She had said ten, before. And damn, that *was* a small fraction.

"Are any of the life-bringers connected to men outside the island?" North asked her.

"No. The bonded brutals were targeted for the strength our life-bringers added to them."

Right; the mated fae were supposedly stronger than the unmated.

"It is a privilege to add your human female to our number of life-bringers. When we've settled on the mainland again, we will immediately test the rest of you, to determine your class."

"How do you test for that?" Sunny checked. "Wait for a period or something? None of us have had those since we left Earth."

The leader looked at her like she'd spoken another language.

Sunny grimaced. "Bad joke?"

"There is a ritual—a blood exchange. Vevol speaks through her leader—which is me—after a number of sacrifices have been made."

I tried not to gag.

Animal sacrifices?

"What kind of sacrifices?" North growled, apparently thinking the same thing I was.

"Plants are crushed and burned. Feathers and scales, pulled. Hair is cut."

I noticed North tucking her forever-long hair behind her shoulders, as if to protect it.

Something told me her mate wouldn't let anyone sacrifice her damn hair if she didn't want them to.

We all relaxed a bit at the answer, though.

"What if North has more brands than you?" Sunny asked.

I nearly groaned, and saw North flash her a glare.

"Then I will abdicate to North," the leader said smoothly. "Assuming she is a harsh, and not a life-bringer. The life-bringers have their own ruler."

"Where is she?" Sunny checked, looking around at the women who seemed nearly done with packing their things.

I was doing the same.

"Hidden away, as she will be until we know she and the others are properly protected and have multiplied across our land." The leader's voice was hard, with that answer. "Now, we shall go."

"What's your name?" I asked her.

"Fovea," she said, pronounced fo-vee-uh.

"You don't give out your full names, though, right?" North asked.

Fovea looked at her, aghast. "Of course not."

Well, at least one thing as we knew it hadn't changed.

THE WOMEN FINISHED PACKING SOON after that, and then the ex-humans and I shifted with all of them.

Rather than taking them to the edge of the lake, where we had camped with the Wild Hunt guys, we were heading right back to the new Stronghold. That had been North's call, after talking to Priel, and I thought it was a good one. If we stopped on the edge of the lake for a few days, the women would have the time and space to recreate their awful class system while trying to incorporate us into it, which none of us wanted.

I flew Sunny and North back to the lake, landing on the beach so they could climb off and run the rest of the way. North was already in Priel's arms before her feet hit the dirt, and he was growling at her. Probably cursing, too.

They were so damn adorable.

January and Lian were gone, already headed back to the Stronghold. Them getting there early was also good call, I thought, so that the fae ladies wouldn't try to abduct her in the name of life-bringers everywhere.

Ervo stood next to the other unmated men, glowering at me.

His usually-calm façade had vanished, and visible fury replaced it.

I tried to take off before he could reach me, but Sunny wasn't far enough for me to spread my wings yet, and his massive hand wrapped possessively around the back of my thick, scaly neck.

"You fly with me, female," he snarled at me.

I jerked away, shifting forms as I did.

That turned out to be a bad call, because that hand he had wrapped around the back of my neck was much more threatening when I was so much smaller than him.

"No way. Look." I gestured to the sky, at the literal *hundreds* of women above us. "I'm even less special now. No one will threaten me."

"The other women are an unknown factor, and I don't trust them with your safety," he said. "You *will* ride me."

I almost laughed, but managed to stop myself.

The bastard definitely didn't know he was making a sexual command.

"That is not your call, *Vi*ervo," I said, emphasizing the first part of his name. The part that made the word a magical connection between us. "And besides, the women up there are watching for the strongest, fiercest men to *breed with*. You don't want me *riding you* right now."

He stepped closer to me, his grip on the back of my neck tightening as my face tilted upward so our eyes met.

My chest rose and fell rapidly, my body flushing under his attention.

His voice was measured when he finally said, "Those females change nothing for me. You will fly on my back, or you won't fly at all."

My eyebrows shot upward. "Is that a *threat*?"

"No, *Mariah*. It's a promise."

My heart plunged into my stomach, and a tingle rolled up my spine. Absently, I realized we were the only ones left on the beach. "How did you learn my name?"

"I listen," he said calmly.

Fury had me clenching my fists. "If you ever use that to control me, the *female brother* connection we have will end."

I felt eyes on my back, and Ervo's jaw clenched. "Your hellhounds have arrived."

Of course they had.

"Will you ride me, or will you walk at my side?" The phoenix asked me, his voice still level.

I fought the urge to knee him in the damned balls. "I'll ride on your back, but this is the last time. Understand?"

He didn't answer me—instead, he tugged me up onto his strong, feathery back as he took off from the ground, hauling me into the sky with him.

Adrenaline had my heart pounding in my chest as I leaned against his neck. Though he wasn't on fire, I was pretty sure that even if he had been, it wouldn't burn me.

He hung back behind the rest of the group, but followed them steadily as we flew. My fingers dug into the soft, golden feathers on his neck, my eyelids lowering a bit at the warm comfort of the contact. I hadn't realized how stressed I was until I was relaxing against his literally-hot body.

It didn't register for me as we flew, that we were getting further and further behind the other group, until we were nearly at the Stronghold.

He waited until the others had begun landing and everyone was distracted, before veering off smoothly to the right.

I sat up, but he began weaving around the tallest trees so rapidly that it made my heart pump. The man was silent, his movements so sharp and controlled that it made my head spin.

If I thought he'd give me an answer, I would've asked him where we were going.

Instead I remained quiet, gripping his feathers.

He and I didn't agree on many things—if any—but I definitely didn't fear for my life with him. I'd never trusted anyone to keep me safe the way I did Ervo.

If anything, the further we got from the new Stronghold and the fae women, the calmer I felt.

ANOTHER FEW HOURS PASSED, and night engulfed us completely by the time Ervo finally slowed.

We were at the top of a tall mountain that was absolutely covered in trees, and my exhausted eyes traced the view slowly.

It was gorgeous, just like the rest of Vevol.

Ervo dove toward the trees, then shifted suddenly. A shriek escaped me as we plummeted—and cut off completely when his feet hit the ground.

When I realized I had been held firmly in his arms the entire time, I let out a huff. "Where are we?"

"My home."

I looked around the place while still in the man's arms.

It was wide and open, with bookshelves lining every inch of the walls other than the small kitchen, and a bathroom. The corners of the home were made up of tree trunks, and I realized I could see the forest around and below us from the patio we had landed on.

A monster-sized mattress was the only piece of furniture other than the bookshelves, and it sat in the middle of the room.

"Why are we at your house?" I asked him, as he carried me toward said mattress. My stomach rumbled angrily, and I grimaced.

His jaw set, and he placed me carefully on the bed before striding toward the kitchen.

"You can't haul me away to your treehouse and then ignore me when I ask you why," I argued, standing up.

That bed smelled *way* too much like Ervo for my sanity.

He pulled out a pot and pan, his movements jerky as he filled one with water, grabbing ingredients after he set it on the stove.

Finally, he said through clenched teeth, "It's been ages since I've seen you, and then you vanished into thin air. I'm on the last shred of my sanity, and could break the fragile peace that exists right now should I snap."

I blinked. "Why are you on the last shred of your sanity?"

He didn't answer right away, continuing to cook in jerky movements that made me worry he might cut off a finger or something.

After a few minutes passed, I decided he probably wasn't going to tell me.

I changed the question as I strode over to the nearest bookshelf. "How long is it going to take you to calm down, then?"

"A few days, I'd guess."

Well, that wasn't so bad.

"If you tell me why you're so bent out of shape about me being out of your sight, maybe I could help," I remarked, tugging a book off the shelf and flipping through the pages even though I was too tired to focus on the words.

He didn't answer for a few minutes.

The smell of sizzling food made my stomach growl again.

Ervo's voice was strained when he said, "You're mine."

"Your girl-brother, yes," I mumbled, my gaze stuck to the pages as I realized what I'd found on his shelf.

A poetry book.

I *loved* poetry.

The emotion, the lyrical quality of the words, the way everything flowed...

The right poetry just made me feel things so, so strongly.

Why did Ervo have a poem book, though? He definitely didn't seem like an emotional man.

"Exactly," he said with a growl.

"So you're worried that me—your sister—is in danger when you can't see me physically in front of you?" I asked absently, my mind buried in the poem in front of my eyes.

"Yes."

I glanced up at him, and saw him stirring the food violently. "Don't destroy the beans."

"They're not beans," he growled back.

Well, he was touchy tonight. Showing me all the emotions he usually kept hidden.

"It calmed you down when we shared a bed back in the hellhounds' territory. Would that help you get your shit together faster?" I checked.

"It would," he said stiffly.

"Okay, we'll both sleep in your bed—on separate sides of course—and try to leave in the morning so no one comes looking for me. How does that sound?"

He jerked his head in a nod.

His shoulders didn't seem relaxed at all, but when we'd shared a bed after the abduction, it really had chilled him out instantly. I didn't even think he had slept, but he'd been like a new man when I woke up.

And since I definitely didn't see *him* as a brother, I had no problem with it.

He finished cooking while I tried—and failed—to focus on the poems in the book I'd found. Afterward, we ate together, sitting on the edge of his mattress.

And then we silently slid into spots on opposite sides of the bed.

I clung to my edge, and was quickly overwhelmed by the calming scent of the man next to me. It knocked me out in little more than a heartbeat.

THREE

I WOKE up sweating all over Ervo.

My tank top had ridden up to just below my boobs, so over half of my bare chest was plastered to his. A massive, hot hand was draped over my ass—which was thankfully still covered—and the other had slid beneath my top and curled around my ribs. His fingertips were pressing into the rim of my nipple, and damn, I had no idea that could be a turn-on.

Ervo's breathing was steady, though, his body so relaxed that I didn't think he was awake yet.

...which meant I had time to salvage this shitshow.

I was on top of him, on his side of the bed, so clearly my sleep-self had decided to be a needy bitch. This whole thing was my fault, and I needed to end it.

Quickly.

I carefully wiggled my arms out—one from underneath his back, and the other from between our bodies.

His breathing was still steady, phew.

Now, to deal with *his* arms...

I huffed out a breath as I glanced backward, at the one on my ass.

How dare he hold my butt so possessively while declaring that he didn't want to be anything but friends?

Or *siblings*?

I knew he was into me—he just wouldn't admit it.

So, I eased his arm away from my ass as I rolled slightly away.

Instead of letting go of me—like a normal sleeping person—his fingers dug into my crack.

I inhaled sharply.

The ones on the other hand tightened on my nipple, and I squeaked.

Ervo's eyes opened slowly, and collided with mine.

My lips parted as I watched his brown skin redden, just the tiniest bit.

He was blushing.

Blushing, blushing.

Holy shit, why was that so adorable?

He slowly released my nipple, and withdrew his hand from beneath my tank.

The fingers in my crack moved even slower than the others, but finally, he removed that hand too.

I rolled off of him and hurried to the bathroom before either of us had to say anything.

Though I didn't need to, I grabbed the bar of scratchy soap by the sink and started scrubbing at my hands quickly. They weren't dirty, but it gave me something to do, and sort of distracted me from my problem.

Which was waking up in bed with a man I had ultimate, strong, hot feelings for. And his hands had been touching me, in ways I really, really liked.

And...

Shit, I needed to focus on my soap. If only it wasn't so *soapy*.

Eventually I gave up on my hands, used the facilities, and finally emerged from the bathroom.

Ervo was already cooking again.

My stomach growled hopefully as I went back to the book of poetry I hadn't managed to focus on the night before. I feigned thumbing through it as I called across the room, "How are you feeling?"

"Better," he admitted. "Much better."

Thank the damned heavens.

"Think we can go back today, then?" I asked.

"Yes."

Phew.

That was a major relief.

I wasn't sure I could manage another wake-up like today's without rubbing myself all over him like an animal in heat.

"We'll eat, and then head out. If we're lucky, no one realized we were gone."

"I can tell them we got lost," I said, though I questioned myself immediately afterward.

Ervo's silence told me no one would believe that, but he didn't bring it up again, so I didn't either.

I kept my eyes on the book while we ate, reading silently, and then slid it back on the shelf while he took my plate back to his sink for me. When I offered to clean up, he gave me a simple, neutral, "No."

So, I watched him.

And wondered how the hell I'd gotten unlucky enough to have feelings for the one male in all of Vevol who only wanted me to be his sister.

WE LEFT when he finished with the dishes, and this time, I flew on my own. I could smell his scent on my scales, as we flew, which did strange things to my head. I tried to ignore that, though.

THE STRONGHOLD WAS a chaotic mess when we arrived. The female fae seemed to have set up shop inside it and around it, so the thing was surrounded by their colorful tents.

I'd put money on the life-bringers being locked inside, though.

Ervo didn't try to stop me when I slipped away from him, weaving around the tents on my way to the door. People were coming and going, and no one paid me a spare glance, so I didn't even have to lie about getting lost.

When I finally made it into the building, the human chick who was usually guarding it was gone.

In her place were four big, mean-looking fae ladies.

They glared at me, but waved me in.

I silently headed up the stairs, my chest feeling tight as I went.

I found Sunny and Dots back in our room already, both of them sprawled across their beds like we'd never left.

And shit, I *hated* that idea.

The Stronghold had started feeling like something of a prison, recently.

"You guys are staying here?" I asked them.

Sunny made a face. "We don't have a choice. The fae chicks are calling the shots now, and they're not letting any of us out of here until the ritual to determine whether or not we're life-bringers. I think the fae guys are going to man-up soon and have a talk about things not being the same way they used to be, but who knows when that will happen."

Shit.

"Where are North and January?" I checked.

"Their mates swept them away like knights in shining armor," Sunny grumbled. "Ours, as you can see, did not."

No kidding.

"Where did Ervo take you?" Dots wondered.

I grimaced. "He was all stressed. Took me to his treehouse. We ate food, slept in the same bed, and then he was good to go."

Dots's expression grew apologetic, and Sunny just snorted.

"He's so clueless," she said.

"Right?" I dropped to my mattress. "It was nice to get out of here for a few days when we went after the other ladies, though."

"It really was. I want to live in a tree house, far from here," Dots said with a sigh. "One with a really good view. It would be nice to wake up to silence, and just look out at the forest every morning."

"Amen," Sunny agreed, holding her fist out to Dots. Dots bumped it.

Her words made me ache for the same thing—but not just any treehouse.

The one I wanted, I could clearly envision. With so damn many bookshelves, and a massive bed that smelled like utter heaven, and food sizzling on the stove while a gorgeous monster of a man stirred violently...

Okay, maybe I was getting a little too particular.

"I need to figure out a way to make him realize that he doesn't just see me as a sister," I admitted.

"Girl, what you need is to take a page out of North's book," Sunny said.

I flashed her a confused look.

"What she did with Clevv? Started looking for another mate, just to ignite the yummy possessiveness? I'd do it myself, if I wasn't so damn positive that Teris would hand me lube as I walked away."

Dots rolled her eyes. "He wouldn't do that."

"Yeah, he would."

My forehead wrinkled as memories of Clevv sprung to mind. "That whole thing didn't work out well for North—or the rest of us."

Sunny shrugged. "We're all still alive. North and Priel are mated. Clevv's in the ground. Things were rough for a minute, but it did work out."

I grimaced. "I don't know..."

"You have all those hellhounds who think they owe you their lives," Dots said. "What if you tell one of them that a kiss to make Ervo jealous is his way to repay you, and that he has to walk away afterward without looking at you again?"

That... well, it wasn't the worst idea I'd ever heard.

Then again, we had come up with a vast number of shitty ideas in the years we'd been locked in the Stronghold. Most of which involved the fae men in some way, and never ended up happening.

"I'll think about it," I finally said.

"Doooo ittt," Sunny put on a thick, fake fae accent, and I snorted.

Dots laughed.

"We so need a way out of here. I can't take another few weeks of this." Sunny gestured around us. "I miss the bastard who doesn't even want me as his mate. How screwy is that?"

"Not screwy," Dots said. "You care about him. Caring about someone isn't a problem."

"Right, but I care more. Which *is* a problem."

"Then maybe you really *should* kiss another guy," Dots suggested.

"Eh." Sunny made a face. "I don't know."

"We don't have to decide anything today. Maybe we should try to escape and see what all is going on out there," I suggested.

I'd been in such a hurry to get away from Ervo that I hadn't considered I'd be locked in the Stronghold again when I walked in, honestly.

"We tried a few hours ago and got shut down. The unseelie girls did too. They're hiding out in their own rooms, and they seemed just as annoyed as us. Except the mated ones; they seemed kind of relieved to have some protection from the guys they're paired with."

"Do the men have anything to say about the female fae's thoughts about mating?" I checked.

"We got thrown in here before we could find out," Sunny said with a shrug.

I grimaced. "When is the thing to determine whether or not we're life-bringers going to happen?"

"Tomorrow, I think. The harsh ones are really excited about it."

I made a face, but didn't move to get up.

Guess it was going to be a long day.

TIME CREPT by so damn slowly.

When the afternoon came around, I was peering out the window, trying to locate anyone who might stand a chance at getting me out of there. I'd already attempted to get past the harsh ladies downstairs, but no dice. They weren't budging.

After our last adventure, I was done sitting on my ass. I wanted to live, dammit.

Sunny was throwing a pillow in the air and catching it, bored out of her mind.

"Alright," Dots finally said. "I didn't want to do this, but Nev taught me how to use our nature magic. I can break us out of here. It will probably piss off the female fae, though, and this is a dangerous time to do that."

I whipped around, staring at her.

I gaped at her. "You've known this since we got here?"

"Why do we care about pissing them off? They're going to find out that we're life-bringers and try to lock us up somewhere!" Sunny exclaimed.

Dots's face turned pink. "If we go out there, we're going to have to rely on the Wild Hunt to protect us from the fae women. I didn't want to put them in that position."

"And you don't trust them completely," Sunny said with a sigh.

"They're violent." She lifted a shrug. "It's a personal rule not to trust anyone violent."

"The harsh women seem just as dangerous," Sunny pointed out.

"I've never been hurt by a woman," Dots said simply. "But you guys are right; I'm tired of hiding away. Vevol is beautiful, and I want to live in it. Not just sit around watching movies about humans living lives that will never be ours again. I want to build myself a house in the trees, and decide my own destiny."

"That was basically a Disney movie monologue, but I support it," Sunny told her with a grin.

Dots blush crept over her shoulders and down her arms.

"Alright, let's get out of here," Dots said, turning toward the wall.

I watched carefully as she walked up to it, putting her hands on the stone and closing her eyes.

One minute passed, and then another.

There was no sign that she was figuring anything out, but we waited.

Finally, there was a groaning noise, and an uneven crack appeared in the wall.

It slowly, slowly, widened.

Twenty minutes must've passed before it was finally large enough for one of us to fit through. A quick glance out the window showed that we had the complete attention from pretty much every visible man outside; the women were all busy collecting shit to sacrifice, or guarding the door.

I was sure they'd be pissed when they realized we were sneaking out, but screw them.

They'd locked us up.

"I can't jump out of that thing," Sunny hissed. "I don't have wings, remember?"

"We can jump together. I should be able to shift fast enough to carry us both out of here, and I'm sure my hellhounds will follow us, so we'll be fine."

"Where are we going to go, though?" Dots asked, breathing rapidly after the effort of using her magic. "What if we get separated?"

"Then we meet at the old Stronghold," Sunny said firmly. "Let's do this. It's risky, but it's only a matter of time before the other women realize where we're going and try to stop us. So... let's scram."

She was right.

"You first," Dots told me.

Sunny wrapped her arms around my waist as we wormed our way through the crack in the wall. A sharp bit of stone sliced through the back of my thigh, making me wince, but I didn't stop.

We were getting the hell out.

I waited on the ledge, letting my gaze skim the small crowd that had gathered below us and in the sky above us.

My chest swelled, and I realized what we had to do.

"Do you trust me?" I asked Sunny.

"As long as you get us away from these crazy chicks," Sunny hissed. "I'm not ready to be anyone's baby mama."

Make that two of us.

"Agreed!" Dots called from behind us.

"Then we fly straight into that crowd, toward all of the men who look like seelies," I said firmly.

The seelies wouldn't let anyone control them, and hopefully, that meant they wouldn't let anyone control us.

"If you say so," Sunny grumbled.

She was plastered to my back, then, gripping me like a lifeline, so it was time.

I let out a slow breath, and jumped.

Time seemed to slow around me as my body elongated and transformed. Sunny shrieked as she struggled to hang on to my widening belly.

A massive phoenix dropped out of the sky and plucked her off of my back, hauling the cursing Sunny as he flew level with me.

I looked over at Ervo, gratitude swelling in my chest.

Dots caught up a moment later, lining up on my other side.

It was time to make a decision.

I really didn't want to, but...

I was doing it.

Tucking my wings, I dove downward. My body spiraled toward the ground like a real damn fae's.

I shifted just before I landed, and my feet hit the ground. They did so with way too much force, and I accidentally launched into some guy a few feet away from me.

He crashed to the dirt, and I landed right the hell on top of him.

"Sorry," I groaned.

He laughed wildly in response. "That was badass, Mare."

The man knew my nickname.

Of course he did.

There were so many more men interested in all of us than we had ever even met.

A pair of massive hands grabbed me by the waist and hauled me off the male fae's chest. I was set on my feet, facing a narrow-eyed Ervo.

"What are you doing?" he asked me.

I noticed Teris and Nev near Sunny and Dots, too.

"The female fae locked us in our room and refused to let us leave the Stronghold," I told Ervo, forcing my voice and expression to remain even. "We assumed that the seelie, of all people, would understand how shitty it is to be controlled."

Growls of agreement rolled through the large group gathered around us.

This was working in our favor, so I needed to go with it.

Quickly.

Raising my voice, I added, "The fae women want to use us as baby incubators. They don't want to let us choose mates, and they've already said that they won't allow us to stay with whoever they decide we need to have sex with to make the baby. You know that we used to be human; that we believe in steady, committed relationships. Will you protect us from them?"

Louder growls echoed through the masses.

"Just because the female fae think things need to happen the way they used to doesn't mean they're right," I continued. "If you want real mates, then you need to stand up for yourselves. Tell the Wild Hunt and the unseelie council to fight for you. You're not just sperm donors; you're strong men, who deserve not to be used by these women."

The growls became *snarls* of agreement, and I turned away from Ervo so I could see more of the men.

"What if this starts the war North warned us of?" one of the fae called out.

"Some things are worth going to war over," I said simply.

Roars and shouts of agreement followed.

My gaze collided with that of the man I had literally crashed into.

He seemed nice...

And my conversation with Sunny and Dots was still lingering at the forefront of my mind.

I needed to do something to show Ervo that he cared more about me than he realized. Possibly by making him jealous.

So I strode toward the guy I'd crashed into, and wrapped my hand around his arm.

"Will you fly with me?" I asked him. I wasn't perfect at telling the different types of fae apart, but I would've put money on him being either a phoenix or a dragon. He just had that look. "After being trapped all day, I want to be in the sky for a bit."

His eyes brightened. "It would be my pleasure."

I glanced over my shoulder, looking for Sunny and Dots. They were both grinning at me.

"I want to get out into the forest too," Sunny declared. "Is there a basilisk here who wants to teach me how to be a damn good snake? My lessons were lacking." She flashed Teris a look, and his jaw clenched.

Someone nearby shoved his way through the group. "I want to," he said, his wavy blond hair falling into his eyes. The way Sunny grinned when she took in all that golden skin told me that she most definitely approved.

"I'd like to build a house," Dots admitted. "Can someone teach me more about the magic I'll need to know to do so?"

The man nearest to her surged forward. "I can."

She smiled at him, and he beamed back at her.

Out of the corner of my eye, I noticed Ervo standing statue-still. His fists were clenched, and his eyes were dark.

My chest hurt.

I hated that I was hurting him, but what was the alternative? This flight would either help him realize that I wasn't going to wait forever for him to figure out that he was interested in me... or it would help me move on.

I was really hoping for option one.

"Ready?" The fae I'd chosen asked me.

"Yes."

He grinned and launched into the sky, shifting into a huge emerald dragon almost immediately after leaving the ground.

I followed him, the reflection of my own sapphire scales bouncing off of his and sending disco-ball-like strips of light over the trees.

All of the fae knew about mine and my friends' agreement with the Wild Hunt. They knew that Ervo and I weren't really together.

But they must've noticed the way he watched me fly away from him, and the furious calm in his eyes.

Four

We flew for around an hour, until January and Lian caught up to us. She gave me what must've been the phoenix version of a grin as we flew together for a few minutes, and even without discussing it, all four of us headed back to the neutral territory that housed the new Stronghold.

I did the whole spiral-to-the-ground thing as we reached it, but screwed it up worse the second time around, and plummeted head-first.

A pair of massive hands plucked me out of the air before I collided with the ground, yanking me against a gigantic chest that I knew a lot better than I should've.

I couldn't help but laugh when the world spun around me while he flipped me over and set me down on my feet. "Thanks." I grinned at Ervo, as I took a step backward to move away from him.

Or at least, tried to.

His grip on my waist was too tight, holding my chest to his with too much force, for me to pull away.

Our eyes locked together, and the fierce anger inside his made me shiver.

"Mare!" January flung her arms around me, hugging me and Ervo both. She had never been a hugger until recently. But then again, she had only recently gotten pregnant. And discovered real happiness.

"Oof," I huffed, being squeezed against Ervo's chest by two people at once.

The thick hardness of his gigantic erection pressed against my lower belly, but of course he didn't acknowledge it.

So I didn't either.

She released me a minute later, and Ervo did too.

I stepped away, straightening and flashing a smile at the fae man I'd flown with when I saw him beaming. Though I didn't know his name, I was fairly certain he didn't think the flight was any more serious than it had been. We hadn't touched or anything.

"We heard that you're starting a war," January said with a grin.

I shook my head. "Hopefully not a war. I just refuse to be locked up in there any longer." I tossed a hand toward the building. "The female fae want to use us like animals for breeding, assuming we pass their Life-Bringer test."

"Which you probably will, assuming you had a period back on Earth," January said.

"Exactly."

"I already got the same offer. They'll feed me, clothe me, and take care of me, all for the small price of ditching my mate." She rolled her eyes at me. "Maybe they don't know how good the sex is."

"Or how nice it feels to have the arms of the man you love wrapped around you," North said, strolling up to the group. Priel's arm was around her waist, holding her close to his chest.

I turned toward her. "Have you seen visions of anything shitty?"

She shook her head. "Not yet. It'll probably take a few days though, if any of this has changed the future." She gestured around us. "But I agree. Whether or not I have a baby should be my choice, and I'm sure as hell not walking away from Priel. The consequences can be damned for this."

"Naomi snuck out of the Stronghold with the other unseelie women shortly after you, Sunny, and Dots did," one of the male fae told me, from across the group. "They saw us agree to protect you and climbed out the same way you did."

"Suddenly they see the value of men who refuse to bow to authority," January said drily.

"Late is better than never," North said with a shrug. "And anyway, I'm sure the seelie aren't complaining about having more women around."

Murmurs of agreement rolled through the group.

"Where are they all?" January asked.

"Most are learning to make homes, with Dots. They didn't realize they could also be taught that magic," another fae man explained. "The mated women set up a meeting with their unseelie, to let them know the decision they've made. Because Naomi is the only permanently mated one, they think that threats to bond with other males will force the unseelies to side with them."

"There are a *lot* of fae women, though," I admitted.

"Most of whom believe that sex is only meant for making strong babies, and only for the Life-Bringers," North countered.

Priel snorted. "Twenty human women who know sex can be enjoyable are more valuable to us than two-hundred fae females who'd cut our cocks off before climbing them."

North smacked him on the arm, but grumbled agreements seemed to echo through the group.

"The best scenario would be the fae women realizing that things are different now, and that the men aren't going to act as stud-horses for their babies," January said. "Maybe if we can show them that mated couples can be happy together, they'll understand."

"We have precisely two examples of that," one of the fae men pointed out.

"Five, if the rest of the seelie girls continue their charade with the Wild Hunt," another countered.

I felt Ervo tense behind me.

"More pairings will happen naturally as time progresses and the women are allowed their freedom," Lian said. "The charade has ended, and will not resume. Each woman deserves the right to choose if she will be pursued—whether born a fae or transformed into one. We can't force the females from the island into complying with our views any more than they can force us. Our efforts would be better spent preparing the next group to go to Earth for the coming Winter Solstice."

Reluctant murmurs of agreement followed his words.

"January and I will attend the meeting with the unseelies. When we know how they will approach the situation, we'll speak with the fae females and let them know that the human women have been taken into our protection," Lian added.

"We'll come too," North told him.

No one protested that, so the four of them took off...

Leaving me alone, with so damn many men.

"Thank you for flying with me," the man I'd crashed into earlier said, still grinning at me. "It was the highlight of my century."

My face heated. Mostly out of guilt that I'd only done it to make Ervo jealous. "You're welcome. I had fun, too."

"Can I bring you a cake, later?" he asked me.

A barely-audible growl vibrated the chest of the phoenix behind me.

I hesitated.

Agreeing to that would be telling him that I was interested, or even just considering being interested in him.

The memory of Clevv's claws digging into my skin had my agreement dying in my throat.

"Ask again after things are settled with the female fae?" I said, instead.

He beamed at me. "Of course."

Knowing that he wasn't going to walk away from me, I nodded, and then turned and begun striding in the opposite direction as if I knew where I was going.

Ervo followed me, of course.

I felt more sets of eyes on me, and a quick glance to my left and right proved that I'd regained my hellhound guard dogs.

Damn, I needed to figure out a way to shake them. Somehow, they always managed to catch up to me soon after I landed. I knew they could move fast, but it was frustrating to never be able to get away from them.

An idea hit me, and I halted.

Ervo stopped as soon as I did, his chest meeting my back firmly and his hand landing on my hip.

The touch made my stomach twist.

"I figured out a way for you to pay your life debt," I told the hounds in the forest around me.

They emerged from the trees, and Ervo's grip on me tightened.

"My life is at risk because of the female fae," I told them.

They tensed, like they expected me to ask them to start murdering the women.

"I want you to talk to the harsh ones. Follow them. Get to know them. Become their friends. They haven't been around men in a long time, and it sounds like things were really different back when they used to be a part of fae society. So you can repay me by building friendships with the women, to help them understand why humans want real relationships with the men we bind ourselves to, and so that they don't try to lock us away or anything."

There was a beat of silence.

"This is far too simple a request," one of the hellhounds finally rumbled.

My lips curved upward. "Have you met them? They *hate* men. You'll have to bribe them with so much cake, it'll probably make you sick. Or at least sick of cooking."

"You are far too kind to us," one of the hounds said. "But if this is your wish, we will comply."

I think they had realized that following me around and protecting me wasn't an easy task given that I had wings and they did not.

But also, I was being honest. If they could positively impact the female fae, it could only work out in our favor.

"It is. You can report to Ervo about your progress, since he has a vested interest in your debt as well," I said, smoothly handing him the responsibility for a group of men that I had never wanted in the first place.

He didn't physically respond behind me, and I knew him well enough to know that if his body didn't show his emotions, his face wouldn't either.

"Very well." The hound bowed to me.

One by one, the rest of them did too.

Then they silently made their way into the forest, leaving me and Ervo alone.

I could hear people talking in the distance, but no one was close enough to hear us, or see us.

And Ervo's hand was still on my hip, his hard chest against my back.

I knew he wasn't going to keep quiet about the flight earlier, and waited.

Sure enough, his breath brushed my ear a moment later as he said calmly, "So you'll forget that you're mine when the opportunity arises to fly with another male, yet put me in charge of a situation I would've avoided by ending the lives of the men involved?"

"You want to be my brother," I told him, staring out at the forest just in case he was tall enough to see what I was looking at from where he stood. "Brothers deal with that kind of thing, not the dates their sisters go on."

His fingers dug into my skin, just soft enough not to hurt me. "And was that a *date*?"

There hadn't been any conversation, or physical contact or anything, so I wouldn't really say that it was a date.

But... it wasn't *not* a date.

And technically, we *had* been alone together.

"It was."

"When did you decide to start *dating*?" He hissed the words at me, and I took a damn lot of pride in the fact that I was affecting his perfect, calm façade.

"I've been thinking about it for months." My voice was the neutral tone his usually took, and honestly, I was giving him the truth. "I want a mate. Someone who looks at me the way Lian looks at January. Humans find their person by dating, so that's what I'm doing now."

His grip on my hip grew painful, in a way that I loved, because it meant that I'd gotten under Ervo's skin.

I forced my breathing to remain steady as he lowered his lips to my ear and said in a deadly voice, "I followed you, Mariah. As I will on every one of these *dates*. Had Iver touched you, even the tiniest brush of his wing against your scales, I would have ripped his heart from his body and dropped both from the sky so fast that Vevol herself couldn't stop me."

I couldn't stop the shiver that rolled down my spine.

No one on Earth had ever called me Mare. I had always been Mariah, until Ana learned my full name when I arrived in Vevol and gave me the nickname. The fact that Ervo had discovered that somehow, was messing with me.

I hadn't given it to him myself, I realized, so he couldn't use it against me. Even if he wanted to.

His voice was slightly louder, and a hell of a lot harder when he added, "Should any part of another male touch your skin again in any way, he will meet his demise. You belong to *me*."

I kind of hated myself for being turned on by the words. And the way he gripped my hip. And the way his chest pressed against my back.

And... well, just *him*.

The whole damn man was a turn-on, and I didn't know what to do about it.

"That doesn't sound like brotherly love," I breathed to him. "You wouldn't kill North for touching Priel."

"Perhaps not." His lips brushed the shell of my ear, and I shuddered.

The movement dragged my ass over his front, and my eyes widened as his erection pressed against me.

"But I will destroy anyone who so much as *considers* touching you."

His teeth caught my earlobe, tugging on both of my piercings before he finally straightened and stepped back. When he released his grip on my hip, I ached for his touch, but didn't turn around to look at him.

The overwhelming feeling that things had just changed hit me—and they hit me hard.

Ervo hadn't hauled me back to his house, or screwed me against a tree...

But he had just admitted that his feelings didn't sound like brotherly affection.

And threatened anyone who might so much as consider touching me. Which wasn't a first, but it felt different that time.

More like... a dare.

As if he was challenging me to try it, to test him. To see if he'd defend me as brutally as he claimed.

But I still remembered the last time he had tried to kill someone for being involved in hurting me.

The way I'd landed on my knees, in front of him.

The way he'd snarled at me that I should never kneel for a man.

The way he had let the hellhounds live, despite his clear hatred for them and what they'd let Clevv do to me.

And shit, even thinking about Clevv and the way he had met his end made me nauseous.

I wasn't going to let my thoughts linger there, though.

I was going to meet his challenge, and I was going to meet it head-on.

Ervo didn't like that I'd been alone with another man. He'd followed me, like a damn stalker. And afterward, he had tracked me down and tried to stake a claim on me.

But he hadn't asked me to be his mate yet.

He hadn't tried to kiss me again, or to make me smell more like him.

He hadn't insisted that I spend every night in his bed.

He knew that he cared about me, and wanted me, but he didn't understand how much.

And a smirk stretched my lips when I realized what I was going to do to help him figure it out.

MY PLAN BUBBLED SILENTLY within me as I found Dots and most of the unseelie girls. They were all talking to pairs of fae men, each lost in their conversation.

I was sure it hadn't been easy to get the unseelie girls to walk away from each other long enough to have real conversations with the men, but imagined that the idea of that knowledge and power was worth more than their cliques to them.

"Mare!" Dots waved me over, flashing me a grin. There were two men with her—neither of which was Nev—but I crossed the distance between us and gave her a quick hug.

Like January, she was a hugger.

I never had been, back on Earth. Mostly because it wasn't an option for me. My family weren't that kind of people.

Even if they had been, I wouldn't have wanted to hug them. There was no love lost between us—because that love had never existed.

But I'd discovered, in Vevol, that I had an affinity for any physical contact, really. There was something about touching someone else, whether a brush of a hand or a fierce hug, that made me feel as if I mattered to them.

And I'd grown awfully addicted to mattering to people. Well, to mattering at all.

I supposed that was because I had never felt that way on Earth.

"Do you want to learn the magic too?" she asked me.

"Of course. What if you're not there to break us out of the next Stronghold?"

She grinned, her face pink and her expression happy. I envied that happiness of hers, which had always seemed to come so easily. I knew she'd been through hell, so it wasn't as if she'd just been blessed with a simple life and a happy spirit. But still, the way she smiled made me wish that I could feel as upbeat about everything as she did.

I wasn't an unhappy person... but I could be happier.

I knew that better than I wanted to admit, especially since everything had happened with Clevv and the hellhounds.

Ervo's gaze remained on me, and I could feel his eyes as if they were his damn hands on my back.

I ignored them, though.

"Can you guys find two more fae to teach Mare?" she asked the man she was working with, then looked over at me. "Turns out, it's easier to be taught by people who are the same kind of fae as you. The phoenixes connect with Vevol differently than the dragons do, for example."

"I never considered that," I admitted.

Then again, there was much about Vevol that I hadn't considered. Mostly because I'd never had the information I would need to do so, or a way to get that information.

Two dragon men jogged over less than a minute later, and Dots gave me one last quick hug before we separated, focusing on our lessons.

Or at least, *trying* to focus.

I found it difficult to pay attention to much of anything when a pair of hot eyes watched me so closely, waiting for someone to touch me so he could come out of the shadows and destroy them.

Five

When North, January, and everyone else who had attended the meeting with the unseelie leaders returned, they were grinning.

It turned out that despite the unseelie's coldness and overall unpleasantness, they weren't willing to abandon the females they had for the ones who only wanted to use them for baby-making.

They had met with the female fae and let them know that the classification ceremony thing wasn't going to happen that day, and that the human women had chosen to remain with the men.

The fae ladies were apparently not thrilled—particularly their leader—but for now, they had accepted our decision.

I was sure that their leader wouldn't accept it for long, but figured we had plenty of time to worry about that in the future.

"Can I talk to you?" I asked North, ducking away from Dots, Sunny, and the group of men surrounding us.

"Sure." She looked a bit surprised by the request, but the two of us walked into the forest, stopping when we were far enough that no one would overhear us.

"Can you see Ervo?" I murmured to her, having turned my back to him so he couldn't read my lips or anything.

"Yes." She studied me curiously.

I bit my lip. "Try not to visibly react to what I'm saying, but I think Ervo is realizing that he wants to be more than brother and sister. I flew with another guy earlier, and when I came back, he got sort of caveman-like. I want to push him, but he's made it clear that he'll kill any man that touches me."

North's expression remained neutral. "Damn."

"Yeah."

Her lips quirked upward slightly. "So I take it there's a plan?"

"Yes, but I need your help. Could you ask Priel to find me some men to go flying with, or hiking with, or something? And just make sure they know they can't touch me?"

North grimaced. "I would if I could, but he won't get involved in any of his brothers' love lives. I already asked him why Teris is so against mating with Sunny, and he told me that he has no idea and isn't going to poke around. It's their business, not ours."

I grimaced. "Damn."

"Yeah. I'm sorry." She made a face. "You could ask January, though. I'm pretty sure Lian is known for bugging them all and worrying over everyone like a mother hen. His focus has been on her since the pregnancy started, but he might be up for it."

I nodded. "I'll think about it."

"You could also achieve the same level of possessiveness by just flirting, though. Spending time with the guys is sure to piss Ervo off, but walking up to them, and smiling at them? Priel hates it when I look at another guy too long." She flashed me a grin. "Did he threaten to kill them if *you* touched *them* yet?"

My eyes widened.

"It's a loophole, for sure. Ervo seems like someone who plays by his own set of rules. If his rules aren't technically broken, he'll know he has no ground to stand on. And he'll probably add that to the rules, but until then, it's fair game."

"You're right," I admitted, biting my lip. "He didn't freak out at that guy when I crashed into him."

He'd just picked me up and set me on my feet, away from the guy.

"You can get pretty damn flirty with a couple of touches. Fluff your hair, make your clothes a bit disheveled, accidentally run into someone..."

My heartbeat picked up. "Sunny thinks I should just kiss someone."

North's eyebrows shot upward. "I tried the kissing thing with other fae. Do not recommend it."

My excitement fizzled out. "You're right. It's a terrible idea."

Sunny strolled over to us, and we scooted back to give her space. "You guys look like you're coming up with an evil plan, and I want in," she declared. "I'm so *damn* tired of Teris."

North explained, "We're trying to think of a way to make Ervo jealous. He finally started admitting that he might have feelings for Mare outside of the brotherly thing he's been clinging to."

Sunny's eyes lit up. "Oh, girl. This is my thing. I've got it."

We waited.

She knew she had us on the edge of our seats, figuratively.

"Dance party." She spread her hands through the air, as if she could see the headline. "We make sure the fae understand that everyone's just having fun, no one's forming bonds or anything. And we turn up the music, and we shake our asses. The unseelie ladies will feel the girl power in it, and they'll be so down. It's perfect. And you'd better believe that stone-cold phoenix will be sitting in some tree, watching you grind against some sexy basilisk."

North snorted, but I grinned.

"It would work," North admitted. "But grinding on someone other than your mate would have to be outlawed. These guys are virgins; do you know how much over-excited jizzing would happen if there was grinding?"

Sunny cackled. "The more the merrier."

"No," I said, though I was laughing too. "We can't do that. Maybe we make it a looking but not touching thing?"

"Or, we tie the hands of any fae who wants to come in, so he can't grab any of the good bits. Then, any physical contact is up to the woman involved," Sunny said. She was still grinning wickedly. "Come on, we can totally make this happen."

"Alright, I'm in," North agreed.

So yeah, that's how I ended up on the party planning committee, throwing together a rave.

. . .

I DIDN'T KNOW where the music was coming from, but it was so loud it shook the trees.

The fae had pulled out some kind of wine that tasted stupidly good, and made us feel kind of buzzed.

And Dots and Sunny had indeed managed to block off the area—with the help of a handful of fae dudes and a wall of tall, thick stone. No one on the outside could see in, unless they were in the sky or trees.

Every fae dude who came inside had his hands tied around his back. Sunny was using rope that they could easily break, but everyone had been warned that breaking the rope meant leaving the party.

So, the rope stayed tied.

And damn, did the party begin.

Every single one of us ex-humans were there, and it was safe to say that the unseelie chicks surprised all of us with their level of enthusiasm—and their dance moves. I assumed their excitement was because this was the most human-like thing they had done in a long time, but it could've been something else.

I didn't know them well enough to really say.

The fae men danced their asses off too, despite the rope binding their hands. I refused to let myself look around for Ervo, because I'd already seen him in the sky, watching from above.

It was time to get my flirt on, though.

I was determined to do this.

Sunny and Dots were running the entrance, tying hands and letting people in. Despite Sunny's excitement, she hadn't seemed to have any desire to join the dancing crowd, just beaming at her creation from the side.

North was grinding up against Priel off to one side, and they both seemed to be enjoying the party tremendously. January and Lian were in a similar position, though she was staying far away from the wine since we had no idea how it would affect her baby.

And... I was putting this shit off.

Taking a deep breath, I turned toward the crowd, and forced myself to head straight into it.

The men outnumbered the women insanely, so it wasn't hard to find one of them.

I put a hand on the shoulder of the first one I found, and unconsciously looked up at the sky.

The unfamiliar fae man turned toward me with a grin, following my gaze as his smile grew knowing. "Ervo's been obsessed with you for a while," he called out to me. "And you stare at him just as much as he stares at you."

"I didn't know anyone had noticed," I admitted, having to yell over the music.

He laughed. "We're hopeful, but not stupid."

I smiled sheepishly. "Sorry."

"Don't apologize." He shrugged playfully. "It is what it is."

My smile became a grin. "Would you mind if I danced with you to make him jealous? As long as you don't touch me, I don't think you'll be in any danger."

He laughed again, louder. "Hell yes. I've never seen him lose his cool! Bet I'll get a kick out of it!"

I laughed too. "Probably!"

I'd learned how to dance ballroom-style as a kid and teenager, but it wasn't as if I could drag the fae man right into an elegant waltz. Everyone else was just sort of shaking their ass or rubbing up against each other, which seemed awkward, so I wasn't really interested in it.

Then, as if on cue, the booming music became a slow, vibrant love song.

I glanced over at the entrance, and found Sunny grinning like a madwoman, giving me a thumbs-up.

Another laugh escaped me, but I set my hands on the fae's shoulders, stepping up close so our chests brushed.

Waltzing was out, but I could just hold onto his shoulders and sway like it was a high school prom.

A roar echoing through the trees above us had me grinning wildly, and the fae in front of me too.

"How long do you think we have before he dives down and tries to eat me?" the man I was dancing with yelled.

I couldn't even answer; I was grinning too widely.

The stone walls around us moved, stretching up higher and higher. They rapidly formed a dome, shutting us off from the rest of the world, and I noticed a line of fae men along the sides of it, working under Sunny's orders.

That chick was an evil genius.

"Guess someone's got your back!" I yelled to the guy.

He just laughed.

A few seconds later, booming fae laughter meshed with the music as a furious, disheveled-looking Ervo shoved his way through the crowd. There was fire blazing off his shoulders, reminding me that he was, in fact, a phoenix.

As if I could've forgotten that.

"Thanks for the dance!" I told the fae, stepping away with a grin as the song ended.

"Any time," he called back, matching my grin with his own.

I spun to face Ervo as he reached me. Though I opened my mouth to say something, he just grabbed me by the waist and threw me over his shoulder before striding right back in the direction he had come from. His hands were on the backs of my thighs, acting as a fae seatbelt, holding me tightly to him.

"I can walk," I called to him, as he made quick work of the distance between us and the exit.

His fingers only dug deeper into my thighs in response.

Soon enough, we were outside the party's dome, and Ervo was shifting forms, dragging me up onto his back as he took to the sky. My fingers tangled in his feathers, gripping him hard as I leaned against him.

He must've gotten some kind of power trip from flying with me, because the bastard was making a habit of it.

Though frankly, I couldn't say I hated it.

We only flew for a few minutes before he landed in an empty strip of the forest. The branches and leaves swayed in the wind around us as he set me on my feet, then stalked toward me.

I walked backward until my shoulders collided with a thick tree trunk.

Ervo's chest was heaving as he towered over me, his eyes and voice lined with fury. "What the *fuck* was that?"

"I danced with someone. Like I did a *million* times on Earth." My voice was harsh, but I wanted it to be.

If we needed to argue for him to get it through his thick skull that he wanted me, then I would argue fiercely.

"This isn't *Earth*," he snarled at me. "And you don't belong to *Woza*."

I retorted, "Actually, I don't belong to anyone. Pretty sure I'd remember it if I had sex with one of the fae."

Flames reignited on his shoulders, and his fists clenched tightly, but he was silent.

Or at least, he was silent for a minute.

As exhilarating as his jealousy had been at first, I was starting to feel kind of guilty for pushing him. I cared about him, after all.

And the way I was pushing him wasn't helping either of us.

I finally said, "If you'd like to have a rational discussion about the potential feelings we might have for each other, let me know. If you are truly not interested in being my mate, walk the hell away from me, Viervo."

The guilt in my chest was turning into anger, and growing fiercely.

He seriously thought he could just keep everyone else away from me without actually being with me.

Clearly, I had let him walk all over me for way too long.

And yet I was still standing there, just letting him—

"I have made my interest in you clear from the beginning, Mariah." His voice was low and furious. "I may have failed you on more than one occasion, but I have fought like hell to redeem myself in your eyes. I've protected you. Cared for you. Tried to make you see that I would give my life for you. And yet still, I find you pressed against another male, gripping him with the hands that should stroke *my* form." By the time he got to the last sentence, his snarl was ferocious.

"What are you talking about? Every time I asked you if you were interested in me, you called yourself my brother. I had brothers on Earth, and they sure as hell didn't want to touch me. Or kiss me. Or do anything remotely sexual with me. Family is blood, and you told me you would protect me like a *sister*!"

His eyes burned into me. "Family is *chosen* in Vevol, Mariah, and I *chose* you. Your scent didn't drive me to madness; I picked you for your quiet passion, for your mind, for your fire. Do you not think I would sacrifice myself for Lian or Priel? Or Nev, or Teris? I sure as fuck wasn't claiming you as my blood. I was claiming you as my female; as the woman I wanted to be my mate."

I blinked at him.

And blinked again, slower.

"I think we had a misunderstanding." I broke the tense silence between us. "I thought you were telling me that I belonged to you like a sibling. Like you had affection for me, but not attraction."

"I can assure you that is *not* the case." He stepped closer, pressing his erection against my belly with the motion. I sucked in a breath, and the motion made my breasts press against him.

"Well you should've said that earlier," I finally whispered.

He growled, "And you should've *asked me*. Had I known you thought I found you unattractive, I would've cleared that up in a heartbeat."

Honestly?

I believed him.

I really, really believed him.

"So what now?" I asked him.

We had acknowledged that we were interested in each other, but... what did that mean for us? Where did we go from there?

"I don't know," Ervo admitted. "I've never done this before."

I bit my lip. "Neither have I."

He blinked at me. "You've never been with a male before?"

Oh, damn.

This conversation was happening already.

Yikes.

"No. I mean, um, yes. I've been with a guy before. A few guys. At different times—I'm pretty vanilla, honestly," I said hastily.

His eyes darkened.

Shit.

"I've never been in a relationship before, I mean. It was always just sex, and I never really enjoyed it. I have a hard time climaxing, I guess. One of the guys made me feel really bad about it once, and I never bothered again. That was before I came to Vevol, though, so like... I don't know, seven years ago? Shit, that makes me sound like a loser, but—"

His lips landed on mine, softly. Not hesitantly, but not certainly, either.

The kiss surprised me, but I slowly moved my mouth with his, sliding my tongue against the seam of his lips as my hands curled between us.

When he parted them for me, my tongue slid into his mouth, and we both groaned as it met his.

One of his hands wrapped around the back of my head, tilting me more so he had better access as he took over the kiss. The way his tongue stroked mine was slow and sexy, like there was nowhere else he wanted to be, and nothing else he wanted to be doing.

Like he wasn't dying to get to the sex already, but just wanted to stay where we were and enjoy kissing me.

His other hand wrapped around my thigh, and he used the grip to hoist me up a foot or two. I squeaked into his mouth, wrapping my hands around his shoulders when he set my pelvis a little above his, so the thick length of his erection was pressed against my core.

He halted, pulling away. "Is this okay?" he asked me, his chest rising and falling rapidly. His eyes had shifted a little, I realized, as I saw what looked like sparks and coals rolling through his irises.

"Extremely okay," I breathed, leaning my head back against the tree and accidentally smooshing his hand a little.

He didn't seem to mind—probably because he used that same hand to drag my head back to his.

I gripped his face as he kissed me slowly, exploring my mouth so unhurriedly that it started to mess with my mind.

Didn't he want more?

Didn't he want *me*?

Didn't he—

"Ohhh," I moaned into his mouth as he slowly moved his hips, dragging his erection over my core.

He halted, and then pulled his lips from mine.

I couldn't help the soft groan that escaped me at the absence of his tongue.

"You're drunk," he growled at me, as if he'd just realized it.

"Not really. Only had a few glasses," I whispered, tugging his face down toward mine. His palm left the back of my head, landing on my hand and pressing tightly so my fingers dug into his cheek.

"I don't even know if you consciously want this," he said to me.

Hurt curled in my abdomen. "That's not fair. I've been trying to get you to notice me for months."

"I always noticed you." His voice was low. "We can't do this until you're sober, Mariah."

My eyes narrowed at him.

"Where are you sleeping tonight?" His gaze jerked in the direction of the rave my friends and I had put together. "Whose home are you sharing?"

Fury coursed through me, and I yanked my hands away from his face. "Put me down."

He growled at me, but a moment later, set me on my feet.

Too angry to tell him that he was being a jackass, or that he'd offended me by just assuming so easily that I'd sleep with another man, I just walked away from him.

He stalked behind me. "Mariah."

"No," I shot back. "You don't get to '*Mariah*' me and assume it works like an apology. It doesn't."

He huffed out a breath, catching up to me quickly and walking at my side. "I shouldn't have said that."

"No, you shouldn't have. I had a few drinks, yes, but I am *not* drunk. And it's not like I was kissing a bunch of guys or even flirting with any of them. I told that fae at the party that I wanted to make you jealous so you would pull your head out of your ass, and he agreed. He was *not* into me."

"Male fae are into anyone with breasts," he argued.

"Well, he knew I wasn't interested in him, because I told him that plainly. So back off," I shot back.

He walked beside me in silence for a few moments before finally admitting, "I've been bordering on insanity for too long. I'm sorry."

"Trust is a required part of any relationship, Ervo. I don't expect you to trust me completely after five minutes, but it's a dick move to accuse me of planning on sleeping with someone else right after making out with you."

He let out a slow breath. "I assumed you were rejecting me, all this time. When you scoffed at my explanations, it seemed like a rejection. Keeping my cool in the face of repeated reminders that the female I wanted wasn't interested in me was not easy. It'll take me time to wrap my head around all that's happened, to see that I was wrong."

My throat swelled.

I understood why he had felt that way. Hadn't I felt it too?

"I'm sorry," I admitted.

"As am I."

There was another brief silence, but this time, it wasn't uncomfortable. With the music playing loudly in the distance as we walked toward it, it was actually kind of peaceful.

"I asked about your sleeping arrangements because I wanted you in my bed again. I should've just said so," he told me, slipping his hands in his shorts' pockets.

"It was nice, wasn't it?" I asked him softly.

"Blissful torture," he murmured.

My lips curved upward at the poetic description. "I'd like to share a bed, too. Do you have a house here?"

"I do not. While the others focused on building, I couldn't bring myself to fly far enough that I couldn't see you through your window."

My face warmed. "Well, we can figure something out."

I wrapped my hand around his bicep, biting my lip as I tried to feel it up without being a total freak.

But damn, that thing was huge.

"Why are we going back to the party?" I asked him.

"I saw something strange, before I got distracted. Just need to make sure it's nothing." He pulled his arm closer to his body, tugging me along with it.

My lips turned downward. "What was it?"

"A few of the fae women, headed toward the building. Probably just going to see what's happening."

"Shit." I picked up the pace.

"There are plenty of men there. I'm sure they're fine," Ervo told me, though he jogged beside me when I started running.

Running and I were not friends, but sometimes, it was worth the sweat, heavy breathing, and mental discomfort.

THE PARTY WAS STILL BOOMING when we reached the opening of the dome, and I relaxed when I saw that everyone was still having a good time. There were no female fae to be seen, and all was well.

So what were the fae women up to?

Six

Ervo pulled me into his arms and relaxed against one side of the wall that marked the party's entrance. We watched everyone for a few minutes, and my lips curved upward when I saw Sunny still on the edge of the group, chatting with the fae who seemed to be in charge of the music.

Teris was leaned up against the wall opposite ours, watching the party. There were a few guys stationed in chairs at the entrance, making sure that none of the men went in with their hands untied, so I assumed that was the reason Teris hadn't gone in.

I'd never had a conversation with the sabertooth fae before. In his beast form, he looked a lot like a tiger the size of a bear, and those damn teeth… shudder.

I wanted to talk to him, but Ervo was holding me tightly enough that I didn't think it would be the best idea. In a few days, when he calmed down, maybe I could ask him what his deal with Sunny was. And why he wasn't into her.

But the way his eyes tracked her every move told me there was probably more to the story than that. He wouldn't be watching her so closely if he was as disinterested as she thought, would he?

I studied him for a moment.

January told me once that she thought he looked like a choir boy, but I had spent more than my fair share of time with choir boys. Those bastards would put on a charming face one minute, and stab you in the back the next. Teris didn't look like one of them to me at all.

He was tan, with light brown hair that was cut short on the sides but longer on the top. When I'd first met him, he hadn't had any tattoos, but now, markings stretched over his left fist and climbed all the way up to his shoulder before wrapping around his throat. I would've had to get closer to see what they were depictions of, but I didn't move.

Like all of the other fae, he was ridiculously buff. But unlike many of them, there was something calm about him.

"You're staring at another male, Mariah," Ervo said into my ear, making me shiver as his arms tightened around me. "Have you forgotten who you belong to again already?"

I turned my head a bit, and he dipped his toward me so I could explain. "Sunny thinks he's not interested in her, but he hasn't looked away from her," I said softly. "I'm curious as to why he's always turning her down."

Understanding flooded his gaze. When I lowered my head, his lips brushed my ear. "Teris won't settle for less than love. Unless he feels that his female loves him, he won't consider them mates."

Damn.

"Don't tell her that, though," he nipped at my ear, tugging lightly on both of my diamond earrings with his teeth. I bit my lip, looking at the man a little differently.

I supposed that wasn't entirely surprising. The fae didn't do casual hookups, but even among the possessive guys, there would be differing degrees of emotions when it came to permanent relationships.

I could definitely respect the desire to make sure someone loved you before binding your life—and mind—to theirs permanently. I had felt that way for a long time, too. And I supposed I hadn't really taken the time to think about how things would happen between me and Ervo if we finally admitted how we felt to each other, but... well, I needed to make sure neither of us would want to change our minds afterward.

People always changed in time. That was the only real thing you could be certain of when it came to a relationship—that both of you would change.

So I needed to make sure that I understood Ervo's past and he understood mine, to be as certain as possible that we would want to live with whoever we both became over the next however many years.

Change wasn't bad, but having the wrong ideas about it could be detrimental.

And despite my attraction to Ervo, and the fact that I trusted him, I didn't really know him. I didn't understand his hopes and dreams. I hadn't admitted my darkest secrets to him.

And those things definitely needed to come before we decided to have sex, since that would bond us permanently.

As far as Sunny and Teris went, I could understand his hesitance. Sunny put a lot of effort into making sure that she never came across as too serious, or too emotional. With sarcasm and humor, she carefully controlled the way people saw her.

Despite their many opposites—her jokes and his silence, her sass and his seriousness—I knew that Sunny had been through something shitty enough to make her wish for an escape from her life. She chalked it up to family drama whenever anyone talked about it, but that was basically just another way to say that she didn't want to get into it.

Suddenly, Teris's nostrils flared, and Ervo went still against my back.

In the blink of an eye, Teris was barreling into the crowd.

Ervo launched off the ground, shifting and hauling me high into the trees too fast for me to argue. He set me on a thick branch, and snarled at me, "Don't move."

And then he was diving back down toward the dome, spiraling toward the ground.

I blinked down at the world below me. Heights didn't scare me anymore, thanks to my wings, but...

What was happening?

I hadn't smelled anything abnormal.

Had there been a problem with something?

Why else would Teris have charged into the group like that, and Ervo have left me in a tree?

I could see the dome's entrance from where I was, and no one had gone in or out, but my stomach clenched.

What if Ervo was in danger?

If this had something to do with the female fae, the other girls and I would be safe. They wanted us alive, at least until they discovered whether or not we were life-bringers.

But they didn't care about the men.

My gaze caught on a small movement below, and I watched a line of fae women sprint toward the dome.

The music cut off before they reached the stone building and disappeared inside.

Panic flooded me.

Ervo was in there.

They wouldn't care about keeping the men alive, but I did.

A female fae emerged from the building, with an ex-human woman hanging over her back, unconscious.

My eyes widened, and my lips parted.

Shit.

Another fae woman emerged, with another human woman on her back.

There were no sounds that told me anyone was fighting.

No screams, or yells.

Just an eerie silence.

When another woman came out with Dots hanging over her shoulder, my stomach clenched.

I had to do something, didn't I?

But what?

Flying down there would be absolutely stupid. I wanted to live my life for real, not get myself captured. So obviously, that wasn't an option. No way in hell could I fight the female fae.

The men seemed to have been incapacitated in some way—otherwise how would the women have gotten the ex-human girls from them?

If the men had been knocked out somehow, they wouldn't be able to follow the fae women, to see where they were taking the other ladies.

So that was what I could do, without getting myself captured—I could figure out where the female fae were taking the other ladies.

Though more fae women were emerging from the dome, I only gave them one last glance before quietly and carefully making my way to my feet.

The trees in Vevol—or at least in the part of the forest we occupied—were massive. Most of the tree trunks were as thick around as small cars. A lot of the branches were as thick around as I was, and all of them overlapped with branches from other trees.

That meant I could climb from tree to tree.

Theoretically.

My balance wasn't great, though. It never had been. I was the girl who spent her weekends relaxing in the bathtub with a book, trying not to drop the damn thing in the water, not camped out at the gym. I had been pretty damn good at riding horses throughout the majority of my Earth life, but it had been ages since then, and branches were nothing like horses.

If I shifted forms, it would be much easier. But the chance of being spotted in my dragon form was a lot higher, so it was time to play Tarzan.

There were a ton of branches around me, stretching in all different directions, so I wasn't going to have to operate on balance alone.

And the ladies at the front of the group were only getting further away, so...

I couldn't avoid this any longer.

It was go time.

Not gonna lie, I silently hummed Mission Impossible music as I loosely wrapped my fingers around the branch above my head.

I think the music was my brain's way of avoiding the panic that was threatening to cut off my damn breathing.

And, since I couldn't think of another excuse, I started walking.

Luckily, the branch remained mostly steady for the first half of its length. As I reached the second half, it started to sway.

Panic made my breathing pick up, but I forced myself to continue moving steadily even as the branch narrowed.

Knowing that I could shift if I needed to took away the fear of crashing to my death, but there was still the fear of *plunging* before I managed to shift...

And getting caught by the female fae.

Luckily, my reflexes and speed both seemed to have improved when I became a fae myself, because as I continued moving, I got more comfortable on the branches. I started walking faster, and then eventually, started jogging. The female fae moved more quickly than I did, but there were a bunch of them, so I didn't get too far behind.

When they finally stopped moving, I was coated in a thin layer of sweat, my heart pounding lightly as I loosely hugged the nearest tree's trunk, still standing on one of the branches.

The sun was rising over the trees as I watched the last two fae women disappear into a cave that looked like nothing but a crack between two rocks.

Guess we knew where they stood when it came to letting us have personal freedom.

I'd seen them haul January and North in, too, which meant there would be at least two raging mated men when they realized their women were gone. From experience, I knew the rest of the seelie would probably rage with the Wild Hunt guys. Those bastards were always looking for an excuse to fight.

I'd never seen the unseelie council up close, or had a conversation with any of the other unseelies, but I had to think that at least a few of them were protective of women. Particularly the ones who had exchanged vows with ex-human women.

If not them, the Tame King still had to react. Him and his queen, Naomi, had sealed their bond through sex. They didn't get along, but that didn't change the fact that they were mated.

My eyes widened as I watched the crack between the two rocks seal, merging the rocks and completely concealing the evidence of their hiding place.

I stared down at it for a few long moments, trying to memorize the location. Knowing that my senses were better in my dragon form, I carefully walked a few feet from the tree's trunk, and then shifted.

Though the branch strained a little beneath my new weight, it didn't crack or break as I studied everything around me.

Taking in the smells, sights, and sounds, I forced myself to pay attention to everything.

I was going to find this place again, with the men, and get the other women out.

There was no other choice.

Since I didn't know if there were any other female fae out guarding the forest or searching for me or anything, I shifted back to my human form and then started on the long journey back through the trees.

No way in hell was I getting dragged into their cave when I was the only one who knew where my friends had been taken.

BY THE TIME I made it back to the dome, I had been hearing roars and snapping tree branches, smelling blood, and seeing men soar over my head as well as sprint below me for about half an hour.

None of them appeared to be in their right minds, possessed by their fury, so I didn't call out to any of them.

The level-headed men would probably have stayed near the dome, to try to figure shit out, I hoped.

It seemed like it had only been thirty minutes or so since they started waking up, after all.

When I reached the tree Ervo had left me in, I debated attempting to climb down for a full minute before my tired, stressed-out mind admitted that was a stupid idea.

So, I shifted and glided down to the ground. I saw Nev in a group with a few other fae I didn't recognize, but since he was the only member of the Wild Hunt within my view, he was the man I headed toward.

They all noticed me coming, and cleared enough space for me to land—albeit clumsily.

I crashed into a pair of guys after I hit the ground, but this time, didn't earn any chuckles.

Things were too intense for that.

"What happened? Where did they take you?" Nev asked me, as the men I'd hit released me and stepped away. They gave me plenty of space, so Nev was the one I was nearest to. "They disguised their scents somehow."

I appreciated that he was level-headed, despite the anger he was probably dealing with. He and Dots were the friendliest of the remaining unmated seelie couples; they actually seemed to get along the way friends would. They didn't discuss their pasts or anything, from what I knew, but they didn't argue or have problems with each other.

"Ervo smelled something in the air and then hid me in a tree," I explained quickly. "I followed the fae women from above. I saw where they took the other girls—I can lead you guys there." My heart was pounding quickly, oblivious to the hunger that rumbled my stomach.

Relief crossed Nev's face. "Damn. We owe you." He turned to the other guys. "Spread the word. Gather everyone you can, and make sure someone finds Lian, Aev, and Priel. We'll head out as soon as we can."

The seelie usually hated being given orders, but the laid-back way Nev gave them and the tension of the situation ensured that they didn't argue.

The men exchanged a few words before dividing, some taking off on foot while others shifted.

"Where did Ervo go?" I asked him, wrapping my arms around my middle as my stomach growled loudly.

"I don't know," Nev admitted, gesturing me toward a bare patch of dirt. "I've never seen my brothers react like this. I knew the mate bond was intense, but the way they woke up..." he shook his head. "They lost their minds. It makes me wonder if my feelings for my female aren't what I think."

"Not everyone reacts the same way to stress. I don't think losing your mind to panic is a sign that you're in love with someone, or—"

A familiar roar above me made me jerk my head upward, cutting my words off completely.

The massive phoenix spiraled toward me much more smoothly than I'd done when I attempted the same thing—but instead of crashing, or even landing, he grabbed me with his gigantic claws and soared into the sky with me.

Despite the shriek that escaped me as I was ripped away from the ground, no panic accompanied the flight upward. His grip on me was tight without being painful, and I knew that in either form, he was stubborn enough not to drop me even if he was shot out of the damn sky.

A few minutes later, I realized where he was heading.

Back to his treehouse.

On any other day, that would've been fine. Welcome, even.

But this wasn't any other day.

"Viervo!" I called, hoping the use of his full name would shock him into listening to me. "I followed the female fae and saw where they took the other women. We have to get the other guys and go after them!"

The phoenix roared at me.

But, a few minutes later, he spiraled back into the trees.

My side met his chest as he landed on a thick branch, and a moment later, my feet were on the smooth wood and my back was pressed against it too. Ervo's hands lifted to the trunk on either side of my head, and I tipped my head back so I could look him in the eyes as he glowered down at me.

His chest heaved, rising and falling rapidly against me.

"I told you to stay in the tree," he finally said, his voice furious and uneven. "I told you to stay in the fucking tree, Mare. And then I woke up, and you were gone. And you never gave me your name yourself, so I couldn't try to call you to me. And—"

I put a hand on his chest, directly over his pounding heart. "I followed them. I couldn't stay put while they were all being taken away. Didn't you find my scent in the trees?"

His responding grimace told me that he either hadn't looked, or hadn't found it.

"Did Priel and Lian use North and January's names?" I asked.

"It didn't work." Ervo's eyes shut, his breathing still harsh and uneven. "We think the female fae's ceremony stopped it." His eyes opened again, and damn, they were pissed. "You *left*."

"I had to do something. You vanished into the dome, and it was so silent." I gestured in the direction of the place. "I was terrified, okay? But I knew I couldn't fight them, and I needed to do *something*."

"You scared the hell out of me," he snapped. And then he took a deep breath in, and let it out slowly. "But I'm proud of you."

My throat swelled. "Me too," I admitted quietly.

His hand wrapped around the back of my neck, and the other arm slid around my waist as he pulled me to his chest and hugged me hard. My arms went around him as I hugged him back even tighter, holding him fiercely.

We stood like that for longer than I expected, but shit, I hadn't realized how much I needed it.

"We're going to help the other men get their females back," Ervo eventually said in a low voice. "And then I'm not going to let you out of my arms for an entire week. Understand?"

My body warmed further. "I understand."

Seven

There were hundreds of men gathered when we finally landed back by the dome. The dome, which was in pieces, now. I supposed that was probably for the best.

At the front of the group, Lian was pacing, and Priel was arguing with Aev. Their eyes were shifted, and there was something much more wild-looking about all three of them.

Lian surged toward us when we landed, snarling, "Where are they?"

"Control your temper when you speak to my female or I'll control it for you, brother," Ervo growled back.

Considering the phoenix was barely keeping his own anger under control, I found the threat kind of ironic. But then again, when had Ervo not been protective of me like that?

"My mate and the child she's growing have been captured by women who would keep them away from me for the rest of their lives, and apparently have the magic to do so," Lian said through gritted teeth. "Excuse me for having a *temper*."

I put a hand on Ervo's abdomen, stepping up next to him and quickly saying, "It's okay. I get it. The fae women took our ladies to a cave whose entrance was a crack between two rocks, and then sealed it with magic after they went in. I'm sure you've already figured it out, but I'm pretty sure they're performing the sacrifice-ceremony to determine whether or not the women are life-bringers."

"And they undoubtedly have a plan to keep our females from us if they are," Priel growled.

"Maybe," I agreed. "But North is probably going to be the lead life-bringer after they've finished their identification ceremony, which will change things. If worst comes to worst, we can use me as bait."

"No." Ervo's voice was hard.

"We'll rip their fucking throats out before that," Lian said darkly.

"Okay, let's not do that," I said quickly. "Let's just get to them and see what happens."

"None of the women die, human or fae," another man growled from somewhere nearby."

I nodded. "Agreed."

And with that, we took to the sky.

ABOUT THREE-QUARTERS of the way there, Lian suddenly vanished from where he had been flying beside me.

I blinked rapidly at the place the missing dragon had been.

Below us, I heard a few growls. When I looked down, Priel was also gone.

Shit.

Aeven, who was a sabertooth, was gone when my gaze moved to where *he* had been.

We flew faster, then, worried that the women had been hurt in some way.

TWENTY MINUTES LATER, we were standing in front of the cave. It was still sealed up tight, and I couldn't hear a damn thing.

When I started walking toward it, Ervo stopped me with a hand on my hip. His chest met my back, and he murmured, "You're not going anywhere near that."

And then he pulled me more tightly against him.

Well.

Okay, then.

Honestly, I was too exhausted to complain. And even if I wasn't, my nerves were absolutely shot.

One of the unseelies I didn't recognize prowled toward the stone boulder and put a hand on it. A moment later, the stones split the way they had been before.

The unseelie man looked toward us.

As if in slow motion, I watched as a massive spear cut through his chest from behind.

My heart dropped into my stomach and horror blossomed within me.

The man looked down at the weapon sticking out of him, and then slowly sank to his knees, revealing the female fae leader, Fovea.

Shock rolled through the group.

The male fae fought frequently, but not like that.

Not stabbing someone in the back.

Ervo dragged me backward, and men surged forward, blocking me from her view.

"Give us the final human female and we will release your kings," Fovea said calmly. "Keep her from us, and more of you will die."

Silence reigned among the fae men.

I desperately wanted to see inside that cave, to know what was happening to my friends. To help them, in whatever small way I was capable of.

But I remained where I was.

And stayed silent.

"You have one hour before my spear finds another brutal male heart," the female leader said, before stepping back into the cave. She put a hand on the stone wall, and the hiding place resealed itself.

A few of the unseelies silently picked up the body of the dead fae.

My eyes watered for him.

For the way the life had drained from his eyes.

The way his death could've been completely avoidable...

I couldn't let that happen again.

"They won't kill Aev, Lian, or Priel," Nev said, from a few feet away from us. "The women seem to take care of each other, even the harsh ones. Killing the mated men would end the human women, so I don't think they'll do it."

"And they won't kill me, if I go in there," I added.

"No." Ervo's voice was hard, but even. "You're staying right here."

Murmurs of agreement rolled through the group, but I noticed that Nev's wasn't one of them.

"Did Priel or Lian give any of you their full names?" someone asked Nev. I was pretty sure the question was geared toward all of the seelies.

Teris scowled. "Of course not."

"I'm not watching anyone else die," I said to the group, raising my voice. "I'm going in there."

"Not a fucking chance." The phoenix's voice was a snarl.

Nev caught my eye, and tipped his head toward the forest. I nodded, turning and walking in that direction.

Growls and arguments began to break through the previously-calm group, but Nev was my focus for the time being.

We walked for a few minutes—Ervo never releasing his hold on me—until stopping with Nev and Teris.

"I have an idea," the basilisk said to us in a low voice. He looked at Ervo. "But you're not going to like it." He looked at me. "You probably won't either."

Great.

"I'm listening," I said anyway.

He dipped his head in a nod. "We need someone on the inside to communicate with. As it stands, we have no idea what we'd face if we walked in now. Many of us could use Naomi's name, but that would only lead to bloodshed. It has to be a male on the outside, if we want to control the situation."

I was pretty sure I knew where he was going with this, and was entirely certain I didn't like it.

But I remained silent anyway, hearing him out.

His attention was entirely on me as he said the next part. "If the two of you sealed your mate bond, you could communicate. Ervo could remain out here, and you could go inside and figure out what's going on. You could tell him, and we could get our girls out."

I was right about his idea.

Honestly, it was the only real call.

Even if it meant mating with Ervo this long before I felt ready, before we knew each other, before… well, before we did anything that should logically come before mating.

Friendship.

Sharing our thoughts and dreams.

Understanding each other.

Playing around without actually sealing the bond.

"And then what?" Ervo growled. "The fae women are going to try this shit again, now that they know it works."

"Not if we kill their leader." Nev's expression was wicked.

"No." This time, my voice was the even one. "Fovea has so many brands; we don't know how Vevol will respond if she dies. And there are already few enough women. We underestimated them this time, but it won't happen again. They don't know where the Stronghold is, or the location of anything else that you guys have built since they were hidden away; we can go somewhere else until we can make them understand that they don't get to control us. No one else needs to die."

Even as I said the words, I remembered the ruthless way the leader had ended that male fae's life.

In the female fae's minds, they were still at war with the men. It would take something drastic for them to see things differently.

But for now, Nev was right about his plan.

It was the best way for us to get out of the current shitty situation with as little death as possible. Just a Band-Aid over a much larger problem, but a Band-Aid nonetheless.

"I'll do it," I said quietly, looking at Ervo. "We can't leave the other girls in there, and no one else needs to die. It's not fair to them."

Even as I said the words, my heart clenched.

This wasn't the way I wanted things to happen. I'd wanted to make sure we were on the same page about everything—to make sure we knew each other perfectly, to the point where having sex would feel incredible, even if it ended up just as bad as it had been back on Earth.

To make sure he really, honestly loved me.

"I don't care what's fair to them, Mariah. It's not fair to *you*," my phoenix growled back.

"What's not fair about it? I get to mate with the guy I've been trying to make notice me for months," I said, though the words were a bit weak.

Honestly, I wanted to wait.

But that wasn't an option.

And I didn't think I would ever regret a choice I made to free the girls who had become my family.

"Are you in?" I asked him.

"Of course I'm in," he scowled. "But I'm not just going to watch you walk into a cave I might not get you back from."

"I'll give you my name."

His eyes narrowed. "I want you to want this, Mariah."

"I do," I said bluntly.

It was the truth.

It was faster than I wanted, but I *did* still want it.

"I'll leave you two to figure it out. Take as much time as you need; there are some unseelie bastards our world would be better off with—" Nev began, but cut himself off when the ground beneath me rippled.

I looked down in time to fall through the portal that had appeared beneath my feet as a familiar female voice said my name.

Mariah.

Ana's word rippled through the air as I landed on my ass in a room I didn't know.

The air was cold and humid, the stone beneath me rough and icy.

A group of the other ex-human women were lined up against a wall beside me, with something that looked like blood smeared on their faces in lines that had to be some kind of ancient glyphs. I tried to look at all of them, to see if my closest friends were there.

Sunny and Dots were missing—I realized that, and counted the rest of the women quickly.

Fourteen.

Five were missing, then, because there were twenty of us in total, myself included.

They all looked absolutely terrified.

At the end of the row, North was on her knees. There were tears streaking down her face, and January and Ana had their arms wrapped around her, like they were holding the dark-haired oracle in place.

Ana's gaze met mine and her lips formed two words, her expression dark and panicked.

Those two words made my stomach clench.

"I'm sorry."

Ana didn't apologize.

She wasn't a bad person—I'd known her four years, and probably knew more about her than any of the other current seelie ladies did. She had been in the military, and horrible things had happened to her. Without any family to call her own, she had spiraled when she was released from duty.

And now, she was *apologizing* to me.

A heavy thud sounded on my right, and my head jerked in that direction.

I was still on the ground, on my hands and knees.

And now, Priel's bleeding, unconscious body was less than a foot from my face.

The man looked *horrible*.

There were cuts on his face, and arms, and chest. None of them looked shallow, and all of them bled profusely.

My stomach rolled.

Was this because of me?

My gaze lifted to the woman in front me.

Fovea.

Fear and hatred welled up inside me as one.

"Now, before the steam fades," Fovea commanded the other women in the cave. I hadn't looked around, but the room felt wide and open.

Three women surged toward me, catching me off guard so I didn't have time to fight, or move.

Two of the woman grabbed me—one harshly taking my arms and pinning them behind me. The other grabbed my face, gripping my hair and chin as she held my head still.

The third woman kneeled in front of me, a dagger in one hand and a small bowl of blood-like liquid in the other.

My head was held firmly in place as the fae woman dipped the tip of the dagger in the liquid before lifting it to my face.

She dragged that knife over my flesh, cutting and tracing an intricate pattern of some kind over my face.

The sting made my eyes water, but I didn't let myself move. Not while the knife was so close to my face, to my eyes and nose.

One final, slow drag of the knife over my bottom lip was the last of the markings.

The woman finally lowered the dagger.

Those holding me didn't release me.

A small surge of power rolled through me, and then into the room.

Fovea's face darkened. "Another harsh. Put her with the others."

I was yanked to my feet and then dragged across the room and deposited on the opposite side of the row from North and January.

My eyes landed on another, much smaller row.

One consisting of only five women.

Sunny and Dots were among them.

If I was harsh, and the others were too, then the five of them had been declared life-bringers.

But...

I tried to look down the row, to see January.

She was pregnant. Her abdomen had rounded slightly, and the other symptoms were present too.

The harsh women weren't supposed to be able to grow babies, though.

Right?

"We have no need of harsh females who cannot obey orders," Fovea said coldly to the rest of the female fae in the room. "We take our life-bringers, and go."

My eyes collided with Sunny's.

Despite her usual feigned confidence, she looked terrified.

If I were facing the forced breeding process the same way she was, then I would be terrified too.

The female fae began to move.

Three of them grabbed Dots, Sunny, and the other new life-bringers.

So many others surrounded those five.

"Stop," North said, nearly snarling the words. "If I'm harsh, then I can challenge you for leadership."

Every fae in the room froze.

"How many brands do you possess?" Fovea hissed.

"Seventy-one."

A sharp inhale seemed to cut through the room.

"Impossible," Fovea finally snapped.

"I have more than you, don't I?"

"An equal number," the fae woman spat. "We will count them."

"Yours *and* mine," North growled.

"Find an ettisho," Fovea ordered one of the women.

She disappeared into a small crack in the wall, barely fitting through.

The room was tense and silent.

I could hear roaring and snarling outside, coming from my right. In the opposite direction from where the other woman had disappeared.

Were there two entrances to the cave?

One minute passed, and then another.

It couldn't have been more than five by the time the woman slinked back into the room holding a long, thick red stone in her hand. The shape of it reminded me of a disposable water bottle.

Fovea removed her clothes, stripping out of the long, dress-like top and then removing the thong-looking underwear she'd had on beneath it.

North stepped away from our group and took off her own tank top and shorts.

The women faced each other, looking like complete opposites. One short and pale, with dark hair, burning reddish-orange eyes, and a slim figure. The other, tall and dark, with white hair, bright blue eyes, and so much muscle she somehow managed to look like both a model and bodybuilder at the same time.

When the female fae gave the stone to Fovea, I noticed that her palm was covered in something that looked like extremely-pigmented red chalk.

Fovea snapped the stone in half, giving one piece to the woman who had retrieved it before looking at North. "Who will count for you?"

North didn't hesitate. "Mare."

My heart clenched, but I stepped forward.

We needed to look strong. I didn't know why she thought I could do that—or why she hadn't chosen Ana, who would start a fight with anyone or anything if she thought it would help even slightly. Or January, whose pregnant belly ensured that no one would attack her, even if they had the same question I did about how she was growing a baby if she was a harsh.

I accepted the other half of the stone from Fovea anyway, stepping back into place beside North. The texture of it was almost exactly the same as chalk.

Fovea stretched out an arm, and the woman beside her dragged the end of the stone over her first brand and saying aloud, "One."

The women glared at us.

It must've been our turn.

"One," I said, after running my own fae-chalk over North's first brand.

The fae women went next, repeating the motion on another brand, and calling, "Two."

The process was simple, and the pace picked up as we continued going back and forth, counting carefully.

Everyone was holding a breath when we finally reached the end.

Fovea's last brand was traced on the back of her right ankle. "Seventy-one."

I chalked the final brand on the top of North's left foot. "Seventy-one."

The fae woman whose name I didn't know carefully re-inspected every single inch of Fovea's skin, moving her braids as needed, and even peering at the leader's scalp while looking for one last, hidden brand.

None was found.

With a dark expression, the fae carefully set her chunk of the chalk—ettisho—on the ground. "Seventy-one," she repeated.

I followed her lead, carefully looking over North's skin. The girl's hair was already stained reddish-black thanks to the chalk I'd gotten in it as I moved it around earlier, but I didn't hesitate to move it again, looking for just one more marking.

One last brand would change everything. It would force the harsh to accept peace—and to release our women.

But I didn't find one.

So, with my heart pounding in my ears, I slowly lowered our ettisho to the ground and then stood back up, saying, "Seventy-one."

Silence rang through the cave. The men outside had stopped fighting ages ago. I didn't know where they were, or what they were doing—but none of us dared to bring it up.

Priel was still unconscious, though the blood had dried on his skin after his wounds healed themselves.

Earlier, I'd noticed Aev and Lian, both also unconscious, dropped unceremoniously in the corner of the room furthest from the women. A few female fae guarded them—though I was pretty sure they were threatening more than protecting.

"How do we determine the leader, then?" North asked, her voice hard.

"A fight, to decide which of us can better protect our life-bringers. Under the full moon," Fovea said, through a clenched jaw. "The victor leads. The loser becomes second-in-command."

My throat swelled.

Either way, North was going to have some say in how the fae women ran things.

"I don't know how to fight," North said, her own jaw tightening.

"Then I suppose you have three weeks to learn. Until then, I retain full control." The female fae's eyes narrowed at North, but I noticed them flick to January, and linger on the curve of her abdomen for a long moment.

Finally, she gave her women one last command.

"Leave the unwilling protectors. We go now."

The first of the harsh women shifted their fingers into claws, many of them also gripping weapons, as they moved fluidly toward the crack in the wall that the woman had slipped through to get the chalk.

The speed and unity with which they moved was kind of impressive, but I didn't miss the way their gazes went.

The same way the queen's had gone; to January.

And to the swell of her belly.

They had lived for hundreds of years, at least. Always being taught that they couldn't create life, and that they were made to protect those who could.

A shiver rolled down my spine as I realized how they must've felt, seeing a harsh woman growing the life they had always protected so fiercely.

They must've wondered whether or not they could do the same—and fought the urge to drag January into their arms and protect her the way they had always protected their own pregnant females.

Fovea wanted to retain the sliver of control she still felt like she held. She didn't want to bring it up—or voice those thoughts.

But she had to be having them.

Anyone would've, in her situation.

And something told me that because of those thoughts, everything was going to change.

We just had to survive until then.

Eight

Ervo

"Hold your positions. They're coming," Nev hissed. "Screw this up and we castrate you."

He'd stepped into the leadership position after all hell broke loose, and though I wouldn't admit it aloud, I was grateful.

I could feel the rope of my sanity fraying, piece by piece.

When my female had disappeared, called away by the full name she had never given me, I could've ripped that fucking cave apart with my bare hands. I tried to, even—but my brothers stopped me before I got anyone killed.

Now, I waited with the others.

The waiting might be the end of me, but it was safer for my female.

So I waited.

Mariah's damned hellhounds had emerged from the forest shortly after she vanished, interrupting the fighting to report to me what they'd found when they followed the female fae:

A back entrance to the cave.

It was small—too small for any of the males to fit through.

But they'd listened in, and heard my Mariah declared a harsh fae.

And heard North challenge Fovea's leadership.

We weren't sure what would happen—but we had listened to every tense moment that had gone down in the cave, carefully morphing the crack in the stone to amplify the noise.

Mariah's counting had calmed the fury coursing through my blood, just enough to let me remain in control. The repetition of her voice, reminding me that she was alive and whole, kept me anchored.

And when Fovea finally commanded her females to retreat, we were prepared.

Our masses parted, a quarter of the men remaining at the front entrance to the cave, in case the women decided to use it.

We waited silently, following the plan Nev had set into motion.

All of us remained hidden as the women began to emerge, never looking far enough into the trees to see us, in part thanks to the memis leaves that Vuvim had ordered all of us to use to conceal our scents.

As much as it rankled to obey the unseelie general, the basilisk knew how to remain hidden better than anyone else, so we followed his orders.

The hellhounds and basilisks silently stalked all of the female fae into the forest, until the last one finally emerged.

And then, our men attacked.

No blood was spilled—we'd prepared the same damn koveko they had, and used it to knock them out just as swiftly as they had used it on us. But rather than cowardly filling a dome with poisonous gas, we'd soaked cloth with the plant's liquid.

The cloth was pressed to their lips and noses, so they knew exactly what had happened and who had bested them.

The bitches had caught us off-guard, but it wouldn't happen again.

Not on my mate's life.

I didn't bother assisting with the female fae, not when so many of my brothers were looking forward to the fight.

No—I didn't give a damn about the victory.

The only thing I cared about was inside that cave.

Teris's hands were planted to the stone beside mine and so many of my brothers as we slammed our power into the rock, commanding Vevol to give us what we wanted. A fierce crack echoed through the forest's canopy as we focused our magic to open the cave completely, revealing the rest of the females we had failed to protect.

As soon as the gap was wide enough, I abandoned the magic, surging into the cave.

Blood pounded through my body so loudly that it drowned out all noise as I saw my female on her knees, beside North. They leaned over Priel, but a single glance told me that his chest still rose and fell steadily. His coloring was normal, too—so the bastard was fine.

Just poisoned, like the rest of us. And slightly worse for the wear, according to the dried blood on his skin.

With his mate beside him, he would recover quickly.

My Mariah's eyes lifted to me just before I reached her, hauling her up off the ground and yanking her fiercely to my chest.

I wouldn't release her.

Never again.

I'd tie the woman to my side for every day of every remaining century we would live through.

She was *mine.*

And I'd failed her yet again.

Her lips moved as I stalked out of the cave, shifting and launching us into the sky. I couldn't hear her—not while the adrenaline pumped through me so ferociously, not while the panic and fear I had felt were still flooding every pore I possessed.

Not when I'd come so close to losing her.

Nine

Mare

I THOUGHT I had seen Ervo lose control before, but I was wrong. The fury that had possessed him before was nothing like the one that had claimed him now. He couldn't even seem to hear me speak as he grabbed me out of the cave and took off into the sky.

My fingers were buried in his golden feathers again, but this time, he was on fire. The flames didn't burn my skin, simply stroking my flesh and warming me completely.

Despite the tension and fear that had overwhelmed me in the cave, I felt calm on his back, flying through the forest with him.

Nothing that had happened in that cave made sense. I still had so many questions, too.

But before I got answers to any of them, I was going to have to figure out how to calm my phoenix down.

My face heated when I realized I'd started thinking of him as mine. But...

Wasn't he?

He'd never looked at another woman the way he looked at me. He'd never touched one of them. Never pinned them to a tree and told them they were his.

Never lost his shit when one of them was in danger.

So maybe he was kind of mine.

And maybe I was kind of his.

No decisions had really been made on that front, though. Our conversation during the dance party had been a huge step in the right direction, but things weren't finished. Not even close.

Exhaustion begun to settle into my bones as soon as we were far enough from the cave not to see or hear anyone else.

I leaned against him, barely managing to keep my eyes open so I didn't fall asleep and plummet off his back. He probably wouldn't let me, but I didn't know if he was back to his right-mind yet, so I wasn't going to risk it.

The forest was silent and peaceful as we flew for hours, and the sun was setting when we finally reached Ervo's house.

I gripped his feathers tightly until they morphed into skin, and then loosened my hold on his muscles.

He walked me straight into the kitchen, his hand spread under my ass to hold me upright as he pulled out a pan and started cooking.

"I need to sleep," I whispered to him, so exhausted I was dizzy.

"After you've eaten."

I sighed, dropping my forehead to his shoulder.

Every time I started to doze, he'd squeeze my ass, waking me up.

A few minutes later—which felt like much, much longer—he was carrying me and a large plate of food to the bed. When he sat down on the mattress, he set me down next to him and put the plate on his lap.

One of his hands stopped me when I started lowering my back to the bed. The other hand scooped up a spoonful of food, lifting it to my mouth. I was too exhausted to even look at it and see what it was, so I shook my head at him.

"Eat, and I'll let you sleep." He pressed the spoon to my lips. "Your stomach stopped growling a few hours ago; you've got to eat."

I groaned, but the sound didn't earn me any compassion.

So, I finally opened my mouth.

He slipped the spoon inside, removing it so I could chew and swallow. The man had another bite ready by the time I was done with the first, and when he wouldn't take no for an answer, I accepted it.

Slowly, I made my way through the entire plate he'd made for me.

When I was finally done, I fell asleep before my head even hit the pillow.

WHEN I WOKE UP, I felt severely disoriented. There was drool on my chin, and sweat soaking my sheets and pillow.

The smell surrounding me was incredible, but something about the situation felt wrong.

I finally cracked my eyes open and looked around.

I was... in Ervo's bed.

But where was Ervo?

Carefully, I picked my head up and looked around the room.

I found the man in the kitchen, stirring something violently.

"How long was I asleep?" I rasped to him.

"Over a day," he growled back.

A glance out at the forest beyond the balcony told me it was probably the middle of the night.

The blankets next to me weren't warm, and the yummy scent on them wasn't fresh.

Hmm.

"Did you sleep next to me?" I asked.

"No."

I frowned. "Why not?"

"You weren't awake to give me permission." His voice was clipped. "And I don't need the sleep."

Like hell he didn't.

"Why wouldn't you need sleep?"

"I failed to protect my female yet again. I need training—not rest."

Oh.

There was no reason for him to feel guilty about what had happened with the female fae, but...

Well, I wasn't surprised that he did.

"How did you fail me?" I asked him.

"You were pulled from my arms and into that cave, where anything could've happened to you."

"You didn't have my name," I pointed out.

That was my fault, honestly.

"I should've earned your trust enough to have it," he growled back.

Whatever he was stirring in that bowl was getting a lot of attention, because the man still hadn't looked over his shoulder at me.

Clearly, I needed to do something.

My mind whirred with possible options, but I didn't want to think or overthink about that.

I just wanted to... act. To feel.

To live, like I'd wanted to for so long.

And living meant acting without thinking, sometimes.

So I walked into the kitchen, and slid between the massive man and the batter he was whipping.

And then, I wrapped my arms around his middle.

He went still when I pressed my head to his chest. I was so tiny next to him, but I didn't mind that. Not in the slightest.

"I need you to hug me back, Viervo," I whispered to him.

Slowly, his hands unclenched from the bowl and strange-looking whisk.

And when he took a step back, walking me with him, his arms wrapped around me too.

My eyes closed, and I leaned into him. He was so warm, and smelled so nice.

The beat of his heart against my ear calmed me, too.

There were still problems between us that we needed to resolve—mainly, the months he'd spent thinking I was rejecting him. And the months I'd spent thinking he was rejecting me. And the fact that despite our interest in each other, and the way I trusted him with my life, we weren't really *friends*.

"Thank you for being there," I said quietly to him. "For getting me out of the cave, and bringing me here."

There was a long moment of silence between us, but it was so, so comfortable.

His arms tightened around my back. "I should've done more, sooner."

"What happened down there needed to happen," I murmured, hoping it would help him realize that he'd done more than enough. "North challenged Fovea. They're going to fight during the full moon, and she's going to lose. But when she loses, she'll become second-in-command, and we'll have some say in how the fae women function. The female fae realized that January is a harsh who's pregnant, which means there's a chance they could get pregnant too. I feel like that's going to change everything for them."

"You still should never have been in danger like that."

Damn, he was persistent.

I needed… to distract him.

Somehow.

So I changed the subject. "Have you eaten?"

Sometimes food could be the best distraction.

"Yes."

I scrambled for another distraction.

The only one I could really come up with was… well, me.

"I'm going to shower. Do you think you could come and stay by me while I do?" I checked. "I don't want to be alone right now."

Though I wasn't looking up at him when I asked the question, I could feel his stare.

He didn't answer.

I waited a minute, and then another.

His cock was hardening against my abdomen, and damn, I loved that.

"Yes," he finally growled.

Phew.

I fought the urge to do some kind of terrible victory dance.

I would enjoy the *hell* out of distracting him with my naked body.

"Perfect." I brushed my lips over his nipple, fighting a grin at the way his erection throbbed against my belly.

When I started to step away, he didn't release me.

I lifted my gaze to his. "You have to let go, if I'm going to get in the shower."

His reluctance was evident, but he finally released his hold on my waist.

My hips swayed heavily as I strode to the bathroom. Ervo's hand snaked around me, gripping my hip tightly as he stepped up right behind me. My ass brushed his erection with every motion, and his chest was rumbling when we made it to the bathroom.

He leaned with me when I stretched into the shower to turn the water on, and then stepped back with me when I did the same so I could strip my clothes off.

The man inhaled sharply when my tank top went over my head.

He took another two steps back until his ass met the sink, his hands gripping the edge of it like it was the only thing stopping him from reaching over and grabbing *me*.

I slid my shorts down my thighs, dropping them on the ground and then reaching up to my hair. I'd spent an insane amount of time trying to keep it smooth and under control back on Earth, because my family required it. So, since I'd come to Vevol, I simply let the curls do what they wanted and put them up in a puff on top of my head.

I actually thought the style suited my face more than any of the ones I'd fought so hard to maintain before. And the fae version of shampoo never seemed to dry out my hair, leaving it soft and bouncy.

My curls remained pointed to the sky even after I tugged the hair tie out and tossed it toward the sink. Ervo caught it before it landed, lifting the fabric to his nose and inhaling lightly, then slipping it over his wrist.

When I shook my hair out, pushing it down with my fingers, most of the strands finally fell around my shoulders. Sunny had been a hair stylist back on Earth, so she always trimmed it for me before it got too long. I wasn't a fan of ultra-long curls because they were a pain in the ass, and would make my puff extremely huge. She'd taught me how to cut her hair too, so we always joked that we kept each other looking hot.

Ervo's gaze was molten, his jaw clenched as he watched me step into the shower. It didn't have a door at all, or a wall to block anything out. But it was pretty damn huge, so I didn't think the water would splash outside of the area.

Feeling him watch me that closely, knowing he was watching my every move, made me hot.

My eyes closed, my head tipping back as the warm water moved over my skin. Ervo growled, and I glanced over at the sink in surprise when I heard a loud cracking noise.

Shit.

He'd legitimately cracked the side of the sink.

I studied him, as he stared at me.

He was always so controlled. And I understood—I had spent most of my life hiding in the shadows in an attempt to avoid being noticed.

Sometimes, keeping your expression neutral and your mouth shut was the only way to survive.

Ervo seemed to have adopted the same mindset as I had—but to an extreme.

He was always worried about me, taking care of me, and never caring about himself.

If we were ever going to have a shot at being together, though, he needed to open up a little. Admit what he wanted.

If looking at me naked was intense enough for him to break the sink, there had to be some desire behind it. The desire to touch me, or taste me, or hold me, I would suspect.

"Why aren't you in here with me?" I asked him, closing my eyes and lifting my face back up toward the running water.

"I wasn't invited," he said, his voice low.

"You didn't ask for an invitation."

Silence answered me.

I gave him time to process what I'd said, remaining quiet as I reached for the soap on a small shelf against the far side of the shower.

"It's my job to provide for you," he finally said. "Not to take what I want."

"Don't you think providing warm hugs and soft touches is part of that? And what about orgasms?"

His chest rumbled at that.

"Besides, asking if you can get in the shower with me is *not* taking what you want. I could say no. Any time that I could say no, you're not taking from me."

He rumbled louder, but said nothing.

I grabbed the bar of shampoo, but when he spoke, stopped it a few inches from my curls.

"Can I wash your hair?" he asked roughly.

Finally.

"Sure. You'd have to get in here for that, though." I gestured to the open space around me.

He rumbled more loudly, and stepped toward me.

I realized what he was going to do an instant before he did it, and blurted, "No clothes allowed, phoenix."

He paused outside the shower and said in a low voice, "I don't want you to feel pressured into anything."

A snort escaped me. "I just *convinced* you to get in the shower with me, and you're worried about pressuring me?"

His Adam's apple bobbed as he swallowed.

"Shorts off. Ass in the shower," I ordered him. "Or I wash my own damn hair."

He finally stripped his shorts down those thick thighs.

I watched him closely, waiting to see the erection I'd felt so many times.

And *damn*, it did not disappoint.

My body heated further as he stepped under the water with me, and I might as well have caught on fire when his hands landed on my waist, easing me a few steps closer to him.

He stopped me before his erection met my back, unfortunately.

And then he snagged the shampoo bar from my hand, rubbing it between his palms before lifting them to my scalp.

A groan escaped me when those long, thick fingers massaged my head.

His chest was still rumbling so much I could practically feel it.

"So do you want me to let you set the pace?" I asked him, barely managing to get the words out while he continued slowly working on my head.

"What do you mean?" His voice was gruff, and if I'd needed any help in that department, would've been a big ole' turn-on.

"You want us to be mates, right?"

"We *are* mates." His answer was quick, and harsh. Like he couldn't stand the thought of me questioning that.

"I'm talking about the physical stuff. Like, is it okay if I kiss you any time I want? Or touch you when I want? Or do you want me to just follow your lead and let you make the rules? I know you've never done anything sexual before, so all of this is new for you. I don't want to make you uncomfortable," I explained.

There was a long moment before Ervo finally admitted, "It would be almost impossible to make me more uncomfortable than I am right now."

...Oh.

My stomach twisted.

I'd made him unhappy, when I pushed him to get into the shower with me.

I stepped away from his hands quickly. "I'm sorry. I shouldn't have pushed you to get in here with me. It's too soon—I should've realized it was too soon." I spun away from him, every beat of my heart making me more nauseous.

I'd probably made him feel violated. Or—

"No, Mariah. It's not too soon. Not even close. That's not—I didn't mean uncomfortable that way." He let out a long, slow breath. "Seeing you like this, touching you like this... it's intense for me. All of the blood rushed to one fucking place, and that's not entirely comfortable. That's all I meant." His hand landed gently on my waist.

Understanding flooded me. "You're uncomfortably horny, you mean."

"Exactly."

I glanced over my shoulder, hoping to see his hand on his cock, but no luck.

"You said you were worried about my discomfort. I was trying to say that touching me, kissing me—they wouldn't make me any more uncomfortable than I am. I already want you with every breath I take."

It occurred to me that Ervo...

He wasn't great at putting his thoughts into words. At least not in the way I would understand them.

If I took what he'd just said at face value, he'd just told me that I was making him uncomfortable by touching him—which was an unpleasant thing in my understanding. But based on what he'd already said, I didn't think he meant unpleasant.

"I'm going to need you to be more direct than that," I said simply, stepping closer to him.

His gaze searched my face. "I want everything with you. *Everything*, Mariah. I ache for it—for all of it. For your hands and lips on every part of me, and mine on every part of you. I don't deserve it—I've failed you too many times. But that knowledge doesn't stop the wanting."

Understanding swelled in my chest.

He wanted me. Wanted to kiss me, to touch me. To be kissed by me, and touched by me.

He just didn't think he was worthy of it.

And feeling unworthy was definitely something that could make a person clam up without admitting their desires aloud.

If things were going to progress for us, I was going to have to prove to him that I didn't find him unworthy. And considering that he thought I'd been rejecting him for months, that probably wasn't going to be an easy feat.

My mind flashed back to that moment in the forest, when I'd been terrified that he was going to murder that whole damn pack of hellhounds. I didn't care for them either, given all that had happened, but I didn't believe in mass murder.

I'd sunk to my knees before him, and begged. "*Please*, Ervo."

The look of barely-contained fury in his eyes, as he hauled me back to my feet, was one I doubted I'd ever forget.

His words, I knew would linger in my mind for the rest of my life. *"You are far too important to ever kneel for a man."*

He had let the hounds live, but he'd only done it for me.

And with those words in my mind again, I understood exactly what I needed to do, to know whether or not he believed he was worthy of me.

I needed to kneel in front of him.

Not today, in the shower. He would snarl those same damn words at me if I tried that.

But it was something to aim for.

A goal, a progress marker.

And damn, I had always loved a good goal.

Usually they were reading goals, though.

With a plan starting to bubble and boil in my mind, I simply said, "Okay," and turned my back to him. "Will you finish washing my hair?"

"Of course." His voice softened, and his fingers slid back into my hair.

And as he massaged my scalp until my whole damn body was jello, I plotted.

Ten

When I shut the water off, Ervo grabbed a towel. He wrapped it carefully around me, then grabbed the second towel and used it gently on my hair.

"I'm pretty sure you're supposed to dry yourself off with that one," I said playfully, making him chuckle softly.

"I'd rather it smell like you before I wrap it around myself."

My face warmed a bit.

My plan was so damn worth it.

I had to take things slow, of course, move in baby steps… but like I said, it was worth it.

When he was satisfied that my curls were dry enough, and his towel smelled enough like me, he removed it from my hair and wrapped it around his waist.

I'd already rolled my towel up above my breasts, so it would stay in place on its own.

"I'm going to wash my clothes," I told him, grabbing them off the ground and carrying them to the sink. "I know you guys usually just burn the smell and germs off everything, but I like it when they smell fresh, like soap." I slid them into the sink, turning the water on.

"I need to finish your food," he told me, though he leaned up against the wall of the bathroom instead of leaving. His eyes followed my hands as I scrubbed the clothes quickly with soap.

The sexy bastard had no idea what the first step of my plan was, and that made me stupidly excited.

"I'll help you cook. But you have to eat too," I warned him. "And sleep next to me afterward. I'm not very tired, but it's still the middle of the night. We don't want to end up exhausted during the day."

"Fine. But when we wake up, I have to train," he warned me.

"Deal." I flashed him a quick smile, and his expression grew soft.

A few more minutes passed, and I continued scrubbing my clothes. He finally stepped out of the bathroom, and I heard fabric rustling as he got dressed. The shorts he'd been wearing earlier were still on the floor of the room, so I grabbed them up off the ground and threw them in the sink, washing them too.

When the clothes were as clean as they'd get, I draped them over the edge of the sink to dry, then padded out of the bathroom.

Ervo was cooking in a clean pair of shorts. They were a deep red color instead of his typical black, and I stared at his ass without a shred of shame for a moment before finally crossing the treehouse.

"What can I do?" I asked him, leaning up against the countertop.

He glanced over at me, and then did a double-take when he realized I was still completely naked.

"You can't cook naked," he rumbled at me. "Go read a book."

"I *can* cook naked, and will," I said calmly. "We already agreed. Give me something to do."

His jaw clenched.

He finally handed me a bowl of something that looked vaguely familiar, and a strange whisk that matched the one he'd been using when I woke up. "Whip this until it's smooth."

"Okay." I grabbed the bowl, dragging it to an empty spot in the kitchen, and then got to work whipping it. Though I didn't look over at Ervo, I felt his eyes on me every couple of seconds. He growled softly a few times, and I forced myself not to grin in response.

The whipping took a while, but I didn't mind it. I'd always liked cooking.

"What are these ingredients?" I asked him, as we worked. "We only ever had a few things delivered to us."

"Our visits were unwelcome, so we brought supplies that wouldn't go bad for a long time," Ervo explained. "Nothing goes bad quickly in Vevol—not plucked fruit, or pulled vegetables. But the things we brought you would last years, in case you decided to stop answering the door. Many of the men hoped to use fresher ingredients to sway the females into meeting with them, but you know how well that worked."

Yeah... not well.

It took a little prodding, but as I asked questions, he described the source of every single item we used. They all came from various plants, used in many different ways. My mind spun as I tried to remember all of the names, flavors, and uses for each of the plants.

"I might need a guidebook or something," I admitted, as Ervo plated the food we'd made.

"You can always ask again."

"I don't like asking. It's a pride thing." I shrugged lightly. "And I always feel like I should be able to remember after one time. It's frustrating, because I'm shitty at memorizing fae names and whatnot."

"You don't need to know anyone's name but mine," Ervo said bluntly.

I snorted, and his lips curved upward just slightly.

We took the food to the bed, and he stopped at the edge of the mattress, watching me slide up onto it. His gaze lingered a bit too long, but I didn't let him know that I'd noticed.

My toes brushed his calf as we ate together, quietly enjoying the food we'd made. Ervo wasn't a man of many words, rarely starting a conversation himself. If I spoke, though, he never ignored me. And I liked that a lot.

I noticed his eyelids looked like they'd started getting heavy while we ate, and a small sliver of worry tugged at me.

He wasn't taking care of himself.

"We can do the dishes after we sleep," I told him, grabbing the empty plate from his lap.

"I'll do them now," he murmured to me, trying to take the plate back.

I moved it further away. "I want you to hold me."

He swallowed roughly, and jerked his head in a nod.

After I set the plates down next to the bed, I slid closer to him. He'd already settled on his back, so I carefully draped half of my body over his.

His chest rumbled, and those big hands of his landed on my lower back and my shoulder blades, not minding my slightly-damp hair.

"Where did you learn my name?" I asked him softly, enjoying the warm strength of his body against mine.

"There was a letter in your room when I visited a few months ago, the one time you allowed me in. It was from Ana." He stroked my lower back lightly.

Ah.

"She wrote to me before she left. Apologized for being so quick to decide my nickname for me. I think she felt bad for strong-arming all of us for so long, but we weren't angry at her. She cared about us, and most of us didn't have people like that on Earth."

His fingers pressed a bit harder into my shoulders and back.

"How did you know how to pronounce it?" I wondered.

"Sunny and Dots were talking about Christmas music a few weeks ago. There was a singer who's known for it, with the same name. I connected the dots when I heard them say it."

Ohh.

That was actually pretty clever. And I was impressed that he'd gone to such lengths to learn my name. It must've meant a lot to him.

"As you know," I said quietly, "My name is Mariah. Mariah Lenore Kingston. My family is very well-known, on Earth. Famous, honestly. My father is an actor, my mother a high-profile lawyer. That probably doesn't mean anything to you, but basically, they were powerful. And they made it very clear to me that I was not."

Ervo went still beneath me.

Statue-still.

I waited for him to ask me what had happened. What my life had been like.

But he didn't.

I had a plan to make him more comfortable with me, but spilling sensitive information about my life without a request wasn't a part of that plan. If he wanted to know something, he was going to have to ask me.

So I didn't say anything else.

My eyes closed, though. I was extremely relaxed with his body against mine.

I'd started to fall asleep when the phoenix finally murmured to me, "Thank you, Mariah."

His arms tightened around me, pulling my bare skin closer to his.

I dragged my thigh up to rest against the underside of his erection, and earned a rumble for it.

"Will you tell me more about your family?" he murmured to me, just before I fell asleep. "I'd like to know how you ended up here."

The question definitely woke me up.

I sighed softly. "It's going to make me sound pitiful."

"That's not even remotely possible."

"Fine. I told you my family was famous. They wanted me to be like them; perfect. One of my older brothers graduated early and became one of the youngest surgeons in the country. The other one was a famous actor by the time he could talk, and his fame only grew from there."

I went on, "I hated crowds, and couldn't stand acting as a little kid, so I threw huge tantrums. Eventually, no one would hire me. When my parents hired the same tutors for me that they did my older brother, all of them agreed that I wasn't willing to learn, too busy with my head in a book. My parents decided I was a failure, and reminded me of it over, and over, and over again."

Ervo's body was deathly still, but his hand started to stroke my back slowly. I could tell it was taking him effort to stay still.

"I had one friend, growing up. Stacy. We were both failures to our parents, but we were there for each other. We both loved to ride horses, and would meet up most days and ride together. There was a storm—and a freak accident. Stacy died, and my parents decided to sell all of the horses. I'd just lost my best and only friend, and they took away the only other thing I really loved. I wasn't even eighteen at the time. I spent months trying to prove myself, so they would let me buy my horse back, but I wasn't allowed to work, and I was still in high school, so I couldn't just leave."

My voice grew softer. "After I graduated, they refused to give me money for college because of my many failures. I applied for jobs, so I could move out and go, but they made sure I didn't get those jobs. Didn't have transportation, either. I was completely at their mercy."

I continued, "The depression became overwhelming, and my thoughts grew very, very dark. A few days after my twentieth birthday, they lit the candles for the damn social media pictures. And as I leaned over, the only thing I could think to wish for was a new life. And then, like a miracle, you guys appeared in my parents' house—and you brought me here. Vevol was never a prison for me; it was a second chance."

Ervo was quiet for a long, long time.

He continued stroking my back, and I waited until he was ready to speak.

"I'm sorry about everything you went through," he finally said, his voice low and soft. "And I'm proud of all you survived."

My eyes watered. "Thank you."

He pulled me slightly closer to him—and I hugged him slightly tighter.

And we fell asleep just like that.

THE SUN WAS BARELY PEEKING over the horizon when a rough rocking motion dragged me from sleep.

I found myself in the exact same position I'd fallen asleep in—my bare body draped over Ervo's half-naked one, and my thigh pressing against his erection. Only, his erection had wormed itself free of the shorts he had on.

His hips were jerking slightly in his sleep, one of his fists clenched in the sheets, and the other on the pillow.

I wished they were in my hair.

His face was twisted in a snarl, and I could see the tip of him glistening.

He was having a wet dream.

And he was *close*.

This was about six steps further along my plan than I was supposed to be, but...

Screw the plan.

After what I'd admitted to him last night, I was feeling about six steps further along than before too.

I slid down his body, biting my lip as I approached his gigantic cock.

I'd only given two blowjobs before, and I was pretty sure I'd done them wrong. But...

I was going for it.

Ervo wouldn't know if I was doing it wrong anyway, and something told me he wouldn't care at all if I was.

My fingers wrapped around the base of him, and his body went still.

I didn't look up, but I felt his eyes on me.

The touch must've yanked him from his dream—and now he was watching me.

The show was going to get a hell of a lot better, too.

I lowered my lips to the head of his cock, and slowly wrapped them around him.

He throbbed in my mouth.

I lifted my tongue to the underside of him, dragging it slowly up that part of his length.

A fierce roar met my ears, and he lost control.

He thrust deeper into my mouth, his pleasure flooding my tastebuds with the flavor of him.

Damn, getting him off that fast made me feel powerful.

"Mariah," he growled at me, cupping my face with a massive palm and tugging my lips up off his cock.

"Hmm?" I licked the mess off my lips, and a ferocious snarl shook the bed.

He was on his feet a heartbeat later, stalking to the bathroom.

I blinked at his ass—or where it had been a moment ago.

Had he just ditched me?

Did he not enjoy that?

I'd already started realizing that his reactions to things made zero logical sense to me, so I didn't let myself jump to conclusions.

Instead, I climbed off the bed and followed him to the bathroom.

He'd left it unlocked, and now the shower was running. His shorts were on the ground, and he stood beneath the flow of the steaming water. One of his palms was on the wall, the other on his cock, giving me a sexy-as-hell side profile as he stroked himself roughly.

His face turned, his eyes molten as they watched me stare at him.

His hand halted on his erection, though.

"Don't stop for me," I said, folding my arms over my chest.

His eyes shut momentarily, and he let out a slow breath.

He opened them again… and he slowly resumed stroking himself, up and down, while he stared at me.

Damn, that was hot.

My body flushed as I watched him work his cock.

I wished I had an easier time orgasming, so I could sit on the edge of that damn toilet and just get myself off.

Unfortunately, my body didn't work that way.

I could still have fun, during sex. It was still enjoyable. I'd just never orgasm.

Which… was pretty damn frustrating, actually.

I pushed those thoughts away, though, as I watched Ervo touch himself. The roll of his hips, the rough motions of his hand on his cock. The curve of his ass, and the movement of his body.

Hot damn.

I was absolutely soaked by the time I watched him erupt, snarling and jerking as he painted the shower with his pleasure.

His chest heaved as he finally released his grip on himself, and then slowly stepped back under the water. His eyes remained locked on my figure, practically burning my skin, as the water cleaned him.

He didn't even bother grabbing soap before he stalked out of the shower, and over to me.

I didn't know what I expected him to do—but it wasn't to grab me by the hips and haul me back to his bed.

The man didn't even seem to notice the water dripping from his skin as he dropped me on the bed, scooting me to the very edge until my ass was hanging off.

Those massive, hot hands were on my thighs, then, spreading me open.

My face burned as he stared.

But my back arched when his fingers opened me up completely, so he could look at every part of me.

He lifted a thick finger to my folds, and dragged a slow circle around my most sensitive part. A cry escaped me, and he held me in place even as I arched harder, and higher. "This is your clit?"

"Yes," I panted.

His finger slid down my center, and traced a slow circle around my entrance.

The touch nearly made me whimper.

"And this is where my cock goes." This one wasn't a question, but a statement.

"Mmhm." I tried to stop my hips from rocking, but failed for the most part. Ervo held me firmly where he wanted me, though, as he acquainted himself with my most intimate parts.

"It stretches?" he asked, sliding just the tip of his finger inside me and tracing the opening.

"Yeah," I breathed.

His finger slid deeper, feeling around slowly in my channel, and his chest rumbled as my body clenched around him. "Are you sure it won't hurt you?"

"Depends," I managed. "If you stretch me with your fingers, first, I'll adjust faster. Without pain."

The rumbling in his chest grew lower, and louder. "What a hardship."

Even with his finger buried inside me, I caught the sarcasm in his voice and laughed breathlessly. "Good perspective."

His thumb dragged over my clit, and I arched.

"You said you have a hard time climaxing," he said, as he slipped a second finger inside me.

I breathed in sharply at the sensation. "Don't want to talk about that right now."

"We *need* to talk about that right now if I'm going to make this good for you. And I'm *going* to make it good for you."

The ferocity in his voice told me that wasn't debatable.

"Explain," he said.

When I didn't, his fingers went still inside me.

A groan escaped me. "I hate you."

"You don't." He stroked my clit lightly, making me squirm.

"I've only had an orgasm once. With a vibrating thing. I have to have something inside me stimulated at the same time my clit is. It doesn't make sense, and I've never really figured it out. But I—ohh." I choked on my own saliva as he started moving his fingers again, sliding them deeper.

There was a look of intense focus on his face as he slowly explored my inside walls.

My hips arched and rocked, but he didn't pay my clit the attention it wanted while he took his time learning my body.

Many of the touches made me move and pant, but I couldn't tell one from another as far as what it was that my body wanted to get off.

"You're killing me," I moaned, when he'd finally made it over every inch of my channel. "I need more."

"I know you do." He stroked my clit a few times, making me cry out and rock my hips more. "Let me take care of you, Mariah."

"I just want to lose it," I moaned.

The pleasure had started becoming too much, and I needed that ever-elusive release.

My stomach was clenched, my whole damn body tight. And—

He leaned in, sucking lightly on my clit as he stroked some part of me.

The climax hit me—and it hit me hard.

I screamed, bucking against his face as he dragged the orgasm out, and out, and out.

My eyes were stinging when the pleasure finally faded, my hips still rocking a bit.

And his gaze—it was satisfied like I'd never seen it before. "No man has ever brought you pleasure?"

"Never," I whispered, my throat swollen a little.

"Because you were made for me." He lowered his teeth back to my clit and slowly, softly, *torturously* dragged them over the sensitive skin. "You'll never go a day without a climax again."

"Is that a promise?" I asked, my voice slightly rough from the screaming.

"A vow." He slowly slid a third finger into my channel, stroking whatever he'd found that made me go off like a damn bomb. The reaction wasn't as intense this time, but shit, it still made me rock. "I want you to drench my fingers one more time before I feed you, Mariah."

"Like I could ever say no to that," I practically whimpered.

His growl of approval made my head spin—and then his lips and tongue made me scream.

Eleven

I SPENT the next few hours in a daze.

Ervo was still determined to train, so he led me down into the bottom level of his treehouse—which I hadn't known existed at all. It was built into the trunk of the tree itself, a massive, multiple-story obstacle course.

And upon seeing it, I realized why he moved so much faster than most of the other seelies I had seen him fighting before.

They were all naturally strong and fast, but he trained—and he must've done it often. With crazy-looking wooden and stone devices, he practiced over and over. Honing his skills, preparing for a fight.

I tried to remember all of the steps in my plan, though it had kind of been blown out of the water by what happened earlier. If we were ever going to become actual mates, we would need to become friends.

And though we were making progress, I didn't really think we were anywhere near that.

Though I did trust Ervo to keep me safe—and to be possessive—I didn't really know how to make myself believe that he wouldn't change his mind about wanting me.

The orgasms had been enough to prove to me that he didn't see me as a female brother, at least.

But wanting to bang someone's body and understand their mind were completely different, so...

I didn't really know what to think.

Deciding just to continue along with the plan I had originally crafted, I told Ervo I was going to the bathroom and climbed back up the spiral staircase that led back into the living area of the treehouse. I did use the bathroom—and then I headed to the kitchen, and started cooking. It was about time to eat, again anyway.

Less than two minutes after I'd started the food, Ervo was already storming into the room. His body gleamed with sweat, and hot damn, he looked good.

"What are you doing?" he asked me in a low, growly voice. His hands landed on my hips, his front pressing to my back.

"Cooking for you. I might not be as good as you, since I'm still trying to learn all of the ingredients, but I can make damn good Vevol-style beans and rice." I flashed him a smile.

He narrowed his eyes at me. "It's *my* job to cook for *you*."

I turned around to face him, feeling an argument coming on.

"Mates are partners. In my world, that implies that they both do things for each other," I countered. "And sharing duties includes the cooking. I should be allowed to cook for you."

"In my world, a male's duty is to care for his female's every need," Ervo growled back.

"In your mind, maybe, but not in your world. Have you seen the other partially-mated couples?" I tossed a hand in the direction everyone else was, though they were a long way away. "Most of the men basically ignore their women when they're not following them around or feeding them, and the women ignore the men too. If you and I work out, we'll only be the third successful, happy couple on this whole damn *planet*."

"*If* we work out?" His voice grew dangerously low.

"Yes, *if*. I still don't know you, and you don't know me."

"I know you." His answer was too quick, too angry.

"What's my favorite color?" I asked.

He blinked.

"What do I do when I'm stressed?" I pressed.

His expression darkened.

"What am I the most afraid of?"

Ervo stepped back, away from me.

I waited to see if he was going to say anything.

When he didn't, I added, "I don't just want a mate, you know. I want a friend. Someone who will become my family, my world. And I know even less about you than you know about me. Honestly, the only things I *do* know about you is that you'll protect me with your life, you're an extremely skilled fighter, and apparently that you like to read."

His jaw clenched tightly.

I waited.

The smell of something burning caught in my nose, and I spun back to the stove, grabbing the spoon and stirring the food rapidly.

When I glanced over my shoulder a few seconds later, Ervo was gone.

I FORCED myself to remain calm and not to let my heart ache too much as I finished cooking. Ervo had left, but his mind worked differently than mine. He might not see it as abandoning me in the middle of a conversation, or refusing to discuss something I found seriously important.

His plate sat on the counter while I ate, leaning up against the cabinets.

The sound of beating wings caught my attention, and I stepped out onto the balcony with my plate, glancing up at the sky.

My forehead wrinkled when I noticed Ervo flying long, slow circles above me, like a vulture watching its prey.

He made no move to fly back to me, so I just strode back into his house and returned to my food.

If he didn't come back down and talk to me soon, then...

Well, then I was going to leave.

Because if Ervo wasn't willing to talk about what I wanted in a mate, or what he wanted, then I was probably going to end up even more heartbroken in this situation than I had expected a few days earlier.

I couldn't stay away from my friends forever, anyway. After all that had gone down in the cave, everyone was going to need a little time to process, but then we needed to regroup. To figure out what we were going to do.

And... I didn't even know what had happened to the female fae.

I'd seen the men trap them, saving Sunny and Dots before they could get spirited away as life-bringers, so I knew they were safe. But I didn't know what had happened since then, or what was currently happening.

And I felt shitty about that.

Ervo had needed time to calm down, to see that I was alright. And I understood that; I'd needed time too.

But I couldn't hide in his treehouse forever.

I'd give it an hour, I decided. Give him an hour. To work through his thoughts, and decide how he wanted to proceed.

I finished my food, then placed the empty plate in the sink. As I walked over to the bookshelf, I eyed the sun and tried to remember how high it was so I could attempt to gauge how much time had passed.

My gaze flicked back to the plate of food I'd made for Ervo. It was already cold; if he left it any longer, it would be nasty.

Despite my effort to prevent it, my mood darkened at the way he had rejected my effort.

As if he could read my thoughts, the phoenix spiraled down toward the treehouse. He landed steadily on the balcony, before striding into the kitchen.

My eyes were glued to him as he picked up the plate and fork.

And his were trained on me as he began to eat.

I forced myself to look away, not to let him see how much his actions had cheered me up.

He hadn't rejected my food... he just wasn't used to the idea of letting me cook for him.

That felt silly to me; what did he think I was going to spend all of my time doing, if he fed me, and clothed me, and protected me? Sit on my ass constantly?

I had gotten enough of that in the Stronghold. It had been relaxing, at first. And I would always enjoy reading.

But I was tired of sitting around. I wanted to make something of myself, to be useful. To do something with my life.

I thumbed through a book as Ervo finished his food and then washed the dishes, picking up the mess I had made. To me, that was partnership. One of us cooking, and the other cleaning. Or both of us cooking and cleaning together.

Then again, it didn't seem like he really wanted a partner.

What he did want...

Well, I wasn't quite sure.

Sex?

Hugs?

Kissing?

He'd never told me, so how was I supposed to know?

I was starting to get a little frustrated, completely unfocused on the book in my hands, when Ervo finally shut off the sink.

My stomach clenched as his soft footsteps carried him toward me. He turned before he reached me, and pulled a book off the wall. And then silently, he handed it to me.

"What is this?" I asked, as I put the other book down with one hand and accepted Ervo's with another.

"I'm not skilled at expressing my emotions aloud," he admitted. "Or opening up. I prefer to keep my thoughts here, where they belong." He tapped his temple. "It will take me time to get used to sharing. And you may need to remind me, to push me." He stepped closer, taking my free hand, and lifting it to his chest. "But I want to be what you want. I want to know your favorite colors, and the things you're afraid of. What exactly I can do to make your eyes light up, too. I fear I might scare you away, should I voice my questions or ask what I'd like to."

My throat swelled. "You have a better chance at scaring me away by murdering people than by asking me whether I prefer long or short hair."

His eyes softened slightly. "I'm sorry."

"For what?"

"For removing Clevv's head while your eyes were on me." His hand pressed against mine lightly on his chest, even as I shivered with the memory. "I don't regret protecting you, or removing a threat from our world. But I will always wish I had done so away from you, so you wouldn't have to live with the horrors of our life here."

"I need to be stronger, anyway," I whispered back.

"You don't." His voice was firm.

His hand lifted my palm from his chest to his lips, where he brushed a kiss over my knuckles.

"I feel like I need to go back to the new Stronghold," I admitted, though I wanted to stay and talk more. To hear him tell me what he was thinking, and why he was thinking it. "North challenged Fovea to a fight. I need to be there with them, to make sure my friends are okay. We became a family."

He let out a slow breath. "Alright. You stay at my side when we get there, though. And fly with me."

"You know I have my own wings," I teased him gently.

"I know you fit perfectly on my back." He brushed another kiss to my knuckles. "We share a bed while we're there, as well. You stay at my side—and there's no *dating*." His voice grew sharp with that last addition. "Or crashing into other men."

A little laugh escaped me. "Okay, I actually didn't do that on purpose."

"I know. It's still not allowed."

His eyes were hot, daring me to disagree.

I rolled mine at him. "Fine. You're going to have to teach me how to land properly, then."

"That, I will do happily." He dragged my knuckles back to his lips. "And my vow stands."

Ohh.

My face heated at the reminder of said vow.

"Does it bother you that I'm a harsh? That I might not be able to have kids?" I asked him, as suddenly as the thought occurred to me.

"Why would it? I never imagined a future with children."

"I don't know. I guess it's something everyone at least considers, back on Earth." My face was still warm. "I always wanted one or two kids. I'm not sure how I feel about the new development that I might not be able to."

"Many things have changed since the female fae were last a part of our society. January is a harsh, yet pregnant. I don't think the division between harsh and light is as written in stone as Fovea believes." He stroked his thumb over my knuckles lightly. "Are you sure I can't convince you to stay here with me for a few more days, Mariah?"

I let my gaze slide over the treehouse.

It was a relaxing place, and the view was beautiful.

But... my friends were going through some shit. And they might not have really needed me, but that didn't mean I didn't want to be there for them.

"Next time," I said instead.

The man's lips curved into one of the expressions he rarely gave me:

A sweet, genuine smile.

I hoped I'd see more of those in the near future, because his smile was gorgeous.

"I'll hold you to that." He pulled me closer, wrapping his free arm around my waist.

"You never told me what the book is," I reminded him, shaking it in the small space between our chests.

"Just bring it with us," he murmured, grabbing me a crossbody bag to hold it in before he caught my lips in his.

The kiss he gave me was soft enough to make my body swell with happiness. I had the same feeling again—the feeling that he wasn't kissing me just to talk me into having sex with him, but that he just liked *kissing me*.

When he wasn't driving me crazy, the man was perfect.

Hell, maybe he was perfect even when he *was* driving me crazy.

We kissed until we were both breathing fast, and then Ervo pulled me onto his back and launched us into the sky.

THE SUN WAS GOING down when we reached the new Stronghold.

There were no female fae standing outside, guarding the place, anymore. The building had grown overnight, though—it was at least three times as big as it had been. And the women had to be inside, I assumed. Why else would they expand it?

I saw a flash of golden hair in one of the windows as a woman walked past it, and wondered how they felt, leaving their beautiful tropical island and colorful tents to move into a cold stone building.

It had to be difficult, I thought.

There were a few male fae in the trees and sky around the Stronghold, but I didn't think they were guarding the women, or trying to protect themselves from them. Just watching them.

Probably to make sure the leaders didn't sneak off to gather more of that poisonous fruit that knocked people out.

One of the men in a tree waved to me and Ervo, and I waved back.

The angry rumble from the phoenix beneath me made me roll my eyes a little —but smile a little too.

We flew further, until we were near the back of the land the men had claimed. I'd seen Priel and Lian through the trees, not too far away. And where those guys were, North and January would be too.

Ervo landed smoothly, pulling me into his arms. "You're mine, female," he warned.

"You never said I wasn't allowed to wave at people," I countered.

"I need to make a damn list," he grumbled. "Crashing into men. Waving at them. Smiling at them."

A snort escaped me. "You're ridiculous."

"If that word also means sexy and possessive in your language, then yes, I am."

I laughed. "If that's what you want to tell yourself, then sure."

His lips curved upward just the tiniest bit as he tugged me closer, lowering his mouth to brush against mine.

My fingers wrapped around the back of his neck as he kissed me, gently at first and then more fiercely, more intimately.

It didn't pass my notice that he'd done it as soon as we landed. The bastard was claiming me, in front of however many fae were around us.

If I had to guess, it was a lot of them.

Ervo wasn't really the kind of guy to make a small statement, after all. Cutting heads off dramatically instead of just slitting throats or stabbing chests made that pretty clear.

As long as it didn't include murder, I didn't mind his tendency toward dramatics. With the murder… I understood him and his culture enough to know why he'd done it. And not to hold it against him, even if the memories of it still made me nauseous.

His hands were on my ass when he finally pulled away, eyes gleaming wickedly.

His expression was usually so neutral, so unreadable, but I supposed I'd started learning to read its nuances.

Or maybe he'd just gotten more expressive when he realized I wasn't rejecting him over and over.

"Ready to find your friends, Mariah?" he asked me.

"Mmhm." I nodded… and then rested my forehead against his chest for a long moment.

His soft rumble only made me squeeze him tighter before I finally released his waist, took his hand, and then headed off.

Twelve

We found Priel and Lian teaching a fighting class.

It definitely caught me by surprise.

Every one of the ex-human women other than me, Sunny, Dots, and Naomi were lined up.

They seemed to be going through some kind of drills—Priel would bark out positions, and all of the women would follow while Lian and a few other men walked around, correcting them. Some of the ladies moved faster and smoother than others, but I figured that was to be expected.

Outside of making the orders, Priel's sole focus was on North. For once, I knew that wasn't just because he was her mate, but because he was her trainer.

It was because she was the one who was going to have to fight Fovea. And Fovea had *centuries* of experience under her belt.

Even if North wasn't going into the fight with a plan to win, she needed to know how to survive.

Ervo's grip on me tightened as we watched the women move through the motions a few times. My gaze lingered on January—who kept flashing glares at Lian every time he walked over and started to say something to her.

I'd spent enough time with my own fae male to know that he was probably trying to talk her into stopping.

And knew her well enough to know that her answer was probably along the lines of, "Not a fucking chance."

It had been hard for the men when we were stolen away from them. I understood that, and didn't blame them for their reaction.

But they probably didn't realize it had been difficult for us, too.

And really damn eye-opening.

Even the tallest and heaviest of us ex-humans was smaller than any of the fae males and females by a long, long way. Most of us had only recently learned how to shift forms. The extent of our strength and speed wasn't something we'd ever had a reason to test.

We'd spent years hiding from the fae, and it showed. But in the years we were hiding, they were fighting each other. Flying, and running. Learning, and living.

We were centuries behind them, at best.

I started stepping toward the group, but Ervo's grip on me held tight.

"No," he said simply.

I flashed him a warning look.

His fingers squeezed mine deathly tight. "I will protect you. You don't need to fight."

"Do you want me to be helpless?" I asked him.

His gaze held mine, but he remained silent.

"All of you know how to fight. How to survive in Vevol. And I'm helpless right now, Viervo. I don't want that to be my life."

If he did...

Well, then I wasn't so sure we would have a future after all.

There was a long, long pause.

The other women were still going through the motions, but I waited silently, hoping the man holding my hand would come to the same conclusion I had.

Finally, he loosened his grip on my fingers, and then released me altogether.

"We'll discuss it more later," he told me in a low voice, though the end of the remark sounded a bit like a question.

"We will," I agreed.

He lifted my fingers to his lips and brushed them over my knuckles. "Be careful, Mariah."

"I will." I stepped up closer to him, pressing a soft kiss to his lips to show him that I appreciated him fighting his instincts on this. "You can come give me tips, like the other men are doing."

He was trying—and that mattered a hell of a lot more to me than I could say.

He tugged my crossbody bag over my shoulder and set it on his own as I stepped back, turning toward the group. When I joined the group, stepping into place a few feet from Ana at the back of the line, she flashed me a grin.

As I returned the expression, I felt more than saw Ervo position himself just a few feet from me.

He was taking me up on my offer.

"This is one of the warm-ups," Ana explained quietly, as I tried to mirror her movements. "It's more about stretching and making your body move in new ways. We'll pair up soon for hand-to-hand combat. The men aren't allowed to fight us yet."

"Who decided that?" I wondered.

"North and January. The rest of us agreed."

Huh.

"Where's Naomi?" I asked. "And Sunny and Dots?"

"Dots walked away the minute this started. Sunny said she wasn't interested either, and followed. Naomi's decided that she's done with Aev, and is staying with the fae women right now. He's kind of losing his mind about it, so things are tense with the unseelie."

Hmm.

I was surprised that Sunny hadn't been interested. It seemed like the kind of thing she'd jump at the chance to do. But I could ask her about it later; the unseelie having issues was a bigger deal.

"Tense how?"

"Right foot back further," Ervo told me in a low voice. "Both of you."

We both scooted our right feet back further, in the strange lunge we were pulling off. Ana definitely moved through it easier than I did, but I chalked that up to her having experience already.

"Some of them have started breaking away, joining the seelie. They saw the connection between your happy little couples and want what they have," she explained.

Ah.

"The council is fighting," the girl in front of us, Blue, added. When she looked at us over her shoulder, I flashed her a small smile. She had light skin and bright blue hair (hence the nickname), changed from blonde by Vevol's magic shortly after she was brought there. We hadn't been close during the one year we'd been at the Stronghold together, not the way I was close with Sunny and Dots, but we'd still spent an assload of time together.

"About the people leaving?" I checked.

"About everything," she explained. "Iyvan tells me things, in exchange for cake. He's a shitty cook, and the dragon on the council."

My eyebrows shot upward. "I thought you guys considered the men the enemies."

"Most of us do," one of the girls I only vaguely recognized called out, from a few people away.

"Some of us are horny bitches," Blue agreed.

I lifted an eyebrow. "I thought you were only offering cake."

She flashed me a grin. "Gotta start somewhere, right?"

My gaze flicked to Ervo, whose expression was neutral. I could've sworn there was an ember of amusement in those dark eyes, though.

"We've started grudgingly accepting that we have to work with the bastards," Ana admitted. "Some of them, at least."

The dirty look she shot to the trees told me there was at least one in particular that she wasn't interested in working with.

"We heard you were giving Druze a run for his money," I told her, curiosity taking hold of me as I struggled to get through the motions. Ervo had stopped correcting me, but I think he realized that I was too interested in the gossip to focus at the moment.

She scowled. "Not gonna talk about that."

"He thinks they're true mates," the woman on her left offered. I recognized Rosalie, with her dark brown skin and white-blonde hair. She and I had been at the Stronghold together for three years, so we knew each other well too. She and Ana had always been really close, which was one of the reasons Ana had gotten more bitter and anxious to leave the Stronghold through the last year she spent there.

"What?" I gaped.

"You look like a damn fish," Ana grumbled at me, a lazy attempt to change the subject.

"You know how the unseelie are, though," Rosalie reminded me.

I didn't really know, but nodded anyway.

And luckily for me, she explained what she meant.

"They're only looking for the power boost that comes with taking a mate. They can use Vevol's magic easier after mating, and impact nature much stronger than they can when they're single." She rolled her eyes. "As if that's a good reason to tell a woman she'll be in your bed tomorrow."

Something told me that very specific situation had happened to her.

"Ever since they learned about sex, they've been unrelenting. Trying to schedule visits. Offering to train us. Actually putting in effort to talk to us," Ana grumbled. "I blame January."

A snort escaped me. "It *is* kind of her fault."

"I heard that," January yelled back from the front of the group. "And the consequence is growing in my uterus right now, making me puke way too often, so fuck off."

Laughter rang out through the group.

"What else are the unseelies fighting about?"

"The control the council and Aev have maintained, and the fact that they acted like they knew everything when they didn't realize something as big as sex existed." Blue said with a shrug. "Which encompasses their whole way of life. A third of their people have already peeled away and joined the seelies—including the generals, who are their best fighters and the heads of their army."

Hot damn.

I glanced at Ervo, who lifted a shoulder in a slight shrug.

I guess he'd been too distracted worrying about protecting my ass to pay attention to the unseelies.

"The way the king handled things with Naomi was the real reason for most of us," one of the men walking through the group said. "He had two decades to convince her he was worthy of her trust, and yet failed to do so. And when he discovered that the seelie king had earned his female's trust so quickly, learning about sex in the process, the council *required* Naomi to mate herself completely with the king, or they'd declare war. It was a violation of the trust of every female under our protection—and every male who would treasure a mate."

Damn.

I'd felt terrible for the woman when January explained to all of us what had happened, but when he put it like that...

It was even worse.

"Will more of them join the seelie?" Blue asked the man, studying him thoughtfully.

"More are leaving every day," he admitted.

"Enough distractions," Priel growled at the group. "My female has to fight the damned harsh leader in a few weeks, so we don't have time for this shit."

North stepped up to him, grabbed him by the arm, and kissed him on the mouth.

I think all of us stared for a minute, before we peeled our gazes from them and focused on the forest and the men inside it.

My eyes landed on Ervo's... and his gaze was soft.

"Pair up," Priel finally barked.

The girls all grabbed the person next to them.

I had the feeling they'd determined their partners when they first started training, and without me, they had an even number.

"You train with me," Ervo said, hooking a finger in the waistband of my shorts and tugging me closer. My side met his chest, and he lowered his lips to my head, leaving a kiss there.

"That's not going to happen," Ana said, flashing him a scowl. "It's against the rules, and the rules keep the peace—and keep all of us safe. Mare can join our group."

The look on the phoenix's face told me that Ana was about to get her damn head cut off. If not literally, then some other way.

I quickly stepped in to keep the peace.

"The seelies live to break rules, and Ervo and I are basically engaged," I said simply.

Her scowl deepened, but she jerked her head in a nod.

She had always been protective over the rest of us, and while it made things tense at times, it was appreciated.

I turned toward Ervo, and his eyes were practically gleaming. "You don't need to fight for me, Mariah."

"Why shouldn't I? You're constantly fighting for me."

There was a long pause before he finally said, "I suppose I don't know."

A laugh escaped me, and I stepped closer to him. "If you get to protect me, then I get to protect you too." I leaned in closer, and he dipped his ear toward me. "Even from tiny, angry human chicks you could easily squish with one of those giant hands."

He snorted, grabbing my hips and dragging me closer. "You weren't insulting my hands a few hours ago."

My face warmed. "Go to hell."

A booming laugh escaped him, and I swear, every man in the forest turned to look at Ervo, surprised that the phoenix was so openly happy.

He just grinned down at me.

And then he kissed me.

Afterward, he taught me how to throw a punch.

It may very well have been the best day of my life.

We practiced fighting for the next few hours, getting more information from the other women during every break we took. The sun finished setting, but none of us was exhausted enough to call it a day until it had been dark for a long while.

I learned that the fae women had been locked in the new Stronghold until they vowed on Vevol not to try to steal *the human females* from the men again. When they had stopped guarding the place, the female fae hadn't emerged.

Loud, sometimes-angry discussions had been heard almost constantly from outside the walls since then, but no amount of spying could figure out what they were arguing about.

Most of the girls assumed it had to do with January being a pregnant Harsh, though. January included.

WHEN THE DAY ENDED, everyone ate dinner together in the massive kitchen/eating area that the male fae had been working on. Afterward, we all parted ways. I looked for Sunny and Dots for a bit, but couldn't find them, and was exhausted after all that fighting.

I'd look for them in the morning, I decided, as Ervo led me through the forest. He was looking for a suitable place to build us a house. I didn't think me and my tiny control over their earth magic would be much help when it came to creating a place to live, but a few of the other men had volunteered to help.

They walked with us, discussing which of the human women might be open to receiving cake soon—and which of the fae women they hoped would change their minds about hating men. They treated me like I was already Ervo's mate, not bothering to flirt with me or be anything but slightly friendly. Not flirting with me was probably a good call for them, considering the annoyed expression on my phoenix's face.

He'd wanted to build the house on his own—but knew I needed to sleep sooner than he could have it done, which was why he'd asked for help.

It was interesting to hear which of the fae women the guys found the most beautiful. As I'd expected, they thought Fovea was insanely sexy, with her big muscles and all that power. But they actually weren't interested in her—the ones they wanted to mate with were quieter ones, on the outskirts of the group. Ones I couldn't remember, even though I tried to.

The guys mentioned multiple times how attractive the *strong* women were, AKA the female fae. It was entertaining... but also made me kind of self-conscious about my lack of muscles.

When Ervo found a pair of trees that he thought was suitable, way on the outskirts of the space, he asked me if I wanted to help with the building. I wasn't skilled with my magic, but when I said I wanted to help, he tugged me up onto his back and started scaling the tree.

The others followed us. None of the men struggled to climb the trees, despite their smooth, shiny bark.

Ervo deposited me on one of the thick branches, and then tucked a few of my fingers into the waistband of his pants.

"Stay close," he warned.

"I'm a professional at walking on tree branches now," I reminded him. "And I have wings, too. So you don't have to worry about me."

His lips curved upward just slightly. "And yet I still do." Leaning closer, he brushed a kiss to the top of my head before walking a few feet down the branches, meeting up with the others.

They discussed quickly what they were making; a simple wooden cube, enclosed on all sides, with a small doorway that led onto a thick balcony for landings. Ervo would add windows and whatever else we needed later, but for now, he wanted privacy.

Since I didn't really know how to guide my magic, he explained to me that I should just let myself feel everyone else's power and add mine to it, making sure mine flowed the same way theirs did.

It didn't make a whole lot of sense to me, but I'd figure it out as we went.

The men put their hands on the tree, and I felt a surge of magic roll through the air. Following suit, I closed my eyes and tried to connect my trickle to the verifiable river of power.

When my power collided with theirs, I felt my magic itself growing thicker and stronger, and I pushed the power to follow the men's commands—to grow and change the way they wanted it to.

Around us, I felt the tree move. It stretched, and thickened, and obeyed.

A few minutes later, the men cut off the stream of magic, and I followed suit.

When I opened my eyes, I found us in a treehouse that resembled Ervo's, with trunks in all four corners, but this one was much smaller—and much wilder.

Tree branches and thick leaves draped across the space a ways above my head, having grown into the new smooth ceiling. A thick branch was embedded in one of the walls, too.

And out on the balcony, I could see leaves all around us.

It was absolutely gorgeous, and unique.

Ervo and I thanked the other men, who just offered us grins and congratulations. Without the massive building full of fae women, I knew our relationship would've been received differently.

But now that there were so many more options, things were changing. And despite everything, I thought maybe those changes were for the better.

"I'll clean up the walls and ceiling," Ervo told me, studying the places the branches had grown into it.

"No, don't," I said quickly. "I love them."

He looked at me in surprise.

"I like that it's not perfect. It makes it seem more real. Natural. Alive." I flashed him a quick smile.

He studied me for a long moment before nodding.

A massive yawn stretched my whole damn face, and Ervo pulled me into his arms, holding me tightly to his chest.

Thirteen

"You need to rest," he murmured to me. "I'll find us some pillows and blankets. Wait here, where I know you're safe."

"Fine." I sighed dramatically, and he lightly tickled my side. A squeal escaped me, earning a soft chuckle from the phoenix before he strode out onto the balcony and disappeared into the forest, heading out to find pillows and blankets.

The space was comfortable, despite being empty. Ervo had explained that you could create a mattress with Vevol's magic, but it was really time-consuming and pretty exhausting. So, we were going to crash on the ground until we were certain enough that we were staying in the treehouse near the Stronghold for the long haul.

Some of the other girls wanted to get away from the rest of the fae, to put more space between them and the men, but I liked being near the action. I'd always enjoyed my friendships with the other women, and I had spent enough time alone on Earth to be certain that wasn't what I wanted in Vevol.

Ervo had assured me that he didn't mind living near everyone else, as long as it meant he was with me. And damn, that made me feel good.

He had set his bag down against one of the far walls at some point in the day, so I crossed the room and picked it up.

We hadn't created any of the floating lights that the fae could make with their magic—they were also exhausting and time consuming, according to Ervo. But I could see just fine in the dark, since I was technically a fae.

I tugged the book out of the bag, still curious about why Ervo had handed it to me and told me to bring it along. The action had been very deliberate, and happened while he was admitting that he wasn't good at voicing his thoughts and emotions.

Opening to the first page—usually a title page on Earth, but some of the books I'd found in Vevol had no titles—I stared down at the paper.

The words on it were handwritten in simple, perfect glyphs. Whatever magic translated our words for the fae and the fae for ours worked on written language too, and I watched the glyphs of the fae language transform into my own.

And into a poem.

There was no title, for the book or poem, and my eyes immediately scanned the words.

She's mine,
It whispers,
The wind against my face.

She's mine,
It bellows,
The scent in my nose.

She's mine,
It snarls,
The beat in my chest

She's mine,
It roars,
Though I don't hold her yet.

. . .

MY MOUTH WAS dry when I finished reading.

My heart beating rapidly.

I reread the poem once, and then again.

Ervo had written it. He had to have written it. The book smelled of him, the handwriting was just as neutral and perfect as I would've expected his.

And the words...

Hadn't he already showed me he felt that way? When he had grabbed the back of my neck and told me I was flying with him? When we'd been captured, and he had allowed a hellhound to fly on his back with me, because the alternative was to let Clevv or one of the others carry me?

When he had removed the head from the body of the man who had hurt me?

I flipped to the next page.

A pounding heart
A fractured mind
Nearly lost, nearly broken
For she's not yet mine

A soft smile
And the gentlest touch
Not for me, not yet,
Though I ache so much.

My cold and brutal
Her warm and kind
Not in my arms,
But always in my mind.

I fear for the future,

I fear for my life
If I can't hold her soon,
Make her my mate,
And my wife.

SHIT.

Holy shit.

My body trembled.

I had thought of the phoenix as too calm.

Too emotionless.

Too cold, and cruel, and brutal.

But he felt things just as strongly as I did.

No; he felt them even stronger than I did, if the poetry was anything to go by.

I was the one who had judged him harshly, and coldly. He had been showing me that he cared in his own rough, untrained way. He'd never been with a human woman; he'd never watched a romance movie, or been told what we liked and wanted.

He'd said again and again that he wanted me. That he was mine.

And I hadn't listened.

My eyes watered as I flipped the page again.

To lose myself
In that smile,
That laugh,
Those eyes.

To fall to pieces
In those arms...
How I long for it,
How hard I try.

. . .

Despite this distance,
Despite this pain,
I continue reaching for her
Again, and again, and again.

She is not mine.
I am not in her bed.
And yet I am hers
As I have always been.

Tears dripped down my cheeks, and I wiped them with my arm before they could fall to the pages of the poem book.

I had rejected him.

I hadn't seen him, not really.

I had *hurt* him.

And yet he had still protected me. Taken care of me as much as I had let him.

Been mine.

I flipped to the next page.

And the next.

And the next.

When Ervo finally landed, I dropped the book on the floor and crossed the space between us quickly. He saw me coming, saw my tears, and alarm flashed over his face. He dropped the pillows and blankets on the balcony—just in time to catch me as I crashed into him.

"What happened?" he demanded, gripping me to his chest tightly as his gaze swept the room, looking for an enemy of some kind to rip apart.

I clutched him fiercely. "I hurt you," I said to him, tears still dripping down my face. "I'm sorry. I'm so, so sorry. I didn't realize—I didn't know. I'm sorry.

His body relaxed a little as he realized why I was crying, and he carried me back into the small house and sat down on the floor with me. There was no door yet, separating our balcony from our house, but I didn't care. "I didn't give you the book to make you cry," he said gently.

"You wanted me to understand," I said, my forehead pressing to his neck.

"No, you wanted to get to know me. The book seemed like the easiest way to make that happen," he explained. His hand stroked my back softly, calmingly. "Don't cry about the past, Mariah. We're here, now. Together. Safe."

"I should've realized sooner," I said, still leaking tears. "We lost so much time."

"We have forever." He continued stroking my back. "All is as it should be, and you are everything I need. I would suffer that pain again in a heartbeat and wait as many more centuries as I needed, to have you here, in my arms. I may not know your favorite food, or what you miss most about Earth, but I know of your quiet strength. I know that you take joy in cooking for the sisters you claimed. I know that your eyes water sometimes, when you read—and that you love books as much as I do. I know that I love you."

The urge to kiss him, to physically connect with him, became unbearable. I pulled away from him, lifting my mouth to his as his hand slid beneath my tank top, stroking my bare back just as lightly and gently.

Our lips collided, and I dragged my body closer to his, sitting on his lap and straddling him. I wanted to *feel him*. I wanted his hands on my skin, his body on mine.

One of his hands pressed into the stone beside us, and I ripped my mouth away from his when I felt the house shake.

His tongue dragged slowly over my collarbone, then worked with his lips as they moved over my throat, making me rock against him as I watched a plank of wood grow slowly over the doorway, until it blocked us completely from whatever eyes were in the forest.

"I want to be your mate," I told Ervo.

His lips halted on my throat.

His erection throbbed beneath me.

"Tell me your favorite color," he said a moment later, then sucked lightly on my sensitive skin.

"Blue, like the water in the lake that surrounded the female fae's island."

He sucked lightly on my throat again, his hands sliding further up my back beneath my tank top, and making me arch slightly against him.

"I don't know why you wanted to come to Vevol, outside of escaping your family" he murmured.

"Because I was tired of being worthless. Of living pointlessly. Of meaning nothing to everyone I should've mattered to."

His eyes lifted to mine, burning with anger. Not anger directed at me, I knew, but at the family I had mentioned.

"I want you inside me," I told Ervo. "Tomorrow, we can talk more about my past. About yours, too."

His fingers curled into my spine. "I won't do something you'll regret, Mariah."

"I'll regret tonight, if you don't take your damn clothes off."

He chuckled softly, and stripped my tank top over my head, leaving me bare from the waist up. His eyes moved slowly, hotly over my skin. While one of his hands remained on my back, the other found my front and slowly slid up my ribs, over the curve of my breasts, against the tight peaks of my nipples. "Let me take care of you tonight. In the morning, we can discuss mating."

He slid down my body, and sucked my clit between his lips.

I stopped thinking.

Nearly stopped breathing, too.

And when he made me lose control with a scream, there was definitely no arguing from me.

When we talked about mating, after I came down from my high and returned the favor to Ervo, we agreed that we would wait to become mates until we had spent more time getting to know each other.

He wasn't willing to risk me regretting our decision—and I respected that tremendously, because I felt the same way, even if I was still willing to take the risk.

So, we stayed up late talking about our pasts instead. Ervo explained that he had experienced a tremendous amount of boredom throughout his life, but that he loved cooking and reading, and enjoyed training. He told me stories of adventures he'd gone on with his brothers, but there was an undercurrent of sadness below each of them.

His life had felt pointless before he met me, he admitted. And that was a huge part of the reason that he had become sort of obsessed with me.

Luckily for him, I loved that obsession.

. . .

THE NEXT FEW weeks passed quickly, exhaustingly, and similarly.

We trained all day, spending some time practicing magic, too. And though we were learning at a decent pace, there was a *lot* to learn.

In the evening, Ervo and I talked about nothing, everything, and poetry. We always talked about poetry. He'd recite poems he'd memorized to me—and I'd recite ones I'd memorized for him.

And then he'd make good on his vow not to let me go a day without climaxing.

Again.

And again.

And again.

It was absolutely blissful.

Fourteen

The night before North's fight, Ervo and I laughed together about a story he told me of him and the rest of the Wild Hunt getting lost in a cave and having to use their magic to tunnel out. It took multiple days, led to multiple fights and injuries, and the men still complained to each other about it every now and then.

When our laughter faded, he rolled me to my back.

His lips captured mine as he leaned over me, his body pressing into mine as we kissed, and kissed, and kissed.

I would never get over the way he kissed me.

The way his mouth made love to mine, as if there was nothing else he'd rather be doing.

And it hit me that I didn't just want to use our tongues, and hands, and lips anymore.

I wanted *him*.

And we'd waited long enough.

He went up on his hands and knees, sliding down until his head was between my thighs—but I stopped him.

"No." I grabbed his face. "I always think too much, about everything. I think, and I hide, and I ignore, until it's too late to make the decision I knew I wanted to make from the damn beginning. I don't want to live that way anymore. I'm tired of hiding and waiting. This is what I want. *You* are what I want. The next poem you write in that book will be one about how I *am* yours."

Those embers in his eyes seemed to ignite, to burn. "Is that so?"

"*Yes.*"

"And if you wake up in the morning with regret, what am I to do?" His rough, calloused thumb dragged over my nipple, making me shudder. "If you look at another male and wish you had taken his cock instead?"

I scowled at him, sitting up and smacking a palm against his shoulder. It made a loud slapping noise, and I immediately felt bad. His eyes only burned hotter, though.

More excited.

My blood pumped faster, too.

"Then you pin me to this damn treehouse and fuck me until I remember that I'm yours," I shot back. "But none of that shit is going to happen. I haven't really looked at another guy since the first time you kissed me in the Stronghold, and—"

His lips captured mine, his hands sliding to my ass as he lifted me higher, pulling me closer and ripping my tank top over my head.

I groaned against his mouth when he tugged my shorts down and then tossed them aside.

My legs spread further without the fabric over them, and I lowered my hands to his erection.

He growled into my mouth when I gripped his length through the fabric, and when I pushed his shorts down his hips, he lifted his ass—and me with him—long enough to tug them down.

And down.

And down.

His hot erection met my clit, and I moaned. His fingers latched onto my hips as he dragged me against him, making me pant.

"You're mine?" he growled at me. It was still a question, though his fingers were sliding down and digging into my ass as he continued grinding me on his hardness, creating delicious, delicious friction.

My mind went back to that first poem in his book.

I was shitty with names. With facts, too.

But quotes and poems seemed to embed themselves in my heart, in my mind.

My breaths were coming out rapidly as I reached between us. He stopped moving—nearly stopped breathing, too. I pushed his tip against my entrance, and lowered myself down just a little.

The pressure was intense as he stretched me, as I waited to adjust, but that didn't stop me from repeating his poem back to him—and changing it, as I did.

My breath brushed his lips, our eyes locked and his body trembling with the effort it took him to remain still, to let me set the pace.

"I'm yours
I whisper,
My breath on your face.

I'm yours,
I bellow,
My scent on your skin.

I'm yours,
I snarl,
Heart pounding in my chest

I'm yours,
I roar,
Forever and more."

With every line, I sank further.

And further.

And further.

And when he was buried completely inside me, stretching me so tightly and hitting every damn nerve I possessed, the poem was over.

Yet we were only just beginning.

His eyes burned into me as his hand slid between us, feeling us. Tracing our connection. Stroking my clit, and his hilt. He was throbbing, his body shaking, and I knew he wouldn't last long.

But I also knew he wouldn't be done after the first climax.

"Say it again," he rumbled, as he slowly stroked my clit.

I was riding him, completely in charge of the moment, but I knew how easily it would be to overwhelm him. I knew, because I was nearly there myself.

And I knew he didn't mean for me to say the whole poem again, but the first line.

"I'm yours," I breathed to him, as he stroked me.

"I'm yours," I repeated, as my hips rocked uncontrollably.

"I'm yours," I panted as I neared the edge, with his cock filling me, stretching me, sending electricity through every damn inch of me.

"I'm yours," I cried, as I finally reached the edge—and lost control completely.

Ervo snarled, thrusting into me hard and fast as I climaxed, and climaxed, and climaxed.

The pleasure was so fierce, so intense, so much *more* than I had ever expected.

And I felt it settle between us as I reached that high—the bond that the fae all wanted so fiercely.

The connection.

The power.

The emotions.

Ervo's thick, hot pleasure.

His heavy, proud joy.

His grateful, disbelieving awe.

His curling, fraying fear.

The fear was small, but it was there. Time would unravel it the rest of the way, though—I would make sure of that.

"She's mine," his voice said in my mind.

Not to me—but in my head nonetheless. It was a simple, overwhelming thought.

"She's mine," he repeated to himself, like he couldn't believe it.

"I'm yours," I whispered back, feeling his body go still.

His erection was still buried inside me, but this was no longer just a physical experience—if it had *ever* been just physical. It was an emotional one; a strong, intense, powerfully-spiritual one.

It wasn't just our bodies that had connected, but our minds and souls, too.

"Fuck," he murmured into my mind.

A soft laugh escaped me, and the motion made him throb inside me.

Still hard—of course he was still hard.

"This is going to take some time to get used to," he admitted to me.

"For someone as quiet and secretive as you, of course it will," I teased back lightly.

He throbbed inside me again.

And again.

"Something tells me you'll make sure that changes, Mariah." His hand stroked my ass slowly, making my body tighten. I was still horny—I still wanted him, wanted more.

"No secrets," I agreed, my breathing picking up. Since he'd finished inside me, I was already literally drenched—and leaking.

Neither of us gave a damn about that, though.

Ervo gripped my thighs, and with one powerful motion, rolled us over. My back met the warm wood, and I breathed through the sudden overwhelming pleasure of the new angle.

He pulled out far enough to tuck something between us—something warm, and thick, and ridged—and then thrust in again.

My body arched hard, my mind spinning at the pleasure.

"What's that?" I hissed into his mind.

He pulled out, sliding it away from my clit and holding it up for me to see. It looked like... a piece of one of my scales. It was about an inch thick, and had been whittled or something. It was flat on the one side, but the other had smooth bumps and ridges.

"You pulled off one of my scales?" I was surprised.

"No; they shed like hair." He tugged lightly on my puff, and I tightened around him, earning a heady rumble. *"I pick them up every time you lose them. The idea of another male with one of them is... maddening."*

Ohhh.

"Maybe it will be less maddening now that I'm entirely yours?" I asked, rocking my hips a little and making him growl.

"Unlikely." He tucked it back between my thighs, and his pelvis pinned it to my clit.

A groan escaped me at the feeling. *"So you turned it into a sex toy?"*

"The first of many," he agreed, thrusting in and out lightly. *"Damn, Mariah."* The words were gravelly. *"You're so tight."*

Pleasure rolled down my spine, and I cried out as I shattered.

Ervo roared as he pounded into me, harder and faster than he had the first time. The movements dragged my orgasm out for what felt like forever, making the pleasure go on and on and on.

We were both panting when he dropped his forehead to mine, the sides of our noses meeting.

"You're incredible," he told me. *"Absolutely perfect."* He rolled us over again, so I was on top. His erection was still inside me, still throbbing a little, but his hands stroked my bare back, ass, and thighs without asking for anything else.

I was pretty sure he was waiting to see what I wanted, if I wanted more.

And I did want more—but the way he stroked my legs reminded me how skinny they were, and how attractive the other guys had found the fae women and their massive muscles.

My face warmed.

"Does it bother you that I'm not strong?" I whispered to him.

His hands paused on my skin. *"What the hell does that mean?"*

My face heated further. *"Back when we made the house, the other guys were talking about how gorgeous the fae women are. I know you value strength—that it's important to you guys. And I've spent the last few years reading books, watching movies, and playing board games, so I'm not exactly muscular. Even before that, I didn't have big muscles or anything. The training is helping a little, and I used to ride horses, which kept me healthy, but that was the extent of my exercise. I—"*

The fingers on one of his hands slid between my ass cheeks, and I let out a squeak as he dipped them into the slickness leaking out of me, and then dragged them up to my back entrance.

My body responded to the unfamiliar, intimate touches, tightening and heating.

"Do you feel that?" he asked me as he lightly slid a finger into uncharted territory.

"Of course," I hissed back, my hips jerking slightly of their own accord.

"Not my fingers, Mariah; the way your body responds to mine. The way you arch against me, with just a simple touch. The way my cock throbs for you, and only you. I don't give a fuck about any other women—I care about you, and your happiness, and what makes you feel good. Your strength is different than theirs, but it's still strength. And frankly, I find your soft, kind humanness far more appealing than any amount of fae muscles."

My face warmed, but my body relaxed.

At least, as much as it could with him still stretching my back entrance the way he was, while his erection throbbed inside me.

"Thank you."

"I find it ironic that you're thanking me for wanting to fuck you, Mariah."

I snorted, and he gave me a soft, rumbly chuckle.

"Get used to it," I teased him. *"Because I'm not going anywhere."* I rocked my hips slowly, dragging him in and out of me, and earned a low growl.

"Even if you did," he said, hauling himself to a seated position and dragging me up with him. My fingers dug into his shoulders at the sudden change in sensation, and I struggled to keep breathing. *"I would follow you."*

"I know you would."

His pleasure hit me through our bond when I said that—and it hit hard.

It meant a lot to him that I knew he would follow me. That I trusted him to protect me.

"Say the words again, love," he growled, sliding me up and down his cock slowly; blissfully yet excruciatingly slowly.

"I'm yours," I murmured.

His breath hitched, and his thumb dragged over my clit. *"And?"*

"And you're mine."

We stopped talking, then, and the pleasure *consumed* us.

It was absolutely perfect.

And when I finally fell asleep against Ervo's chest in the early hours of the morning, I knew without a shadow of doubt that I had finally started *living*.

Fifteen

Ervo

My fingers stroked her hair.

Her shoulders.

Her throat.

Her spine.

The curve of her ass.

The perfect thickness of her thighs.

The patch of curls over her core.

She slept like a rock after hours spent lost in each other's bodies, and yet I wasn't tired.

Or rather, I wasn't tired enough to stop touching her.

Feeling her.

Holding her.

Squeezing her.

She was mine.

She was *everything*.

I'd thought I needed her, before.

But that need was nothing compared to the attachment I now felt. The *devotion*.

This woman...

I had changed for her.

I knew it. I had softened. Smiled. Laughed.

And I'd enjoyed it.

I'd enjoyed *her*.

Not just her body, though that was certainly a pleasure unlike anything else.

But I enjoyed her heart, and her soul. Her jokes. Her happiness. Her stories. Her thoughts, spoken aloud just for me.

All of those things I had wanted, before, without realizing how they would truly affect me.

But now that I had them, I would do anything. Everything. Whatever it took, I would do it, to keep her safe.

To hold her in my arms.

Because we belonged to each other.

Fate hadn't intervened on our behalf—hadn't dragged us together through any fated mate bond.

Instead, we had chosen each other. And to me, that was worth so fucking much more.

Sixteen

Mare

Ervo's hands were moving softly and steadily over my back when I woke up. My lips stretched in a smile, my body already recovered despite the ridiculous amount of time we'd spent making love the night before.

And my mate's cock was already hard against my inner thigh, letting me know that he wanted me.

That he always wanted me.

"Hey," I whispered, lifting my face from his chest so I could look at those gorgeous eyes.

They were soft, and crinkled at the corners.

Because he was happy.

My heart swelled.

"Hey." His hands slid down, cupping my ass and giving it a soft squeeze.

A quiet laugh slipped from me. "Last night was fun."

"I can think of far better terms to use than fun, Mariah." His hands slid over my thighs, parting my legs more and sliding me downward until his erection was nestled right where I wanted it.

"Not all of us are poets," I teased him.

He frowned.

Shit.

Had I offended him?

"Do you hear that?" he asked me, easing us both to a seated position. His gaze flicked to my lips, and he said, "You haven't offended me. I think I hear drums."

"Drums?"

I strained my ears, trying to listen, and finally heard a rapid beating noise. It was faint—just barely there at all.

"You're right." I stared at him with wide eyes. "What does it mean?"

"I don't know. I was under the impression the fight wouldn't happen until tonight." He stood up smoothly, grabbing my clothes off the ground. With one smooth motion, he slid my tank over my hair without wrecking it (though honestly, it was probably already a mess given all that had happened during the night).

"I can get myself dressed," I pointed out to him, as he bent over to help me into my shorts.

"Do you know how many months I spent imagining helping you into—and out of—these clothes, Mariah? Let me take care of you."

"Alright." My eyes followed his every movement as he stepped back, grabbing his own shorts and pulling them on. "You're gorgeous."

He shot me a hot look. "Don't tempt me to strip those clothes off you again already."

I flashed him a grin.

He took my hand, towing me toward the balcony and lighting us both on fire in the process.

"What was that for?" I checked.

He tugged me onto his back as he shifted and dove off the edge, flying toward the drums.

"Couldn't walk you in front of the other fae smelling like sex. And the fire is easier than showering," he explained.

I eyed my arms—and then looked between my legs.

We hadn't cleaned up after last night, so yeah, that was definitely a good call. I was clean, as far as I could tell, so apparently it had worked.

The drum-beating grew louder as we neared the Stronghold.

We got a glimpse of the organized lines of fae women—set up in straight, simple rows, with a handful of ladies working on a group of massive drums near the Stronghold's walls. Fovea was at the front of the women, furthest from the building, and had two others flanking her.

The fae men had formed their own unorganized mass, and faced the women head-on.

I could see Lian and January together in one of the trees off to the side, tucked away where the women wouldn't notice them. North and Priel were at the front of the male fae group. The rest of the ex-human women were scattered throughout the crowd, each of them surrounded by multiple men on all sides.

Protected.

Ervo shifted and landed in one of the trees nearest to the dividing line between the male and female fae, just as the drum-beats ended. He set me on my feet, and pulled me close.

There was a heavy moment of silence before Fovea spoke, her voice magnified by the magic of someone near her.

"Brutal fae males, and human females," Fovea said. The words rang through the forest, and if we hadn't already scared off all the birds by the fact that we were damned predators, I was sure they would've hit the skies. "After days of discussion and consideration, we have made a decision."

More silence followed.

I nearly rolled my eyes.

Fovea was putting on a damn show, and she knew it.

"I will mate with one of your strongest brutals; a member of your Wild Hunt. We will determine whether or not the female harsh truly can bring life by attempting it ourselves—and whether there is merit to these new ways your human females have introduced."

Shocked murmurs rolled through the crowd.

Ervo's chest rumbled unhappily at my side.

My gaze landed on Sunny and Dots. The blood had drained from both of their faces, leaving their skin ashen.

My stomach clenched for both of them.

Her voice rang out one last time. "Bring me your Wild Hunt. The unmated among them will fight for the right to be my mate."

The drum-beating resumed, slower this time.

"They assume you're still unmated," I murmured to Ervo.

"And we will prove them wrong." He swept me up against his chest, and then dove out of the tree.

My arms and legs wrapped around him, and I bit back a scream as we spiraled to the ground. He landed lightly—so lightly that I didn't even understand how—and then strode toward the line with me clinging to him like I didn't have my own damn wings.

I tried to get free, but he held me firmly as he walked.

The whole crowd was silent as we joined the other Wild Hunt members who had already gathered.

Lian had January's waist in a death grip as they stood side-by-side.

North looked like she had physically put herself between Priel and the other women, and his arms were around her middle, holding her tightly to his chest as if he was holding her back from them, stopping her from charging at them.

Nev and Teris stood near me and Ervo, while Sunny and Dots had shoved their way up to January's side.

And, I realized, they were all looking at me and Ervo.

My face heated, but when I whispered for him to put me down, he whispered back a simple "no" and his grip on me tightened.

I gave up on fighting him, rolling my eyes toward January as if to say "men".

Her lips twitched toward a smile.

"There are only two unmated members of the Wild Hunt remaining," North said to Fovea. "You can ask them if they would be willing to fight for the right to mate with you, but it's their choice. We're seelie; we don't force anyone to do a damn thing they don't want to."

Growls of agreement rolled through the crowd.

Fovea's eyes glittered with anger.

I didn't think she was excited about the prospect of taking a mate, honestly.

Nev, I thought, would probably fight. He was the strategic one, so he could definitely imagine the potential good that could come from having a male fae connected to the females. And he and Dots both considered themselves just friends—though she seemed to believe it more than he did.

From what I knew of Teris, he was waiting for love, but spent plenty of time staring at Sunny and protecting her.

So... he probably wouldn't fight.

"You both smell faintly of other females," Fovea told the men, flashing her teeth at them threateningly.

"We participated in a charade of a mating to protect the females," Nev replied calmly. "And I would count myself privileged to fight for the right to mate with you, should you still be interested."

Her eyes softened, just slightly, and she looked to Teris.

There was a tense moment of silence.

I think everyone was waiting for him to say no.

To choose Sunny, the way she had so clearly chosen him.

But when the man finally spoke, he said, "It would be an honor to fight for you."

Sunny's sharp inhale was loud enough that my attention, and that of many others, jerked to her.

She quickly shuttered her reaction as well as she could, clenching her jaw and hiding her emotions.

My eyes caught on the glowing green eyes of a massive basilisk in the tree nearest to her. His scales were the same color as the tree around him, but he seemed to have moved, so the colors didn't line up properly.

And he was glowering at Teris like he was considering swallowing the sabertooth whole.

Neither Sunny nor Dots noticed him, though, and I was quickly distracted by the upcoming fight.

Fovea flashed the men a white-toothed smile, and everyone began clearing space.

Ervo hauled me back a few feet, remaining beside the rest of the Wild Hunt.

What was left of it, anyway.

Dots and Sunny turned around and walked away.

I ached to follow them, to make sure they were okay, but I knew Ervo wouldn't let go of me.

And ultimately, if I followed them, it would make it look like I didn't think they could handle their shit. Which neither of them would want, even a little.

I noticed the camouflaged basilisk disappear into the trees, and my eyes tracked him for a moment before I lost him.

Was he following them?

Was that going to be a problem?

I'd have to worry about them later.

Ervo finally set me down again, tugging my back to his chest and holding me tightly to him. I knew that if I let him, he would've put me behind him. But if he did that, I wouldn't be able to see a damn thing.

The fae women started the drums again, until Fovea gave a loud call to start the fight.

And then, Teris lunged.

He and Nev had to have fought dozens of times, if not hundreds. Maybe even more. The way they moved together was practically a dance, and I couldn't pull my wide eyes away as they shifted between forms naturally and rapidly, using claws and fangs as weapons.

Their movements were so fast and smooth that I couldn't even tell who was winning.

Or *if* one of them was winning.

They were like brothers, so I knew they wouldn't fight to the death. But...

It was still nerve-wracking.

I looked up at Ervo, and he leaned his head down so I could whisper to him.

"Which of them is winning?"

His eyes didn't leave the fight, and he didn't answer immediately. A few seconds passed before he murmured, "It's an even match. Neither have sustained an injury that will slow them yet. When that happens, it will end quickly."

Oh.

That made sense.

It took time for wounds to heal; a bad one would cause a delay, and a delay would give the other man a chance to take the victory.

Though Ervo's ear was beside my lips, my next question went to his mind. *"Do you think they both want to win?"*

I didn't know if he'd see through my question, but I'd explain if he asked.

"You still wonder about Sunny and Teris," he said quietly.

"I do," I admitted.

Ervo considered it, still watching the fight. I watched too, though I was still clueless as to what all was happening.

Clearly, I needed a *lot* more training.

"Teris hasn't been pulling punches and doesn't seem to plan on letting Nev win. Then again, Fovea is skilled enough to recognize it if he was, and would likely call off the fight. So I don't know whether or not that means anything," he murmured. *"But when a fae male is certain about a female, he won't consider fighting for the right to mate with another."*

"That's what I thought." And what Sunny seemed to think too.

The fight went on for another ten minutes.

Honestly, my adrenaline died down.

Both men were in their beast forms and nearly covered in dried blood, yet neither of them had made a significant enough dent in the other to end the fight. And—

Nev's fangs finally scraped Teris's throat.

The sabertooth lunged, but stumbled.

"Basilisk venom," Ervo said to me. *"A full bite can knock out a fae for an hour."*

Damn.

The stumble was the opening the basilisk needed, and Nev's jaw clenched down on Teris's shoulder.

The sabertooth bucked and fought until the second he hit the ground.

Cheers and roars rolled through the crowds around us, the adrenaline of the fight getting to the male and female fae around us. I didn't cheer, though—and neither did North or January, from what I could tell.

Fovea's eyes gleamed with excitement, and the group of female fae looked similarly thrilled by everything that had just gone down.

Nev shifted back, striding toward Fovea in his gigantic fae form, man-bun still on top of his head without a damn hair in place.

As soon as he reached her, he wrapped a hand around her waist, tugged her body to his, and kissed her.

More cheers went through the crowd—hoots and hollers, from both men and women.

The kiss turned into a makeout session, and the cheers only grew louder until Fovea finally stepped away, visibly flustered as she licked her swollen lips.

A satisfied Nev stepped up beside her, taking her hand. She was reluctant to give it to him at first, but when he slid his fingers between hers, she didn't pull away or protest.

When I saw them standing next to each other, I kind of thought the pairing might work. He was calm, collected, and conniving; she was fiery, fierce, and focused. Together, they could be a real force to be reckoned with.

Or maybe, really damn good leaders.

Nev dipped his head toward Fovea, murmuring something to her.

Her eyes narrowed at North, but she murmured something back that seemed to relax Nev.

"Before I make the victor my mate," Fovea said, raising her voice again. "Myself and the other female fae wish to offer the humans an agreement."

Ervo's arms tightened around me.

When I looked at North, her gaze was hard.

We all waited, silence flooding the forest.

Fovea went on, "I propose that we call off the coming fight. And that rather than declaring North my second-in-command, the female fae recognize her as the leader of the human harsh... who are the protectors of their own human life-bringers."

Priel let out a heavy breath of relief.

Honestly, I think most of us did.

North made the fae wait a minute though, before she finally called out, "We accept your proposal and guarantee that you won't be attacked, should you choose to move out of the Stronghold."

Fovea dipped her head. "We will consider your offer."

Then she released Nev's hand and crossed the space between us, stopping in the middle of the empty patch of land.

North pried Priel's arms off of her, striding over to meet the fae woman at the center of the field. When Fovea offered her a hand in a very-human gesture, North accepted it, and shook.

The whole crowd seemed to calm as the women returned to their own groups. And when Fovea shifted to her dragon form, huffing at Nev after he threw a leg over her back and climbed up onto her, cheers erupted from the female fae.

We all watched them take to the sky, and then in a random, insignificant fashion, the groups dissolved.

"I need to find Sunny," I told Ervo.

"I know." He stroked my hip before he released me.

"We dodged a bullet with that one," North told us, as she, Priel, Lian, and January stepped over to us.

"I think January's baby deserves the credit," I admitted.

North snorted, and January grinned.

"I didn't think Teris was going to fight," I said, looking over at the man's unconscious form.

"He's going to have to do some serious groveling if he wants to be with Sunny," North agreed.

January grimaced. "I don't know if any amount of groveling can make up for this."

There was a decent chance she was right.

"Is Dots going to be hurt too?" North asked me.

I shook my head. "I don't think so. I'm going to go find them, though."

"I'll come too," January agreed.

"Same," North said.

"No, you're helping me drag Teris's ass to his house," Lian corrected his mate. "I'm not leaving you alone until the damned female fae have proven that they're not going to try to abduct you or our baby again.

She made a face, but nodded.

"And North needs to sleep," Priel said, grabbing her hand.

"Are the nightmares back?" I asked her.

She shook her head. "I haven't had a single one, through any of this female fae stuff. But the women aren't evil—they're just different. I'm sure more issues will arise, but we'll figure them out. Having Nev connected to Fovea will make it easier. He's one of the only fae I know who actually thinks before he acts."

Priel snorted. "Thanks, Gorgeous."

"I resent that statement," Lian drawled.

January grinned. "Get some sleep. And some not-sleep." She winked. "And Mare, don't forget to find some of the birth-control fruit if you don't want to end up like me. Congrats, you two."

My face heated.

As Priel dragged North away, she reached into his pocket and pulled out a small fruit I had never seen before. She tossed it toward me, and I caught it right before it hit me in the face.

...if her coordination was anything like mine, it was probably a good thing she hadn't had to fight Fovea.

"They taste like ice cream if you stick them in the fridge," she called out. "And it works for men and women both. I'm happy for you guys!"

"Thank you!" I called back.

"You're going to eat that, right?" Ervo murmured to me.

The slight alarm on his face was enough to make me grin. "Yes, I am. I'm not ready for a baby. We have a lot more to learn about each other before we get there."

"Agreed." He peeled the fruit for me as we walked, handing me pieces of the strange thing and eating some of it himself too. It had a weird texture and taste, but in a good way. I could definitely see what North was saying about it tasting like ice cream when it was cold.

We had to ask around to figure out where Sunny and Dots were, but eventually found them on the outskirts of the fae land, near a large tent that I was fairly certain housed Aev, the Tame King.

Seventeen

The women were doing yoga, of all things, when we found them.

Dots seemed pretty good at it, but Sunny's downward dog could've seen much better days.

"How are you doing?" I asked Sunny, as Ervo murmured to me that he was going to find me something to eat—and asked me to wait there for him.

I knew he was giving us as much privacy as his possessive, overprotective self could manage.

"We are so zen," Sunny hollered, still in her attempt at downward dog. "So damn zen."

My lips curved upward. "Convincing."

She lifted one hand off the blanket they were using as a yoga mat and flipped me off.

I grinned back as she finally collapsed onto the blanket, and let out a sigh. "Really, I'm fine. I've been in denial for a while, but I'll move on. I think the tiny mate bond has been making me more into him than I really am."

Hmm.

That was quite the theory, but I didn't know if it was true.

Or possible.

"At least our party planning was successful for you." She forced a smile onto her face. "You got the guy."

"Apparently we were both just miscommunicating." I shrugged lightly. "Do you have a plan for how you're going to deal with your sabertooth issue yet? You know I'll help you carry it out."

"Oh, there's a plan. It's just small right now." She raised two fingers, with just a little gap between them.

A tiny bit of movement in the trees dragged my gaze up to one of them, and I studied it, looking for any sign of the basilisk from earlier. When I couldn't see one, I brushed it off as my imagination.

Sunny looked up at the tree too, following my gaze. "What?"

"I thought I saw something. There was a basilisk in the trees, right next to you, when Teris... you know. He looked like he wanted to murder the sabertooth. I thought it might be the same guy."

Sunny shrugged. "All of the fae are protective of us. If I wasn't so damn obsessed with the bastard who keeps rejecting me, I would already have hooked up with one of them."

"Lies," Dots called, from a weird pretzel-like yoga position that I didn't have a name for. "These are the lies you tell yourself. If you were really that into casual sex, you would've already dumped his ass ages ago."

Sunny flipped Dots off, and she laughed before making a pained noise.

"Are you okay?" I asked her, concerned.

"I'm fine. There's some pain in my chest and stomach that started when the mate bond broke—I'm assuming Nev already kissed Fovea or something. It'll fade, hopefully."

"We should never have agreed to those damn bonds," Sunny muttered.

Dots slowly stretched into a new pose. "Stop lying to yourself, Sunny."

"Just leave me to my lies, woman. I need them to survive until I get out of here long enough to move on."

Dots's new pose was even more complex than the last one. I'd never seen her do yoga in the Stronghold, but it wasn't really surprising that she was into it. "Getting out of here does *not* sound safe."

"I'm a massive snake, and snakes are creepy as hell. I'll be fine."

"More lies," Dots sang.

Sunny tossed a pebble at Dots's ass. "Lies keep some of us sane." She looked at me. "Tell us about your sexathon last night before Dots destroys the lies keeping me from losing my mind, Mare."

I laughed. "How did you know it was a sexathon?"

"The trees are full of fae, and fae talk. Especially when it has to do with sex."

She wasn't wrong, though it made me blush really damn hard to know that someone had heard us.

"The sex was great," I admitted.

Both women stared at me.

They wanted more details, so I kept talking. Not about the sex, but just... him.

"He loves me, and I know I'm safe with him. I know that even if I piss him off, he's still going to be there. Either to drag me back to his house and cook for me, or to distract me, or to kill someone, as dark as that is. I thought we wouldn't really be friends until we knew everything about each other, but that's just not how it went."

"Oh, to be in love," Sunny said with a sigh. "I might be willing to kill for that."

"I think that's the first semi-true statement you've shared," Dots remarked.

Sunny tossed another tiny rock at her ass, making her grin. "I just want someone who puts me first, you know? Like, if I want to kiss him and the world's not in the process of ending, he should drop what he's doing for two damn minutes and kiss me. Is that too much to ask?"

"No, it's not," I said. "And I think you deserve that, and more."

"I know. I just thought for a while that Teris might be falling for me."

I hesitated.

Sunny's eyes narrowed suspiciously. "What do you know?"

Guilt twisted my lips in a grimace. "I was sworn to secrecy."

"Tell that flaming bastard to fuck off and give me the truth, Mare. I've known you longer."

Dots snorted. "Because that determines everything?"

"In this situation, yes."

I nodded. "Let me ask him."

Reaching out to Ervo, I asked, *"Can I tell Sunny what you told me about Teris?"*

I felt Ervo considering it, and he agreed. *"Most male fae know how he feels about the subject. The females might as well too."*

"Thank you. Sunny was going to be pissed if I didn't tell her."

Ervo's chuckle in my mind made me fight a smile.

"Okay, so Ervo told me that Teris won't settle for less than love. And that unless he knows that the woman he's interested in is in love with him, he won't consider them mates, and he won't believe that they belong to each other."

Sunny blinked. "So he thinks my feelings aren't strong enough?"

I shrugged. "Maybe."

"He thinks my feelings aren't strong enough, so he rejects me. Like *that* would make me love him." She laughed bitterly. "He can go to hell. Maybe while he's burning there, he can ask Fovea to mate with him again."

"Sunny," Dots warned.

"Too salty, I know. But seriously, fuck that guy." She stood up. "Girls, it's time to plan another party."

Dots and I exchanged slightly-worried looks.

"Don't worry; this time, we'll invite the fae chicks so they don't bomb us with that damn poisonous fruit again."

"I don't know if that's a good idea..." I warned.

"It's a *great* idea." She flashed me a fanged-grin, and now that I knew about basilisk venom, that was slightly concerning.

But Sunny was hurting, as much as she tried to pretend that she wasn't.

So, in the end, we helped her plan her damn party... the secret parts, we had to do through written notes, so the fae in the trees wouldn't hear.

THE PARTY WASN'T GOING to go down for a few more days, so that evening, Ervo whisked me back to our treehouse. The close one, not the far one.

We made love against the wall, and though I tried to be quiet, I failed.

I was pretty sure that was Ervo's goal, though.

We snuggled up together on the floor and started talking about my family again. It was going to take me a lot longer to move on completely from everything I'd experienced, but he listened without complaint while I ranted, just holding me and stroking my back.

After a moment of silence, I admitted quietly, "Sometimes, I feel bad that my life wasn't as horrible as the other girls' who are here. I know most of them probably survived worse, and I wonder if I should've just figured out a way out of my life instead of making that wish. There are people who deserve to be here more than me—and who probably need it more than me."

"Pain is not a competition, Mariah. We all suffer. We all struggle. We all ache. Your difficulties were neither worse nor better than anyone else's; they just *were*. And now, they're done. And you're mine."

I tried to blink away the water pooling in my eyes. "Thank you."

"You don't need to thank me for being possessive," he teased me softly. "I take great joy in it."

My lips curved upward. "You're funnier than I realized when you were all neutral and grumpy, you know."

"There's a weight over my chest that feels lifted, now that you're in my arms," he admitted to me. "I always felt like I was missing something. The loneliness threatens to eat you alive, as a fae. That changed some, with the arrival of the human women, but these past few months have been a true awakening for all of us. I see now that all of my loneliness was meant to show me how lucky I am to hold you like this—and that in all of my waiting, my soul was looking for yours."

"You didn't know I was yours when you first smelled me, though," I murmured.

"Probably because I strong-armed it into choosing you."

I laughed softly. "Well, I'm glad anyway."

"As am I." He continued to stroke my back as he changed the subject. "What did your horses look like? You never explained them to me, and I struggle to think of an Earth animal that a person could ride."

Oh, geez.

My mind drew a blank as I struggled to come up with something to compare them too.

"I'm going to need to draw them, I think," I said.

He grabbed his poetry book, then, opening it up to a blank sheet for me. I wasn't a great artist, but I sketched the outline of a horse for Ervo, and he nodded slowly when he saw it. All he said was, "Interesting."

"Do you have animals like them here?" I asked him.

"Not quite." He tugged the book from my hand and pulled me back into his arms a little too quickly, but I honestly didn't think much of it. "Tell me the poem again," he said, distracting me. "Our poem."

His hands stroked my hair, and my body relaxed entirely as my eyes closed and I recited the poem I had changed when we mated.

"I'm yours
I whisper,
My breath on your face.

I'm yours,
I bellow,
My scent on your skin.

I'm yours,
I snarl,
Heart pounding in my chest

I'm yours,
I roar,
Forever and more."

WE FELL asleep in each other's arms soon after, and I decided in the moments before sleep stole me, that I hoped every day would end like this one.

And that if even a fraction of them did, I would be the happiest version of me that had ever or would ever exist.

Eighteen

Ervo

"Where are we going?" Mare asked me, for the dozenth time since I'd woken her up before the sunrise and dragged her into the sky with me. She was flying beside me, though I had tried to convince her to ride on my back.

Apparently, my female hated surprises.

"You'll see," I reminded her again.

She groaned at me, but continued flying by my side, brushing the edge of her smooth, scaled wing up against my feathers time and again, as if reminding me that she was still there.

We flew deeper into the mountains, until we finally neared the place the pawe liked to graze.

"We shift on the edge of the valley," I warned Mare quietly. *"We must stay calm, and act as if we're not predators."*

"Okay..." She was dying to know what we were doing, and I fought hard to hide my excitement at her upcoming reaction.

She was going to be thrilled enough that her eyes would gleam, the way they did when she was so happy she had to fight off tears. I didn't understand why they watered as much as they did, but she'd helped me see that it wasn't always a bad thing.

Now, I took joy in the moments when she was happy enough to cry.

"Follow me closely," I added, putting out my flames and diving toward the valley's edge.

Her shock vibrated through my mind when she saw what we were there for. She spiraled down to the ground, landing beside me perfectly, just like I'd taught her to the day before. This was only our third day of being mated, but so far, I was utterly obsessed.

Despite her perfect landing, she pressed herself against my chest, her palm covering her mouth as her eyes watered. She stared at the creatures on the grass in front of us for a few silent minutes.

I remained quiet for her sake, letting the wind tug at us while my female worked through what she was seeing.

"What do you call them?" she finally whispered.

"Pawe." The word was pronounced paw-way, though it would sound different on her lips than mine.

"They're horses," she finally whispered. "Bigger, weirder horses. Just like fae are bigger, weirder people."

A soft chuckle rumbled my chest, and she clutched me tighter, looking up at me with so much excitement that my lips curved upward.

"I love you, Viervo. You know that, right?"

"I do, but I'll never protest hearing the words on your lips." I brushed a kiss to her forehead, and she went on her tiptoes to press her mouth to mine quickly—once, and then again. "And you know I love you?"

"I know." She pulled away, her eyes bright and watery and happy.

Pride coursed through my veins at how easily I had pleased her—at how quickly I had realized that she would love the creatures here.

"Can I get closer?"

"As long as you stay slightly behind me. They're gentle creatures, unless you piss them off. I've seen two of them rip apart a dragon in his beast form who didn't show them proper respect," I explained.

Her gaze grew alarmed. "Maybe we shouldn't."

"They know me," I assured her. "And soon, they'll know you as well."

She looked uncertain, but nodded

My fingers caught hers as I stepped just in front of her, and she stayed behind me as I slowly led her toward the creatures.

Greeting the pawes and letting them carry you through the mountains was the surest way to discover more of Vevol's secrets. My brothers and I had done so a hundred times or more—and with every journey we discovered a new cave, hot spring, or otherwise-hidden location.

They treated us as well as we treated them.

I supposed they were like our females, in that way.

We approached the large male I always greeted. Though he had a name, as all living things in Vevol, I had no way of knowing it. And even if I did, he wouldn't have given it to me.

He was a wild creature, made for hidden coves and undiscovered paths; not an animal to be tamed.

My eyes met his, and I dipped my head toward him.

He dipped his back.

My gaze slowly moved over the other pawes, making sure none of them were close enough that me and Mariah might encroach on them.

When I was satisfied that my female was safe, I slowly stepped up to the male's side and lightly stroked his thick, strong neck. He huffed at me, and I chuckled softly.

"This is my mate," I said to the pawe. "My Mariah. She'd like to greet you, if you're willing."

The beast studied her for a moment before nodding his head at me.

Pride swelled in my chest.

I slowly led her around to the front of me, trusting the creature now that he had agreed.

She nodded once at him, like I had, and he tossed his head at her.

Telling her to get on his back.

"We would enjoy a journey," I told him, lifting Mariah off the ground with one arm as I set my other hand on the beast's back. In one smooth motion, I'd lifted us both up together. He was massive enough that our weight barely affected him, and the moment we were on securely, he took off.

Nineteen

Mare

Wind streaked through my hair as we bent over the creature's back, and joy coursed through me as tears stung my eyes.

So many memories—I had so many memories about riding horses. The best ones from my time on Earth included the strong, powerful creatures.

I had loved them so much, and I had missed them even more.

And the man behind me had seen that, and brought me to meet them, because he realized what they meant to me.

I'd never been loved like that before, by anyone.

And it felt like a privilege to be loved that way. I didn't know if I really deserved it, but damn, I was glad Ervo was mine.

Eventually, the pawe slowed. Ervo thanked it, and eased me off the creature's back before he bowed his head toward it. We were in the middle of the mountains, and my eyes landed on a small, shaded lake.

The sun was shining over us as Ervo led me wordlessly to the shady lake. I think he knew I needed time with my thoughts.

He sat down with his back against a tree, and pulled me into his arms. I relaxed against him, letting my mind return to Earth. To my memories of Stacy and my horses. To the family I'd left behind, and the one I'd gained when I came to Vevol.

Everything had changed for me when I came here.

And all of it, for the better.

Especially in the last few months.

I hadn't really gone through with my plan—hadn't slowly convinced Ervo that we were equals.

But he knew.

And I did too.

"Are you okay?" he asked me, his voice a soft murmur.

"Better than okay," I whispered back. "Thank you so much."

"Any time, Mariah." His lips brushed my forehead.

I bit my lip, another smaller, easier plan bubbling up in my mind. Really, it was the shattered remnants of the old one.

"Would you mind standing up for a minute?" I asked him.

"Sure." His hand ran over my arm as he eased me away from him, rising to his feet. "Why?"

I rose to my knees.

His eyes narrowed at me, and I knew that day was flashing in front of his eyes. The day he had told me never to kneel in front of any man.

"If I want to be on my knees in front of my mate, I should be allowed to," I told him, as I undid the fastener on his shorts.

His eyes narrowed further as he realized what I was about to do.

And further when I dragged his pants down to the grass.

And even further when I wrapped my fingers around the base of his cock, leading it to my mouth.

And then they shut, when I closed my lips around him.

He groaned deeply as I slowly bobbed my head further down his length, gliding him backward, taking him into my throat.

When I looked up, his eyes were open again. Open, and hot as hell.

I dragged his hand to my head, so he could cup me. So he could set the pace.

And finally, he started to move.

His hips rocked as he worked my head over his length, his touch as gentle as always. He groaned and growled and swore as I sucked him, until the taste of him had soaked my mouth and I knew he was only seconds from exploding.

And then, with a grin, I slid my mouth off of his length.

He snarled at me, but didn't finish the job himself.

He was too busy watching me strip my tank top over my head for that.

"Make love to me," I told him, as I slid my shorts down my ass and then got down on my hands and knees.

He sank to his own knees behind me, cupping my core with one hand and finding my clit as he dragged me to him. "Today was supposed to be for you," he growled at me, as he lifted my hips upward, moving me until my slit met his cock.

"It is," I breathed.

All thoughts ceased to exist as our bodies merged, but the connection was more than just physical.

We were mated—down to the fucking soul.

He was mine.

I was his.

And even if I could've made another wish, for another new life, I wouldn't have considered leaving him.

Because in Vevol, I had everything I needed—and the man I loved.

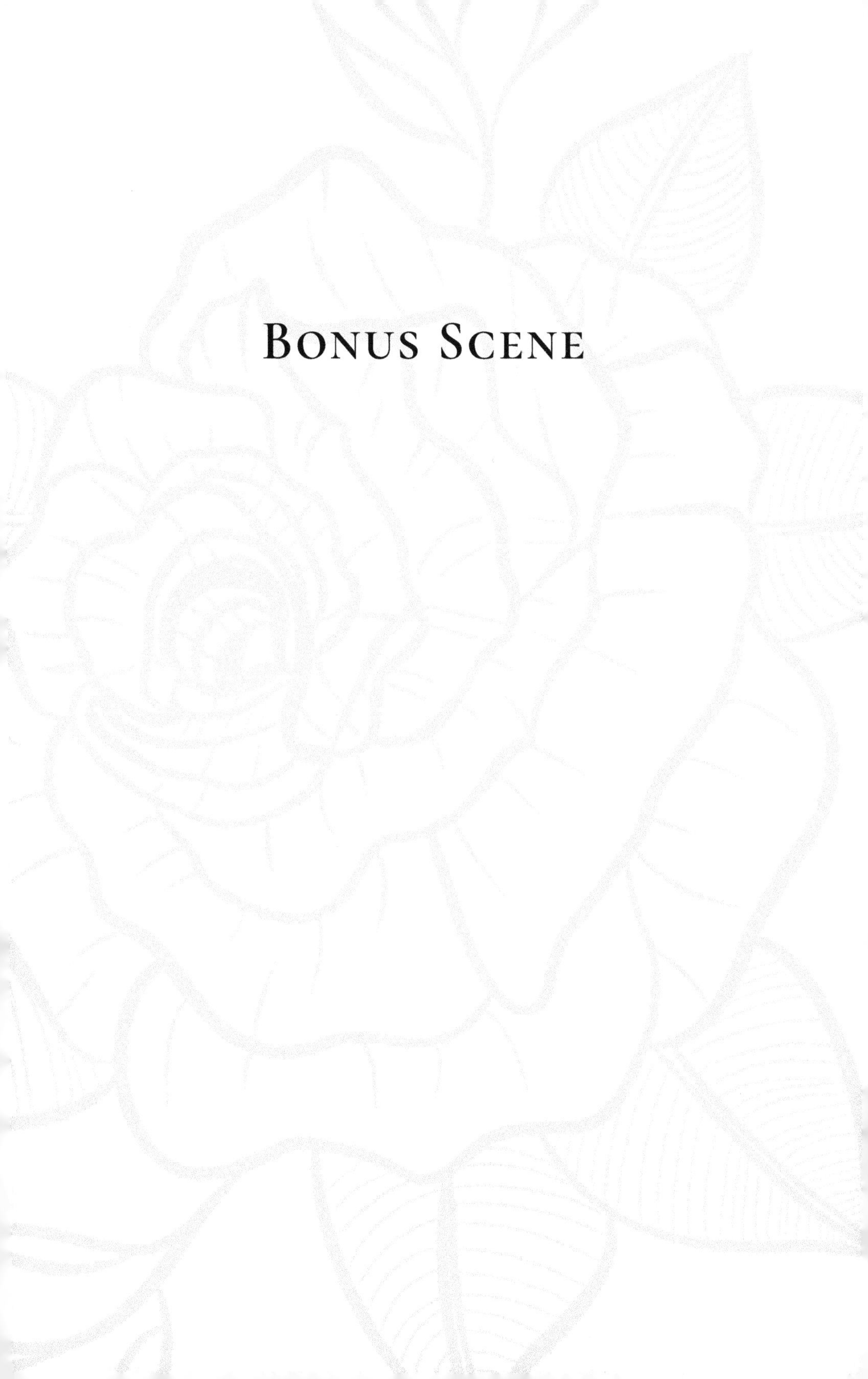

Bonus Scene

The Vicious Fae's Love

Wild Hunt 4

To the books and people that help you heal

One

THE FOREST WAS silent around me as I slipped between the trees. Off in the distance, I could hear the pounding music of the raging party I'd planned and put together. Dots and Mare would keep it going all night, giving me the time I needed to disappear without a male fae tailing me.

One male fae in particular.

The sabertooth one who had turned me down time, after time, after time.

It was pretty ironic, really. I'd wished myself away from Earth to get away from an abusive boyfriend... and yet had managed to fall for a fae guy who was as close to abusive as the fae could get.

Which, honestly, wasn't very close.

Teris hadn't been cruel to me. He definitely hadn't hit me.

But the constant rejection and disinterest was just too damn much.

I was done.

So... I was leaving.

Teris would've been following me, too, if Ana and Rosalie hadn't agreed to start a fight just outside the party. All it took to distract my temporary-mate was one little punch. He was always looking for a fight.

So really, the escape was a team effort. But if you told any ex-human chick that you wanted to get away from a man, they'd just ask how they could help.

I guess I was that way, too… though I'd much rather play match-maker than match-breaker.

Since I moved much faster in my basilisk form, that was the one I currently occupied. The shorts that the other girls always wore didn't work well when I shifted, since I didn't have any legs in my beast form. So before I left, I'd altered them into a miniskirt. It was, admittedly, more scandalous than the shorts. But I was a sucker for a good scandal.

The other basilisks had showed me the best way to get around the forest in our beast forms; we were thick enough and strong enough to keep up with the others for the most part on the forest floor, but in the trees, we thrived.

Long torsos helped with that, I supposed.

So I was sliding through the trees, my movements both fast and silent.

If I was going to get away from Teris, speed and silence were necessary. Despite his lack of desire for me, the bond connecting us still irked him. Which meant he still felt the need to protect me. And possess me.

Honestly, I should've kissed another guy to break the bond before I left, but…

I just couldn't.

Maybe that was out of some twisted sense of loyalty, but it was loyalty all the same.

I spent twenty minutes in the trees, until I reached my first checkpoint:

A river.

Teris would track me easily by scent, unless I did something to cover it. And since I wasn't willing to snuggle up with some random dude, the river was my best shot at hiding myself.

When I reached it, I dove in and was careful to lower the length of my body down deep. I'd heard the men talking about tracking basilisks in water before; they said there were signs of us in the sand and stones for a few hours afterward. Our weight would leave a large dip.

So I spent fifteen minutes headed in the wrong direction, deep in the sand at first and then rising up higher and higher so the tracks would grow lighter.

After that, I turned around and swam hard against the current. I was careful; I couldn't afford not to be.

Not if I wanted to get away from him.

And I didn't just want to—I *needed* to.

I *needed* that space.

I *needed* to move on.

The female fae had once mentioned a lake in the mountains where the women went to give birth. A place of healing, which was exactly what I needed.

Time to heal, move on, and recover.

Another fresh start.

So, that was my focus.

I swam harder.

AFTER A FEW HOURS, I decided it was finally safe enough to get out of the river.

The dirt felt warm on my scales after so much time in the frosty water, and a shiver rolled through me. I ignored the cold, and the hunger rumbling in my belly.

When my tongue flicked outward, I caught a strange smell—an unfamiliar one, but an incredibly appealing one.

My eyes scanned the trees.

Someone was here.

The smell was too strong, too good, for me to be alone right then.

I shifted back to human form, ignoring the way my skirt rode up high on my damned vagina. I'd need a little more fabric to make it more *appropriate*, but I currently had nothing of value to offer in trade for said fabric.

"Who's there?" I demanded. My voice echoed through the trees.

A flicker of movement in the corner of my eye had me spinning around.

The largest basilisk I'd ever seen—so probably the same size as Nev—slid out on a low-hanging branch.

The color of his scales changed as he moved, blending in with the background he followed, and my eyes widened.

"Who are you? How did you find me?" I demanded.

The basilisk finally shifted—sliding out of the tree and landing smoothly on thick thighs.

Like all of the fae, he was massive.

His hair was dark and wavy, short on the sides but long and messy on top. His skin was a gorgeous dark gold color, and his eyes... the vibrant green was bright enough that they almost glowed. Shimmering vine-like tattoos snaked over his arms and torso, wrapping partway over his neck. They were the magical kind that some of us got after becoming fae, not the ink kind that some of the guys gave themselves.

My eyes trailed downward, stopping when I saw him wearing the shorts most of the basilisks sported. They were small and stretchy, but not fireproof like most of the other shifters' clothes. How the strip of fabric survived the shifts, I didn't know. They basically resembled boxer-briefs, honestly.

The man's package was straining against his shorts, and when I realized that was probably because I was *staring at his junk*, I jerked my eyes back to his face.

His calm, expressionless face.

Damn, he was gorgeous.

I cleared my throat.

Guess I was going to have to embrace the fact that I'd totally just checked this guy out.

"Who are you?" I asked, more calmly this time. "And how did you find me?"

I didn't recognize him, though I'd spent time with a ton of basilisks and other types of shifters. There were a lot of fae that I'd never met, but as far as I'd known, they were currently all gathered together.

At the party.

Which I had planned for that very reason.

"Remmo," he said. The word was more flowy than some of the other fae's names, sounding like reh-mo. "I followed you. It was a good plan, keeping to the river." He stretched a hand toward it.

So he *had* been among the other fae.

Panic welled in my chest. "Did Teris follow me too?" I demanded. "Who else is behind you?"

Remmo blinked. "No one else followed. I masked my scent as well."

Relief had me sagging. "Good."

He studied me. "Are you afraid of the sabertooth?"

"No, I'm not afraid of him. He's not interested in me, and I have feelings for him. So... I'm leaving. Just for a while. So I have time to get over him."

"*Get over* him?"

I supposed the term might not make sense to a basilisk who hadn't spent much time with humans. "It's like moving on, I guess."

His lack of response told me he didn't understand that one either.

"I don't want to have romantic feelings for him anymore," I clarified.

The man's body stiffened.

Shit.

He didn't want me to move on, did he?

"If you're friends with him, just jump back in the river and swim away," I snapped. "I asked him to mate with me, and he said no. A dozen times. Mare thinks he's waiting for love, and is trying to test me or something, but he can just fuck off."

The fae relaxed slightly. "I understand. You seek distance in hopes that your feelings will fade."

I nodded emphatically. "Exactly."

"And what if they don't?"

I scowled. "I'm going to the healing lake. If that and the distance can't fix me, then I just won't go back to the Stronghold."

The man was silent for a moment.

Those green eyes were staring into my soul, and I didn't like it at all.

Especially because he smelled *so damn good*.

"Don't judge me," I said defensively. "If you were interested in a woman who didn't want you, you'd do the same thing."

"I wouldn't leave her and seek healing, no."

"Maybe not. But you'd probably start to resent her at least a little, don't you think?"

There was a long pause.

He wasn't going to answer me.

I spun on my heels and stalked into the forest.

He caught up immediately and walked beside me, his steps much quieter than my own. Soon, I'd need to shift back and start moving faster. But… it was nice to have legs again, honestly.

"I offended you," Remmo said, as we walked.

"You're judging me," I grumbled.

"I'm not. I haven't been in your exact situation."

"And how do you know my *exact* situation?" I looked over at him, slightly suspicious.

"There's gossip."

Dammit.

He was definitely right about the gossip.

I huffed. "Fae bastards."

He made a noise of agreement.

"What do they say about me?"

"You're in love with Teris. When you asked him to mate with you, he walked away without a word. The distance between you grows larger by the day."

"Well, they're right." I heaved a sigh. "I'm not in love with him, but everything else… yeah."

"Why would you mate with him if you feel no love?"

"I don't really think I can love anyone at this point," I said bluntly. "And honestly, after what happened with North and Clevv, I'm not going to feel safe until I've banged myself into a secure relationship with someone who will protect me. I might not love Teris, but I trust him to keep me safe. Or at least I did. Now, he's just hurt me too many times."

Remmo was silent for a few minutes as we walked together. He smelled *really* good. Like… suspiciously good. Stupidly good. Like I wanted to grab him and lick his face to see if he tasted as good as he smelled.

Which I *obviously* wasn't going to do.

Probably.

He finally said, "The sabertooth will be able to track you, as long as you're connected. The barest hint of your scent will sing for him."

"It didn't work that way when we were captured by the fae chicks," I pointed out.

Although, Teris *had* been able to track me when Clevv's hounds took me...

"The female fae used leaves to erase your scents," he said simply.

I didn't really trust him.

But I wasn't willing to risk him being right, either.

So I stopped walking.

He stopped too.

Kissing him would be a mistake, most definitely. I didn't know the guy, at all.

But... I was still considering it.

Just a little.

"What kind of fae are you?" I asked him.

He hesitated too long.

"Unseelie, then," I stated.

"I was unseelie, until recently," he admitted.

"How recently?"

"Last week."

Damn.

I didn't love most of the unseelies I'd met. They were colder, more boring.

More calculating, too.

And they *liked* rules.

But he smelled good, and I had to do *something* if I was going to stop Teris from following me. I'd never met a fae that I felt right about kissing to break the bond before, but Remmo sort of felt right.

Or at least not wrong.

So... kissing it was.

"Can I kiss you?" I asked him.

Teris would've said no. At the beginning, we had made out a few times, but that part of our relationship ended quickly.

Remmo just blinked at me.

And then blinked again.

I scowled, spinning around and stalking away.

Screw him.

I wasn't *that* unappealing.

A hand wrapped around my wrist after a few steps, sending a warm electric current through my skin. A quick tug later, my front was pressed against Remmo's.

One of his hands was wrapped around my waist, the other, cupping my face.

Damn, he was tall.

And big.

"Why do you smell so good?" I hissed at him. "This can't be—"

He cut me off with a kiss.

It was just a smash of his lips on mine, but... if he was unseelie, I didn't even know if he'd seen anyone kiss before.

Yet he didn't pull away.

His fingers tightened on my skin, like he wasn't ready for it to end.

So...

I did a thing.

A probably-stupid, possibly-would-regret-later, thing.

I slid my tongue along the seam of his lips, and when they parted, plunged it into his mouth.

A groan escaped him, and he dragged me closer.

Tighter.

And shit, I was right about him tasting good. He was better than good—way, way better than good. Not like candy, or ice cream, but like fresh water on a hot day, like rain in the desert.

Like mutual attraction, after constant rejection.

One of his hands slid into one of my curly puffs and I didn't even care, because he felt and tasted so good.

And when the other hand dragged me closer, my legs wrapped around his hips.

My back hit a tree, and he pressed me against the smooth bark.

I kept kissing him, our tongues and lips dancing and fighting and enjoying the hell out of each other.

Remmo had definitely figured out how kissing worked.

Definitely.

His erection ground against me as his hips jerked, and I rocked against him harder, encouraging him.

And when he snarled into my mouth, soaking both of our pelvises with his release...

I just.

Kept.

Kissing him.

Eventually, I was going to have to stop.

But hot damn... not soon.

Not.

Soon.

Except then, I heard a crash in the forest.

And a *furious* snarl.

My head jerked backward, smashing against the tree, and I winced. My lips were so damn swollen, it was glorious.

And my eyes locked with Remmo's bright green ones.

"We have to go, now," the man whispered against my mouth.

I jerked my head in a nod.

"Do you trust me?" he asked.

I snorted softly. "No."

His lips curved upward, just slightly. "Well, try."

And a moment later, part of his massive torso was wrapped around me. Everything went dark as he held me tightly, wrapped in his warm scales... but for whatever reason, I wasn't afraid.

We remained still for a long moment.

I heard growling, but no fighting.

Until finally, Remmo's body launched, carrying me steadily with him.

I was placed on my feet a moment later, and gaped down at an unconscious Teris.

"How did you do that?" I asked him.

He flashed me a fanged grin. "Did no one teach you about venom?"

"No, they sure as hell *did not*."

"I'll teach you on our way to the lake. After a dip in the river, and a lesson about concealing your scent." He gestured toward said river. "We've only got about an hour before the sabertooth is conscious, so we need to get moving."

I probably should've said no.

I probably should've walked away.

But when he held out his arm, I took it.

Two

I SHIFTED BACK to my basilisk form as I slipped into the river, just because it was easier to roll around in my big ole' snake form.

Remmo did the same, and I shivered a little when his massive side brushed up against mine. Not a bad shiver, either. Somehow, even with the cold water wrapped around us, he shocked me somehow.

I wasn't sure why that kept happening, but figured it was just another weird fae thing. It had never happened when I touched Teris, but he hadn't really liked me. Remmo seemed to at least a little, so maybe that was what the shocking was all about.

He finished washing before me, and shifted back to his man form as he slid out of the river. While I followed him out and shifted too, he plucked a few huge leaves from a large bush that was nearly identical to about a billion others I'd seen in Vevol.

"What's that?" I checked.

"This is how we conceal our scents. Now that they've begun to meld, Teris won't be able to track us." He crumpled a leaf in his gigantic hand before he handed it to me, and I sniffed it.

My eyes watered at the strength of the smell, and I jerked it away from me. "That reeks."

"Yes. It's strong enough to wipe away all other smells. The scent you leave behind when coated in the memis will only be faint, and will smell like the many, many bushes stretching across our lands."

Huh.

That was actually pretty cool.

Maybe I should've asked a fae to teach me about plants while the other girls were fighting. So far I'd only learned about a few, and they all could do cool shit. Like North's birth control ice cream fruit, and the koveko that could knock people out.

I ignored my watering eyes as I quickly dragged the leaf over my exposed skin and clothing the same way Remmo was.

"If you were covered in this stuff, why did you still smell so good to me?" I asked him. "Also, you never told me why you *do* smell so good."

"The effect of the memis wears off over time. And ultimately, each fae is affected differently by the scents of those around them. Some say that Vevol speaks to them through their nose."

A snort escaped me. "They can't *actually* say that."

His lips curved upward. "Some do." He lifted the memis leaf to his hair and dragged it over the pretty, damp waves. I followed suit, though it made me cringe. The last thing I wanted was this stink clinging to my hair.

Well, maybe not the *last* thing. But one of the lasts.

"Well do I smell good to you, too? Or is it a one-way thing?" I checked.

"It's certainly not one-way." He stepped closer to me, kneeling in front of me as he inhaled. I knew he was just checking to see if I'd properly hidden my scent, but the sight of him on his knees in front of me made my cheeks hot anyway.

Some small part of me wondered if maybe he was my fated mate. The way he smelled... shit, it was incredible. But that shouldn't have been the only sign, if we were mates.

According to what little I'd been told by January—and the stories I'd heard *from* the other girls *about* the other girls—when a male fae had met his mate, he knew she was his the minute he caught her scent. He could track her anywhere, with ease, which was why the big, dramatic Wild Hunt shit had been created in the first place.

If I were Remmo's mate, he would've already grabbed me and declared me his. He definitely wouldn't have been able to stay calm while listening to me say that I was in love with Teris, because every fiber of his being would insist that he should beat his chest and make sure everyone knew I was his.

So... I wasn't Remmo's mate.

And he wasn't mine.

But he still wanted to be friends, and apparently we smelled good to each other.

Why not see where it went?

Maybe hanging out with him would help me get over Teris.

Or maybe he'd end up murdering me and hanging my body from a tree. Only time would tell.

Either way, it had to be better than sitting on my ass, waiting for Teris to decide that he wanted me.

"Tuck this in your shirt," he explained to me, grabbing a fresh leaf.

I blinked at him, eyes still watering a bit. "What?"

"...here." He tugged my tank top away from my skin a bit and stuffed the leaf downward.

Until his fingers met the tops of my tits, sending another tiny shock through my skin.

Then he froze.

I lifted a brow at him, watching as his eyes grew rounder.

And rounder.

"Not expecting to find boobs there?" I drawled, when a few more seconds passed and he still hadn't moved.

He jerked his hand away. "I didn't expect them to be soft."

"Pretty much all of me is soft. Here." I grabbed his hand and stuffed it back in my shirt. His fingers slowly wrapped around my tit, as if he couldn't stop himself from gripping it. "I'm not all muscley like you." I gestured to his abdomen. "My belly's soft. My thighs have hella squish. My arms are flabby." I lifted an arm, shaking it around a little. "It's probably not that attractive to you, but—"

His finger tightened on my breast. "It's *fucking* attractive to me."

I blinked.

He didn't release me.

I supposed I *had* been the one to stick his hand in there. He was probably worried he'd offend me if he let go. Or maybe he'd just realized how much he liked tits.

"Okay." I pulled his hand from my shirt, and as soon as I gave the slightest tug, he let go. "So you want this leaf in my top. And another one in my skirt?" I gestured down to the damn thing that had slid up nearly to my waist and barely covered my lady-bits.

"Yes." He handed it to me.

I dutifully tucked them away. "Now, we're good to go?"

"We are. Stay close behind me; I know the fastest way to get there."

Honestly, it was a huge relief to hear that he was going to lead me. It took a whole damn lot of the pressure off me if he knew where we were going and how to get there.

So when he led, I followed.

WE SPENT the rest of the night in the trees. It was kind of incredible to watch the sun rise over the forest from where we were. I kept glancing up at the sunrise even as exhaustion started to slow me down.

I looked up right as we slid from one branch to another—and totally missed the gigantic one I was aiming for. A startled scream escaped me as my huge, scaly ass plummeted.

Electricity flickered through my veins as a thick tail curled around me, halting my fall.

Remmo dragged me easily into the tree, and I shifted back into my human form. My legs straddled the branch, my heart pounding like hell as I struggled to breathe.

"I'm fine," I said to myself. "I'm so fine. So, so fine."

A shock to my back made me shudder as a large, warm hand pressed to my skin. Remmo slid around me, kneeling in front of me with his lips turned down in concern. "You need to rest. I should've realized."

"I was looking at the sunrise," I admitted. "That's why I fell."

Because I'd been looking at the sunrise… and trying to keep up with the fast, gigantic bastard.

His hand stroked my back lightly. "I'm sorry."

"You don't need to apologize. It's not your fault." My eyes closed, and I let out a slow breath. "I think we're going to have to stop so I can sleep. Is Teris going to catch us?"

"No. The memis covered our scents. The sabertooth will likely head back to the Stronghold to tell the others that I stole you from him. They'll assume I'm taking you back to my den."

"Oh, the other girls will tell everyone that I left on my own. I'm not sure what they'll say when he tells them about you…" I bit my lip. "Is your den near the lake?"

"No. It's a long way in that direction." Remmo pointed back in the direction of the Stronghold, and I assumed he meant it was further that way.

"Okay, then we should be fine. As long as you don't care if he tells people that you stole me away."

His eyes gleamed. "I don't care."

"Sweet." I let out another long breath. "Should we find a cave to sleep in or something?"

His lips curved upward slightly. "You know little about being a basilisk."

"Thanks," I drawled.

Remmo chuckled. "We were made to sleep in the trees. Our bodies coil naturally as we rest. You never need to find a cave; there are no predators in this forest that would dare approach you while you rest."

That calmed me a little. "Can you show me?"

"Of course." His hand stroked my back lightly before he stood.

His body shifted as he stretched up toward a branch a few feet above us, and I watched in fascination as his long body wrapped smoothly around it.

The position didn't exactly look comfortable, but I figured it was worth a try.

Shifting forms again, I slowly looped myself around the thick branch. Its bark was cool against my scales, which made me shiver a bit. But when I was fully wrapped, and forced my breathing to grow even, I realized I did feel comfortable.

Really comfortable.

Even as I relaxed, my long body remained wrapped just as tightly around the branch.

My eyes shut, but my tongue snaked out to sniff the air. It had been really damn hard to get used to that at first—the tongue-sniffing thing—but I'd learned that I could smell a lot more in my basilisk form than my human one.

And the taste of Remmo's scent in the air, around me, calmed me further.

I hadn't asked him about the electricity, I realized, even as I started to get sleepy.

But with the wind blowing lightly through the leaves around us, flooding the air with Remmo's yummy smell, I was too comfortable to shift back and ask him.

THE LIGHT STROKE of a tail against my curled body wrestled me from sleep.

I lifted my head, groggily looking up at the basilisk above me. His scales had shifted to the same colors as the branch he was wrapped around, and I stared at him in fascination.

He slowly unwound from the tree, and his scales changed again before he landed on my branch and shifted back to his man form. His hand stroked the back of my head, and a shiver rolled through me. Not just because of the electric shock, but because of the warm touch.

I nuzzled my cheek against his side, encouraging him to keep touching me. I'd never been touched by someone while I was in my basilisk form, and the feeling was fascinating.

"We should start moving," he murmured to me, as he stroked my scales. "If we make good time today, we can make it to the lake tomorrow night."

Tomorrow night?

Damn.

It was further away than I'd realized. I'd been told which direction to go in, but I hadn't asked or figured out how long it would take to get there.

Maybe I was really, really slow... but I'd managed to keep up with the others on every other occasion, so maybe it was just far away.

Rather than changing forms to ask questions or get answers, I just bobbed my head.

Remmo continued stroking my scales for a few more minutes before he shifted back to his basilisk form, and we started moving again.

We made it halfway through the day before my hunger grew too great. I refused to even consider eating an animal—not gonna happen, ever—so I stopped on a branch and waited for Remmo to notice that I wasn't behind him anymore.

I thought it would be at least a few minutes, but he stopped almost as soon as I did, coming back to me.

As he returned, I shifted forms so I could explain.

"I need to eat," I admitted, patting my stomach. "And I can't hunt for an animal. I *won't*."

He dipped his head, and descended down the tree's trunk. I shifted back and followed him, and soon enough, we were on the ground. Both of us transformed to our human forms, and my feet dug into the soft, damp dirt as I looked around.

Honestly, it looked pretty much the same as the other parts of the forest I had seen.

"There's fruit this way," Remmo explained to me, leading me around a gigantic tree. I followed him, trying not to stare at his ass.

We probably needed to have a conversation about the kissing... and the tit grabbing.

But I wasn't looking forward to that conversation, so I kept my mouth shut for the moment.

We found the tree a minute later, absolutely loaded with massive purple fruits. They looked like mangoes, with their shape and variety of colorings, but the smell was very different. And they were much, much bigger.

"What are these?" I asked him, as he plucked one from the tree and brought it to me. He cracked the thing as he reached me, and I realized it had a shell.

"Fromil. They are one of the most common fruits in Vevol; did you not have them at your Stronghold?"

"We didn't." I shook my head, watching as he pried the two halves of the shell apart. The fruit inside looked sticky and purple, but smelled incredible.

"The seelie didn't feed you well?" he asked me.

"Nah. Mostly just rice and beans—or the fae version of it. If we wanted anything else to eat, we would have to go on dates with the fae. Give them a chance to talk to us more, and whatnot. I kissed a fae once for the seelie version of ice cream, but that was before I realized it would start a tiny bond between us. He must not have enjoyed it, because he didn't bother coming back afterward."

Or… maybe the other guys hadn't *let him* come back afterward.

It had been so long ago that I didn't know, or really care.

Remmo looked kind of annoyed as he handed me my half—which was nearly the size of my head—and then broke off a chunk of the shell near the edge. After he showed me how to scoop the fruit into the shell bit and eat it that way, he handed the shell bit to me.

Our fingers brushed as I took it, and I shivered at the electricity.

"Why does that happen?" I asked the basilisk.

"Why does *what* happen?" His gaze was on his own fruit, as he snapped a piece of the shell off and used it to begin eating.

The way he was pointedly looking away from me made me suspicious.

"The electricity, every time we touch."

"Ah." He continued eating.

I waited.

And waited.

"Fill your stomach so we can begin moving again," he said, a few minutes later.

"I'm not hungry anymore." I set the fruit on the ground.

I was being dramatic… but also, I really *wasn't* hungry anymore.

Did my lack of hunger have something to do with the electricity?

I should've been a lot hungrier while we were traveling than I had been, which was kind of suspicious.

"Sunny…" he watched me carefully as I stood up. I think he realized that I was about to walk away from his ass, because he admitted, "Try not to panic, but I believe the shocks are because of the mate bond."

I frowned.

I hadn't felt that with Teris, but... Teris had barely touched me. And only when he had to.

When I tried to remember if North or January had said anything about being shocked, nothing came to mind.

So there was no way to prove him right or wrong.

"Why didn't you just say that?" I sat back down. "And why did you think I would panic?"

He studied me for a moment before admitting, "You made the decision to kiss me very suddenly. I didn't double-check to make certain you were sure you wanted to go through with it. So I thought perhaps you might regret breaking your bond with Teris."

Oh.

"I make almost all of my decisions suddenly. It sometimes leads to regret, but I've accepted it." I grabbed my fruit, and scooped a thick chunk of it into my shell bit. "I don't regret kissing you, though."

I might have imagined it, but I thought his shoulders relaxed a little.

"The shocks between us are supposed to calm both fae involved. The magic of the bond refreshes us, sustaining our bodies without food or water."

Huh.

So that *did* explain why I wasn't really hungry anymore.

"That's pretty cool," I admitted, finally taking a bite of the fruit.

Damn, it was delicious.

He made a noise of agreement, and I studied him before speaking my thoughts. "North kissed Clevv. Did you hear about that?"

His face darkened. "The male who assumed a woman belonged to him to the extent that he justified hurting another? Everyone heard about that."

"Right. Well... do you think Teris is going to try something like that? Does breaking a mate bond make someone insane?"

He considered it. "Did Priel attack any females when North broke the mate bond with him?"

"I don't know. I didn't ask her about that. Probably not, since none of us were near them."

"Then we'll assume that breaking a mate bond doesn't destroy sanity, and learn the truth when we return to the Stronghold."

I grimaced. "What about when I have to break the mate bond between us, Remmo? I don't want you to lose your mind."

His body went very, very still.

I stared at him, unsure why he'd frozen.

And I waited a few minutes, eating silently while I did so.

"We will cross that road if we get there," the basilisk finally said, his voice strained.

Not wanting to further disturb the man, I just nodded.

Three

WHEN WE WERE BOTH FULL, Remmo taught me to leave the rest of the fruit near the edge of the tree's branches. He said there were animals in the forest that weren't strong enough to open the fruit's shell on their own, who would finish what we hadn't. The ones most-likely to come for it were called geggins.

I wanted to stay and watch, and by some miracle, Remmo agreed.

We slid into the trees, hiding silently. His scales shifted to match the branches and leaves around us, hiding him almost completely, and I stared down at the fruit.

A bit of time passed in peaceful silence.

My eyes lit up when slowly, a pair of animals crept out of the trees. They looked almost like small monkeys with really, really long hair—and long ears, too.

They picked the fruit up with small, odd paws before they disappeared into the forest with it.

Remmo gestured for me to follow him when they were gone, and I did—with a massive grin stretching my scaly face.

WE TRAVELED for another day and a half, sleeping in the trees for a few hours when night hit, before we finally reached the lake.

We'd crossed the border into unseelie land at some point—which I knew because of the thick snow on the ground and in the trees. I'd never liked snow on Earth, but now that I didn't seem to get cold very easily, I didn't mind it.

The lake was small, surrounded by trees with massive leafy branches that intertwined, concealing the water completely from the view of anyone who might've flown above.

Remmo shifted forms as we approached it, and I did the same, still taking everything in with wonder.

"It's beautiful," I murmured, my eyes devouring the snowy hills that gave way to a partially-frozen lake.

"It's very cold. Are you sure you want to get in?"

Was it just me, or did he look slightly worried?

"Yeah. I'm hoping it'll help with the heartbreak," I admitted. Though honestly, now that I was away from Teris, and the bond wasn't stretching between us, I felt...

Free.

And I definitely didn't miss him.

Part of me wondered if my affection for him had all been because of the bond. But then again, I was always drawn to his type. The bad-boy kind who would make you chase them, and then when you finally convinced them to give you a chance, made you feel like shit about pretty much everything.

I felt pretty damn ashamed for letting myself have feelings for a man who cared about me so little.

Remmo said nothing as I waded through the snow, headed toward the lake. If it had been any further, I'd have shifted to my basilisk form just to make it easier.

But I reached the shore soon enough, and found the man still beside me. Apparently he had followed me.

"I think I need to do this alone," I told him.

"When I know you're safe in the lake, I'll give you space."

It wasn't much of an agreement, but I nodded anyway. It was kind of sweet that he was going to protect me... even if I was a little worried about the connection he might be feeling between us.

It wasn't like I could fall in love with the guy. And as far as protection, I didn't know how much of it mating with him would provide. Teris was a part of the Wild Hunt; if someone challenged him, he'd kill them, even if he needed the rest of his brothers to help.

But as far as I knew, Remmo was far from any position of leadership. He'd just abandoned the unseelies to become a seelie, a move that I understood, but a move that would probably put him at the bottom of the totem pole.

Unease rolled through me.

Had I accidentally created another Clevv? Another man who would do anything and hurt anyone to get back the woman he wanted as his mate?

If so, he had me exactly where he wanted me.

Far from my friends, far from all the other fae who might consider protecting me...

Shit.

I'd never been great at making wise decisions, but this one might take the worst-choices cake.

At least Remmo smelled good, I supposed.

And kissed really well.

Even if he hid me away in the forest forever, I'd probably enjoy it. That was good to know.

He watched silently as I stepped closer to the water.

"Do you think I need to take my clothes off to heal better?" I asked him, nervous about getting any closer.

"Definitely."

He answered too quickly, and when I glanced over, saw his eyes gleaming.

A laugh escaped me.

He just wanted me naked.

"A man after my own heart."

Logically, clothes wouldn't matter. But... I'd never taken the stretchy fabric swimming before.

"Does this fabric dry fast?" I asked him.

"If you have fire."

Which neither of us did.

"I'll warm you, if you wish to leave the clothes on," he assured me.

Letting him warm me up probably wouldn't be a hardship for him. At least, not for *most* of him.

Still, I figured it was probably the best idea just to take the damn things off. So I walked over to him, tugging my tank top over my head. He seemed to stop breathing as I put it against his chest, his hand rising stiffly to catch the fabric.

I slid the skirt down to my feet next, stepping out of it and handing it to Remmo too.

"Just think of all the advantages you'll have over all the other men when you're trying to win a mate after this," I called to him, as I strode to the water. Something about feeling his hot stare on my bare body made me feel more confident, more certain.

"How would this situation be an advantage?" Remmo's voice strained.

"I already taught you how to kiss!" I exclaimed, stepping a toe into the water and then halting abruptly as a shiver tore through me.

Wow.

Wow.

Wow.

That was cold.

"I taught you how to be less awkward around women, too," I called. "And I'm in the process of training you not to be shocked when you see tits. And vag."

"I think I'd need a closer look to get a proper lesson," he called back. "Maybe the next lesson should be on how to bring a woman pleasure? That would really set me above the rest."

A laugh spluttered out of me. "I think you might just be as snarky as me, Remmo."

"I'll cherish the compliment forever, Iloli." His sarcasm was heavy, and made me grin.

I forced the rest of my foot into the water.

Shit.

Shit.

Shit.

Shit!

That was freaking *ice.*

I continued the conversation to distract myself. "Ill-ole-ee? What does that mean?"

"Your mismatching eyes; it's a word for someone possessing them."

I blinked said mismatching eyes. One of them was black, and the other was silver. On Earth, it was called heterochromia, and I definitely hadn't had it there. I'd thought it was cool when they changed in Vevol, but never thought it meant anything.

He had walked closer, I realized, because his voice was easier to hear over the wind and the lightly-moving water.

"No one's told me that before," I admitted.

"The seelies don't find it significant, so I'm not surprised."

My foot went numb in the water, but I wasn't brave enough to stick the other one in.

He remarked, "You're only putting off the inevitable. Just jump in and all of the discomfort will hit you at once."

"Rip off the bandaid, you mean," I mumbled.

"What's a bandaid?"

"Never mind." I pushed some hair out of my face. "You're right. Do the unseelies consider my eyes significant?"

"They do. Jump in the water, and I'll tell you why."

I huffed at him. "Asshole."

"I would also like to inspect that part of you, yes."

A snort escaped me. "Seriously, you're the male version of me."

"You're still avoiding it, Iloli."

"And you're still being a dick," I shot back.

But then I forced myself to stop thinking—and I jumped.

The water engulfed me.

It was a shock to my whole damn system.

I didn't move, at first. Just felt myself sink to the bottom of the icy lake. Small, smooth stones met my ass, and I let out a slow breath of air as my body adjusted to the cold. On Earth, I knew that snakes couldn't create their own body heat, but I wasn't an Earth snake. And, as I remained under the water, my lungs beginning to strain against the pressure, I got used to the temperature.

When I finally kicked off the ground, swimming up to the surface, I didn't feel like I was dying anymore.

I was shivering wildly, though.

"Do you feel healed?" Remmo asked me.

"No." My puffs had deflated, and now my hair was plastered to the top of my head, dripping freezing water into my eyes. "Tell me about the word, please? I'm going to swim around and see if the healing thing works."

"A fae's eyes only become mismatched when he has developed ultimate control over himself. It's the goal of all unseelies—to become iloli."

My nose wrinkled as I continued to tread water. "Why do they want ultimate control over themselves? And how could I have that?"

"There is power in self-control that the seelies refuse to recognize. Vevol's magic sees it when someone develops that control, and changes them. As for how you developed it, I suppose I would need to know your past to say."

My frown deepened. "I don't think I really have self-control. If I see cake, I eat it. Period."

He chuckled. "Not that kind of self-control, Sunny. It's the ability to see yourself honestly, and control your emotions thoroughly."

"Well, I definitely don't have that either."

"Don't you?" His voice was slightly amused, and I felt like the question was rhetorical. "It applies to your physical forms as well. Some fae struggle to see both halves of themselves as one; your eyes declare that you do not."

I guess he was right about that part. I'd still felt like myself, even the first time I shifted into my massive, creepy snake form. Honestly, I felt pretty damn powerful when I was scaly.

"I still don't know why all of the unseelies would aim for that," I admitted.

"Because otherwise, we were aimless," he said simply. "We had no females. There was no potential for love, or children. This world held nothing for us, and yet here, we were trapped. Becoming iloli was a goal that united us in a time of pure loneliness and emptiness. Perhaps it meant nothing to the seelies, who were content to spend their time fighting each other, but the rest of us wished for a higher purpose."

Huh.

When he said it like that, I guessed it made sense.

"How many of you became ilolis?"

"Not one." He chuckled lightly. "If it hadn't kept us alive, I'd say our effort did more harm than good, which is part of the reason why many of us are defecting to the seelie side. Our search for perfect control seems to have affected the females on our land negatively."

The words felt like a nudge.

Maybe my ultimate control was doing more harm than good for me too.

"On Earth, I always had to walk on eggshells," I admitted to him. "My family was abusive, and then my boyfriend was too. I got away from him for a while, but then he found me. I thought he was going to kill me. I had to learn how to wear a mask, to play a role, just to stay alive. That's probably why I have the eyes."

"Then they are the eyes of a survivor, and you should wear your title with pride." The man's voice was low. "What is this abuse?"

Oh damn.

Something told me this was not a wise conversation to have with a man I'd gone and kissed, starting a mate bond with.

"Never mind," I said quickly. "I don't think the healing is working, and I'm really damn cold. Think I'm going to call it."

"Call it what?" He looked slightly confused—but also suspicious.

"It's a human saying. I'll explain another time." I swam to the edge of the lake, planting my feet on the smooth, slick stones that felt like they were actual ice cubes beneath my feet.

My frozen, pointy tits distracted him from asking more about my family as I carefully made my way out of the water, much to my relief.

When I made it out of the water, my skin was stinging something fierce.

Holy shit.

Holy shit.

Holy shit.

I started jumping, pumping my arms, trying hard to get warm.

"What are you doing?" Remmo sounded amused.

My teeth chattered when is started to answer him, so I closed my mouth tightly.

He set my clothes down, crossing the space between us and quickly wrapping his arms around me. The electric shock felt like nothing since I was so frozen.

But daaaamn, he was warm.

Incredibly warm.

Blissfully warm.

It was just for body heat, I told myself, as I snuggled closer to him.

Just body heat.

"I can shift forms and wrap you up if you'd like. It would be the fastest way to warm up," he murmured to me.

"Yes," I moaned.

With another sexy chuckle, he shifted smoothly. His massive body wrapped around mine like a living cocoon, the way he had when Teris had been coming after me in the forest. Only this time, it was just for warmth.

Another moan escaped me as the air around me warmed quickly, and I plastered my naked front to his scales.

He was like a damn grill. Just cooking me right up to the perfect temperature.

Ohhhh, that felt good.

So good.

I warmed up quickly—and fell asleep almost immediately afterward, like the cold had shut down my damn brain.

MY OWN SNORING woke me up sometime later. I choked on the noise as I jerked my head up off his body, looking around the darkness deliriously before I saw the scales.

Remmo's scales.

Right, I was in a snakey cocoon. For warmth's sake.

Now, I was sweating balls.

"I'm awake," I said groggily, patting the basilisk on the side. Or butt. I supposed there was no way to know what part of him it was at that point. "You can release me."

He slowly unwound, and I found myself standing in the middle of a large circle of green grass. I'd been asleep long enough for his body heat to melt all of the snow under him, apparently.

And... I was still naked.

Remmo left me in the circle after shifting to his man form, and he strode over to the edge of the lake. When he returned holding a bundle of black fabric, I realized he'd been retrieving my clothes for me.

"Thanks." I flashed him a small smile, accepting the clothes even though I was terribly sweaty. The only way to take a shower would've been to jump back in the lake, and that was a no-go.

"You look uncertain," he observed.

"I'm sweaty." I made a face, dropping to my butt on the grass without putting the clothes on. "And I don't know what to do now, since the healing lake didn't work."

"You don't feel any better?"

I considered it.

When I thought of Teris, there was only a tiny bit of that lingering embarrassment. No attraction, no sadness. Some regret, yes, but not regret that he hadn't wanted me.

Regret that I hadn't ditched his ass sooner.

"Maybe I do," I finally said.

"Would you like to talk about it?" He sat down next to me on the grass, keeping his eyes on the lake out in front of us even though I was naked next to him.

I knew that wasn't a rejection of any kind. He had made it clear that he was attracted to me, but since the moment was sort of emotionally intimate, he was being respectful of my space. Our bodies didn't touch at all, and I knew I could just tell him no if I didn't want to talk about it.

But I'd never really talked to anyone about my feelings for Teris. I kept my guard up, always.

Something about Remmo made me feel like I could let it down a little.

"Mostly I just wish I had stopped caring sooner," I finally said. "When I think about the way I kept waiting for him to change his mind, the way I kept offering myself to him… I just feel embarrassed." The words were barely above a whisper.

Remmo stayed quiet.

My face heated. "I was so stupid."

"The only stupid one in the situation was the male fae who wasn't interested in the perfect female who offered him everything." Remmo's voice was low, and calm.

My eyes stung a little.

"He knew, when he formed that bond with you, whether or not he wanted to mate with you. He was the one who said no, time and time again, so he was the one who should have broken that connection when he realized that he didn't want what you clearly did. You should be proud of yourself, for your honesty."

"Have you seen the pity everyone looks at me with?" I asked him quietly. "They don't think that."

"What you've seen in their eyes is not pity, Iloli. It's respect and mutual understanding. Do you not think we understand rejection? Nearly every male fae has waited in line to meet a woman who didn't want us—sometimes for days, or weeks. Are we not more pitiful than you, when you only sought to deepen a mating bond with a man who had already accepted you enough to start it in the first place?"

A moment of silence passed between us.

My thoughts and emotions were all over the place.

As difficult as it was to wrap my mind around, I could honestly see his point.

It would take me time to feel the same way though, I guessed.

"Which woman did you wait in line to meet?" I asked him.

He chuckled. "Viv was the third woman brought from Earth, and the first to come to the unseelie land after five entire years in seelie territory. Naomi and Mina had already been claimed by Aev and Konn. Every single unseelie waited in line to meet her—myself included."

"Which others?" My curiosity grew. I didn't know why, but I felt sort of... protective over Remmo. I didn't like the idea of him waiting in line and then being rejected by the unseelie chicks over and over again.

"Only a few."

"You're being purposefully vague," I pointed out.

"Do you wish to tell me every one of the times you propositioned Teris?"

Well...

Dammit, he had a point.

"Fine. I'll give you one, and you give me one?"

He dipped his head in a nod.

"The very first time Teris and I kissed was in the Stronghold." I stared out at the lake, remembering the moment too vividly. "I was making jokes about hooking up with Priel, before that. He had an easy grin and his tattoos were cool, so I hoped maybe I could mate with him. He wanted North, though, and they're hot together, so I'm glad they worked out. Teris wasn't all that interested in me when we drew names. I know that the guys rigged the drawing, so they could pick who they would be with, but I think the other guys really wanted the other girls, and Teris just didn't care. Nev thought he was really into Dots, then, and all the other couples are now together, so it fits."

I sighed. "Anyway, I kissed him. And I didn't bother with a soft kiss; I just went for it. He kissed me back, for a bit. When he pulled away, I asked if he wanted to mate with me. His exact words were, 'not right now'."

Remmo's body was tense.

Really, really tense.

I wasn't sure why. Maybe he just felt really uncomfortable for me.

I felt uncomfortable for me too.

"In hindsight, I should've realized that was the first of many rejections. But it had been a really long time since I kissed a guy, so I just felt hopeful."

A moment of silence passed between us.

I waited for Remmo to share something.

And waited.

And waited.

Finally, the man said through gritted teeth, "Jia was after Viv. I spent months waiting my turn to meet her. Not in line, but on a list. When the day finally came, she refused to walk through the door. I caught her scent enough to know she wasn't for me, but the hit to my pride was heavy."

Damn.

"You know, I think I'm going to try getting back in the lake," I said.

Mostly because he was still really tense, and I didn't want to keep talking about Teris.

"Do you want to try too?" I checked.

"I don't need healing," he said stiffly.

"Oh, I know. But you're basically a heater, so I thought maybe we could go in together and see if you can keep me warm."

He jerked his head in a nod. "I'll swim."

"Cool." I left my clothes in the ring of grass, standing up and holding my hand out for the fae.

He stiffly stood, accepting my hand. When I slid my fingers between his, he relaxed just a little, and I bit back a smile.

I didn't bother believing we were going to become mates, but he definitely wasn't rejecting me.

Four

"Ready?" Remmo asked me.

"I guess. Hold me while we go in?"

He chuckled, dragging me into his arms. His body was warm against mine, and there was no way to ignore how good his hard muscles felt against my soft curves.

My arms went around his neck as he wrapped his around my back and then used that grip to lift me off the ground.

He took two massive steps toward the lake, and then launched us into the water.

A scream bubbled up in my throat as the icy liquid engulfed me. Remmo's grip remained tight, though, and I adjusted to the water a hell of a lot faster with the man's body pressed up against mine.

We broke the surface a moment later, and my legs wrapped around his hips as he started to tread water for both of us.

Our gazes collided, and when I saw how bright his gorgeous green eyes were, I couldn't stop the grin that spread across my face.

"Colder than you thought?" I asked him, my teeth chattering a little.

"No." He squeezed me closer to him, and I leaned into his heat, pushing my frozen face against his neck.

"How are you still warm?"

He chuckled. "I was never human."

"I feel like that's an insult," I mumbled against his neck.

"It certainly isn't." His hand moved slowly over my back. "Tell me of your life on Earth."

My eyes shut, and I sighed. "I was a hairdresser. Women would come in, and I would cut or color their hair. I didn't love it, but it was something to do, and I was good at it. After I ran from Holden, my coworker Chloe helped me start fresh."

"Holden was your boyfriend?" The words were gritted out through clenched teeth.

"Yeah. He was a real bastard. But me and Chloe started a new life, and things were good for a while, until he found me again. I thought he was going to kill me." My voice grew quieter. "Being taken to Vevol... it honestly saved my life."

His grip on me tightened. "How did you wish yourself here?"

"An eyelash." My lips curved upward just slightly. "When I was little, before my mom died, she always said that you should wish on every eyelash you lose. I wished for a way out, and the Wild Hunt saved me. It was a miracle."

"Did you have feelings for Teris before your agreement with them? Did his scent ever appeal to you?"

"No. I only saw him maybe twice, and I never noticed him smelling good or anything."

His grip remained tight.

"Why?" I asked.

"I was curious if there was anything fateful about your companionship," he admitted.

"Oh, we definitely weren't fated mates. I saw how Lian reacted, when he first met January. He never left our front door, and kept calling her his. Teris never did any of that shit."

Remmo's fingers pressed against my back, and I wrapped my arms a bit tighter around him. With his skin against my face, his incredible scent had flooded every damn pore I possessed. I was relaxed in a way I'd never felt before—and happier than I'd been in a long time, too.

"How do you do that thing with your scales?" I asked him. "Where you blend in with the trees?"

"It's a simple, constant connection to Vevol's magic," he explained. "Most fae cannot focus long enough to keep it going for more than a few minutes, which makes me an outlier. For me, the connection has always been instinctual."

Huh.

"Did your power increase after you kissed me? That's supposed to be part of the bond, right?"

"Yes. It is, and it did."

At least he had benefitted from the temporary bond, so I didn't have to feel bad about putting him on the spot earlier.

Then again, I did still feel kind of bad.

"I probably should've given you more of a choice, with the mating thing," I admitted.

"What do you mean?"

My tips twisted in a grimace. "Suddenly asking if I could kiss you wasn't exactly the classiest way to go about asking if you'd be willing to temporarily bond with me to get me away from Teris."

A moment of silence followed the confession.

When Remmo finally spoke, he said simply, "My answer would've been the same even if you'd given me more time to consider, or phrased the question differently."

It probably shouldn't have, but that made me feel slightly better.

"And for the record," he added, his voice lower. "Should you ever want to kiss me again, there is no need to ask. My answer is always, without question, a yes."

If I hadn't been surrounded by literal ice water, my body would've heated. "I'll keep that in mind."

"Should I apologize for my lack of control in the forest?" he asked me.

It took me a minute to figure out what that one meant. "Oh, how you lost it when we were kissing? No, I get it. You're a virgin, and anyway, that was hot. You made me feel sexy for the first time in like, forever."

"You are extremely sexy." One of his hands slid down to my lower back and curved around my ass cheek, giving it a nice squeeze. I grinned against his neck, and he chuckled.

"Do you think we're healing?" I asked him.

"Not particularly. But I'm still enjoying this." His hand remained on my butt.

"Me too." I let out a slow sigh. "My friends are probably going to show up here looking for us soon. They knew I was headed this way, so when Teris tells them about you, they're going to spill the beans."

"We could leave, then." His voice wasn't urgent, and I knew he was putting the choice in my hands. "If we disguise our scents, we can stay away as long as we'd like to. When we return, it can be on our terms."

On *my* terms, he meant.

And damn, I liked the way it sounded.

"I'd need a way to write the girls a note," I said.

"There is plenty of untouched snow."

I made a face. "It's not very permanent."

"We could portal to Earth, and bring paper back with us."

Now he was talking. "How do you make an Earth portal?"

He chuckled. "I can teach you."

Excitement flooded my veins. "Deal."

"We'll have to get out of the water, first."

"I'm ready."

Really, really ready.

He hauled me out of the lake, not bothering to ask me if I wanted him to put me down. And he didn't release me until we'd reached the ring of grass, where my clothes were still sitting.

"Would you mind wrapping me up first?" I asked him, as he set me down. I was already shivering—and still not a fan of being cold.

"That is another question whose answer is always yes." He shifted forms, and quickly, I found myself engulfed in warm scales. Remmo was colder than usual too, but as I leaned against his side, we both heated up together.

I patted his scales when I was nice and toasty—before the sweating started this time—and he released me.

After I was dressed, I followed him into the forest a little, away from the lake.

The snow squished beneath my toes uncomfortably, and I tried not to wince with each of the steps.

Sometimes, I wished I was one of the shifters with fire. Or wings.

Though, as I was learning, there were cool parts about being a basilisk too.

Remmo explained, "The portal will open for only a moment, and you won't be able to step through—only to reach. You need to will the space between the worlds to thin, and then open, as you tap into your magic."

"Can you show me?"

He flashed me a smile. "Of course."

Remmo's hands went out in front of him. His eyes closed for a moment, and I watched in shock as the air in front of him slowly rippled, and then changed.

A simple shelving unit appeared in front of him, with stacks of paper reams on it.

It was a *store.*

An *actual store.*

It had been nearly four years since I'd been on Earth, and seeing something as simple as a store was seriously trippy.

Remmo reached into the portal, grabbed a ream of paper off the shelf, and tugged it right through the portal.

It closed, and my jaw was still hanging open.

He tucked the paper beneath his arm, then held his hand out and closed my jaw as the portal shut itself.

I batted his hand away. "You stole that!"

"Earth has plenty," he said with a shrug.

"You can't just take things off shelves," I protested.

"Would you like me to return it?"

I blinked. "I... I don't know. I never considered whether or not it was ethical to take shit from Earth."

"This is the way we got everything the females needed that we didn't already possess."

Damn.

"Well you already stole it, so I guess we might as well hold on to it," I said with a grumble. "You probably can't make that exact same shelf appear anyway, can you?"

"It's unlikely."

"Next time, we'll just figure something else out. Do you have anything we can use to write with?"

"There are many stones that work on your paper." He bent over, running his fingers through the dirt for a moment before he came up with a chunk of rock. I accepted it, and when he handed me a sheet of paper, set it up against the tree and wrote a quick message.

I WENT WITH REMMO WILLINGLY. We'll come back when I'm ready.

<3 Sunny

I SCRIBBLED the same thing on a few more sheets of paper, just in case one or two of them blew away or something. It didn't rain very often in the forest outside of the rainy season that was approaching in the next few weeks, so the chance of the notes getting wrecked wasn't huge.

We put them around the lake, pinned half-beneath rocks and stuck to trees with some kind of sap that Remmo got out of one of the trunks. He healed the tree afterward with his magic, of course.

When that was done, I looked at the lake one last time.

Though I wasn't sure whether or not it had healed me, I did feel stronger than I had before I came there. More capable, too.

Something told me that was more Remmo's fault than the lake's, but I ignored that voice in my head as we concealed our scents with the stinky leaves, then shifted forms and slipped back into the forest.

Remmo had offered to show me a pretty cave system that only he and a few of his closest friends knew about, so off we went.

. . .

WE TRAVELED through the rest of the day, stopping for the night inside one of the trees with the shell-fruit called fromil. I ate more than my weight in that shit before wrapping myself around a branch to sleep.

Part of me considered asking Remmo if he'd mind letting me sleep in his cozy snake cocoon, but I decided that was probably too mate-like, and we were just friends.

Friends who had made out, sure, but still.

Just friends.

AFTER TWO MORE DAYS OF traveling, we were deep into unseelie territory, nearing the ocean at the back of the land. Remmo explained that it was called the Salt Shore, and that there was some kind of force field preventing the fae from going past the beach.

He told me about some monsters trapped inside a frozen cave nearby, and that made me shudder. I cut him off before he could give me any details about them, because I did *not* need to start having nightmares again.

The force field on the beach, though, was really damn strange. I questioned him about it when we stopped for the third night, but Remmo didn't seem to know anything beyond what he'd told me.

Halfway through the fourth day, we shifted back to our human forms. We'd been sliding past small ponds and lakes that looked like they held all kinds of little creatures, which sort of disturbed me.

Mostly because I hated bugs.

But come on, who *likes* bugs?

"The cave is up here, through a small pond," Remmo explained to me.

"Are there bugs in it?" I checked.

"Probably." He flashed me an amused look. "You're a basilisk, Iloli."

"I know. But I hate bugs." A shudder rolled through me.

He chuckled, and I found myself opening up a little more.

Talking a little more.

"It usually takes me time to get used to new people and places. Being this comfortable with you is actually kind of out of character for me." I studied him closely. "You're still planning to head back to the others after we explore a bit, right?"

"Of course."

I slipped my hand into his, and his shoulders relaxed as I parted his fingers with mine. The touch was sort of intimate, but it just felt right with him. "Okay, let's do it."

"We have to go underwater to find the cave. I can swim us both down there, if you'd prefer," Remmo offered.

I nodded my agreement, and we started walking.

Two minutes later, we were peering into another pond, our feet still melting into the deep, untouched snow.

On the surface, the pond looked just like all of the others. I glanced at my companion. "Are you sure about this?"

He flashed me a smile. "Extremely. I wouldn't put you in danger."

As stupid as it probably was to do so, I believed him.

He gave my hand a light tug as he slipped into the water, and I slowly followed him in. My eyes widened when I was engulfed in warm water.

"Ohhh, that's nice," I groaned.

He grinned. "Now you trust me?"

"Ish." When I made a face, he laughed.

"I'll take it."

I was grinning too as he pulled me into his arms. Since I'd seen all the bugs, I wasn't going to take my clothes off. "Do you guys have leeches?" I asked him.

"I don't know what a leech is, so I'm not sure."

I wrapped my legs around his waist, holding onto him more tightly as he swam out to the middle of the pond. "They're like... long and squishy, I think. I've only heard of them, never seen them. They're supposed to be in water, and if you go near them, they like, latch on to you and suck your blood or something."

Remmo's eyebrows lifted. "We don't have anything like that."

I let out a relieved breath. "Good."

He chuckled, and I held on tighter. "Get ready to hold your breath. It's a short swim to the next cave, but I want you prepared."

Aww.

That was kind of sweet.

He counted for me, and on three, dove down. I held my breath, shutting my eyes tightly as he swam.

After a few seconds, I peeked one open. When the warm water didn't burn them, I opened wider, peering in surprise at the creatures swimming around us. The water was clear blue, and there were *things* everywhere.

They looked like fish, but moved slower, and more elegantly. Their fins were long and streamed out behind them as they swam, and they weren't too big or vicious-looking.

Still, I resisted the urge to reach out and touch them. They might have hidden teeth.

My eyes followed a rough stone slab as we approached it. There was a thick hole in the center of it, and I assumed that was where we were going. Remmo proved me right when he swam through it a moment later, and then immediately kicked his legs, carrying us upward.

Our heads broke the water's surface, and I stared up in fascination at the cave above us. There were all kinds of things hanging from the ceiling. I'd never been inside a cave before, but I'd heard of stalactites and stalagmites. I assumed these were them—stretching downward, and growing upward, in unique shapes and spirals.

"This is only the first cave. We'll submerge many more times before we reach the one I want to show you," Remmo murmured to me. "Let me know when you're ready.

His hands landed lightly on my back as he waited, and the only sound in the cave was both of us breathing as I looked at everything, again, and again.

"It's so beautiful," I finally said. "I've never seen anything like this. It's just... untouched."

"Vevol is full of places like this. Hidden away, for those who care to look." His hand stroked my lower back lightly.

I spent a few more minutes looking at everything before I finally told him I was ready to go.

He counted down, and then dove again. We swam slightly further this time, past more of the creatures. I noticed that a few of them seemed to be glowing a little bit, but when we surfaced again in the second cave, could only just barely see that glow.

The second cave was a bit darker than the first, but the formations I could see stretched on for what looked like forever.

"It's like an entirely different world down here," I whispered.

"It is." His nose brushed my forehead, and I found myself leaning a bit closer to him, fighting the urge to rest against him as I looked at everything.

When I gave him the okay, we dove down again.

Five

We wove through cave after cave. Some part of me started to get nervous as we went deeper and deeper into the system, but honestly, I trusted Remmo.

Or at least, I trusted him not to take me deep into a cave and leave me for dead.

"Are you sure this is safe?" I asked him, as we surfaced for the fifteenth time. The caves had grown deeper and darker and more confusing, every time, though still stunningly beautiful.

"I wouldn't bring you if it wasn't, Iloli." He tugged a piece of hair off my forehead, tucking it back under the band that still held one of my wrecked puffs in place. "What do you fear?"

"Not being able to get out," I admitted.

"Ah. Here." He swam over to the nearest wall, and placed my hand on the stone. "Tap into your magic, and ask Vevol to show you the way out."

I obeyed, shutting my eyes and searching for that nature magic. It took a bit of effort to find it, since I wasn't exactly a professional, but when I did, a tingle rolled through my shoulders and down my spine.

When I felt that tingle, I silently urged the magic to show me how to get out.

A series of images slowly rolled through my mind—me, swimming back through specific formations.

And when I opened my eyes, I saw what looked like a trail of magic beneath the water. A closer look showed me that they were the fish-creatures—the glowing ones.

They had formed a line, leading me back through the same gap in the stone that Remmo and I had just slipped through.

Awe swelled in my chest.

"Vevol won't let you lose yourself in her secrets," Remmo assured me. "The seelies should have been teaching you these things while they had you."

"The unseelies didn't teach the other girls this stuff either," I murmured back.

"They refused to leave their safe places, or to allow us inside."

"So did we," I admitted.

"Then I have much to show you." He pulled another strand of hair off my face. "Starting with how to tie your hair back more efficiently."

A laugh escaped me, and I saw the playfulness in his eyes. He was just teasing me.

"I wish it had been you," I said suddenly.

He tilted his head, not understanding me.

My face warmed. "With the Wild Hunt, when I formed that bond. I wish it had been with you."

Understanding flooded him, and he squeezed me against his chest lightly. "I'm here now, Iloli. And I'm not going anywhere."

I bit my lip, nodding my head.

I knew there was shit coming our way. When we got back to the new Stronghold, Teris would be there. So would the other fae, who knew a lot more about Remmo than I did. Things would happen that I wasn't necessarily ready for, and I might end up walking away from the man who'd become my friend in the past week or two.

But in that cave, in that moment, he was all I wanted.

And I was going to embrace it for now.

HE COUNTED DOWN, and then dove again.

This time, when my head broke the surface, I could already see the glowing.

My lips parted as my gaze scanned the space around me.

There were no words for the beauty that surrounded us.

The cave was long, open, and nearly pitch black, with what looked like naturally-occurring pillars stretching from the ceiling to the ground. The pillars held up a rough ceiling, covered in more of the beautiful shapes that the other rooms held.

But the room's shape didn't capture my attention.

Because there were so many pillars—and each of them, as far as I could see, was wrapped in vines and flowers that glowed in soft blues, and pinks, and purples.

Some kind of glowing bugs drifted around the space slowly, with wide wings that glittered in the light.

Remmo lifted me up onto the stone floor, setting me down on my ass and murmuring, "Don't touch anything that glows. They all hold poison. It won't kill you, but it will make you sick."

Honestly, they were so beautiful that the warning of poison didn't even faze me.

I stood up as Remmo slid out of the water, and even his gorgeous abs didn't get a second glance as I started to move slowly through the cave.

His hand caught mine, and I slid my fingers between his as we continued to silently walk around, exploring everything.

"This is incredible," I finally breathed. "Thank you for bringing me here."

"Of course. You should've seen far more of Vevol's beauty already." He squeezed my hand lightly, and I squeezed his back.

He was right; I had been in this world for a really damn long time without seeing any part of it.

And now that I'd begun, I wanted to see more.

We reached what looked like the end of the cave, and my heart fell a little.

"Here." He tugged on my hand lightly, leading me to the far-left side. "Follow close behind me. The walls here won't hurt you if you touch them."

I tucked my free hand up against my chest anyway as I walked at his back, trying to see over his gigantic shoulders but failing epically.

I noticed the walls grow tighter around us, and sucked in a breath as Remmo turned sideways to fit.

Still, I did the same, trying not to let myself start feeling claustrophobic as we went.

My breathing picked up anyway as the space got tighter.

And tighter.

And tighter.

I was already hunched over, and struggling to keep moving.

"Stay with me, Iloli," Remmo murmured to me, as he continued leading me through the tight tunnel. It was much tighter for him than me, but that didn't make me feel any better.

I nodded roughly, forcing myself to continue.

"Almost there," he promised, when my breaths grew shallow as the panic grew thicker.

I nodded again.

Almost there.

Almost there.

Almost there.

He finally stepped free of the tunnel, and eased me out of it too.

His arms engulfed me, and I took in a staggering breath as he hugged me tightly to his chest.

It should've made me feel more trapped, but as he held me while I shut my eyes and just focused on breathing in Remmo's scent, my heart rate slowed.

I was alright.

Everything was okay.

"Thanks," I whispered to him. "I think I'm good now."

He slowly released me, and I brushed my lips over his cheek in a quick kiss without thinking about it.

He went still, and as my face warmed, I turned to look out at the room he'd led me into.

My mouth parted when I saw a massive tree that seemed to be growing *into* the cave's walls and ceiling. Stone entwined with branches, stretching through the entire massive space that the cave offered. The ceiling was hundreds of feet above us—and the cave seemed to grow even higher than it. There had to be millions and millions of thick leaves attached to the thing, all glowing a deep emerald green color.

I could see small animals of some kind, climbing around. A few of them were eating some type of fruit that looked as if it were growing on the tree, but wasn't glowing.

"I believe this tree to be one of the goddess Vevol's power sources," Remmo told me, as we both continued staring at the monstrous tree. "If you tap into your magic, you'll feel how it swells here."

"It's a sacred place, then," I said, as I kneeled on the stone and put my palms to the cave floor. My eyes closed as I searched for my magic, and when I found it, I took a sharp breath in.

It didn't feel like a stream anymore.

It felt like a heartbeat.

As I lingered, I could hear the steady rhythm.

Da-dum.

Da-dum.

Da-dum.

"This world really is alive," I whispered.

"It is." His voice was soft.

"Would you mind if we stayed here a while? I think I want to keep listening."

"We'll stay as long as you'd like," he assured me.

I remained where I was, eyes closed and palms on the stone while I listened to and felt the heartbeat of Vevol. It was calming... and it made me feel peace.

Da-dum.

Da-dum.

Da-dum.

The magic held me in rapture for what could've been minutes, or hours, and I didn't move until my stomach rumbled to let me know that it was time to get up again.

"I'll grab you some fruit." He brushed his hand lightly over my head as he passed me. The contact shouldn't have made my lips curve upward, but it did.

When he came back with some of the tree's fruit, he sat beside me. I finally removed my hands from the stone, accepting the food.

"What do you call this one?" I asked him, as I lifted what looked like a massive, silver pear to my lips.

"It has no name. I've never seen it anywhere else."

I paused before taking a bite. "Is it safe?"

"Yes. Feel with your magic; Vevol will warn you of anything that will harm you."

I reached my magic to the fruit, as instructed, and felt nothing that might have resembled a warning. So, I took a bite.

The texture was odd, and reminded me of biting into an orange slice. The flavor was slightly sour, too, but even more sweet.

"Yum," I said through a mouthful, making Remmo grin before he bit into his own fruit.

We made quick work of it, and then placed the fruit's core at the base of the tree, for the animals that lived on and inside it. Remmo assured me that they would either eat it or take care of the remnants, and I believed him.

He caught my hand, and led me around the tree as we stepped away.

"Where are we going now?" I wondered.

"Not leaving." He flashed me another grin. "There's a waterfall, and a warm pool. I thought you'd like to see it."

I'd finally dried from our last swim, but... he was right, I wanted to see it.

And probably swim in it, because why the hell not?

My hair was already a wreck anyway, and he didn't seem to care.

"Are you judging my sad puffs right now?" I asked him, extremely seriously. "Because if you are, I might have to kill you and throw your body in the waterfall."

"You might as well sacrifice me to the tree if you're going to go to the effort of killing me," he drawled back.

I snorted, and he grinned.

We continued climbing over massive roots. "You didn't answer my question."

"No, I'm not judging your hair. I think it's cute." He tugged on one of the puffs, and I realized in horror that they probably looked like pigtails.

That sure as hell wasn't cool, so I tugged the hair bands out quickly. My hair fell around my face, and since it was dry, went about to my collarbone. As soon as it got wet, that shit was going to get long, though.

"Want me to hang on to those?"

"Sure." I handed them over, and he slid them onto his wrist.

The motion was kind of... intimate.

And really sweet.

But I wasn't going to let myself think about that.

We finally made it around the tree, and followed a slow-moving river to a large rock formation. Sure enough, at the top, there was a trickling waterfall that led into a small stream. The stream was wide enough for two people, and wrapped around the rock formation in a way that kind of reminded me of the lazy river at a waterpark I'd gone to on a field trip in middle school once.

It was more pretty than overwhelmingly-gorgeous, but the steam rising off the water definitely drew me in.

Magical hot tub?

Yes please.

"The stream only runs in a circle, so don't worry about getting swept away. If you do, it'll just bring you right back," he told me, as we headed toward the water.

"Damn. Vevol doesn't mess around." I dipped a toe in, and shivered at the glorious heat. It wasn't just warm like the water in the caves; it was hot.

And the exact opposite of the frozen lake, I supposed.

It was a good kind of opposite, though.

I jumped in, earning a surprised laugh from the man I'd left behind as I cannonballed, splashing water all over him. The stream's pull was pretty strong, but since I'd already been warned, I didn't fight against it.

Instead, I sucked air into my lungs, lifting my chest and abdomen to make myself float. The world was silent as I stared up at the ceiling, being towed around by the blissful water.

Already, I'd decided that this stream was a hell of a lot better for *healing* than that frozen lake. At least when it came to a broken heart.

I had hardly thought about Teris in ages.

A pair of hands grabbed me by the waist on my second lap around the lazy river, and I shrieked as Remmo pulled me under.

He let me wrestle myself free, and laughed when I clung to him.

"That was a dick move," I told him, though I was fighting a grin. Those gigantic hands gripped my hips while the stream continued carrying us around.

"Was it?" he teased me, eyes glittering.

"It was."

"I suppose you'd better punish me then."

He didn't even realize the sexual undertones to his words—or the way my already-hot body was flushing.

I could imagine him tying me to a bed, putting those big, sexy hands on my body while he *punished me*.

It should've scared me, or brought up shitty memories from my past.

But it just turned me on.

"I can think of better punishments," I breathed.

The moment was just perfect—and the man was too.

He hadn't pushed me into anything.

He hadn't asked me for anything, or refused anything when I asked him, either.

He hadn't kept secrets from me, or dodged questions, or rejected me.

He was just there.

Constantly.

Unquestionably.

There, and mine.

So I grabbed his face—and I kissed him.

The soft press of his mouth to mine was everything.

And the way his tongue snaked into my mouth was even *more.*

His grip on my thighs slid up to my ass, pulling me tighter to him while our tongues moved together. They were slow at first—intimate.

And then growing hotter, needier, more desperate.

We were burning, together.

Blazing.

And I never wanted it to end.

His fingers moved up my body, sliding beneath my tank top.

I jerked my head away from his long enough to peel the fabric off my skin and then throw it to the side of the river.

He growled as one of his hands slid over my bare back, the other moving up my ribcage, finding one of my breasts and grabbing it in his hand.

I hissed as his fingers dragged over my nipple—and I arched when he pinched it, recapturing my lips as he did.

My bare chest was plastered to his. His hand, my skirt, and his shorts were the only things between us as he held that grip on my tit, not releasing the soft, sensitive skin.

He pulled me closer to him—stretching my legs open further as he dragged my core to his erection.

I moaned into his mouth when the length of his cock was pressed against my slit, putting pressure exactly where I wanted it. I rocked against him as the pleasure gathered, our lips still fighting for dominance as he squeezed me and touched me and worked me.

"We're not mating," I panted to him.

"Not mating," Remmo growled back, confirming my words as his hand finally left my tit long enough to drag my skirt down, and down, and down. His shorts followed it to the shore, both landing with a plop.

My fingers dug into the soft, wet waves of his hair as he grabbed my bare ass, setting me up against his erection again while we kissed. The water was so hot—and we were both so damn wet—as he pushed me beneath the waterfall. The pull of the stream was nearly nothing as he pinned me to the warm stone wall. Water fell behind him, and dripped on both of us, but we were all hands and lips and bare skin.

He ground his cock against me, right where I needed him, and my breathing was staggered as I wrenched my mouth away from his, my head tilting back as the pleasure swelled, and swelled, and swelled.

"Need your fingers," I panted, hips arching desperately against him.

He dragged me away long enough to slide two thick fingers into my channel, groaning at the feel of me wrapped around the digits as he pulled me closer again. My inner thigh pinned his cock to his abdomen.

His fingers were so huge that I moaned, still rocking against him, needy and right on the edge of release.

He didn't know my body, though. Didn't know what I needed.

I slid my own hand between my thighs, teasing my clit. And just that tiny touch was enough to set me off.

I lost it with a cry, my body tightening around his fingers as my hips moved uncontrollably. Remmo snarled, his cock jerking against my leg as he found his release.

We both panted as we came down from the high together, his fingers still buried inside me. He made no move to pull them out—and I sure as hell didn't ask him to.

"Teach me how your body works," he said against my shoulder, when our breathing had finally calmed down enough that we could speak.

Shit, he smelled *so* good.

I shouldn't be horny anymore, but I still totally was.

"Maybe later," I mumbled, licking his neck a little just to make sure his skin still tasted as good as it smelled.

It did.

It really freakin' did.

"*Now*, Iloli."

The command in his voice, for the first time since I'd met him, was too hot for me to deny him.

"Get out of the water, then."

He crossed the river, hauling both of us out without a damn problem.

Six

His fingers finally slid out of me as he set me down on a strip of smooth, warm stone. My body tensed at the feeling of emptiness that followed the loss.

Remmo parted my thighs and stared down at me with a wrinkle between his eyes like I was a puzzle he needed to solve. His fingers opened my folds further, and those eyes burned hotter.

"This is my clit." I slid my fingers down there, circling it to show him exactly where the pleasure button was. "If you don't touch this, I don't get off."

"Like this?" His finger slowly circled the skin the way I'd showed him.

"Yeah." I groaned out the word; it felt way better when he did that to me than when I did it to myself. "You can do other things to it too, just start slow. It's really sensitive."

"And this?" He slid a finger into my channel, still circling my clit lightly.

"That's where the cock goes," I said breathlessly. "It's not that sensitive. Feels good to have something inside it, but I've never gotten off that way."

"You will." His words were simple, but certain.

I didn't bother arguing with him, not while he was touching me like that.

"Are there sensitive places inside?"

"Supposedly. I've never—shit." A hiss escaped me as he ran his finger roughly over some sensitive part of me.

Apparently I *did* have a g-spot. Maybe she didn't want to make herself known until I made it to Vevol.

"Lighter! Lighter!" I about screamed the words as the pressure grew too much.

His touch slowed immediately, his forehead knitting with concern. "You're okay?"

"Wow. Yeah. Just too intense," I panted.

Understanding crossed his face. "And this is your ass?" He ran a slick finger over my back entrance, and I shuddered.

"Yep."

His eyes lit with interest at my shudder. "You like that?"

"Honestly not sure," I managed. He was still playing with my clit, and thinking was becoming more difficult by the second.

"I'll need time to try everything," he said, studying my abdomen as he focused on my clit again, though his thumb was still rubbing lightly over my back entrance. "To figure out what you like best."

"Or I can just tell you. No learning required."

"No." He didn't bother with an explanation.

And, not going to lie, the way he'd just gotten super bossy was hot as hell.

That was probably my bad-boy preferences coming back to bite my ass, but for once, I didn't mind one bit.

"Tell me how you touch yourself," he growled, lightly working my clit.

He kept changing the motion—trying new patterns, new movements—and it was all incredible.

My fingers tried to dig into the stone beneath me, but there was no grip to it. Remmo noticed the motion, and lowered his head closer to my core as he dragged my hands to his hair.

I gripped him tightly as he worked me, his breath moving slowly and hotly over my skin.

"Tell me, Iloli."

"In bed—I usually do it in my bed," I breathed, struggling for air as he dragged me closer to the edge. "It was easier when I had my own room. Haven't been able to in a while."

"Tell me who you picture while you do it." His growl was low, and something told me that the wrong answer here would screw up everything.

Luckily, the truth wouldn't piss him off.

"No one. I don't picture anyone. I don't—my brain doesn't work in pictures. It's just the feeling. The words. It takes me a while to get there, but—*ohhh shit, Remmo.*"

I was getting close. Way too close.

"Say it again," he commanded.

"Which part?"

"My name, Iloli. Say my name."

"Remmo." The word came out in a groan as he picked up the pace on my clit, sliding two fingers on his other hand slowly into my channel. "Oh shit. Oh shit. Oh shit. Oh shit." I was wailing, or yelling, or moaning—I didn't know. The feelings moving through me were like nothing I'd ever felt. So much stronger, I didn't even know what to do or say or think. "What are you doing to me?"

My back arched, and I screamed. I felt a gush—and then Remmo was snarling. It scared me at first—until I saw him jerking his cock, and felt him lose control all over my thigh.

When I finally opened my eyes, the heat in his gaze as it continued moving over me ensured that my very-relaxed body was still turned on, just a little.

"Fluid came out of you," he said to me, and my face warmed.

I'd been fairly sure that was what had happened. I'd heard of it, but never experienced it before. And hot damn, it was incredible.

"Sorry. I—"

"No." His voice was harsh. His fingers gripped my legs, holding them open further. "You don't apologize for the best moment of someone's life, Iloli. You were perfect. And you're going to explain to me everything you know about sex, while I clean you up."

I supposed that was fair.

And I was really damn glad that he felt that way... because I'd never climaxed like that before.

. . .

REMMO and I talked about the logistics of sex for a while. He was as good a listener as he was a teacher—asking me all kinds of questions that I never would've come up with myself. I had answers for most of them, though.

Eventually, he ran out of questions, so we retrieved our clothes and found a comfortable spot to lay down near the tree. It had to be night time by then, but the cave still felt special. Honestly, I had no desire to leave any time soon.

I wasn't sure about laying in Remmo's arms to sleep, and gave him an uncertain glance as we both sat down.

"You keep looking at me like you expect me to drag you back to the waterfall and make love to you, Iloli," he drawled.

I snorted as I lowered myself to my back on the warm, smooth stone. "I guess I do."

"Why? I haven't pressured you into anything."

"Yeah, I know. You're great. I just..." I trailed off, staring up at the glowing leaves above me. "I guess I still don't know what I want."

"Your heart still yearns for Teris?" His voice was low and grave.

"No, I don't miss him. I'm just afraid of letting myself fall into another bad relationship." My voice was quiet. "I've never been good at knowing what's right for me. Part of me wishes my fated mate would swoop out of the trees and declare me his, just so I didn't have to wonder anymore."

Remmo was silent for a moment.

A long, long moment.

He finally said, "Fate is not always correct. There were many fated couples in the unseelie land who despised each other."

"I know. But if it isn't my choice, then when everything goes to shit, I'll know it's not my fault."

There was a long pause before he spoke again.

"You assume that all relationships will fall apart?"

"If I'm in them, yes," I whispered, letting my eyes shut tightly. "I told you that before."

"I suppose I didn't take it seriously."

My lips curved upward a little sadly. "Well, I do make a lot of jokes."

He chuckled softly. "You do."

"You're okay with only being friends?" I asked.

"I am thrilled just to be at your side, Iloli."

"Even if we don't make out again, or get each other off, or have sex?" I pressed. "I don't think I'm ready for this thing between us to get any more intense than it is. We might need to take a few steps back."

"Even then, Sunny. Being next to you is more than enough for me." His murmur was quiet, but truthful.

My eyes stung, and I couldn't come up with any words to say.

When the side of his hand bumped mine lightly, I took the opportunity to take it and slide my fingers between his. He let me grip him tightly, and both of us were silent for so long that I fell asleep.

THE NEXT FEW days passed by slowly—but in the very best way.

Remmo patiently taught me the ins and outs of Vevol's magic. When I needed a break, we'd eat fruit and chat about the wild places he'd seen. Every time he told me about something new, I found myself wanting to see it.

Not alone—with him.

Which I didn't allow myself to overthink, though I was tempted.

When we weren't talking about Vevol, he was questioning me about Earth. I started to dodge the questions about my life—so he stopped asking them—and instead told him about the books and movies that I had loved so much. I'd tried bargaining with some of the seelies for movies and books in particular that I wanted from Earth, back when we lived in the Stronghold, but they never brought the right ones.

So, my largest fictional obsessions lived only in my memories.

And Remmo's, too, as he listened to me explain in detail every single plot twist, turn, and slide in every damn series that I loved.

To his credit, he asked all the right questions. And he was properly stunned when he found out that Darth Vader was Luke Skywalker's father, so I decided he was officially my favorite audience in Vevol.

A few days morphed into a few weeks, and neither of us was in a hurry to leave. I fought hard to keep things platonic, since I didn't want to crush his heart when I eventually decided to break the mating bond.

Honestly, he was the best friend I'd had in a long time.

Other than Dots, but I considered her family.

But eventually, I decided I needed to emerge and prove to my friends that Remmo had in fact not murdered me. So, after three weeks and a handful of days in the glowing cave, we headed back out.

"This time, you lead the way," Remmo told me, his eyes glittering.

It brought him way too much joy to see me using my magic. I'd explained to him two weeks earlier that many popular young adult novels featured powerful chicks who ended up losing their magic at the end. It had always bothered me that they came out weaker than the strong guys they were in love with.

Remmo had been hell-bent on proving that things would work out the opposite way for us since then.

And honestly, I was slightly obsessed with the fact that he didn't just want me to *be with him*. He wanted me to be *powerful,* and *capable*.

"Alright. No staring at my ass," I warned him.

He flashed me a vicious grin. "Good luck enforcing that one."

I rolled my eyes at him, but couldn't fight my own grin.

After a quick push of power, the glowing fish-things were forming a line, leading us out.

Remmo followed closely behind me as we swam through cave after cave, weaving our way back out of the sacred place.

When we emerged, the sun was shining overhead. I shielded my eyes, groaning at how bright it was after so much time in the dim cave.

Remmo chuckled. "There's a fish just under your foot."

I jerked my feet up with a shriek, and earned a booming laugh for it.

"Damn you," I grumbled at him, peering down into the water.

He was right though; there were not-fish everywhere. They were actually called novocannes, but he found the word "fish" to be kind of hilarious, so he'd taken to calling them that, even though they were clearly not fish.

"Come on, Iloli." He hooked his fingers in the waistband of my skirt and towed me toward dry land.

"The dirt is going to feel weird after so much time on the stone," I remarked, letting him lift me out of the pond.

I could've done it myself, but there was something really damn appealing about letting him take care of me that way.

"The trees, too," he agreed, setting me on my feet. I didn't bother adjusting my skirt; that bitch was always riding up my ass. It would get some serious modifications when we were back at the Stronghold. "Ready?"

"So ready," I drawled.

His lips quirked upward.

I set my hands on his shoulders when he started to turn away, and he halted.

"Thank you," I said.

His eyes met mine.

"Seriously, Remmo. Thank you. These have been the best weeks of my life, and I say that with zero sarcasm for once."

His lips curved upward further. "They've been the best weeks of mine, as well." His hands lifted to cup my face. "You are brilliant, and funny, and beautiful in every way there is. Thank you for letting me come with you."

I rolled my eyes, though I was biting my lip to fight the grin pulling at my lips. "Now you're just being cheesy."

He chuckled. "Sometimes the truth is cheesy."

And then he pulled me into a hug.

My arms wrapped around his back, and I squeezed him fiercely.

Everything was going to change when we made it back to the Stronghold. I think we both knew that, as much as we didn't want to admit it. I would be back with my friends, and Teris would be there. And...

I had no idea what was going to happen, honestly.

"What are we going to do when we get back?" I whispered to him.

"I'm going to kick Teris's ass when he attacks me," Remmo said calmly. "And then, we'll figure it out."

My whole body clenched.

Shit, I hated that idea.

"I won't let him attack you," I said.

"You won't have a choice. I kissed the female he was mated to, so there will be a fight."

"No, Remmo. I—"

He squeezed me tightly, cutting me off. "I knew the consequences when I kissed you, Iloli. Let me face them." His lips brushed the top of my hair, and then my forehead too. "Are you ready to get moving?"

"No." I let out a puff of air. "I'm going to think of a way around another damn fight."

"Think while we move," he said, giving me a quick, soft smile before he shifted forms.

Though I wanted to curse him out and stay right where I was until I had the answer I wanted, I shifted too, and off we went.

As THE DAY PASSED, my mood darkened.

Because I'd come to a realization I hated—and developed a plan that made me want to barf.

Teris would beat Remmo in a fight if it came to that. And the sabertooth bastard was vicious. He'd kill my basilisk if he got the chance.

The only way to avoid that would be to reestablish my bond with Teris.

That thought made me nauseous. Really, really nauseous.

But I couldn't watch Remmo die.

The only alternative I came up with would be to mate with Remmo. If our lives were connected, Teris wouldn't dare hurt my mate.

But Remmo and I...

We were just friends.

I wasn't in love with him, because I refused to let myself feel that. Or anything near that. The only people I'd ever loved had hurt me in every damn way there was, so...

No, love wasn't an option.

Mating wasn't, either.

Even if I had wanted to mate with Remmo, I couldn't do that without knowing the gossip about him. He hadn't told me anything more about his past than I had mine—so we knew some things about each other, but not a ton.

As far as I knew, he was just one of the many cold unseelies trying to learn to control themselves perfectly up until a few months earlier.

But what if there was more to him? What if he'd dated one of the other girls or something, and hadn't told me?

My paranoia had me making up stories by the assload, so yeah.

Mating was a no-go.

Which meant I was going to have to kiss Teris.

Seven

"What are you thinking about?" Remmo asked me, as we ate a dinner of the shelled fruits called fromil and some strange vegetables that almost reminded me of longer, skinnier, blue carrots. According to Remmo, they were called covais.

I rarely ate silently, but I hadn't talked much since I decided that I was going to have to reform my bond with Teris.

"Nothing," I lied.

As much as I didn't want to, I knew I was going to have to distance myself from Remmo. The basilisk wasn't going to accept my decision to kiss Teris without a fight. We hadn't talked about that, but I just *knew*.

"Iloli," he warned.

He rarely called me Sunny. I kind of loved that. No one had ever called me Sunny before I came to Vevol, anyway. Ana was the one who'd made up the damn nickname, and honestly, I was kind of excited for the day that I finally told someone my real name. Hopefully, the nickname would die a fast, bloody death.

"I don't know. I guess now that we're headed back, I just..." I hesitated, mostly for dramatic effect. "I'm thinking about Teris."

It wasn't a lie.

Not completely.

I *was* thinking about Teris.

Just not in the way I had implied.

Remmo's jaw clenched.

Damn, I loved how much he hated my ex-relationship with the sabertooth. He was getting more and more possessive, and even if it was probably cruel of me, I was absolutely obsessed with that.

"Thinking what?" He gritted the words out.

"I don't know." I shrugged. "Just thinking."

His eyes burned into me, but he said nothing else.

So *I* said nothing else.

And we went to sleep with a tension between us that I hated—but one that I was going to have to embrace if I wanted the basilisk to live.

We could still be friends, after all. Even if I was temporarily mated to Teris. It would take him time to forgive me, but Remmo *would* forgive me.

THE NEXT DAY, as we traveled, the tension only grew. And that night, neither of us spoke.

It was horrible.

Tears stung my eyes as I stared down at the world beneath me, my long body wrapped around a thick tree branch.

I hated the distance between us.

In the past few weeks, Remmo had started to mean a hell of a lot to me.

And I didn't want that to change.

I heard the leaves above me rustle just slightly, and then the man's low voice met my ears. "Can I hold you, Iloli?"

My throat was swollen, but I bobbed my scaly head.

A moment later, a thick, scaly body was wrapping around mine, holding me to the branch completely. He was so damn warm.

My eyes closed as his head rested on the top of mine. The weight of it was comforting, rather than painful.

And just as I fell asleep, I could've sworn I heard a low, silky voice whisper into my mind,

"You are mine, Iloli."

It was probably just a dream, though.

WHEN I WOKE UP, I realized that our bodies had wrapped around each other, getting all tangled.

Though I wanted to stay like that forever, I had started recognizing a few of the scents in the forest, and knew we were getting close to the Stronghold.

So I slid away from Remmo, mentally preparing myself for the hell that was coming my way.

I had to kiss a man who wasn't attracted to me.

I was going to hurt the fae I had started to consider my best friend.

There was no point in putting it off any longer, so I slipped away from Remmo, knowing he would have no problem catching me.

Sure enough, he was at my side less than a minute later.

We travelled in silence, the only sounds resulting from me brushing against leaves and other things. Remmo was as quiet as always, never making a noise unless he decided to.

WE REACHED the Stronghold around lunch time.

When I smelled something delicious cooking, I assumed that the massive, new-ish kitchen at the center of the land the male fae had claimed was the source.

I headed that way, figuring that if we were going to have a confrontation, we may as well do it where there was food so we could eat afterward.

As much as I enjoyed fruit and veggies, it would be nice to have something else.

I hadn't reached the kitchen—or started descending the branches—when I glanced over and realized that Remmo was gone.

Panic flared in my stomach, and I halted.

My tongue flicked out as I tasted the air, looking for my friend. His heavy, yummy scent was easy to follow, so I turned around quickly, rushing in the direction he'd gone.

A ferocious snarl met my ears before I reached the end of the scent trail, and my panic grew fiercely.

Teris.

That sound had been Teris.

I threw myself out of the trees, tapping into Vevol's magic to soften the landing the way Remmo had taught me, and landed lightly on my feet.

Male fae were all around me, building something. I didn't even stop to look what it was as I sprinted in the direction of Teris's snarl.

When I found him and Remmo, the men were circling each other, both in their beast forms.

A thick arm blocked my path as I tried to throw myself between them, and I opened my mouth to yell at the person before I realized it was Ervo.

Mare was tucked against his side, her expression worried.

"You're okay?" she whispered to me.

"I'm fine." I tried to shove past Ervo, but his arm wouldn't budge. "Move," I hissed, eyes glued to the men.

They were moving slowly, both of them shifting back to their man forms, and both wearing furious expressions. I barely recognized Remmo's cold anger, after so much time with his peaceful grins.

"They can't fight," I whispered desperately to Ervo. "Teris will kill him."

The expression Ervo shot me was almost... curious. And definitely not as panicked as it should've been. "Who do you think that male is?"

"Remmo."

His expression grew thoughtful, but he said nothing.

Mare was saying something, but I didn't hear her—I was too focused on my plan to prevent the fight.

If I could get to Teris, it would work.

It would have to work.

...unless Remmo challenged the sabertooth for the right to bond with me or something, afterward.

I wasn't going to consider that outcome though, because I couldn't think of any other way to stop the fight.

And the men were still circling, so I had time.

I lunged away from Ervo, shoving through the group of fae men that surrounded Teris and Remmo.

Remmo's sharp voice cut through the ring at the same time I finally reached the front. "Don't let my female get any closer."

A pair of beefy arms grabbed me by the biceps, hauling me off the ground and holding me between two gigantic men.

A glance upward proved that I didn't recognize either of them.

And since they had listened to Remmo, they were probably unseelie.

But why had they listened to Remmo?

Wasn't he just one of the many unseelies?

"Sunny is not yours, Vuvim," Teris growled, as he and Remmo continued circling.

Vuvim? Was that Remmo's nickname or something?

Wasn't *Remmo* his nickname?

"She belongs with the wild fae. With the females she has chosen as sisters. With *me*." Teris's words were low and angry, and where his fingernails were, claws had cut through.

"If that were true, it would be your scent on her skin. Beneath her clothing. In her hair." Remmo's voice was silky and dangerous without being rough or snarly.

And yet he spoke the exact words that would ignite every ounce of possessiveness the sabertooth had ever felt for me.

Teris roared.

"Stop!" I yelled the word, and everyone's attention swung to me.

I was still dangling off the ground, held up by two damn giants.

"Stop. No one needs to fight. I'll do whatever I have to, to prevent the fight, okay? I don't want anyone bleeding."

Remmo's gaze slid over me.

And while he was looking at me, Teris lunged.

I screamed as his claws tore through the space Remmo was—or the space Remmo had been, a second earlier.

In that breath, the basilisk had vanished.

My panicked gaze scanned the trees, looking for him. For his scales.

Remmo wouldn't have run from the fight, would he? That didn't seem like—

Teris rolled out of the way just in time to avoid a slash of Remmo's fangs where his neck had been a heartbeat earlier.

"Fight without your venom, or don't fight at all, Vuvim," Teris snarled at Remmo.

My head spun.

On Earth, when things got violent, I would shut down. My breathing would slow, and I'd disappear into myself. My emotions would cease to exist, and I would feel nothing until it was over.

It was an automatic response I had no control over, and as the fight continued, that's exactly what happened.

My breathing slowed.

My thoughts went silent.

And everything that happened in front of me meant less, and less, and less, until I was numb.

Numb to the swinging fists.

Numb to the blood.

Numb to the shifting back and forth.

Numb to the close calls, to Teris's snarls, to Remmo's cold, controlled fury.

Numb to the sight of the sabertooth sinking to his knees with Remmo's arm around his throat, and the sabertooth losing consciousness.

Numb as I was lowered back to my feet, and the men on both sides of me stepped back.

Numb, until a pair of warm, familiar hands landed gently on my face. There was blood on them, but I don't think the basilisk even realized.

"We have much to discuss, Iloli," he murmured to me.

"No," I whispered.

Remmo blinked.

"No." My voice rang in my ears.

My heart pounded hollowly in my chest as I pushed his hands off my face and stepped back.

When he came closer, to cover the space I'd put between us, I took another step.

And another.

And another.

"He called you Vuvim," I said.

"Many do. In your language, it translates to something along the lines of *ghost*. It's different enough that the translation magic doesn't work on it."

"Who *are* you?" My voice shook.

"You know the answer to that, Sunny." His eyes were gentle, but I was still walking away from him—and he was still walking toward me.

"To the unseelies, who are you? You said you were seelie."

"Before our faction began to break, we were organized in many ways. The council headed the government. The generals were over fighting. I was the basilisk general."

My lips opened, and then closed.

I stopped walking.

He stopped too, leaving just a breath between us.

"You called me your female," I said.

His head dipped. "The mate bond connects us."

"You made them *hold me back*."

"We've spent weeks together, Iloli. I know when you're scheming. You didn't think I could beat Teris—you were going to bond yourself to him again. I couldn't allow that."

"*Allow* it?" My voice raised. "That wasn't your decision to make."

"It was my life you were trying to protect, so yes, it *was*." His voice went lower with every damn word.

"I don't even know you," I said, eyes stinging and head shaking.

"Sunny!" Dots called out. My head jerked in her direction as she jumped out of a tree and then landed lightly on her feet. Her long, straight golden hair was already being tugged in the breeze as she threw her arms around me. "What happened? I heard fighting. Why were you gone so long? So much has changed. Your note said something about—" She cut herself off when she noticed Remmo. "Oh, damn."

"Dots, meet *Vuvim*." My voice was cutting. "Can I get a ride out of here?"

"Sure." She eyed me, then looked at Remmo. "Nice to meet you, I guess."

He didn't even bat an eyelash at her, saying in a low voice to me, "We are *not* done here."

"Maybe you aren't, but I am." I grabbed Dots' shoulder, and she caught the drift, shifting rapidly and hauling ass off the ground.

Remmo remained where I'd left him, his gaze tracking me and my friend as she glided through the trees.

MY EYES SHUT, and I tried not to let them water as she soared through the forest. After a while, she landed on a large wooden platform that nearly blended into the trees it was nestled between. I recognized the spot she'd chosen for her house, but the platform looked almost exactly the same as it had the last time I was there. I'd expected her to make more progress on it than she had.

"What happened when you left? I am so confused." She plopped down on her ass on the platform, but I didn't sit.

I started pacing, grabbing at the wild puffs of hair on top of my head that I really desperately needed to shampoo and condition. Being in and out of the water so much had *not* made my hair feel great.

"The plan went perfectly, but when I got out of the river, Remmo came out of the trees. He was gorgeous, and he told me that my plan was a good one, but that I still smelled like Teris and he would be able to track me. He offered to show me how to hide my scent, and the moment was all steamy, and I just... I asked him if I could kiss him."

I went on, my voice raising and my words coming out faster as I continued. "And I thought he was rejecting me, but then he kissed me, and it was so damn good. And he smelled incredible, and there was electricity... and then Teris showed up, and Remmo knocked him out. And when he offered to take me to the healing lake, I said yes."

I was rambling—and pacing—and gesturing wildly, like a crazy person.

Dots just blinked at me.

"And the water was so cold, and he warmed me up, and I wasn't ready to go back to Teris, and he offered to show me a cave in his land. I agreed, because I was stupid, and happy, and he was my friend. And the cave was incredible, and things got steamy, but not too steamy, and—"

"Breathe, Sunny." Dots lifted her hands. "Just breathe for a minute, okay? In, and out."

I tried to take slow, deep breaths, but mostly failed.

It did help me calm down a little, though. Not enough to make my heart stop racing, but a little.

"So he followed you away from the party, and then you kissed him?" she checked.

I nodded, though it hadn't really occurred to me that he had *followed me*.

"And then you went to the lake. It didn't heal you, so you weren't ready to come back, and he took you to a cave?"

"Yeah. A hidden cave system." I let out a slow breath of air, really trying to calm myself down. "We stayed for a few weeks, and he taught me how to use my magic. And then we came back."

"So you're okay?"

I nodded. "I'm okay."

"And he didn't do anything shady?"

"No. He was a perfect gentleman."

"Good. So, why are we freaking out about this?" She gestured between us and the place we had been with Remmo. "You *want* to fall in love."

"Because I thought he was just one of the random unseelie, and that I was going to have to kiss Teris so Remmo wouldn't get murdered. And I don't even know if I *can* fall in love. But apparently he lied—or I just didn't ask enough questions? He's not random at all. He's one of the unseelie generals, so... like one of their best fighters?" I squeezed my eyes shut. "What the hell do I even do here?"

"You don't have to decide anything right now." She lifted a shoulder. "I think you have a right to take time to figure out what you want.

"No, you don't get it. He can blend into trees and shit. He taught me how to do it too, but I can only do it for a few minutes. Most basilisks can only do it for a few minutes, but he can do it for as long as he wants. Apparently he's called Vuvim because it means ghost—and with his scales, and how quiet he is, he practically is one. He could be listening right now and I wouldn't even know."

Dots's eyebrows shot upward, and her gaze scanned the trees. "Seriously?"

I nodded jerkily.

She stood up. "Well, let's go to the Stronghold for a few hours."

My eyes nearly bulged from my head. "With the crazy-ass fae chicks? Are you insane?"

"Things have changed a lot since you left. Me and the other seelie ladies went with Priel to open the portal to Earth on winter solstice, and crazy things happened. North's brands lit up like lightbulbs, and portals erupted all along the beach. Human women fell through all of them—so we have seventy-one new human ladies."

She continued, "North is down to just one brand, so now she can only see the future. She and Priel went back to his place immediately afterward, so she could rest, and haven't come back. The female fae stepped up and are taking care of the new humans, teaching them all kinds of things about Vevol. Mare is in charge of making sure they don't brainwash the new women against the men. And the fae expanded the Stronghold again, for the new ladies."

My eyes nearly burst from my head. "Are you kidding me?"

"Nope." She popped her lips on the 'p'. "Aev, the Tame King, is kind of losing his mind, since Naomi left him a while ago. Things are tense with the unseelies because of that. Nev and Fovea are going at it like bunnies, and the fae ladies are all sniffing around the guys. I don't even think we're considered attractive at this point, with all of them around. It's actually pretty perfect."

I grimaced. "Holy shit."

A minute passed as I tried to absorb everything. It hadn't occurred to me that I would be gone during the winter solstice, but the timing did line up. And since North had so many brands, with just the one extra ability, that did make sense too...

Shit, though.

Maybe I shouldn't have spent so much time in that cave.

Then again, I was much stronger and more capable now than I had been when I first left with Remmo.

Finally, I asked, "You seriously think it's a good idea?"

"I think there are no men allowed in the Stronghold, Nev included, and we're life-bringers. If we ask the female fae for a few hours of protection, we'll make their day."

She brushed dirt off her ass.

I heard rustling in the trees, and caught a familiar smell.

My eyes widened as Remmo slid out, shifting forms and remaining in the tree without taking a step onto Dots's house-platform. He would consider it her territory, and therefore, off limits.

Unless he thought I was in danger, at least.

"What do you want?" I demanded.

"You need to stay where I can see you. Away from the female fae," he said in a low voice. "I don't trust them."

"Well, I don't trust *you*." I glanced at Dots, and she dipped her head just the tiniest bit.

Remmo noticed the movement, and lunged.

Dots was too fast—she grabbed me and took to the sky.

And the one thing Remmo couldn't do, was fly.

DOTS MUST'VE BEEN PRACTICING with her wings, because she was a hell of a lot faster than I remembered. And with our tiny head-start, we reached the Stronghold just in time for me to yell to the female fae mingling outside that we needed protection—

And just in time for them to form a female wall, dividing us from the man calling my name from the trees.

EIGHT

DOTS WAS right about things having settled down—and about the influx of women.

The female fae and new humans down in the living area were downright friendly. Some of them even smiled. It was bizarre, but in a pleasant way.

When we asked if they had clean clothes and an empty room we could borrow for a bit, they were more than happy to lead us up the stairs and get us settled in the exact same room we had once shared with Mare. The crack in the wall had been repaired, which made us both grin.

One of the mattresses had also been removed, so now there were just two beds, both of them on frames. They had colorful blankets and comfortable-looking pillows on them.

Someone brought us a few pairs of the female-fae-style clothing, and we both held them up to ourselves, checking each other out with grins.

Their clothes were much fancier—and prettier—than the ones the seelie had given us.

Honestly, I was excited to try them on.

But first, shampoo and conditioner.

"Tell me everything while you shower," Dots ordered.

I agreed, and we stepped into the bathroom. She sat on the counter while I scrubbed myself down in the shower, letting the conditioner sit in my hair while I talked, and talked, and talked. Dots asked questions, and I answered all of them.

Even the ones I didn't want to answer.

By the time I finished talking, she was being way too quiet.

"What are you thinking?" I asked her, shutting off the water and reaching for the robe I'd noticed hanging nearby before I got in.

She hesitated.

"Girl, I am so done doing yoga with you if you don't tell me right now," I grumbled.

She sighed. "Have you asked him if he's your mate?"

I blinked. "What?"

"It's just that the electricity was the first thing January noticed between her and Lian. She was talking to the new human ladies a few days ago, and she said there was electricity when they touched. And when he introduced himself to her, he gave her his whole name. That sounds kind of like what happened with you and Remmo."

I blinked at her again.

And again.

And finally said, "We had already bonded ourselves to each other, though. We never touched before that. And Mare loved the way Ervo smelled, too, and they weren't fated. I didn't directly ask Remmo if he thought we were fated mates, but he didn't act like we were fated. And he had plenty of opportunities to tell me, if he thought we were."

"Well then why was he following you in the first place?"

I blinked again. "Stop giving me hard questions, Dots."

Why *had* he followed me?

I didn't think I'd asked him that.

She flashed me an apologetic grin. "I'm sorry, but you asked me what I think. I think it sounds like you're probably fated mates."

I sank to the toilet, my robe remaining tucked closely around me as I used the damn toilet seat like it was a chair. "There's no way. You saw how the other guys were—they wouldn't take no for an answer. And they were all, 'me Tarzan, you Jane'. And—"

"And every man is different," she pointed out. "Remmo is unseelie. He'll respond differently to everything for that reason. Plus, you weren't around any other interested guys, so there was no need for possessive Tarzan stuff."

"Yeah, but he didn't lose his shit when I mentioned Teris. He asked me about him, sometimes. He'd get pissy if I mentioned missing Teris or anything, but not if I just talked to him. And—"

"We went all out for that party, Sunny. Every one of us was there, and no one saw you slip out. I was watching. The only possible way he could've followed you is if he literally stayed right next to you the entire time. Why would he do that, when you were in love with Teris and there was a whole building full of single fae and human women who might actually want him? If he wasn't your mate, why would he bother?"

"I don't know." I brushed a hand over my face, wiping away a bunch of stray water that hadn't yet dried completely. "And it's Summer. My real name—it's Summer. I'm tired of being called Sunny."

She smiled. "I'm Dakota."

I held out a hand, and she shook it, pretending to be dainty. "Nice to meet you," I drawled.

She put on a thick, fake fae accent. "The pleasure is mine."

I snorted, and she laughed.

We both grew quiet, then. "What am I supposed to do, Dots? Dakota?"

"You don't have to decide right now," she reminded me. "But ultimately, I think you need to have an honest conversation with him."

"But what if you're wrong? What if we're not mates, and I just screw everything up even more by asking him?"

She frowned. "We could go talk to January to get more details if you want. Or one of the other girls. Naomi is living here right now, so it wouldn't be hard to ask her."

I nodded.

Good; this was a good plan.

"First, we should sleep," I told her.

She flashed me a grin. “Trying to avoid it, huh?”

“Yup.” I finally got off the toilet. “Remmo followed me here, so I know he’s probably waiting outside. And I might as well make him sweat a little while I hide out in here, after the lies he pulled. He sure as hell didn’t tell me that he was an unseelie general.”

“We should ask around about the Vuvim thing,” she agreed. “Maybe we *should* go find January and Lian.”

“I can’t leave, or the bastard will probably follow us there,” I reminded her.

“Depends how dedicated he is.” She lifted a shoulder.

I thought back to the cave.

To the way he’d looked at me.

To the way he’d taught me how to access my magic.

To the way he’d wrapped himself around me in the tree on the way back, when he either heard or smelled my tears.

“He’s dedicated,” I finally said.

Her lips curved upward. “Good.” She grabbed the female fae tops off the counter, and held them both up. “Which one of these suckers can handle those melons you call tits?”

I snorted a laugh. “They’re stretchy. I’m sure they’ll survive. Do you want pink, or green?” One of the tops was a soft rose color, and the other one was a deep, emerald green. The color reminded me of Remmo’s eyes, so I was hoping she picked it to save me from feeling like I was dressing for him.

“Pink.” She handed me the green, then dangled the tiny pair of panties that came with it off her fingertip. “You going to try these little things?”

I grinned and snagged the green ones from her hand. “I bet they don’t ride up like my shorts or skirt, so you can be damn sure I am.”

“If Remmo’s as possessive as the other fae guys, he’s going to lose his shit when he sees you out in public in them,” she said with a laugh.

“I don’t know, I was wearing that skirt for ages, and you could see all the goods most of that time,” I said, gesturing to my lady bits.

Dots—Dakota—laughed harder. “You guys were alone. He was probably just enjoying the show.”

I cracked a grin. "Damn straight."

She wiped at her eyes, since they were watering a little. She almost always got teary when she laughed a lot.

I tugged the panties on—yeah, they were basically a stretchy thong—and then wormed my way into the dress-like top that all the fae women wore. The fabric was light and comfortable, and I liked the way it flowed.

"Are you going to wear the female fae clothes?" I checked.

She ran her fingers over the fabric. "Part of me is nervous about looking pretty," she admitted. "I know we're kind of sexy in the tanks and shorts, but it's not the same."

My humor faded.

The darkness that we'd both experienced settled over both of us. "I know." My hands smoothed over the dress. "We need to find you a new fake mate. You felt better when Nev was protecting you, right?"

"I did," she admitted. "But I want to protect myself, to learn how to fight. And I don't want to lead anyone on. But when the violence starts..."

"You can't," I finished for her.

"I can't," she agreed glumly.

"Don't give up. You'll get there."

"I hope so," she murmured.

"And hey, if you don't, I'm positive that we can find you a fake mate."

She made a face. "I'm tired of faking things. I just want to live."

"Then put the damn dress on and we'll talk someone into kicking ass for us if we have to."

Dots—Dakota—swapped her tank top for the dress, leaving her black shorts on under it instead of going with the tiny underwear.

I grabbed a comb out of the bathroom and started gently working it through my curls. They were actually a lot less tangled than I anticipated, and I yawned widely. "Do you think the fae chicks or the new humans will judge me if I take a nap?"

Dakota shrugged. "So what if they do?"

I flashed her a grin. "That's the spirit."

She rolled her eyes, but couldn't hide her smile. "I've got to head out. I was put on spy duty by the Wild Hunt guys. It's not super serious, but I'm keeping an eye on Aev, making sure he doesn't do anything stupid. They don't think he'll expect it from a woman. I rotate with one of the other unseelie ladies, but she only takes over for a few hours a day so I can sleep."

"Damn, girl. Look at you." I whistled, and she grinned.

"It's nice to be useful."

I shooed her toward the door. "Alright, working woman. Get out of here."

She laughed. "Remmo's not going to come for me or anything, is he? How mad is he going to be?"

"Not mad. At least, not at you. Remmo doesn't do the rage thing that some of the fae dudes do. His is a calm, calculated anger. I guess I understand why some of the girls prefer unseelie now."

She nodded. "I definitely get it too. Aev is kind of a wild card, but I feel safe enough around him because I've never seen him rage or fight. Even while he's losing his mind, he's just... quiet."

I lifted an eyebrow. "You talk to him?"

Her face reddened. "Only a little. We've sort of been becoming friends. I'm pretty sure he knows I'm spying on him, but doesn't care. He's mated, so it's not like anything can happen between us." She brushed her hair over her shoulder. "I'll see you in a few hours, Summer."

I grinned at her use of my real name. "Same, Dakota."

Her lips curved upward. "You should spread the news about my name, by the way. I'm tired of being Dots."

"I'll get right on it."

"Me too." She winked at me before she slipped out, shutting the door behind her.

I felt eyes on me, and my gaze lifted to the window, whose view I was standing directly in. All I saw out there was trees, but I scanned them closely, looking for a sign of scales.

A pair of green eyes appeared in the middle of an otherwise-normal branch, and I breathed in sharply.

Remmo was there.

Of course he was there.

I might have walked away from him—or flown away—but he had made it clear that as far as he was concerned, nothing between us was finished.

There was no curtain to drop over the window, so I simply plopped down on the furthest bed from it and dragged the blankets over my head.

As hard as I tried to sleep, I just couldn't.

After half an hour of tossing and turning, while Dots's—dammit, Dakota's—words ran through my mind, I finally dragged my ass out of bed.

I didn't let myself look over my shoulder to see if Remmo was still outside as I left the room.

After a stop downstairs to inquire about Naomi's location, I was back up the stairs and knocking on the door across from the one that was temporarily mine.

The damn windows all over the place ensured that if he tried, Remmo would be able to see exactly what I was doing, which messed with my mind.

Naomi opened it just a tiny bit, peeking out at me and looking around the hallway before she opened the door and gestured for me to hurry inside.

Like always, she looked perfectly put together. She was wearing the same thing Dots—Dakota—had put on; the female fae dress-shirt, with the seelie shorts. Unlike my green one and Dakota's pink, her dress was a deep, shimmering golden color that made her look like the queen everyone declared she was. It made her tan skin and blue eyes look even more striking. And the script-looking magical tattoo sleeve climbing one of her arms looked more elegant next to the pretty dress.

Her room was almost identical to mine, but unlike it, hers had a curtain over the window and only one bed in a corner of the space.

"How did you talk someone into giving you a curtain?" I asked.

Her lips quirked upward. "The unseelie kept stationing people to watch me outside. I started changing my clothes right in front of the window, and the next day, a curtain was delivered. I'm sure it was probably from one of the guards; one of them is really protective of me, in a way Aev has never been."

I laughed. "Damn, you're an evil genius."

"Nah, just used to dealing with the fae. Especially my guards." Her small smile faded a bit. "What's up? Are you okay? We've never really talked before."

That's how it was with a lot of the ex-human women. We all knew of each other, but hadn't really gotten to know anyone unless we'd been in the Stronghold together. Or in the seelie's version of it, I guess.

And now that there were so many more of us, I was sure it would only get worse.

"Yeah, I'm fine. I just had a few questions about fated mates that I hoped you could answer."

She nodded, crossing the room and taking a seat on the edge of her bed. "Sure."

I wrapped my arms around my abdomen. "Okay, so, you probably heard how I ran away from Teris?"

"Yes."

"I went through the river, so he wouldn't be able to track my scent. When I got out of the river, one of the fae came out of the trees. Remmo."

"Is he seelie?"

I shook my head. "The unseelie call him Vuvim. I didn't know that though—he introduced himself as Remmo."

Her eyes went wide. "The basilisk general? He thinks you're his mate?"

"I don't know. He had followed me, but I didn't ask him why. In the moment, it didn't occur to me. He said he used to be unseelie but had recently defected. I thought he was just one of the masses, you know? I didn't even know the unseelie had generals, and he definitely didn't start by telling me people called him *the ghost*."

Naomi grimaced. "The only reason a fae male would introduce himself to a female with his entire name is if he's already decided he belongs to her. Have you tried to use it? To see if it's really his name?"

"No."

"Well, don't do it in here or the female fae will kill him," she warned. "And if you're really fated mates, your lives might already be connected."

My throat swelled with panic. "So what do I do?"

Naomi lifted a shoulder. "You can accept him, like January, North, and Mare did. Or you can turn him down and try to fight fate. But ultimately, none of the men with fated mates have ever walked away. All of us who've been claimed or started bonds with someone that seems chosen by fate have those men permanently tailing us. Even if we fight it, or the men fight it, there's no way out." She hesitated. "Well, no *easy* way out."

Shit.

"Then why are you in here?" I gestured to the room.

She grimaced. "Because Aev and I don't like each other, and the unseelie are falling apart."

My eyebrows shot upward, and I waited for more of an explanation.

Naomi admitted, "We've never gotten along. He's cold and unfeeling. I'm not big on sharing my emotions, either. The sex was terrible. He doesn't listen to me unless there's literally no other option. I could go on... but it's unnecessary. When I walked away, he didn't use my name to get me back. I think he hates me as much as I hate him."

"Damn. Well, you just might be my hero for leaving him, then."

Her lips curved upward slightly. "Thanks, I guess." She leaned back on the bed, planting her palms on the mattress. "So, you and Vuvim. Is he kind?"

The fact that she picked that question first, when she could've started with any others, didn't pass my notice.

And dammit, my throat swelled. "He is."

"Good." The word was simple, but powerful. "What are your questions?"

"I just want to be sure that there's a real possibility that we're fated before I ask him," I admitted. "I don't want to offend him. We were out in the wild together for weeks, and it was the best few weeks of my life. I like him—a lot. And I'm pissed that he lied to me, but I'm going to forgive him for it. Not yet, but it's pretty damn inevitable."

"Does his scent call to you?" she asked. "Does it stand out enough to you that you could follow it even if he wasn't next to you?"

"Yes." I bit my lip.

"When you met him, did you immediately feel like you could trust him?"

"Yes."

"When he touched you, were there sparks from the very beginning?"

"I'm not positive. There were sparks as soon as we'd kissed for the first time, though."

She nodded. "It takes longer for the sparks to develop between chosen mates. I'd say you can be ninety-nine percent sure that you're fated."

My world nearly spun. "Really?"

"Yes. Lily and Jenna, two of the girls who've been here the longest, have been pretty sure that they're fated for almost fifteen years. They couldn't do anything about it or find out for sure until we got out of the unseelie land, but now that we're free, they've sealed their bond."

I raised my eyebrows. "Damn."

Naomi continued, "They have the same mental connection that the other mated couples have, now. And they've started questioning everyone over the last few weeks, so they can put together a list of the identifiers for everyone else. All this to say, we've been talking about it. It seems like when all of those factors align, a couple is fated."

"Shit. Are there any fated male couples? I've never heard the guys talk about that."

"There are. They've only just started admitting it to themselves and everyone else." She gave me a quick smile. "It's sweet to see everyone working things out. Everyone except me and Aeven, at least."

I grimaced for her. "I'm sorry."

"It's not your fault. And I've been talking to Fovea—she thinks she knows a way to separate me from him. She did it for one of her life-bringers once. Before the war and everything, after the guy she was paired with went insane. I can't talk about details, but... there's hope." Her cheeks were pink, and her eyes were bright.

"Fovea does seem like the type who would know that shit."

Naomi laughed. "Yeah. You should see her, now that she's with Nev. She suddenly understands the benefit of having a mate, and is furious on my behalf that Aev and I didn't work out."

I snorted. "Thank Vevol for the female fae, I guess."

"I guess so."

The subject changed, and we chatted for a bit longer before I headed back to my room.

Knowing that Remmo and I were probably, in fact, fated...

Well, it screwed with my mind, that was for sure.

But it did make me feel better about ditching him outside.

Because one thing was certain:

If we were mates, he had known about it from the moment he slid out of the trees. And maybe even before then.

Nine
Remmo

I remained in the forest, just outside the Stronghold, while my female proceeded to pretend I didn't exist.

One day passed, and then another, and another.

But I was a patient hunter.

I would wait an eternity for her if I needed to.

Eventually, she would emerge from the Stronghold.

And then, she would be mine in every way there was.

My brothers came to me with requests for help with their problems, but I sent them all on their way.

Because I was no longer Vuvim; not now that I had a female to protect, and teach, and love.

Now, I was her mate. And she was the most important thing in my world.

TEN

SUNNY

I SURVIVED a week with the female fae before I couldn't take the avoidance anymore. Dots—dammit, Dakota—only came by to sleep in our temporary room at the Stronghold for a few hours each day. So, I distracted myself from the green-eyed basilisk in the trees outside by playing cards.

Though I was absolute shit at every fae game and most of the human ones I learned, I spectacularly defeated both fae and ex-human women at every damn game of poker we played.

But by the time that week ended, I finally couldn't ignore the truth anymore.

I missed Remmo.

...I missed him a *lot.*

So, on the morning of day eight, I thanked the female fae for their hospitality —got invited to a round of a fae dice game that I would most certainly lose if I took them up on it—and walked out of the Stronghold.

My eyes scanned the trees when Remmo didn't emerge immediately and scoop me into his arms or something. Not gonna lie, my heart fell a little bit.

But I could smell his scent all over the forest around the Stronghold, so I knew he was there.

And I was going to find him.

I wandered around a few minutes, inhaling his yummy smell, until I heard his voice.

Not gonna lie, it nearly stopped my damn heart.

Maybe I missed him even more than I'd realized.

"As I have told you, I have no interest in leading any number of unseelie," Remmo said harshly. "How many times do I need to repeat this?"

Another man responded, "Your female has yet to even acknowledge that she's yours, Vuvim. What do you think you'll accomplish, waiting out here in the —" he cut himself off abruptly, and then muttered, "What the hell?"

I thought I saw movement in the trees above me, but before I could call out to Remmo, a massive basilisk had me wrapped up tightly, trapped completely in his warm scales.

His smell was intoxicating.

I didn't let him know that, though, as he squeezed me.

"Can't breathe," I hissed.

He hissed back, and wrapped tighter.

Something told me this was payback for putting stone walls between us for a week, and I didn't hate it.

Not at all.

After a few minutes, his grip finally loosened, and then he was both unwinding and shifting forms. My face met a warm, hard chest a moment later, and a set of gigantic arms held me fiercely.

I went up on my tiptoes so I could bury my face against him, and he lifted me up off the ground to make it easier for me.

My eyes stung as I nuzzled up against his neck.

I'd been trying not to miss him—and failing miserably.

"Why do I smell your tears?" He practically growled the words at me. "Are you hurt?"

"No." I batted my eyes, trying to get rid of the damn evidence.

"Iloli." His chest rumbled unhappily.

"I just missed you," I said with a sigh. "I tried not to."

I could practically feel the anger leave him as his tense body relaxed.

"As you should've," he grumbled. "Never do that again."

My lips curved upward slightly. "No promises."

"I'll tie you up in my den if you so much as consider it."

"Sounds kinda kinky," I whispered.

He chuckled. His hand smoothed over my back, slowly and steadily, as he murmured, "We need to talk."

Dammit.

This was the conversation I'd been hiding from for an entire *week*.

Time to face the music, I guess.

"I know."

"Are you going to introduce me to the female you're mooning after?" The second male voice grumbled. I peeked over Remmo's shoulder, but didn't see anyone.

"My *mate*, you mean? No." Remmo drawled.

I pulled my face away from his neck, though. He kept my chest pinned to his with his grip on my back, but didn't try to stop me from leaning away and looking at the other man.

He was gigantic, as expected, and his expression was as grumpy as his voice. His features were harsh, his skin black and his hair a mass of loose curls on top of his head.

"I'm Sunny," I told him.

"*Summer*, according to Dakota." Remmo corrected me with another growl. "I should've been the first to know that."

I shot him a threatening look. "She's basically my sister, so she deserved to have it first."

I looked back at the other guy and flashed him a smile. "And you are?"

"Korrik." He grunted the word, which I assumed was his name.

Remmo's fingers dug into my back. "Do not smile at my brothers when I'm angry with you, Iloli."

I flashed him a scowl. "I'm angry with you too, bastard." His eyes gleamed wickedly, and I turned back to Korrik. "What did you say about a civil war?"

“That is not your concern,” Remmo told me in a low voice, before growling at his friend. “Leave us.”

“I know you’re not trying to bench me after spending weeks teaching me how to use my magic,” I shot back to Remmo.

He sighed heavily.

Korrik took the opportunity to speak. “The remaining unseelies wish to elect the generals as the new council, because they’ve forsaken Aev’s. Other than me, the rest of us won’t consider taking a new leadership position without Vuvim.” He gestured toward Remmo.

“You’re a general?” I asked. “What kind?”

He glared at me.

“She doesn’t know the question is inappropriate,” Remmo said sharply. “She has never been unseelie.”

He nodded reluctantly. “I am the sabertooth general. Oren is the dragon, and Devv is the hellhound.”

“All of us defected, so our previous roles mean little,” Remmo said. “And as I’ve told the other generals, taking Aev’s throne after he’s lost his female would likely lead to him losing control. And if Aev loses control, the snow melts, which is not an option.”

“Why does it matter if the snow melts?” I asked.

“The klynnas will escape.” Korrik’s voice was harsh.

“What the hell is a klynna?” The strange word was pronounced clin-uh, and I had never heard it before.

“Wild beasts that are large enough and strong enough to kill fae,” Remmo admitted. “The monsters I told you about, who are trapped on our land. The only time the unseelie and seelie worked together was to imprison them. Vevol gave Aev his ice magic as a way to trap them, because they were massacring us. It takes dozens of fae working together to down a klynna, and the damn things come back to life a few days after you kill them unless you tear them to shreds and separate the pieces. Even then, over time they will resurrect.”

Holy shit.

Someone should’ve included that in the nonexistent *Welcome to Vevol* guidebook.

"So we have to figure out a way to chill Aev out before you guys can become unseelie leaders," I said. "To keep the snow around."

Korrik grumbled, "The only way to stabilize the king is through his female, and I doubt she will return to him."

"She's not going back," I agreed. "The female fae know how to break her bond with him. Apparently it's pretty complex, but it sounds like a sure thing."

The men's faces became grave.

Korrik said, "Then we'll need to prepare him, so he can maintain his hold on the ice. Did she tell you when it's going to happen?"

"No. But you can't tell him—he might try to stop her."

"Aev doesn't wish to be mated to Naomi any more than she wishes to be mated to him, Iloli." Remmo's voice was careful, but his grip on me remained firm.

Korrik just grumbled, "He sure as hell won't force her to stay bonded to him. I'll get the other generals together and figure out a way to prepare Aev for what's coming. If he can maintain his hold on the ice, then I'll be back to convince you to lead." He gave Remmo one last glance.

"You know my answer," the basilisk said simply.

Korrik heaved a sigh, and walked away.

Leaving me still pressed against Remmo's chest.

I peeled myself off of the man. He looked down at me and then tugged me right back, asking in a low voice, "What are you wearing, Iloli?"

"A female fae outfit." I tugged at the skirt part of the dress, which flowed nicely thanks to the slit up the middle. "Cute, huh?"

"Those are extremely small underwear."

"Nice observation skills. Gold star." I patted him on the chest. "Now, let go of me."

He pulled me closer. "I'll find you shorts to go under it."

"The shorts don't shift well. Always getting caught on things. And you saw how well my skirt worked, so thanks, but no thanks." I tried to ease away again, and he pulled me even tighter.

"Stop trying to get away from me. We need to talk."

I nodded. "Preferably not while any female fae who wanted to watch could see us."

He glanced over toward the Stronghold. "I have a den a short distance from here. I haven't visited in a while, but I'm sure it's still standing. There's no kitchen, though."

"I miss fresh fruit anyway. Let's go."

He still didn't release me.

I stared up at him, and waited for him to look down at me. When he did, there was a crease on his forehead. Reaching up, I smoothed it out. It came right back, immediately.

"If I let go of you, are you going to try to run from me again?" he asked, voice low and cautious.

"No." My answer was truthful. "I've done enough thinking and running in the last week for at least a year. If you let go of me, I'm just going to follow you to your den, so we can talk. Even if it leads to arguing."

His lips curved upward slightly. "Something tells me you plan on yelling at me."

I flashed him a grin. "It's a possibility. If you can't take it, walk away now."

He chuckled. "That's not going to happen." His lips brushed my forehead, like he couldn't resist, and then he released me. "You need a shower. You smell like the female fae."

I made a face at him. "Shut up and show me the way to your den."

He laughed. "Alright. Pay close attention, because I plan on having you back there frequently. And adding a kitchen."

"Stop stressing about the kitchen thing," I told him, as he shifted forms. My hand stroked his scales lightly, and he wrapped around me when I shifted too. Our bodies warmed each other as they tangled, and if I was in my human form, my face would've warmed.

I didn't know how the conversation was going to go… but honestly, I was kind of looking forward to it.

Finally, I would have answers.

Eleven

It took about an hour to reach his den, but that felt like a reasonable amount of time—and a good, solid distance from everyone else—to me.

If we decided to be more than friends, after all, I was going to want privacy.

Allll the privacy.

And allll the sex.

Though, I needed to not think about that until we had some more conversations about important shit.

Mainly the mate stuff. Because I'd been remembering every time I asked him a question that gave him the perfect opportunity to tell me what we were to each other, and he didn't take me up on any of them.

I didn't know we had reached the den until he slid through an extremely-well-disguised hole in a tree the size of a grocery store, and his gigantic body disappeared.

I peered into the hole, blinking down into the wide, hollowed-out tree.

There were a series of thick branches jutting out on the inside, positioned strategically so a basilisk could use them to work their way down to solid land.

Remmo was already at the bottom when I slipped inside and started making my way to the ground, but he waited patiently for me. The bastard always wanted to see me trying new shit and learning things. I supposed that was probably a good quality for him to have, even if it made things difficult for me sometimes.

He had a large shelled fruit open and waiting in his hands when I landed on my feet.

"I'm really not that hungry," I told him as I shifted and looked around.

The space was wide, but not too wide that it wasn't cozy anymore. There was plenty of space for a huge mattress, a fridge, and what looked like a large, weird couch. A small shelf of books was beside the couch. A bathroom doorway was off to my left side, and everything was spaced out so much that the place felt huge.

"Just eat, please?"

As much as I wanted to say yes and make him happy, I knew there were things to discuss first.

It was time for me to start asking the shitty questions and making him uncomfortable, because he had been keeping too much from me.

I put a hand on my hip. "*Why* do you want me to eat?"

He grimaced.

"No, we're not doing any of that shit." I poked his face. "This expression tells me that you don't want to answer me. If you want me here, eating your food, giving you a chance to explain why you were hiding *so many things* from me for so long, you give me the whole entire truth. Without a damn grimace. One lie, one half-answer, and I'm out. Completely."

He nodded slowly. "Alright." When he gestured toward a piece of furniture that sort of resembled a couch, I walked over there and sat down. As soon as I was sitting, he set half of the shelled fruit on my lap, and handed me a piece of the shell to use as a spoon. "Keep this over those damn underwear or I'm not going to be able to think straight. And eat it, if you want me talking."

I loved it when he got bossy with me, but rolled my eyes at him anyway just to egg him on.

"I want to see you eating, because it's been days since I got to feed you myself to make sure you're getting enough," he said bluntly. "When you were in the Stronghold, I worried about you."

Aww.

Okay, that answer passed all the tests.

"Alright." I took a bite of the fruit, and he watched me. His eyes drank me in, like he couldn't get enough of the way I looked. When I'd swallowed the bite, I finally asked the question I'd had jumping around in my mind for days...

"Why did you follow me away from the party that night?"

Twelve

The gleam in Remmo's eyes told me he'd been waiting for that question. But the reluctance in them told me that he wasn't sure how I was going to take the answer.

"The full truth," I reminded him. "I want to know everything. Especially if anything you told me while we were on our little adventure was a lie."

He nodded. "Alright. If you want the full truth, we need to go back a few months. To the day you and the other unmated seelie women moved into the new Stronghold."

"Okay." I took another bite of the fruit, knowing he'd stop talking if he didn't think I was upholding my end of the deal.

"I was waiting in the trees, hidden, when you and the others arrived. As always, I was scouting for my people. I saw you shift, and turn right to Teris. I smelled your scent in the air immediately. And as soon as I smelled it, I felt it pulling at me, commanding me to move closer, to meet you, to surrender myself to you, to make you mine. But the moment I started to reveal myself, I saw the way you smiled at Teris. And I caught a hint of his scent tangled with yours."

I stopped eating, and just stared at him.

Remmo stood up, off the cushion he'd sat down on, and began to pace slowly. "I returned to my perch, and I watched until I understood the situation entirely. Until I'd realized that out of all the men in Vevol, *I* had been blessed to be fated to one of the females we all yearned for. And that the woman I wanted

—the one whose scent sang to me, whose smile made my chest ache—was in love with another man. *My mate* was already taken."

My throat was so damn dry when he looked up at me, focusing on the fruit on my lap. "Eat, Iloli."

I took one bite, and when that didn't satisfy him, took two more.

Finally, he continued. "I didn't know how to respond, at first. Didn't know what to do. Should I challenge Teris? Kill him for the right to claim *my* female? And risk breaking your heart in the process? I couldn't do it. So, I didn't return to my people; I couldn't leave your side. When my brothers found me, they realized the situation and urged me to go down and speak to you. To tell you that you belonged to me, and that you needed to leave Teris. But I couldn't bring myself to do that, either. I wanted it to be your choice, if you chose me. And I refused to be the man you settled on simply because the sabertooth didn't want you."

My stomach was a damn ball.

But I forced more fruit into my mouth.

"The night of the party, I'd already figured out the entirety of your plan. I knew you'd never seen me watching you from the trees, so you wouldn't bother looking for me when you left. I followed you until I heard Teris a long way behind us—and then I knew I had to warn you, or you wouldn't get away from him. So I introduced myself."

"With your full name?" I asked quietly.

"Yes. It's always been yours to have," he said simply. "I didn't plan on kissing you. I just couldn't stand to see your plan fail because of that damn bond with Teris."

"But why didn't you tell me, then? I was already leaving him, so what was the point in keeping it a secret?"

"Because you were looking for a reason not to be in love with Teris, and I didn't want to be that reason." He ran a hand through his hair—looking disheveled for the first time in ages. "I didn't want to be your excuse, or your ticket away from the sabertooth. I wanted to be your friend. Your lover. Your *mate*. If I told you what I was to you then, you would've seen the opportunity. You would've used me as an excuse. And I would've let you, because I was yours. As I have always been yours."

I opened my mouth to argue.

To tell him that he was wrong, that I wouldn't have kissed him and told Teris that I'd met my fated mate so he and I were done.

But... I couldn't honestly say that was true.

So I closed my mouth for a few minutes.

And I waited.

"I wanted to tell you so damn many times, Iloli. You must believe that. I ached to feel your hands on my skin, to feel you sleep in my arms. But every time I opened my mouth to do so, I heard your words. I remembered your pain. And I put it off a little longer, so I could first prove to you that I wanted to be more than *just* your fated mate. Fate means almost nothing; friendship, companionship, and love are what matters."

I put the fruit down next to my feet, no longer hungry in the slightest. "What about in the forest, on the way back to the Stronghold? You knew I thought Teris was going to kick your ass."

He nodded. "Anything I said would've been taken as me trying to reassure you that I was stronger than you thought. I didn't need to convince you of anything at that point; I needed to prove myself to you. When you saw me beat Teris, I knew that you would have no choice but to accept the truth about who I was."

"Vuvim?" I asked with a small grimace.

"To others, yes." He dipped his head in a nod. "But not to you."

I closed my eyes and let out a slow breath. "I was so stupid."

His hands caught mine, and when I opened my eyes, I found him crouching in front of me, holding my fingers tightly. "No, Iloli. You were hurting, never stupid. I was giving you time, and space, preferring to be by your side as your friend rather than your fated mate."

"Until we got back to the Stronghold," I pointed out.

"Even then. I wouldn't handle it well if you broke our bond or chose another male, but I still didn't intend to ask you for more than you were ready to give. And the same is true now, too. If you still want to be just friends, we will be just friends."

"You and I were never good at the just friend thing," I said with a sigh.

"Sure we were. It's been weeks since we so much as kissed."

I lifted an eyebrow at him. "How many times did you check out my ass, or boobs? And how many times did I stare at your abs or your butt?"

"I hope these are rhetorical questions, because I haven't been keeping count." He dragged my hands to his chest, setting my palms there.

We still hadn't really talked about my past.

I hadn't explained abuse to him, though he may have figured it out.

And... I couldn't give him what he wanted.

"I still can't fall in love with you," I told him quietly. "I don't think it's even possible for me."

"Then I will take whatever you want to give me, and I will proudly call you mine." His eyes were warm and steady.

For whatever it was worth, I believed him.

I just wasn't sure that was enough.

"Even if I tell you I want us to live in separate houses? That I want space, and you can't stalk me in the trees anymore?" I asked.

The warmth in his eyes faded slightly.

He didn't answer right away.

"We could still share a home, as friends," he finally said.

I heaved a sigh. "You're still fae, Remmo. And ultimately, that means you're still going to want a relationship with the kind of intimacy that I don't know if I'll ever be ready for."

"You were ready to mate with Teris," he countered. "You wanted the protection he could provide. I could protect you better than him, if we were to mate. And with the bond completed, my instincts would become easier to manage. I could learn to give you the space you require."

"I don't want to spend the rest of my life disappointing you," I argued. "I don't want to wake up every day, and look at you, and know that if you were with someone else, she could give you everything I can't."

"Then what's the alternative, Iloli? You are my female, and the reason my heart still beats in my chest. My entire world, too. Even if I were to try, I couldn't move on from our connection. And I *refuse* to try. I will love you, regardless of your feelings for me. You have never lied to me or led me on in any way; I know what you're willing to offer me—and I would be *privileged* to have it."

"I don't want you to start resenting me next month, or next week, or next year," I argued.

"I have lived alone for centuries. How could I resent the woman that provides me companionship? You could ask any of my brothers; I am not the resentful type."

"Unless it comes to Teris," I pointed out.

"I don't resent him—I want to remove his head from his body. There is a large difference."

I snorted, pulling my hands away from his chest and leaning back. My knees nearly touched his bare abdomen, and the way our eyes was almost level was kind of overwhelming for me.

"I'll think about it," I agreed. "If we do become mates, the physical stuff could only be about getting off, though. You can't talk about loving me while you're inside me—that will mess with my head."

"I understand." His voice was a little gravelly when he said that, and I ignored the resulting warmth in my lower belly. "Now, I need you to eat." He placed the fruit back on my lap, and I grimaced.

"Seriously, I'm not hungry.

His words mimicked mine. "*Seriously*, I need to see you fill your stomach." The backs of his knuckles brushed my cheek, and he rose to his feet.

My eyes landed on his erection, straining against his pants. And then followed his ass as he strode over to the bookshelf.

"What are you doing?" I asked.

"I've kept journals for as long as I've been alive. I need to go over my notes about the klynnas. We tested their speed, strength, and agility. The others won't have things down as accurately as I do."

"You have centuries worth of journals right there?" My eyebrows lifted into my forehead.

He chuckled. "No. Most of them are in my main den, but it takes much longer to get there."

"Did you hide it in a glowing cave?"

"Not quite." He flashed me a smirk as he grabbed a stack of journals near the bottom of the shelf. "I don't *think* the notes are here, but if I'm lucky, they will be."

"What was that face for?" I gestured to his face with the pointy end of my shell-spoon.

"I think you'll like my den when you see it, that's all." He opened the first notebook.

"*When* I see it?"

"Yes. You are my female; my home is as much yours as it is mine, now." He flipped through the pages of the book, and I watched quietly.

"How dangerous are they? The klynnas?"

"Dangerous enough that I still have nightmares about the brothers I lost to them centuries ago," he admitted.

Shit.

I tensed, considering asking him to try teaching me how to fight, so I could protect myself. He'd been a really damn good teacher, when it came to everything else.

But I still shut down when I saw violence. I still went numb.

It wasn't healthy.

But if he saw the way I reacted, how would *he* react?

"That sexy little brain of yours is spinning, Iloli. Just speak your thoughts to me; you know I will listen."

Damn him for being right.

And damn me for trusting him to listen.

I opened my mouth to lie, but the truth came pouring out.

"I want to learn how to fight. I don't want to be helpless anymore. But when I see violence, my brain just stops functioning."

His eyes lifted from his book. "You want me to train you?"

"Maybe? I don't know. It might not work."

"It would work." His voice was thick with certainty. "If I train you alone, there will be no violence to see. Just you and I, moving our bodies."

The words weren't even that suggestive, but my mind steered us straight back to that warm waterfall, and the makeout session we'd shared.

My face was hot when I spoke again. "We could try it. I don't feel as sure about us succeeding as you seem, but I'd like to try. If the klynnas get out, I don't want to be helpless."

"I won't leave you defenseless," he said firmly.

"I know, but I also don't want you or anyone else babysitting me. I *want* to learn how to fight. I just don't want any shitty memories coming back, or to have to numb myself to any more of my life than I already have."

His hand landed gently on my thigh. "I'll teach you, Iloli. Do you want to start now, or take a few days to think about it?"

I made a face. "I've been avoiding shit for a week now. I'm tired of putting things off."

He chuckled, setting his journal down on the couch. "Now it is."

"Where do you want to do it?"

"There's plenty of space in here. I'll just move the couch."

I hopped up, taking the rest of my shelled fruit to the fridge and tucking it away. There were a few other fruits and vegetables stored inside it, and I noticed a few of the round *birth control fruits*, as me and the other women had taken to calling them.

"You planning on fucking me?" I asked him, grabbing one of the fruits and holding it up.

He let out a booming laugh. "Those have been there since before I met you."

Huh. I sniffed them, but they smelled fine. "How do they last so long after being picked?"

"It takes years for fruit to go bad here. Is it different on Earth?"

"Yup." I put the fruit back and shut the fridge. "Are you dying for a baby? I know some of the male fae are desperate for it; I've heard them talking."

"Those males should chase the female fae, then. The only thing I'm *dying for* is a completed mate bond that prevents Teris from looking twice at you," Remmo said, as he settled the couch into place against a previously-bare stretch of wall. "Having our scents permanently intertwined is what calls to me. If we decided to have a child, I would figure out how to be a good father. But all I truly want is you."

Well, that sure as hell made my heart nice and toasty.

He stepped away, turning around and surveying the room before dipping his head once. "We'll need more space when we begin to wrestle, but for now, this will work."

Did he say *wrestle*?

Maybe I needed to rethink my choice in trainer.

His gaze lifted to me, and scanned me slowly.

My face heated.

"We'll need a pair of the seelie's female clothing for you to practice in. The dress isn't practical for fighting—and those panties will be the death of me if you're constantly changing positions."

A snort escaped me. "Alright. You want to head back to the Stronghold today?"

"Not particularly." He ran a hand through his hair, disheveling the waves as he mentally ran over the options.

"How about we just chill until tomorrow?" I suggested. "We can eat fruit, and I can help you look through your journals if you're cool with it."

He nodded, and his shoulders relaxed slightly. "That sounds nice." He paused. "I do need you to shower, though. You don't smell like yourself."

"The scent is probably embedded in my clothes too," I pointed out.

"I'll scrub it out of them. You can wear some of my spare clothing while they dry."

Figuring it wasn't worth an argument—and not hating the idea of feeling and smelling Remmo's clothes on my skin—I just nodded.

His eyes followed me as I crossed the room, and even when I shut the door to the bathroom behind me, I felt like his gaze was still on my skin.

Being just friends was going to be really damn rough.

I stripped out of my clothes and turned on the shower, glancing over my shoulder at the door. Though I was kind of itching to slip my fingers between my thighs and relieve some of the pressure there, I was pretty sure some remnant of the scent would linger, somewhere. Either on me, or in the bathroom.

And if the scent was there, Remmo would find it.

Which was why I hadn't tried anything, in the time we'd spent together.

My imagination had run a bit wild in my showers at the Stronghold, but this wasn't the Stronghold. And if I was going to tell Remmo that I expected us to be nothing but friends, I couldn't get myself off in his bathroom three minutes later.

I *did* have morals.

Slipping into the shower, I groaned as the hot water rained down on my skin.

It felt so damn good.

Even if my morals prevented me from getting off, I could sure as hell enjoy a hot shower.

WHEN I STEPPED BACK OUT, Remmo was sprawled out on the couch. His body was relaxed, and his scent flooded the air deliciously. He'd put on a soft-looking pair of sweats, and I tried not to pay attention to the tent in them, because it would totally turn me on.

A pair of clothes were folded and sitting neatly on the floor outside the bathroom door. I murmured a thank you as I grabbed them and stepped back inside.

He'd seen me naked enough times that modesty was pretty pointless, but now that I knew what we were to each other, I knew I needed to be more careful. I didn't want to hurt him, after all.

His white long-sleeved button-up draped over my body, falling to the middle of my thighs as I tugged it into place. It was much more comfortable than it looked, surprisingly. I pressed the soft fabric to my nose as I inhaled.

A groan escaped me when the scent of Remmo, embedded so damn deeply into the fabric, filled my lungs.

How could I have ever thought the way he smelled to me was anything other than a sign of our connection?

A pair of pants still remained on the ground, but I knew those things would be way too big for me, so I didn't bother.

I debated putting the panties from my fae dress back on, but decided against it. Going commando felt kinda scandalous, and that made my blood hot.

Opening the door, I peeked my head out. "What should I wash the clothes with? Just soap?"

"Soap will work," Remmo agreed, though his voice sounded a bit raspy. And when I followed his gaze, I found my nipples saluting him through the semi-sheer fabric. They were not only pointy, but a hell of a lot darker than the fabric, so he could definitely see them.

I stepped back into the bathroom, grinning to myself.

This was even more scandalous.

I should've wanted to keep things squeaky clean. I should've been acting like a damn saint.

But I didn't think I even possessed either of those settings, so screw that.

I'd embrace the scandal, and see what happened.

Thirteen

Remmo's eyes tracked me as I walked to the couch, my dress hanging up in the bathroom. I plopped down on the opposite side of the furniture from him, and held a hand out for a journal.

Silently, he gave me one.

His eyes were still glued to my figure.

I pretended not to notice as I tucked my feet up beneath me and started to read.

...maybe I didn't just want to be friends after all.

Maybe I wanted to see how long it would take him to lose control, and pin me to a wall, and fuck me.

Maybe I wanted to see the strong, perfectly-controlled fae lose control of his calm façade and command me to strip, to sit on his cock, to give myself to him.

That was my new goal, I decided, as I flipped through the journal looking for details about the monsters.

The journal didn't seem to hold anything personal at all; just a summary of what Remmo had seen while he was spying on people, and a plan of action in case the people he'd been tracking decided to attack.

Nothing about the klynnas at all.

Still, I kept flipping the pages, scanning the words he'd written in his pretty, elegant handwriting.

After some time had passed, I looked over at Remmo and found his attention also fixed on a journal.

Just to nudge him a little closer to that edge I was hoping to push him over, I stretched my legs out.

The movement immediately made his attention jerk back to me. And his eyes followed my legs as I lifted them toward him. "Is it cool if I put my feet up here?" I asked him, lowering a foot to the middle of his thigh.

"Yes." His eyes followed my feet as I settled them on his lap—being careful not to accidentally bump the erection straining against his shorts.

I'd get to the bumping later.

First, I needed to get him comfortable with this.

One of his hands landed lightly on my feet, and I shivered a bit at the warmth that wrapped around them. His gaze lifted back to my breasts until my shivering stopped, and then he dragged his attention back to his book.

And he read.

He was going to be a tough one to crack, but damn… I was going to have fun pushing him.

We read until we were too exhausted to keep our eyes open, making it through five of the journals between the two of us.

"I'll sleep on the couch," he murmured to me, as I slowly rose to my feet.

"No. It's your house; if there's only one bed, you're sleeping in it. There's plenty of space for both of us," I said, grabbing his hand in mine.

He was silent as I led him to the mattress, and even more silent as I climbed to the far side. There was only one pillow, right in the middle of the mattress, and my inner temptress cackled.

Remmo slid beneath the blankets, not going anywhere near the pillow as he stiffly looked over at me.

"We can share the damn pillow," I grumbled at him, fighting hard to hide my thrill with how perfectly the situation was going down.

"It's yours," he said in a low voice.

"Actually, it's yours." I plopped my head down far away from said pillow, giving him a taste of his own medicine. "I'm not using it if you're not."

His chest rumbled unhappily. "You are my mate. Taking care of you is my role."

"And taking care of you is mine," I countered.

A moment of tense silence passed.

And then another.

"We share the pillow, then," he said, as he reached the same conclusion I had.

"Alright. Don't feel bad if you accidentally touch me during the night, either. If we're sharing a pillow, it's bound to happen."

He said nothing to that, but we both scooted to the center of the bed, facing away from each other.

My ass met his lower back, and he froze.

I closed my eyes and made my breathing level out slowly, as if I was falling asleep, even though every inch of me was wide awake.

The circumstances in which I was forced to learn that skill were unfortunate ones, but I wouldn't let those bad memories cloud these moments with a man I trusted and liked.

Unlike mine, his breathing wasn't level.

He moved slightly, rolling to his back and putting a bit more space between us.

Dammit.

A few minutes passed before he let out a long, slow breath.

A few *more* minutes passed before I heard fabric rustle.

His weight left the bed a moment later, and I didn't hear a damn thing as I watched him slip up and out of the tree silently.

I gave him a minute before channeling my inner *Vuvim* and shifting myself, sliding up and out the same way he had.

My head peeked out through the exit, my eyes scanning the trees—and then stopping with my head tilted completely back, staring up at the man a handful of branches above me.

He was completely naked, one hand pressed to the smooth bark of the tree, and the other stroking his cock.

My mouth dried.

I think my body almost glitched out and shut down.

He was silent, but his head tilted back and his chest rose and fell rapidly. His strokes grew harder and faster, until the wind carried his low groan to me as he lost himself to the release, and I knew I had to move.

I was back in bed faster than I'd realized I could get there, in the same exact position I'd occupied before I followed him up.

My breathing was even, despite my racing heart, and I forced even that damn disobedient organ to calm as I waited for Remmo to return.

A few minutes later, his weight shifted the bed silently. His body rolled toward mine, until his front was spooning my back lightly—just barely touching me.

His skin was even warmer than usual, and I itched to ask him what he was picturing when he was in the trees. To make sure that when he'd stroked himself, he'd done so to the mental image of me.

But I stayed silent.

And a few minutes later, his breathing leveled out. In his sleep, he rolled closer to me, pressing a covered, still-hard cock to my ass as he cradled me against him.

Eventually, my racing thoughts calmed, and I fell asleep with his body pressed to mine.

WHEN I WOKE UP, we were in exactly the same position we fell asleep in. Remmo's chest was still rising and falling steadily, and I felt more well-rested than I had in ages.

Probably because I went from living in a cave, to hiding out with the female fae, and was now accepting my connection to Remmo at least a little bit.

I needed to pee, so I carefully rolled away from the basilisk.

He remained where he was, his breathing still steady. He'd never slept that soundly when we were in the forest or in the cave together, so I was kind of surprised that he didn't move.

Maybe he was just comfortable.

I climbed off the bottom end of the bed, slipping into the bathroom and closing the door quietly. When I was done, I headed back to the bed, and found Remmo rubbing at his eyes with the back of his hand.

"You okay?" I checked

"Yeah. Just been a long time since I slept that well." He yawned widely, remaining where he was.

Hesitation had settled in my middle, but I forced it to subside as I climbed back to my spot in the bed. Remmo was on his back, so I plopped down on my back too. My side met his, but neither of us reacted to the touch.

I was itching to ask him about what I'd watched him do the night before—and whether or not he'd been imagining me when he did it. Logic told me I was definitely the motivating factor, but self-doubt and past experiences made me question said logic.

I didn't want to be the needy chick who asked questions about that shit, though.

"Why did you sleep so good?" I asked, instead.

Hoping he would somehow admit to jerking off before coming to bed with me.

"Being here in my home, where I know we're both safe, puts me at ease," he admitted. His hand found mine, and his fingers slid between mine.

That was all he was going to give me.

Unseelie bastard.

I was going to have to be more blunt.

More... honest.

I supposed he probably wanted that, even if it was going to kill me a little on the inside.

"So, being just friends is a little hard on me, physically," I began.

As soon as I said that, my brain started screaming at me to abort the mission.

But it was too damn late.

"What are your thoughts about us touching ourselves?" I asked, fighting the urge to cringe at my own awkwardness.

My brain was still screaming at me to change the subject.

To take it back.

To walk away.

I forced myself to remain calm, even though he made me wait for what felt like an hour (but was probably only two minutes) before he answered.

"If we are keeping our hands to ourselves, I think it's to be expected," Remmo finally said.

"Same." I nodded.

And couldn't come up with a tactful way to tell him that he'd better not be imagining any of my friends when he jacked off, or I was legitimately going to kill him.

I felt him look at me, and forced my gaze to remain on the ceiling a long, long way above us.

"You look stressed," he told me.

"Thanks," I drawled.

His chuckle didn't relax me one damn bit. "If you have a question, just ask it, Iloli."

I huffed. "It's fine if you touch yourself, obviously. I'm not your boss or anything. I just don't like the idea of you thinking about another woman while you're doing it. So—"

He rolled toward me and set a possessive hand on my abdomen.

Whatever I'd been about to say died in my throat.

"Do you know what I picture, when I touch myself?" His voice was low, his eyes hot. And he didn't wait for my answer before speaking again. "I picture us back in that cave. The way your bare body felt against mine, the way your core wrapped around my fingers. The desperation to know how you taste—to feel your body hold my cock instead. I picture the way it happened—and the way I'd like it to happen the next time."

My lower belly was painfully hot. My face was, too.

Even though the only damn part of me he'd touched was my stomach.

"You are the only female for me, and I'm sure as fuck the only male for you now. If you so much as *consider* imagining another male's cock, hand, or mouth anywhere near your body, I will refuse to leave your side long enough for you to slide those little fingers between those thighs. Are we clear?"

Shit, I loved it when he got bossy like that.

"I'm going to need an answer, Iloli." His voice was low. "Without a joke this time."

"The only hands, mouth, or tongue that I want on my body is yours. Even in my imagination," I admitted. "So yeah, we're clear."

"Good." His fingers dug into my belly lightly, like he wasn't ready to pull them off of me. "Now, we need to get to the Stronghold for your clothing."

I nodded, climbing out of bed.

His eyes were hot on my skin as I slipped back into the bathroom to change back into my stretchy clothing. I left his shirt where my other clothes had been, and when I stepped back out there, he was waiting for me with more fruit in his hands. Since we'd been touching so much, the occasional zing of electricity had left me feeling plenty satisfied.

When he broke the fruit in half and handed me one of the pieces, though, I took it. And after we'd both eaten, we headed out.

BECAUSE I KNEW where we were going for once, he didn't stay ahead of me. Instead, we traveled through the trees together.

After a short stop at the Stronghold—during which I was convinced by some of the new ex-human girls to plan another dance party soon—we returned.

And from there, started training.

As much as I dreaded it, it really wasn't that bad. He started me the same way the other women had apparently started—by moving through a number of motions meant to warm me up. They definitely made me sweaty, but the real *warmth* came from watching Remmo move through those same motions.

He'd call out a pose, and I'd have to strike it. Despite my multiple jokes about it—all of which he laughed at, like a damn good mate—it was a real workout for my untrained ass. All of the time I'd spent traveling with Remmo helped me get somewhat in shape, but nowhere near strong enough to be ready for the fighting that was apparently coming my way.

When I was suitably warmed up, he made me drink some water. Then he stepped up behind me, hands landing on my hips as he straightened my stance. "Do you want to learn how to fight fae, or just klynnas?"

"Just klynnas." I didn't hesitate on that one.

I was not interested in fighting my friends, or anyone else. I just wanted to be able to defend myself from those damned monsters.

"A klynna is like a dragon mixed with a phoenix. Fire, scales, feathers, and claws. I'll need to review my notes to make sure I'm remembering perfectly, but typically, the goal was to knock them from the sky long enough to rip out their hearts. Remove both hearts, and it buys you a few hours."

My lips parted in horror. "Only a few hours?"

"Yes. Even their hearts can regrow. It takes the venom of eight basilisks to knock a klynna out, so typically, we would need ten basilisks, each paired with two protectors. Another two dozen fae would be distractions—tearing at its wings, attracting its claws, and such. If you want to train to fight a klynna, you'll need to focus on agility, stability, and strength. And you'll need to knock out a few of the other fae with your venom, to make sure you know how to use it."

I sighed heavily. "Why do I feel like you're trying to tell me that I either need to learn how to actually fight to be ready for that, or get really into doing yoga with Dots?"

He chuckled. "Because if you want me to allow you anywhere near a klynna, you'll need to learn how to actually fight *and* get really into yoga."

"Overprotective bastard," I grumbled.

"Understandably protective mate," he corrected me, his fingers stroking my hip lightly. "The rest of us have had centuries to learn how to defend ourselves and the others around us. It's okay if you don't want that for yourself; no one will be angry with you if you choose not to fight."

I would be angry with me, though.

And something inside me would die if I had to cower in the trees while my friends risked their lives to kill those monsters—while Remmo risked his life.

"I'm not a fighter," I said softly. "The damned female fae and their ceremony proved that. I'm just... when shit hits the fan, I go silent. I shut down."

"And that's what the training is for. It prepares your mind, as well as your body." He tapped my temple, and then my collarbone.

"It never looked like it took a whole lot of thinking when the seelies fought," I countered.

"The seelies see themselves as little more than wild animals when it comes to a fight. They rely on instinct. Those of us who fight with our minds succeed more consistently than those who lean on brute force."

Huh.

I guess he had a point with that.

Though brute force did seem to succeed a good portion of the time, too.

"Fine. You can teach me." I heaved a sigh. "But if I shut down, you can't freak out at me. Just give me a few minutes and I'll snap out of it eventually."

"We'll start with a punch." He lifted my hand, forming it into a fist for me. "Like this." He guided my arm through the motion. "The power comes from here, not here." He patted my abdomen, and then my arm.

I'd heard similar things in movies and books, so I didn't doubt him. Not that I had any reason to, anyway.

We went through the motions, and with him standing behind me or to the side of me while I moved my body and received his critiques, it didn't trigger me at all.

But when he stood in front of me with pads over his hands, thin ones that he'd created quickly with his magic, my stomach clenched.

"Now, you'll follow my instructions as we go through the kicks and punches," he said. "I need to see how you move before we keep going."

I swallowed my fear and nodded.

But the moment my fist started swinging, my brain stopped.

I didn't even feel it connect.

My thoughts shut down.

My breathing slowed.

A pair of green eyes filled my vision, and a pair of soft hands cupped my face.

Remmo.

"I'm right here," he told me.

I heard it, but I felt nothing.

"I need to take a shower," I said, fighting the panic. Trying to ignore the way my chest was caving in, the way my body had numbed itself to the potential pain it saw in my future.

Arguing—fighting—standing up for myself in any way?

It always led to pain.

Which was why I relied on jokes. On sarcasm. It distanced me from anyone who might want to hurt me.

Confrontation was... not my friend.

Hell, it was my weakness.

One of so damn many.

"Iloli," Remmo said, but I didn't see him. I might as well have been looking straight through the massive, gorgeous man. "Sunny. Summer."

"I need to take a shower," I repeated, stepping away.

He released me—but when I walked silently to the bathroom, he followed.

Fourteen

There was no shower curtain. No door to hide me from Remmo when I stripped.

My clothes went over my head anyway.

He had seen me naked before, so it wasn't a first.

I stepped under the scalding hot water and closed my eyes. The way it hit my face wasn't enough to pull me out of the darkness I'd just found myself engulfed in.

A pair of warm hands landed gently on my hips, and I tensed at the contact. My body was already ready—waiting—for pain.

Instead, I was carefully pulled to a warm chest, and wrapped in a pair of strong arms. Remmo's grip was tight enough to make me feel safe, but loose enough not to make me feel trapped.

I pressed my cheek to his bare chest, inhaling his scent as the water fell on both of us.

He said nothing, just holding me. And the calm, steady beat of his heart against my ear slowly relaxed my shoulders.

I was okay, I admitted to myself, after a few minutes had passed.

I was okay.

Things were different now.

Remmo was my fated mate; he couldn't have hurt me even if he wanted to. And after all that time we'd spent together, I knew without a doubt that he didn't want to. And that his anger was not the brutal rage of the men I had known on Earth.

When Remmo got angry, he grew quiet. Efficient. Vicious. I'd seen it, when he was fighting Teris. He hadn't caused any more harm than he'd needed to—and he hadn't done anywhere near as much damage as he could've.

Even when I suggested mating with another man, he never got really mad. He definitely never raged.

And even if he *did* rage, I was confident that he wouldn't take that fury out on me.

I trusted him, I realized, in a sharp moment of clarity.

Not just to keep me safe—but to treat me well.

And that was a first for me.

"I'm sorry," I whispered against his chest, knowing he would hear the soft words even over the sound of the shower.

"You have nothing to apologize for. You warned me this might happen—and I am in no way hurt or offended." His soft answer calmed my nerves more than I'd expected it to.

His hand began to move over my back, gently. The motions soothed me, and I let myself relax in his arms. My chest was bare against his, and he was hard against my lower belly, but the moment wasn't one of desire or attraction.

Just raw, honest intimacy.

I was fragile, and he was strong.

Strong enough for the both of us, maybe.

I wanted to be strong too, but... it would take time.

"You'll still train me?" I asked him quietly.

"Of course. And the more naked interruptions, the better."

A snort escaped me.

We really did have the same sense of humor.

"In all seriousness, we have all the time in the world, Iloli. If we need to spend the next month practicing the same one movement, getting you comfortable with the mental implications of it, then that's what we'll do." He continued to stroke my back lightly. "And should you ever want to discuss what memories make you react this way, you know that I'm here."

"I know," I admitted.

And I did.

If I wanted to talk about something, Remmo would listen. Always.

"Can we just work on the yoga shit for the rest of the day?" I asked him. "I need time to wrap my head around all of this."

"Of course."

We stayed in the shower for at least another ten or twenty minutes, me clinging to Remmo and him holding me firmly against him. When I finally felt like I could handle the real world, I shut off the water, dried myself off, and put my workout tank and shorts back on again.

And then, we got back to work.

THAT NIGHT, after we were done training, I showered again—by myself, that time. I'd gotten sweaty as hell, and my muscles were yelling at me. Remmo assured me that my fae healing would take care of everything in the next hour or two, leaving me fresh and recharged by the time we started training again tomorrow.

I came out of the shower wearing his white shirt again, and his eyes followed me from where he sat, sprawled out on the couch with one of his journals.

After padding over to him, I curled up next to him, setting my feet on his lap and *accidentally* brushing his erection with one of them.

He didn't mention it, silently offering me a journal. I made it about a quarter of the way through it before I fell asleep, too exhausted from the day to focus.

I wasn't sure how long I'd been out when I felt a pair of sturdy arms lift me off the cushions.

Even though I was mostly-asleep, a mental image of the way he'd slipped out of bed the night before came to my mind. So when he set me down, I rolled halfway on top of him—making him go still, until his arms locked around my back and my waist, holding me securely against him.

He inhaled my scent and held me tight while I pressed my nose to his neck, nuzzling right in as if that was where I belonged.

I fell back asleep quickly, and neither of us moved a damn inch all night.

. . .

We didn't talk about the snuggling-session as we ate breakfast and then got back to training the next morning.

When we went back to the punching after lunch, I shut down again. But that time, Remmo calmed me outside the shower, just holding me in his arms until I'd relaxed enough to breathe and think and process normally. After another hour or two passed, we tried again, with the same result.

And after we were done training and I'd taken a quick shower, we ended up on the couch together again, until I fell asleep the same way I had the night before. When he carried me to his bed—our bed—we slept together in it.

The lines between friends and mates had blurred dramatically, but I was still waiting for him to make the first move, because I wanted him to want me.

And because the training exhausted me both mentally and physically, to the point where I couldn't even consider pushing myself out of my comfort zone when it came to Remmo.

So I didn't.

And we trained.

And spending all of our time together must've been one hell of a cock block, because there was no way in hell he'd had a chance to jack off since that night—and he had to be getting as horny as I was, even if we were both ignoring the hell out of those feelings.

Two weeks passed in that fashion, before slight movement woke me up in the middle of the night.

It took me a few minutes to get my eyes open, but when I did, I found the bed empty.

I stared at the spot Remmo had filled for a long moment.

A long, long moment.

And then my head craned up toward the sky.

Toward the tree branch, where I knew he had probably gone.

I could've left him to it.

Could've gone back to sleep.

But… I wanted him.

In my sleepy, vulnerable state, I had no choice but to admit that to myself.

I'd wanted him for weeks.

Hell, I'd wanted him since the first time he kissed me in the forest, like there was no one else for him and nothing else he would rather have been doing.

So I slid out of the massive white shirt I'd been borrowing every night, shifted forms, and headed out.

At the entrance to our house, I peered up.

Heat flooded me when I found Remmo in the same position he'd been in the last time—one palm to the tree, the other on his cock.

Stroking, roughly.

I wanted him to see me, so I let out a slow, soft hiss.

His head jerked to the side, and when those bright green eyes collided with mine, he went still.

And remained still as I slid up into the tree, shifting as I reached his branch.

He stayed where he was, his breathing ragged and his body tense while I stepped around him, placing myself between his chest and the tree's bark.

When I pulled his hand away from his erection, he released it without protest.

I'd been hoping he'd get overwhelmed with lust and would just grab me and kiss me and screw me. But that hadn't happened… and I was tired of waiting for it.

It was time to take things into my own hands.

Literally.

My fingers wrapped around his erection, and he let out a strangled breath.

"Iloli," he said, voice low and rough.

Instead of answering, I kissed him. Just lifted my head up, and captured his lips in mine.

And damn, did he kiss me back.

While our lips and tongues fought, I moved my hand slowly over his cock—which was already wet with something, probably saliva—making him groan. One of his hands wrapped around my lower back, sliding down to my ass and gripping it tightly.

The other hand finally left the tree, grabbing my thigh and lifting me up so the hand on my ass could slip to my front and find my core.

I took a sharp breath in, pausing the kiss when his fingers found my clit.

I'd already taught him what I liked and showed him how to make me feel good.

And I knew him well enough to be confident that he hadn't forgotten one damn detail of that experience.

His teeth dragged over my lower lip, reminding me to kiss him, so I tangled my tongue with his again as he touched me. As I touched him.

And moments later, he was sliding two fingers inside me, stretching me while he worked my clit.

The pleasure built sharply, hotly, until I was unraveling. Remmo snarled while I cried out, our noses pressing against each other and our lips only a breath apart.

We were both panting as we came down from the high, our chests nestled together while they rose and fell rapidly.

"Shit," I managed, leaning my head back against the tree trunk. "That was hot."

"It was." His low, rough voice heated me all over again. It didn't hurt that his fingers were still buried inside me, either. Or that mine were still wrapped around his erection, and the evidence of his pleasure was on my hip and the side of my ass.

His forehead met mine softly, and both of us closed our eyes as we enjoyed the comfortable silence of the forest around us.

Guilt was eating at me, though, so I quietly admitted, "I have to tell you something."

His body tensed. "You still have feelings for Teris?"

"What? No. Nothing like that." I opened my eyes, pushing his soft, wavy hair out from between our foreheads. His eyes opened too, and I saw seriousness in them. He was worried about what I was going to say.

He might be pissed when he found out, but I was pretty sure he'd be less pissed than if I *did* have feelings for Teris. Which I definitely didn't.

So I said, "I saw you touch yourself up here, that night a few weeks ago. I shouldn't have watched, but I did."

He was silent for a moment, and so, so still. His eyes were still piercing mine, but giving away none of his emotions.

I explained, "You were so hot, I just couldn't look away. I feel terrible for doing it without asking for your permission or telling you afterward. I know it was shitty, I just—"

"My body is yours to see," he said. "Had I known you were watching, I would've worked harder to put on a show. Nothing about that is shitty, so let go of the guilt."

As if to prove that he truly felt that way, his already-hard cock went harder in my hand.

My body heated.

He asked, "That's why you made sure I wasn't imagining anyone else?"

"Yes."

His eyes closed, and he let out a slow breath.

I heaved a sigh, my body still trembling a bit from all the attention he showed it. "I have something else to confess."

He opened—and narrowed—his eyes. "Is it about Teris?"

I rolled mine at him. "No, it's not about Teris. *Nothing* is about Teris anymore."

"You shouldn't be afraid to tell me. Even if it's about Teris."

I scowled at him. "It's *not*."

He leaned forward and captured my lips in his. Not for any real reason, as far as I could tell. Just because he could, and I'd basically given him permission by interrupting him and grabbing his erection.

The kiss was slow, and soft, and then he released me with a murmur of, "Tell me already, Iloli."

I nodded, moving his head too since our foreheads were pressed together again already. "I've been testing your self-control ever since we got here. I wanted your damn self-control to fail. I wanted you to go wild, to pin me to a wall and screw me until neither of us could walk straight."

I spoke faster as I continued. "I was hoping that if I just waited you out, and slept on top of you so you couldn't sneak away and jerk off, that you'd tell me what you wanted. It was stupid, I know, because I said I just wanted to be friends. And I know you're unseelie, so I shouldn't have expected you to just fail at self-control. But I still kept hoping."

A long moment of silence passed.

He carefully slid his hand out from between my thighs, and wrapped it around my hip. The slickness on it made me feel hotter, but I ignored that.

"I am not a mind-reader, Iloli," he finally said, his voice low and his erection pressing into my thigh. "If I had known you felt that way, I would've acted on my desires long ago."

I nodded again. "I know. I just... I don't know. I guess I feel like I'm always pushing you, and I don't want to have to push you to like me. I've had to do that with every other guy I've ever been with—at least at the beginning. And they never treated me right. I'm just tired of it."

"You've never had to push me to like you," he countered.

"Don't you remember when I asked you to kiss me in the forest? You stared at me like I'd grown a second head."

"No. I stared at you like my fated mate had just asked me to kiss her, when I didn't know how to kiss, and as far as I knew, she was in love with another man."

I guess that was pretty fair, actually.

"What about the river, when I was naked? I put your hand on my tits, and you were shocked."

"All of this was new for me," he said, growling quietly at me. I was getting him a little worked up—which I loved. "And I have never been someone who takes unnecessary risks, Iloli. I wait until the time is right, with everything. But with you, there's no clear timeline. No directions to follow, no plans to be made. I pushed you too—don't you remember the way I wrapped you up in my scales, when your body was bare and shivering? Or when I convinced you to go with me to the glowing caves, or when I dragged you into the small river there?"

"I basically attacked you in that river," I pointed out.

He scoffed. "If that was an attack, then consider me at your mercy for the rest of our damn lives."

A snort escaped me, and his expression softened slightly. "Fine. Maybe we push *each other*. But you never tell me what you really want—so I think I push more."

"Then I will do better at expressing my desires clearly. Though in my defense, I think my cock declares my thoughts better than I can with words."

I laughed softly. "I guess you have a point."

He nodded, and brushed his lips over mine once, and then again. "You sincerely doubt my interest in your body?"

"Yes. No. I don't know. Not really, I guess." I shrugged. "I'm just kind of a mess."

"My mess." He stroked my hip possessively as he murmured, "Do you know what I was picturing, when you found me up here?"

More heat swelled inside me. "No."

"In my mind," he said, and then set my feet down on the ground. I released his erection as he turned me so my back was to his chest. His hands lifted mine to the tree's trunk, placing my palms flat on the smooth wood, above my head. "You were positioned like this." He lifted my hips easily, setting my core against the length of his cock and wrapping my legs around the backs of his thighs.

"Oh yeah?" I breathed, feeling his erection as it pressed against my slit. "What were you doing?"

"Fucking you, hard." His voice was in my ear. "And you were yelling, like you did in the cave. Screaming to the whole forest that you belonged to me." He moved his hips slowly, dragging his cock over my clit in a way that made me hotter—and drenched him.

"Prove it," I said, as he continued moving just enough to make me absolutely insane.

He chuckled, his hand sliding between my thighs to catch his cock and hold it there, making sure it was still moving against me.

Rubbing against me.

Bringing me back to that damn edge.

And suddenly, I accepted the fact I'd been avoiding for the last few weeks.

The fact that I wanted to be Remmo's. And that I wanted him to be mine.

Permanently.

"I want you inside me," I breathed to him.

"We need to talk before we become mates," he said, though his voice was gravelly again.

"About what?" I tossed back.

"Love."

"You said you would give me whatever I wanted. That you'd take whatever I had to offer. This is what I have to offer, Remmo. *Me*."

He growled at me when I slid a hand between my thighs, pushing his to the side and taking his cock.

"We're already mates," I told him. "You and I both know that, right?"

"Yes." The word was nearly a snarl as I pressed the head of him to my slit.

"I want you. We can figure all the other shit out later." I moved my hips in a slow circle. "Do you want this?"

"More than I want to breathe," the man's teeth caught on my throat, and I sucked in a breath as I lowered my hips, taking the head of him inside me.

Damn, that was a stretch.

He lifted my hand back to the tree, stepping closer until my tits and nose met the smooth wood.

"Slow," I warned him, as he gripped my hips and started to pull me closer. My breath came out in heavy pants as he moved me down, and down, and down, filling me in a way I'd never even imagined was possible.

"Wait," I moaned, my hips moving just a little as I adjusted to him. His chest rose and fell rapidly against my back, his hands moving from my tits, to my thighs, to my clit, like he couldn't decide which part of me to hold. "How's that?" I asked him, sucking in a shallow breath after the words had left me. "Good? I can't see your face."

"Incredible." His voice was strained, but his hands grabbed my hips again, and so, so slowly, he pulled me away from the tree. And inch by inch, turned me around on his cock, until my legs were wrapped around his waist and our eyes were locked.

His greens burned into my black and silvers, and I was still struggling to breathe.

"Tell me how you feel," he said, not a question but a command.

"So good," I whispered, moving my hips lightly. "So, so good. You're everywhere—filling me so damn well."

His eyes heated, lowering to the place our bodies connected.

He used his grip on my hips to slowly, so slowly, lift me up off of him a little. We watched together as his massive cock slid out of me inch by inch—and then as my body took him again, the skin hot and wet.

It was all overwhelming. *So* overwhelming. I could feel myself getting close to the edge—could feel my body starting to demand more.

"You are so damn pretty." His hand lowered to the place we were connected, and he dragged a thick index finger over the sensitive flesh he was stretching so much. "Especially when my cock is inside you."

A breathless laugh escaped me. "That makes me more attractive, huh?"

He chuckled, low and gravelly. "You have no idea." His finger dragged up to my clit, and he slowly, *lazily*, circled it.

My hips jerked, and I cried out.

"You can be louder than that, Iloli. I want this whole forest to hear you." He was still playing with my clit. The bastard wasn't moving his hips like I wanted him to—wasn't giving me the hard, fast sex he'd promised.

But this was so damn much better.

I was moaning and panting as I rocked on him, his spare hand helping my hips as they rolled, and circled, and moved. The sensation of fullness was unreal, and the way he touched me was overwhelming. It was too much—it was all too much.

My fingernails dug into his shoulders, cutting into his skin as I lost control of my body. It moved desperately, of its own accord. When the orgasm hit, my head tilted back as I cried out.

My shoulders hit the tree's trunk as I came down from the high, sucking in air. "Too much," I groaned to Remmo. "This is too much."

His finger left my clit, and he started to pull out. Even though he hadn't reached the edge, I knew he would walk away if I told him to—that he wouldn't touch me again if I didn't let him.

"In a good way," I panted, sinking back down on his cock. "Give me more."

His teeth grazed my throat as he started to move—thrusting, like I wanted, with his thumb still on my clit. He remembered what I'd said to him in the cave about how to get me off—and he wanted me to feel good.

His free hand dragged both of mine up above my head, pinning them there as he recaptured my lips with his own. Our mouths fought and danced, swollen skin on swollen skin, while our pleasure spiraled higher and hotter. He knew my body, and I knew his, and when we finally shattered together?

It was life-changing.

I felt the power roll through us and the forest, like Vevol herself was telling her world that we were mates. I'd felt it a tiny bit before, when the other couples did the deed, but that had been before Remmo trained me.

Now, I felt everything.

The mental bond settled between us, our thoughts and emotions connecting and heightening each other. He felt my excited dedication—and I felt his thick, hot joy as our foreheads met, both of us panting together.

Neither of us would ever be alone again.

There was still shit to figure out, but we *would* figure it out—because now, we were mates.

Permanently.

Undeniably.

In every way that there was.

His lips crashed into mine again as we remained in that tree, our bodies merged together, and I sure as hell kissed him back.

Fifteen

Remmo

I stared down at my Iloli, watching her bare chest rise and fall as she slept. She was nestled in my arms with her back against my chest, and was exhausted from both the training and the love-making. So after we had mated, I'd dragged her back to bed.

Of course, when she'd refused to sleep, I wore her out again. And again. Not with my fingers, this time, but with my cock.

And damn, I'd never get enough of watching her eyes dilate and hearing her cries as she shattered.

Or feeling her body clench around me as I lost myself inside her.

I wondered if I'd ever regain control of that particular part of my anatomy, as it strained against her ass, already rearing to go again.

It was unlikely, I decided.

And I didn't hate that idea at all.

But I did hate the fact that whatever she had experienced in her past had hurt her so badly that she didn't believe herself capable of love. Likely at the hands of Holden, the boyfriend who had nearly taken her life. Eventually, I would get the full story of that.

But even without the full story, if I could get through the portal between Earth and Vevol, I would've already enjoyed watching his soul leave his body.

Because I couldn't, I focused on my mate.

It was probably for the better, as much as I hated to admit it.

My Iloli was wrong about being unable to love. I'd seen the way she cared about Dakota—the way she claimed they were like sisters. There was love required for a bond like that.

And I'd felt her blooming love for me through our bond when it settled into place.

She didn't realize it yet, but she was just as in love with me as I was with her.

Soon, I would get her to share her past with me.

And then I would prove to her that I loved her—and wait patiently for the day that she realized she loved me too.

But for now, the fact that we were in bed together, without a shred of fabric separating our bodies while she slept peacefully in my arms, was more than enough.

Sixteen

Sunny

I WOKE up to Remmo's hand stroking my lower belly—and was immediately confident that he was doing so in an effort to stop himself from stroking me lower.

"You can wake me up for sex any time you want," I mumbled to him. "Waking up with your face between my thighs would be hot."

He gave me a rumbly chuckle as his fingers slid down to where we both wanted them. "Noted."

I let out a soft groan as he slowly dragged his finger around my clit, like he was a damned professional already.

Knowing him, he'd probably written out every sexual experience we'd shared so that he could analyze them and figure out how to maximize my pleasure.

His passion for understanding things was really damn attractive to me.

"Close your eyes," he murmured into my ear.

My first instinct would've been to argue, if he'd been anyone else.

But he wasn't anyone else.

He was Remmo, and I trusted him.

So I shut my eyes.

His hands were parting my thighs a moment later, and I moaned when the heat of his tongue found my clit.

The way he licked me was slow and luxurious, his hands holding me open and his thumbs dragging lightly over my inner thighs, making me squirm.

He'd opened his emotions to me somehow—I could feel his heavy desire, his thick pleasure, his hot enjoyment. Feeling him inside me like that was so damn intense, I didn't even have the words.

"How did you do that?" I asked him, and he understood exactly what I was referring to.

"I explored the bond while you were sleeping."

Why that made me even more turned on, I couldn't say.

"It has multiple faucets. The thought and emotion sharing are only the beginning. We'll keep experimenting with it."

I groaned at him as he slid a finger inside me, dragging it over my g-spot and making me see stars.

I was so damn close.

"It should not be hot when you talk about experimenting," I moaned aloud.

His low chuckle made me jerk my hips, and he dragged his teeth over my clit.

The sensation sent me over the edge, and I shattered with a loud cry.

"Wait, wait," I groaned, pushing at his face when he tried to keep licking me. "Give me a couple seconds."

I released his head, and he lowered his nose to my clit, resting it against the swollen flesh. "You smell incredible, Iloli. I didn't think your scent could get better, but it has."

"Thanks, I think." I sucked in massive gulps of air. "You're too good at that for someone who was a virgin up until last night."

He chuckled again. "You taught me how to please you. I only listened." He dragged his nose slowly against my clit, and I groaned.

His chest rumbled, and his tongue descended again, starting just as slow as it had the last time.

My breathing was rough, and my fingers dug into the sheets. He lifted them to his hair—and I buried them in the thick, soft waves, gripping tightly while he continued kissing my core, dragging his finger slowly over my g-spot at the same time.

It took longer to get there in round two, but shit, he got me there. My wail was louder when I went over the edge that time—and his heady satisfaction curled between us through the bond, making my mind spin.

He gave me another moment, resting his nose on my clit again. I could *feel* how much he liked my scent, and that was really damn hot for me.

"How do I share my emotions with you?" I asked him, as my heartbeat finally slowed a little. The fact that he seemed more than content to just sit there, giving me pleasure without taking any for himself, made me feel really damn loved.

"Find the bond, in your mind," he murmured against my clit. It would've made my hips jerk, if he hadn't just exhausted me so thoroughly.

I forced myself to look for it—to find that bridge between my mind and Remmo's. When I found it, it didn't feel like a bridge. It felt like... a pulse. Like our heartbeats had intertwined, connecting us so much more fiercely than I'd ever imagined.

"Good." His approval made my heart swell. "Feel how my end is open, and yours is closed."

It wasn't a question, but an instruction. He was the best teacher I'd ever had, in every damn way.

It took a few minutes, but I followed the bond. When I found his side, I understood what he meant about it being open. His steady confidence and pride flowed through, along with a few snippets of thoughts brushing past me.

They were soft, and wordless. Not so much as thoughts... more like things his mind was noticing subconsciously. I tuned in carefully, and the sensations he was feeling rolled through me.

The sweet, sexy smell of my pleasure.

The damp, soft slickness of my skin beneath his hands, against his face.

The hard, pulsing need in his cock.

The satisfied pleasure that accompanied him being able to make me shatter again, and again.

An image hit me, almost like a video from Earth—one of my body, from the spot Remmo occupied between my thighs. I was arching, my face twisted in pleasure, as I cried out while I lost control.

Slowly, I withdrew from his mind.

"Don't think I did that right," I whispered, though my body was now hot and needy all over again.

Shit, I wanted him.

"Try again." His thumbs stroked my inner thighs. "After you've done it, I'll reward you."

"With what? Chocolate?" I was a little breathless as I teased him, but he still met my small grin with his own gleaming eyes.

"Something better." He dragged his tongue over my clit, torturously slowly before repeating, "Try again, Iloli."

He wanted to feel my emotions, to slip into that stream in my mind.

And… maybe I wanted him to, too.

I nodded, closing my eyes and following the bond again.

This time, I found myself on my end of the connection. And where Remmo's had been wide open, there was some kind of invisible force field over mine.

I felt it there, though I couldn't press up against it or anything.

"The feelings will be intense when you first take it down," he murmured against my core. "I nearly lost control all over your backside."

A soft laugh escaped me. "You should've woken me up."

"You needed rest." He inhaled my scent slowly, and I felt wisps of his joy, and his pleasure.

"Then you should've just jerked off all over me. I wouldn't have minded."

His low growl and the wave of desire that rolled through the bond was enough to make me arch my back, gasping a little as he said, "The wall first, Iloli."

I focused on the damn wall.

There was no way to physically remove it, so I drew my attention to my emotions—to my desire, and the heat I felt, and the happiness soaking every damn inch of me—and I threw it all at the wall.

It shattered, and I cried out.

My back arched as my emotions collided with Remmo's in a thick wave, our thoughts merging.

He worked my clit with his tongue, dragging out the climax until I'd collapsed on the bed, moaning and moving my hips against the oversensitivity I was now feeling thanks to my mate.

"You're incredible," he growled against my core. My eyes were still closed, but our emotions warred—so damn much pleasure, and need, and satisfaction. It was all *so much.*

Remmo stood and dragged my ass off the edge of the bed. When he set his cock against my slit, a long, tortured groan escaped me.

His need and mine had woven together.

His thoughts and mine were moving as one, responding to each other.

Even the scents we were smelling and the sensations we were feeling were merging together, connecting.

His cock slid inside me, and my back arched again. His fingers were no longer on my clit—but I didn't need them. Not this time.

He'd been right about that, in the cave, I thought.

And that thought was washed away by the fierce, joyful pleasure coursing through both of us.

This was perfect.

This was everything.

We moved as one, and neither of us lasted long.

We lost control together, and as he filled me with his pleasure, I felt a release like the one I'd only had in the cave—and screamed.

And screamed.

And screamed.

It was unreal.

Insane.

So damn powerful, I could barely think, breathe, or function.

We were both wet when Remmo dragged me back into our bed, holding me close. The invisible shields in our minds were slowly, naturally, building themselves back up. But we didn't care. We knew how to take them down—and our bodies needed a break anyway.

"That was unreal," I whispered to Remmo. "Absolutely insane."

"It was incredible," he murmured back, pressing his lips to the top of my head while his hands moved calmly over my back and hip. "I wonder what else we can do."

A laugh escaped me. "Let's just enjoy this for now."

He chuckled, and the rumble of his chest against me made me smile. "Sorry. I wasn't trying to lessen it."

"I know you weren't." I closed my eyes, snuggling tighter against his chest. "I need to start eating the birth control fruit."

"The unseelie call them lilano." He continued stroking my skin. "I'll start eating them too."

"Good call. Since I'm a life-bringer and whatnot."

He chuckled. "I haven't quite figured out what Vevol intended when she created them. If the harsh can also bear children, then it's not that. Do you know what they were originally called? No one would give us any details."

I forced my mind back to the day I'd found the fae women on that island, with Dakota, Mare, and North. "Light. The protectors were harsh, and the life-bringers were light."

"A suitable title for you, then." He sounded thoughtful. "I think Vevol will reveal their true nature in time."

"Seems like she loves to be vague," I agreed.

He gave a murmur of agreement. "Are you ready to shower and train?"

I groaned. "Not more training."

He laughed. "You're the one who wanted to learn, Iloli. I offered to protect you instead."

"I know. Just let me grumble."

"Alright. Grumble away." He picked me up, crossing the room and opening the fridge a few inches from my bare body. I shivered as the cold air met my skin, but he closed it a moment later. He tucked the cold fruit between our chests and grinned playfully when I shuddered against him because of the cold.

"Bastard," I complained, though I was still snuggled against him.

"Insult me all you want, Summer. I'll still feed you fruit and wash your skin," he teased me, stepping into the shower and turning the water on. It was already hot when it rained down on us, and I groaned at the blissfulness of it.

He adjusted our position so he was holding me with just the one arm on my ass. With the other hand, he easily peeled the fuzzy, lumpy red skin off the birth control fruit—the lilano. I tilted my head back, and he fed me a piece of the fruit.

I bit down, and was surprised by the creamy sweetness of it. "Shit. North was right; it's basically ice cream."

"Is it?" He popped a piece into his mouth. "Most unseelie love lilano. They grow all throughout the forest in our land, as you probably noticed while we were traveling."

"I did," I agreed, taking another bite of the fruit when he put it to my lips. It had filmy dividers between segments, like an orange, but otherwise it was completely foreign. "The seelie told us they stopped eating them a long time ago, because the fruit changed the texture of their semen."

Remmo snorted. "Why did they care about that?"

I laughed. "I don't even know. If they were trying to have kids, it would matter. Considering that they were single for centuries, you wouldn't think it would even cross their minds."

"The seelie aren't very logical, but what many of them lack in critical thinking, they make up for in passion. Sometimes, I've envied the simpler way they live and see the world," Remmo admitted.

"Technically, you joined them," I pointed out to him. "You are seelie."

He made a noise of disagreement. "I only joined them to spite Aev and his council. They required one of the women to mate completely with her male, on the threat of starting a war, and Naomi went through with it. Forcing any female to mate with someone is not only cruel, but extremely far from the rules all of us followed."

"Then it sounds like Aev is going to get what he has coming for him when Fovea breaks Naomi's bond to him," I said.

"I suppose. He hasn't truly been himself since that female showed up, though. All of the blame doesn't belong on his shoulders." Remmo continued feeding me the fruit as we talked.

"How so?"

"From the beginning, he knew Naomi was his mate. And she despised him, loudly. Her whole world had just changed, which we all understood, so he gave her the space she requested. But that space only grew wider, and being forced to remain away from your fated mate is very difficult on a male fae. It goes against your nature, and feels like you're tearing off your own skin. He fought the bond for a very, very long time. Long enough that his personality seeped away, replaced by the desperation of ignored instincts."

I grimaced. "How did you do that for so long, then?"

His lips curved upward. "I didn't."

I blinked. "I thought you've known we were mates for a while."

"Since you moved to the new Stronghold," he agreed. "I saw your feelings for Teris, and respected them, even though it nearly killed me. That doesn't mean I stayed away from you."

I remembered something Mare had said, then.

About a basilisk in the trees, during Nev and Teris's fight for a mate.

She had thought she saw something a few times...

And Dakota had said the same thing, on a few different occasions.

I had chalked it up to all of the male fae being overprotective, but apparently, I was wrong.

"You followed me," I said.

"I protected you as well as I could, while your heart belonged to another." He put another piece of fruit in my mouth, and I chewed slowly.

"You're lucky I'm used to all this fae shit, or I'd think that was creepy instead of kinda sexy," I finally told him.

Remmo chuckled. "I'm lucky for many, many reasons Iloli." He tossed the fruit's peel toward the sink, and set me down on my feet. "Can I wash you?"

"Sure."

He handed me the second lilano while he grabbed the bar of soap, moving me out of the water long enough to start scrubbing my hair. "I'll get shampoo for you the next time we're back at the Stronghold, assuming you don't wish to stay and make a den there."

"You're too good to me," I groaned in response, relaxing against his body while his long, strong fingers massaged my scalp.

"I have to prove myself worthy of you somehow," he said, his voice playful.

But the words... they sounded honest.

I turned toward him, ignoring the soap in my hair and on his hands. Setting my palms on his face, I tugged him down toward me, until he was looking me almost straight in the eyes.

"If there was ever anything to prove, you proved it when you stayed in the trees because you thought I was in love with Teris. You chose what you thought was my happiness, over your own. And that's love, in its purest form. I've seen a shitload of broken, screwed-up love from people who didn't deserve a damn thing from me, and you are not one of them. When you looked at me, and you knew that I was your mate, and you stayed where you were because you thought I wanted Teris? That tells me everything about who you are, in here." I set my palm on the center of his chest.

The emotions in his eyes were thick, just like the ones in my throat.

When he finally dipped his head in the smallest nod, I released him, turning back around. He went back to massaging my scalp, his touch still gentle.

My hands trembled a little as I resumed peeling that damn lilano, though.

"If one of us needs to prove themself worthy, it's me," I mumbled, my eyes stinging a little.

I hated that I couldn't give him what he deserved—that I would always choose myself first. That I didn't know how to be what he needed, or how to love as fiercely as his mate should.

His lips brushed my ear a few minutes later. "If remaining in the trees when I thought you loved Teris proved my feelings for you... then what did you prove when you were willing to bond yourself to a man who had done nothing but hurt you, because you thought it would save my life?"

He straightened without waiting for my answer.

Which was a good thing, because I didn't have one.

My hands continued to tremble as I finished peeling the lilano and ate my half of the fruit while Remmo continued washing my hair.

And as hard as I tried to come up with a response to his question, I couldn't think of a single one.

Well, fine.

I could only think of one.

And it was the same damn thing I'd told Remmo:

It proved that I loved him.

But that was ridiculous.

Wasn't it?

Seventeen

If Remmo noticed that I was uncharacteristically quiet as we trained that day, he didn't mention it.

Honestly, the chances of him not noticing it were pretty slim. He was Remmo. He noticed everything.

There was a reason they called him *Vuvim*, after all. And from what I had gathered, they did so because he was a damn good spy when he wanted to be.

So he was being quiet to give me space.

Because he knew he'd dropped one hell of a bomb on me in the shower that morning, and that I'd need time to process it.

Because he knew *me*.

And that kind of scared me.

So, after we finished training that night and stepped back into the shower together, scrubbing our own bodies silently, I gave in to my basest fears. I blurted out, "Let's go back to the Stronghold."

Remmo looked at me, lifting an eyebrow. "Why?"

"It's been a while since I've seen Dots. Plus, I want to see how all the newbie humans are doing. And I want to know if Fovea is pregnant yet. And—" I cut myself off when he placed a hand on the center of my chest, directly over my heart.

"Don't lie to me, Iloli." His voice was gentle. "I scared you, earlier."

"You didn't *scare* me. Just... maybe overwhelmed me?" I bit my lip. "And those things aren't lies. I am curious. Dots—Dakota, dammit—was put on spy duty. She's spying on Aev, and I can see tall, dark, damaged, and silent totally being her type. She's probably crushing on him, and won't admit it to anyone but me."

I turned away from Remmo, closing my eyes and scrubbing my hair. There was so damn much sweat in the strands. "Plus, we should probably be there when Naomi breaks her bond to him, so we know if he loses control of the klynnas. You're probably the unseelie expert on fighting them, since you seem to be the expert on everything. And you know we need to see if I can actually swing a fist at someone other than you, because I know you won't let me hurt you, and I don't know that about them. Oh, and—"

I inhaled sharply when his hands landed on my hips, and then one of them slid down to my core.

He slowly traced a finger around my clit, and I found myself grabbing his arm, holding it like it was a damn anchor.

"Are you distracting me with sex?" I asked him.

He stepped forward once, so his erection met my backside, and then again, so I was pressed up against the shower's wall.

Not gonna lie, I was starting to really enjoy being sandwiched between two hard things like that.

"Yes." He nibbled on my earlobe, still stroking me, and I groaned.

"Cool."

His rough chuckle made my lips curl upward slightly. "If you need time to process, I will give you time. Space, too, if necessary. But don't lie to me, Iloli. Never." He pinched my clit, and I cried out.

Remmo eased up on the sensitive flesh, and his other hand wrapped around my thigh, lifting me up off the ground.

I felt his side of our bond open, and gasped as his emotions came flooding toward me—his concern, his possessiveness, his need, his love.

My eyes stung.

He lined the head of his cock up with my slit, and slowly slid home.

The stinging in my eyes grew fiercer as he filled me, his emotions still raging through me.

Concern, possessiveness, need, love.

Concern, possessiveness, need, love.

Concern, possessiveness, need...

Love.

One of my hands reached back, looking for his hair, and I felt the ripple of his carnal satisfaction through the bond as I buried my fingers in the strands, tugging and pulling on them like they were my damn anchor.

He started moving, our hips working together as he thrust in and out. His fingers left my clit, sliding up to wrap around my breasts as he pressed me harder into the wall.

We weren't fucking—we were making love.

And my damn eyes were still stinging.

His words were rough in my ear when he said, "You are my everything, Iloli. Our bond is still new, still forming. But you can be damn well sure that I won't let you walk away from me. You are my Summer—my light—my mate. And there is nothing you could do, think, or say to change that. Nothing."

I cried out when he pushed me over the edge, saying into my mind the one thing that he knew I needed to hear.

"I love you, Iloli."

And though I didn't say the words back, his hot satisfaction as we came down from the high told me that he might've felt the same thing I was feeling.

That he might've realized I was probably falling in love with him too...

If I wasn't already head over heels.

WE WASHED EACH OTHER QUIETLY, our bodies humming with the relaxation that had set in as we detangled from each other.

"Going back to the Stronghold is probably a good idea," Remmo murmured to me, as he helped me rinse shampoo out of my curls. "Not so you can get away from me—I *will* break down any walls you put between us, now—but for all of the reasons you gave. We need to make sure Aev isn't going to break when Naomi destroys their bond, and we need to be prepared in case he does.

Enough time has passed that I think you'll be able to throw a punch at someone other than me, too. And I know the perfect test subject."

I lifted an eyebrow at him over my shoulder. "Do I even want to know?"

He chuckled. "Probably not."

We finished washing, and I shut off the water. "You don't have a den we can stay in there, do you?"

"No," he admitted.

I shrugged. "No big deal. We can make one. It probably won't be as fancy as this, but we'll survive until we get everything figured out back there. Though, if you're going to be one of the generals again, we'll need to live there so we don't have to commute."

He flashed me a warning look. "I am not going to be a general again. I have no desire to be a part of their new council."

"I know you don't." I put my palms on his chest, stepping up closer to him. Neither of us had grabbed a towel yet, but we weren't in a hurry. "But that's probably why you'd be so good at it."

He shook his head, and cupped my face between his palms. "You are my priority. I haven't earned your trust enough to hear the stories of your past, or your whole name, so we definitely aren't at a point where I can consider taking on new responsibilities. And that is not my way of blaming you or guilt-tripping you; it's simply a fact. You come first."

"Was that a sex joke?" I whispered to him.

His lips curved upward slightly, and then he kissed me. When he pulled away, he said, "You know I love you?"

I bit my lip. "I know."

"Good." He kissed me again, and then released my face and stepped back, turning to grab our towels.

"We could do it together," I said, suddenly feeling kind of vulnerable. He handed me my towel, wrapping his around his waist. "Be on the council, I mean. If your council supports women and cares about our opinions, you would have a better chance of avoiding a repeat of the last council's mistakes. And now, there are a lot of women. Some of them will probably want to be unseelie. As sexy as the *wild seelie* thing is, there's a lot more security involved when there are rules being followed, and when rule-breakers have an authority figure to answer to."

He considered it, taking my towel and wrapping it around me because I wasn't moving fast enough. I rolled my eyes at him, and he flicked my nose lightly, making me snort.

"It's a good idea," he admitted. "Or it would be, if I was interested in joining the council. Which I am not. They would listen to you, though. You are Iloli; the very thing all of us were striving to become for so long. The men respect you."

My face twisted in a grimace. "They don't respect me. I was the pathetic girl who kept panting after one of the only straight men on the planet who wouldn't say yes to a woman asking him to mate with her."

He chuckled. "We've had this conversation before."

I scowled at him.

"Most of us were the pathetic men who kept panting after women who didn't want us too, Summer. You showed us that women struggle with the same feelings we do; that sure as hell earned you the respect of most of the men. Add your wicked sense of humor, these gorgeous mismatched eyes, and the fact that you wear the scent of Vuvim as your personal perfume?" His eyes gleamed as he stepped closer to me, his fingers wrapping around my backside, slipping beneath the towel and squeezing. "You will soon be my people's obsession. No one will dare mess with you."

"The council should be approachable, though," I pointed out.

He lifted an eyebrow at me. "Why?"

I blinked.

Honestly, I didn't have a good answer for that one.

"The council should be *fair*," he corrected. "Perhaps the next time they approach me, I'll suggest they ask my mate to fill my position."

"Don't do that," I warned.

"Why not?"

I scowled. "I don't know. Just... don't."

He chuckled, and kissed me. "Come to bed with me. I want to feel you wrapped around my cock again before we fall asleep."

I pushed at his face—and then dragged it back to me, and kissed it.

More sex?

Yes please.

I was one hundred percent convinced that it was the best distraction from my uncertainty and uncontrollable emotions.

We left early the next morning—me dressed in my tank top and shorts. Since I planned on fighting, I decided I didn't really want to risk flashing my vag at any random men or women in the female fae outfit.

Plus, I was pretty sure Remmo would end up beating someone's head in if I wore those tiny panties, and I'd rather avoid that outcome.

We stopped to eat a few lilanos on the way, and still made it before most of the fae were awake.

Dakota flew down from her perch in the trees as we arrived, throwing her arms around me for a huge hug and giving me a fierce grin as she looked between me and Remmo. She was back in her seelie tank top and shorts, with her long, straight hair blowing in the wind. "Decided to make things official, huh?"

"She finally talked me into it," Remmo drawled, wrapping an arm around my waist and tugging me to his chest.

Me and Dakota both laughed.

The grin she gave me was so damn genuine that it made my throat swell. "I'm sure."

"So has Naomi broken the bond yet?" I asked her, as we all started walking further into the forest.

"Nope. It'll break during the full moon, so we still have a few weeks. Aev agreed to step down as king a few days ago, and the unseelies are pestering the generals to become the new council. They're waiting for you two, though."

Remmo grimaced, but I nodded.

After we'd talked to his friend in the forest, I figured that would be the case.

"How's North doing, after losing all those brands?"

"Mare visited her last week and said that she and Priel are doing great. She's relieved to have the brands removed so she doesn't have to lead, but she's having a harder time focusing her future-sight now," Dakota explained. "They're staying in his cave for a while, but will come out if we need them. The chaos here doesn't really suit them, so they're happier there."

I nodded. That, I could definitely see.

Unlike them, I liked the chaos, though.

Dakota did too, even if she wouldn't admit it.

"I can ask a few of the fae to help you make a house here, if you're going to stay?" She flashed me a hopeful smile.

"We're going to stay," I agreed. "But I think we can handle it. The power will feel a little different if we let someone else build it." I glanced at Remmo, to make sure we were on the same page, and he nodded.

Was it just me, or was there a little pride in his eyes?

"Awesome." Dakota grinned at me.

"I'm going to find you someone to fight with," Remmo told me, leaning in and kissing my forehead. "I'll be back for you soon."

He was giving me privacy to talk to Dakota—which I appreciated tremendously, mostly because I knew he was possessive enough that he'd have a hard time walking away from me.

But he respected my need for space, and that meant a lot to me.

"You're learning to fight?" Dakota asked me, surprise lacing her voice.

"Yeah. It was rough at first—the memories." I shivered, and she shuddered. "But we're pushing past it. I still suck, but I suck a little less. Remmo thinks I'll be able to throw a punch at someone other than him now. I don't know if he's right, but it's worth a try. I don't want to be useless if the klynnas get out."

"I don't either," Dakota admitted. "Aev and I have sort of become friends. I'm hoping if I'm with him when the bond breaks, maybe he'll be able to stop himself from releasing them."

I nodded. "I hope you're right. How are the new humans adjusting?"

"Better than the rest of us did. I think having the female fae around and never having to run for their lives from the fae men during the Wild Hunt's charade made the adjustment easier for them. Most of them still refuse to try shifting, but that's their call anyway."

"I don't blame them. That shit was scary when we first got here." Changing the subject as we continued to walk, I said, "Remmo wants me to take his place on the unseelie council. He won't join the other generals—he wants me to be his priority, because I still haven't given him my name or the details about my past."

Dakota grimaced. "Would he join them if you told him?"

"I doubt it. He's really not interested—and he thinks I'd be better for the job." I rolled my eyes at her, but she shrugged.

"I actually think you'd be good at it too."

I shot her an incredulous look. "What are you talking about?"

She gestured toward a group of male fae, who were cooking something up at the kitchen. Two of the unseelie chicks were with them, not flirting but just talking. "Who are they?"

I rattled off the men's names, followed by the women's.

She pointed to the left, where a group of fae men were participating in some kind of rowdy wrestling competition. The fact that Dakota hadn't turned and ran in the other direction from the fighting was a huge sign of growth for her, but she didn't acknowledge it. "Who are they?"

"I don't see why knowing their names has anything to do with leading," I countered.

She gave me a pointed look.

I heaved a sigh, and told her all of their names.

"You know the fae. You like them. More than any of the other women here, I would say. And they all know you, because of the thing with Teris and now the thing with Remmo. They like you."

"That's what Remmo said, but I still don't think they can respect me for chasing Teris," I argued.

Dakota laughed. "The male fae *wish* they had an opportunity to chase a woman the way you chased Teris. They understand how much it sucks to get rejected. I think they like you more for it."

"He said that too," I replied glumly. "You think I should do it?"

"I think you should do whatever makes you happy," she said simply. "You would be a good council-member, but that doesn't mean you're obligated to do it. You could just hear them out, and see if you think you'd enjoy it. If Remmo's not going to do it, you're probably the second-best thing in their eyes."

"I guess that's reasonable," I admitted. "Even if it stings a little to be second choice."

She grinned. "Remmo would probably know, huh?"

My face heated. "I should apologize to him for that."

"You didn't know he existed, so it's not your fault. Don't apologize for things outside of your control." She waved me toward her. "Come on, Aev's tent is up here. I've got to check in with him."

My eyebrows lifted, but I followed her.

This was an all-new Dakota... and I didn't hate it.

Not at all.

Eighteen

"Aev," Dakota called into the trees. "Come down and meet Summer!"

An annoyed growl came from the branches over our heads, and my eyes widened when a monstrous sabertooth came prowling down one of the thick branches. The branch dipped lower with his weight, but he didn't even seem to notice. In their beast forms, the sabertooth bastards looked like monster-sized tigers, stripes and all, with huge-ass tusks.

"He hasn't been spending much time in his man form since he got the news about the bond breaking," Dakota explained to me, gesturing for him to come down again. He growled at her, but it wasn't an angry growl. More like an annoyed one.

He smoothly jumped down from the branch, landing lightly.

"This is my best friend, Summer," Dakota told the king.

Or ex-king, I supposed, since she said he had stepped down when the unseelies basically commanded him to.

"Hi." I waved.

He sniffed the air, and his expression grew surprised.

"She's mated to Vuvim," Dakota explained.

He looked at me with new eyes, and dipped his head toward me in what looked kind of like...

Respect.

Dammit, Remmo was right about that. Did he always have to be right?

Aev stepped closer to Dakota, and she scratched his head lightly.

My eyebrows shot into my forehead, but I didn't say anything. Not a damn peep. Mostly because I didn't even know what to say or think.

I didn't know Aev, but...

Naomi and him hated each other. And they were *mated.*

Granted, they were about to get magically separated. But still.

It was just different.

Then again, so were me and Remmo. I had been partially mated to Teris when we paired up.

And I knew that Aev and Naomi had never wanted each other or loved each other. It sounded like they had basically been in an arranged marriage that made both of them miserable.

"Have any of the new human girls paired up with the fae?" I asked Dakota, changing the subject. She was still scratching Aev's furry head, almost absent-mindedly.

"Nope. Mare and the female fae are making sure they understand that the fae don't do casual—and that having sex with one is permanent. I think seeing Naomi and Fovea working together to break a bond has probably sobered them up to that fact. And January's baby bump probably helped."

Aev gave an unhappy rumble, and Dakota scratched his ears a little more enthusiastically. He leaned into her touch.

I tried not to eye them suspiciously.

I really, really did.

But definitely failed.

She noticed, and laughed. "Don't panic, we're just friends. Neither of us is planning on taking a mate after the Naomi thing blows over. Too much stress."

I wasn't convinced, but wasn't about to say that aloud. Luckily, Dakota changed the subject, asking me how Remmo was training me. I explained the method to her—how we'd started, and how the shitty panic attacks had gone, but how I'd moved past them thanks to Remmo.

"Damn. That sounds awful," she admitted.

I laughed. "It was. But I feel better, having all that shit off my shoulders."

"I get that."

Remmo took that moment to step out of the trees—and I grinned at him until he lifted his hands in surrender. "Don't be mad," he said.

I was ninety-nine percent sure that every time someone said that, it meant they were about to say something that would definitely make you mad.

"What am I not supposed to be mad about?"

"The person you're going to throw a punch at is Teris."

"Teris?! I'm going to kill you," I muttered to Remmo, as he stepped up to me and buried his nose in one of my puffs for a minute. "If you mess up my hair, I will double-kill you."

He chuckled. "Hear me out, Iloli."

I shot him an extremely un-thrilled look, but waited.

"Teris is the safest person for you to try throwing a punch at, other than me," he explained. "With me, you feel safe enough to do it. With him, you're still angry. Punching him will feel like self-defense."

"I'm *not* angry with him anymore, but that would actually trigger me *more*," I argued. "Do you know how many times I would've defended myself, if I knew how to fight? How different my life would've been?"

"No." Remmo's voice was steady, and his expression soft. "I don't. But I do know that we've worked through those triggers, and will continue to do so until they no longer exist."

"That's never going to happen."

He flashed me a wicked smile. "Then I suppose you'll have to snuggle naked with me every day for the rest of our extremely long lives while you calm down from the panic. What a *hardship*."

I snorted, even though I was trying to be angry.

Dakota laughed. "He *does* have your same sense of humor."

"Yeah, yeah. We're perfect together and whatnot," I grumbled, stepping away from him and looking at Teris. "Alright, where are we doing this?"

"Not in front of me," Dakota said helpfully.

"No. I have an audience of unseelie gathering. The other generals will be there in case I lose control," Remmo said.

I flashed him a frown. "Why would you lose control?"

"Because you're going to be throwing punches at *Teris*," Dakota pointed out. "His protective instincts will be hard to ignore."

Oh.

Right.

I should've known that.

As far as Remmo was concerned, Teris had already hurt me a lot, over a long period of time. Not physically, but emotional pain sucked a lot too.

And given that he felt like I was his to protect, it would be difficult for him to fight those instincts if he saw me facing off against Teris.

"Alright, fine," I said with a sigh. "You'll owe me, though."

"I'll pay in orgasms, tonight," the basilisk murmured into my mind, flashing me a wicked grin.

I couldn't help but mirror the expression.

"I feel like he just told you something dirty through your bond," Dakota said, tapping her temple.

"I'll admit to nothing," Remmo said smoothly, as he slid his hand down to my lower back and began leading me away.

"They call him the ghost for a reason," I called back to Dots.

She just laughed and called out, "I'm happy for you!"

I waved over my shoulder at her, but honestly...

I was happy for me too.

MY HAPPINESS for myself vanished when Remmo walked me right into the middle of a massive group of fae.

"Why are you doing this to me?" I groaned into his mind.

He chuckled silently. *"You wanted me to train you, and I'm not doing it half-assedly. If you want me to let you walk into a fight where actual injuries are being dealt, you have to face your demons."*

"Teris isn't a demon. Just a dick."

"Better to start with dicks than demons."

I sighed heavily. *"You and I are not friends anymore."*

"I'll change your mind later," he said, and when I looked up at him, the bastard winked at me.

We stopped at the inner-edge of the group, just before a wide, empty circle in the center of the gathered men who were all talking and growling excitedly. There was practically energy coming off of them.

Hopefully they were excited to watch me punch Teris, not to see me get my ass handed to me.

And not to see Remmo rip Teris's head off.

I shuddered at the thought.

"No heads are getting ripped off. See the men over there?" He gestured toward the guys just behind us, and I recognized Korrik. He was one of the generals, so the others next to him had to be generals too. *"They'll make sure I don't kill Teris unless he physically hurts you."*

"So he's not allowed to punch back?" I asked.

"No. He'll just take your punches, so you know what it feels like when your fist collides with skin."

"Probably a good call," I said glumly.

Remmo's hand landed on my side, and he turned me toward him. My chest met his as he tilted my head back and kissed me, hot and deep.

He caught me off guard with it—but I sure as hell kissed him back. Cheering erupted in the crowd around us, and it occurred to me that we were the first successful unseelie couple.

There were three seelie ones... but the seelies were wild. They were messy.

Seeing one of their generals in love with his mate, kissing his woman, had to be a confidence boost for the faction of fae that had been falling apart.

Hopefully it would be enough to hold the remaining unseelies together until they had a new council.

When he released me a few minutes later, his eyes were gleaming. *"If that bastard tries to talk to you or touch you, you remind him who you belong to."*

"I will." I bit my lip to hide a smile.

Okay, the possessiveness... it was really hot.

Really, really hot.

He squeezed my ass, earning more hoots and hollers from the fae around us before I stepped forward.

My stomach clenched as I balled my fists, trying to get myself ready.

This was going to be rough, but I'd survive it. The worst thing that could happen was a panic attack or a full-on mental-shutdown, but Remmo knew what to do in those cases.

He'd have my back, and he'd get me out of there if he needed to.

Everything was going to be fine.

I reminded myself of that as I stepped up to Teris, fists still clenched the way Remmo had taught me.

"This is just to get you ready for more fighting," Teris told me gruffly. "Don't pull your punches. Your tiny fists aren't going to hurt me."

I wanted to glower at him.

To tell him that I hated him.

But... I didn't hate him.

Honestly, I didn't feel much of anything for him anymore.

He was in the past. And my future? Well, it was filled with the gorgeous green eyes of the basilisk that I loved.

That thought hit me hard in the chest.

I loved him.

I *loved* Remmo.

I hadn't thought it was possible... but he was my best friend, and as surprising as it was, I was in love with him.

Because I wanted to tell him, and because I wasn't the kind of person who held that shit in and waited for a perfect moment, I turned and ran back to Remmo, throwing myself into his arms. He lifted me off the ground, hugging me tightly.

"You okay?" he murmured aloud.

"I'm in love with you," I breathed back. "I love you, Remmo."

He chuckled, and squeezed me tighter. "I know you do, Iloli. Now get your sexy little ass out there and face your dick."

I snorted.

He squeezed my butt in response, and released me with a grin.

The fae around us were cheering again—louder.

They'd probably all heard every word of our conversation, but I didn't care.

And I was grinning as I walked back to Teris, with my head held high.

"Ready?" I asked him.

"Yup." He only looked slightly annoyed by my conversation with Remmo—so obviously, I had made the right decision. If I kissed Teris in front of Remmo, he'd lose his shit.

I stopped a short distance in front of the sabertooth, and widened my stance like my man had taught me. My fists formed the correct position, and with one smooth motion, I punched Teris.

Not hard—I really wasn't great at hitting hard—and right in the abs.

He didn't even flinch.

But excitement coursed through me anyway.

Because I hadn't shut down.

I hadn't panicked.

I looked over my shoulder at Remmo, and found him grinning and giving me a thumbs-up.

So I punched Teris again, a little harder.

And a third time, even harder.

When he still didn't flinch, barely even bothered by the hits, it encouraged me. I kept going, kept punching him, showing myself that I could do this. That I could fight, without losing my mind or losing my shit.

That I wasn't broken at all.

When I finally stepped back, practically beaming at my ex—well, not at him, but just beaming in general—I offered him a hand.

He eyed my hand, not sure what to do with it.

"Humans usually shake hands after fights," I said.

It was honestly just a theory, but I was going with it. It wasn't like Teris knew any better.

He awkwardly took my hand and shook it harder than he needed to. I released him with a simple, "Thank you."

He grunted in agreement, and then turned and started to walk away. After a few steps, he paused.

And then slowly turned back around and covered the distance between us. His hands slipped into the pockets of the strange ripped pants he always wore. "For what it's worth, I'm sorry," he said. "And I hope he makes you happy."

His voice sounded honest, and I knew he wasn't one for lying or wasting words.

"He does," I said honestly. "And I'm sorry too. I should've walked away a long time ago."

He dipped his head in the smallest nod, and then turned and strode through the crowd.

Remmo was hauling me up into his arms and tossing me into the air a moment later. Laughter cut through me as whoops rippled around us. Every unseelie I saw was grinning, and many of them were cheering—cheering for me because I'd faced my demons.

Or dick, I supposed.

My eyes stung anyway. "You're going to make me cry," I told him, grinning despite the way they were watering.

"Happy tears are allowed, Iloli," Remmo said with a smile. "And now, we're going to go scrub your hand until it doesn't stink any longer."

A laugh escaped me, and similar sounds rolled through the fae around us.

It hadn't occurred to me before, what us being together would mean for the unseelies. All they'd ever had was unhappy couples, so we were the first for them.

Hopefully, the first of many.

Remmo set me down, taking my hand and lacing his fingers through mine.

"Brothers," he called to the group. "This is my mate." His voice was proud, and it hit me then, what the unseelie offered each other.

Not just rules to follow, and a goal to pursue... but a united brotherhood.

A *family*.

The seelie were connected through their wildness, but there were dozens and dozens of small groups among them, like the Wild Hunt.

The unseelie were *united*. They supported each other in their efforts to improve, and had each other's backs in a way the seelie just didn't.

Neither way of living was wrong... but I was starting to find myself really damn in favor of the unseelie one.

Our shoulders were slapped—lightly, in my case—and congratulations rang from every damn set of lips as we made our way out.

And then to the nearest river, so Remmo could scrub everyone's scent off my skin but his.

Nineteen

We spent an hour in the river, playing around the way we had in the glowing cave. And kissing; there was plenty of kissing.

When we finally emerged with swollen lips and massive grins, we found the other four generals waiting in the forest.

Wanting an answer.

Remmo draped an arm over my shoulders, dragging me closer to his chest. "You're bringing me the same request I've already turned down half a dozen times, aren't you?" he drawled to the other generals, though he was grinning a bit.

"We are," one of the men admitted. "Aev officially stepped down already. Have you reconsidered? We won't lead without you, particularly now that you're the only one of us with a mate." He gestured toward me.

I saw Remmo's eyes gleam, the way they did when he was planning some nefarious shit. *"Don't even think about it,"* I warned him mentally.

He flashed me a vicious grin. "I have too much to teach my female about our world to consider joining the council. But I do have an alternate proposal for you."

I bit back a sigh.

The generals waited.

Remmo nodded his head toward me. "The unseelies like my Iloli. They respect her. She has a unique perspective that no others in our faction can offer—and if she becomes a leader, some of the new females she's befriended will probably follow her to our group. She probably also knows most of our men's names already."

"I *don't* know most of their names already," I corrected him. "The unseelies keep to themselves more than the seelies do. Or I guess, most of them just don't mingle with the seelies." I did know the names of most of them who had defected before I took off with Remmo, though.

And a lot of them had defected.

So maybe I *did* know most of their names.

I wasn't going to say that aloud, though.

"You *do* know most of the seelie's names," one of the generals said thoughtfully. "They all like you. Having a fae on the council who the seelies actually like would be useful."

He actually looked like he was considering Remmo's suggestion.

"We'll think about it," Korrik grunted. "And see how the others feel."

"When you come to the same conclusion I have, let us know. I'll try to convince her that you're worth it." Remmo winked at the men, before steering me away from them and further into the forest. The snow was a little deeper there—it was icy against my toes, but between my heat and Remmo's, it wasn't a huge deal.

"You're never going to convince me," I warned him, after we were far enough away that they wouldn't hear us.

He chuckled. "I already have, Iloli. You won't be able to turn them down when they ask." His hand stroked my bicep, his arm still draped over my shoulders. The sun was low in the sky already, I realized—and we still needed to work on our house.

"Time to pick a tree?" I asked him, scoping out the forest above us.

"Unless you wish to build near Dakota." His words were simple, like he didn't care either way.

And honestly, I knew he would be happy anywhere.

But… dammit, he was right. He'd already convinced me why I should side with the unseelies.

"We'll build here, on the unseelie side. I know there's some of everything in the middle of the neutral territory, but on this part of the outskirts, it's just unseelie, right?"

"And one seelie bastard who lives to make our lives hell," Remmo admitted.

"Then it's perfect," I said simply.

He lowered toward me, and kissed me. "It'll take us a few hours to build a place large enough to sleep in, so pick your tree."

I peered up at the branches above us and pointed to one at random. "How about that one?"

Remmo hesitated.

I lifted an eyebrow at him.

"The trees in that direction will have better sunlight, at better hours," he explained, pointing in the opposite direction from my tree.

I snorted. "I don't give a damn where we live, Rem. You pick for us."

The grin he gave me was really damn heart-stopping—and so was the kiss that followed it.

We shifted, and he led me around the trees until he picked one that was suitable. When he'd decided, we both shifted back. I sat straddling the branch, and he did too, with his back pressed against mine.

"Do you want to choose how it looks?" he asked me.

"Nope."

He flashed me another grin. "Thank you."

"Any time." I winked at him, and he reached over to squeeze my boob before he grabbed the tree again.

"Follow my magic with yours," he told me, not bothering with instructions as to how. I already knew how, because he had already taught me.

I closed my eyes, and when I felt him tap into his magic, I did the same. Inhaling sharply, I breathed, "Do you feel that?"

"We're much stronger, now that our bond has formed," he admitted.

"Much, much stronger."

"Mmhm. Focus, Iloli."

I laughed, and he reached back and squeezed my boob again before *he* focused.

We both quieted, our whole attention moving to the magic flowing through us and into the house Remmo intended to build.

And slowly, as the sun sank behind the mountains and trees, bathing the sky in darkness, our home grew around the branch we were sitting on.

When the magic stopped and I opened my eyes, we had a simple cube-shaped house, with a small box for a door. It would take a lot longer to turn it into everything we wanted... but we had all the time in the world.

"Come to bed with me, Iloli?" Remmo asked me, slipping off the branch that cut through the middle of our house and landing smoothly on the wooden floor seven feet below it. It didn't struggle to hold his weight, or move in the slightest—so I took his hand when he offered it to me.

I landed lightly in his arms, and flashed him a tired grin. He returned it, and I just...

Loved him.

And wanted him.

My shoulders met the stone wall of the house a moment later, my feet finding the floor, and then I was sliding downward before Remmo could stop me.

"I haven't taught you everything about sex yet, you know," I told him, as I tugged his shorts down his thighs. Those gorgeous green eyes of his were hot when I looked up at him.

"Haven't you?"

"Not this." My fingers wrapped around the base of his cock, and my lips wrapped around the head.

A low, savage groan escaped him as I licked the underside of him, surprising myself with the taste that flooded my mouth. He actually tasted... kinda good. Not chocolate-level good, but nowhere near the weird-ass flavor of the Earth guys I'd been with.

One of his palms met the wall, and he buried the other one in my hair. With everyone else, I was fiercely protective of my curls. But he manhandled them all he wanted, and it had yet to bother me in the slightest.

"Shit," he said through clenched teeth, digging his fingers deeper into my hair.

"Good?" I asked around his cock, looking up at him as I bobbed my head, taking him deeper into my throat.

"Too good." The words were gritted out, and I could tell he was fighting to stop himself from taking over the situation. My man was as loving as it got—but damn, he liked to take control when things got hot. And I was totally, completely here for it.

I continued bobbing, and sucking, and working the base of him until he was growling at me, dragging my mouth off his erection and lifting me into his arms. My back hit the wall as his cock found my entrance, and then he was surging into me, stretching me and filling me.

I sucked in a breath at the tight fit, at the intense fullness.

Shit, it was *so* good.

His fingers were on my ass, spreading me wider—and I arched when one of them found my back entrance.

"Oh damn," I groaned. "That's unexplored territory. You sure you want to go there?"

He chuckled, rumbling against my chest. "We're one now, Iloli. For better or worse."

"I like the sound of that," I managed, as he began to rhythmically move his hips.

And to slowly fill my back entrance with his finger.

My breathing grew ragged, my body tight and tense as he explored a part of me I'd never let anyone touch.

And holy hell, it was intense.

So, so intense.

It didn't take long to get me there—and then I was screaming to the forest, screaming my pleasure as Remmo dragged me over the edge.

Reminding me why we were perfect for each other, why we were mates.

And why I loved him.

"You're so good to me," I panted, coming down from the high.

He'd lost control too, though his eyes were still gleaming in that wicked way that told me he wasn't done with me yet.

And shit, I *loved* that look in them.

"Never thought I'd find a guy as horny as me," I admitted, as he lowered us to the ground together. He was still buried inside me—though he'd removed his finger from my back entrance, and was now drawing shapes on my bare back and ass with his hand.

If I had to guess, he was probably drawing out his plans for the new house. Or den, I supposed.

He chuckled in response. "You never thought you'd find a fae, either."

My lips curved upward. "That's true. I'm glad I did, though. Really, really glad. And I'm glad that out of all the men in this forest, it was you."

"As am I, Iloli."

Our voices had gotten softer, and as much as I didn't want them to, my thoughts had turned inward.

And they'd slipped right into my life on Earth.

Remmo hadn't asked me for details about it. He wasn't self-conscious about not knowing them, either.

But... I wanted him to have them. To understand me. To know that I felt just as strongly about him as he did about me.

"My name is Summer," I told him softly, barely audibly at all.

"Hello, Summer. You're the most beautiful woman I've ever seen," Remmo murmured back. His fingers still moved on my spine, though if he'd been drawing plans for the house, he seemed to have given up on them. "That's what I intended to tell you, the first time we spoke. I had it planned out. 'Hello, Sunny,' I would've said. 'You're the most beautiful woman I've ever seen, and I think you may be my mate'. It would've been smooth, don't you think?"

I laughed softly. "It would've been perfect. You already *knew* we were mates, though, didn't you?"

"Of course. I figured a softer start would probably have a better chance of success, though."

Another laugh escaped me. "Probably a good call."

He murmured his agreement. "But then I saw how you felt about Teris, and I thought, what chance did I have? None of the women favored the unseelies. You were too wild, and too beautiful, to ever consider a man your people called Tame."

"You're not the Tame King," I countered.

"Perhaps not. But isn't that what you thought of all of us?"

I considered his words. "I guess it was."

"It's in the past now, though." His words were soft, and his voice calm. "Thank Vevol."

"Would you have come out of the trees and talked to me that day, if I hadn't smelled you?" I asked him, growing more curious.

"Probably not," he admitted.

My throat swelled. "Then I'm really damn glad you smell so good."

"Me too." His lips brushed the top of my head once, and then again.

And though my thoughts were on my Earth life, and he could probably feel some semblance of the war going on within me, he said nothing.

Just gave me the silence and peace that I needed.

"Remmo," I finally said, my eyes stinging a little. "Can I tell you about my past?"

My voice wobbled a bit.

His hand stopped moving on my back. "Of course, Iloli."

"It's dark," I warned him quietly. "You'll probably want to hit something."

"Then I'll go find Teris, after you've said all you're willing to." His voice was light, but serious too.

And I couldn't help it—I laughed softly. A few tears dripped onto his chest, and he resumed stroking my back slowly.

"My home was never a happy place, or a safe one," I whispered, beginning the story of a broken girl, from a broken home, who made choices that only led her into a more broken life.

But when that story ended, a magical one started—one of fae who were kind and gentle, despite their beastliness. And one of a family I chose, who chose me back.

That story didn't end—not even when the next one began.

The love story that I would repeat for anyone who would listen... and for the children that Remmo and I eventually decided to have.

They would never grow up in a broken home like mine.

They would know what it was to be loved by so many people.

The same way I did, after coming to Vevol.

TWENTY

REMMO

MY ILOLI WAS right about me needing to hit something after hearing her story. My brothers needed the practice anyway, though.

She watched on, anxiously at first, but she pushed through the stress until she could watch with a different set of eyes.

A warrior's eyes.

And afterward, not only was she more confident in my ability to protect herself, but she was asking me questions about the moves. Asking me to teach her more. To continue training her.

I'd never agreed to anything as rapidly as I did that.

Because whether she knew it or not, Summer was already a warrior. She had been for a long, long time. And whatever our future held, it would be nothing like her past.

I'd fill our house with love—and cake—and anything else I could possibly think of to prove to her, day after day, that I loved her. That I'd care for her.

That I was hers, and she was mine.

"You're thinking too hard," she teased me, as we walked toward the river so I could scrub the blood from my skin. Though her voice was playful, there was still vulnerability in her eyes. She worried that I saw her differently now that I knew what she'd survived.

And I did; but not in the way she thought.

Now, I understood her strength more than I ever could've before.

"Part of me is," I agreed, dragging our intertwined hands to my erection and pressing the back of her hand against it.

She laughed, and the way her happiness lit up her eyes filled me with pride.

I was so damn proud of her. Proud of her for surviving the hell she had been through, and for remaining strong in the face of all of it.

Had I known all that she'd lived through, I would never have pushed her to continue trying in those moments of panic during the time we'd spent training in our den. But despite my yearning to protect her, I was still proud of her. Maybe even more-so because of the way she'd pushed through it all, and come out stronger.

"Bet I can fix that," she said playfully.

"Think so?" I dragged her into my arms, then jumped into the river. She spat out water and was laughing hard when we surfaced.

"Bastard," she teased me, as I held her in my arms and grinned at her.

My mate.

My Iloli.

My everything.

I kissed her, to make sure she knew that she meant the world to me.

And when she pulled her shorts to the side, making room for my cock, I slid inside her until I was buried right where I belonged.

She needed the reassurance that I still found her as fun and sexy as I had before... and I just needed *her*.

So we made love in the river and then on the riverbed, after we accidentally went under too long, and came up sputtering for breath, our bodies still connected.

And then back in our treehouse, the den we had created together.

She had survived hell—and I would make sure her life in Vevol was as close to heaven as any fae or human could get.

Bonus Scene

Join my email list to read a bonus scene about Sunny and Remmo's trip to his old den! It's NOT necessary to the story at all, just a fun little extra for newsletter subscribers.

BONUS SCENE

You'll receive updates on book releases as well as any upcoming deals and promotions. No spam!

If you'd like to subscribe to text notifications about new releases, text the word BOOKS to the number (855) 293-3564

The Barbaric Fae's Soul

Wild Hunt 5

To the books and people that don’t make your heart ache.

One

Dakota

I FORCED my breathing to remain steady and my thoughts to remain bright as I approached the massive tent that I knew Aev occupied. Once at the center of the other fae, it had been moved back further and further as more men abandoned the unseelie side of the neutral territory that all of the fae in Vevol resided in.

Now, most of them had returned.

And yet the tent was still far from the nearest unseelie.

In it, was the man who'd once called himself their king.

His people had abandoned him for something outside his control. Now that his mate was about to destroy the bond between them by changing her name, and therefore her identity altogether, he was going to be hurting.

No one knew if he'd be able to hold together the prison he'd created with the ice magic only he possessed... but there was nothing anyone could do to help him with it.

Which was why I was there.

No one knew that I was. Not even Sunny—dammit, *Summer*. Remembering our real names was difficult after so many years of nicknames.

But anyway, I knew what it felt like to have your mate bond snapped. Mine hadn't been complete, but the pain of it breaking had been excruciating.

Aev and I had become friends of a sort, in the time I'd been assigned to spy on him. The seelie fae were wild enough that they usually didn't bother with assignments, but I'd asked for something to do. Something to make me feel helpful.

And when I found the ex-king spending almost all of his time in his beast form, in an effort to fight the pain of the mating bond he was attempting to ignore, I ached for him. And befriended him.

The thought of what Aev would soon be feeling made my eyes sting.

And the threat of those monsters his magic held back, potentially being unleashed on our land, was enough to make me shiver.

My breathing stayed even as I walked right into the tent without knocking. I halted in the doorway, stopping in my tracks as my lips parted and my face grew so hot it might as well have been on fire. The thick flap of fabric that worked as a door met my back silently, but I didn't budge.

Aev was in his man form, for the first time in weeks.

And he was on his knees, with one hand braced against a large wooden chest. His pants were around his knees, the curve of his ass on perfect display—and his hand was wrapped around his cock.

Stroking it.

My open lips rounded, my eyes widening.

I should've been triggered.

I should've turned and ran the other way.

But all I could think, as I watched the man touch himself, was *he's stunning*.

There was something just... elegant about him.

I'd only seen him in person a few times before, and he was always the same. Big, and silent, and gorgeous.

Some part of me—some stupid, ridiculous part of me that must've completely forgotten about the hell I'd been through at the hands of nearly every man I'd ever been involved with—wanted to help him.

It wanted me to sink to my knees beside him.

To wrap my own fingers around his length and show him pleasure like he'd never experienced it.

But I didn't.

And I wouldn't.

His breathing picked up, as he continued stroking himself.

This was a horrible violation of his privacy. I needed to leave—I *knew* I needed to leave.

But I couldn't make my feet move.

His fingers dug into the wooden chest, his strokes growing rougher, and heat flared in my lower belly.

He was about to lose it.

My toes curled into the soft carpet beneath them, and desire swelled inside me.

I hadn't been attracted to someone like this in so many years, if *ever*.

I moved my foot slightly, parting my legs just the tiniest bit, and Aev's head jerked toward me.

His hand stilled as our eyes collided. My soft browns, and his vibrant blues.

There was a moment of tense, heavy silence.

He had to be able to smell my attraction to him.

I could sure as hell smell how turned-on he was, though it had nothing to do with me.

And—

His head jerked backward as his spine arched harshly.

An anguished roar escaped him.

Panic swelled in my chest, in place of the desire I'd felt. The searing pain had only lasted a second for me, when Nev sealed things with Fovea, but the ache... the ache had gone on. And on. And on.

Even now, I felt it.

And Aev's would be much worse.

...unless I took it away.

His fingers dug into the wooden chest so hard that the wood began to morph.

His chin dropped to his chest, his breathing ragged and pained.

My heart began to beat faster.

I had only been coming to sit with him. To hug him, if he needed a friend. To distract him, with silly stories about a happy life that I'd been pretending was mine on Earth. As far as he knew, I'd had everything I ever wanted handed to me on a silver platter. I hadn't lied about my life, but I'd left out the painful parts.

So I couldn't seriously be considering doing what I was thinking of doing.

...could I?

My feet carried me over to the man.

The *king*.

Fate had gotten things wrong, with him and Naomi. They were both cold and icy—and someone icy needed to be with someone different. Someone bright enough to put on a smile and pretend that everything was still good, even when life was crumbling.

Someone like me.

... I could take his pain away.

My knees met the ground, and my fingers wrapped around his cock.

His head jerked upward, pain swimming in those gorgeous, bright blue eyes.

"If we create a bond, the pain will disappear," I whispered to him. "It doesn't need to be permanent—we can just do it to stop the hurting."

His jaw tightened.

I waited for him to say no.

To reject me.

To choose pain.

But instead, he jerked his head in a nod and released his grip on his erection, leaving it to me.

His hand on the wooden chest remained in place as I slowly dragged mine down his massive length. I'd never touched a fae cock before, but they weren't really different from human ones—just bigger.

A low, rumbly groan escaped his chest, and I released him for a moment when I reached the end of his length.

My hand lifted to his mouth, and the look he gave me was a question.

"Your tongue," I said.

His eyes burned me.

And I'd never felt as powerful as I did when the unseelie king slowly dragged his tongue over my palm.

Or when I wrapped my fingers back around his erection.

Or when I pulled them down in a long, slow stroke.

His other hand was clenched in a tight fist, resting on the ground. The normally-tan skin was pale, because it was clenched so hard.

Naomi wouldn't have wanted him to touch her, I realized, as I stroked him again.

And again.

And again.

She would've wanted him to hold back. To keep his desires in check.

I wanted him to let go.

So I released his erection again, just long enough to pull my shorts down my thighs and then toss them to the ground, leaving me in just the simple tank top I almost always wore.

His eyes were even hotter than they had been as they took me in while I caught his erection again.

I opened my thighs wider, and as I stroked him, I slid my hand between my legs.

I'd never done *anything* like this before.

I'd never been *brave* like this before.

But... I'd never felt *excited* like this before, either.

Or *hopeful* like this.

I groaned as I felt the swollen flesh between my thighs.

A snarl escaped him, and he clenched his fist even tighter, as I touched us both.

Thunder sounded over our heads—the first rainstorm of the wet season we'd been waiting for.

"Do you want to touch me?" I asked Aev, as his hips began to jerk a little. He was close; I could tell he was.

"I don't know how to make you feel good," he growled at me, even as his fingers slid between my thighs.

His erection started to throb, and I halted my fingers, making him snarl at me.

"You're too close," I told him, our eyes locking again for a moment. "Just wait. We can finish together if you wait."

His jaw clenched so tightly it had to hurt.

I parted my legs further, giving him better access as I took his huge hand in mine. Separating his fingers a little, I guided his index to my clit, and then sucked in a breath when his warm, rough finger moved over it at my command. "This is where it feels the best. Be gentle."

He slowly dragged his finger around the sensitive bud, and my breathing picked up rapidly.

His eyes dilated as he watched, and he repeated the motion.

"Not here?" He slid another finger inside me as he continued making those small circles, and a noise escaped me. One I didn't think I'd ever made before.

"Both feel good. But my clit mainly, if you want me to climax."

He bobbed his head, and I started to stroke him again, slowly.

A hiss escaped him, his hips jerking as he picked up the pace of his fingers on me and in me. And it shouldn't have felt good—it should've brought back bad memories. It should've made me run.

But I'd never done anything like this before, and it felt too incredible to consider stopping.

Cries started to escape me. Foreign-sounding cries of hot, growing need. I was close, I was *so* close.

Aev's hand closed around mine on his erection, abandoning the wooden chest to stop me as I pumped him.

"You first," he said roughly. "You finish first."

The words were hot.

So damn hot.

My back arched, and for the first time in my life, I was hit with a pleasure so strong, so intense, that I screamed.

My hand jerked over his erection frantically, pulling it toward me as I shattered, wanting him to lose it with me but having little control over myself. And he didn't disappoint.

His roar shook the tent as he painted my abdomen with his pleasure. And the pain that had been nagging at me, aching in my bones, since Nev mated with Fovea? It vanished as a new, strong bond fell into place.

Our chests were both heaving as we opened our eyes to look at each other.

My body burned with the memory of what we'd just done as realization set in.

I whispered, "I was coming to make sure you were okay. I didn't mean to interrupt, or to breach your privacy, or—"

"Don't apologize." His voice was hard.

But not cold.

With one hand, he opened the wooden chest he'd warped, and pulled out a loose white shirt. I watched in silent shock as he carefully used it to clean me off. And then he looked down at my core, and realized he was still holding it with one hand.

Buried inside it, too.

His fingers slowly slid out, and my breathing hitched as he cleaned the sensitive flesh with that shirt.

He nearly did the same to his hand—but then he looked at it.

And looked.

And looked.

And finally, lifting his gaze to mine, he dragged that hand up to his mouth, and wrapped those thick, lush lips around the finger that had been inside me.

My desire swelled hotter.

The tent must've been flooded with the scent of it.

Of *us*.

And when his chest rumbled at my taste, my breathing was already picking up again.

"I know you might still have feelings for her," I said in a quick, harsh whisper. "I know it's just sex—or just almost sex. But if you want, we can—"

He jerked to his feet.

His cock was still erect, the tip still dripping, but all of the blood had drained from his face, making his tan skin look ashen.

"The klynnas." His voice was barely loud enough for me to make out the words.

They were enough to put me on my feet in a heartbeat.

"I let go," he said, his gaze jerking to me. "When the bond broke—I couldn't hold the ice. And then you were—and I—"

He didn't finish.

I didn't need him to.

It was as much my fault as it was his.

"What do we do?" I asked softly.

"We warn the others." He grabbed my shorts off the ground and put them in my hands. "*Now.*"

I yanked them on as he literally *ran* out of the tent, with me rushing behind him. My tank top was still slightly damp with his release, so I grabbed the shirt on my way out too—although I realized the error of that as soon as I'd pulled it over my head and covered myself with the sticky fabric.

We both smelled and looked like exactly what we'd just done... but there were bigger problems on the horizon.

So we ran, as the skies dumped rain on us, and panic coursed through us both.

The constant ache I'd been dealing with since Nev mated with Fovea was gone, I noticed, as I followed Aev. The man was stupidly fast, and I was getting further behind him, but I didn't ask him to slow down.

Honestly, my head was still spinning with the shock of what I'd done.

I'd planned on sitting by him, assuming he'd be in his beast form.

Petting his furry, sabertooth head.

Telling him that he would be alright in the end.

Helping him breathe through the ache that would be his constant companion after the loss of his mate bond.

Not, well, screwing him. Or getting close to it.

The word felt dirty, but what we'd done hadn't felt that way. It had just felt good, and right.

The huge, sticky, now-soaked shirt I was wearing did not, though.

Every male and female fae in the massive kitchen and eating area stared at us as we approached. There was a massive wooden canopy stretching over the entire space, keeping everyone dry.

My face was probably bright red, but once again, there were bigger problems.

"Is the ice intact?" one of the men demanded, striding out to meet Aev. I recognized him as Korrik, one of the old unseelie generals, who had become a part of their new council. He had dark skin and thick, curly hair. He almost always looked angry, and was never cheerful, but also never cruel.

Everyone else behind him was deadly quiet.

We all knew there was a possibility that Aev would lose control when Naomi broke the bond—no one was under the impression that breaking it would be easy on him.

"I lost my grip on the ice covering the stone that blocks the entrance," Aev told the man, his voice low and his body tense. "If it's still in place, I can no longer feel it."

Korrik swore and raked a hand through his hair.

"I'll go check the prison to see if it's intact," Aev said. "For now, prepare to fight. Keep the skies clear, and the basilisks ready. Has Vuvim returned?"

Korrik shook his head. "Not yet. He and Summer are still retrieving the journals, but they should be back any time now."

Aev dipped his head. "Send scouts out in all directions. Watch for the beasts' shadows. I won't be able to return until I've checked the cave completely, so I can seal it shut if any of them haven't made it out."

"Goddess be with you," Korrik rumbled, clasping Aev on the shoulder.

"And you as well." Aev shifted and streaked off into the forest, without so much as a glance back at me.

I didn't expect him to look my way.

I *shouldn't* have expected it.

I knew that.

But my cheeks still flushed redder, and hotter.

Korrik inhaled, and went still for a moment before he looked at me.

I ignored my instincts, which screamed at me to step away from him.

Men were dangerous.

They were the enemy.

At least, my instincts seemed to think so.

I knew better, though. I'd even befriended some men, and my fear of them had calmed.

"Aev hasn't been himself since Naomi. Did he force you?" Korrik asked me, his voice barely audible.

My whole damn body was probably blushing. That always happened when I got really self-conscious, for some annoying reason. "Of course not," I said. "The desire was mutual."

Korrik let out a slow breath, and I don't think I imagined the relief behind it. "Use your fire to clean yourself. Aev doesn't need any more rumors circulating."

He turned, striding back to the group and calling out orders.

I... hadn't even considered my fire.

Of course I should've considered it.

Why hadn't I?

After a moment of focus, flames rippled over my skin and burned away the evidence of what had just occurred. Ave's shirt turned to ashes, and I forced myself to stop considering the consequences of what I'd just done.

Of the bond I'd just created.

We were only friends. Nothing more. Our connection put an end to our pain, and that was all.

So I strode into the group of fae and asked, "How can I help?"

Two

Aev

For the first time in two decades, my mind was completely clear. There was no instinct driving me toward Naomi's side. No silent, invisible pressure to chase a woman who didn't want me. No rejection clouding my thoughts and making me feel like I needed to capture and claim the woman fate had paired me with, or else continue suffering the constant burning pain in my chest that had lingered for so long.

With that clear mind, I should've been thinking about my people.

Or about the terror I may have just released upon all of us.

Or at the very least, about the fact that my power was currently so weak that I couldn't even feel the icy prison I'd built with my own magic.

Instead, I was thinking about the golden-haired phoenix who had taken my cock in her small hand, because she wanted to take away my pain.

About the way her hot flesh had felt against my fingers.

About the trust in her eyes.

The desire.

I had once hoped that Naomi would look at me like that, but the hope had fizzled out years and years ago. Our mating was one neither of us had enjoyed—and I was really damn glad that she'd discovered a way out for us both.

Dakota and I had only spoken in our human forms a few times while the seelie had her spying on me, because I'd rarely been out of my beast form. When we had talked, we'd discussed the pain she had been in since Nev broke their bond. She was happy for the male, and hadn't been hurt that he picked another woman. But there was a constant pain that lingered on the frayed edge of the bond they'd once shared.

Had I been free to do so, I would've offered to exchange simple vows with her, to free her from that pain. Because I wasn't, she had simply been preparing me for the agony that would likely accompany my broken bond as well.

She didn't know that I'd been in pain because of that damn bond since the beginning of it, though.

As I ran through the forest, my lungs filled and emptied completely. My heart beat normally. And my mind—it was gloriously quiet.

I had considered, in the moments before accepting Dakota's proposal, that another mate bond could be just as bad as the one I had already dealt with.

That I may not want to tie myself to another woman.

But the pain had been excruciating, and I knew Dakota. I'd heard her stories of her life. I knew that she was gentle, and kind.

And that if I asked her to, she would kiss another male to break the bond between us, and wouldn't hold it against me in any way.

Unlike Naomi, she cared about me.

And that was a difficult thing to wrap my mind around, considering the way the last two decades had gone.

Now that I was running, though, I was able to look inward, at the new bond in my chest.

It felt so much different than the old one.

Mine and Naomi's connection had felt forced. Like fate had slashed her claws through both of us, binding us through pain and blood and hatred.

The bond with Dakota felt like...

Fresh air, and freedom.

Damn, it was blissful.

All of Vevol looked and felt different, because finally, I could breathe again.

Dakota didn't want a true mate, and I didn't either. But this bond between us was taking away our pain. And since it didn't feel like a cage, or a prison, I had no desire to be free of it.

So I lowered my head toward the ground, tapped into Vevol's magic, and ran faster through the melting snow I'd given up on holding in place.

If I couldn't keep the icy prison in my grip, there was no point in dividing seelie from unseelie.

And if the klynnas had escaped, we were going to need every set of hands Vevol had—seelie and unseelie alike.

Three

Dakota

"Aev is checking the prison right now," I told Fovea, when she answered the door to the Stronghold. Her lips turned down in a deep grimace, her hands and arms spotted with something dark red that I really hoped wasn't dried blood. She turned her back to me and led me deeper inside.

"Do we trust the king to do that?" the woman asked over her shoulder, without turning to glance at me.

Irritation swelled in my chest, but I forced myself not to acknowledge it.

Frustration had no real value, especially in a situation like this. Usually, I was fairly hard to annoy. But for whatever reason, I was protective of Aev.

"Yes. He was the one who held the prison together for so long; what reason would he have to lie about this?"

"I don't think he's lying, but he should be in a great amount of pain." She glanced over at me, concern knitting her eyebrows.

Oh.

I blushed, and my whole body probably went pink again, like it always did.

"I kissed him," I lied.

It was close enough to the truth.

I added quickly, "I've been in pain since my fake mate bond with Nev broke, so I told Aev that if he was hurting too, we would make a temporary bond to save him from that pain. We're friends. And it worked."

Fovea's eyebrows raised. "That's actually a good idea."

At least she hadn't judged me.

She brought the subject back to the monsters that may or may not be free. "Nev and I have discussed the klynnas. There was nothing like them in Vevol before the war, which leads me to believe that they were a punishment for the male fae, because of their decision to attack each other. I have been trying to reach the goddess, to determine some way around the male fae's method of repeatedly killing the creatures, but she has yet to connect with me."

"Has anyone gone to ask North if she's seen anything?"

"No. Her future-sight will take decades to develop, if not centuries."

"Still, she might be able to figure something out," I reminded Fovea. "I can go to their cave. I think I'm the only one who knows where it is, other than the Wild Hunt guys."

She flashed me a concerned look over her shoulder. "Nev asked me to stay out of the skies. Soaring over the trees makes us easy pickings for the klynnas. We don't know if they've escaped yet, but if Aev can't feel the prison anymore, it's likely."

I grimaced. "Maybe we can send someone else."

"We'll discuss it with the men," she said.

I didn't think she could possibly say anything that would surprise me more than *that.*

We stepped into the third-floor living area, and my eyes widened when I saw Naomi sprawled across a couch, absolutely covered in what was either blood or… blood-colored body paint?

I was going to go with the body paint thing.

The room was full of fae women; some were spreading another layer of the body paint over Naomi's skin, some were testing her vitals with fingers over her wrist or throat. Most were just watching, though. There were a bunch of the new human women too, lined up along the edges of the room.

"What's wrong with her?" I asked quietly.

"Changing one's true name is a dangerous practice, but it's the only way to break a mate bond," Fovea explained, stopping beside me and letting her gaze move over the woman. "We've removed her previous name from her, but now she's lost to the goddess as she tries to establish a new one."

"Damn. So she's on some kind of... spirit journey?" I asked, thinking back to one of the Disney movies I'd seen as a kid. The term sounded kind of familiar, but it had been so long since I watched it that I couldn't say for sure.

"That's an accurate description, actually." Fovea sounded kind of surprised. "Do humans often go on these?"

I shook my head. "Not that I know of. I was just guessing."

"Ah. Well, yes. There's no way to say how long her journey will last. When we changed the name of my life-bringer, she was with the goddess for eight days."

"Eight days?" My eyebrows shot upward. "Then what's the body paint for?"

"It's clay, mixed with her blood. Blood activates the clay, and the magic in it slows her body's processes to keep her alive without sustenance while she's on her journey."

Okay, that was pretty cool.

I'd have to remember it, in case I ever got horribly injured. Which... would hopefully never happen. But the abuse survivor in me refused to believe that I was past all of life's horrors. Even if none of the fae hurt me, there were a million other ways that life could bite me in the ass. And being prepared reduced the stress of waiting for the inevitable.

In my life, pain had always been inevitable. It was why I tried to stay happy—because I had to enjoy the good moments while they lasted.

"My harsh and I will prepare for battle," Fovea told me, her expression dark. "And pray for a way to avoid it."

I dipped my head. "I'll tell the men."

"If you see Nev..." she trailed off, her gaze focusing on the wall across the room. "Tell him not to bother asking me to stay out of the fight," she finally said.

I studied her for a long moment.

She seemed so much calmer than she had when we first found the fae women in the forest.

"You look happy," I said to her.

Her lips curved upward, just the tiniest bit. "I suppose I do." She looked at me, then. "Don't delay. We have no time to waste, if these klynnas have truly escaped."

Right.

I nodded, and then headed out.

If she was pregnant, I was pretty sure the rest of the harsh ladies would make her sit out. And she would probably let them, because they valued the ability to bring life so much.

That made me think it was probably safe to say that she hadn't gotten knocked up yet.

I couldn't help but wonder how things would change for the rest of the female fae, when she ended up pregnant, though. If she did.

But my focus was on the klynnas.

Despite Fovea's warning to stay out of the sky, I shifted forms and flew back to the men. As long as I remained beneath the treetops, I didn't think anything above could see me at all.

A dragon shifter I didn't recognize launched out of the trees and flew above me after I passed him—shielding my body with his, I guess.

The fae were overprotective, but flying above me like that was next-level. Which only made me more nervous about the klynnas.

He remained over me until I landed beside the new unseelie council and Nev and Teris. The dragon shifter landed with me, and he gave me a concerned look when he did. I recognized him as one of the unseelie, but I didn't know his name. "You have to stay out of the skies, Dakota. Flying is dangerous when the klynnas are free."

Being scolded by a man made me naturally inclined to act quiet and agreeable, but I was trying to kill those instincts, so I pushed them away.

"Can they see through the trees?" I asked instead of nodding or backing away.

"No, but their sense of smell is strong."

"I'll be more careful, then," I said, just to placate him.

He dipped his head.

"Are the female fae preparing?" Nev asked me.

I think we all knew he was really checking on Fovea. The two of them weren't a normal mated couple in the sense that they didn't live together or spend most of their time together, but I was pretty sure they would get there.

They seemed to like each other more than they'd admitted, and everyone in the forest had heard them having sex way too often at the beginning of their mating. The sounds had only stopped when Nev finally finished building a house for them.

"Yes. The harsh are all getting ready to fight—Fovea included. She told me to make sure you knew she wasn't going to sit out."

His lips curved upward slightly. "As I expected."

He was totally into her. Which I didn't really understand, given that the female fae had murdered one of the unseelies. And someone who was violent once could always become violent again—or kill unnecessarily again.

That was probably why I felt safe around Aev, though. Because I'd never seen him even threaten to hurt anyone.

Then again, the unseelie as a whole were less violent than the seelie. They could fight, but I'd never seen them fight each other for fun or to establish dominance like the seelies did. And that also contributed to my comfort. Aev was the unseelie king for a long time; their reduced violent tendencies could be related to him, maybe. I didn't know the men's history enough to say for sure.

The council and wild hunt guys began discussing their plans—how many basilisks they had gathered, how they were going to reinforce the trees' branches to further block us from the klynnas' sight, and things like that. I listened closely, but didn't know enough about the creatures or Vevol's magic to have anything to contribute to the conversation.

It sounded like they were fairly confident the monsters were free, though. And since Aev was pretty sure too, I felt like that was probably a safe bet.

"If our oracle was here, she could warn us about incoming attacks," Nev said, partway through the conversation.

I perked up; I had said something along those lines to Fovea, hadn't I?

"She could give us locations, and time to clear out the other human women," Korrik agreed. "Assuming she's figured out how to use her sight."

"It should be easier to control without all of those brands. According to Fovea, the mass amount of magic makes it nearly impossible to do anything on purpose. She plans to be on the beach when the next portal opens, in hopes that Vevol will remove some of her brands too," Nev explained. "It'll still take time for North to figure the magic out, but the odds are better now."

I blinked.

Fovea wanted to get rid of some of her brands? I hadn't seen that coming.

Then again, the women had gone through a whiplash-like number of changes in the last few months, so I supposed it wasn't completely out of left field.

"Lian won't take January to get North, though. Not while she's pregnant and the klynnas may be in the skies," Teris countered. "And Mare will be needed here, to help with keeping the human females from panicking while the harsh women fight with us. Ervo won't leave without her."

"You'll have to go after Priel and his mate," Nev agreed. "I can't leave Fovea, and no one else knows the location."

Teris grimaced.

He loved fighting more than any of the other fae I knew. I would've put money on him being excited about the klynnas' freedom, rather than afraid.

So I spoke up. "I can go. I've been to North and Priel's cave before; I know where it is."

Too many sets of eyes turned to me.

My cheeks heated, and I knew it was only a matter of time before my entire body was pinkish red, stained by my damn blush.

"I can't fight, anyway. There's no reason to send someone who could be helpful when I'm here," I added. "And I want to be useful."

"It's not safe," one of the generals said. The hellhound one—Taven, pronounced tah-vin. "We can't send a female phoenix alone through the forest."

"North could save lives," I pointed out. "And when Aev left, he ran that way." I tossed a hand in the direction he'd gone. "North's cave is that way." I gestured in the opposite direction. "By the time the klynnas catch me, I'll have reached North and Priel already."

"We don't know that for certain," another of the men argued.

"I'll go with her," one of the new unseelie council guys said. He was Oren, the old dragon general. The man was tall and tanned, with golden blonde hair that fell to his shoulders. Honestly, he reminded me of a Greek god, but I didn't say that aloud. "I can fly above her; the klynnas will see me as a better target if they approach."

My eyes widened in horror. "No."

"Better me than you," Oren told me, his green eyes piercing as they locked with mine. "And with the king's scent on your skin, something tells me that I'd be dead anyway if I let you fly away without protection."

My face grew hotter. The pink on my skin had probably become a patchy red as I said quickly, "He abdicated. He's not the king. And we only—the connection is just—he was in pain. Kissing stopped the pain. That's all."

"You can't go alone," Nev said firmly. "There's no question. Take Oren, or take someone else. Otherwise, Teris goes."

Teris's scowl told me how much he appreciated being thrown into that role. And honestly, I wanted to go. I loved being out in the forest, and being helpful made me feel good. Especially since I'd refused to learn how to fight.

So I finally nodded. "I'll go. But only with an unseelie, one who can't fly, so I can get away from him if I need to."

No way in hell was I going to end up trapped with *anyone*.

Nev and Teris looked at the group of unseelie generals.

"Taven?" Oren asked.

"No. I'm still assigned to protect the queen," the hellhound general said in a hard voice. "I won't leave her side."

Without questioning that weird, slightly-possessive comment, Devv (the phoenix general) said firmly, "Naomi is not our queen. Summer is the closest thing we have to that right now—and second would be Dakota, who carries Aev's scent."

The silence that followed that remark was heavy, and my skin burned with embarrassment.

I'd need to break my bond with Aev. I didn't want to have the pain, but if he kissed another woman... well, then he'd really be free. From both me, and the pain.

I should never have done what I did in his tent, no matter how intense those moments had been. It wasn't worth everyone's judgment, or the embarrassment, or the awkwardness of watching him walk away from me.

If only there was a way to break the bond without one of us hurting.

"Still, I will not leave Naomi. She needs my protection," the hellhound general finally said. "The female fae can't be fully trusted."

Devv dipped his head, and the rest of the eyes turned to Korrik, who was the sabertooth general and thus the last unmated one who couldn't fly.

"I can have one of my top men go with her," Korrik said.

"No. It needs to be one of you, in case Aev flips his lid when he gets back and finds her gone. He trusts you," Teris growled at the generals.

Korrik didn't look happy about it, but he finally agreed. "I'll go."

Suddenly, I was regretting my offer completely.

It was too late to take it back, though, so...

I was going on a road trip of sorts with grumpy old Korrik.

Yay.

The men discussed their plans for a few more minutes before Korrik gestured toward the forest. And without *goodbye*s or *good luck*s, we both disappeared into the forest together. Me, flying so low that dodging trees took up most of my focus, and Korrik moving through the trees like he was a damn basilisk.

At least I was doing something useful, instead of sitting on my ass and waiting for a klynna to attack.

Four

Aev

The longer I ran, the more I regretted not bringing Dakota with me.

Honestly, the woman was just a ray of damn sunshine. She laughed easily, and smiled even easier. When something went wrong, she didn't yell or panic, just calmly took it in.

She was so full of life that her entire body blushed when she was embarrassed, or excited. So full of life that when she grew too sad, or too happy, her eyes even watered.

I'd never been the enthusiastic type. My nature was laid-back, calm, and steady.

And something about her joy made the world brighter.

I couldn't have brought her with me unless she volunteered to ride on my back, though. The skies weren't safe for a phoenix if the klynnas were free, and I would never risk her that way.

It had crossed my mind to ask her, but I'd already been heading away—and I knew the invitation to ride on my back would strike her strangely, given her desire for independence.

Whether she would accept or not was beyond me, but in the moment, I didn't want to risk her being uncomfortable. Not after she'd given me the most intense sexual experience of my life, just to take away my pain.

Eighteen hours of running alone were enough to make me regret not asking, though. While I felt free, it would've been nice to be free with company.

And even if we couldn't speak, everything would have been better with her beside me.

I STOPPED RUNNING when I could finally feel the melting snow around the cave. My claws dug into the dirt as I sank into my ice magic, and slowly, I used Vevol's power and my frost to create a mental image of the prison.

Sure enough, the stone we'd closed the cave with had been turned to rubble.

And the inside was completely bare of everything but loose, fallen feathers and scales.

That was all the confirmation I needed, so there was no point in delaying my return. The cave was empty, and the klynnas were free. I hadn't heard or seen them yet, but past experience told me they would head for their nests before they went hunting. Their prison had been too small for laying eggs—and their numbers, too low.

The males would take their females to their nests, hidden throughout the mountains, and ensure that the women and their eggs were safe before hunting us down.

But they *would* come for us.

And we needed to be ready.

So I turned and headed back.

Dakota's swaying golden hair and bright smile filled my mind as I ran. I needed to stop and sleep... but I was itching to return to her too much to bother.

She had been about to offer me more of herself, when I realized I'd lost control of the klynnas. I was sure of it. And whatever she offered, I wanted to take. The more distance I'd put between us, the more certain I was of that.

THE GENERALS WERE RUNNING practice drills with our people, the harsh female fae, and the seelies too, when I made it back to the Stronghold. Though I was exhausted, I was alert and searching the trees for any sign of Dakota, as I had been since I'd approached.

One of our dragons, Juret, was in the sky, acting as the klynna.

Oren and Devv were watching from the trees, barking orders when someone did something wrong.

Vuvim and Summer were on the ground, watching together. They had returned, apparently.

The drill continued as the generals climbed out of the trees—minus Korrik, I noticed. The Wild Hunt men, except Priel, met us too. Those of them who were mated brought their females. And Fovea abandoned the drill, leading a few of her women down to our group as well.

Though my first instinct was to ask where Dakota was, I knew she was safe. My men wouldn't have let her put herself in danger. So I explained the situation, instead of inquiring about her.

"Without the mate bond, I am much weaker," I said bluntly. "It'll take time to adjust to the new length of my power. I couldn't feel the prison until I had nearly reached it. When my magic finally met it, it was empty. The klynnas are long gone—back to the mountains, to rebuild their nests, if I had to guess. When the males have ensured the safety of their mates, they will be in our skies, hunting us down."

Nods went around the group.

Everyone seemed to have expected the news, which meant that hopefully, they had been preparing.

"The oracle should be here soon. With any luck, she'll be able to use her magic to pinpoint where and when the attacks will be," Oren said.

"Do we need to start building homes under the ground?" Sunny asked. "Or at least fortify the Stronghold somehow? Only a few of the new human girls have even tried shifting; they're basically sitting ducks."

"My life-bringers have focused their magic on tunneling downward," Fovea agreed. "It's not safe for them or our humans on the land."

"I can help them," Sunny offered. "I'm pretty useless up here, and there's no way Remmo will let me fight one of the klynnas yet."

"Not a chance," Remmo agreed.

"I can help too," January added.

"So can I," Mare put in. "We can use the opportunity to try to teach the new human girls to channel Vevol's magic, too."

Nods went around the group.

I itched to ask where Dakota was again, but still remained silent.

She was probably in the trees, spying on someone else for the damned Wild Hunt. Or perhaps already helping the other life-bringers tunnel downward.

"Until we've heard and seen the first klynna, we continue training," Oren said. "If we're going to avoid carnage, we need to be working as a united team, rather than three separate groups."

Everyone in the circle exchanged grimaces.

There *were* three separate groups. And each of us had extremely different ideas and preferences. Getting our people to work as one would be a headache.

But a headache I didn't have to deal with, since I'd finally been freed from both my mate bond with Naomi and the throne I'd never wanted.

"None of us want to die," I said simply. All of their gazes turned to me, but I was used to the stares. "We all need to forget how we classify ourselves, and focus on the desire to live. We are not unseelie, seelie, or harsh right now. We are fae. And we want to survive."

A few people nodded.

Some looked at me a bit differently.

Done with the conversation—and with waiting for someone to just tell me where the hell my female was—I stepped across the distance between us and grabbed Vuvim by the elbow. "Where is Dakota?"

Nothing happened without Vuvim noticing, or finding out about it soon after.

"She went to retrieve the oracle and her mate," Vuvim said, though his gaze grew slightly curious. "Why do you wear her scent?"

"She left?" My voice lowered, and I stepped back, turning my gaze to the other remaining generals, who would've had to approve her leaving. "Which of you let her go?"

They gave me nothing but silence in response.

Assholes.

"No way. Did she kiss you?" Summer demanded, though she looked absolutely thrilled. "I knew she had a thing for you."

I had no idea what *had a thing for you* might mean, but I supposed kissing was probably the most appropriate thing to claim we'd done to connect ourselves.

"Yes, she kissed me. I was in pain after the bond broke, and Dakota took pity on me," I said. It was only a half-lie. I lowered my voice, and felt my power flood the words as I asked again, "*Which of you let her go*?"

"All of us did," Taven finally growled. "She was the only one who knew where the oracle was other than Teris, and he wanted to stay and fight."

My icy glare landed on the Wild Hunt's sabertooth. "You let my female risk her life so you could *stay and fight*?"

"A female you're willing to leave behind isn't one you should claim as yours, *Tame King*," Teris drawled back.

The words didn't surprise me.

I had not been myself in a long time. Since Naomi began rejecting me, I had started fading. Every damn male fae knew that.

But I was no longer fading, or *tame*.

And it was time to make sure the damn seelies knew that.

Covering the distance between myself and Teris in two steps, I grabbed the man by the throat. He didn't bother trying to stop me, or to prove that he didn't consider me a threat.

But even without the power boost of a completed mate bond, I was stronger now than I had been in centuries. Because now, I wasn't holding an ice prison and the snow that covered half of our world's distance.

My ice stretched quickly over his throat and down his shoulders. He was already covered in a thin layer of it before he realized the danger he was in.

His brothers ripped his body from my grip, everyone around us staring at me.

It had been a long time since I defended myself.

Since I *lived*.

Ervo had the ice melted off Teris's face in a moment, and then the other sabertooth was swearing and glowering at me.

I said in an even, cold voice, "Dakota is my friend, by her own choice. We are bonded, *by her own choice*. I left her here for *her safety*, when bringing her with me would've been nothing but selfish. Call me whatever you want when I'm gone, but when I'm in front of you? You insult me, and you'll realize why my bastard friends forced me to become the king."

There were many eyes on us. The training exercise had ended, but I didn't give a damn who saw me.

I was no longer ruled by Naomi's dislike.

I was free, now.

"Where is the cave?" I asked Ervo, who was still behind Teris, working on melting the ice wrapped around his friend's body. He was one of the more reasonable seelie leaders.

Still, he said nothing.

"You should be able to follow your connection to her," Summer said from behind me. I turned to face her, and she flashed me a grin. "You can track your mate by their scent, if you pay close enough attention. It'll be in the air, just barely."

I looked at Vuvim, and he dipped his head in a nod.

"Thank you," I said, nodding back at Summer. "I'll return with your sister, and the oracle."

Her grin only grew wider. "Thanks."

I shifted forms and ran in the direction of the seelie's land, altering my course when I caught the tiniest hint of Dakota's scent in the air. Though I didn't know how she managed to smell like sunshine, I took in every drop of that scent like a drowning man seeking air.

Five

Dakota

"What the fuck were you thinking?" Priel snarled at me, pacing the room.

I took a step back.

I wasn't necessarily afraid of him, but instinct told me that there was a very large, very dangerous man in front of me, and he could easily take his anger out on me physically.

"Easy," North growled back at him, grabbing him by the massive arm. "This is *not* Dots's fault. She didn't know the klynnas were tuned into Aev's scent, or that they made nests in these mountains. *I* didn't even know that."

"It didn't occur to any of you?" Priel demanded, turning his glare to Korrik.

Korrik only shrugged. "We didn't know if they had even escaped. And if there are klynnas coming for your mate, shouldn't she see them before any of us?"

Priel took a threatening step toward the man, and I took another step back.

North put herself between me, Korrik, and her furious mate, and his chest met her back.

We'd travelled through the night. It had been midday when Korrik and I had noticed a shadow above us as we approached the entrance to Priel and North's cave—and we had rushed inside just in time. The thing's monstrous claws had barely missed Korrik's body.

That had been an hour ago.

Priel was still raging.

"I'm still trying to figure out my magic," North said as she held Priel back. His hands landed on her waist, and she relaxed slightly. "I don't have anyone to teach me, so it's all trial and error. But the point is, I didn't know the klynnas even existed. So what are we supposed to do now?" She looked over her shoulder, at Priel.

He was still pissed off, but his expression softened slightly when she looked at him like that. "There's nothing we *can* do. Korrik and I can't take down a fucking klynna. We'd need a dozen basilisks, and a heap of other fae. We've got to sit here, and hope like hell that they can't decimate this mountain."

My eyes widened in horror. "Could they do that?"

"I don't know." Priel's voice was grim.

"If I were to take Dakota's clothes, I may be able to distract it long enough for you three to get away," Korrik said, with a heaving sigh.

"His scent is barely on her at all," Priel argued. "Not enough for them to follow her clothing if she was nearby and the smell was on her actual skin."

"Unless you broke the mate bond, right?" North asked. Her gaze was on mine, and panic clutched my abdomen.

Aev probably didn't want the bond. He hadn't even looked back at me when he took off into the forest. But... breaking it would hurt him.

And the last thing I wanted to do was hurt him, after he had spent so many years in pain because of Naomi. Both of them were at fault for that situation, but he was the one who had suffered the most, because he was a male fae.

"I don't want to do that unless we have no other choice," I said quietly.

"I don't either," Korrik agreed. "If we kiss or exchange vows, Aev will probably kill me."

North rolled her eyes. "He let Naomi break their bond without so much as an argument. I think he'd understand in this situation."

"That's not true. He *wanted* the bond broken," I corrected her.

"We can wait until they start ripping the mountain apart," Priel growled.

Unlike us, he hadn't gone off topic.

"Fine," Korrik agreed. "When they start trying to take the mountain down, Dakota and I form a bond. Then, I take her clothing to distract the klynna long enough for the three of you to get away."

I didn't like that plan.

Hated it.

But what was the alternative?

Since I couldn't find one, I stayed quiet.

And we waited.

A DAY and a half passed quickly, and tensely. I slept a bunch, getting comfortable on one of the couches because there was no way I was getting in North and Priel's bed.

North and Priel painted together, communicating silently, and Korrik paced. He looked exhausted, but stressed too.

When I woke up late during the second night, I heard Priel and Korrik discussing their plan in low voices, and remained quiet.

"Aev is going back to his old self, now that he's separate from Naomi?" Priel asked Korrik.

"Yes. He seemed much better in the few minutes before he left for the cave. Lighter. More commanding."

"More like the king," Priel said, and sounded sort of grim. "If he doesn't have to hold the prison anymore, he'll have a hell of a lot more magic. Even without his bond to her."

"If we can stay here long enough, he'll probably come after her. The mate bond should drive him to it. Those damn things are constantly pushing men toward their bonded female."

"That's not a bad thing," Priel growled.

"Not always." There was a tense moment. "Aev killed a klynna with his ice once. Before Naomi, obviously. And it came back, like they always do. But it was just him. He froze its heart in its chest. If we buy enough time, he might be able to do the same to this one."

"That's a possibility we can't afford to wait for." I heard a creaking noise that made me think one of them had leaned back in a chair or something. "You'll have to lead it to the lake. You remember that those bastards won't touch the water."

"I remember. It's a solid day's journey, though. A damn lot of running with a klynna on my tail."

"It's too bad you don't have wings," Priel agreed. "You'd be more likely to make it there, if you did."

"Dakota didn't want any of the winged fae with her. Didn't feel safe enough." He didn't sound angry about that fact—just stated it bluntly.

It was true, but my face heated anyway.

I wished I could trust the male fae more than I did. But... I didn't.

"Our humans have all been through their own hells," Priel said. "They're survivors, like us. If I'd been dragged into their world, I doubt I'd make it as long."

Korrik chuckled. "On that, we can agree."

The men continued talking, but the subject changed to the past, and stories of the times they'd worked together to kill klynnas. The camaraderie surprised me, but then again, I knew that the drama of the monsters returning was going to force the fae to get along. Male and female, seelie and unseelie.

Nothing united people the way a fear of death could.

My mind kept going to Priel's words, though.

Someone with wings would have the best chance of survival.

Someone with wings could outrun the monster.

For the sake of my conscience... it was going to have to be me.

At least that way, Aev wouldn't have to deal with pain unless I managed to get myself killed.

I accepted that, and starting preparing myself to act as bait.

WHEN THE MEN decided to call it a night, I waited silently.

After I was certain that they were out, I crept into the kitchen and quietly had one last meal of fruit. All they had was the birth control fruit Summer called lilano, but I ate a few of them as near-silently as I could.

If I was going to be flying the monster all the way to the lake, I needed *something* in my stomach.

My feet were silent on the tile as I grabbed a clean paintbrush off one of the tables, dipped it into the white puddle on the paper-plate-like leaf that North had been using as a palette, and then lifted it to the wall. Priel had covered something with black paint earlier, making a fresh canvas, so I went over to that spot and quickly painted the words,

I'll meet you back at the Stronghold.

Though I hesitated at first, not sure how I should sign it, I finally signed it with my full name.

They couldn't use it to summon me if I didn't speak it to them aloud, I didn't think.

I set the paintbrush down in the paint puddle, hoping that would keep it wet long enough for North to salvage it, because I couldn't turn on the water and risk the noise.

With that done, I padded silently to the cave's entrance, and then slowly made my way out.

The klynna had gone silent above us a few hours earlier, but when Korrik had checked outside, he saw it sitting on a set of trees directly in front of the cave, waiting.

I'd never seen one before, so when I stepped up to the entrance and peered outside, my lips parted.

I'd expected the creature to look like a monster.

Size-wise, it was. The thing was the size of an airplane.

But it was the most gorgeous airplane I'd ever seen.

It was scaled from head to toe, its coloring starting a light red and growing darker until it was a deep, glittering crimson at the tail. Its wings were a feathered masterpiece, with the same ombre-like style as the rest of its body. When it moved, the feathers blew a little in the wind, revealing gleaming scales beneath them.

It was strong, elegant, and absolutely stunning.

And it was going to try to kill me when I took to the sky.

That was pretty damn terrifying.

I glanced backward, over my shoulder. Though I couldn't see into the cave from there, I remembered what Priel had said.

If you had wings, you would have a better chance.

And I let out a slow, shaky breath.

This was the best chance for all of us to escape. I'd flown a lot, in the past few months; I was just as fast as the other phoenixes, despite my size in comparison to their gigantic male ones.

I had a chance at making it out of this alive. More of a chance than Korrik did, so I couldn't let him take the fall for me.

And overthinking about it wasn't going to get me anywhere.

So I swallowed my fear, and acted.

My feet were light on the stone beneath them as I tapped into Vevol's magic, using her power to launch myself into the air and take off. Wind rushed against my face, through my feathers and the flames of my magic, and I pushed myself to move faster than I ever had before.

The klynna roared at me, its massive wings shooting it into the sky at my back, but I didn't let myself pause or look or slow down in the slightest.

I didn't have time.

My heart pounded, my wings pumping.

And I could *feel* the monster in the sky behind me.

Trying to catch me.

But I remained far enough ahead that it didn't touch me, despite its snapping teeth and swinging claws.

I was going to survive.

All of us were.

After a few hours, my energy started to fade.

I should've expected that. Flying at full speed for long periods of time wasn't something I'd ever done before. Usually, I would slow long enough to find my rhythm. Thanks to the desperation coursing through me, I couldn't find it.

My body ached.

The stress of being chased by a monster that would eat me like a snack was wearing down on me.

But I kept flying anyway.

The alternative was death.

A FEW MORE HOURS PASSED BEFORE I knew I was about to meet my end.

I'd slowed too much—and the klynna was catching me. Though I'd passed dozens of rivers and ponds, I'd need deep water to really escape the monster, so I couldn't have risked stopping.

Not when my life was on the line.

The klynna's teeth suddenly clamped down on my wing, and an awful scream pierced the air as it shook me wildly.

A snarl sounded below me, but the pain was too intense to focus long enough to look for the source.

Out of nowhere, ice traveled over the creature's face, blocking its nostrils and forcing its jaws apart. The ice freed me from the monster's grip, so I tucked my injured wing and dove toward the ground.

Shifting forms just in time to use my magic, I landed hard on one of the branches. The world spun around me, but was steady enough that I saw Aev in a tree not far from me.

The klynna did too.

It dove like I had, roaring and throwing fire toward Aev. The sabertooth's sleek, furry body smoothly dodged the attack.

When the airplane-sized monster landed on the dirt, taking out a few huge trees in the process, the ground shook. I grabbed the branch I was sitting on so I didn't slide off the huge, smooth surface of it.

The movement sent hot pain through my back, and when I looked over my shoulder to see the injury, my stomach clenched.

That was a lot of blood.

The skin was knitting itself together already, but it was a damn good thing I was fae.

A huge cracking noise had me jerking my head back toward the man who'd saved my life.

Horror flooded me when I looked at him.

The klynna was breaking through the branches, blowing hot fire everywhere in an attempt to get to Aev. Luckily, there was enough pollen in the air to prevent the world around us from burning.

I knew he could kill it—he had killed one by himself, a long time ago, according to Korrik. But what if his magic was different now? He hadn't had time to adjust to the change to it since losing his bond with Naomi. And the klynnas had been hidden away for so long that he could've forgotten how he killed that one.

If he *did* forget, then what?

I didn't want to consider that, so I pushed the thought away.

I needed to get back in the fight, to distract the monster and give Aev a chance to figure out if he could end it or not.

Carefully, I made my way to my feet and glanced down at my back one last time. The skin had finished healing, and I didn't feel any residual pain.

There was no time to muse about how incredible that was.

I shifted forms and launched into the air, and was hit with a whole new dose of adrenaline now that it wasn't just my life on the line.

With Aev at risk, I was alive again.

Desperate, again.

Aev leaped to a new branch as the klynna crushed the one he was on.

I barreled toward the klynna, just in time to watch as the monster tried to grab Aev in its jaws.

Ice flooded its mouth, giving the fae time to throw himself out if its path. He hurtled toward the ground, and it was a long way down, but he could cushion his fall with magic.

I heard Aev roar as I swept down into the klynna's view, catching its attention.

Its gaze tracked me, and by some miracle, it didn't bite at me again.

Not that I stayed in place long enough to give it the chance.

The klynna's attention jerked back to Aev, who was on the ground and looked... broken.

Too broken to get up.

Panic swelled in my chest as I spiraled toward him. I couldn't grab him in my claws—I'd slice through his skin. I'd have to shift, and soar back into the sky quickly.

It might not even be possible.

The klynna might beat me to it, or take us both out.

But I couldn't let Aev die.

I timed it wrong and stumbled when I hit the ground.

My small, human eyes collided with the huge, furious ones of the klynna only a few feet from us.

Aev's arms wrapped around my waist, gripping me tightly.

But instead of snapping its jaws or blowing fire, the monster went still.

"Please don't kill us," I whispered to it.

It blinked its massive eyes.

The urge to lift my hand out toward it and try to press my palm to its warm nose was overwhelming. I didn't understand why I felt that way, and I ignored it in favor of survival.

The klynna took one massive, ground-shaking step back.

And then another.

Wind assaulted us as it spread its wings and then launched into the sky, leaving me gaping after it as the trees and ground shook around us.

Six

"How did you do that?" Aev rasped from behind me.

I hurriedly turned around so I could face him, looking him up and down for injuries while he replied, "I'm fine. Just broke some ribs, and an arm. It'll heal in the next five minutes or so."

I gaped down at him. "You *just* broke some ribs? Broken ribs are incredibly painful."

His forehead wrinkled. "When have you broken your ribs?"

Right.

He only knew the pleasant parts of my life.

"What do you mean, how did I do that?" I changed the subject as I gestured over my shoulder, carefully feeling around his chest as I attempted to check his injuries. I could see bruises in four different places, and assumed they were all breaks. "I have no idea why it flew away. Maybe it's going back to bring its buddies so they can eat us together?"

"Your magic connected to the klynna's. I felt the pulse of power through our bond." He tapped the center of his chest, and winced at the pain. "It felt like... light."

"Light like a feather? Or light like sunshine?" I checked, as I eyed his arm. If it needed to be set, he must've already done it, because it looked like it was already healing properly.

"Like sunshine. The same way you smell." He closed his eyes as I continued pressing my fingers lightly to his skin.

"How can I smell like sunshine? What does sunshine smell like?"

"I don't know," he murmured back. "Like you."

I snorted, but said nothing else for a few minutes. Though I didn't want to take my hands off of his muscular form, I forced myself to pull my fingers away from his skin. "The bruises are gone."

"Pain's almost gone too." He was breathing more deeply now, and he had relaxed a bit.

I realized I'd never seen him calm like that before—not in the few months we'd known each other.

"You know the Wild Hunt sent me to spy on you, right?" I asked him quietly.

Now that he'd risked his life for me and we had a tiny mate bond, it didn't seem honest to keep that from him.

His lips curved upward slightly, his eyes remaining closed. "I know. It didn't matter to me."

Good.

Phew.

He opened his eyes, and they narrowed at me. "You were supposed to be with Korrik."

My face reddened. "I was the bait."

"You were *what*?"

"The klynna smelled you on my skin and hunted me to North and Priel's cave. We didn't realize they would be looking out for your scent, or else I would've stayed back at the Stronghold. It caught us when we got there, and waited outside for us. Korrik, North, and Priel decided that I needed to start a bond with Korrik so the klynna wouldn't chase me, and then give him my clothes, which smelled like you, so he could bait the monster into following him so the rest of us could escape."

He blinked.

I went on quickly, "I heard him and Priel talking about how Korrik would have a better chance of surviving if he had wings. I was the only one with wings—and they only followed us because of me. I couldn't let him risk his life for me. So, I left them a note to meet me at the Stronghold, and snuck out after they went to sleep."

Aev slowly closed his eyes.

And let out a long, deep breath.

I opened my mouth to tell him that it was the only reasonable option, and that the general's life wasn't worth any less than mine—but before I could speak, he lifted a finger to my lips.

I closed them.

His voice was low and raspy when he said, "If I hadn't been here, you would've *died*, Dakota."

"I didn't, though," I whispered back.

His eyes opened, and they were angry.

My entire body went stiff, my stomach churning with fear.

He slid a hand onto my face, cupping my cheek in his gigantic palm.

My fear dissipated, and I stared down at him.

"You never risk your life again, okay?" he finally asked, his voice strained.

I blinked. "I don't think I can promise that."

Not when the klynnas were in the sky, and I had somehow *connected* with that one.

"You were exhausted. I saw it in your body's position, and the klynna did too. You're good in the sky, but those of us who have been alive for a long time have more endurance after running and flying for centuries. You put yourself at a huge, unnecessary risk. I know you didn't want someone else to risk their life for you, but the fact is that you're more important than Korrik. We have almost exactly twice as many men as we have women right now; our society can handle the loss of a man, but not a woman. We need you."

My defenses rose, though I didn't really feel attacked the way I had when my mom or dad or ex-boyfriend would insult me. He hadn't even really insulted me... just calmly stated the facts and made me feel bad that way.

"My life is as valuable to me as I decide it is," I told him, standing up and moving away from him. "I would rather risk myself than have someone else's death on my conscience, and that's my decision to make. Not because I'm a life-bringer, but because I'm a person. If you can't respect that, then you need to back off."

He sat up, and the motions were smooth enough that I assumed he was done healing. "The fact is that Korrik had a much higher chance of survival than you did. And regardless of your gender, the only person who should risk their life is the person with the highest chance of surviving."

"Does that mean that the next time a klynna shows up, you're going to stand back and let me deal with it myself, since I seem to have the highest chance of surviving them now?" I countered.

He didn't answer immediately, but stood slowly, so he could face me.

I took another step back, and he didn't try to stop me. "I didn't think so. If you can't respect my right to make decisions that will impact my life and peace of mind, our friendship is over, and the temporary mate bond we've built will be broken as soon as we're back at the Stronghold." My voice was shaking a little when I got to the last sentence.

Aev slowly lifted his hands in surrender and took a step back himself. His lips had formed a tight line, his forehead smoothing icily. "I overstepped my boundaries; I understand. It won't happen again."

My heart was pounding fiercely in my chest, but it stumbled a beat when I realized what I was doing.

I was treating him like Naomi would've.

Like I'd wanted to treat my ex, and my parents, but always been too afraid to.

He didn't deserve that. And I didn't want to be that person.

I could still set boundaries and clear things up without hurting him, or putting distance between us.

"You didn't overstep," I said quietly. "You protected me, and I appreciate that. I'm sorry that I risked my life, but the endurance thing didn't occur to me. I really thought I had a better chance of surviving the klynna than Korrik did, and I knew they'd never give me the time of day if I brought it up."

Aev's eyes softened slightly, though he still seemed a bit colder and more closed off than he had been earlier. "The council and the Wild Hunt don't often take your opinions or feelings on important matters into consideration. I apologize for that."

My face reddened. "It's okay, I'm used to it."

His forehead wrinkled, and I knew I'd let too much slip again.

"We should probably get going." I gestured toward the sky.

He dipped his head in a nod. "The skies are too dangerous. Will you ride with me? On my back?"

My probably-blotchy, red face, heated further. "I guess. But if there's a klynna, you have to let me try to deal with it."

He let out a rough laugh. "Already dying to risk yourself again?" The words came out playful, not harsh.

I rolled my eyes at him. "I just don't want to watch the damn thing kill you."

"We'll conceal our scents." He gestured toward one of the many bushes with leaves that could wipe out a person's smell. Sunny had taught me how to use them one day, after I asked her. She knew all kinds of shit about Vevol thanks to her mate, and was happier than I'd ever seen her. "I can move silently enough through the forest that they won't be able to sense us, or track us."

I bit back a sigh. "Alright."

His lips curved upward a bit. "You sound extremely excited."

A quiet laugh escaped me. "I love flying. It makes me feel strong, and free. I don't want to be reduced to a passenger."

He smiled.

The expression was so gorgeous that my breath caught.

"You'll feel the same way when we run together."

"Would you, if we flew together?" I countered.

I knew how men were. They didn't want to be upstaged, ever. And riding on the back of a woman? None of the men I'd ever known would've been caught dead doing that.

"Flying with you would be a privilege. One I'd remember proudly, until the day my soul leaves my body." His fingers skated lightly over the back of my hand before he gestured toward his left. "We'll rinse off in the river first."

When he shifted forms, I eyed him, trying to figure out how I was going to get all the way up on top of him. He smoothly lowered to his stomach, making my job much easier, and I slid a leg over his back.

My fingers slipped into the silky fur I'd spent too much time petting over the last few months, and I leaned my chest to his neck while I got settled into place. As I wrapped my arms around his neck, I lowered myself against him.

He didn't move, and I thought he might be waiting for me to tell him I was ready. He was probably worried about spooking me; he'd seen the way I reacted when things freaked me out. I just... left.

The alternative was panicking, so leaving felt preferable.

Because of my reactions, though, his caution was understandable.

"Okay," I whispered. "Go slow at first. I'm not sure I'll be able to hold on tight enough for you to move fast."

He snorted at me, and my lips curved a little. He seemed different, now. Calmer. More open.

Freer, maybe.

If anyone could understand the relief of freedom, it was me.

I clutched his fur like a lifeline as he rose smoothly to his feet. He took a few slow steps first, and to my surprise, I didn't so much as budge.

Aev picked up the pace a little, and my body didn't sway or slip or anything. I could feel his heart beating against my hands, which was kind of intense, but I liked it.

He trotted for a few minutes, and I grew more comfortable on his back. I thought he would stop when he reached the river, but instead, he launched us into it.

I held my breath as we submerged, and gripped his powerful body with my arms and legs while he rolled us a few times.

Before my lungs started to strain, he burst back through the water and then landed lightly on the dirt.

He shook off, and a loud laugh escaped me. When he flashed me a toothy grin, I laughed again. "You're just a big golden retriever, huh?"

He licked my knee, giving a rumbly chuckle before he carried me over to the nearest scent-tranquillizing bush and rubbed up against it. The soft leaves hit me in the face, and I tugged a couple of them off, running them over my arms and legs and chest.

Aev shifted too, and I squeaked when I found my thighs wrapped around a chiseled abdomen and my arms around those massive biceps.

He grinned at me over his shoulder, and our lips were only a breath apart. "This'll only take a second."

If he kept looking at me like that, I wasn't sure I would react well. He was just too damn gorgeous.

Part of me wondered if I only felt that way because of the bond, but my affection for the man had been growing for two months. We were just friends —but I liked being his friend.

I liked it a lot.

So I stayed silent as he turned back toward the bush, grabbing a few leaves and running them over his body the same way I had. He was more thorough than me—but he was the one the klynnas wanted revenge on.

"Is it safe for us to go back to the Stronghold?" I asked him. "With the klynnas after you?"

"I'll just have to keep my scent concealed," he said, like it wasn't a big deal. I supposed it only took a minute, and the effect lasted hours. "Staying out here isn't an option. Korrik will send a search party for you if we don't get back so everyone can see that you're safe and sound. And there was the development of your connection with the beasts—we need to tell them about that. Maybe North will be able to see something related to it."

That was so many words for the usually-silent man. I loved seeing him that way, honestly.

"You seem different," I told him, biting my lip as I waited for his response.

He chuckled and tossed his leaves to the ground, but the soft breeze picked them up and towed them away before they could hit the dirt. "I feel better than I have in two decades, because of you." His hand squeezed the back of my knee, lightly. My body flushed, but I hoped he was oblivious to the heat blooming within me because of his touch.

Aev didn't know how he'd affected me in that tent—or how he was still affecting me.

And he had left without a backward glance when he realized the prison might be down.

"Not because of me," I countered. "Because Naomi broke your bond. She's in some kind of a coma now, on a spirit journey."

"Good for her, I suppose." The man shrugged a gigantic shoulder. "I don't particularly care what she's doing, so long as I'm free of her."

I rolled my eyes. "Liar."

He raised an eyebrow. "I've been trapped with that woman for two decades, Dakota. If I'd known there was a way out, I would have taken it *years* ago. We didn't hate each other; we didn't feel anything for each other. There was nothing but pain for me in this world because of that bond for *twenty years*. Even the sex was terrible, and based on what happened between you and I, something tells me it shouldn't have been."

Any desire I'd felt vanished when he mentioned having sex with her. I'd known they'd done it, I just felt... possessive, maybe?

Or protective?

That sounded better.

I was going with protective, even if it was kind of a lie.

"You just slipped away," he told me, studying me with interest.

"I'm in the exact same place I was thirty seconds ago, actually." I was choosing to ignore the fact that he was referring to emotional slippage, not physical.

"In here, you slipped away." His forehead bumped mine.

I lifted an eyebrow, trying to ignore the heat crawling over my face and shoulders and arms. "You're delusional."

A laugh escaped him. "Now I know I'm right. Your body tells your truth." He brushed the backs of his knuckles over my cheek, and my skin only heated further. "If we're going to be friends, you have to tell me when I do something to push you away. My only experience with women is misery."

A snort escaped me. "That sounds like my only experience with men."

His forehead creased. "You said nothing about men when you told me stories of your life."

Dammit, I needed to watch myself much, much closer.

It was time for a hard-assed subject change. Really, I should've told him we needed to start running, but I was so comfortable. And I liked talking to him, more than I wanted to admit. So I blurted, "It's weird to think of you and Naomi having sex. I've been here for so many years, and the fae are always... celibate, I guess? I don't know. It's stupid."

Understanding flooded his gaze. "It's not stupid. I would feel more than *weird* in your shoes if our situations were reversed. If you'd been mated to Nev..." He grimaced. "I don't particularly want to know how I'd feel about that connection. I already want to break his nose for choosing Fovea over you. Who the hell wants to be mated to a murderous fae bitch?"

I grinned so widely that my face nearly split in two. "I think that's the perfect description of her. But he mated with her to establish a connection with the female fae, and hopefully persuade them to refrain from said murderous activity because of it. He talked to me about it afterward, and I wasn't upset. Well, maybe I was upset about the pain that followed the bond breaking, but that wasn't his fault." I rubbed at the center of my chest, where the ache had been for so long.

"You kept your pain too quiet. Someone would've forged a bond with you to remove it from your shoulders," he said, his voice a bit chastising.

"I know. But I didn't want something fake again; at least with us, we're friends, you know?"

He nodded. "Our bond feels more like a home than the prison my last one was."

"A home?" I teased.

He flashed me an amused look. "Yes. The connection feels as natural to me as breathing."

"For me too," I admitted.

It was strange, but I wasn't going to question it. Not after everything both of us had been through.

"We need to get moving," Aev told me, brushing his hand over my knee again like he just couldn't help it. "But we may as well get the awkwardness out of the way first." His eyes were locked with mine, and his expression was so quietly intense that I didn't dare look away. "Honestly, I was in terrible pain when Naomi decided she would rather cement our bond than go to war with the seelie. Despite what some people seem to think, no one forced her to make that decision. I probably would've refused her if I'd been in my right mind, but I wasn't. I haven't been in a long time. That kind of mental strain and physical pain… it splinters your mind." He shook his head a little.

"You don't have to tell me this," I said quietly.

"I do, because I don't want you feeling discomfort with this topic," he said bluntly. "Or wondering how it happened, either. I hoped that her agreeing to sex would mean that she would finally consider me as a partner. That perhaps the pain would end. But it only gave me more guilt, and rage, and detached unhappiness. After hearing the bits and pieces of the sex discussions that are now happening, and seeing brief glimpses into her mind, I became even more certain that Naomi wanted nothing to do with me. The pain grew worse, then. I felt… barbaric, almost. Reduced to my primal instincts."

My throat swelled. "What do you mean, bits and pieces about the sex discussion?"

He grimaced. "A true sexual experience should be like the one you and I shared in the tent, not like the one Naomi and I suffered through."

My eyebrows lifted. "Can I ask for details?"

"I already promised to give them to you." His fingers began rubbing over my knee sort of rhythmically, and I wondered if maybe the movement was keeping him calm. "She made one of the men blindfold me, so I couldn't see her, and told me not to touch her skin. She sat on the edge of the bed, and guided me an inch or two into her body—it wasn't soaked, or soft, like yours was. I could smell her tears in the air. We were both relieved that the bond kicked in immediately, without requiring any kind of pleasure. I withdrew from her as fast as possible and left the room." He shut his eyes. "Fuck. It was terrible for the both of us. I didn't realize it could feel *good*, the way it did in the tent."

I was horrified by the experience he'd described. *Absolutely fucking horrified.* "I've been in bad sexual situations, too," I told him, my eyes stinging. "Really bad ones. You both consented, as messed up as the situation was. That doesn't always happen on Earth."

His eyebrows furrowed. There was more confusion than anger, at first. But it slowly morphed, and his voice was deadly when he asked, "A human male forced himself on you?"

My eyes stung more, but I nodded. "I don't want to talk about the details, but I know how it feels to be helpless in those situations. And I'm sorry that you do too."

He pulled me off his back and wrapped his arms around me, hugging me fiercely tight. I clung to him, trying to stop the tears that were falling against his warm, perfect shoulder. "I would destroy them, if it were possible," he said in a low voice. "I would make them suffer for hurting you."

A shudder ripped down my spine. "Please, don't talk about violence."

He rested his cheek against the top of my head. "I'm sorry. I'd sooner end my own life than raise a hand to you, though. I hope you know that."

Honestly?

I *did* know that.

Someone who could suffer for as long as Aev did, without physically hurting the woman who had caused him so much pain? He knew how to control his temper. To control his fists, too.

And I trusted him more because of it.

"Maybe we can take away more of each other's pain later," I told him quietly. "In your tent again. Just as friends—just to enjoy it."

"I'd love nothing more," he murmured, his hand stroking the bare patch of skin between the bottom hem of my tank top and the top of my shorts.

We stayed like that for a little while longer, before we finally headed back.

Seven

Aev was right about running. There was something incredibly freeing about it. About feeling the wind on my cheeks, and feeling his body move beneath mine. About the way I grew to trust him more, as he carried me through the trees.

It was sometime in the middle of the night or early hours of the morning when we finally got back to the Stronghold—and people were arguing loudly, near the massive kitchen that many of us ate at.

Aev didn't bother heading to his tent, instead carrying me straight into the belly of the argument.

"Dakota!" Summer came out of nowhere, plowing into me and nearly knocking me off of Aev's back. A laugh escaped me as he tilted the other way, righting me almost effortlessly. She squeezed me tightly, and I hugged her back just as fiercely as I slid off the sabertooth.

After my conversation with Aev a few hours earlier, I was feeling kind of emotional.

And tired; really tired.

Aev shifted and stepped up beside me, his hand landing lightly on my lower back as Summer released me.

"I knew you could outfly the klynna," she told me, flashing Remmo a dirty look. "*Some of us* weren't so sure, but I believed in you."

My eyes caught on a serious-looking North, a pissed-looking Priel, and a furious-looking Korrik. The latter of which was storming toward me like hell was on his heels.

I took a step away from him, and the back of my shoulder met one of Aev's pecs.

"He won't hurt you," the king murmured to me.

I knew he wouldn't.

Mostly.

But my body still relaxed more with his words.

"I didn't outfly it," I admitted to Summer, and everyone else who was listening in. There were still other conversations happening nearby, but murmurs quieted them.

"You froze it?" someone asked Aev.

"No. It nearly ended us," he said. "But Dakota's magic connected to it, and when she ordered it to leave, it flew away."

That wasn't exactly how it had gone... but I had a feeling he wanted them to see me as strong, and powerful. Saying that I ordered it to leave made me sound a lot less pathetic than saying I'd begged it to.

The fact that he was protecting me like that made me really damn glad I'd trusted my instincts when it came to befriending him. Those instincts were scarred bitches, but sometimes, they did well.

And this was definitely one of those times.

Thanks to Aev's revelation, you could've heard a bird fly over the trees, because the forest was so quiet.

"How?" Korrik finally asked.

But he wasn't looking at Aev.

He was looking at *me.*

Talking to *me.*

Waiting for an answer.

Because he respected me to give one, I realized.

And damn, that made my chest warm.

Maybe I liked unseelies more than I had realized.

"I don't know," I admitted. "I didn't do it on purpose. I spoke to the klynna, and for some reason, it listened."

More silence followed that revelation.

"It's because she's a life-bringer," Fovea said gravely. "Vevol blesses them in many ways."

"How would *life-bringers* control the monsters?" Summer argued.

"The same way a wish could open a portal to bring us here, I'd imagine," North said, stepping closer to me and Summer. "None of it's logical. There's magic woven into every fiber of this world, and Vevol has more power than we can imagine."

"So what do we do, then?" Summer asked. "I don't want to throw myself in some monster's path to see if I can convince it not to eat us."

"You won't." Remmo's voice left no room for question.

"I won't risk my life-bringers either," Fovea said. "And we cannot use the new human females as bait; we haven't classified them yet, and most are still unwilling to shift."

"I'll do it," I offered.

Everyone looked at Aev.

I didn't even wonder if they were looking at me.

His fingers pressed against my back a little, but he said nothing. Instead, he turned his gaze to me.

So everyone else did too.

"I can't fight, so I might as well be useful in some way," I said with a shrug. "If I die, then at least I'll die trying to protect the rest of you."

That last part was probably a mistake to say aloud, because I *felt* Aev's mood darken rapidly behind me.

"We'll start discussing options for the first klynna attack," Remmo said smoothly, trying to reduce the sudden tension.

Aev dipped his head in a nod. "Dakota needs to rest. Send someone for me if one of the beasts approaches."

He started walking, his hand still on my back. I could've stepped away instead of moving with him, but I stayed by his side instead.

"I don't know where your house is," he admitted to me, as we walked.

It surprised me that he hadn't brought up what I said earlier, but I wasn't about to question that.

I pointed. "At the edge of the other houses, in that direction. It's in the trees, so it's easiest to fly there."

"No flying while the klynnas are out." He tugged one of my hands up over his shoulder and shifted quickly.

My chest sank against his neck like it was the most natural thing in the world, my fingers sinking into his fur. Despite his icy magic, he was always warm and comfortable.

"Do you need me to show you?" I called out to him, as he ran.

He shook his head smoothly, and I gripped his fur a bit tighter as he leapt to the nearest tree and scaled it with ease. His body righted as he landed on a branch, and then he was slipping through the trees like he belonged in them.

And of course, he found my treehouse without a problem.

He stopped just outside of it, giving me time to slip off his back before he shifted and studied it. "It's missing a roof. And walls."

"It's not done," I said quickly, face heating up. Soon enough, my whole damn body would be covered in the red blotches of my blush.

My "house" was just a smooth platform made of pure black wood, with a simple box full of pillows and blankets off to one side. I'd started on the walls a few weeks back, until I got distracted, so they were a few inches tall.

"The rainy season is about to start, Dakota." His chest rumbled unhappily with the words. "This isn't a safe place to live. Especially with the klynnas roaming the skies."

"Okay." I held up a finger. "I was put on spy duty, remember? I've been busy entertaining a moody sabertooth. Besides, I'm basically made of fire. I can survive rain. And potentially klynnas, too. So... it's perfect."

He lifted an eyebrow at me, and said nothing.

I huffed at him. "If I asked one of the men to help me, they might've expected something in return. And Summer told me that it will feel different if anyone else's magic creates it except mine. So, I can't accept help. I want it to be *mine*."

He grimaced. "All I have is the tent someone set up. You can stay there, or you can sacrifice the feel of the magic to let a few others help with this place."

I shook my head. "I'll just stay with the female fae."

They weren't trustworthy, but they wouldn't let anything happen to me. They were obsessed with protecting life-bringers, after all.

His body stiffened.

I stepped away from him, heading toward the edge of the platform. His fingers closed around my wrist to stop me, and I couldn't help my body's reaction.

I just... froze.

His grip was soft, unlike the memories of the ones flashing through my mind in that moment. If I'd tugged, he would've let go.

But that didn't make the moment any less triggering.

"You're trembling." Aev's voice was low, and slightly worried. He released me, stepping between me and the ledge of my house and lifting his hands up as if in surrender. "Dakota."

"Don't call me that." My voice was sharp.

I took a step back, and another. My chest was rising and falling rapidly as memories assaulted me. Focusing my thoughts, I tried to drag myself out of the past and back into my current reality.

I wasn't on Earth anymore. I wasn't in danger. No one was going to hurt me.

But... it didn't feel that way.

It felt like the forest was closing in on me.

Like there was pressure in my chest, pain in my heart.

Concern knitted the king's forehead. "What's happening?"

I sank to my knees, pressing my palms to the smooth stone and tucking my chin to my chest. The trees rustled, and in the corner of my eye, I saw a gleam of familiar-looking scales. The basilisk shifted into her fae form, but I didn't look at her, just silently repeating thoughts that I hoped would calm me.

I was fine.

Everything was fine.

The words were basically a plea.

"She's having a panic attack," Summer said calmly. "Don't move."

Aev remained where he was as my best friend—who was practically my sister—kneeled beside me and wrapped her arms around my middle, tugging me to her chest.

I resisted her grip at first, all thoughts silent as the panic enveloped me. But finally, the awful fear eased a little, and I grabbed her. Clung to her.

"You're safe," Summer told me, her voice gentle but firm. "No one's going to hurt you here."

I squeezed my eyes shut as the panic finally started to fade.

Pathetic, my dad would've called me.

Dramatic, my mother would've said.

Ridiculous, my boyfriend would've sneered.

They were wrong.

They were all wrong.

I had to believe that.

Especially because I could feel Aev staring at me.

Staring, and hopefully not thinking the same exact things they had always said.

"Sorry," I whispered, to both him and Summer.

"I *know* you didn't just apologize for having feelings," she shot back.

My lips curved upward a tiny bit.

"Sleep will help with the stress," she told me. "I'd offer my place, but we both know you don't want to crash in my sex den."

My tiny smile grew a little. "I don't."

"Blue offered her house. She and Presley share it. I don't think you know them any better than I do, but it's closer to the action than the Stronghold is. And you know you can't sleep here."

"I know," I admitted. "Their place would work, if you're sure they don't mind."

"Girl, you just offered yourself as a damn *human sacrifice*. They can survive without their house for half the day. And by the way, if I didn't trust your magic, I would already have kidnapped your ass and dragged you out of here for your own safety."

A quiet laugh escaped me. "As expected."

"Mmhm. Come on; I don't know how much time we'll have until the next klynna passes. If they're really hunting for Aev, it may not be long."

I nodded, letting out a shaky breath and sitting up straighter as I untangled my arms from around her.

"Have you been concealing your scent?" Summer asked Aev.

"Yes. Every hour." He didn't hesitate; he had been vigilant about jumping into those bushes.

"If you hurt her, I *will* convince my mate to kill you," she warned him.

"He didn't," I told her quickly and quietly, without meeting Aev's gaze. "It was just memories."

"Good. Remmo likes him." She looped her arm through mine and said over her shoulder, "The generals want to talk to you. If Dakota's going to throw herself in front of a klynna, they want to figure out if you'll be able to help buy time for them to get her out."

"I'll do whatever I can to make it easier for her," Aev said in a low voice. "And I'd like to know the plan. You'll keep her safe?"

"Of course."

Aev shifted, and though he moved too silently for me to hear him leave, I saw the flash of orange out of the corner of my eye as he slid into the trees.

I wished he had touched my hand or something before he left. But why would he, after I lost my damn mind to a panic attack? He probably wouldn't want to touch me at all.

"I think I'm going to need to form a bond with someone else," I said quietly. "He has his own baggage; he doesn't need to deal with mine too. And he definitely doesn't need more drama in his life."

"Oh please. You've been nothing but good for him, and you know it. Everyone has issues; all of us who are here wished to get away from Earth for one reason or another. And last I heard, you were just friends anyway." She lifted an eyebrow at me.

My face heated. "We are. Friends with benefits."

She snorted. "With a fae?"

"He's uniquely qualified not to want anything serious."

A laugh escaped her. "You're delusional. He was absolutely terrified that he'd caused you pain or screwed shit up between you two. Maybe he doesn't want anything serious *yet*, but he's a fae. He will. And you will too, because it feels really damn incredible to be adored as fiercely as the fae love."

"Summer," I said with a sigh.

"Come on, I'll give you a ride down. You need sleep, girl."

I groaned, but when she shifted, I slid onto her gigantic, scaly back and wrapped my arms around her neck.

And when she took me to a simple wooden house on the floor of the forest, tucked between two humongous trees, I simply slipped inside and climbed into the first bed I saw.

She was right; sleep would help.

But as I drifted off, I couldn't help but think that Aev needed to rest too.

EIGHT

AEV

"YOU NEED to talk to that damn woman," Korrik growled at me, as I landed beside him and shifted forms. "She could've *died*."

"I already did. She overheard you and Priel talking about winged fae having a better chance of outrunning the monsters, and wasn't willing to let you sacrifice yourself for her if that was the case." I slid my hands into my pockets, letting my fists clench.

My skin itched.

Not the way it had when Naomi refused to see me—nothing like that. It itched because I'd scared Dakota somehow, and I hadn't had the chance to apologize.

Because Summer had held her, instead of me.

Because I wanted her to trust me. To rely on me. To cling to me the way she had clung to Summer.

Because I wanted to understand what her panic attack was, and how I could avoid doing anything to cause another one.

Because I wanted to rescue her from that fear, or those memories.

...The itch was foreign, but not unwelcome.

Not unwelcome at all.

"Damn." Korrik grimaced.

I added, "Keeping secrets from the females doesn't do anyone any good. They need to understand the full gravity of every situation, so they can decide for themselves. If you had one simple conversation with her, Dakota would never have risked her life the way she did."

"Well now I understand why they picked him as king," a woman muttered. "He's the only one with common sense."

I glanced over and found the oracle standing beside her hellhound. Priel growled at her, and she batted at his shoulder lightly. When he tugged her closer, she went up on her tiptoes and kissed his cheek. "You're still hotter," she whispered to him. "But you're kind of controlling."

"Kind of?" he rumbled back.

Her laughter cut through the air.

"How strong is your magic, Aev?" Vuvim asked, and I lifted my gaze to the basilisk general. He had refused to join the new council, but that didn't mean he'd lost anyone's respect. Even the seelies would hear him out when he spoke.

"I'm still figuring that out. The mate bond multiplied it fiercely enough that without it, I now feel weaker than I am," I explained. "And it's been centuries since I had the chance to use it on anything but the prison."

"Theoretically, it's still strong enough to temporarily kill a klynna?" Vuvim checked.

"It used to be, so theoretically, yes."

He nodded.

"If Dakota is putting herself in front of it, I won't be focused on trying to down it," I warned him. "I'll be preparing to freeze its mouth and throat long enough to get her away from it in case she fails."

"That could give us enough time to get basilisks in place," Oren said thoughtfully.

"They have fire," Teris pointed out. "They can break through the ice almost instantly."

Our last fight had proven that to be true.

"It'll distract a klynna long enough to get Dakota away and flood the skies with our warriors," Fovea said. "So it's definitely better than nothing."

"I may be able to do more damage after she's safe," I added. "Assuming I can practice enough to get a real feel for my power again. The last time I killed one,

I did so from the trees, while it dove past me. Replicating the situation well enough for me to kill it would be difficult at best, but I can at least delay it."

"You saved our asses," Korrik said unhappily. "And we may need you to do it again."

"There are enough of us that hopefully we can avoid a repeat," Oren said.

Murmurs of agreement rolled through the crowd.

"We'll continue running our drills on the ground," Fovea added. "If they're going to attack us, we'll be ready for it."

The group parted, but I strode forward and caught Oren by the arm before he could leave. "I need you to carry Dakota into the sky," I told him in a low voice. "I don't trust any of the seelie to keep her safe."

He dipped his head. "Assuming she agrees to it."

"I'll talk to her."

I released him, but he grabbed my arm the same way I'd grabbed his. "I'm surprised you accepted a bond so easily, given what happened with Naomi."

"Dakota is nothing like Naomi. And besides, she only offered to take away both of our pain. A broken bond causes a constant ache."

"You will still yearn for her," he said, studying me.

My lips curved upward. "I'd yearn for her even without the bond. And if I asked her to break it right now, she would. I am not trapped, brother; I have been freed. She freed me."

Oren's voice was solemn as he said, "Should you need someone else to take the bond for your sanity, I am willing."

Considering the way my bond with Naomi had deteriorated me, he was making a very serious and very generous offer. It was unnecessary, but that didn't make it any less significant. "I'll keep that in mind. Thank you."

"For what it's worth, I'm glad your first bond was broken. You're more alive than I've seen you in decades."

I laughed, rich and deep. "I *feel* more alive than I've been in decades."

He released my arm. "Perhaps fate sometimes tests us."

"Or perhaps it only drew me to Naomi to stop the wars before she was injured. Regardless of the past, it brought us here. And this is a much better situation for all of us." I gestured toward the forest.

"I suppose so." Oren looked thoughtful.

"I need someone to practice on. Care to offer yourself up?"

He chuckled. "Only because you've learned how to smile again."

I slugged him in the arm, grinning, and we turned and strode into the forest together.

Nine
Dakota

I wasn't sure how much time had passed when I sat up, blinking sleep from my eyes. A glance to the side proved that both Blue and Presley were out cold in the other bed—identifiable by Blue's blue hair and the shimmering reddish-brown tattoos running down Presley's pale arm.

Paper crinkled next to me, and I lifted it to read the note Summer must've left.

Went back to my sex cave. Yell if you need me!

-S

I folded the paper and slipped out of bed, padding toward the door. I opened it as quietly as possible and then shut it the same way after I was through, rubbing the sleep from my eyes.

When I looked around again, I realized it was early in the morning. The sun hadn't even started to rise yet, but I could hear a few people up and moving already.

It felt weird to be away from Aev after we'd spent so many hours together.

Had he slept yet?

I started to walk toward his tent without really thinking, and then halted when I realized I could smell him—in the opposite direction I'd been heading.

He smelled… pretty good, actually.

I headed in that direction, curious about where he'd gone and what he'd done while I was asleep.

And also feeling bad that I hadn't apologized to him for freaking out on him earlier. I needed to at least *sort of* explain myself. Hopefully he hadn't already decided that he was done being friends with me or anything.

I finger-combed my hair as I quietly made my way through the forest. I could feel eyes on me—and felt something weird on one of my boobs. When I tugged my tank top off my skin and peered downward, I snorted. There were a few scent-hiding leaves tucked between my breasts.

When I thought about it, I vaguely remembered Summer waking me up long enough to command me to stick the leaves in my clothes at some point while I'd been asleep.

Tugging the leaves out, I tossed them to the ground. The wind would carry them off somewhere.

Though I could feel some in the back of my top too, when I reached back, I couldn't quite reach any of the leaves. So, I gave up on trying to retrieve them, and instead lit myself on fire to burn them away.

It didn't take too long to track Aev's smell to the source. I stepped around a massive tree, and halted in place when I saw two men moving together, chests heaving and faces grinning as they spun and whirled. When one slashed, the other dodged. When one lunged, the other rolled.

It almost looked like… a dance.

No one was bleeding.

They both looked happy.

I expected it to trigger me, seeing the fight.

But strangely enough, it didn't.

There was a pinch on some invisible nerve, but the panic didn't come.

Aev's head jerked toward me, and before our eyes had even collided, he'd thrown a smooth tuck-roll-thing and landed on his feet in front of me.

"You're alright?" he checked, his gaze sweeping over my face.

"I'm fine. Do you have a minute?" My eyes flicked to Oren, who he had been fighting with.

"Of course."

"Find someone else's ass to freeze next time," Oren told Aev. He studied me for a moment before he turned and walked away.

"Have you slept?" I asked the ex-king.

His lips curved upward. "Nah. It's been a long time since I felt this alive; I don't really want to sleep through it."

I nodded, even though my first instinct was to protest, to tell him that he still needed to rest. Because how long had it been since he slept? The circles under his eyes had circles of their own.

"About earlier..." I bit my lip, trying to figure out what to say and how to say it.

"I hope you're not about to apologize." He slipped his hands into his shorts' pockets.

"I *am* about to apologize. I should've warned you, at least. The triggers are random, and the panic is fierce. I'm a lot better at fighting them than I used to be, but when I get tired, the panic gets more uncontrollable. I'm sorry I didn't let you know sooner. And..."

I sighed. "I'm sorry that I didn't tell you the full truth about my past. I was trying to keep things light and happy, because of everything with Naomi. I like to pretend the shitty things never happened, because it's easier to stay positive that way. But I should've warned you, so I'm sorry."

"I understand. You were keeping me sane, you know. Giving me something to think about other than the pain, for the first time in a long time. And I appreciate that immensely."

My lips curved upward a little bit at the honesty in his voice. "Then you're welcome, I guess." I paused, and then let myself blurt my thoughts. "You really do need to sleep."

He chuckled. "I'll sleep when I know we're not at risk anymore. It's been so long since I had this much access to my ice. Between the time, and the downgrade in magic after losing the mate bond, I may as well be starting over entirely. The council and Wild Hunt are relying on me to keep you alive if you can't control the klynna, and I have to be ready."

"You'll be more ready if you've rested. How many days has it been since you slept?"

"A few."

I stepped closer to him. Though my instincts were all over the place, I didn't fight the urge to lift my hand to his face and slowly drag a finger over the thick circle beneath his eye. He went still with my touch; I don't even think he dared to breathe. "We're friends, right?" I asked him.

He gave me the smallest nod.

"Friends listen to each other when they say they need to rest."

"Do they?" His voice was low, and gravelly.

"Yes."

"And what would you be doing, if I was sleeping? I can't risk missing the fight with the next klynna, Da..." Aev trailed off, and didn't finish.

I remembered telling him not to call me Dakota, when I'd been triggered.

"When you grabbed me and said my name like that, it reminded me of my ex-boyfriend," I admitted to him. "He would never let me walk away from him, so it brought bad memories back. I didn't mean that you shouldn't call me by my name, I was just panicking. I'm sorry."

"I don't want to remind you of him."

"You don't." My lips curved upward sadly. "It's just trauma."

"I'll think of a nickname for you," he said simply.

"You could just call me Dots. I've been answering to that for a long time."

"No. It's too playful for the woman who would approach me in my tent the way you did, just to take away my pain."

My face heated. "It wasn't just to take away your pain. I was being a little selfish."

"Then I enjoyed your selfishness immensely, and would welcome it at any time." He gently caught my hand, since my fingers were still on his face. "Come to my tent with me, and I'll rest without complaint. Not for long—just long enough to ease your conscience."

I should've said no.

I should've come up with an excuse.

But honestly? I didn't want to.

So I nodded.

And his lips curved upward.

He released my hand, and we headed off toward his tent together. Both of us were silent, and neither of us bothered shifting forms.

"You and Oren weren't fighting the way the seelie fight," I said quietly, as we walked through the forest that still seemed mostly asleep.

"The seelie are more violent than us, and Oren and I weren't truly fighting; he was testing me, to see if I could freeze him while he burned and attacked me. It was a mental exercise more than a physical one, and unfortunately, I didn't succeed."

"Oh. How did you learn to move like that?"

"Lots and lots of practice." He flashed me a white-toothed grin. "You know, you could learn to protect yourself without any violence. There are fae who prefer not to trade punches, and they train their bodies through gymnastic movements rather than fighting ones."

"Is it like what you and Oren were doing?" I asked him. "It almost looked like you were dancing."

"It does resemble a dance," Aev agreed. "You perform the same motions—you just teach your body to pull back, rather than attacking. It doesn't prepare you for the physical or emotional consequences of an actual fight, but it would give you more control over your body."

"That would be amazing," I admitted. "Feeling strong and in control... I've always wondered what it would be like."

"Then I will find one of my men to teach you," he said simply.

"Why can't you?" I looked at him, frowning slightly.

He focused on the trees, straight ahead. "I didn't think you would want me to."

"I'd feel safer if it was you. I know that's probably hard to believe after my panic attack, but it's true. My panic has nothing to do with you; it's just memories."

"Then when we've dealt with the klynnas, I'll train you." His hand carefully took mine, and I slid my fingers between his. Neither of us looked at each other.

"After you rest," I reminded him.

He chuckled. "After I rest."

We reached his tent, and he maintained his hold on my hand as he opened the flap, letting us both inside. It had only been a few days since we'd been in there together, but it looked and felt so different since the last time.

His bed was in the opposite corner from the place he had been kneeling when I walked in on him that night. And though both of us glanced at that wooden chest with the morphed lid, neither of us commented on it as we walked toward the bed.

Aev released my hand when we reached the mattress. "You'll stay close?"

"I will."

He sat down on the edge of the mattress, and his gaze went back to that corner.

My face warmed as the memories flashed before my eyes. Good memories, this time.

No one had ever made me feel like that before. That sexy, or powerful.

"Should you ever want a repeat of that night," Aev said in a low voice, "The answer is always yes. Any time. Any place. You say the word or touch me, and I can guarantee I'll be ready in a heartbeat. Maybe sooner."

A soft laugh escaped me. "I'll keep that in mind."

He slid under the blanket on the mattress. "My bed is available, too."

"Is it?" My voice was soft and playful.

"Always."

My lips curved upward as he slid beneath the blankets, tugging them over his thighs as he rolled to his stomach. His eyes shut, and it occurred to me how strange this moment was.

We were just friends, and yet, the sexiest moments of my life had been spent in this tent, with the stunning fae in front of me who was lying on his stomach like a normal person.

The stunning fae who I trusted more than I'd trusted any other man in... well, maybe my entire life.

Nev and I were friends, but he was kind of sneaky. And as he proved when he mated with Fovea, he had plans that didn't include me. It was hard to trust someone like that. And even though I knew none of the other Wild Hunt guys would hurt me, I wasn't under any kind of impression that I could sit next to them and tell them about my past without being judged.

I knew that most fae men would probably be freaked out by my panic attack in the forest the day before. And maybe Aev was freaked out too—but I didn't think he was.

"You're staring at me," he said quietly, a few minutes later.

"I'm just thinking," I whispered back.

"Loudly."

I smiled. "I'll work on it."

His lips curved upward. "You don't need to. Think as loudly as you want."

I lifted my gaze off his figure anyway, as my thoughts continued to spin.

Aev's breathing grew even as he fell asleep, and... well, I was a little tired of standing. There were cushions on the other side of the room, but I'd feel awkward sitting on the cushions.

And I was still tired.

Maybe I could get a little more sleep.

He *had* offered me half of the bed.

So I slowly slipped under the blankets, carefully remaining on my side of the mattress. Our bodies didn't touch, but sharing the space still felt intimate.

Even though I'd just slept for a bit, I closed my eyes, and somehow managed to fall asleep again.

When I woke up, there was a massive arm draped over my waist, and my cheek was resting against the side of Aev's face, with my hair pooled on the mattress beside us. I really needed to cut a few inches off so it wouldn't tangle as easily, but I hadn't managed to convince myself to do it.

His hand was moving slowly on my upper back, over my tank top, so he wasn't touching any of my bare skin.

"Your breathing changed," he murmured to me.

My lips curved upward. "Did it?" My voice was sleepy, and that made the moment feel a little vulnerable. I forced my eyes to stay closed. "Sorry, I must've climbed on you while I was sleeping."

"Don't be. I could get used to waking up like this." He moved his cheek a little, and the stubble on his face brushed against my skin, giving me goosebumps.

"Me too," I admitted.

His hand continued moving slowly over my back, still not touching my bare skin. I supposed he was being respectful, but I itched to feel him really touch me.

Any awkwardness from before we'd fallen asleep had pretty much faded. It was hard to feel uncomfortable when we were so completely relaxed in each other's arms.

"You can touch my back, you know," I whispered, after a few more minutes of overly-appropriate contact. Neither of us seemed to be in a hurry to get up.

"I didn't want to make you uncomfortable."

Happiness swelled in my chest. "Thank you."

A moment of silence followed, and his hand slowly began moving over more of my back. It still went over my tank top, but now he was touching more of me, not avoiding my skin altogether. It felt good, but still wasn't exactly what I wanted.

I hesitated for a few minutes before finally saying, "Despite what happened in your tent, I'm not usually very forward when it comes to new things. If you ever want something, it's best just to ask me."

"I'll keep that in mind," Aev said.

His hand moved up to my shoulder blade, and he slowly started to trace the marking there. It had appeared a little after I got settled in the Stronghold, a masterpiece of red roses and thorny vines that stretched over more than half of my back.

A thought occurred to me, one I'd been itching to ask a fae but had never really felt comfortable enough to bring up. "Do you have roses here?"

"Roses?"

"The flowers on my back."

"We call those drelaes, but they aren't purely flowers. They're..." He trailed off, considering it. "Well, predators. They consume bugs, and any small animals that get close enough."

My eyes nearly bulged out of my head. "What?!" I turned, trying to see my tattoos again, to check if they really looked like roses. When I started looking closer, I realized that they did look slightly different. "Do they have vines, too?"

He gave me a small smile, his pretty blue eyes bright and calm. "The vines are a part of them. They can move around the forest with them, climbing the trees." His finger traced one of the long, spiraling vines, until it disappeared into my tank top.

"Well, that's terrifying." I grimaced deeply, dropping my head back to rest against the side of Aev's. "Why do I have carnivorous flowers on my back?"

"There's usually some kind of message in the magical markings."

"What kind of message? Like, words?"

"No. It's usually symbolic, and the meaning makes itself known to the wearer at some point in their life." He didn't sound nearly as bothered by the marks as I felt, and he was still tracing them on my shoulder.

I frowned. "I don't even want to know the meaning behind mine."

"Why not? The meaning could have to do with anything. Like you, drelaes are beautiful, and they look fragile but are among the strongest plants in Vevol's forests."

I sighed. "Maybe I do want to know the meaning. I thought they were roses, and it was some kind of omen about my future."

He chuckled. "What's unique about roses?"

"I don't really know. Usually men buy red ones for women they care about. My boyfriend only ever bought them for me when I was sporting the bruises he gave me. He'd apologize, and bring me flowers, and say that he'd never hurt me again. We'd both act like we believed it was true." My eyes shut, and I let out a slow breath. "I fantasized about stabbing him with the thorns on them so many times. It wasn't even realistic—the thorns aren't that big. But I still thought about it. Do you think that makes me a bad person?"

"I think if that makes you a bad person, you should embrace the title. I've already fantasized about doing far worse to that man, and I don't even know what he looks like."

My lips curved upward sadly. "I tried to get away from him, a few days before I made the wish and got brought here. I didn't stab him—I slipped away. But a friend I thought I could trust had warned him, and he was waiting for me. He hurt me, worse than ever before."

I continued, my words coming out faster as I did. "I was in the hospital when the fae came for me. He was talking to the nurse—acting like the perfect boyfriend. He'd told them that I was mugged, and they bought it. Or at least pretended to. I looked at the clock, and it was 11:11, and I wished with every fiber of my being that I wouldn't make it to 11:12. And then the portal opened, and the Wild Hunt grabbed me. My eyes met my ex's as the guys took me through that portal, and the relief I felt was just... everything." Tears leaked down my cheeks as I told the story, but I didn't try to wipe them away.

Aev's fingers had paused on my back.

"I don't know why I'm telling you this. I've never even told Summer this before," I confessed. "But I didn't wish for another chance at life—I wished for death, Aev. I don't deserve to be here. I *never* deserved to be here. Not when there are other people who would've fought harder or wanted it more. That's why I put so much effort into staying positive—because I owe everyone else who *does* deserve to be here. I don't even know what kind of person it makes me, to have wished for that."

Aev was silent for a moment. It was only a heartbeat, but it felt like a century. "It makes you a drelae, Dakota. Beautiful, and fragile, with long, thorny vines."

I snorted, tears dripping on Aev's pillow, now. "Please. Maybe I'm a drelae without the flower part. Just a bunch of thorny vines."

He laughed quietly. "Maybe I should call you Thorns, then."

Despite the seriousness of the conversation a few moments ago, my lips stretched in a soft grin. "Thorns? What a compliment."

"It *is* a compliment. Your thorns make you strong." He resumed tracing the shape of my markings.

It occurred to me, then, the difference between Aev and my ex. Aev and I weren't together—not really. But while my ex had always wanted me to be weaker, and smaller, and quieter, Aev just wanted me strong.

And I wondered if maybe, at the end of the day, that's what love was supposed to be like.

"We should probably get up so you can train some more," I admitted.

"Probably," he agreed.

But neither of us moved.

And my lips curved upward again, just a little.

Ten

Aev resumed tracing my marking, and my thoughts quieted. My body had been completely and utterly relaxed before we talked about everything, but now, I was kind of keyed up.

"How much of your back does your marking cover?" he asked me, sounding almost absent-minded. He stiffened as soon as the words were out. "Sorry. I don't mean to push."

"You don't need to apologize; that's not pushy. If you ordered me to rip my shirt off or ripped it off for me, that would be pushy. But in the right situation, maybe a little sexy too."

He laughed—a deep belly laugh, one I'd never heard from him. And that laugh made me grin, widely. "Sexy, huh?"

"Sure. Give it a try, I bet you could do it right."

He laughed again—this time, a little bit in disbelief. "I'm not ripping your shirt off, Thorns."

My grin widened.

I probably shouldn't have, but I loved the nickname. I'd been Dakota, and I'd been Dots—but I sure as hell had never been anything nearly as badass as *Thorns*.

"I gave you two options. A command would work too."

"I don't want to make you uncomfortable," he said, laughter in his voice still.

"Well, I'm the one who walked in on you jerking off. I'm pretty sure you owe me a lot of discomfort to make up for that one," I teased. "And I already offered, so obviously this one's on me."

"I suppose that's a valid point." He grew quiet for a moment.

My humor faded in the silence, and I started to wonder if I'd made him uncomfortable. That hadn't been my intention—and he'd seemed playful, hadn't he?

"Thorns," he finally said, his voice soft and silky. "Take off your top so I can see your markings."

My lower belly clenched at the sexy tone of that command, and I slowly eased myself up, off his chest. Those gorgeous bright blue eyes were hot, and my lips curved upward. "If you insist."

His eyes burned into me as I reached down to the bottom hem of my tank top, and slowly pulled it up, over my head.

The man beneath me went completely and utterly still as I dropped the fabric next to us on the bed.

His eyes were trained on my face, his jaw clenched and his body so, so tight.

"Do you want to touch me?" I asked him, both hot and curious at the same time.

He was so hard to read, sometimes. So used to shutting himself down, to staying quiet, to making himself smaller for Naomi.

"Yes." The word was barely a breath, and he still didn't move.

My lips curved upward a little more, and I lifted my hands to my breasts. They weren't huge or tiny; I appreciated their averageness, though.

His eyes dipped to my nipples when I dragged my thumbs over them slowly.

Finally, he was looking at me.

"Am I pushing you too much?" I asked, biting my lip when he still didn't try to touch me.

"No. That's not even possible." His voice was low, and rough.

"Okay." I slid myself backward a little, until my ass met the rock-hard erection I'd been wondering about. He let out a long breath when I rocked lightly against him once. "Too much?"

"Still not possible." His voice was strained.

I finally released my breasts. "This is way too one-sided, Aev. I'm the one who instigated things the first time; now I feel like I'm violating you or something."

His hands slid up to my waist, holding me in place before I could get off of him. "I don't know what I'm doing," he admitted.

"I know. Naomi treated you like shit. That doesn't mean you can't touch me."

"This has nothing to do with her. I just..." he let out a harsh breath. "I don't know what you'd like. What would feel good. And if I let myself touch you, I don't know if I'll be able to stop."

There was vulnerability in his eyes, in his voice.

And I loved that.

"You're afraid of losing control," I said.

"Unfortunately." He heaved a sigh.

I laughed. "You don't need to be afraid. Tell me what you want, and I'll tell you if it's too much. I like to get bossed around when things get hot though; I should probably admit that."

His eyes gleamed wickedly. "Do you?"

"A lot."

"Good." He dragged his thumbs over my bare hips, and I shivered. "I want to taste you," he said, voice low. "Your mouth, first. And then every other inch of you. I want to watch you lose control on my tongue."

Oh damn. "I think I could handle that," I said, my breathing picking up a little as I rocked my ass lightly against his hardness.

"I want my fingers buried inside you again." He dragged his thumbs over my hipbones, and I rocked a little more. "So I can feel you tighten when you shatter."

"Okay," I managed to get out.

His voice got lower and more growly as he continued. "I want those pretty little nipples in my mouth, while I touch you. I want your legs around my back, my hands on your ass, while we get as close to fucking as possible."

"Really?" I breathed.

"Yes." He dragged his thumbs over my hips. "That all sounds okay?"

"Stop teasing me and do it already," I demanded.

A dark laugh escaped him. He rolled me over in one fluid motion, and then lowered his face to mine.

"Last chance to back out," he murmured, his lips brushing my mouth as he spoke.

"For you too," I countered, my chest rising and falling hard against his.

His lips curved upward for a moment, his eyes growing electric before he pressed his mouth to mine.

He was new to all of this, so I didn't hesitate to part my lips and slide my tongue into his mouth. We groaned together as we tasted each other, and shit, Aev learned the right way to kiss me, *fast*.

The hand he wasn't using to hold his body off of mine buried itself in my hair, gripping the back of my head as he kissed me.

Thunder cracked overhead, but I barely heard it at all as Aev's mouth made love to mine. He may as well have been consuming me, and if he was, I wouldn't bother stopping him. The rain started to pour, drowning out the sounds of anyone around us, but we didn't bother pausing.

Aev's hardness pressed against my core, and my legs wrapped around his back, pulling him as close to me as he could possibly get.

A huge drop of water splattered on my cheek, and I paused.

Aev slowed and then pulled away, opening his eyes.

I peered around him, tugging one of my swollen lips into my mouth as I stared up at the top of the tent.

Rain was falling through the fabric, and Aev was already on his way toward being drenched. The water that had hit my face must've come off of *him*.

"It's just rain," he told me, retaking my lips.

I kissed him for another minute before I pulled away to laugh at the fact that he was dripping all over me. His lips stretched in a sheepish grin as he wiped rain off my nose.

"Sorry," I told him, still grinning.

"Not your fault. We both need a more secure place to live." He wiped more rain off my face as it dripped out of his hair and onto me.

"Aev!" Someone yelled from outside the tent. "The klynnas always hunt in the rain. We need you and Dakota out here."

His smile faded.

Mine did too.

"He's right," Aev admitted, slowly easing himself off of me. His erection tented his pants, and I tried not to let myself drool at the sight.

He handed me my tank top, and stepped back as I tugged it over my head. There was hesitance in his gaze when he looked at me, and I couldn't help but worry that I'd just screwed things up between us.

"Still friends?" I asked him.

"Of course, Thorns." He flashed me a small smile, and I returned it.

Hopefully, all was still well.

THE MALE FAE looked like they were preparing for war when we emerged from the tent. None of them had any kind of armor on, but they stood in organized groups, solemnly watching the sky as water poured from the clouds above the trees

Aev didn't hold my hand, or otherwise acknowledge what we'd just done. The swelling in my lips had already gone down, too, so there was no evidence that we'd been making out for who knew how long.

He strode off to speak with a few of the unseelie leaders, looking more like a king than he ever had in the time I had known him.

Oren left the group just as Aev joined it, and the dragon general stepped into place beside me as we headed toward the four mated ex-human women and their men. They were in their own circle, on the opposite side of the area from the other leaders.

"You'll be flying with me," Oren said.

"I'll be flying myself," I countered, my eyes moving over the crowd of fae in front of us so I didn't have to look him in the eyes.

"You'll need to focus on the klynna. You can't do that and be ready to get yourself out of the way if you fail. Every second matters."

"I don't fly with anyone," I told him, finally meeting his gaze. The man looked frustrated, and I didn't blame him. But that didn't change my opinions in the slightest.

"The king is the one who asked me. You'll have to bring it up with him." Oren tucked his hands in the pockets of his shorts.

My defenses rose. "Aev doesn't get to make that decision for me."

"You started a mate bond with him. Bonds create attachment that didn't exist previously. If you don't believe that attachment gives him enough authority to care about your safety, you need to break the bond before the emotions grow any stronger." Oren's voice had an undercurrent of anger in it, which caught me off guard.

And made my defenses swell.

I argued, "We created a bond to get us both out of pain. Nothing else."

"If that was true, you wouldn't smell of each other's pleasure."

"Back off," I hissed, as we approached the other ex-human women. My heart was beating irrationally fast, but I knew that was because of the conversation.

"If you refuse to care about Aev like a mate, break the bond," Oren said.

He walked in the other direction as I joined my friends and their mates. It was still raining on us, and my hair was plastered to my back and chest, with a few strands stuck to my arms as well.

"You look sick," Summer said, her forehead creasing as she grabbed my arm and tugged me toward her. "What happened?"

I glanced at Remmo, who was beside her, but deep in conversation with Lian. January, North, and Priel were talking, and Mare and Ervo looked like they were having an intense discussion.

"Oren said Aev asked him to fly me to the klynna," I admitted.

The creases in her forehead deepened. "So?"

"You know I don't fly with anyone. I don't trust them." I wrapped my arms around my abdomen.

"I know. But I want you to survive this insane plan, and you have a much better chance of doing that if you don't fly yourself."

"He told me I should break my bond with Aev," I said, frustration welling in my chest. "He acted like I'm the bad guy."

Summer's eyebrows shot upward. "What the hell?"

"I don't know." I wrapped my arms tighter around my middle. I'd felt like that a few times, but I'd chalked it up to my past. "Do you think I am?"

"Of course not." She scowled. "But you *do* need to fly with someone."

"What are we talking about?" January checked, as she and North stepped up to me and Summer.

"Dakota wants to fly herself to the klynna." Summer tossed a hand toward the sky.

"Well, that's a shitty idea," January said with a grimace. Her hand lowered to her abdomen, and I glanced at the curve of it. She was definitely visibly pregnant now, but her bump wasn't huge. Since no one was certain how long an ex-human and fae pregnancy would last, we weren't sure how much longer she had, but she didn't look like she was about to pop anytime soon. The fae life-bringers assumed she was about halfway through the pregnancy.

"I don't want to fly with someone I don't trust," I corrected Summer, shooting her a dark look.

She shrugged. "Who do you trust enough to fly with, then?"

I blinked.

"No one, huh?" Summer said pointedly.

My lips pressed together.

She was right.

I really didn't trust many people at all. And since Aev and Summer couldn't fly, there was no one.

"I could fly you," January offered. "I know we're not super close, but I at least don't have a dick."

"Girl, you're pregnant. We all know that's not an option," Summer tossed back.

January heaved a sigh.

I glanced at North, and frowned when I saw her focused on something beyond us. When I looked in that direction, I saw nothing but trees.

"She's trying to see the fight," January told me.

Oh.

"Has it worked?"

January shook her head. "Her magic should be getting easier to control, but it isn't."

That was a little concerning.

"Mare," January called out, pulling our dragon chick from her conversation with Ervo. She looked over at us, giving us the tiniest smile. "Can you fly Dots up to meet the klynna?"

"No." Ervo answered before Mare could, glowering at all of us. "There are plenty of unattached males who can do that."

Mare gave him a look. "It's my choice, Viervo." She turned her gaze back to us. "But honestly, I'm not the best choice. There are a lot of fae who are faster and more skilled at flying than I am."

Summer looked at me. "If Aev asked Oren, he's probably a good pick, as shitty as he treated you. Aev probably has other friends who would be just as good, too."

I shook my head. "I won't fly with them."

I didn't even know if I was willing to fly with a man at all, but after our conversation, there wasn't even a question about Oren. I wouldn't fly with him, period.

"What about Lian?" Summer asked, looking at January.

"No. I'll be protecting my female and the other life-bringers in the Stronghold," he said, from a few feet away.

I tightened my arms around my abdomen. "I'll ask Fovea."

"The female fae are far less trustworthy than the males," Remmo countered. "Devv would do it. Summer knows him well."

"I do. I could ask Devv," Summer offered, looking at me.

Waiting.

My throat tightened. "I'll think about it."

"You don't have time to think about it," Summer warned.

I jerked my head in a nod, turning and striding away from the group. My head was spinning, and I just needed to get away from them. From everyone.

I forced myself to walk at a normal pace as I slipped into the forest, between the trees, toward the Stronghold so no one would come after me right away.

Eleven

I FOUND myself walking back to Blue and Presley's place. It was one of the only human-looking houses in the forest, since the majority of the fae seemed to prefer caves or treehouses.

They were both sitting on top of the slanted roof of the house, their legs dangling over the edge and their heads tipped back so the rain would land on their faces.

"What are you doing?" I called out to them.

"Living!" Blue yelled back. "Come join us!"

I hesitated.

Presley waved me toward them, so I walked over. They had a smooth wooden ladder attached to the building, and it looked like it was a part of the structure.

Though I wasn't entirely certain it was safe, I climbed up. They had carved the ladder steps a bit, making it rough enough that I didn't slip.

When I reached the top of the ladder, I realized the roof of the building was rough too. They must've made a habit out of sitting up there, since they'd bothered making it grippy enough that they wouldn't slide off.

I'd never had a conversation with either of the women, as far as I could remember. But I tended to keep to myself unless I absolutely had to socialize.

"Doesn't the rain feel nice?" Blue called. She was beside me, and Presley was beside her.

"I guess." I tilted my head back like the other two women were doing, my eyes and mouth closed to the rain falling on us. Because it was being filtered through the trees, it wasn't falling steadily at all. There would be multiple drips, and then big gushes. It was weird, but sort of refreshing too.

"You look stressed," Presley noted, after a few calm, quiet minutes had passed. Though I was still stressing a little, the quiet peace of the moment had relaxed me.

"I formed a temporary bond with Aev," I admitted. "As friends."

Blue said, "Yeah, everyone knows."

"Oren told me that I need to break it before I hurt him."

Presley whistled. "Dick."

"Is he, though? What if I'm wrong?"

"Oren thinks mate bonds are curses," Blue said. When I looked at her, I found her already looking at me. "He told me he's my fated mate, but he's not willing to be destroyed by a bond. His words, not mine. I would take what he says with a grain of salt."

I grimaced. "I'm sorry."

"Don't be." Her lips curved upward, and she turned her face back to the sky. I did the same, closing my eyes to the falling rain. "Life is beautiful here even when it's shitty, don't you think?"

"I do." I let out a long, slow breath. "It's hard to let go of the past, though."

"Memories can be a real bitch," Presley agreed.

"Amen," Blue muttered.

I bit my lip for a moment before admitting, "I'm supposed to fly with someone, but I never have before. I don't like touching people, let alone trusting them with my life that way."

Both women lifted their heads so they could look at me, so I did the same and looked at them.

"I can fly you," Presley said. "I spend a lot of time in the sky. I haven't been flying for centuries like some of these bastards, but I do fly with the men a lot, and have had them putting me through drills and stuff. So I'm nowhere near a beginner."

"I can't ask you to risk your life," I countered.

"You didn't ask, I offered."

When I hesitated, she added, "I'm not a basilisk or a life-bringer, and the guys won't let me fly as a distraction with them, so carrying you would give me a way to help. And you wouldn't have to be uncomfortable with some fae dude, so it's a win-win situation."

"I bet Aev won't like it, though," Blue said.

"They're only friends, remember?" Presley flashed her a devious grin, and Blue laughed.

My lips curved upward too.

My gaze caught on something out in the forest, and my eyebrows shot upward when Naomi stepped out from between some trees.

I hadn't known she was awake.

Then again, I had been gone a while, and then asleep for a bit...

"Hey, Nai," Blue lifted a hand and wiggled her fingers. I'd never heard anyone use the nickname for her—just the *Nay* part of her name—but I'd only talked to her two or three times, and she'd seemed cold and unhappy every one of them.

Honestly, the woman looked terrible. Her tan skin was splotchy, and her long, dark hair was tied in a single braid that hung over her shoulder. Rainwater dripped down her face, and her simple, seelie-style tank top and shorts were plastered to her skin.

I couldn't remember ever seeing her dressed that way before, but I thought it actually kind of suited her.

Naomi waved back, climbing up the ladder and scooting toward me. When she was sitting next to me, her face tilted to the sky and her eyes closed too.

"Are you feeling any better?" Blue asked her.

"Getting there." Her voice was quiet, and raspy. "No klynnas yet?"

"Nope. The guys think it's only a matter of time, though, since the rain will wash Aev's scent into the ground or something. I don't really get it," Blue explained.

Naomi sighed, but didn't ask any more questions.

My stomach clenched, and I wondered if I should say something about Aev. If I should warn her, or make sure she was okay with it, or something. But the separation between them had been mutual—and mostly her call, from what I knew—so I didn't think I really needed to ask her about it.

"This is awkward," Presley whispered. "Can we just bring up Aev already?"

Blue snorted. "Smooth, Press."

"Aeven and I were a horrible match," Naomi told me, without lifting her face to look at me. "I never had feelings for him, romantic or friendly. He's not a terrible person, so I wish you the best, but it's not awkward for me if you're with him. He smells just like everyone else to me now that my name's been changed, so our fated mate bond is well and truly broken, and I have no desire to ever have a conversation with him again."

I let out a relieved breath. "Alright."

"Do you feel like you have closure?" Blue wondered. "I feel like there's no closure with me and Oren, you know? Like we're supposed to be together, but we're not, and... I don't know. I guess I'm just not sure."

"I don't feel like Aeven and I were ever close enough to need closure. At least not on my side of things. I hurt him more than he hurt me, though. Don't let fate make your decision for you, Blue. Love is a choice. Mating should be one too."

Her words struck me, hard.

Before I had time to really think about them, though, a shadow passed over our heads.

Shit.

The klynnas.

A sabertooth streaked through the trees, and I recognized him without even seeing his eyes.

Aev.

"We have to go, now," I told Presley, standing swiftly. The roof wasn't the safest place to do that, but we needed to get our asses into gear.

"Where?" Naomi asked.

None of us answered her—Presley just grabbed me by the arm and launched into the sky, shifting on the fly.

Aev snarled at us, but Presley was smart enough to dodge him as she hauled ass toward the rest of the fae, who were all ready for a fight.

I didn't know exactly how this was supposed to work.

I should've had a serious conversation with whoever was in charge of making the plans, instead of letting my panic lead me away from everyone else.

But I didn't do either of those things.

So, I'd just have to figure it out as we went.

Presley reached the organized groups of fae just as the klynna above us roared.

It was warning us, I thought.

Giving us a chance to hand Aev over.

Which, obviously, we weren't going to do.

Oren gestured for Presley to follow him, shifting and launching himself into the sky. She didn't hesitate to do so, her nose on his gleaming golden tail as his massive, scaly form flew upward.

I still smelled enough like Aev to catch the creature's attention, I hoped.

Presley and Oren wove through the trees rapidly, gaining altitude until they broke through the branches and up into the sky.

My heart pounded hard, but I felt no panic.

The last time, I had locked eyes with it, and pleaded with it. It hadn't obeyed me; it had answered my plea.

So I wasn't going to try to *command* the creature to do anything. It was too large and too intelligent for that.

I needed to look it in the eyes and *ask* it to leave without killing anyone.

Without killing *Aev*.

The klynna roared when it saw Oren—and dove toward us when it saw me. It looked a lot like the first one I'd seen, covered in scales and with strong, feathery wings, but the coloring was that of a sunset back on Earth, with gorgeous oranges, reds, golds, and pinks.

Despite its beauty, I knew it wanted me dead.

Presley dove back into the trees for a moment, cutting off my view of the creature.

"I need to see its eyes!" I yelled to her. The flames running over her feathers burned white and blue and green as she burst back into the sky.

The klynna was already barreling toward us.

We wouldn't have much time, but we'd have to make it work, because there was no other alternative that I could accept.

Presley zigzagged through the air and forest, leading the monster on a chase away from the Stronghold and slowing it down as it broke through branches and trees. I saw glimpses of other dragons and phoenixes in the skies behind the creature, waiting to attack if we needed them. The heavens poured water on all of us as we flew, but it didn't slow Presley.

Though her efforts only put the tiniest amount of space between us and the klynna, I knew I had to make it enough.

She flew in a quick, sweeping loop, and then launched straight at the monster.

Its massive pink eyes locked with mine, and its jaws opened.

A snarl below us was followed by ice blossoming in the creature's mouth. The ice blocked its fire, growing larger and thicker and wider.

I didn't have time to think about that, or even notice it, so I didn't let myself.

I just called out, "Please, don't hurt us. The king only trapped you to protect his people. Please just leave, so no one has to die."

Something inside me seemed to settle into place. I could almost feel the creature's determination sliding, and then vanishing.

The klynna chomped down on the ice in its mouth as Presley dove beneath its belly. She spiraled into the trees, hauling ass away from the creature, and further away from the Stronghold just in case it didn't listen to me.

The monster roared, but then its shadow left us.

And when Presley broke through the trees again, so we could find the beast, we saw its tail as it flew away from us.

"Holy shit," I whispered, my heart thrumming in my chest.

Presley let out a puff of air that sounded like an agreement to me.

A snarl beneath us had my attention jerking downward.

Presley let out another puff of air that sounded like a sigh, before she dove back into the trees, moving slower now that our lives weren't at risk.

She was on the forest floor a minute later, and Aev leapt to the ground, his massive paws shifting into feet before he landed.

I slid off Presley, pretty damn sure he was storming toward me, not her.

She shifted too, but stayed back.

Something told me that if anything went to shit, she'd take my side.

Oren landed a few feet away from Aev, too.

My body tensed, expecting the king to yell at me, with that fury in his eyes. I waited for him to tell me I'd screwed up, or ream me for my many mistakes.

Instead, he yanked me into his arms and squeezed me tightly.

My arms were trapped between us, and the stress in my middle dissolved as he hugged me fiercely.

"You scared the hell out of me," he said roughly.

My eyes stung at the emotion in his voice.

He... wasn't angry.

He was scared.

And relieved.

"I should've stayed with everyone else and asked what the plan was," I whispered back.

"We'll do better next time. Be more ready."

I blinked back tears.

I'd given him the chance to put the blame completely on me, and he'd settled it on both of us. Even more than that, he had sort of... done away with it, by turning it into a lesson that we'd learned.

After slipping my arms out from between us, I wrapped them around his back, and held him. Not quite as tightly as he held me, but I didn't have the same strength he did.

"We'll tell the others what happened, in case they didn't see everything," Presley said. When I peeked past Aev, I saw her grab Oren's arm and start dragging him away. "Take your time."

"He might need backup," Oren growled at her.

"She's not Naomi," Presley tossed back.

Oren didn't have anything to say to that, and I shut my eyes, taking in a deep, shaky breath.

"Well that was terrifying," I finally whispered, when I knew we were alone.

"Terrifying is far too weak a word."

My lips curved upward, just slightly. "It could've been worse."

"Of course it could've been worse. I could've lost you." There was a growl in his voice that made me shiver.

The rain seemed to have stopped, but my mind was moving too quickly to pay attention to that. And of course, it had gone back to the very thing that had stressed me out earlier, even after almost dying.

A prime example of my shitty traumatized brain, I supposed.

I couldn't help it; I blurted my thoughts. "Oren thinks the bond is pushing you to feel more for me than you would otherwise. It creates attachment, he says."

Aev didn't answer immediately. His lack of response told me he probably agreed.

And if he agreed...

Well, then we needed to fix it.

"I don't want you to fall in love with me because of a bond," I said quietly. "I don't want you to lose your mind because of our connection if the next klynna kills me. We're just friends—and as your friend, I think we need to break the bond to protect you."

Aev's body was completely still against mine. He barely seemed to breathe. "What do you suggest, then?"

"I can ask the female fae. One of them might be willing to kiss you, to remove the connection. I—"

"I *won't* touch another woman. And I doubt vows would be enough to break us at this point." His voice was hard, and...

Maybe cold, too.

My throat swelled. "I can talk to Teris. He's probably in pain after ending things with Sunny. I know he wouldn't fall in love with me, too, so he'd be a safe choice."

"I don't trust Teris." Aev's voice was harder, and colder.

"I'm not saying we shouldn't keep doing what we're doing." I released my grip on him, and he stiffly let go of me so I could take a step away. "I'm saying that I don't want to hurt you. And I don't want our connection to turn into what you had with Naomi."

"You bring me to life when she darkened and deadened me, Thorns," he said, those gorgeous blue eyes burning me furiously. "Our connection is nothing like that."

"But I don't want to hurt you." I tossed a hand toward the trees. "What if that klynna had killed me?"

"I would've ended it brutally, and spent the rest of my fucking days freezing its heart in its chest over and over again." The words were a low growl, but more than that, they were a promise.

"That's not healthy," I protested.

"Then what is it?" He stepped toward me, carefully taking my face between his hands. "Tell me, Thorns. What is this fear in my chest, this need in my belly, this desperation in my mind?"

"It sounds like—" I cut myself off, not allowing myself to finish the sentence.

Because it sounded like *love*, and I had no idea what that would mean for us.

A tense moment passed before his lips brushed mine once, and then again. With the third kiss, he didn't pull away. He *captured* me.

His tongue slipped into my mouth, his hands tilting my face back further as he slowly stroked into my mouth once, and then again.

My body came to life against his, my fingers digging into his back as he kissed me slowly, and intensely.

"Take your shirt off, Thorns," he murmured against my lips.

"Do it yourself," I countered, breathless as he pulled away. His fingers slid beneath the hem of my tank, and smoothly lifted it over my head.

I didn't hear the fabric hit the forest floor as he stepped back, letting his eyes trail over my bare torso.

His hands left my face, sliding slowly down my breasts and over my ribcage. He stroked my skin, content with holding and feeling and gripping me.

"You're perfection." His words were a low, smoldering stroke, and my eyes closed as I reveled in them. His fingers dragged over my nipples, and my hips arched. "I want to taste you," he told me, thumbs still teasing my nipples slowly. My hips were swaying a little, moving against the erection I could now feel against me. "Give me permission, Thorns."

"You can taste me." I stepped closer to kiss him again, and he kissed back without pause, or hesitance, or fear.

But then he pulled away, sliding down to his knees in front of me.

With one smooth motion, he lifted me by the backs of my thighs and pinned me to a tree. His fingers dug into my skin as he leaned in close enough that his nose brushed my damp core. A growl rumbled in his chest as he inhaled the scent of me, and his hands slid up to the waistband of my shorts.

"Take them off," I breathed, knowing he was going to ask.

His fingers dipped beneath the fabric, and my chest rose and fell rapidly.

My heart beat erratically, my fingers slipping into his hair as he pulled the fabric down, and down, and down.

Aev's hands stroked my legs slowly as he lifted my feet one at a time, freeing me from the hold of the fabric.

My eyes closed when my shorts were on the ground and Aev's nose slowly brushed my clit, making me shiver.

"Eyes open," he warned me, his breath light on my sensitive skin.

I forced my eyes open, and they collided with his. Our gazes remained connected as he dragged the tip of his tongue over my center.

A moan escaped me as he focused on my core, his gaze hot while he opened my legs and spread me wide for him.

"You are so fucking beautiful," he told me, chest rumbling. The honesty behind his words was enough to make me want him more.

I opened my mouth to thank him, to tell him that he was gorgeous too, but then his tongue was on me.

And the words died in my throat as he slowly stroked my clit.

My brain might as well have short-circuited at the fierce pleasure of it.

My legs shook as he dragged his tongue around my clit again, and again, and again. He realized I wasn't going to be able to stand for much longer, and gripped my ass as he lifted me off my feet. My legs wrapped around his head, and he held me up without a problem. I rocked against him, making sounds I didn't know I was capable of as he feasted on me.

And when I lost control, climaxing harder than I ever had before, he dragged his teeth over my clit, prolonging the pleasure as much as possible.

"Holy shit," I panted, dropping my head against the smooth bark of the white tree behind me.

"You're fucking delicious," Aev growled into my core. If I wasn't so sated, the words would've made me wet all over again.

He wasn't in any kind of hurry to set me down on my feet, and I didn't want the moment to end, but...

We had been having an important conversation before he kissed me and then distracted me so completely.

I eased one of my legs away from his face, and he lowered my feet to the ground one by one. "We still need to talk about the bond," I warned him, though the words were halfhearted.

"I want it," he said simply. I tried not to notice the tent in his pants as he stood up and then stepped away to retrieve my clothing. "I want *you*. Permanently."

"There's more to it than desire," I countered. His hand brushed my breasts before he slid my tank top over my head, tugging it back into place as if he knew my body as well as I did.

Though we'd only just started getting acquainted that way, he'd definitely paid attention when I was telling him what I liked.

Definitely.

"It's *our* bond," he told me, kneeling in front of me again and easing my feet into my shorts before pulling them back into place. "Oren can mind his own damn business."

"He's worried about you."

"And the fact that *you're* worried about it tells me everything I need to know." He took my face in his hands, stepping up close so our chests pressed together and his erection met my stomach. "I want this, Thorns. I want *you*. Let me want you."

Goosebumps broke out over my skin.

Let me want you.

I had imagined having a real, healthy relationship, back when I was on Earth. I had tried to picture what it would feel like to be loved. To be with someone who was interested in me, who wasn't locked in the awful cycle of abuse. I'd wondered what it would feel like to be wanted.

But those dreams had nothing on the actual reality of having a massive, dark-haired, blue-eyed fae pressed against me, telling me to *let him want me*.

My eyes stung. "I won't survive it," I whispered. "If this isn't real, I won't survive that. We need to break the connection, so I can know whether or not your feelings are real. You might not want me without the bond."

"That's an impossibility." His thumb moved slowly over my lips, and I leaned in closer until my forehead met his. My eyes closed, and he dragged his thumb on my bottom lip. Something about the motion was ridiculously erotic, but I didn't act on it.

"Then it won't affect you if we do it."

He scowled. "Watching you kiss Teris would sure as hell *affect me*, Thorns."

At least we were finally in agreement that Teris would be the one I made a temporary bond with. I trusted him not to develop feelings for me, because he hadn't with Sunny.

"I'll start with the vows," I said. "It might work."

He didn't look convinced, at all.

I eased his hands away from my face. "I don't want things between us to go any further until I know for sure that your feelings are yours, Aev."

"Aeven," he said roughly. "My name is Aeven."

My throat swelled, and I nodded.

But I didn't give him my name.

He seemed to have no problem committing to me, deciding that he wanted me, but it wasn't that simple for me. He and Naomi had been toxic to each other, but they'd never loved each other.

I had loved my ex, and he loved me too.

But he had hurt me anyway.

Again, and again, and again.

That made love feel like an untrustworthy emotion to me, and I had no idea what that meant for me and Aev.

But I didn't even know whether or not his feelings for me were real.

So… after I figured that out, I'd decide what to do about the love thing.

Twelve

Aev shifted, and I let him give me a ride back to everyone else. The crowds of fae had somewhat dissembled, and everyone seemed to be breathing easier now that they knew we had a shot at protecting ourselves from the klynnas.

Too bad it involved life-bringers risking our lives.

Aev slowed as we approached everyone, and I slipped off his back. He growled at me, but it wasn't an angry growl; more of an annoyed one.

Something told me that since he'd decided he wanted me *permanently*, he was only going to get more… fae-like.

Possessive.

Protective.

Then again, he was already both of those things. He had run into the forest after me, when he realized I was going to find North. And he had risked his life to keep me safe a few times, too.

Summer came out of nowhere and nearly tackled me in a hug. A laugh escaped me as I hugged her back, just as tightly as she hugged me.

"No more risking your life," she declared.

"You know my answer to that," I teased her.

"I refuse to accept it." She squeezed me tighter.

I laughed again.

"Did you have to save her ass?" Summer asked Aev, who I realized had shifted back to his man form.

"No." He didn't even hesitate.

"He had to ice the klynna's mouth, or it would've roasted us," I corrected him.

"Presley would've dodged the flames," Aev countered.

"Wait, Presley flew you?" Summer's eyebrows shot upward. "Hopefully she doesn't have a fated mate to lose his shit about that."

"She doesn't," Presley called out, from where she sat on a thick tree limb nearby. "Totally unattached, thankfully."

I grinned.

Summer snorted. "Just wait, you'll end up like me eventually, completely attached and one hundred percent okay with it."

Remmo strode up to us then, as if on cue. "How close was it?"

The words were directed to Aev.

"Too close." The sabertooth's voice lowered. "We'll need to find other life-bringer volunteers. Thorns can't be risking her life every time one comes around. There has to be a rotation."

"Blue said she'll do it. Rosalie, too. *Thorns* can teach them." Summer winked at me, and my face heated. Of course, it was followed by the rest of me, as my whole body blushed. "Remmo still isn't on board with me doing it, so I'm benched for now."

"No, I most certainly am not," the basilisk agreed.

"There's not much to it. You just have to make eye contact with them, and then you feel it, here." I tapped the center of my chest, hoping to distract them from the whole nickname thing.

"They'll have to go with you next time," Summer said.

I waited for Oren to protest, since he was Blue's fated mate, but I could see him from where I was. He pressed his lips together in a tight line, but said nothing.

"I'll talk to Fovea about classifying the new human females. They can't spend the rest of their lives in the Stronghold with the klynnas in the skies. We'll need them," Korrik said with a sigh. "Unless you want to deal with her?" He looked at Summer.

She made a face. "I'll pass."

It was on the tip of my tongue to offer to do it myself, but...

I needed to talk to Teris.

And probably to get some rest afterward, if I was going to be ready for the next klynna. That whole thing had been intense, and extremely exhausting.

Before I could do either of those things, though, I needed to talk to Summer alone.

"I'll take care of it," Oren said, though he was grimacing.

I gestured for Summer to step off to the side, and felt Aev's eyes on me as she followed me away from the others. I wasn't under any kind of impression that we were alone or had real privacy, but what I was going to have to do wasn't private anyway.

"Aev is getting possessive," I told her quietly. "He thinks he wants us to be permanent. I don't trust his feelings, because of the bond."

"Girl, he's a fae. There's no way around the possessive thing. Remmo doesn't even want me to help deal with the damn klynnas yet, and I respect his feelings too much to fight with him about it."

"I know, I know. It just..." I bit my lip. "I don't trust love, you know? People in love still hurt each other."

Understanding welled in her eyes. "I understand completely. But just like you're not Naomi, he's not your dad, or your ex."

"I know. But the bond creates emotion, right? So who's to say it won't ruin everything tomorrow? Or that he'll realize he doesn't have actual feelings for me?"

"The bond doesn't create emotion, Dakota, it creates *attachment*. In a healthy relationship, that attachment is a good thing. In Aev's relationship with Naomi, it didn't work, because there was no emotion to back it up. That made it toxic. But if there's love, or even just some small amount of affection, it only makes your connection stronger."

I sighed, brushing some loose hair out of my face. "He acted like my mate, Summer. What do I do with that?"

"Did it trigger you?" she asked.

I shook my head.

"Do you trust him?"

I bit my lip, not wanting to give her a nod.

She gave me a massive grin. "Then just enjoy it. The possessiveness can be really damn sexy, you know."

Aev's words rolled through my mind.

Let me want you.

Even this much later, they still gave me goosebumps.

"I think I'm going to ask Teris to bond with me temporarily," I told her. "That's why I needed to talk to you—I needed to make sure it wouldn't affect us." I gestured between us.

Her eyebrows shot upward. "Don't you remember Clevv?"

"Aeven isn't Clevv." My voice came out harsher than I intended, so I tried to smooth it as I explained, "I need to know if his emotions are real."

"I have no feelings for Teris anymore, outside of disdain. But I'd like it to be known that I—who am typically the maker of risky, dramatic plans—think there's no way this plan could work out well for any of you. I still support you, if you really want to go through with it, but I have to put it out there."

"I'll put it in the records." I winked at her.

She flashed me a grin, though there was a wrinkle in her forehead that told me she was nowhere near completely convinced. "Good luck, girly."

"I'll need it." I stepped away from her, scanning the groups of fae around us until I found the Wild Hunt guys. Mare, North, and January were with them, but Nev and Fovea were missing. That didn't surprise me; she had yet to start befriending his friends as far as I could tell.

Teris was with them, the only unmated male in the group.

Aev fell into step beside me as I headed toward them. Though I itched to tuck my hands into my pockets or something, to keep them occupied, my fireproof shorts didn't have any.

"You shouldn't watch me kiss Teris," I told him.

"Of course I should. Kiss him while I'm not there, and you're cheating on me, so I have to kill him. Kiss him while I'm watching, and you're breaking a mate bond. I'll still want him dead, but I should be able to control myself at least."

My face, neck, arms, chest, and shoulders flushed again with his words.

I hadn't thought of it like cheating, but... it kind of was.

Even though I hadn't committed to him, outside of friendship.

The logistics of that depended on whether a mate bond was a relationship and a commitment, or just a simple physical connection. After what I'd found out about it creating attachment, I was starting to think it was more of a relationship.

"Clevv lost his mind when North broke their bond," I said quietly.

"I was very much sane when Naomi broke mine. Don't worry about me." He wrapped a hand around my elbow, stepping closer to me, and our footsteps slowed as we walked together. "We will need ground rules, if you're serious about doing this, though."

"What kind of ground rules?"

"I need to understand exactly what I can and can't do." His voice lowered, because we were approaching the Wild Hunt guys.

"Hey, Dakota." Mare flashed me a big smile, moving away from Ervo to hug me. I hugged her back, and Aev released my arm. When I stepped beside him again, his hand lifted to my lower back, and rested there.

"There's the woman of the hour," January said with a grin.

North looked out of it, like she was lost in her magic again, but Priel had her back pressed to his front, and didn't look concerned. He was definitely the worrying kind—like all the other mated fae men—so I knew he would've been fussing over her if he thought something was wrong.

"Presley was the real hero. I just had to bark an order at a klynna," I said, lifting one shoulder in a shrug.

"Don't sell yourself short," Mare countered. "We all saw how massive those things are."

She was right; they were pretty terrifying. But also, really beautiful.

The other women questioned me about how everything had happened, and I explained my side of the events. Aev stepped up a little closer to me as I spoke, and his hand wrapped around my hip until he was holding me securely, with my side resting lightly against his.

"Can we talk, Teris?" I asked quietly, after the conversation had shifted and January and Mare were talking vibrantly about something, with their mates speaking too. It hadn't passed my notice, the way Aev had reverted to his silent, aloof self while we were talking to the Wild Hunt guys. But I supposed it was natural after so many years of dealing silently with the pain his mate bond had caused.

"We can figure out rules afterward," I told Aeven quietly, as he and I followed Teris away from the others.

He dipped his head, though he absolutely did not look thrilled by the developments.

"What do you want?" Teris looked wary, and I didn't blame him. Honestly, I felt for him. He and Summer had been a terrible match, and I'd never really thought their personalities meshed well.

"Are you still in pain from the bond breaking?" I asked.

"Yes. Were you?" His gaze flicked to Aev, and I couldn't read whatever emotion was in it.

"Constantly," I admitted. "Until we bonded." I gestured between myself and Aev, not about to enable Teris to ignore the gorgeous king next to me. "I need to ask for a favor. You can say no, of course—but it would buy you a little time without pain."

His eyebrows lifted, and he looked at Aev again.

When Aev just set his jaw and said nothing, Teris looked back at me and asked, "You want to break your bond?"

"Yes. Temporarily." I tacked that last bit on hastily at the end, needing to make sure things were clear. "Because the mating bonds seem to create feelings. I want to make sure Aev's feelings for me are real."

Teris scowled. "Mate bonds *don't* create feelings. If they did, I'd have accepted Summer's advances long before she got with the scaly asshole." He tossed a hand in the direction I assumed my best friend and her mate were. "A bond makes you possessive to the point of insanity, but doesn't do a damn thing otherwise."

"You were barely bonded for a few months," Aev countered, finally speaking up. "You cannot possibly imagine the long-term effects of an ignored bond. The pain becomes mind-numbing, and the rejection, soul-sucking."

He probably had a point there, but I didn't want the men to start arguing.

"Everyone's experiences are valid," I said simply. "The bond turned Clevv insane, so obviously it affects everyone differently. There's no clear description of what it does and doesn't do, because it affects people's minds. Men's in particular."

"He chose to embrace the insanity. We know how to fight it." Teris gestured between Aev and himself. "How long would the temporary bond last?"

"How long did it take for your possessiveness to fade?" I checked.

"About a week."

"Then at least that long. If Aev's feelings fade with the bond, longer." I glanced over at him, and found his expression dark.

"I don't want to be the rejector in a long-term bond again," Teris warned.

"Should my feelings fade the way Thorns seems to think they will, Oren already volunteered to connect with her. I'm sure there'd be a line of others thrilled by the opportunity, if we were to ask around."

"She might even have a fated mate in one of the unseelies," Teris pointed out.

The blood drained from Aev's face, and his eyes lifted to the trees, scanning them slowly. There were a few fae in different positions, watching our interaction and some of the others. The fated mate thing was probably a bit of a trigger for Aev, and I felt bad about that.

I slipped my hand around his bicep in an effort to calm him. All it did was remind me how ridiculously strong the man was. Seriously, those biceps were massive. "If I had a fated mate who was interested in me, he would've already come forward. I've been single for a while, remember?"

"That's true," he said, though he continued scanning the trees.

Would he get all barbarically possessive, if I told him I was his?

Would he want to claim me in every way, to show the other men that I was taken? Or would it calm him?

Why did the idea of that give me goosebumps?

"I'll do it, as long as no one's going to try to kill me for it," Teris finally said, looking at Aev. "Then again, it might be fun to fight the tamed king." He flashed him a smirk.

Aev's lips curved upward wickedly. "You'd find me a much harder target to hit now that I have my ice back."

Teris lifted a shoulder. "Only one way to find out."

"Not while Thorns is here," Aev said simply.

The ease with which he turned down the fight made my heart swell, even if I felt a little bad that he couldn't do what he wanted around me. His fight with Oren hadn't been triggering for me, but he knew that I usually avoided all semblance of violence. That shit was brutal on my mind.

"Alright. Let's get this over with," Teris said, gesturing for me to come closer.

"That's exactly what you want to hear from a guy you're about to kiss," I drawled back.

"It sure as hell better be how he feels," Aev said. Despite the warning in the words, his voice was perfectly pleasant.

"As soon as you feel the bond break, pull her away," Teris instructed the ex-king.

"I will."

I stepped up to Teris, wishing there was another way out of the bond that didn't involve *kissing someone*.

"I'm sorry," I whispered to both men. This whole thing was going to be shitty for both of them—and it was completely my fault.

"I'd do the exact same thing in your shoes," Teris said bluntly.

"And you know I wouldn't go along with this if I didn't understand your fear," Aev said.

Teris tucked his hands in the pockets of his pants as I stepped closer to him. I'd never seen any other fae wearing long pants before—Teris was the only one. And there were rips in the fabric that looked intentional, so I wasn't entirely sure why he bothered. But anyway, keeping his hands to himself was probably a good call, if we wanted to avoid bloodshed. I'd never seen Aev hurt anyone, but between his ice magic and the way I had seen him fight, he was undoubtedly skilled enough to do it.

"Are you really sure about this?" I asked Teris, grimacing.

"Are you?" he countered.

I let out a slow breath.

No, I was not.

But Aev's hands landed on my hips, anchoring me and telling me he had accepted it.

So I went up on my tiptoes, and kissed Teris.

It was an awkward press of lips on lips at first, but I knew that wouldn't be enough to create a bond—or break the one I'd made and strengthened with Aev already.

So I parted my lips, and slipped my tongue into his mouth.

Teris kissed me back, but the motions were just... polite. There was no feeling behind it. It was the awkward motion of mouth on mouth and lips on lips, without any passion, or desire.

A minute passed before I finally felt the bond start to shift—and I was already pulling back from Teris when Aev tugged me away, pulling me into his arms and holding me tightly to him.

His chest was heaving, his bright eyes burning into mine as he held me tightly, gripping me in his arms.

Though I itched to press my lips to his, to replace the feel of Teris's mouth on mine with a real kiss that would make me warm and happy, I knew I couldn't.

So I just hugged him back, tightly.

"Let me know when you're ready for that fight," Teris told Aev. Our new bond had changed his scent slightly, making him smell more appealing, so I could tell by the change in smell when he walked away.

Aev made no effort to release me—and I didn't ask him to.

A few minutes passed before his breathing finally started slowing to its normal pace.

"I'm sorry," I told him again, my voice quiet.

"Don't apologize for doing what felt right," he murmured back, his voice straining a little. "I may not like it, but I do understand. And now, I would like to talk about those rules."

"Okay." I bit my lip. "I'm not sure where we can go. Your tent is dripping, and my house is..." *Not a house yet.* "Do you think some of the other guys would help build it? We can't wait until I have the time to do it myself. I don't want to bother anyone, but we need somewhere to go, now that it's the rainy season and all. I'll be fine with the magic not feeling completely like my own if it means somewhere dry to sleep."

Aev looked up at the trees.

A male fae leapt smoothly from a branch far over our head, and then landed lightly on his feet. Two more followed.

"We'll grab more help and meet you there," one of the men said. I vaguely recognized him, but didn't have a name to go with the face.

"That's okay, we don't need anything big," I said quickly.

My protest was ignored, and all three men headed off in different directions.

Thirteen

Aev pulled me onto his back as he shifted, and I wrapped my arms around his neck, burying my fingers in his fur as I pressed my face to his warmth. The contact was soothing, and he still smelled nice, even without the added level of whatever the bond provided that had made him smell extra good to me.

He smoothly made his way through the trees, heading directly to the platform I'd created. It was on one of the far edges of the fae land, not on the seelie or unseelie side, but somewhere between the two. I hadn't wanted to claim either group as mine—and I still didn't want to, even though Summer kept trying to convince me to join the unseelies.

When he landed on my platform, I lifted my head from his fur and looked around with wide eyes.

There were already fae around us—nearly two dozen men.

We really didn't need that many, I thought, but didn't say it aloud.

Most of them were kneeling down with their palms on the smooth stone platform, and their eyes closed. It was already a few feet bigger on every side than it had been the last time I was there, and the tree branches above our heads seemed to be shifting.

The one man who wasn't kneeling strode over to us, wearing a friendly grin. Aev shifted forms, wrapping his arm around my waist. The gesture was possessive, but in the best way.

The fae nodded at Aev, but looked at me when he asked, "What do you want it to look like?"

I glanced to the side as another handful of men arrived. We had to be up to nearly thirty of them—some were in the trees, at that point, not fitting on the platform even though it was still growing rapidly.

"Uh... walls and a roof? I'm not picky."

"Give Firo permission and he'll make you something that doesn't even resemble a house, Thorns," Aev warned me, his voice light.

I laughed. "Do your worst, then. If you've got the manpower, I'd like a bathroom, too."

"One bathroom and some walls, coming right up." Firo winked at me, then strode back into the group of men.

I had to do a double-take when I looked over and realized that the group had more than doubled. There had to be nearly a hundred fae men there. My eyes were massive and round. "Holy shit." I scanned their faces, but only recognized two of them, and both were members of the new council. "Are they all unseelie?" I asked Aev.

"Yes. I was a good king, before Naomi." He released his hold on my waist. "I'm going to throw my magic in with everyone else's."

I caught his arm before he could leave me. "Can I help too?"

"Of course." He flashed me a small, tense smile.

The broken bond had to be bothering him, and I felt shitty for that.

We kneeled on the platform along with everyone else, and when I felt the flow of magic from all of the other fae, I sank mine into it too.

The power's flow was overwhelming. It felt like a massive gust of something strong, natural, and *alive*. Like I'd connected to a current of over a hundred other living souls.

Summer had told me that the unseelie were family. That they believed in each other and supported each other in a way the seelie just didn't. I hadn't thought she was wrong... I just hadn't cared before.

Now, I understood the draw of that.

The strength of it, too.

To not only not have to face the world alone, but to do so with so many other people, was surreal. I couldn't even imagine a life like that.

But if I was with Aev, that was what I'd have, wasn't it? His friends. His family.

Maybe that should've scared me, but the idea made me hopeful, honestly.

It would be nice to have people to trust. Someone to ask for help when I needed it. The Wild Hunt had been on my side when I was temporarily mated to Nev, and it had been good, but even then, it hadn't been like this. If I'd asked some of the seelies for help, they would've helped. But I was terrible at asking, and afraid of leading them on or making them think I wanted more than just help.

If Aev's feelings were real, everything could change for me, in a really incredible way.

Then again, given where I was and what I was doing, everything had *already* changed.

But what if those feelings weren't real?

I didn't want to admit it to myself, but that would hurt like hell.

Maybe I didn't know what I wanted after all.

Maybe I wanted him to want me permanently, too.

I couldn't tell how our magic was being used, not while I was tangled in the intense mass of power.

Time moved quickly, and I felt our magic change its focus multiple times as Firo focused us to do exactly what he wanted.

When the magic finally slowed, I realized Firo had stopped directing, and I slowly withdrew from the waning flow.

I pulled my magic free, and looked around me. My eyes widened as I took in the newly-crafted space stretching around us.

It seemed to be shaped like a slice of a cylinder, encircling part of the tree's thick trunk. When I looked upward, I saw more levels and layers above us. The floors were all done in smooth, dark wood, with the walls made of sleek white. Scattered through the white, there were pops of the greens and blues that the more exotic-looking trees sported.

On one of the floors, I could see a mattress. On another, a kitchen. On a third, a few couches. The one we currently stood on had the bathroom I'd requested.

"Well?" Firo spread his arms out. "What do you think?"

"It's incredible," I admitted, still trying to take everything in. "Thank you."

"For our queen? Any time." He winked at me.

I blinked.

Their Queen?

They couldn't really think that, could they?

But Aev was better, now that he was freed from Naomi. If his state of mind determined whether he'd become king again, he could definitely qualify now.

I looked at him, and found him shaking his head. "I was removed from the throne, and I don't want it back."

"You never wanted it to begin with," Firo countered. "And everything is different now." He gestured toward me and Aev, still kneeling side-by-side.

Aev stood smoothly, offering me a hand. I accepted it, and he pulled me smoothly to my feet as he told the other man, "I won't agree with you."

"You don't have to." Firo winked, and then looked at me. "It's nice to meet you, even if you smell like a seelie."

A laugh escaped me. Teris was undoubtedly to blame for the smell, but I didn't want to say that.

Firo stepped away, grabbing another male fae's hand and weaving their fingers together. I realized that some of the fae were already filtering out, talking calmly amongst themselves and waving when I looked over at them.

"Should we thank them?" I murmured to Aev, as they started making their way out.

"They know I'd do the same for them, so no thanks are required," he told me with a small smile.

I must not have looked convinced, because he gave me a quiet, rumbly chuckle before he called out, "Thank you." His voice carried through the space, but all he got in return were some hands thrown up in recognition.

No one seemed to plan on sticking around to chat, which I honestly appreciated. If I was going to befriend them, it would take time, and I wasn't ready at the moment.

Soon enough, the house was empty, and I heard one last door shut. There was one on the floor we were currently on, and from the way everyone had left, I assumed there was one on every other floor too.

"Should we lock everything up?" I asked Aev, not ready for a serious conversation quite yet.

"I would say yes, but with the klynnas roaming, they may need you. We'll need to leave most of them open." He stroked my knuckles with his thumb as he tugged me toward the strategically-placed branches that would lead us up to a higher floor. When he shifted forms and tugged me onto his back, I didn't resist the contact, burying my fingers in his fur again.

Though some part of me hoped he was carrying me to the couches, it didn't surprise me at all when he stepped onto the level with the monstrous bed, striding right over to the brand-new mattress and the blankets stretching across it.

He shifted back and set me down on the bed, then locked the door nearby before coming back to sit next to me. I was on the edge, with my legs dangling off the side. He turned, sliding one knee further up the mattress so he could face me.

Reluctantly, I did the same.

"You look terrified," Aev said, his voice low but edged in humor. "How bad can a few rules possibly be?"

"I don't know." I lifted a shoulder. Honestly, my mind was going back to all the things I did that had pissed my ex off. Talking out of turn, having a personality, laughing at jokes... everything I'd done had made him angry.

Hopefully, none of that was what Aev's rules were about, or we were going to have a big problem on our hands. I wasn't going to deal with that shit again. "Tell me what you're thinking, and I'll let you know."

"The main rule I need is for you not to touch other men."

I...

What?

I blinked. "I don't usually touch random men. Or people. I hug my friends sometimes, but other than that, it's just you."

He said bluntly, "I know. But I need us to agree on that, because without the bond connecting us, I feel like I'm losing you. And you're not only the female I want, but my friend, as well."

Oh.

Well, then.

"Okay, I won't touch other men," I agreed.

If all of the rules were like that—about our relationship, setting boundaries as to what would make us both feel the best about our connection, I could handle rules.

I hesitated to voice the one I wanted to make, though.

"It's your turn, Thorns."

I heaved a sigh. "This is going to sound really insecure."

His lips curved upward a little. "And mine didn't?"

A soft laugh escaped me. "Alright. I just... I don't want you to be alone with Naomi. Obviously I'm not going to ask you not to talk to her or anything, but if you're alone with her, it'll make me feel like something's going on between you two again."

He frowned at me. "That's not insecure at all. We were mated, as shitty a time as it was, so that's a reasonable boundary."

I let out a breath of relief.

"I'd like us to live here together." He gestured to the building. "Not because my home is currently drenched, even though it is. But because I feel far more certain that I have a chance at convincing you to fall in love with me while we're sharing a home."

I lifted an eyebrow.

"You wanted insecurities. There's another one." He winked at me, and my lips curved upward in a grudging smile.

"I was already planning on living here together." It was my turn, and since we were already delving into awkward topics... "You have to share a bed with me, if we're doing that. I liked sleeping together, the way we did in your tent."

"Done." He didn't so much as bat an eye, not that it surprised me. "I'd like to know before you risk your life again, like you did when you went to find North or hopped on Presley's back."

I scowled. "I did what someone needed to do, and no one else could." I gestured toward the forest around us. "If we're making rules like that, you're not allowed to chase me if I walk away from you because I need time to think."

"Like hell I'm not." He leaned toward me, and I fought the urge to lean in closer. Instead, I made myself lean back. "You want me to go a week without kissing you, or tasting you, or touching you, because you don't believe my feelings are genuine. That physical contact makes me feel secure in this—in us. I've agreed because your comfort and trust matter to me, but while I'm already forcing myself to leave distance between us, it's unfair to expect me to let you walk away every time you feel uncertain."

I glared at him. "It'll take a week just for the bond to vanish, Aev. It'll be at least another week after that until we know whether or not you really want me —maybe longer. And there's a damn good chance you won't want me. So why should we bother doing any of this?"

"Because our bond brings me to life," he growled at me. "And because it makes you feel safe."

My mouth was open, ready to lay harsh words down, but those words stopped in my throat when what he'd said clicked.

It makes you feel safe.

He was right, wasn't he?

Nothing ever made me feel safe. Not walls, not promises. Definitely not love, relationships, or anything related to them.

And yet, our connection had done exactly that.

It had made me feel safe.

And for me, safety was massive. Crazily massive.

I rubbed at my eyes with one of my hands. "You're right. I'm sorry; talking about risking my life kind of pissed me off, but I understand why you asked what you did. It's just that I don't really want to risk myself, you know? I've only done it because someone had to, and I was the best option. And I know you disagree, but I have to do what I feel like is right. I'm not always going to be able to check in with you before that stuff happens."

He grimaced, but nodded. "I understand. It frustrates me too, but it is what it is. We don't really need rules—I just need some way to know that what we have between us means something to you, too."

Oh.

My throat swelled. "Our friendship means a lot to me. I haven't really had time to wrap my head around letting us be more, but I'm getting there. Or at least trying to, anyway."

"I can accept that." He caught my hand and lifted it to his lips, brushing a kiss to my knuckles. "I know I can't kiss you, or taste you, but can I still touch you freely?"

"Of course. I love it when you touch me."

He brushed his lips against my knuckles again.

The door beneath ours opened. "Dakota?" Summer called out.

"Yeah?"

"There's a klynna headed this way. Everyone's ready to fly with you."

Shit.

Aev's expression grew solemn.

Though neither of us wanted to face another of the damned monsters, or risk our lives again, we both stood, and went hand-in-hand.

Fourteen

"Lead the way," Rosalie said with a grin, as I slipped onto Presely's back. Rosalie was sitting on Devv's back already—he was the phoenix on the new unseelie council, so he was the old phoenix general. The fae man was tall and tan, with long golden brown hair that he kept up in a bun most of the time, but he was currently in his beast form. Though he was burning freely, his flames didn't bother her, since she was a hellhound.

Blue was on Oren's back, and though she looked nervous, she didn't grip him too tightly.

"Right now they're only watching, trying to feel the same connection you do," Summer explained to me, from where she stood with Remmo. Her back was to his chest, and he was eyeing the sky, his expression neutral. "The guys will be watching Presley, making sure to stay out of her way, so don't worry about them. Just stay alive and kick klynna ass."

My lips curved upward. "The goal is to *avoid* a fight."

She flashed me a quick, tense grin. "I guess."

I knew she was making a joke to try to relieve some stress from the situation, and I appreciated that.

I leaned forward, wrapping my arms around Presley's fiery, feathery neck as the klynna roared. This one was louder than the last one; even its roar shook the ground beneath us.

"Here goes nothing," Rosalie muttered, before Presley launched into the sky.

My heartbeat picked up as we soared toward the monstrous creature. The underside of its scaled belly was every shade of blue I'd ever imagined, and then some.

There hadn't been time to process what I was about to do—that I was going to have to repeat everything that had happened earlier. But I couldn't let myself embrace that fear. Not while we were soaring toward the beast in the sky.

I controlled my breathing as Presley flew a quick loop around the creature, catching its attention.

Its head jerked toward us, and when its massive jaws parted, ice filled its mouth so fast it was forced open even wider.

Its furious eyes collided with mine, and as our energy collided, I yelled out a fast, "Please leave, and tell the others to stop hunting us!"

The creature roared, shooting fire toward us before it soared upward, and then away. Presley had to spiral sideways to dodge the fire, but managed to do so without getting burned.

"Well, that wasn't so bad!" Rosalie yelled, from a few yards away.

"Could've been worse," I called back.

The next one probably *would* be worse.

I didn't think the creature would really listen to me when it came to telling its friends not to come after us, but figured it was worth a shot.

And I hoped we'd bought ourselves a few hours or so, though it hadn't been all that long since the last one appeared.

We all landed, and the fliers shifted back while Rosalie questioned me about how I'd done what I'd done. Blue seemed uncharacteristically quiet, though I supposed that having Oren stand so close to her might've been messing with her mind, considering what they were and what they weren't.

I was exhausted, but when my stomach growled, Aev slipped his hand in mine and towed me toward the massive outdoor kitchen.

Some of the fae nodded at him as we passed them, and I was fairly confident they were unseelies. Their whole attitude was so much different than the seelies, and I wanted to ask him about that. Most of our friendship had been established by me talking, not him. And it made things feel sort of uneven between us.

Maybe that was part of the reason I was so uncertain about his feelings for me. Or so hesitant to let things progress past friendship.

While he grabbed us both plates and loaded them up, checking with me on what I wanted before putting it on my plate, I decided I'd bring it up to him after we ate.

Despite all of the people greeting him with nods and friendly smiles, asking him how he was feeling, and grinning at me too, he carried our plates to a table on the outer edge of the group. When he set our plates down beside each other, instead of across from each other, he did so in a way that our backs would face the other tables. It was a simple and polite way to tell people that we wanted space, and based on what I knew of the unseelie, I figured they would respect it.

Despite my quiet uncertainty about how I would bring up my worries to him, I dug into the food without hesitation. I was hungrier than I'd realized.

When we finally slowed, I noticed Aev studying me.

"What?" I asked him, my face, neck, and chest heating. Trying to calm myself, I nibbled on a few of the vegetable chips that could be made by baking thin slices of one of the veggies I didn't know the name of. I'd never been very interested in cooking, truthfully.

"You're avoiding looking at me," he said. He didn't sound irritated, or frustrated. Just curious.

I bit my lip. "Sorry."

"Don't apologize, just tell me why." He brushed the backs of his knuckles over my cheek, and I wasn't sure if he did so because there were crumbs, or just because he wanted to touch me. I was pretty fine with it either way.

"Oh." I looked away again. "I just... I realized that you know me a lot better than I know you. Before your bond broke, you were usually in your sabertooth form. Since then, things have been crazy, so we haven't spent a whole lot of time talking."

My ex would've flipped his lid if I dared talk to him that way. Bringing up something that could be construed as a weakness for him? Bad idea.

But Aev just considered my words for a minute. When he spoke, he admitted, "You're right."

I blinked.

Definitely wasn't used to being told that by men.

"I'll do better," he told me simply.

I blinked again.

Wasn't used to being told that, either, unless it was in reference to bruises on my skin after he had lost his temper.

"Really?" The word slipped out before I could stop myself.

"Of course. Your feelings matter to me, Thorns." He caught my hand, slipping his fingers between mine. "I would never have agreed to the temporary bond with Teris if I didn't believe that."

I liked how he emphasized *temporary*, and I loved that my feelings mattered to him.

That *I* mattered to him. Not just as a potential mate, but as a person, with thoughts and feelings that were just as important as his.

He took our trays back, and cleaned them quickly before putting them away. When he came back to me, he held out a hand. "Come with me?"

I didn't hesitate to take it, but didn't stand up quite yet. "What if there's another klynna?"

"We'll stay close."

I stood, and he pulled me onto his back as he shifted forms.

AEV WOVE through the trees quickly, and ten minutes later, we were far enough away from the gathered fae who were still ready in case they needed to fight a klynna, so they couldn't hear or see us. Since we were still close enough that we could get back to them quickly, I wasn't worried about the distance.

He shifted back when we were nestled in the crook of a massive V-shaped tree branch, with just enough room at the bottom of the V for both of us to sit comfortably. Our backs were to the branch, our knees bumping and our pelvises only a few inches from each other.

"When the war with the seelies ended, all of us were lost," Aev said quietly. His hand caught one of mine, and he held it on his knee, stroking my knuckles with his thumb. "It occurred to me that we needed a goal. Something to pursue, to unite us, before we were lost. We had separated from the seelie because they refused to follow rules, leaders, and boundaries—but those things kept us sane."

"Summer told me that you were all trying to become ilolis," I admitted, though I wasn't entirely sure that was the proper way to use the word. It was Remmo's nickname for her, so I at least knew that it was the correct term.

"Yes. When a fae has complete control, one of their eyes changes, like hers." He gestured to one of his eyes. "It seemed as good a goal as any. Until the seelies began bringing females to our world, it united us. We made plans, and traded stories about our efforts to change. It was fun," he said simply.

"But then Naomi arrived, and hell broke loose. The council and I had to create new rules to prevent our fae from going rabid in an effort to steal her from the seelies. The rules meant little to the more lonely, more desperate males. I had hunted a group of them into seelie land, hoping to stop them before they started another damn war, the night I met her," he continued.

My eyes widened.

I definitely hadn't heard this story before.

"I was a hands-on king. That was why they chose me—the bastards practically forced it on me. Because when others might send someone else into seelie territory in their place, I would just go after the rule-breakers myself, and knock their heads in until they saw their errors." His lips curved upward, just slightly, but there was something sad in that smile. "This group actually managed to get past the seelie. I don't know how—afterward, they refused to open their mouths, and the seelies wouldn't admit how they'd been defeated. But my unseelies had Naomi tied to one of their backs. She was fighting them, until the moment our eyes met."

My own eyes had to be wide as plates.

Maybe if I hadn't known the outcome of their love story, it would've been romantic. I was still dying to hear what had happened, even knowing how things had ended, but it wasn't the same. It was more of a sad excitement than a sweet one.

"Don't leave me hanging." I bumped Aev's knee with my own, and he chuckled.

"I don't want this to make you doubt me."

"It won't." The answer was completely and totally honest. "You're not into her. She's not into you. You never have been. Fate is like the wind, or the sunshine. It's there, but that doesn't mean it's always right, or necessary."

His eyes softened. "That's a beautiful perspective, Thorns."

I lifted a shoulder, not sure how to reply.

"Then again, your beautiful perspectives are one of my favorite things about you." He squeezed my hand. "The moment our eyes met, I felt the bond kick in. She called us soulmates—she felt it strike, too, but she was furious about it, and made that clear through the entire journey back to my land. She despised that she'd been dropped in an unfamiliar world, without even one other female, and that fate was then pushing her to bond with me."

He continued, "I was lost as to what to do with her. She despised me, and I'm not one to push myself on people. If she didn't want me, she didn't want me. But the bond kept digging its claws into me. I faded over time, as I stayed away from her. My desires disappeared, replaced entirely by desperation. Everything that made me a good king vanished too. And yet my people still backed me, still believed in me, because of who I'd been in the past. It wasn't until they saw how the Wild Hunt males wooed their females that they questioned me. Then, they started to see me as weak for not being able to win over my fated female."

"But she didn't want you, and you didn't want her," I said quietly, understanding setting in.

"No, I did not." His expression was neutral, but sad. "It's a strange thing, being told you're supposed to be with someone who doesn't appeal to you. It makes you wonder if you're wrong—and question yourself, on every front. Now that I've gotten to know you, I understand why her personality wasn't attractive to me. I don't want someone angry, or cold, or harsh. I want someone light, playful, and kind, even when she has every reason not to be." He squeezed my hand again.

"Wow." I leaned my head back against the tree. "I'm sorry. I can't imagine going through that."

"As I can't imagine what you've suffered." His thumb stroked my knuckles.

We were both quiet for a moment, until I broke the silence. "Tell me a story about the time before you met her. Tell me what you were like."

His lips curved upward. "A much happier topic. I approve."

A soft laugh escaped me, and he settled against the tree a bit more relaxed than he had been. "One of the plots to become iloli involved stripping naked and dipping in a natural hot spring full of electric novocannes. I've never been so afraid I'd lose my cock in my life."

I snorted. "What the hell is a novocanne?" The word was pronounce noh-voh-cah-nay, and I was fairly sure Summer had mentioned them before, though I couldn't come up with what they were for the life of me.

His eyes were bright as he explained them to me—they sounded like some kind of eel-like fish. And I asked him questions, so he continued telling the story, making me laugh at the insanity these fae men had come up with.

I watched Aev come to life as we talked about the ridiculous plots his people had invented, and the grudgingly enthusiastic way he had gone about participating in those plots, however insane or risky they were.

WE'D BEEN SITTING in that tree for hours, and my butt was entirely numb, when I heard the klynna roar above our heads.

Aev's eyes met mine for half a second, and then he had tugged me up onto his back, and we were moving through the trees, headed for the others.

Rosalie took the lead this time, and though I didn't say it aloud, it was a relief not to be the one in charge of catching the beast's attention. She diverted it flawlessly, and we were back on the ground less than ten minutes later.

Soon after we landed, the adrenaline faded, and the exhaustion set in. Aev's arms wrapped around me, and I leaned against him.

"Get some sleep," Rosalie told me, grinning broadly.

Maybe taming klynnas had become her new passion. She could have it, because it definitely wasn't mine.

"It's not even dark out," I protested, gesturing toward the sky.

"It's dark in your house," Aev said, sweeping me off my feet and striding toward the trees.

Maybe I should've protested, but... it was nice to have someone take care of me. On Earth, that had never happened. Not that I could remember, at least.

So I let him carry me away, and tried not to let my mind wrap itself around the fact that if Aev's feelings didn't vanish in the next week or two, I might actually stand a chance at being with someone who could love me the way I'd always dreamed of being loved.

Fifteen

I FELL ASLEEP AS SOON as my head hit the pillow, and woke up in Aev's arms. He was breathing steadily, but I thought I'd heard a knock or something. My face was tucked against his neck, and his arms were wrapped against my back, holding me to him.

Another knock sounded on the door, and I closed my eyes, sighing quietly. Aev's arms tightened around me, and his lips brushed the top of my head once, and then again.

"Gotta get up," I mumbled to him.

"Mmhm." He squeezed me tightly, earning a quiet groan before he chuckled and released me. "I've got it." His lips brushed my forehead, and then I watched his ass as he strode toward the door.

He was wearing shorts, unfortunately for me.

The unseelie had given up on their fancier clothing a while earlier though, so he was shirtless, which *was* fortunate for me.

He opened the door, and went still.

I frowned at his body language.

"Hey. Can we talk?" Naomi's voice floated in—calm, and quiet.

I stiffened.

Aev didn't glance at me. "I'd rather not," he said simply. When he stepped back and started closing the door, she shoved past him and slid into our room.

Naomi glanced at me and bit her lip. "Sorry. I know this is weird."

"It's fine," I said politely, though it was kind of a lie.

She looked at Aev. "Can we talk alone?"

My heart caught in my throat.

What if he actually wanted to talk to her alone?

Our talk about boundaries flashed through my mind, and despite the discomfort of the conversation, I was relieved that we'd talked about it. If he said yes to Naomi, he'd do so knowing that he was making me uncomfortable, and it would be the only red flag I needed to distance myself from him.

"No." Aev didn't hesitate, slipping his hands in his pockets and giving her a flat look.

"Alright. That's okay." She rocked back and forth on her heels a little before letting out a quick, harsh breath. "This is going to be awkward, but we might as well get it over with. While I was in the coma, changing my name, Vevol showed me my past. Mostly, the few interactions you and I had. I realized while she was showing them to me that I was a bitch to you. The situation between us was difficult for me, but you didn't deserve the way I treated you. You were always kind to me, even when me and the bond were both horrible to you. I still think fate made a flamingly-shitty error by pairing us together, but I'm sorry that I made it worse for us. So... that's it. I hope it gives you closure, and you don't curse my name or anything." She took a step back, toward the door. "I really am happy for you guys."

I could see the wary shock in Aev's eyes, and didn't think he was going to say anything to her.

"Thanks." I flashed her a tiny smile, so she knew she was good to leave like she clearly wanted to.

She nodded and then slipped out onto the balcony outside our door. I saw a flash of silver scales as she shifted, diving toward the ground. The skies weren't safe, but those of us with wings needed to get around *somehow*. She could've always just jumped down and tuned into her magic to fall more gently, but I wasn't sure if she even knew how to do that, since she had avoided the fae men so thoroughly.

Aev let out a long breath, and I wrapped my arms around my abdomen, uncertain of what to say to him.

He walked back to the bed, sitting down on the edge of it and then reaching for me. Those gorgeous eyes of his met mine, and I gave him a tiny nod, answering his silent question. With my permission, he dragged me into his arms and held me to his chest.

"You okay?" I whispered, feeling more secure now that he'd reacted by turning toward me instead of away.

"Mmhm." His chin rested on my head as he tucked me closer, tightening his arms around me.

"Do you want to talk about it?"

"Not really." He squeezed me. "But I think you deserve to know, if you'd like to."

My throat swelled.

He'd told me a bunch of stories about how things were when he was the king, but I'd changed the subject away from Naomi. I hadn't wanted to know. And... I still didn't.

"If you ever want to talk about it, I'll always be happy to listen. But I feel like I know enough about how things were for you that I don't need the details unless you want to give them to me."

He squeezed me even tighter. "Thank you."

"Of course." I pressed a kiss to his throat, and his chest rumbled happily. It almost sounded like a purr, and my lips curved upward with that thought.

"Do you want to go for a run with me again? We can let the others know that we're awake first, so they know we're watching for klynnas too," he asked.

"Sure." I smiled against his neck, fairly confident that we were going to end up in a tree again, trading stories about our lives.

He stood, pulling me onto his back as he shifted forms, and a moment later, we were moving through the trees.

A KLYNNA WAS HEADED toward us before we'd even finished talking to the fae gathered, still ready for a fight that may or may not come. Rosalie and Blue had been manning the skies, but Blue looked exhausted, and Rosalie's excitement seemed to have faded.

Rosalie and I sent Blue away to sleep, and I spoke with Rosalie for a moment before we headed into the skies.

"How bad is it?" I asked her.

The klynna was approaching, but we had time.

She grimaced. "We can connect with them enough to send them away, but it doesn't seem to do anything when we order them to stop returning. At this rate, we're going to need a lot more life-bringers. Sunny decided she'll help if they start coming in pairs, but I talked to the last few from our group, and they're not interested in helping out."

I let out a puff of air. "Damn."

"Yeah. I asked Fovea how they're doing when it comes to classifying the new humans, and she said that they've got everything they need collected, but they can't do it for another week because of the moon. Whatever that means."

I bit my lip. "We can probably hold out for another week."

"As long as they don't start coming in twos or threes," she agreed. "It's been happening at least twice an hour, though."

Shit.

The klynna roared above our heads, and we parted ways. I slipped onto Presley's back while Rosalie climbed onto Devv's, and we took to the sky.

THE REST of the day passed in a stressful blur. The klynna attacks increased to three to four times an hour, with the same four beasts returning after the impact of our commands faded from their minds. One of them was the red one I'd first seen outside North and Priel's cave. Another was the sunset-colored one. The third was a masterpiece of blues. And the last one was a gorgeous, glistening black, like obsidian with a hell of a lot more sparkle.

Despite their beauty, it had started to feel like it was only a matter of time before one of them ate one of us.

When Blue was well-enough rested, she swapped places with Rosalie. And when Rosalie had gotten enough sleep, she came back and swapped with me.

Aev stayed in the trees when I crashed in the house for a few hours, murmuring to me that he needed to keep an eye on the klynnas to make sure no one was burned. Because he was sitting in the trees, only using his ice magic to keep me and the other life-bringers from getting roasted by klynna fire, I figured he could handle the repetitive strain of the magic a little longer.

When I woke up, I traded places with Blue.

The klynnas had started coming in pairs, so everything was getting more difficult. Sunny joined our rotation, but we were all struggling to keep up with the monsters. The close calls became closer, and Aev's ice magic became more necessary.

On the third day, they started coming in trios.

I made Aev sleep a few hours with me that day, knowing he couldn't keep it up forever without any rest, despite his protests. A few other fae took to the skies with the other girls, trying to distract the beasts.

Apparently, they saw right past the distractions, and focused on those of us who could control them. After one particularly close call, a furious, worried Remmo retrieved Aev from our bed. My king didn't protest as we headed back to the others, though the circles under his eyes were dark and thick.

We were all tired, but if we could hold out a few more days, we would have more help.

When Rosalie came to trade places with me on the fifth day, so I could finally crash again, it was the middle of the night.

The new humans would be classified in about forty-eight hours, so we wouldn't have to stick it out alone for too much longer.

But as I searched for Aev, planning to make him sleep for at least an hour or two, one of the dragons who had been flying with us swept down from the trees and landed beside me. His eyes were wild, his white-blond hair sticking up in every direction.

He reached for my arm, to stop me, but halted his fingers a few inches from my skin. He must've remembered who I was, and that I didn't like to be touched, I assumed.

Red blossomed on his cheeks, though, and his gaze swept over the trees. "I know she's yours," he said quickly.

When I glanced over my shoulder, I realized he was talking to Aev. The gorgeous ex-king was striding toward me, with purplish circles under his eyes and a clenched jaw. "We're all tired," he told the dragon guy anyway, wrapping his arm around my waist and leaning in to press his cheek to my head. "What happened?"

"All four of them are together now, and it looks like another one joined them. They're flying toward us," the fae explained quickly, his expression somewhere between stressed, apologetic, and afraid.

Aev swore, pulling me tighter to his side.

"Thanks for letting us know." I gave the blond fae the biggest smile I could muster—which wasn't big. It probably didn't even resemble a smile.

The man nodded, and then left.

Aev pulled me into his arms, crushing me tightly to his chest. "You'll be careful?" he murmured to me, voice raspy and exhausted.

"Of course. As soon as they're gone, you need to sleep. Even just in a tree, or cuddled up at my feet in your beast form while we wait for them to regroup," I whispered back. "It's been too long. I need you to take care of yourself."

He swallowed roughly, and I felt the movement against my forehead. "Alright. I'll come to you when you're back on the ground, safe."

We held onto each other tightly for a few more seconds before he reluctantly released me, kissed my forehead, and then made his way back to his own place in the trees.

I knew it killed him to rely on Presley to protect me, but I loved that he trusted me and her enough to let it happen anyway. And despite how many days had passed since the bond had been broken, he'd only seemed to get more attached to me, not less.

I headed back to the other life-bringers and their male rides, and Presley strode up to the group at the same time I did. We all exchanged worried grimaces.

"We've got this," Rosalie said, though her expression told me she only half-believed it.

"They won't know what hit them," Blue agreed weakly. "Me and Oren will take the blue one."

"I'll take the red one," I said, looking at Presley. She nodded in confirmation.

"We'll take the obsidian one," Summer said, looking at the fae dragon she'd been flying with. He was friends with Remmo, and his name was Kiin, but that was all I knew about him.

"And Devv and I will take the sunset one." Rosalie snagged the male phoenix's hand, and I watched them closely. She flashed him a tired grin, and both his cheeks and ears reddened.

"Are you together?" Blue asked Rosalie, her expression growing curious.

"Sort of. It's new." Rosalie lifted a shoulder. "He's a damn good kisser."

His face and ears reddened further, but he was grinning, then.

They were adorable, and the way she bumped her arm against his made me really happy for them.

“Congrats,” Blue said, smiling at them.

“Thanks.” Rosalie smiled back, and there was light in her eyes that I hadn’t seen before.

“How pissed is Ana?” Summer asked, her tired voice playful.

Rosalie snorted. “Not thrilled. But she’s falling for that obnoxious basilisk mate of hers too, however slowly and reluctantly.”

The rest of us laughed.

“Alright, we need to go,” Oren said, striding up behind Blue. When he placed a possessive hand on her hip, my curiosity grew, though her expression didn’t change.

“Let’s do it,” Rosalie agreed. “The fifth klynna is free game. Winner gets a twenty-minute nap.”

Chuckles rolled through the group.

Presley, Devv, Oren, and Kiin shifted forms, and the rest of us slid onto their backs. When they launched into the sky, I braced myself for the adrenaline that was coming.

Sixteen

The wind whooshed around us as I leaned against the back of Presley's flaming neck. The klynnas flew in a massive *M* shape together, with two on top and three on the bottom. The obsidian one and the new green one were on the top, and the other three took the bottom.

Ours, the red, was the furthest from us, so we had to move quickly. It was the same one that almost killed me after I ran from North and Priel's cave, so it had a special place in my heart—and not in a fantastic way.

All five klynnas roared in staggered succession, creating huge gusts of wind that Presley navigated smoothly.

I heard smaller roars and cries from the other dragons and phoenixes who joined us in the sky, catching up to us as we approached the klynna. They had basilisks on their backs, ready in case we needed them to try to knock out the monsters.

The blue klynna breathed fire at us, and since no one was too close to it, Aev didn't bother freezing it before it loosed the flames. We had to dodge a little, but not enough that it felt like a close call.

Blue and Oren spiraled toward that klynna as its fire died, and Blue yelled a command. They were the fastest of us, good at getting in and out quickly.

Their klynna's throat filled with ice as they dove out of the way, and Presley went over the top of it before spiraling down beneath its belly and soaring under it.

Rosalie's klynna roared behind us, but I couldn't see what was happening over there, so I didn't let myself think too much about that—I had to keep my mind on our monster.

Its mouth flooded with ice as we flew over the top of it again, and its head jerked toward us.

I felt the connection as its conscience met mine.

Our eyes were locked, but the bond felt... weaker, somehow.

I called the command anyway. "Please, turn around and leave us!"

I felt the words slide over the creature, as if they were too slippery to set in. The klynna roared, and didn't do as I'd asked.

My eyes widened as I felt the connection grow thinner.

Presley flew another loop around it, since it hadn't turned back or even slowed down. Two of the other klynnas had already broken away from the group, but ours hadn't moved.

We dodged its thrashing legs successfully, flying over the top of it again.

Its eyes collided with mine once more.

This time, when I felt its will connect with mine, I called out, "Please, go!"

The klynna blew fire at us, burning through the ice in its throat in a heartbeat. Presley dove around its belly again, and one of its legs shot out toward us.

Its claws closed around us.

A cracking noise that must've been Presley's ribs made my stomach turn, and she let out a blood-curdling scream.

Shock overpowered my fear as she shifted and slipped through its claws, free-falling toward the trees below us. I watched as Blue and Oren dove toward her, but without the phoenix below me, I was facing the klynna's fury alone.

Its massive claws snapped around me, and I looked down when I felt wetness trickling on my abdomen.

My lips parted when I saw the thick, red claw protruding from my belly, cutting straight through my middle.

The world spun around me, and I grabbed at the claws as pain bloomed in my chest, fierce enough to stop my breath.

The klynna roared, and it barreled away from the Stronghold.

Away from my friends.

Away from Aev.

I saw trees burning, behind me. I saw my friends and the other shifters struggling to deal with the klynnas.

And I saw that no one was following me.

They hadn't realized I wasn't still with Presley, tucked safely in Oren's claws.

They hadn't realized I was alone and injured.

They would, eventually.

Summer would.

Aev would.

But until then, I was on my own.

THE KLYNNA MOVED DIZZYINGLY FAST. Then again, I was already dizzy thanks to the fierce pain that had my mind short-circuiting, but somehow remaining conscious. The klynna crashed through a few trees, taking out chunks of wood as it dove toward a small clearing. It roared when it landed roughly in a patch of dirt that looked well-worn.

I screamed as more pain reverberated through me. My body was on fire—and cold, at the same time.

I could heal quickly, thanks to my magic, but the hole in my middle… it was massive.

I wasn't sure even the fae's fast healing would be enough to save me.

Thunder cracked over our heads, and the klynna roared. It tilted its claws, and my world shifted. More pain cut through me, intense enough to silence my screams and knock me out for a moment as I slid slowly down the sharp length of the creature's claws.

My back hit the ground, jarring me to consciousness. Tears leaked down my face as the klynna roared at me again.

I realized it was raining again, when I saw the water dripping from the klynna's massive face. I couldn't feel the droplets, but they were hitting me. They had to be hitting me.

My chest rose and fell shallowly.

Agonizingly.

Everything hurt.

Everything.

So much that I couldn't even feel anything but that pain.

The klynna roared again as its massive red eyes met mine. I felt the connection that used to exist between us—felt the break in it, the reason that it no longer held.

And then I felt the creature's fury.

Its *pain.*

Not the same physical kind as mine—its was a righteous, angry, sad pain.

"I'm sorry," I whispered to it, though my lips moved so slowly I wasn't even sure whether the words came out at all. "I just wanted to live."

The klynna roared again at me, and I felt the connection between us slowly knit back together.

I felt it grow and swell, as it became something real. Something thick. Something *alive.*

And I felt the creature's pain of being trapped.

Its fear of watching its mate be locked away again by the unseelie king.

Its desire for revenge, for all the years it spent trapped.

My eyes stung. "I'm so sorry," I said to the creature, my voice cracking in my throat. "They thought you would kill them."

The creature roared again—but this time, I didn't feel anger.

Only pain, and echoed fear.

The klynnas thought the fae would kill them, too.

Hadn't they tried to, so many times?

The klynna stomped away from me, and the ground shook beneath me. I was too weak to move—losing too much blood. I could feel my body trying to heal itself, but with so much of my life-force soaking the dirt already, there wasn't enough magic, or energy, left to recover.

I was dying.

Not at the hands of my ex, who I'd thought would be my end so many years ago.

Not at the hands of the fae, who I'd realized could kill me the first moment we'd landed on that beach in Vevol.

But at the hands of a beautiful, elegant creature, who was protecting its family in the only way it knew how.

I supposed if someone was going to kill me, at least the klynna's reason was valiant. It wasn't a death I would be ashamed of—or one I would regret, if there was another life after this.

The klynna came back a moment later. I blinked at it when it dropped a clawful of mud on me. The thick, wet goop splattered on my face, covering my torso and legs.

It took a moment for me to process what had just happened, and why.

My mind was exhausted, and moving slowly.

But then I remembered what Fovea had said.

Blood and mud could keep someone alive.

Whether she knew it or not, my fake mate's new wife had just saved my life.

Her, and the klynna.

My hands moved quickly, shakily, *numbly*, over the mud on my chest.

I had to mix it with the blood beneath me, but there was so much of both that it wasn't a challenge.

I caked myself in it desperately, rushing to cover myself.

To save myself.

Because I might've wanted to die in that hospital back on Earth, before the fae appeared and saved me, but now?

Now, I wanted like hell to live.

To make stupid jokes with Summer again.

To love Aev, and learn what it felt like to be loved by him.

Tears leaked down my face as I hurried to save my own life.

I felt my heartbeat slow, as the mixture began to work—or as the life began to drain from my body. I supposed I didn't really know which one it was. Whether I lived or died was in Vevol's hands.

The klynna plopped down next to me, its eyes on me. Though I wasn't looking at them, I could still feel the connection between us. It was thick, and strong, and real. And something told me that it just might be permanent.

My own eyes closed slowly, despite the fierce effort I put forward to hold them open.

To keep them on the creature, or on the sky, or on the trees.

And I was lost to the pain in my chest, to the mud and blood on my skin, to...

Well, to Vevol.

Seventeen

Aev

My mind fell into a calm, cold place when everything went to hell, the same way it always had. All I could do was freeze the klynnas' jaws, to stop them from burning our fae.

To protect my female.

But there were too many of them.

And my energy was waning—it had been waning for days.

When I reached the end of my ice, I shifted forms and launched through the trees. Flames filled the sky, and my heart pounded hard, my chest aching fiercely as panic flooded every fiber of my being.

I tried to watch the sky, but the flames were too massive.

Too thick, and too bright.

I couldn't see her.

I couldn't see my mate.

My Thorns.

My emotions rattled around in my chest, stronger and fiercer than I knew they could be, as I waited for the life-bringers to regain control of the monsters in the sky.

Minutes passed so slowly they may as well have been hours, days, or weeks.

And finally, the fire faded.

Blue and Oren dove toward the ground, with an injured Presley in his claws.

My heart froze in my chest.

Fear stole my breath, my thoughts, my mind.

I dove too, tapping into Vevol's magic and managing to land just lightly enough not to break any bones. I rolled to my feet, popping up and running toward them.

"Where is she? Where's Dakota?" I demanded, desperation making my heart pound like a drum and my breaths move faster than any klynna.

Blue frowned. "Someone grabbed her. They were both falling—weren't they?" She looked at Oren, who lifted one shoulder. "Everything happened so fast," she added quickly. "And then they just left, without us doing anything. I don't know what happened."

My eyes narrowed at Oren.

He didn't think my feelings for her were genuine. If he'd let something happen to her because of that...

"I didn't see her," he said, his gaze meeting mine. "I was focused on the klynna. You reached the end of your ice?"

I jerked my head in a nod.

My magic was finite—there was only so much of it. And after losing my mate bond twice, and then spending days awake and fighting, it had run out. I needed to rest, to give my body time to recover.

But that didn't matter.

Nothing mattered except Dakota, until she was in my arms, against my chest, breathing steadily with that soft, tiny smile she wore while she slept.

"Someone must've grabbed her," Blue said quickly, though her face was pale and her eyes were lifting to the trees.

"She didn't fall," Presley rasped. Her eyes were closed, her face twisted in pain. Her injuries would heal, but by the shallow way she was breathing, I knew it would take time. "The klynna had her."

My breathing stopped.

My *heart* stopped.

The klynna had her.

"The magic didn't work," Presley added, though her voice was shakier, the words sounding more like breaths. The woman was in serious pain—pain that would likely knock her out again, soon. "It wouldn't turn around. I think it took her."

Fear welled in my chest.

I wasn't connected to her—we weren't bonded.

I couldn't hunt her by scent.

I couldn't *help* her.

"Aev," Oren started to say, but I was already moving.

Running.

Sprinting.

Like a fucking ghost through the trees.

I couldn't find my Thorns, but Teris could. And that bastard would take me to her.

Finding him wasn't difficult; I'd smelled his scent on her skin all week. It had been driving me mad, though I hadn't let her see how much I despised it.

I reached him in less than two minutes, finding him tensed in a tree, watching the remaining fliers in the sky. The klynnas were all gone, but there were still fae above us, watching. Waiting.

Making sure we were truly safe.

I shifted in an instant, snarling, "Dakota was taken. Lead me to her."

The words weren't *tame*.

I would never be that, not when it came to her.

That woman was sunshine, in every fucking way. She deserved a hell of a lot better than me—but I'd love her more than life itself if she let me.

Teris didn't pause, or think.

It was one of the only things I liked about the bastard—the way he reacted in an instant, without considering any alternatives. I'd never been like that, and doubted I ever would be, but I could see the benefit of it.

He streaked through the trees, and I followed behind him. He was faster than me, but he didn't slow, or wait for me. After so many days without sleep, I didn't stand a damn chance at keeping up with him. But I didn't mind that, either.

Because the faster he moved, the sooner he would reach her.

The more quickly he would find my female—my mate, even if she had yet to accept that.

And the better chance there was that she would be alive.

I followed his scent when I lost sight of him—and didn't realize he'd stopped until I slammed right into him.

He didn't growl at me as he jumped to another branch, inclining his head toward something below us.

I looked down, and blinked.

And then blinked again.

Dakota was laying on the forest floor, a long way below us. She was coated in mud, and there was a massive red klynna lying beside her, watching her.

Her chest rose and fell slowly, but evenly.

She was alive.

But I took in the mud—and the red tinge to it.

Blood, too.

Fear swelled within me.

The klynna didn't look like it was trying to kill her. I could see mud on one of its legs and some of its claws—had the damn thing *brought* the mud to her?

It was just watching her.

And she was breathing.

Alive, and healing whatever wound had bled.

Perhaps if I'd had any ice left, I would've tried to fight the beast. But without my magic, there was nothing I could do.

"We'll have to wait," Teris said, and I realized he'd shifted back to his man form.

"I can't," I told him.

He sighed. "It's your funeral, brother."

The words were tired.

Even just a week of fighting the bond's pull would do that to a man. He didn't know how different it could feel, when you loved the woman. When you wanted her so desperately. When you knew you'd give anything to spend your life with her.

"I have to make sure it's mixed properly. That it's keeping her alive," I said. "Leave, if you want."

The man gave me a dead-panned stare, but I only held his gaze for a moment before I jumped from the tree.

My eyes collided with the klynna's as I landed gently.

Its body tensed, but it didn't move.

"She's hurt," I said in a low voice, lifting my hands slowly to show the monster that I meant him no harm. "I need to check her wounds. To make sure the mud is keeping her alive so she can heal them."

Fae healed more slowly with the blood and mud mixture applied to them, but it grounded their soul to their body. It made sure that they couldn't die as they recovered, buying them the time they needed.

The klynna gave no sign that he understood my words, but he didn't growl at me either.

Leaving my hands beside my head, I slowly moved closer to Dakota, one step at a time. I paused after each one, making sure the klynna could see that I wasn't going to attack him.

Finally, I made it to her side, and kneeled in the mud next to her. I didn't give a damn about the mess—but my stomach churned at the sight of the blood staining her skin, and coloring the goop on her body too. It was mixed unevenly, messily, but the slow rate of her breathing told me that it was doing its job.

I carefully began mixing more of the mud into the blood I could see beneath it. When it was the right color and consistency, I lifted it to her body, and carefully coated her chest and abdomen with it. I couldn't see where she was injured, but even just layering the blood and mud would help guide Vevol's magic to my female.

Rain fell on us lightly, but I leaned over her so it couldn't wash away the mud that would keep her alive.

"You're going to make it," I told her, my voice certain despite the slight shake to it. "You're too strong to let yourself fade, Thorns. Too strong to let this be your end. We have a future together, no matter how hard you might resist it or how much you fear it isn't true. My heart belongs to you—and soon, yours will belong to me too."

Though there was no sign that she'd heard me, no evidence of her recovery, I continued layering her skin in the mud.

And I continued speaking to her, just in case some part of her could hear me. Just in case my words would bring her back to me. "You're mine, Thorns. Whether you like it or not, you belong to me. And I'll fight like hell to make sure you know that, every day for the rest of our lives. I was in darkness, and you brought me light. You woke me up. You *saved me*. Now, nothing could take me from your side. Not your doubt, or your fear, or your memories. Because just as much as you belong to me, I belong to you too. You own me, body, heart, and soul. Permanently."

I continued speaking to her and waiting for her, coating her in blood and mud, determined that she would wake up eventually.

I refused to accept any alternative, because as I'd told her, my heart belonged to her. Whether she realized it or not, hers belong to me too.

And that was something I'd cherish and hold tightly to, for the rest of our lives.

Eighteen

Dakota

A low, sexy voice was murmuring something to me when I regained consciousness. I couldn't make out the words at first, but I felt the soft slide of hands on my skin, spreading something thick and wet over me.

The words became clearer as I remembered where I was and what had happened—that the klynna had hurt me. That we'd bonded, somehow. That I'd been dying, and now I was covered in mud.

"Your breathing changed," Aev's low, soft voice murmured.

My lips curved upward, just a little. "Of course you noticed." The words came out as barely more than a mumble, but his chuckle told me he understood them anyway.

"Any idea why the klynna hasn't attacked me, Thorns?" he asked me, still speaking quietly.

I wrestled my eyelids open for a minute, trying to see said klynna, but failed. They were too heavy. "I think we bonded," I finally whispered. "Not a mate bond, obviously, but something else. I can feel its emotions when I look at it, and I think it can feel mine."

There was a moment's pause. Aev finally said, "Well, damn."

A soft laugh escaped me. "Yeah."

"Leave it to you to befriend a klynna, Sunshine." The words were a little playful, and my lips curved upward a bit more.

"They're just trying to protect their mates," I told him, kind of worried he would be angry with me or otherwise unhappy. "They're trying to keep their families safe. You trapped them, and they don't want to be trapped again."

Aev was quiet for a moment, but his hands were still moving slowly over my abdomen. I couldn't feel any pain, but I didn't know if that meant something or not, since I was still covered in blood and mud. "We knew they didn't necessarily want to kill us," Aev finally said. "But they kept attacking if any of us ventured into the skies. We understand possessiveness—I'd say that's obvious. But we couldn't stop attacking them when we knew they would take any opportunity to kill us. It was hunt or be hunted, kill or be killed."

"I don't blame you for doing what you did. I just thought you should know. If we can come to some sort of agreement with them, it'll be better for all of us," I said quietly. "We can't keep doing what we've been doing."

"We most certainly cannot." His words were quiet, but firm. "Where did it hurt you?"

"Its claw went through me," I admitted. "I think I was dying."

"Fuck."

"Yeah." I tried once again to wrestle my eyes open, and finally managed to squint up at the man.

Damn, he was beautiful.

His hair was messy and wild, those dark circles under his eyes were darker and thicker, and there were random streaks of bloody mud on his face, arms, and chest. But those blue eyes were still bright, and there was a strength in the set of his shoulders that made me feel at ease.

That made me feel *safe.*

The sun was rising through the trees, so hours must've passed while I healed. I didn't feel any more pain, luckily. The rays of sunshine bounced off of the gorgeous man beside me, but he didn't notice them.

He was only looking at me.

"Do you think I'm okay?" I asked him quietly.

"If you're awake, you're probably healed." He slid a mud-drenched hand over my abdomen, slowly and carefully. "Do you feel any pain?"

"No."

"Then we should wash you off, so we can see if there's any remaining damage."

Despite his words, he made no move to pick me up or anything.

My lips curved upward, just a little, as he stared at me. His forehead was creased, his hands still moving over my abdomen slowly, like he was trying to check for wounds despite the many, many layers of mud covering me.

I asked, "You're worried about me?"

"Like you wouldn't believe," he admitted, carefully slipping his hand into mine. The drying mud on my fingers cracked at the contact, and the wet mud on his softened mine.

His eyes lifted to the klynna, and he studied it for a moment before he looked back at me. I realized it might react if he picked me up, and turned my head slowly. The mud on my neck did the same dry cracking thing it had done on my hands, but I ignored it as I met the klynna's eyes.

Even without looking at each other, I could feel the bond thrumming through both of us. But when our eyes met, that connection swelled and thickened.

The klynna's emotions rolled through my mind.

Worry for my safety.

Desire to return home, to his mate.

Fear of what the connection may mean.

Certainty that the goddess had intended us to connect, despite the difference between us.

The pure strength of his feelings still surprised me.

"Aev is mine," I whispered to the creature, tightening my grip on the unseelie's hand. "Please don't hurt him."

The klynna blinked slowly, and I felt its agreement before I looked up at Aev. His lips were tilted upward, his gaze soft. "I'm yours, am I?"

"You are." I bit my lip, and his small smile stretched upward. "Right?"

"Yes, Thorns. Always." His lips brushed my forehead, even though I could feel the dried mud on it. The fact that he didn't mind the mess spoke volumes.

He carefully slipped his arms beneath me, picking me up slowly. It took him a minute to pry me out of the mud, but then there was a soft suctioning noise, and I was free.

My face met his chest as I leaned against him, inhaling the scent of his sweat and worry, mixed with mud. He held me close, and moved slowly away from the klynna.

Heavy, ground-shaking footsteps told me that the creature was following us.

"We'll need to let everyone know not to hurt the klynnas," I said quietly, my lips brushing Aev's chest as I spoke.

"The others haven't come back since you were hurt," he told me, running a hand calmingly over the back of my leg. "I think your new friend is keeping them at bay somehow."

Huh.

"Have you talked to anyone else about it?" I asked, because I was a little worried about Summer and Rosalie. Alarm bells went off in my mind when it went there. "And Presley? How's Presley?"

"I'm sure she's fully-recovered by now. Her injuries looked painful, but she was otherwise fine last I saw her. Summer came and checked on you twice, so I know she's alright. Worried about you, but seems to trust me to look after you. She and Vuvim explained how the fight ended, and then let me know that the klynnas hadn't come back, though I would've seen them if they had. They've been dealing with the stressed crowds of fae."

"That's good." I let my eyes close, too exhausted to hold them open. I hadn't been sleeping while the mud and blood worked on me; I'd been unconscious, and healing slowly.

"Stay awake, Thorns. I need to clean you off, to see if we need fresh mud or if the magic has taken care of you.

"Alright." I wrestled my eyes back open. "Are we going to the river?"

"Yes."

I nodded against his chest as he continued walking. "Do you think the klynnas can communicate mentally?"

"It's a reasonable possibility, since mated fae can. Perhaps mated klynnas can, or their minds work on a different level than ours, so all of them communicate that way."

Hmm.

I was intrigued by the thought, but unsure whether I'd find out the truth. After I was clean, I would ask the creature, I decided.

"Thank you for protecting me," I told Aev quietly.

"You had already protected yourself. And besides, I should've seen the klynna fly away with you. I should've noticed you being taken. I couldn't even hunt you here on my own." Frustration flooded his voice.

"Did you have to find Teris?"

"Yes." The word was short, and hard.

My voice was softer when I replied, "Whatever possessiveness was caused by the bond should've mostly faded by now, right?" It had been... five days? Six? Seven? Honestly, everything had been a blur since then, and I wasn't sure how long I'd been unconscious in the forest.

"My desire to protect you has nothing to do with the bond, Thorns." His arms tightened around me slightly, holding me closer. "I've told you that."

"I know. I'm a pain."

He gave me a low chuckle. "You are not."

"Oh, I am. I know I am. But you like me anyway. I don't know why, but I'll take it." I closed my eyes and leaned against his chest.

"It's because you're light, and happy. Because you see the good in nearly every situation, and smile even when there's no good to be found. You're like the sun, Thorns—you make everything brighter. And I know the darkness far too well to walk away from my own personal sunshine."

I opened my stinging eyes. "What am I even supposed to say to that?"

"Kiss me?" he suggested.

I laughed softly. "I think we should wait out the bond a little longer, just to make sure. But I think you're it for me too, Aev. That terrifies me, but it's true. My life has been so much better with you in it."

"I don't see how. Everything has gone to hell since you and I became friends. I even released the klynnas." His voice was grim.

I flashed him a small smile. "That wasn't your fault. And hey, when everything goes to hell, everyone needs someone to hang on to. You became that someone for me."

"So I'm nothing but an anchor to you?" he asked, voice playful.

I laughed. "Exactly."

He grinned down at me, looking so much more alive than he had before our bond. Before he was freed from Naomi. And I decided that she was right—that they were just a horrible match.

Whatever Vevol's reasoning was for pairing them together, I was so damn grateful they were now apart that I didn't even have the words to describe it.

WE REACHED the river a few minutes later, and the klynna plopped down beside it as Aev slipped into the water. It was flowing much faster than it had been the last time I'd seen it, and he frowned at it for a moment before grabbing a long, thick vine off a nearby tree, and dragging it over to the bank with us.

The very end of the vine dangled into the river while he slid into the water, and I clung to him when the cold of it soaked through the mud on my skin and made me shiver.

My flames burst to life as Aev maneuvered me around, tying the end of the vine to my waist loosely before he began scrubbing my skin lightly. The fire had already burned the mud off my arm and legs, leaving my torso to the sabertooth in front of me. He didn't pay any mind to my flames, focused entirely on cleaning my abdomen carefully. He had to roll my tank top up to the middle of my breasts to do so, but they didn't distract him for more than a few seconds.

"Can I burn you?" I asked him, slightly worried.

"If you tried hard, yes. But all fae are fire-resistant, so you'd have to want me burned," he said absent-mindedly, since he was focused on cleaning me.

When my bare skin was in front of him, pale and whole, he let out a long, relieved breath.

"I'm okay, right?" I checked.

"You're perfect." He smoothed a hand slowly over my belly, and my body clenched. "You feel better?"

"I do."

"Good." He leaned his lips to my stomach, and then brushed a kiss to the new skin there. "You scared the hell out of me, Thorns." His arms landed on my hips as he straightened to his full height. The man was so massive, he towered over me.

With my ex, that would've scared me.

With him, it was just... right.

"After we've dealt with the beasts, and you're satisfied that my emotions are genuinely my own, I plan on locking us in our house," he told me, voice low.

"*Our* house?" I lifted an eyebrow.

His tired eyes gleamed. "Yes, Thorns. *Our* house. You told me you want me bossy—so you're getting the king."

My lower belly warmed. "I'll believe it when I see it," I said, mostly teasing him.

He lowered his lips to my throat, and I went still as he slowly dragged the tip of his tongue in a circle around a tiny strip of sensitive skin. A shudder rolled through me, and he stepped impossibly closer. His erection met my stomach, and I found my head tilting to the side, giving him better access.

My eyes closed on their own volition as he sucked lightly on the skin, making my heartbeat pick up. The thought that he could feel that heartbeat on his *tongue* was enough to make me hotter.

My body was throbbing with need when he finally released my throat, lifting his lips to my ear and murmuring, "You'll see it, Sunshine."

When he nipped at my throat and stepped back, I let out a soft groan that made him chuckle. I forced my eyes open, and looked at the klynna that was bonded to me. Its emotions collided with mine, and I felt...

Amusement.

Apparently, Aev's teasing had been funny to the creature, or at least interesting.

The ex-king's arms wrapped around my waist, tugging me back to his chest. "We should get back to the others, so you can show them that you're whole," he told me, stroking the wet, tangled length of my hair like it was golden silk rather than a light brown rat's nest. I didn't complain, though. I actually loved it.

"Alright." I closed my eyes and focused on the flames within me, dragging them outward until I felt them burning away the rest of the mud on my skin, in my hair, and on my clothes. When we stepped out of the river, we were both clean—and I was ready to figure out what was coming next.

Nineteen

Aev ran us back to the group of fae waiting solemnly for the next fight, and my klynna-friend followed in the forest behind us. I asked him to wait when we approached the others, and he remained where he was as we went back and explained to everyone what had happened between me and the creature.

Some people were alarmed by the bond between me and him. Others were fascinated, or excited.

We spoke with everyone for a few minutes before the klynna stomped into our group, shaking the forest with every footstep. Everyone watched silently as he approached. Not as a monster, this time, but as a tentative friend.

I watched the creature move. Despite its size, and the weapon its whole body was, there was a grace to it that reminded me of the fae. Humans moved clumsily, sometimes jerkily. But fae? They just *flowed*. And the klynnas did too, I realized.

None of the fae or ex-humans tried to touch the creature. That was probably wise; the klynnas seemed far too intelligent, and far too dangerous, to treat them like pets. For all we knew, they could be our equals in every way except size.

They all just watched him, and he watched them too.

I stood next to Aev, with his arm wrapped around my waist, holding me to his side. His fingers rested securely on my hip, and I was fighting the urge to lean my head against his shoulder and let myself fall asleep.

"Can you make an agreement with them?" Summer asked me, looking just as exhausted as I felt.

I shrugged. "I can try."

Honestly, I had no idea if it would work. But it was worth a shot, wasn't it?

Aev's fingers pressed into my hip a little harder. I knew he wouldn't like the idea of me taking more of a risk, but I also knew he wouldn't argue with me about it. Not when I was the only one with this connection to the klynnas—the only one who could do it. I had made it clear to him when we set boundaries that I was going to do whatever I felt like I had to, to help keep everyone safe. And he had respected that since then, even if he didn't like that.

He wouldn't let me do it alone, though. Not if he could help it. And I appreciated that immensely.

"If you can convince them not to attack us, you can have any damn thing you want," one of the unseelie council members muttered. I thought it might've been Korrik, but didn't acknowledge the words, since I didn't think I'd ask them for anything.

What more did I need? Now that I had a house, and Aev...

I bit my lip as I glanced over at the king. He stood straight, his expression neutral, but he held onto me tightly enough that I felt like his lifeline.

Maybe I really was an anchor for him.

Aev looked back at me, and his neutral expression softened into something kind. Maybe even sweet. His lips curved up slightly, though I could still see a little uncertainty in his gaze. "It's your call, Thorns."

Pride swelled within me.

He trusted me.

Believed in me.

And if he could, why shouldn't I?

I looked back out at the crowd. At the fae men and women, at the ex-humans. My gaze collided with Nev's, and he gave me a tiny nod. He and I had never been anything more than friends, but that one look told me that he believed in me too.

That he knew I could do this.

I lifted my chin a fraction of an inch, lowering my shoulders as I called out, "If it's possible, we'll make peace with the klynnas. We'll make sure all of us are safe—that our lives can go back to normal."

I wasn't sure there was really an established *normal* in our society of lonely fae men, uncertain ex-humans, and wild female fae, but anything was better than the fear we were currently struggling with.

"We'll classify the new humans as soon as the moon allows, in case you fail," Fovea said from beside Nev.

That was a little negative, but probably a good call anyway, so I agreed.

Then, I looked to Aev. "Ready?"

"Not really." He flashed me a tired grin, and I couldn't stop the matching one from breaking out on my face.

A few whoops and cheers erupted from the unseelie side of the crowd, and someone yelled, "Kiss her!"

I laughed, and Aev's grin widened.

Waiting out the bond no longer felt that important, but I was going to do it anyway, just in case. When I promised myself to Aeven, when I connected our futures permanently, I wanted to be certain that I would never have regrets or questions about that connection.

He pulled me up onto his back as he shifted forms and took off into the trees, with more cheers echoing behind us from the fae who weren't scrambling out of the way of the klynna that launched into the sky. I found myself staring at the gorgeous gleam of the klynna's scales as I buried my fingers deeper into Aev's fur, holding tightly to the sabertooth I'd begun to trust more than anyone else in both Vevol and Earth combined.

Though I could've flown with the klynna, and part of me wanted to, I was so comfortable on Aev's back that I simply snuggled deeper into his fur as the day progressed, wrestling my eyelids open every time they closed.

I MUST'VE FALLEN asleep at some point, because it was dark outside again when Aev stopped. The lack of motion roused me, and I opened sleepy eyes, blinking rapidly as I looked around the forest. There were massive trees on every side of us, different than the ones I'd seen before. These ones were loaded with huge fruits, the same ones Summer had brought back for me from one of her trips with Remmo a few weeks back.

Aev shifted forms, steadying me when I wobbled at the sudden weight on my feet.

Damn, I was still exhausted.

He looked even more drained than me, though, so I murmured, "Sit down. I can grab food."

The klynna landed a short distance away from us, breaking chunks out of a few trees in the process, but we didn't comment on that. At least it hadn't knocked any of the massive things over that time.

I expected Aev to protest my plan, but he gave a tired nod and plopped down on the dirt without a word. He did brush his lips to the back of my hand, though, before leaning his head against a tree and closing his eyes.

I gave in to an urge and dragged my fingers through his hair, earning a soft groan before I turned and strode toward the fruit trees. My legs were more wobbly than I would've liked, but that was to be expected after spending an entire day on Aev's back.

He was already snoring softly when I made it to him with the fruit a few minutes later, so I woke him up gently. It took a minute, but he finally accepted the fruit and ate quickly.

"Sorry I'm so tired," he mumbled, as he set the empty shell of his fruit on the ground off to the side of the tree.

"Don't be. You've been awake a long, long time. Get some sleep." I slid my fingers into his hair again, and he leaned his head toward me as his eyes shuttered. A heavy sigh escaped him, and he finally leaned away, plopping down on the ground on his back. He didn't so much as move a toe before he was snoring again, and my lips curved upward at the soft vulnerability of the moment.

He trusted me, too. Just as much as I trusted him. And that felt really, really good.

I finished eating, and moved the fruit's shells a little more before I walked over to the klynna. He was sprawled out on the ground on his belly, and only peeked one gigantic eye open as I approached him.

I didn't reach a hand out to pet him or anything; he wasn't just some animal. He was an intelligent being, one I was connected to, by some kind of miracle.

"Hello," I said quietly, as I felt its emotions rolling through me.

Tired.

Yearning for his mate, for his home.

Hopeful at the prospect of peace and security.

"I'm ready to move on to the next chapter too, friend," I murmured, wrapping my arms around my abdomen. "It's been a long time, hasn't it? Long enough that change doesn't feel like the enemy anymore."

The klynna snorted at me.

My smile widened. "Maybe that's just me."

He blew a puff of smoke toward me and closed his eye. I could still feel his sleepy amusement, though.

"Goodnight, Redd," I teased him lightly, as I turned on my heels. He needed a name; I might as well give him one.

His conscious brushed my mind, and I heard a single word in my head. *"Rerrwyn."*

My heart warmed. "Goodnight, Rerrwyn."

His gentle approval brushed through my mind, and I felt so much peace as I walked back to a snoring Aev that it was honestly unreal.

I lowered myself to the ground beside him, resting my head against the shoulder on the arm he still had sprawled out wide. As soon as I was settled against him, he made a grumbling noise, and tugged me closer. When he was satisfied that I was close enough, my body was draped almost entirely over his.

His arms wrapped around me, tightening until I was securely in place. "I want a nickname too, Thorns," he mumbled as he tucked my head beneath his chin. My forehead pressed to his neck as my smile widened. I was almost entirely certain that he was still asleep, and wouldn't remember saying that in the morning.

But despite him being asleep, I was also almost positive that the words he'd said were true.

He wanted a nickname too.

All of his friends called him Aev, and always had. It was his name. Naomi had called him Aeven, which was why I'd never used it.

It was only fair that I give him a nickname too.

And despite my own exhaustion, I thought about it while I rested in his arms, completely safe and more comfortable than I'd ever been in my life.

I couldn't think of anything particular at first—he was just Aev to me.

So I focused on the nickname he'd given me.

Thorns.

Because my thorns made me strong.

What made Aev strong, though?

I considered what I knew about him. About his past as king. About how incredible he'd been at it—incredible enough to chase a bunch of horny, lonely unseelie bastards onto seelie land, knowing that he'd likely end up in a fight he wanted nothing to do with.

Incredible enough not to push Naomi for more than she was willing to give at any point during their connection.

Incredible enough to fight the awful pain of an unwanted mate bond for two decades, even when it cost him everything.

Incredible enough to wrap those huge arms around me and hold me tightly while he slept, even after all he had survived.

If we were both drelae, and my strength was in my thorns...

Then his was in his vines. The thick, strong connections that bound him to the trees, to the family he'd chosen, to Vevol herself.

And now, to me.

And as terrifying as that was, I hoped like hell that he would never let go.

IT WAS the middle of the day when I finally woke up. Aev was still asleep, though no longer snoring. Rerrwyn had moved closer at some point, and was plopped down on the ground only a few feet to my left.

I was still draped over Aev's body, with one of his gigantic hands gripping my ass lightly, and the other buried in my hair. The moment felt intimate, but in a way that I absolutely adored.

His breathing was still even, and I knew he could've slept through the rest of the day and probably the night too, without waking up. I should've made him sleep more while we were diverting the klynnas, but when there was no one else with the same ice power as him, it was a hard argument.

My eyes met Rerrwyn's, and he blinked at me slowly.

Though I didn't hear any more words from him, I felt his question.

Was I ready to go?

He was eager to get back home, but he did understand how long Aev and I had gone without the kind of sleep we really needed.

I nodded at him, carefully putting my hands on Aev's chest. It took a lot of effort to peel myself off of him, and he made a grumbling noise when I accidentally moved against his erection a little, but he let me sit up.

His hand tightened on my ass, and my cheeks heated as my gaze jerked to Rerrwyn.

The klynna let out an amused huff, and I relaxed a bit.

Aev squeezed my ass, and a squeak escaped me. His lips curved upward, and I couldn't help but laugh.

He peeked his eyes open, and slowly took in my face. His smile widened as he saw me, and the man looked so much calmer than he had in days. "Hey, Thorns."

"Hey, Vines." The nickname slipped out, and my cheeks flushed.

Curiosity lit his blue eyes brighter, and I bit my lip.

"I like it," he said. "You'll tell me what it means, eventually?"

"Yes, eventually."

He caught my hand and dragged it to his lips, brushing a kiss to my knuckles. "The pull of the bond is gone. I don't feel it at all. And yet, I still want you. In my arms. In my bed. On my tongue. Around my cock, too."

My face flushed, and I felt the heat spread down my neck, over my chest, and across my arms. "Technically, it's *our* bed."

A laugh escaped him—a loud, genuine one that made me smile.

"You're fucking perfect." He dragged my fingers back to his lips. "How much longer are you going to make me wait, Sunshine?"

"I haven't decided yet."

He pulled one of my fingers away from the others, and slid the tip of it between his lips. My eyes widened and my blush spread over more of my skin as he sucked gently on the digit, dragging his tongue over the pad and slowly having his way with it.

It shouldn't have been erotic.

It really shouldn't have been.

But *damn*, it definitely was.

"We need to go," I managed to say, probably squeaking again on accident.

"Mmhm." He slowly finished what he was doing.

Somehow, I was already drenched and dying to let him take that tongue to other, more sensitive parts of me.

But I didn't know if we were ready to reignite the bond yet. A few more days would make me more certain that his feelings were real.

He finally released my finger, nipping at it with his teeth before letting go altogether. "Can I fly with you for a bit?"

I blinked. "You *want* me to fly?"

"Of course I do. You're a phoenix, Thorns."

I knew that.

I *did* know that.

It just surprised me to hear him say it. To hear him not just reluctantly agree to let me take the lead for a while—but to hear him *ask* me to have a turn.

"Do you think it's safe?" I checked, before committing.

"I do. Our friend must've sent his brothers away after he connected with you; they wouldn't have left on their own. And that means he protected you. I trust he'll continue to do so."

Gratitude and pride warred within me.

"How do you do that?" I asked him.

"How do I do what?" He tilted his head to the side a bit, sitting up on his forearms.

"Make me feel strong, without even saying it." I tossed a hand toward him. "You trust me, even when you don't have to. It messes with me."

He grinned at me—a full-on grin, gorgeous enough to stop my damn heart. "You *are* strong, Thorns. I'm not doing anything special. I just believe in you."

My eyes stung, but tears didn't fall. "Well, thank you."

"Always." He wrapped those gigantic arms around me and dragged me back to his chest, holding me tight until my emotions faded enough that I was no longer at risk of tearing up. "I love you, Dakota. I know you still think it might be because of the bond, but I swear to you that it's not. I know myself—I know my emotions. I have for centuries, despite my bond with Naomi draining the life from me. I know that I love you, and I want you to trust that."

"Well dammit, now you're going to make me cry again," I mumbled, eyes stinging once more.

He chuckled. "The way you feel everything so strongly is beautiful, you know."

"It's really not," I said, though I sniffled a few times—and hoped he would disagree.

"It really is." The man didn't disappoint.

My man.

And damn, I loved knowing that he was mine.

"You're obnoxiously good at everything," I mumbled, making him laugh.

He stroked my back while I struggled with my emotions. I wanted to tell him what I felt too, but I was still terrified. And I knew he understood that—that it didn't bother him.

After my eyes stopped watering, we ate, and then took to the skies. And as I flew over Vevol's forests, with Aev having the time of his life on my back, that same thought that had shaken me so hard occurred to me again.

My ex and my parents had always wanted me weak. But Aev?

He was head-over-heels in love with my strength.

Twenty

I FLEW for most of the day, but when exhaustion began to set in during the afternoon, I landed on a thick branch and shifted back. "Would you mind running for a while? I need a break," I admitted.

"Of course not." He dragged me into his arms and hugged me tightly. I knew that if I'd given him the green light, he would've kissed me. "You're so damn sexy, Thorns," he said into my hair.

My face warmed. "Right back at you, Vines."

Aev's chuckle rumbled both of our chests, and I hugged him tighter, wishing we were alone in our house again. As much fun as flying with him had been, I was ready to be done with the trip and just collapse in bed.

He shifted, and I buried my face in his fur as he took off into the forest. Rerrwyn followed above the trees, his massive tail taking out a branch every now and then.

The sun was going down when the forest thinned, and I stared up at the largest cliffs I'd ever seen. They were the color of melted butter, but the edges were jagged and sharp-looking. And perched at different levels of them, I could see the gleam of colorful klynna feathers and scales.

Aev made his way down from the tree we were in, and from the ground, peered up at the cliffs that stretched so insanely far above our heads. The klynnas that had once seemed monstrous to me were nothing but beautiful, now, and the way they brightened the cliffs was a sight I didn't think I'd ever forget.

"Wow," I murmured to Aev, as he shifted back to his man form.

"I can't believe they're not attacking us," he admitted. "Coming anywhere near here was a death sentence, before you."

Before me.

It was strange to think that I'd changed things for these larger-than-life fae that had saved me only a few years earlier.

"I can fly us up there," I said, noticing Rerrwyn still soaring over our heads. A smaller pink klynna had joined him, and my heart about melted when I realized that must've been his mate.

She was rubbing up against him, flying with him. "Look how adorable they are." I pointed up toward them, and Aev peered upward. His lips curved, and he slid an arm around my waist.

"Adorable," he agreed, and I had the distinct feeling that he'd never spoken that word before. That thought made me smile.

"Come on." I tugged on his hand as I shifted, and he slid onto my back. I was big enough in my phoenix form that his weight wasn't difficult to carry, even though the man was ridiculously muscular.

"Be careful, Thorns. If they act threatening at all, fly away. Toss me off your back; I'll be fine," he called out, as I took to the sky.

I nodded, even though I had absolutely no intention to do what he'd said.

If they were threatening, we'd deal with it together.

I flew in a wide circle, moving slowly and trying to look as friendly as possible. Though I didn't quite understand why the immortal, airplane-sized klynnas feared the fae, I still respected that feeling, and didn't want to scare them.

Though a few of the creatures watched warily from their nests, many others gathered near the edge of the tallest cliff. Rerrwyn and his mate landed beside that crowd, and the other klynnas made space for them.

They left a gap at the front of their group for us, making it clear where they wanted me to go. Though they way overestimated how much space we'd need, I appreciated it anyway.

I slowly circled the cliff before making my way to the spot they'd left for us. When I landed, I did so carefully, tapping into Vevol's magic to make sure the landing was gentle.

Aev remained on my back as I looked at the klynnas gathered. Though we hadn't discussed it, we both knew that I was the only one who could communicate with them. And that meant Aev would follow my lead, even if it irked at his protective instincts.

My eyes collided with Rerrwyn's, and he nodded his head while his emotions ran over me.

I was safe.

They wanted peace too.

Letting out a slow puff of air, I shifted back to my human form and stood in front of them. Aev stepped up to me, pressing his chest to my back and holding me around the waist. Though the only thing he could really do to protect me in the situation was drag me off the cliff, I figured holding me the way he was would make him look more like a worried male, and less like the fae men the klynnas despised.

The klynnas made noises I couldn't identify, which worried me a little, but Rerrwyn's emotions told me they were just shocked to see a female version of the male fae who had hunted them.

His emotions shifted, and when most of the other klynnas looked at him, I got the feeling they were having a silent conversation. It made me curious, but there was no way for me to listen in. His emotions remained calm, though, so I didn't think it was anything to worry about.

So many huge heads swiveled back to us.

Aev's grip on me tightened, but I stayed calm, in hopes he would do the same.

My eyes met one of the other klynnas, and her emotions met mine much more lightly than Rerrwyn's usually did.

Hopeful.

Desperate.

Afraid.

She wanted peace, too.

The only time I'd heard Rerrwyn's actual voice in my mind was when he gave me his name, and I knew that names had power in Vevol. If it was his full name

—which I thought it likely was—I could use it to call him to me, at any given time.

Which meant protection.

So, I didn't think we could communicate verbally about everything. The connection didn't feel like it worked that way, and I'd never seen any other evidence that it could.

But I did know that the klynnas could understand when I spoke, because they had turned away so many times when me and the other life-bringers had asked them to.

"We don't want to fight with you," I told the klynnas. Though I didn't yell, or even talk all that loudly, I spoke clearly and confidently. I hoped that would sway things in my favor, if I needed any help to do that. "We all want peace. The fae who used to fight with you had no way of connecting with you like we do now, and they feared you. They regret trapping you, now that they understand your feelings. And now that we can communicate, we hope to eliminate any need for fighting."

The klynnas watched me, and the feeling of Rerrwyn's approval flowed from the creature to me.

"Like you, we just want to live our lives in safety and peace. We want the freedom to choose our mates, and the time to love them the way we want to. We have no desire to hurt you, as your males can proclaim. When we could've attacked in the time you've been free, we never did. Instead, we used what power we had to defend our people without violence. Now, we just want to coexist peacefully. Would you be interested in that?"

Rerrwyn lowered his head toward me—a motion of confirmation, if his emotions were to be believed.

Another klynna lowered her head, too. Another male followed her, and then two more females.

A few minutes passed, but slowly, all of the creatures around us did the same.

Hope swelled within both me and Rerrwyn.

His emotions brushed mine as they all lifted their heads.

He wanted to promise his protection.

And wanted me to promise ours too.

Though the klynnas were so much bigger and stronger than the fae, the fae had trapped them. And they had made them afraid for a long, long time, as far as I understood.

"I know you may need time to consider it, but if you're interested, we can also offer something bigger," I said. "The promise of protection. If you would be willing to do the same for us, then should your people come under attack by any of the creatures in Vevol, we would be willing to help. We aren't as big as you, but we excel at working together."

I added, "I know it'll take time before you trust us, after how long the male fae had you trapped. But I know we all want peace, so I hope you'll consider it."

A few heads dipped.

No one was fully agreeing to it yet, but Rerrwyn's emotions told me that eventually, they would. They hadn't realized before meeting us that the fae felt the same way they did—that they had families they were trying to protect, and that they were afraid for their lives.

"We need to get back to our people," I said, giving the klynnas a quick, small smile. "But thank you for hearing us out. And thank you for agreeing to stop the fighting. I'll bring some of our life-bringers to bond with more of you in a few weeks, for more confirmation that you can trust us."

The klynnas bowed their heads again, and Aev squeezed my hand before I shifted forms. He leaned against me as I turned slowly and then took to the sky.

The wind rustled my feathers as I soared over the forest. Though I didn't think the klynnas would follow me, I wasn't going to land until we were a little bit further away, just in case.

When I glanced back and could no longer see the gleaming colors of the creatures on the cliffs, I finally dove down toward the forest. Aev's hands were soft in my feathers, and having his warm, strong body pressed against my back was really, really nice.

I landed smoothly on a thick tree branch, and he pulled me into his arms as I let out a heavy breath. "I think we did it," I said, against his chest.

"I think *you* did it, Thorns." His lips brushed the top of my head, and his arms tightened around me. "I'm dying to make you mine."

The words were low, but deeply honest.

"How about we wait until we get back to our house? Then, it'll have been long enough that I know the bond isn't affecting you, and I can warn Teris."

He sighed, but agreed. "I'll get you home first."

His hand slid over my ass, and a soft laugh escaped me when he squeezed.

I smiled. "What a *gentleman*."

He chuckled. "I never claimed to be that." He squeezed my ass again. "We'd better get moving, before I convince you to strip right here."

"What happened to being the king?" I teased him.

He growled playfully at me. "Before I strip these clothes off you, then." He squeezed my butt one more time before he towed me onto his back, shifting forms and taking off into the forest. I buried my face into his fur, holding him tightly as he ran.

WE STOPPED for the night a few hours later. I'd been drifting off for a while, and it was already the middle of the night, but I assumed Aev wanted to put more space between us and the klynnas before stopping. And I really didn't blame him for that.

We'd made peace with them, but it was still tentative. When more of them were bonded to more of us, we would all feel more secure in that peace.

After we ate way, way too much fruit, we collapsed in each other's arms. Aev pulled me on top of him before he drifted off, and I decided I loved falling asleep with him.

We woke up when the sun rose, and were back on the road again soon after. Though he stopped running partway through to ask me if I wanted to fly, I turned him down.

I loved running with him. And honestly, I was still a little tired from spending most of the day before in the sky.

We weren't far from home when we stopped for the second night, but decided we'd rather snuggle up than run for a few more hours. So, we ate, and stayed up late talking before we fell asleep again.

The next morning, we ran the last handful of hours back home. Most of the fae were still gathered together, ready for a fight, but I noticed some of the new human women walking around. The older ones were with them, showing them around and being friendly—even Ana.

Aev and I made a quick announcement about the klynnas. After everyone cheered, I headed over to my best friend, who stood off to the side of the group, grinning massively.

Summer hugged me tightly, and I hugged her back just as fiercely. "You look happy," she declared.

"I feel happy," I admitted. "Do you know where Teris is? Aev and I are going to seal our bond, but I want to warn him, first."

"He followed Naomi when she left a few days ago," Summer said.

I pulled out of the hug, and blinked at her. "What?"

"Naomi told Blue and Presley that Vevol gave her some sort of assignment when she was done with her spirit journey." Summer shrugged. "No one's seen Teris since she slipped away, so we assume he followed her."

I blinked again.

And again.

"Like Remmo followed you?" I finally asked her.

She laughed. "If they were fated, he probably *wouldn't* have gone after her. You know Teris doesn't care about fate. He just wants love."

She had a point with that.

I sighed. "How am I supposed to warn him, then?"

"Girl, he knows the bond is temporary. He doesn't need a warning that you're going to bang your king; we all know that's coming." She winked at me, and my face heated. The blush spread over my neck, and chest, and down my arms, and she grinned at me.

I couldn't help but grin back, though mine was a little sheepish. "Alright, fine. Thank you."

"Any time." She gave me one last hug, before Remmo told her they needed to do something, and towed her away from me.

Leaving me with Aev.

He was having a conversation with an agitated-looking Oren, and a few others too. I noticed Korrik talking to Presley off to the side of them—and saw her roll her eyes at him. He fought a grin, and she bit her lip to hide a smile.

The unseelie girls were interacting. They were opening up. And the unseelie guys were, too.

I caught the end of Oren's and Aev's conversation as I stepped up to my sabertooth. "Just give it a chance, brother." He smacked Oren lightly on the shoulder. "If you know you want her, you're already in a much different position than I was in before."

His face was a little red, but he nodded.

Aev's arm wrapped around my waist, and he dragged me to his chest, holding me tightly. I flashed him a smile, and he brushed a kiss to my nose. "Did you find Teris?"

"Apparently, Naomi left on some sort of errand for Vevol, and he followed her." I bit my lip. While I didn't think that would bother him, I also didn't think he'd faced the idea of her with another man yet.

He lifted an eyebrow. "That should be interesting."

And that was the end of his response.

A smile blossomed on my face. "Ready to go home?"

"You have no idea." His hand slid into my hair, and he dragged my mouth to his. He didn't hesitate—his tongue slid between my lips, and he devoured me.

My bond with Teris fizzled out in an instant, and I felt a strong, solid connection to Aev fall into place.

The unseelies around us and in the trees whooped and cheered. When Aev pulled away long enough to throw me over his shoulder, I caught a glimpse of Oren, and saw that even he was smiling a bit.

Aev shifted forms and took off into the forest again, this time, taking me home.

Twenty-One

He closed and locked the door behind us, carrying me with him as he checked every level of our place until every single door was locked.

Instead of taking me straight to the bed when he knew we were locked up tight, he carried me down to the bathroom. My ass met the countertop before he stepped over to the shower, turning the water on. Our gazes met as he turned back to me, and his eyes were hot, but his lips were curved upward in a grin.

"You mind if we shower first? I'm filthy." He gestured to his hair, and I smiled. I used my fire to clean myself up when I started feeling gritty, but he didn't have that advantage.

"Sounds like fun."

He stepped closer to me and slid his fingertips beneath my top, then pulled on it, slowly tugging the fabric up my skin. He was leaving time for me to ask him to stop, while still taking charge like I'd told him I wanted him to.

I lifted my arms up instead, making his job easier.

My tank top landed in the sink a moment later, and then his hands were moving slowly over my abdomen, over my breasts. I closed my eyes as he played with my nipples, his touch soft and slow. My body warmed, and memories of the times things had heated up between us flashed through my mind.

Kneeling in his tent.

Together, in his bed.

His face between my thighs, in the forest.

He was so damn good to me.

When his hands found my hips, I opened my eyes. He pulled me down from the countertop, and set me on my feet.

And then he lowered to his knees in front of me, his hands sliding slowly up my legs.

"I thought you were being the king," I whispered, my whole body hot.

"Even a king should kneel for his queen, don't you think?" Those blue eyes were molten as they collided with mine.

And damn—he was right.

I gave him a small nod as his fingers hooked in the waistband of my shorts, and he pulled them down lightly, slowly, *carefully*.

My body clenched when he freed me from the fabric, the same way he had in the forest that day.

The same way I knew he would for the rest of our lives, if I let him.

And damn—I would let him.

"You're so fucking perfect," he told me, his voice low as his hands slid back up my thighs, parting me for him. Exposing me to him.

There was no urge to cover myself, or hide.

Only fierce desire, and calm confidence.

"So are you," I said, sliding my fingers into his hair.

"You're going to lose it before we get in the shower," he told me, eyes locked with mine. "And then in the shower. And then in the bed, before I finally slide inside you and make you mine."

Heat bloomed over my cheeks as my body flushed.

"Look at that." His words were playful, as he lifted one hand from my core to my nipple. It was damp with my need as he dragged it over the sensitive bud. "Even these pretty little breasts blush with the rest of you."

A soft laugh escaped me, and he grinned at me—fierce, happy, and horny as hell. "You're mine," he told me. "Every gorgeous, flushed inch of you."

And then he kissed my core.

My fingers gripped the strands of his hair like a lifeline as he dragged his tongue up the center of me. I groaned at the feel of it—the warm, slick wetness of his tongue, as he began to circle my clit slowly.

He teased my entrance with a massive finger as he made love to me with his mouth, and my legs opened wider, making room for him.

I was pulling on his hair, *yanking* on his hair, when he dragged his teeth over my clit. I was already so close to the edge that it sent me over. I cried out as pleasure coursed through my body, and he held me steady as my body quivered.

Without removing his mouth or finger from me, he picked me up with an arm around the back of my ass and carried me into the shower. Luckily, our ceiling was really damn tall.

Hot water streamed down on us as my back met the wall when he kneeled again. A cry escaped me as he picked up the pace with his tongue, starting to move his finger slowly inside me.

I was panting when he pulled his face away from my core long enough to growl, "Are there any sensitive places inside you?"

My mind spun, and I tried to come up with words. Mostly, I didn't succeed.

But everything he knew about sex, I had taught him. So he wouldn't know, if I didn't tell him.

I finally managed to explain quickly, "Supposedly, there's a g-spot. A sensitive patch sort of close to my clit, but inside me. I've never found it though, or had anyone else find it." I stumbled over the words a little, but the heat in his eyes told me he didn't give a damn about my stumbling.

He studied me with interest as he began moving his finger inside me, painfully slowly. He was stroking my insides—trying to find that spot. And he didn't even notice the water falling over his head, dripping down his face.

My knees buckled when he found the spot, and a curse escaped me when his hand landed on my abdomen, holding me up.

His lips curved wickedly, still glistening with the evidence of how good he'd been to me, and he stroked it again.

A moan escaped me, and the back of my head hit the shower wall.

He swiped his tongue over my clit again as he slowly teased that spot.

I cried out as he continued touching, and tasting, and stroking. Pushing me closer and closer to the edge.

And when I finally shattered, I did so with a scream, my hips arching desperately against him.

Aev was growling in satisfaction when I finally came down from the high, panting. He hadn't given up on my clit—he was still licking me slowly. I didn't think he was even trying to take me back to the edge yet, though. He just didn't want to stop. His reluctance when he finally pulled away confirmed that suspicion.

I sagged against the wall, completely spent and insanely satisfied. "You're really good at that," I managed.

He chuckled, standing and stepping up to me until our bare chests collided. I frowned when I realized he was still wearing shorts, and then reached down to take them off.

Aev caught my hands before I could undo the fastener on them. "This is about you," he said, eyes hot as he dragged my hands back to his lips and brushed the soft flesh over my knuckles.

"I want it to be about both of us," I countered, tugging my hands back down to his shorts. "You probably don't even know what a blowjob is, do you?"

He shook his head, his gaze focused on watching my hands move against his skin as I slowly unfastened his shorts.

"Then I think it's my job to educate you," I said playfully. My hands found the waistband of his shorts, and I pulled them down slowly. His cock sprung free, and I took in a sharp breath of air as I looked at him.

I'd forgotten how big he was.

How *gorgeous* he was.

His shorts hit the floor, and he kicked them out of the way as I wrapped a hand around his erection. "Damn, Vines. Look at you," I murmured, kneeling in front of him.

He gave me a choked growl as I leaned my face up to his erection and dragged the tip of my tongue over his slit. The taste of his pleasure was so much better than expected—and I leaned in further, wrapping my lips around the head of him.

One of his hands buried in my hair, and the other formed a tight fist on the wall. I got the sense that he was fighting with himself not to grab my face, not to use me the way he probably wanted to.

"It'll be better when you claim me if you lose it in my mouth first," I told him, speaking around his erection. A desperate snarl escaped him, and his hips jerked lightly while his hand in my hair tightened.

I focused on his cock, sucking and bobbing slowly. His hips jerked harder, the movements growing more desperate as he neared the edge.

"Show me how good you'll fill me, Vines," I told him, my tongue bumping the underside of him as I spoke without pulling away. "Show me how much you like fucking my mouth."

The words sent him over the edge.

He roared, bucking his hips wildly. I knew he was out of control—and I loved it so damn much.

His pleasure flooded my mouth and my throat, his erection never bottoming out as he fought not to hurt me, even in his most overwhelming moments.

"Holy fuck, Thorns," he growled at me, chest heaving as he pulled his cock from my mouth with a popping noise and lifted me to my feet. He tugged me into his arms, hugging me fiercely tight. "If your mouth is that good, I can't even imagine what it'll feel like to be inside you."

I laughed, wrapping my arms around his shoulders and pulling myself up further in his grip. "Even better, with any luck."

"I can't wait." One of his hands lowered to my ass, and his fingers slowly traced up and down the slit there. Though he didn't push me for more, just the touch alone was erotic. "I didn't hurt you, did I?"

"No. You were being even more careful than you needed to." I kept my voice playful, so he'd know it was the truth.

"No such thing as too careful with you." He continued exploring me with his fingers for a few more minutes before he finally stepped back and grabbed a bar of soap off a small shelf nearby. The unseelie who'd built our house had really thought about *everything*.

Aev scrubbed himself quickly, and then moved his soapy hands to me. Though I wasn't really dirty, I would never say no to having his hands on me.

By the time I was squeaky clean, I was horny again from his touch.

He rinsed both of us in the water before turning it off. I dried us both off quickly with my flames, and then he pulled me back into his arms with a grin.

My legs wrapped around his hips when he hauled me up off the ground, and his lips captured mine as he strode to the bed. I buried my fingers in the soft, silky strands of his hair as he kissed me, and I kissed the hell out of him right back.

Our mouths were locked when he found the mattress, our bare bodies nearly interlocked. His erection was wedged up against my slit, moving against my clit with every motion thanks to the slickness between my thighs.

Aev lowered me to the bed, and then pulled away. I grabbed him by his hair as he kissed his way down my throat, chest, and abdomen, and he stopped to look at me with his tongue in my navel when I tugged.

"I'm ready now," I told him, and his eyes burned hotter.

"I promised you one more," he said, then dragged his tongue down another inch further.

"Give it to me while you're inside me."

His eyes narrowed at me. "I'm no liar, Thorns."

"Save it for later, then. After we're permanent."

Those narrowed eyes heated. "You're sure about this?"

"Completely." I didn't even hesitate.

I didn't need to.

No one in my life before I came to Vevol had ever wanted me strong. They'd never encouraged me, or believed in me. Hell, maybe they'd never even really loved me.

But Aev loved me.

And I loved him, too.

"I love you," I said. "You probably realized that ages ago, even though I didn't say it. But I love y—oh!" I gasped when his tongue met my clit, his hair slipping out of my grip as my hips arched.

"Love me enough to let me watch you lose control again before I make you mine forever, Thorns," he said, before devouring me.

He played me with his fingers and tongue like I was a damn instrument. He made me move, and cry out, and finally, shatter.

I was panting and groaning when he stood at the end of the bed, opening my legs and stepping up to my core. His fingers moved slowly over me, teasing my clit and stroking my channel, making sure I was ready for him.

Despite the satisfaction coursing through my veins, it occurred to me that this was probably the way he'd taken Naomi.

"Are you sure you want me like this?" I asked him, propping myself up on my elbows.

He lifted his hot gaze from my core. "Positive."

My body burned.

A do-over.

He wanted a do-over.

With a woman he really loved—one who really loved him too.

"Good. Afterward, I want you to take me from behind." I flashed him a sexy smile, and his lips curved up in a wicked smirk.

"I'll take you in every damn position there is by the time I let you out of this house, Thorns. That's a promise."

"Prove it."

Our eyes remained connected as he lined his tip up with my slit. "Ready, Sunshine?"

"Completely."

He slid inside me, just an inch. His fingers were stroking my clit again—he remembered what I'd said about needing that to orgasm, and he wasn't going to forget it, even when he was buried inside me.

The way he stretched me, and touched me, was enough to make my breathing more difficult.

The pleasure continued building as he slid another inch inside me, and another, and another.

I was so close to the edge that the whole damn world was spinning when he was finally fully sheathed inside me. His fingers had stilled on my clit, but I was too close to losing control to care.

He was so, insanely huge.

I was so, insanely full.

And the way his hooded eyes went from staring into mine, to tracing the connection of our bodies, and back to mine, only made me hotter.

"Holy fucking hell, Thorns," he finally said, voice so strained it made my throat swell.

"Feels good?" I managed.

A dark chuckle escaped him, and he throbbed inside me. My hips arched, and he grabbed my ass, holding me in place. "None of that, Sunshine. You'll make me lose it way too soon."

"I'm close," I admitted, and he throbbed inside me a few more times. "You feel so, so good." The last word came out as a moan when he throbbed against my g-spot, and he held me firmly in place as I rocked desperately. "Damn you," I panted, body clenched and screaming at me for stopping.

"I don't want this to end." He squeezed my ass cheeks in those big hands of his.

"We can go again afterward. As many times as you can make me feel good." I was officially gasping for breath, and I didn't even care.

It was too damn incredible.

I jerked my hips, and he wasn't holding tightly enough to stop me. I cried out as the pleasure hit me hard, harder than ever before, and he roared as he slammed into me again, and again, and again, emptying himself inside me. The bond between us swelled bigger and hotter and heavier as our minds connected, but no thoughts or emotions came through on their own.

Aev pulled out, chest heaving and hair a bit sweaty. With one smooth motion, he had me laying on my stomach, and was climbing onto the bed behind me.

I was so drained—but Aev's erection was still straining. Sunny had told me that fae men didn't need to recharge the way humans did, and I hadn't really considered what it meant.

But hot damn, it meant a lot.

Endless desire.

Long sex sessions.

Multiple orgasms for both of us.

My body flushed at the thoughts.

I definitely shouldn't have let him get me off so many times already; I was going to be worn out so much sooner than him.

"I don't want you thinking like that when you're naked in our bed, Thorns," Aev growled at me. Apparently, I was accidentally broadcasting my thoughts. Oops. "When you're too tired, we'll stop. Period. I'll feed you and hold you while you sleep, and when you're ready, I'll take you again. Your comfort matters a hell of a lot more than mine."

My whole body flushed. "Talk to me like that, and I don't know if I'll ever get too tired."

He gave me a low chuckle, and mental images of myself with my ass in the air, taking his cock, assaulted me from his end of the bond.

My body heated further.

"Look at this pretty little back turning red for me," he murmured, stroking my skin slowly as he moved my legs into place. "Lift your ass for me, Sunshine."

I didn't even consider arguing with him. It was too much of a turn-on when he got bossy like that—when he told me what he wanted.

And he was still sending me the filthiest, most erotic mental pictures. If Aev always thought in pictures instead of words, he was going to be a thoroughly distracting mate for the rest of our damn lives.

I'd love every minute of it.

He opened my thighs wider, and I got an x-rated image of my own core in my mind, spread open wide and dripping wet. My entire body managed to heat even more—and then he touched me.

And shit, his mind played the moment like a movie right into mine.

I was shuddering in seconds, nearing the edge, and he thrust inside me without skipping so much as a beat.

It should've taken so much longer, but with the mental stimulation of his dirty, dirty thoughts, I was shattering on his cock in seconds, screaming like hell was on my heels as I did. It was the most intense orgasm of my life—and his pleasure only made it that much better.

"You're going to kill me," I groaned at Aev, my body still throbbing as those images lived on in his mind even after he'd lost control with me.

He laughed—loud, genuine, and happy enough to make my heart ache with happiness too. Now he was imagining me up against a wall, and it was making me dizzy. "You still want it, Thorns. I can feel it, here and here." He tapped his forehead, and then my pubic bone, where I knew I was tightening around his erection. "Let go. Enjoy this." His eyes were bright and excited, and damn, I was excited too.

"Alright, Vines. Take me to the wall." I lifted an arm, and he scooped me up easily, hauling me across the room. "Use my body."

"With pleasure." He nipped at my collarbone as I wrapped my legs around his thighs, taking him back inside me in a quick motion that made us both groan.

AN ENTIRE DAY passed before we finally collapsed in bed together, completely and utterly spent. Benefits of fae healing, I supposed. We'd stopped to eat a few times—the fae who'd built our house had filled the fridge to the brim with the birth control fruits called lilano. They were delicious, so eating them definitely wasn't a hassle.

We'd talked about having kids—neither of us was ready yet, but we were both excited by the idea, so we decided we'd consider trying in a few months.

Then, we talked about life, laying in each other's arms as the exhaustion really set in.

Knowing that the klynnas were taken care of, and the new ex-humans were classified, and we were safe? It made everything feel easier, and calmer.

And that brought me peace.

Not as much peace as the man holding me in his arms, but still.

"Do you still want me to train you?" Aev murmured, as I teetered on the edge of sleep.

"I don't," I admitted.

I didn't want it, but I also didn't feel like I needed it.

I had Aev, I had my friends, I had all of the unseelies now, and I had Rerrwyn, too. If I were to train, I would have to embrace the horrors of my past, and push past them.

But I didn't want to push past them.

I had already accepted them, and left them behind. Facing them again... I wasn't interested in that.

"Then you won't," Aev said simply, as he stroked my back. "I'll protect you, and my men will too. With their lives, because they know what's good for them."

My lips curved upward. "I like that."

"I like you." He brushed his lips over my forehead. "In fact, I love you."

I laughed softly. "I know. You said that about a hundred times while you were banging me earlier."

He laughed, his chest rumbling beneath me, and my smile was so wide it stretched my cheeks. "Because I'm a damn lucky man."

"You are," I agreed, voice sleepy and playful. "And I love you too."

"As you should, Thorns."

Another laugh escaped me, and I snuggled up closer to him. He squeezed me tightly, and I closed my eyes.

Everything had changed when I came to Vevol... and it had all been for the better. I had been scared of everything before, but now, I wasn't afraid of anything. Not even the future.

And that was a damn good feeling.

Twenty-Two

Aev—A Few Weeks Later

"Make sure you hang onto the back of your attractive male companion, no matter what!" Dakota called to the crowd of female ex-human life-bringers, who had paired up with the single male fae. Vuvim and Summer stood beside us, along with Oren and Blue, and Rosalie and Devv. Each couple was holding hands, though Oren still looked a bit uncertain about it.

The stiff bastard would come around, though. His smiley human mate was already making sure of that.

Two weeks before, we'd traveled back to the klynnas' cliffs with all three other couples, so the women could bond with the beasts. We'd needed a few more connections to establish security before we brought a larger crowd of the newer ex-humans. They still scared easily—both the new humans, and the klynnas.

But with four solid bonds between our people, and a caution to the klynnas that each woman would be arriving on the back of a man, we were fairly confident there wouldn't be any problems. Nothing was ever certain, but that was simply a part of life in Vevol, with all of the magic running rampant.

And usually, it made things more interesting.

Dakota called out, "Men, remember to stay in the order we assigned you, so we can keep things organized. We'll be spending a few nights in the forest, so stay civil. You know Aev isn't afraid to kick your asses, seelie and unseelie alike." The chastising look she sent the men made me hold back a snort.

"Don't make me laugh," she warned me mentally, fighting a grin.

Everyone knew my female was the happiest in Vevol though, so her smile and laughter wouldn't surprise anyone. It certainly wouldn't scare them.

They would stay in line with me watching them, though. Even the seelies weren't usually willing to risk pissing off my mate when they knew it would mean coming face-to-face with my ice magic.

"Ready?" she asked me, aloud this time as she flashed me that grin she'd failed at suppressing.

"Ready," I confirmed, grinning right back at her. I swept her into my arms and kissed her.

Whoops and cheers went through the crowd of my men—and some of the seelies hollered, too. The dividing lines between our people were becoming impossibly thin, especially since most of the Wild Hunt men had stopped leading in any capacity now that they were mated. Teris was still absent, but no one was worried about him or Naomi. They would kick each other's asses if they needed to, and if they were gone long enough, we'd send a search party.

I kissed my female again before shifting forms and pulling her onto my back.

As I took off into the forest, I heard swearing and laughter as everyone started shifting quickly so they could catch up with us.

My lips stretched into a grin as I ran, and my mind touched Dakota's. *"I'm really damn glad I have you."*

"I don't even want to imagine life without you anymore," she murmured back.

Her fingers buried into my fur, tugging lightly, and we both focused on the beauty of the forest around us as we ran.

As beautiful as it was, I had Vevol's greatest treasure snuggled up against me, and I'd make damn certain not to forget it.

The Primal Fae's Queen

Wild Hunt Book 6

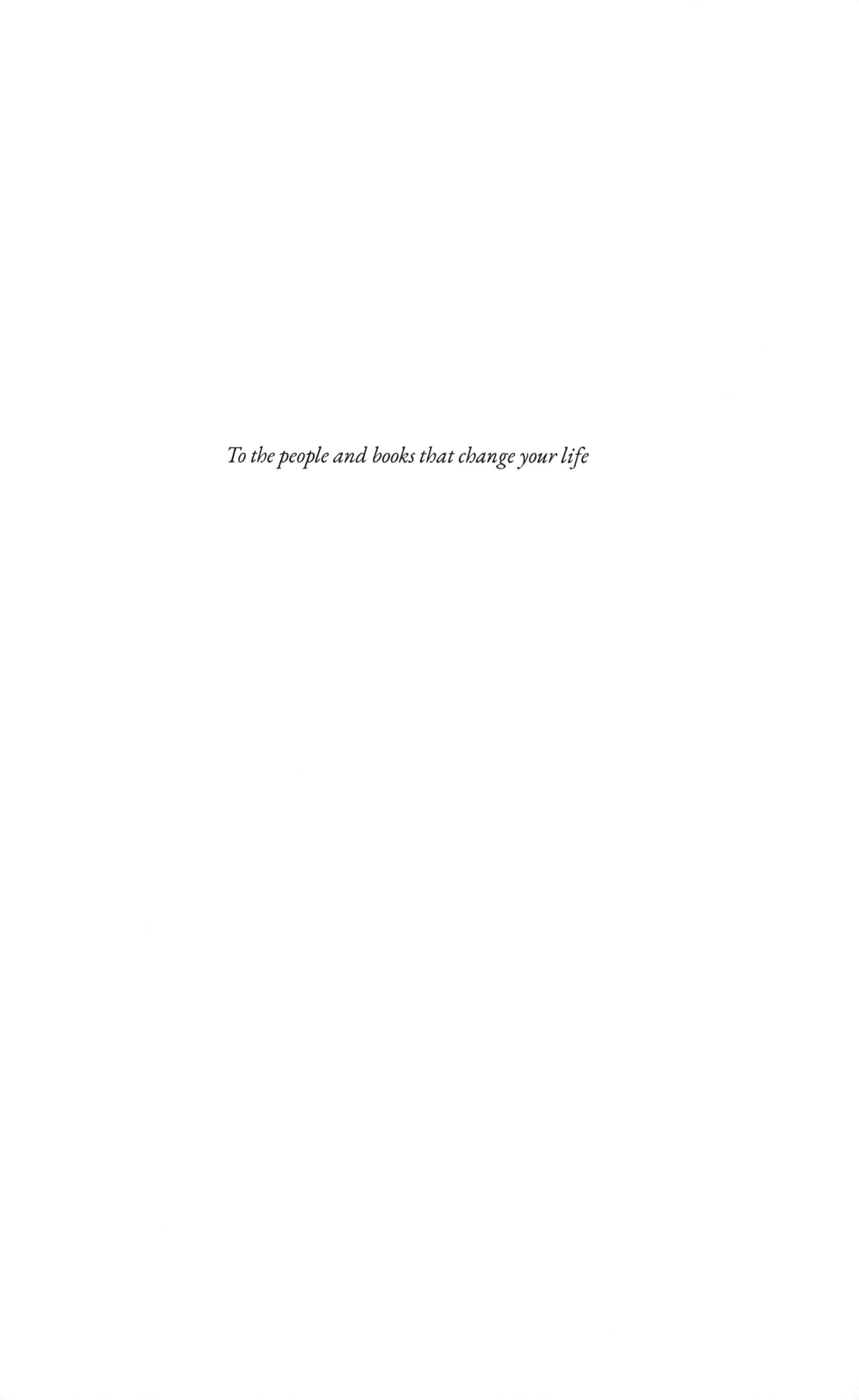

To the people and books that change your life

One

Naomi

The male fae in the trees had been following me for two entire weeks.

It was a sabertooth—I'd realized that much on the first day, when I caught a glimpse of his fur from the sky. Since I was a dragon, it wasn't like he was running next to me; I was flying.

Whoever he was, I had expected him to come out and chastise me for leaving without an escort as soon as I landed to eat and sleep for the night. I'd been tense, waiting for it. Hell, I'd listened to my stomach rumble all day to avoid that conversation.

But when I'd landed, I hadn't seen so much as a flash of fur, or heard a single growl.

Since then, I'd waited for the damn fae to come out and introduce himself every time I landed. Yet he never did, leaving me absolutely clueless as to who he was.

I knew who he *wasn't*, though.

Aeven.

The king was probably knocking boots with his new mate as I flew away from the Stronghold. And honestly, I was happy for them.

But bitter for me.

Because I'd ignored him and hoped like hell that our connection would just vanish, for *two decades*. We'd only interacted on six occasions in all those years.

Six.

When the bond hadn't disappeared, I'd finally figured out a way to split us up entirely.

But then Vevol had shown me myself in a long, painful vision.

And I'd realized that if I would've just swallowed my damn pride and talked to the guy, Aev and I could've made it work together. He was kind, thoughtful, gentle, and playful. And he knew how to step up and take control when needed.

But I'd missed my chance.

I didn't regret that—not really. I'd been struggling for a long time, and he hadn't made even a tiny bit of effort to step in or help. Plus, he and Dakota honestly did seem like a good match. And I was fairly certain that I liked my guys rougher, harsher, and more direct than the king.

But I was still a little bitter that I'd missed my shot. Because if I'd been just slightly less stubborn, I could've been sitting on a hunky fae dude's lap while he rubbed my feet and fed me fruit.

Instead, I was sleeping on the dirt, alone. With some random sabertooth guy stalking me.

I'd tried to come up with who it might be, but drew a blank. The unseelie legitimately hated me for putting Aev through hell. One of their ex-generals had guarded me, but when I left, I was positive he would've seen it as me releasing him from that duty.

Which left the seelie guys.

And the only sabertooth seelie I knew was the one who hadn't bothered putting up a fight when Aev swept me off to the unseelie side of the world two decades earlier. I hadn't heard a peep from him since then, so it obviously wasn't him.

But what kind of guy would've followed me into the forest after all the hell I'd put Aev through?

Maybe he was an outcast or something.

I didn't know.

I was itching to find out, though.

Anyway, I'd been itching about it since day one. After I'd flown to the old unseelie territory, I'd been soaring in massive, slow circles, trying to find the cave Vevol had told me about. But she was a goddess, so her directions were shitty.

When I landed for another dinner of fruit and loneliness on the fifteenth day, I was exhausted.

And frustrated.

I still had no idea where I was, or how to find that damn cave.

Halfway through the massive fruit I was eating—the one I'd always called *purple shell-fruit* in my head, my frustration reached a peak.

I was sweaty.

I was tired.

I was lonely.

And I wanted to go home, even though I still didn't have a damn home after two decades in Vevol.

So I turned my anger to the guy who had been following me.

"I know you're out there!" I yelled at the trees, cupping my hands to make my voice louder. I didn't think it would help all that much, since Vevol's trees were stupidly tall and wide, but I did it anyway. "Come talk to me for five minutes! I need directions!"

For two tense minutes, I waited for something.

Anything.

A sign that I'd been heard.

A sign that I'd been ignored would've worked, even.

But I got nothing.

Anger swelled in my chest.

"You are the fucking worst!" I shouted. Looking around the dirt at my bare feet, I grabbed the nearest rock—it was bigger than my fist—and hurled it at a tree. It collided with the trunk, making a noise that did not resemble an Earthly rock-on-wood *thunk*.

Sometimes, I missed Earth.

And sometimes I wanted to flip it the bird and curse its name.

Then again, I was like that with most places. And people.

And... everything else, too.

I needed an attitude adjustment, but I wasn't sure how to go about doing that. At least I'd swallowed my pride long enough to apologize to Aev; that had made me feel slightly better about some things.

"Trying to kill a tree now?" A deep male voice drawled behind me.

I spun around, clenching my fists and wishing I'd kept that rock.

The man in front of me was...

"Teris?" I blinked at the seelie.

The Wild Hunt's sabertooth.

He was even bigger than I remembered him, and so muscular he might as well have been chiseled out of stone.

While his chest and arms had been free of ink the last time I saw him, one of his arms was now covered in black markings that began on his hand and snaked up over his shoulder and around his neck. They were intricately detailed, but I couldn't tell what they depicted from where I was. Somehow, they made him even more gorgeous.

Why the hell had he followed me, though?

And... why was I so glad it was him?

I didn't really need an answer to that last one. The answer could be found in our history. I just liked to pretend it hadn't happened, because of everything that had come afterward.

He made a show of glancing over his shoulders one at a time, and the expression on his face was so sarcastic that I had to fight a snort. "Don't see anyone else."

"Why didn't you come out sooner? You've been following me for two weeks!" I tossed a hand up toward the treetops.

"Have I?" He lifted an eyebrow.

I rolled my eyes at him, and strode past the bastard, heading back to my shell-fruit.

"Where are you trying to go?" he asked me, following me to my seat. When I sat down, he walked away until he'd stopped and leaned back against a tree at least twenty feet away from mine.

Clearly, he wasn't interested in me. Not that I expected him to be.

"Vevol sent me to the old klynna cave. She needs me to do something there." I grabbed my big-ass fruit and the makeshift spoon I'd created with part of its shell.

"To do *what* there?"

"Don't worry about it. You're clearly not interested in joining my shitty adventure."

"I'm not giving you directions unless you give me the truth," he said bluntly.

"I'm not giving you the truth unless you're joining my team of one." I gestured to myself.

Maybe I was even lonelier than I'd realized.

Teris narrowed his eyes at me.

I stared right back.

Neither of us folded.

I finished my shell-fruit and dropped the shell on the dirt before I stood up and brushed off my ass. I'd taken to wearing the simple tank top and shorts the seelies gave their ladies, just because they were comfortable. Most of us ex-human women had, honestly. Some of the female fae, too.

Teris's eyes followed me as I plopped down in a bush of massive, soft-ish leaves and got comfortable.

He didn't say a word about my invitation-of-sorts, but I didn't ask again.

And neither of us dared to bring up the past.

Because twenty years ago, we had been really damn in love—until I'd found my fated mate, and never seen Teris again. Aev didn't even know that he and I had a thing. No one did.

So yeah, I didn't think Teris was going to agree to join me.

But I also didn't think I was going to find the damn klynna cave on my own.

...Which left us at a stalemate.

But hey, at least I wasn't *completely* alone anymore.

TERIS WAS GONE when I woke up. Since he'd been following me for two weeks already, I figured he was going to continue following me. If he didn't...

Well, I would figure it out.

I'd asked him to stay with me, and he'd refused, so it didn't really matter what I wanted. He was going to do whatever the hell he decided to do, and there was nothing I could do to change that.

After another long day of flying around cluelessly, I landed near some trees. They were loaded with the small birth-control fruits that Blue had told me were called *lilano*. The only male fae I'd ever spoken to enough to learn anything about Vevol was Teris, and that was so long ago. He'd been busy enough fighting off the other men with the rest of the Wild Hunt that asking for names and uses of plants had been the last thing on my mind.

Then again, I'd also been busy checking him out.

And telling him about all the sad shit I'd lived through on Earth.

And… falling in love with him.

Which I really needed to let go of.

I'd managed not to think about him more than once a day or so in the many years since we'd been apart. That was pretty good, right?

Shit.

Maybe it wasn't.

Maybe I had never really moved on.

Seeing him the night before, talking to him, hearing his sarcasm…

It had brought me right back.

I'd move on again, though. I had to believe that.

I plucked a few lilanos from a tree before plopping down on my ass and peeling the first fruit. They were small and round, with bright red skin that was somehow still coarse despite the red fur covering it. There were many bumps and sharp bits protruding from it, but I knew the bumpy bits were good for opening them up. I'd been living on lilanos for long before any of us knew they also functioned as birth control. They were basically healthy ice cream, so why the hell wouldn't I?

While I ate in silence, I considered my options.

Pretending Teris wasn't there would be the easiest, but also the loneliest, and my chances of finding the klynna cave were nearly zero on my own.

Vevol had told me it was in the eastern part of the old unseelie territory, and that I'd recognize it by the swoop of white stone in the mountains around it. But there were so damn many miles of white stone mountains, and they were all covered in massive trees. I'd flown over all of them, and seen many swooping shapes, but I'd never found the entrance to any kind of a cave no matter how much I poked around them.

So, I was stuck.

And if I wanted Teris to tell me where to go, I was going to have to tell him the truth about the mission Vevol had sent me on.

If I did that, he would probably drag me back to the Stronghold kicking and screaming. Teris wasn't like Aev; he wouldn't just accept it if I turned him down or made my own decisions for my own reason. He was wild, primal, and dominant.

Or at least, he had been all of those things when I'd known him. I supposed two decades was enough to change anyone permanently.

Then again, I never would've imagined him as the kind of man who would let me go without a fight, back then. And he'd done exactly that when Aev stole me away, so maybe I hadn't really known him at all.

With all those thoughts running through my mind, I decided that I wasn't quite desperate enough to turn to him yet. I'd keep searching until I couldn't handle it anymore, and if I still hadn't found the cave by then, I'd tell him the truth.

And fight like hell to stop him from hauling my ass back to the other fae.

Another week passed before I reached the end of my rope.

I couldn't spend any more time poking around the damn mountains cluelessly. Or sleeping on the forest floor. Or so entirely alone. It was bringing back memories of that first year I'd spent hidden away on my own in the unseelie version of the Stronghold, and those had been the worst days of my life. Even worse than the Earth ones.

I forced myself to eat slowly, so Teris wouldn't see my desperation. The more confident and comfortable he thought I was, the better odds I probably had at convincing him that I was sure about my plan.

After I'd dropped my lilanos' peels on the ground, leaving them for the small scavengers I'd seen up in the branches a few times, I leaned my head back against the tree and waited.

A few minutes later, I called out, "Alright, I'll give you the truth in exchange for directions to the cave."

There was no immediate movement in the trees around me, but I didn't see any reason to believe that Teris would've headed back to the Stronghold after so much time spent following me through the forest. So I didn't panic.

A few minutes passed before I finally saw a sabertooth slink through the trees. He leapt smoothly to the ground, and I swallowed my sudden surprise at the size of him. It was rare for me to be around male fae at all, so I would've been just as surprised if he were any other creature.

He shifted forms, sliding his hands into the pockets of the ripped pants he always wore.

As far as I knew, I was one of the only people in Vevol who knew why he wore pants instead of the shorts most male fae preferred.

I wasn't about to bring that up, though. Not when I was about to try to pull off telling him half of the truth for the sake of finding the cave.

He leaned up against a tree, remaining even further from me than he'd been the last time we spoke.

"Vevol is dying," I told him. I didn't bother softening the blow; it wasn't something small. The goddess was dying, but she had assured me that she had already ensured that her land would survive. It was just her consciousness that was fading. Which was still a big deal, but not world-ending.

He blinked.

His forehead furrowed.

"The goddess Vevol is dying," I clarified. "Bringing so many humans here and making them fae went against some sort of godly rule. She's fading, now. The last of her magic will go into bringing one last group of humans here through Fovea's brands, and then changing them, to make sure the fae population can start growing again. It'll happen sometime soon, and then she'll be gone."

Teris blinked again, his forehead furrowing further.

All of that was the complete truth, though the whole *sometime soon* thing was extremely vague when I knew exactly what would trigger it.

"Why has she sent you to the klynna cave, then?" Teris finally asked, after a long moment had passed.

"Tell me where to find it, and I'll tell you," I countered.

His eyes narrowed at me.

Mine narrowed back at him. "I gave you answers. You haven't done a damn thing except stalk me, Teris."

He scoffed. "You'd get yourself killed out here on your own, *Queen Naomi*."

The damn audacity of that man made my fists clench.

"It's been almost two weeks, and I'm perfectly fine. Fuck off." I stood up and strode away.

I'd find the damn cave on my own.

A strong hand wrapped around my wrist, and tugged hard. My body spun until my chest collided roughly with Teris's. He grabbed me by the waist, holding my front flush against his.

My head was tilted back, his turned down, and our eyes were locked. While his orbs were a deep, intense teal color, mine were a piercing blue.

"You're in the wrong mountain range. I'll take you to the right one," he said in a low growl. "Tell me."

It was time to artfully mix truth and lie to satisfy him. With our bodies pressed together like they were, making my mind spin, it wouldn't be easy. But I'd manage, because it was the only real option.

"The klynna cave connects to some sort of underground river cavern with a massive tree that Vevol calls her heart. She needs me to get all of the animals who live on the tree to leave, because it will die when she fades. It's her anchor."

The first part was true, but the second part was bullshit.

The tree wasn't going to die.

But Teris wasn't going to find that out.

He studied me, eyes narrowed.

If he'd known me better, maybe he would've picked up on the lie.

And if I hadn't spent so many years so damn miserable, maybe I would've been a worse liar.

Teris finally dipped his head. "Fine. We'll clear the tree. Then, we go back to the Stronghold and warn Fovea about what will happen with her brands."

"Why does she need a warning? Because you have feelings for her?" I shot back, without thinking it through. My heart pounded wildly against his chest, and I could feel his beating hard against mine too. "I know you lost the fight with Nev to mate with her."

His eyes darkened. "I've never *lost* a fight with Nev. We leave in the morning."

With that, he released my hip and shifted forms, disappearing back into the forest.

I sucked in a deep breath of air at the sudden hit of silence. It had felt good to talk to someone, even Teris. Even if he didn't want me. Even if I couldn't stop myself from pissing him off.

But what did it mean, that he'd never lost a fight with Nev?

Everyone knew he'd lost.

Unless...

Had he thrown the fight?

There was no way he could throw it that convincingly, was there? The female fae were warriors; they would see right through it if he hadn't taken it seriously or given his all.

...Right?

Two

When morning came around, and I sat up, Teris was already leaned up against a tree and glaring at me.

"Nice to see you too," I mumbled, rubbing sleep out of my eyes as I untangled myself from the bush I'd slept in. My hair got stuck, and I swore as I tried to untangle the dark, forever-long strands from the branches and leaves.

"I need to cut this shit off," I muttered to myself, yanking, tugging, and ripping at it. It was thick, and much longer than I'd ever kept it back on Earth. But it had started growing much faster after I came to Vevol, which made it too much of a pain to keep up with trimming it constantly, especially since I was terrible at cutting it evenly. I usually chopped it to my shoulders every two or three months, and didn't let it grow past my lower back.

"Don't," Teris growled at me, plucking my hands off the tangled mass.

My words died in my throat as I watched him swiftly free it from the bush, much faster and less painfully than I had been doing it. "Don't what?" I finally asked, as he freed the last few strands and swept a hand down the length of it, making sure he hadn't missed any.

"Cut it." He released my hair and stepped away from me. "I'll stay high in the trees. Blow fire if you need me to slow down. And if you see a damn klynna, you land on the branches with me."

"Dakota made peace with the klynnas," I pointed out, still reeling a little from his words, and clueless as to why he wouldn't want me to cut my hair.

He ignored me, shifting forms and streaking into the forest.

More curses spilled from me as I shifted too, launching myself into the sky and fighting like hell to catch up to the sabertooth. He stayed far enough ahead of me that I had to squint to make his fur out through the branches and leaves, but I worked hard and managed to keep up with him.

And honestly, I was pretty damn proud of that.

We passed a klynna at one point, and I heard him snarling at me when I nodded at it without diving away from it. The thing was so massive that I didn't stand a chance at outrunning it, anyway, and flying away like it was going to kill me wasn't going to do a damn thing to help Dakota's peace agreement.

HALF THE DAY had passed when we reached the mountains I was supposed to be searching. They were made of smooth black stone, rather than the white I'd thought I was looking for. There was a thick column of glittering white rock sweeping through many of the mountains, though, and when I saw that, Vevol's instructions made a lot more sense.

You would think a goddess would be better at giving directions. But since she'd never actually had to travel like a normal fae, I supposed it made sense that she was shitty with geography.

Teris disappeared into the trees near one sweeping part of the white rock column, so I figured that was where we were going, and spiraled down to the forest.

I shifted before landing, but the moment my feet met the ground, a massive body crashed into mine. My back hit a smooth tree roughly, but not hard enough to cause pain.

Teris snarled at me, "We had a fucking deal, Nai."

"Did we?" I drawled back, playing the same damn card he had the first time we talked, even though my heart was beating irrationally fast with his use of my old nickname.

"You saw the klynna. It could've *killed* you."

"Think how much easier your life would be if I was gone," I shot back.

"Don't even fucking suggest that." He grabbed my face in both of his hands, his grip tight but not painful as he tilted my head back so he could glare at me more effectively.

"You didn't care when Aev dragged me off to his land and locked me away for two decades, so why the hell would it matter to you if I faced off with a klynna and lost?" I shot back, wrapping my fingers around his hands and gripping them hard.

His eyes went dark—nearly black. "He was your mate. You wanted him. You chose him, *Queen Naomi*."

That damn insult again.

"*Fate* wanted us together," I spat. "*I* wanted you."

His body went still.

Statue-still.

I ripped his hands off my face, and when I pushed him away, he took a step back.

Deep-seated hurt and long-simmering fury warred within me as I stalked toward the cave. Though I couldn't hear Teris behind me, I didn't think he'd just watch me walk away.

His heart had to be beating at least half as quickly as mine, and mine was moving so fast it felt like it was about to pound right through my ribs and out of my damn chest.

I lit my hand on fire with the magic boiling in my veins as I stormed into the dark cave. The entrance was wide, as it had to be, for the klynnas to fit through it. The edges of it were jagged, which made me think they might have broken through actual stone.

I wondered if maybe the fae had sealed the creatures in with more than just ice and rock—maybe they'd used their magic to grow the prison's walls, too. They would've probably had to, to keep those massive beasts trapped.

My eyes moved over the scraped and scorched walls as I moved deeper into the cave. Honestly, it was more like a hole in a mountain. I'd thought the entrance was wide, but the more I walked, the larger the space got, until it felt like I was in another world altogether.

Teris caught up to me at some point, walking at my side. His eyes were alert, his body tense and ready for a fight.

I hadn't heard a single sound other than our footsteps and the soft crackling of my fire, so I wasn't nervous.

But I was ready to get the hell out of there.

We walked for another twenty minutes before I finally caught a glimpse of the tree we were looking for. It was massive, and glowed slightly gold, loaded with fruit as it seemed to climb through the bottom of the cave and up further into the mountain. Small animals moved over the branches—my excuse to Teris for being there in the first place.

Both of us were silent until we approached the tree.

"I'll start pulling the beovas from the left. You take the right," the sabertooth growled to me.

I assumed the beovas were the small animals, and nodded even though I had no intention of following through with his plan.

He went left, and I walked right, just enough that he wouldn't be able to see me from his side of the tree.

"Here goes nothing," I whispered to the tree, as I stepped close to it and spread my fingers over the smooth, white bark. It was warm against my palms, and that warmth spread through my arms and into my chest. My eyes closed, and I reached my magic toward the tree the way Vevol had told me that I would need to.

The magic within the tree swelled and heated as the goddess's consciousness met mine.

She had no physical form anymore, but I could still feel her. Mainly, I felt her approval, and her acceptance of the fate she was going to face.

Over the past few weeks, she had been weaving her magic more deeply into the land, giving it every last ounce of her power.

Her final acts of rebellion—and protection—were through both Fovea, and me.

And while I dreaded what was coming, because I'd had to connect with the goddess when I changed my name, I was the only option. No one else had the thick tether to her that she needed to accomplish this last thing.

But I would handle it fine.

It would be great.

Maybe if I kept telling myself that, I'd believe it eventually, too.

"Thank you," she murmured into my mind.

She sounded tired—and my throat swelled at the memories of the last time someone had said those words to me, in that same voice.

My mother, on her death bed, after so many years of pain.

Tears welled behind my eyelids, but I nodded, forcing the emotions away. *"Thank you,"* I said quietly. *"You changed all of our lives."*

"It was an honor. If there was another way..." she trailed off, her voice growing faint.

"I know." And I did.

If there had been any way around this, the goddess would've found it. I knew her well enough through everything she had done for the fae, to know that.

"You'll warn them?" she whispered to me.

"Yes, and I'll protect them."

"What about your mate?"

I squeezed my eyes tighter. *"I'll put as much effort as I can afford into the bond this time, like I promised."*

"Thank you." The words were so soft, so grateful, that my eyes stung.

I bit my lip. *"You don't owe me any thanks. I hope that whatever the next life holds for you, it's a good one."*

"And I hope the same for you. Don't turn your back to love again, child. Embrace it."

Her consciousness blew away, then, like grains of sand in the wind. And the moment the last grain was gone, her power hit me.

Hard.

A connection to the glowing tree my hands were on burst to life in my chest, in my abdomen, in my mind.

It anchored itself within me—and then I felt it roll through the rest of Vevol.

I felt it hit each of the fae, and swell within them, changing them.

Making them stronger.

It lingered on Fovea, and I felt her brands burn as Vevol used that stored magic to reach back to Earth and pull another group of women through.

I felt it blossom in the land, making the trees grow larger and thicker and tougher.

I felt it wrap around the animals, making them bigger too.

I felt it collide with the barriers around the edge of the world we'd thought was only ours—and destroy that barrier, opening us up to the rest of the world.

There were no other beings in our world like the ones she'd created, Vevol had warned me. Outside of the fae and klynnas, there were only wild beasts and savage animals.

The final strands of the goddess's magic slammed into me.

My back arched, my fingers digging into the tree's bark as I screamed in pain. She'd warned me her magic would hurt—that her final act of creation would wreck me thoroughly until I was tied to a man strong enough to share the overwhelming magic.

The power grew so intense that I crashed to my knees. My back was still arched, my hands still on the trees.

"What the hell is going on, Nai?" Teris was snarling at me, but I barely registered the words. His hands were on my body—I felt them, and then heard him swear as he withdrew quickly.

Was I burning up?

I felt like I was burning up.

Time passed.

I wasn't sure how much.

Maybe a few minutes?

Maybe a few hours?

When the burning finally faded, I was still on my knees. Every inch of me was shaking.

I needed food.

And water.

And sleep.

Unfortunately, the low growl I heard off to my left (one that definitely hadn't come from the swearing sabertooth who hadn't left my side while I was suffering) told me that it was time to get up and face the music.

I cracked my eyes open, wincing when a sharp pain in my head throbbed in retaliation to the movement.

The pain was much worse than Vevol had warned me it would be.

My eyes moved slowly over the army of monsters in front of us. They were massive—twice as big as any earthly bears, as well as stronger and angrier-looking.

Their fur came in the same colors as the trees; the white, the black, the blue, and the green.

But their eyes were silver, and glowing.

And they were all focused on me.

When Teris stood slowly, I felt the motion at my side more than saw it.

"Wait," I whispered to him, fear swelling within me when I realized he thought the creatures were a threat to him.

They weren't.

They were Vevol's final gift to her fae.

And they were *mine.*

"Stay back, Nai." His voice was low, and hard.

To anyone who didn't know Teris, it would've sounded angry.

I knew he wasn't pissed, though. At least not entirely. He *was* undoubtedly furious with me.

But the man was worried, too.

My monsters only picked up on that anger, though.

And I wasn't strong enough to control them, yet. Not the way I would need to be.

"Stop." I tried to grab Teris's hand and pull him back to me, but he side-stepped me.

The motion was enough to set off the creatures.

I needed to come up with a name for them, but that was the least of my concerns at the moment, because they were all going for Teris's throat.

Vevol's magic had made him bigger, and stronger. In his sabertooth form, he could definitely take on the creatures. And with his fighting skills, he could probably handle a few of them.

But not an entire klynna-prison cave full of them.

I lunged to my feet, ignoring the burning in my body and focusing on the panic in my chest as I shoved myself between Teris and the monsters.

I couldn't let them kill him.

Not when I was the only reason he was even there.

"Stop!" I cried out, voice shakier than expected. Not from fear, but from the exhaustion of whatever the hell Vevol had just done to me to create the army in front of us.

Teris spun me out of the way, dropping me on my ass. I clung to him though, wrapping my legs around the back of him so he couldn't leave, while yelling, "They won't hurt me! Stop!"

Teris snarled at me, but when he looked over and realized the creatures weren't attacking him, he went silent for a moment. They were still growling—they weren't statues who existed only to do what I said. But they had heard me when I told them to stop, and decided to listen to me.

I untangled my legs from around Teris. My knees buckled when my feet hit the floor, and he looped an arm around my middle, holding me up.

"What the hell is going on?" he growled into my ear.

The creatures snarled at him in response, and a few stepped closer to us. Teris's arm tightened around me, and I knew he was preparing to throw me out of the way again. Something told me he'd move too fast for me to fight him, the second time around.

My fingers dug into his thick, strong arms in an attempt to secure myself to him more completely.

"A lot," I said weakly. "I'm not strong enough to control them very well yet. I need to rest."

"Fine." He gritted the word out in response, and then took one careful step toward the cave's exit.

The creatures roared, and some of them took threatening steps toward us.

Teris swore, dragging me back a bit. His ass was nearly to the wall, which would give us some amount of safety—and also trap us more. There were a few of the creatures between him and that safety, though.

"They're going to kill you," I whispered, my gaze sliding over the monsters. The only way to keep him safe would be to make him smell like me.

And the only way to make him smell like me...

Well, he wasn't going to like it. The bastard didn't even want me.

"Way to be positive," he growled back.

I squeezed his arm. "They won't hurt *me*, Ter."

"So?"

I bit my lip, not wanting to say what I was thinking aloud.

His body went still when he realized what I wasn't saying.

"Fucking hell," he muttered. "We're not *mating*, Nai."

I squeezed my eyes shut, just for a moment. I legitimately felt like I could keel over at any damn minute.

"It would be fake," I whispered. "Temporary."

"Mate bonds are never *fake*." His voice was low. "We'll find another way out of this."

I grimaced, because as far as I could tell, there were no other options. But I didn't argue, because it was going to have to be his call. His life was the one in danger.

"Hold on tight," he growled at me.

And then he turned and ran.

Three

Teris slammed a hand against the tree. I felt it in my chest as his magic moved the branches rapidly, widening a gap between the tree's trunk and the bottom portion of the cave.

One of the creatures launched toward as us Teris dove through the gap. My heart dropped into my stomach as we fell, but he landed easily, rolling with me effortlessly before popping back up and jogging away.

The tree reverted to its original form as soon as we were through the gap, and I couldn't even hear the snarls of the creatures we'd left behind.

Teris let out a harsh breath as he looked around the cave we'd landed in. It wasn't massive, but there was a thick river or stream at one side of the space that seemed to be flowing in a circle. On another side, I saw a crack in a wall that I thought we might be able to fit through.

At least, I *thought* I saw a crack.

My mind was spinning like I couldn't believe.

He set me on my feet, and I nearly face-planted until he caught me by the waist, balancing me.

"You look like shit," Teris growled at me. "Can those things use Vevol's magic?"

"It's not Vevol's anymore, it's the fae's," I whispered.

"So they can't."

"No." I closed my eyes.

My ass landed on the ground a moment later, and my back was up against a stone wall. I nearly fell over anyway.

"Stay awake," Teris grunted, before he let go of me.

His hands were on my face a moment later, squeezing my chin lightly. I wrestled my eyes open, and he held something smooth to my lips. When I looked down at it, a little cross-eyed, I realized it looked like a giant pear with silver skin.

"Bite it," the sabertooth ordered me.

Normally, I would've argued.

I was so out of it that I followed the command, sinking my teeth into the soft flesh. The texture was like the pulp of an orange, with a bit of tang to it and even more sweetness.

Slowly, I chewed and swallowed.

"More." Teris turned the fruit.

I sighed softly, but took another bite, and then another.

Slowly, I continued until I'd eaten the whole thing. It didn't have a core or seeds, so that made life easier.

He carried me over to the slow-moving river in the corner that seemed to be flowing in a circle, tucking my back to his front and then leaning over. When he filled a massive hand full of water and lifted it to my lips, I reluctantly drank.

"You're still shaking." He sounded frustrated about that, but there was nothing I could do to stop it. "What the hell was that?"

"I told you Vevol was dying. She needed to use me as a vessel for the last bit of her magic, so she could infuse it into the land and fae. You're bigger and stronger, now. Everyone is. Even the klynnas. The forcefield fell, so our land is open wide to whatever else exists outside."

Teris didn't say anything to that.

I didn't blame him; I didn't know what there was to say.

He carried me back to the wall, and asked, "Will those things hunt you down?"

"I don't think so. I'm not strong enough to control them yet." My eyes closed, my breathing leveling out as the exhaustion set in more firmly. He was still holding me, so I leaned my face up to his neck, letting myself enjoy the contact.

"Yet?"

"Have to take a mate again," I mumbled. "Goddess said so."

"What the fuck?" he sounded almost outraged.

"Magic's too strong for me alone. There's gotta be someone lonely enough to consider me. Won't make it a week without a mate," I rambled, my words growing softer as I started drifting off to sleep.

"Bullshit," Teris snapped.

"Yeah. Might die alone." I sighed against Teris's chest. He felt so damn good—and smelled even better.

That thought slipped out, and I murmured, "You smell good."

With that, sleep took me.

Four

Teris

I HELD Naomi until she was snoring loudly enough that I knew she was most definitely asleep, and then I carefully set her down on the ground. It was uncomfortable, but it would have to do, because the woman couldn't have stayed awake if she tried.

My fists clenched as I stepped away from her, my body trembling as I started pacing the cave.

I hadn't planned on letting her know I was following her. Hell, I hadn't even planned on *following* her. The temporary bond with Dakota had still been driving me mad with possessiveness, and I'd caught a whiff of Nai's scent moving away from the Stronghold, and I'd just... followed it.

And followed it.

And followed it.

When the bond had finally broken, I'd scrubbed Dakota's damn scent off my skin until I was nearly bleeding. I understood why she'd needed the connection —and I would've done the same in her situation too.

But it still just felt *wrong*.

The possessiveness and need for someone you didn't know or love?

It fucked with you.

I could've turned back, after the bond broke. I no longer felt like crawling out of my skin, which was a definite benefit. But Naomi had still been in the sky, and despite the shit in our past, I couldn't leave her alone even when my head was clear. How she'd slipped past that hellhound guard dog of hers was beside me, but I hadn't dared get close enough to her to ask.

My feet moved harshly over the smooth stone floor of the cave. I wasn't good with sitting still; I'd never been great with that.

And having the woman I still fucking loved, who'd chosen another man, in the room with me?

That sure as hell didn't help me calm down.

Especially now that I knew she had lied to me about her reasons for coming to the cave.

And that she was planning on begging some fucking bastard to be her mate.

The memory of her snuggled up against my chest, telling me I smelled good, only made all that shit worse, too.

I muttered a curse when I realized I was still hard just from holding her in my arms and hearing her voice. What the hell was wrong with me? She had made it astoundingly clear that she wanted Aev, even if everything had gone to hell for them eventually.

I'd been careful to avoid hearing anything about the two of them for most of the time we'd been apart, but I'd been told a few things by the king himself when Dakota was asking me to create a bond between us. He'd made it sound like their connection had been hell for both of them.

And that had made me itch like hell to confront her. To ask her why she had chosen a stranger over me. Why she'd never used my name to call me to her, if her mating was hell. Why she'd looked so damn *happy* when the fated mate bond fell into place between them.

Of course, I hadn't done that.

I'd watched her from the trees, like the fucking stalker she had accused me of being.

Because even two decades later, a second rejection from the woman I'd fallen head over ass in love with would still be the most painful moment of my life.

But now, we were together.

Trapped in an underground cave.

I'd never been there before; it was on unseelie territory, so I didn't know the area.

I'd seen one promising way out, though. Hopefully it would eventually lead to the surface, because I wasn't about to carry my female back into the klynna's prison with all of those *things* the goddess had apparently created on her deathbed.

My female.

Fuck, I needed to change my damn mindset.

I'd never been able to convince myself that she wasn't mine, or that I didn't want her. Not when I thought she was in love with Aev. Definitely not when Summer was asking me to mate with her, though she clearly didn't love me.

And not one damn fucker knew.

We'd been careful; everyone wanted her, because she was literally the only woman in our world. I'd kept her safe, and never asked anything from her. She'd told me about kissing, about oral sex, about fucking.

And I'd never told a damn soul.

We'd been planning on trying the first one, the night she was taken from me. Those damn unseelies had knocked me and the other seelie guards out with a mixture of koveko and some other plant that I still hadn't fucking figured out. I'd been checking on them, just about to call it a night and climb into bed with my female. She had just gotten out of the shower, and I knew she wasn't wearing anything but the t-shirt she always slept in. I was going to kiss her, and if she let me, ravage the rest of her body with my mouth.

But the unseelies stole her from me.

I caught up to them at the same time Aev did. He was there to kick their asses—any fool could've seen that.

But then he looked at her.

And she looked at him.

The hope in her eyes... the way she said their souls were connected... it nearly killed me.

I let out a slow breath, shaking my head and yanking my thoughts out of the past.

Twenty years was way too damn long to still be caught up on that. I'd wondered if I could fall in love with one of the other ex-human females the same way I had with Naomi, but none of them even smelled good to me.

The only woman I wanted was the one who didn't want me.

Although...

Things were different, now.

She had said I was wrong about her not wanting me.

I didn't want to let myself hope that we might fall right back to where we'd been. It had been far too long for that.

But we were both unattached.

And she was looking for a mate.

Maybe we could get reacquainted.

Maybe...

Fuck, I shouldn't have even been considering it.

But that didn't change a damn thing about what I wanted.

Her.

I had always wanted her.

My erection was straining against my pants, and I glanced over at her. She slept soundly, snoring the same way she always had two decades earlier.

Fuck, she was beautiful. The most gorgeous woman I had ever seen, even after all this time. The confident lines of her face had softened in sleep, and it only made me want her more.

For a moment, I let myself imagine what it would feel like to be her mate.

To touch her whenever I wanted, to hold her hand when we walked. To carry her on my back as I ran, and fly with her when she was desperate for the freedom of the skies.

To make her laugh.

To tease her.

To touch her soft skin and watch her unravel on my tongue.

That thought had my erection throbbing.

I'd gotten off to a mental image of her in my arms, moaning in my bed, so damn many times. She'd been mine first, so I didn't feel guilty for it.

My gaze focused on her face, for one long moment.

I'd let myself get off to her one last time. To her image, her figure, her voice.

And then, I would either convince her to be mine, or leave her in my past.

With my mind made up, I strode over to the circling river and stepped in. If she woke while I was jerking off, that was the safest place to be, not that I thought she'd be scared by it.

We'd gotten off together twice, before she left me. I had relived those days every damn time since.

My eyes closed as I palmed my cock, with the river's water flowing past me. Her scent was in my nose, filling my senses with the combined smell of us.

I let my mind go back to the best fucking night of my life.

We'd been up most of the night, talking. She'd been in Vevol for a few months, and the time had passed quickly. We'd gotten to know each other slowly, and could talk for hours.

"Want to try something fun?" Nai asked, attempting to wiggle her eyebrows at me. She sat on the kitchen counter, finishing up the late-night snack she'd convinced me to make after hearing my stomach growl. All she had on was a t-shirt and a pair of the tiny panties she claimed kept her modest, and it had been driving me crazy for hours.

"It must be fun for you to do that with your forehead." I ran a finger playfully over the wrinkles she'd created with the motion.

"Oh, it is. Come on." She slipped off the counter and waved me toward her bedroom.

My cock hardened at the sight of her hips, ass, and hair swaying as she walked, but I tried to ignore it. She'd already explained sex to me when she realized I had no idea what it was—and sworn me to secrecy, because there was enough insanity among the males as it was.

"Is this fun going to get me attacked?" I grumbled, feigning disinterest.

She flashed me a grin. "Would it be worth it if it didn't?"

The woman had a point.

She reached down, grabbing the hem of her t-shirt and tugging it up over her head. I nearly tripped over my feet when the shirt hit me in the chest, giving me a clear view of her bare back while that sexy long hair swung around the middle of her spine, drawing my focus to her waist, and the tiny panties barely covering her ass.

"No touching," she warned me.

We didn't know mate bonds existed, but Naomi had admitted to me that she was a virgin. The word meant nothing to me, but she'd explained it. Virginity was a strange concept, but I supposed it made sense for the most part.

She stepped out of the panties, tossing them to me before she slid onto the bed. I lifted them to my nose without thinking eyes widening and cock throbbing as she opened her legs to me, just a little.

There were men fighting outside the small house we occupied, and no one knew I was there with her... and she was bare, for my eyes alone.

I nearly erupted in my pants at the thought, the sight, and the smell of her.

"Take your pants off," she said.

I snaked my tongue over her panties, and her cheeks flushed red.

My eyes closed as I fought to maintain control over myself.

Damn, I was close to losing it.

"I want to watch you touch yourself while I do the same. I heard you in the shower yesterday; it sounded fucking hot," Nai said.

I opened my eyes and dropped her panties. "You're sure?"

"Mmhm." She dragged a finger up her center, and I fisted my cock.

"Fuck," I hissed, watching her stroke herself slowly. One of her hands lifted to her nipples, and I gripped my erection tightly, knowing it'd only take one pull and I'd be gone.

"You're supposed to give me a show," she teased me, her face red and her eyes bright. Her breathing was fast, and her hips were moving with her finger, evidence of her enjoyment.

"I don't want to lose it first," I growled back.

Her lips curved upward wickedly. "You could cover me with your pleasure. I could use it to touch myself."

The mental image of her doing that was enough to set me off.

I dropped to my knees on the bed, leaning over her and erupting with a snarl. She was drenched in me, and so fucking sexy I could barely breathe.

My cock still ached for release, with her looking at me like that.

"Damn seductress," I growled at her. "Show me how you'll use me."

Her eyes heated, and she rubbed my pleasure over her core. I nearly lost it again when she started bucking and rocking, breathing hard and swearing harder.

"I'm so close," she panted. "Touch yourself."

I didn't need another damn invitation.

My hand worked my cock while she moaned my name, the scent of our pleasure on the air, and we lost control together.

And then began again.

And again.

And again.

I SWORE, biting back a snarl as I lost control, stroking myself roughly. Naomi was still snoring, but knowing she was behind me and could wake up at any moment only made the release more intense.

And as my mind cleared and my body relaxed, I made a decision.

Naomi was mine.

She had always been mine.

I'd get the full story about her and Aev...

And I would erase every fucking moment they'd ever spent together from her memories day by day and hour by hour, until the only name and body she knew was *mine*.

Five

Naomi

Teris was pacing the cave slowly when I woke up. He'd never used to like to stay still, so it didn't surprise me that he was up and moving. He no longer seemed panicked, but instead, thoughtful.

"Has there been any sign of the creatures?" I croaked to him.

Damn, I sounded bad.

My body felt like it weighed a million pounds, and my muscles ached terribly, so it wasn't a huge surprise that I sounded as crappy as I felt.

"No. I'm sure they can't find the other entrance to this place. When I tapped into the magic for a way out, it pulled me in that direction." He gestured toward the crack in the wall I'd noticed the last time.

"Cool." I eased myself up to a sitting position—or at least tried to. The physical pain of the movement surprised me, and I would've crashed back to the ground if Teris hadn't caught me by the waist and hauled me up to my feet.

He set me down carefully, and I fought a groan at the intense soreness in my body. I managed to get out a rough, "Thanks."

"You're in pain," he growled back at me.

"No," I protested weakly.

His scoff told me I hadn't even almost sold him on it.

"Where?" He began lifting my arms, stepping around me and checking for injuries.

"Everywhere. It's not actual pain; I'm just really sore," I explained. "The goddess warned me that the magic would take a toll until I had a mate to share it with. I'll survive."

"I can't believe you agreed to this," he grumbled at me, stepping back behind me. The feel of his chest against my back as he wrapped an arm around my waist to hold me up was really, really nice.

I wasn't sure why he was being so nice to me, so I didn't acknowledge it.

Instead, I closed my eyes. "She didn't have enough power left to reach out to Fovea or North, so I was the only option."

"Anyone could've put their damn hand on the tree and let them suck the power out of them. *I* could've done it," he growled.

"The person who took control of the creatures would have to choose a mate within a week. I wouldn't ask anyone else to do it," I snapped back. "I know the cost of mating with someone you don't want, and I wouldn't ask my worst enemy to do it."

Teris's arm tightened around my waist, and I waited for him to say something.

To say anything.

Instead, he lifted me smoothly off the ground and walked toward the crack in the wall.

"What are you doing?" I asked.

"Getting us out of here." He didn't sound angry with me or anything, which surprised me a little.

"I'll walk."

"You couldn't even *sit up*, Nai. If we're going to get you mated in the next six days, we have to move fast."

"Seven," I corrected him.

"You slept nearly twenty-four hours. There's fruit for you in my pocket when you're inevitably hit with sudden, intense hunger."

My lips curved in a ghost of a smile.

He remembered how violently hungry I could get.

"Six days, then," I said quietly, as he moved me beside him, turning both of us sideways as he carried me through the tight fit of the crack in the cave.

"Yup."

The smooth way he moved me through the cave was really damn impressive.

"Do you know any strong seelies who might be interested in mating with me?" I asked him quietly, as he moved us. "The unseelies all hate me for what happened with Aev, so they're not really an option. And Vevol made me promise to choose one of the strongest males, so I wouldn't lose control of the creatures. They're meant to be an army to protect us, in case any monsters come from the other lands now that the forcefields separating us are down."

"What happened with Aev?" Teris asked, dodging my first question entirely.

That wasn't a no.

"Everyone knows the story," I shot back.

"Not me." He stepped free of the crack between the rocks, and pulled me out too. Then, he swept me into his arms and draped me over his shoulder. I winced in pain with the movement. Not because of him, but because every inch of me ached.

I huffed, but didn't open my mouth.

What was I supposed to say to him about Aeven when I'd spent so long hoping that he would show up and sweep me away from the unseelies?

"The last time I saw you, you had just met Aev, and were staring at him like your whole damn world was right now that he was in it," Teris said gruffly.

"I *never* looked at him that way," I shot back, fury flaming to life in my veins with his words.

"I caught up to you in the forest thirty seconds after he did. I'm not *wondering*, Nai. I saw you look at him—and I saw him look at you. Everyone could feel the fucking magic in the air when Vevol connected you two, too." He didn't sound angry about it, but I kind of wished he did.

My own anger had mostly fizzled out with his words, though, and my words were quiet when I replied, "I had no idea what that connection meant. It felt too intense, and that terrified me. If I was looking at him that way, it was unintentional. I asked him to leave me as soon as he'd dragged me back to his house, and he did. I was up for three days pacing the room and wondering why you hadn't chased after me, and if I'd imagined everything between us."

Teris stopped, suddenly.

Just halted, where he was.

My face bumped his back, and I fought a groan at the ripple of pain. Not because of the collision, but because of the muscles.

"I had to use my magic to trap myself in a cave for days, because I knew I'd hunt you down if I was free. By the time I came out, every fucking male was talking about how perfect your *mate bond* was, and how lucky the unseelie bastard was to have you."

My eyes stung.

I hadn't considered what it would look like or sound like to Teris. I definitely hadn't known that he'd seen me meet Aev. I thought he'd just let me walk away without caring enough to come after me, but... that really didn't fit his personality, did it?

"If I hadn't seen you meet him, I would've come after you anyway. But the way you looked at him played in my mind over and over again, and there was no fucking way I'd survive seeing you look at him like that again."

The burning in my eyes grew fiercer. "I thought you just didn't want me."

Teris was moving again—moving fast.

He had me on my feet, with my back pinned to the wall, a heartbeat later. His hands cupped my face, and his eyes burned into mine in another heartbeat. "I *always* wanted you, Nai. *Always*. With every fucking beat of my heart, I wanted you. If I had realized..." He shook his head harshly. "I would've fought with everything I had to get you back, if I'd realized that was what you wanted, even years later. Hell, even *decades* later."

"But not now," I whispered.

His lips twisted in a snarl. "Now, I would fucking destroy any man who dared even *consider* mating with you. You're *mine*. Six days from now, the only bastard you'll be tied to is me."

With that, he eased me back over his shoulder and started walking again.

My throat swelled.

My eyes burned.

But my thoughts were too scrambled for me to come up with anything worth saying aloud.

He wanted me.

He'd always wanted me.

The same way I'd always wanted him.

A damn misunderstanding was the only thing that had kept us apart for two decades.

So much lost time.

And yet I wasn't ready to climb into his arms and declare myself his. If we were going to be together, we'd have to get to know each other all over again and see if we could move on from the past. These new versions of us might not even be compatible... but the prospect of finding out made me really damn hopeful.

THE CAVE TERIS carried me through was absolutely stunning. It was dark, with dozens and dozens of thick stone pillars running vertically throughout the massive space. There were glowing flowers wrapped around the pillars growing wildly, and shimmering bugs of some sort flying lazily around the cavern.

"Don't touch anything," Teris warned me, as I reached a hand out toward one of the flowers we were about to pass. "It could be poisonous."

I snatched my hand back quickly. "Really?"

"Yes. I've never seen these particular flowers, but the glowing ones we have on our side of the world can make you vomit for days."

Damn.

I tucked my hands up close to Teris's back, and tried not to let myself focus on the feel of his muscles moving against my hands.

"Tell me more about you and Aev," he said, as we walked.

I grimaced. "I'd really rather not."

He growled at me. "Not your call, Nai."

I scoffed. "It's *entirely* my call. Vevol showed me every single interaction Aeven and I had when I was changing my name, and it made me feel like the shittiest person on the planet. I fucking *ruined* him."

"The bond did that," Teris growled back. "I know unsealed mate bonds, Nai. Trust me, the damn thing didn't need any help from you.

That was... not what I was expecting him to say.

"According to Vevol, we could've made things work. I just wasn't willing to give him a chance," I argued.

"You didn't owe him a chance. And if you couldn't get away from him, you sure as hell should've trusted me enough to use my name. You should've known I would've gotten you out of there, even if you didn't want to be with me."

"I was stubborn, okay? You know that. I thought you weren't interested in me, so I wasn't going to ask you for help. I dealt with Aev. It wasn't even difficult. When I told him I didn't want to talk, he didn't ask me to talk. We literally only saw each other in person six times in two decades—and one of those was the worst night of my life," I snapped back.

"The night you mated with him?"

I squeezed my eyes shut, and didn't answer that.

"You'll tell me at some point," he growled.

"I'm sure you enjoyed being with Sunny more than I did Aeven," I finally said, changing the subject.

He scoffed. "I know what it feels like to be loved by a woman who means everything to me, and what Summer and I had was nowhere near that. Even with the bond between us driving me insane and her throwing herself at me, we only kissed three times, and none of them meant anything."

I grimaced.

I guess if anyone could understand being the bad guy in a mate bond, it was Teris. He was known for rejecting Sunny—Summer—but everything had worked out for her when she fell in love with the basilisk general, Vuvim, so most people had forgotten about that whole thing.

But their bond had been short—and mine with Aev was so damn long. My forgiveness wouldn't come anywhere near as fast as Teris's had.

"I never kissed Aev," I told him, quietly. "So you're more experienced than me. When we had sex, it was so fast and horrible that I don't think it even counts."

I hadn't even realized Teris was holding the backs of my thighs, but his grip on them tightened enough that I definitely couldn't ignore it any longer. "Tell me." The words were gritted out, and a little angry.

"No."

He dug his fingers into my thighs, and honestly, it felt good. No one had ever grabbed me like that, like they needed me. Even when Teris and I were together, we'd been keeping it a secret. He'd never really touched me—which was a good thing in hindsight, because if he had, it would've started a bond between us.

Although, maybe it was a bad thing in hindsight. Because if we'd had a bond, meeting Aev wouldn't have done a damn thing to it, at least for me and Teris. If anything, knowing that Aev was feeling that connection would've pushed Teris and I to seal the bond we'd already started to free Aev.

And if that had happened… well, then everything would've been different. So damn much different.

But that hadn't happened.

"I will trap your ass right here and hold you fucking captive if you don't tell me, Nai."

I scowled. "You wouldn't."

"Try me." The grit in his voice told me he was being honest.

But I was *not* getting manipulated into telling that shitty story to the man I'd thought wasn't interested in me. If he wanted my answers, he could come up with some sensitive shit to tell me in exchange. He was the one sprouting crap about not letting me mate with anyone else, which meant he was planning on mating with me and would do it to stay alive.

So, there was no risk to me.

Outside of the basic risk that Teris potentially was to my heart, and mind, and every other damn part of me. Including the extremely sensitive bits.

"I'm not telling you," I said flatly.

He stepped up to one of the thick columns, sliding me off his back as he pressed a hand to it. The glowing flowers on it slid to the side as he set me down on my feet, pinning me against the stone.

I peered over my shoulders, one after the other.

The flowers were only a few inches to either side of me, which meant there was a real chance I could hit them if I tried to escape. Which could potentially make me sick for days. Days that I couldn't afford, given the deadline for taking a mate that was approaching.

Teris took my face in his hands.

Those gorgeous, dark teal eyes blazed into mine for a long, long moment.

And then he kissed me.

I'd never kissed anyone. I'd been eighteen when I was pulled out of Earth, and I'd spent the last six of those eighteen years taking care of my dying mother. At the end, things had gotten so bad that I had to drop out of high school to become her full-time caregiver. And I'd cherished every damn one of those minutes.

But they hadn't exactly made me experienced at much of anything else.

And kissing Teris was...

Well damn, it was like nothing I'd ever imagined.

His lips were soft and hot on mine, his tongue sliding into my mouth without so much as a pause of hesitation. He kissed me like he was claiming me, like he was telling me that I was his again.

Like he wanted me, and needed me, and belonged to me.

And damn, I wanted him to belong to me.

Even though there was so much shit to work through, and so many factors we'd needed to deal with... I still wanted him.

Despite the beginnings of a bond falling into place in my chest.

Despite the past we hadn't worked through.

Despite the aching pain in every limb I possessed.

Despite *everything*.

One of his hands slid around the back of my neck. He buried it in my hair and used the grip to tilt my face back, so he had better access to my mouth.

His other hand dragged down my arm and wrapped around my hip. He used it to pull my pelvis to his, so I could feel his erection against my abdomen.

Hot damn, he wanted me.

The kiss grew hotter, and more frantic. I worked my hands out from between us and buried them in his hair, pulling him impossibly closer. The hot growl he gave me as he dragged his hand down to my ass, and *squeezed*, made me moan.

I'd never felt so desired—not since those times we got off together in my old bedroom.

I'd never wanted someone so much—not since that night I was going to invite him into my bed.

He pulled his lips from mine, and I panted hard as he gripped my ass and leaned closer to my ear. "I'm going to touch you," he said, voice low and gravelly.

I jerked my head in a nod, brushing my smooth cheek against his prickly, stubbly chin.

The hand he had on my ass slid into my shorts, and my hips jerked as the hot, rough pad of his finger ran over my clit. His touch was impossibly-light, but I was so insanely sensitive. He continued moving slowly around my clit, circling it, touching me exactly the way I liked.

He couldn't have remembered those times in my bed—could he?

But he must've, because he knew just how to touch me.

"Did Aeven touch you here?" he asked me, before his lips landed on my throat and sucked hard.

"No," I rasped, hips rocking. He rubbed me hard, a reward for the answer, and I cried out as I jerked toward him. His finger slowed, though, touch growing lighter.

"Did he grab you? Hold you?"

"No. I didn't let him touch me at all," I breathed.

"Good." His growl made me so damn hot, and my breathing halted when he slowly dragged another finger over my slit. "Open your legs for me, Nai."

I opened them.

My eyes slammed shut, my back arching toward him desperately as he slid the tip of his finger inside me.

He nipped at my throat. "You're drenched for me."

"Yeah," I managed, hips still moving as he stroked me so damn slowly.

"Tell me how deep he was," Teris said, his lips against my throat.

I went still.

He slowly slid that finger deeper inside me, stroking the walls of my channel while he teased my clit.

A shudder rolled through me, hot and heavy thanks to his touches. His words. His attention.

"This deep?" he asked, voice still low.

He'd only slid half his finger in—but he knew after what I'd told him that I hadn't forgotten anything that had happened with Aev.

"No," I whispered.

His growl of approval made my breathing pick up, and he dragged his thumb over my clit harder, and faster.

I shattered without any kind of a warning.

My desperate cries echoed through the cavern as my hips arched and bucked, intense pleasure rolling through me. He held me close, one hand still gripping my hair and the other still working my clit to drag out the orgasm.

I collapsed against his chest when the pleasure faded, now sweating. His fingers were still on my clit, moving slowly against my over-sensitive skin. He must've remembered how to give me time between orgasms—he must've remembered the nights we'd spent in bed together, even though we didn't touch each other.

"You did so damn good, Nai. You rode my hand so perfectly," he murmured, stroking me slowly.

The words made me warm all over again.

"You remember the night you had me get off all over your core, so you could touch yourself with me?" His voice was in my ear, making me even damn wetter.

"Of course. Do you?"

"Every day." His growl was fierce. "I've imagined how differently things would've ended up if we'd fucked that night, instead of just touching ourselves all night, so many times."

He rubbed my clit hard, and my hips jerked for him, the need building again already. "I've pictured what you'd look like with those thighs spread wide for me while I sank inside those pretty wet folds of yours. I've imagined the cries you'd make, the desperate motions of these sexy little hips, the way you'd lose control around me... every fucking day."

I couldn't breathe.

I.

Couldn't.

Breathe.

And I hoped I'd never be able to again, hoped every moment of my life would feel like this.

Wanted.

Needed.

Desired.

"Does it make you lose it?" I breathed.

"Over and over again." He bit down on my throat.

He slid another finger inside me, and the fullness—it made me choke on nothing.

"You're close again already," Teris said, easing up a little.

"I want to feel you inside me," I moaned.

The words just slipped out. There was no thinking, no pausing. Just the honest desperation of a woman whose only experience with sex had been hellish. A woman who'd just gotten reacquainted with the love of her life, the one she'd thought she lost.

A woman who hadn't felt truly loved since before she met her *fated mate.*

"You will," Teris told me, voice growly and low. "But not until you've drenched my hand and face with your pleasure a dozen times."

My throat dried.

He slid another finger inside me—and worked my clit roughly.

My head tilted back as the pleasure cut through me, and I cried out.

I was boneless when it faded, and exhausted when I draped my face against his shoulder.

"You'll never think about your damn king again after I've made you mine," Teris said, his fingers still buried inside me.

"That a promise?" I mumbled.

"A vow." He nipped at my shoulder. "*Queen* Nai."

I snorted softly.

There were still so many things we hadn't talked about.

So many years we hadn't caught up on.

So many factors we hadn't considered.

And yet the only thought I had was, *I want this to happen again, soon.*

Six

Teris must've learned enough about my mating with Aev to satisfy him, because he didn't bring it up again as he slid his fingers out of me, sucked my pleasure off of them, and then scooped me into his arms and resumed walking.

Despite the erotic moment, I must've fallen asleep almost immediately.

I wasn't sure how much time had passed when his hands were on my face again, waking me up gently. I wondered, passingly, if because he hadn't touched me back then, he was trying to make up for lost time now. Or if he just really loved touching me.

"We have to go underwater," he told me quietly. He was sitting on the edge of a lake of some kind, with his butt on stone but legs hanging in the water. I didn't feel any water on myself, and when I lifted my head from his chest, realized I was straddling him.

I blinked a few times, trying to wake myself up. Now that I wasn't asleep, the ache in my limbs was awful.

His lips brushed mine, lightly. Like he couldn't resist.

"Do you hate me for the bond yet?" I whispered to him.

His lips curved upward. "I was obsessed with you long enough that I don't even feel it."

My heart warmed.

"We do need to get underwater, though. There's a possibility that your creatures may go for the other fae without you to control them."

My eyes widened at the thought.

I had a week to pick a mate... but those things could do a lot of damage in a week, without anyone to guide them.

"We have to warn everyone," I said.

He dipped his head in a nod. "Even if it means going back."

Shit.

I really didn't want to go back and deal with everyone. The gossip there would be, when me and Teris, the only fae villains, showed up bonded...

Damn.

He chuckled. "It won't be that bad."

"They hate me," I admitted. "All the unseelie men. A lot of the seelies too. And the female fae don't understand why I didn't want Aev, now that they've seen him with Dakota."

"The female fae don't like anyone." He slid a hand into my hair and tugged playfully. "And when we show up mated, no one will dare talk bad about you."

I huffed a sigh. "It's not going to work like that."

He changed tactics. "Nev told me before I left that Fovea's scent had started changing. That means she's likely pregnant—and if she is, everyone will have much bigger things to worry about than us finding each other again."

"They don't know we found each other the first time," I pointed out.

"I can ensure that gossip makes its way around, if you'd prefer. If we're star-crossed lovers, we aren't villains anymore."

I gave him a dark look. "We weren't star-crossed lovers."

He didn't respond to my remark, and gripped my waist. "Hold me tightly. I'll be following the magic's trail out, and I don't want to lose you."

"I could ride on your back," I suggested.

The look he gave me was dirty. "You feel much better this way."

My legs tightened around his back, and he brushed his lips against mine one more time before he tucked my face against his chest, and then slid into the water.

We submerged once, and came up for air immediately. The warmth of the water surprised me with its pleasantness, and when I looked down, I saw large fish-like creatures with long, wavy things moving around them.

"What are those?" I asked him.

He glanced down at the water, and frowned. "The unseelies didn't teach you about our world?"

"If I'd been less stubborn and actually talked to them, maybe they would've." I lifted a shoulder.

"They're novocannes. They're in most of the rivers, lakes, and ponds."

Oh.

Fish, then. But the Vevol version.

"They're not going to hurt us?" I checked.

"No, they're harmless." He hugged me closer to him, treading water easily. "If you see anything you don't know the name of while we're traveling, point it out. You've been here far too long to not know the basics."

On that, we could agree.

"Thanks."

He scowled at me—apparently, he didn't believe I needed to thank him.

"Hold your breath," he warned me, and then dove down.

I followed instructions, leaving my eyes open so I could watch as Teris swam us away from the glowing cavern with strong, steady strokes. He carried me without a struggle, but it was kind of a long swim, so I still needed to suck in air quickly when we surfaced.

"Good." He stroked my lower back as I breathed heavily.

"I'm not usually this weak," I told him, my voice a little shaky. "It's the pull of the magic. The goddess undersold the strength of it."

"I know you're strong, Nai. You're a *Queen*, after all." His drawl made me smack him on the shoulder, and that made him grin at me. "I know the magic's affecting you. It's really damn strong if you have to take a mate to balance it out—and even stronger if you only have a week to do that. Vevol might be insane, but she hasn't destroyed us yet."

"*Yet* being the keyword there," I muttered.

"There's still time." He slid a hand down to my ass, and squeezed lightly. "Ready? I don't know how many times we're going to have to do this, but I get the sense we're a long way from getting out."

I sighed. "It's fine. I'm ready."

With that, he submerged us again.

It took me longer to recover every time we went under—and Teris's concern grew with every chest-heaving, lung-straining breath I took.

"I'm fine," I promised, panting like a dog.

Though I had no idea how long we'd been swimming, it felt like forever.

"You're not fine," he growled back. "I don't even think you have six days at this rate."

Harsh, but probably true.

"Vevol probably didn't factor in me exhausting myself swimming through caves," I murmured.

"We're going to have to mate sooner than we planned."

I blinked. "You know you don't have to go through with that. Your possessiveness will probably fade, and—"

"I imagined ripping your king's throat out nearly every day for two decades, Nai. If you mate with someone else again, you'll have to kill me." Honesty rang out in his voice.

"Obviously I'm not going to do that."

"Then you're going to have to let me claim you. And there's no point in waiting for the inevitable when it means you're just going to get worse."

I huffed at him. "You don't have a romantic bone in your body."

He gripped my ass, and squeezed. "You'd be surprised, Queenie."

I smacked him on the shoulder lightly for the nickname again. He squeezed my ass in retaliation. "What's the ink for?" I wondered, trailing a finger over one of the larger shapes on his collarbone. His cock throbbed to life against my core, and my face heated at the attention.

Apparently, he liked it when I touched him.

"The mate bond was nearly impossible to ignore. The pain of the tattoos distracted me long enough to fight the pull of it."

Damn.

My face fell, and I knew he saw my emotions flash across it.

"Aeven would've been a hell of a lot more capable than you of finding a decent enough male for you to kiss to cut off your bond," Teris said bluntly. "You didn't know anyone; he did. Don't feel bad for the bastard when he could've changed his own damn situation if he'd tried."

"It's not that simple," I said quietly. "We were fated. He felt an obligation for me."

"And I feel an obligation to break his nose. Doesn't mean I have to go through with it," Teris growled.

A snort escaped me. "You're the worst."

"Am I really?" he drawled. Though he was teasing me, I saw a little hesitation in his eyes.

He was used to being the villain, too.

"No. You saved my life." I leaned my forehead to his shoulder. "It's going to take another decade to get back to the Stronghold at this rate. We should probably find a cave and just do it."

"That's exactly how I want my woman to talk about fucking me for the first time," he grumbled, adjusting his grip on me so he was ready to dive down again.

I laughed. "Maybe *I'm* the worst."

"No, Queenie. You're perfect. Don't fucking forget it."

With that, he dove down into the water.

While he swam us, his hand slid into the back of my shorts, and his fingers found my clit.

I jerked against him, shocked by the touch—and more than a little turned on by it.

He stroked me slowly while we swam, and stopped when we surfaced. I sucked in air, panting and resisting the urge to rock against his hand. Or his erection. He was rock-hard against me.

"If I'm not going to have the chance to hand-fuck you a dozen times before I take you, I'm at least going to make sure you're really damn ready for me before we find the right cave," he growled at me.

My body flushed hotter. "I swear, you didn't talk this dirty the last time I knew you."

His eyes darkened. "The last time you knew me, I didn't know what it felt like to lose you." He pinched my clit between his fingers, and I swore quietly, arching against him and finding his erection against me.

Damn, I liked the feel of that.

"So you're smarter now?" I asked, voice straining.

"Nah. Just more desperate." He rocked me against his hardness, just a little. "Hold your breath."

I did as he said, and he submerged again, fingers still stroking me as we swam.

When we surfaced again, I was shaking and worked up. "You're dragging this out on purpose," I grumbled, after I'd caught my breath. His fingers were just pressing lightly against me, making me insane.

"Hell yeah, I am." He sucked on my neck, and I arched against him a little. "Tell me how you want me to fuck you, when we find the right cave."

I sighed.

He eased his fingers away from my clit, and I muttered a curse, jerking my hips and forcing myself to focus on his question.

"I don't know," I finally said. "It was dark, when Aev and I... you know. I think I want eye contact. And dirty talk. I just want you to love it." My voice grew quieter as I spoke. "I want to enjoy it too."

"That part's already guaranteed, Nai." He rubbed my clit lightly again, making my hips rock a little. "I want you to give me a position. Standing, with you pinned to a wall? On your back, on the stone? On top of me?"

My body flushed, and my mind rolled through the options as he gave them. When I answered, I did so almost as soon as he was done speaking. "On top of you, at first. I think it would be good for me to have control, this time. To know it's my choice. After the first time, I'd like it if you just took control."

"That would be my fucking pleasure, Queenie." He pinched my clit again, and I swore at him again, jerking my hips. His lips stretched in a wicked grin. "Hold your breath."

I did just in time for him to dive down with me, still teasing my clit.

We surfaced again a few seconds later, in another new cave without any kind of a platform we could get out on.

When I groaned, Teris chuckled. He sucked on my neck again, murmuring, "Just focus on what it'll feel like to have my cock buried inside your needy body, Nai."

When he talked to me like that, it was hard to think about anything else.

We surfaced again, and again, with more shitty luck.

Nowhere to climb out.

Nowhere to climb on top of Teris.

Nowhere to claim him, and let him claim me.

We had really shitty luck.

"I can't stop picturing what it'll feel like to have you wrapped around me," he'd murmur to me.

"I can't wait to have your tits in my mouth and my cock buried inside you," he'd growl.

"I'm going to make you lose it so hard you see the fucking stars," he'd swear.

And I got needier.

And needier.

And needier.

Everything became a blur of his fingers, his words, and heat. He didn't let me lose it—but he let me get so damn close that I was nearly mad with need.

When we finally swam out of the final cave, I barely even noticed the moon over our heads.

My eyes landed on the muddy riverbank, and my body could've orgasmed in relief.

It didn't, though.

It was waiting for my dirty, dirty fae.

"Are you sure about this?" I asked him as he waded out of the pond, still holding me around his waist, and still touching me.

"I've been sure about this for two decades, Nai," he growled back.

And that was more than enough of an answer for me.

Teris set me down on my feet, holding me until I was steady, and then finally sliding his hand out of my shorts. My toes sank into the mud, and part of my feet did too, but I didn't give a damn.

He was taking off his pants—that was all I cared about.

He pushed the fabric down far enough for his cock to spring free—and I nearly groaned at the sight of it. Thick, and hard, and veined... exactly the same way I'd left it, though it was probably terrible to think that way.

"Still good enough for you?" he drawled to me, stroking the length slowly.

I was on fire.

I had to be on fire.

I wanted him so damn badly.

"Perfect," I breathed.

"Then strip for me, little Queen."

Suddenly, the nickname didn't feel like an insult anymore.

"If we're doing this, I want your pants off completely. You know I want your scars, too, Ter," I warned.

He stared at me for a long, long moment before he slowly peeled them down those massive, gorgeous thighs.

Inch by inch, he exposed the scarred skin he hid with fabric, day in and day out. All of the seelies had scars—they all loved to fight. But the sheer number of them on his legs was enough to make a person wonder what Teris had been through. Because he'd lost his memories, and didn't know the source of them, he was self-conscious of them.

But to me, they were just a part of him.

"You're so damn beautiful," I murmured to him, stepping closer and taking his cock in one of my hands. It was softer than I expected—insanely soft.

With the other hand, I slowly stroked his thigh, showing him silently that I wasn't afraid of him. That I didn't judge him.

He closed his hand around mine on his erection. "Keep touching me like that and this'll be over long before I'm ready."

I flashed him a smile. "Is that a challenge?"

He laughed—loud, gravelly, and free. "Not this time."

"Next time, then." I stepped back, my body still throbbing desperately for the big finish that was coming.

"I've waited far too long to see you bare again, Nai. Take those clothes off before I take them off for you," my sabertooth warned.

I stepped back, grabbing the bottom hem of my tank top and tugging it over my head. Teris's hands were on my tits before I'd even pulled the fabric free of my hair—touching, and stroking, and kneading.

"Look at you, little Queen. So perfect for me." Teris pinched my nipples lightly. "The shorts, now."

I stripped my shorts off, bending a little to do so. Teris growled at the sight of me bending toward him, and I considered taking his cock in my mouth.

Before I could make a decision, I was in his arms, and he was ripping my shorts the rest of the way down my legs. He threw them out of the way as his lips crashed into mine, and then our flushed bare bodies were pressed together as he kissed the hell out of me.

The world tilted, and I felt my knees hit the mud when his ass met the ground —and then his back.

He was ready for me.

Letting me set the pace.

But I was enjoying the kissing so damn much that I wasn't in any kind of a hurry.

His hands moved over my body, feeling me and touching me and squeezing me while our tongues warred and danced.

I rocked against his erection as he touched me, taking myself closer and closer to the edge with the hot hardness of his body.

And when I finally moved my hips, lining the head of his cock up with my slit, he cursed against my mouth, "So fucking wet for me."

"Only for you, Ter," I whispered back.

He snarled, fingers digging into my ass and my breast as he squeezed hard. "Not going to last long."

"Neither will I." I moved my hips again, sinking down and taking the head of him inside me.

We groaned into each other's mouths, our lips and tongues on pause as we focused on the more intimate parts of our bodies.

"You really sure about this?" I asked, giving him one last time to change his mind and run in the other direction for me.

Part of me still expected him to change his mind, because part of me still believed he just hadn't cared enough to come after me.

"Ask me that again and I'll tie you to my bed and fuck you until we're both raw, Nai."

The words he growled were so genuinely Teris that my uncertainty dissolved.

His hands landed on my hips, and he tugged. Not harshly, but confidently. Confidently enough that he bottomed out inside me a heartbeat later.

My world spun.

My heart raced.

He filled me up so much.

The feeling was foreign, but incredible.

"Holy shit," I breathed, not sure my mind was still functioning right.

"*Fuck*." Teris wrapped a hand in my hair, using it like a rope to anchor him. The slight pull of his grip on it made me groan.

I could feel the bond we'd created begin to grow inside me.

It felt like it was made of light—and warmed me, as it bloomed, and bloomed, and bloomed.

Teris's emotions crashed into me as the bond finished growing.

His ferocious need.

His fierce happiness.

His deep gratitude.

All of that was just too damn much for me.

My body arched, my head tilting back as the pleasure rolled through me, and I screamed. Teris roared, erupting inside me with a harsh jerk of his hips that only intensified everything for both of us.

His emotions faded away as we came down from the high, both of us breathing hard.

"Fuck, Vevol did a number on you," he grunted at me, dragging my palm to his heart and pressing my hand down hard on it. "That magic has a bite to it."

"She undersold it, right?" I mumbled.

He chuckled, low and rough. *"You're the best."*

The words felt distinctly like a thought, and happiness swelled inside me. The few times I'd heard Aev's thoughts, it had just felt *wrong*.

"If you're thinking about him while I'm throbbing inside you, I must be doing this wrong," he growled into my mind, though I could feel that he was mostly teasing. It would take some time to get past the... well, the past... but we'd get there.

I had to believe that.

"How am I still horny?" I groaned at him. *"We're supposed to be headed back to the Stronghold right now."*

"We'll make this quick, then." He nipped at my throat, and then rolled us over in one smooth motion. Mud was all over both of us at that point, but neither of us cared. The position changed the sensations entirely, and when Teris started moving, I found myself spiraling back into another orgasm so much faster than I expected.

"One more?" he asked me, grinning down at me as we both struggled to catch our breaths.

"Just one," I agreed, then grabbed onto him and held tightly as he sprung to his feet, walking our bare, mud-coated asses to the nearest tree. He pinned me, and fucked me slowly, until we were unraveling together in the most intimate orgasm yet.

Seven

It took a few minutes to clean the mud off—and to find our clothes, then clean them too—before we were finally ready to hit the road.

"Can I carry you?" he asked me, looking at me sideways as he fastened his pants back into place. His face was a little red, and I itched to feel his emotions again, so I could know exactly what he was thinking. Our thoughts didn't seem to automatically broadcast to each other; it took focus.

"Sure. You're probably faster than me," I agreed.

There was something almost awkward between us.

I wanted to figure it out, to sit down and talk about it, but we didn't have time. And honestly, everything had happened between us so fast that I was still kind of worried that I might end up regretting everything.

I'd never told Teris that, of course. It would only hurt him.

But he had to be thinking and feeling the same way, didn't he? We hadn't even had a conversation about our past twenty years, outside of the missing each other thing. And something told me we had both changed more than we realized.

We'd cross that path when we got there, I guessed, because we had no choice but to be all-in now. Although, there were definitely a lot of shitty degrees to a mate bond. I'd been there and done most of them.

Hopefully we could figure out a way past them, because the last thing I wanted was another crappy mating.

I BURIED my fingers into Teris's silky fur as he ran through the forest. The ache in my body had faded for the most part, but I still felt exhausted. I figured I'd need to rest for a while to recover from the impact of the magic, but according to the goddess, we would be fine after we adjusted to the new channel of magic.

I'd never ridden on anyone's back before—at least not of my own volition. The only times I'd ridden with someone had been by force, and obviously, I hadn't been a fan of that.

But running with Teris was completely and absolutely different. It felt the way flying did; like freedom.

I leaned in close to him, holding his fur securely as my lips stretched slowly into a grin.

"You doing okay?" he asked me, his voice calmer than I'd ever heard it. The mental communication felt right, this time. Natural, too.

"I'm great," I admitted. *"This is incredible."*

"A new way to see Vevol?" His voice was a bit playful, and that made my grin wider.

"Mmhm. Riding my man: the best way to tour a new world."

He snorted. *"This world isn't new for you. Or at least it shouldn't be."*

"Not much has happened the way it should've since I got here." The humor faded out of my voice.

"That's going to change now, Queen Nai." His humor didn't disappear with mine, luckily. And he knew that damn nickname would piss me off, or at least snap me out of the funk I was sliding into.

"Again with the Queen thing," I grumbled at him.

"Well, now it's true. Queen Nai of the monsters."

I scowled. *"They're not monsters. Hopefully."*

"Your lack of certainty doesn't inspire confidence," he drawled back.

"Your lack of confidence in me doesn't inspire my certainty, either."

He laughed into my mind. *"Touché."*

I pressed my cheek to his neck, watching the forest around us as he moved. *"So did you really throw the fight for Fovea?"* I asked quietly.

"Of course I did. I know Nev well enough to be sure that he would make a loveless mating work. And even if I didn't, he and I had already discussed the need to find a way to bring us and the female fae together. They were going to keep killing our people if we didn't do something to convince them we weren't at war. Mating with one of the women was the easiest way, we just expected him to be paired with one of the life-bringers, not Fovea herself." His voice was low, but calm. I didn't see any reason for him to lie about it, and Teris had never been a liar anyway.

"You weren't considering mating with a life-bringer yourself?"

He didn't answer immediately, which made me slightly nervous. But then he finally admitted, *"I knew it would've hurt Summer, and I felt shitty for hurting her as much as I already had. It's difficult to be locked in a mate bond you know you don't want, as a male. Because every instinct you have screams at you to protect the female, and claim her, and yet you feel no true desire to do so. It's exhausting."*

"It sounds terrible." And again, I felt much like crap for putting Aev through that.

Not that I needed any help feeling bad for everything that had happened with him.

"Don't start feeling bad again," Teris warned me, his voice getting growly.

"It's impossible not to."

"Any man with half a brain could meet you and know what kind of woman you are, Nai."

"What the hell does that mean?" I shot back, my defenses rising.

"Some females are willing to chase men. Others won't consider someone who doesn't chase them. You're the latter, obviously."

I scowled. *"That makes me sound even worse."*

"Wanting a man who fights for you isn't a bad quality. I'd say it makes you pretty damn sane. If Aeven really wanted you, or deserved you, he would've been knocking on your door every day. He would throw all of his energy into coming up with some way to talk you into seeing him, or even just speaking with him through the damn door. A man who wants you will chase you—because he knows it's worth every breath."

I didn't know what to say to that, so I remained in stunned silence.

"But now the only bastard who gets to chase you is me. And if anyone other males so much as consider looking at you the way I do, they're dead."

They probably shouldn't have, but those words gave me a hell of a lot of goosebumps.

A loud roar sounded somewhere above our heads, distinctly different from the ones the klynnas made, and my head jerked upward.

"It's just a dragon, Nai," Teris said. *"Just one of our fae."*

"But what's it doing out here?" I murmured back, eyes scanning the treetops above our heads as if they could answer my question. *"We're a long way from the Stronghold."*

"Maybe they sent a search party for us."

"No. I told Presley and Blue where we're going. The unseelies are glad to be rid of me, the female fae believe in the goddess too much to go against her, and the seelie probably haven't even realized I'm gone."

"They realized," Teris growled back. He reluctantly added, *"But they'll trust me to protect you."*

I heard another roar, much closer to us.

"It can't be coming toward us, can it? Why would one of the fae attack us?" I asked, growing a bit panicked.

Fighting was not one of my talents. Not at all. I'd avoided the male fae for too many years to let them teach me.

"No. I'm sure there's an explanation," Teris said, though his voice was a bit tense.

He was climbing higher into the trees, toward the highest branches, I realized.

He wanted to see the dragon. To make sure we were right.

Teris leaped up to a bare branch, shifting forms and holding me tightly to his chest when he landed on two feet, peering up into the bare sky.

Our eyes landed on an emerald dragon gleaming in the moon's light, but...

It was different.

The shape of it was harsher. Sharper. Crueler. It didn't have the same majestic sweeping lines that the fae dragons did; it looked like a weapon.

Like a monster.

It roared again—and its eyes landed on us.

Teris swore, throwing me over his shoulder and launching himself off the branch. I gripped his fur for dear life, biting back a scream when I felt the dragon's claws swipe through the air where my head had been just a heartbeat earlier. It was a miracle all my damn hair was still attached.

"It's not a fae," I whispered, horror pounding in my chest.

"No." Teris almost sounded… worried.

But I knew I had to be imagining it.

"Can we outrun it?" I asked.

"We're going to find out." His voice was grim. *"Hold on tight, Nai. As tight as you can."*

"I will."

The monster crashed through the trees behind us. It was smaller than the male fae dragons—so about the same size as me, if I had to guess. But its movements were sharper, like the rest of it. It wasn't strong enough or large enough to break the thick branches, so they slowed it down, but only slightly.

And not enough for us to really get away from it.

We were slowly inching further in front of it, but that couldn't last. I knew that couldn't last.

"I'm going to throw you off my back," Teris warned me. His voice had gone calm—the fighting calm I knew so well.

"No," I said sharply.

"I can take one damn dragon down, Nai. Trust me."

I trusted him.

But that didn't mean I wanted to see him hurt.

"What if they can't be killed, like the klynnas?" I protested.

"The only way to learn that is by killing it. Trust me, and get those wings ready. Only fly far enough to get out of the way, and then hide."

"Okay," I finally whispered.

"This is only our beginning. We're going to be just fine," he reassured me.

I bit back a snort, my eyes watering slightly from the fear. *"This is so damn far from our beginning, Ter."*

He chuckled into my mind. *"Just trust me, baby."*

And despite everything, I did.

When he dropped his head, stopping suddenly, I sailed smoothly off his back. Rather than shifting, I tapped into Vevol's magic—my magic, now—and landed lightly on a thick branch. I was far enough away not to be in danger of catching a stray claw to the face, but close enough that I could still see what was happening.

I clutched the nearest vertical branch when a snarling Teris lunged for the emerald dragon. He dodged the creatures teeth and claws, burying his own massive fangs in the monster's throat as he flew over its neck.

Teris had grown tremendously with the influx of magic from the goddess, I realized, when I saw the size of him next to the dragon. He was absolutely massive. As big as those creatures Vevol had created, at least.

I saw harsh, bleeding lines on the dragon's shoulder as it spun toward the place Teris had landed. The sabertooth didn't even look fazed by the fight, despite the nausea in my stomach and the fear swelling in my chest.

He knew what he was doing.

He knew how to fight.

He was going to be fine.

I forced those thoughts to keep running through my mind as I watched Teris soar past the dragon again, slicing through the other side of its neck.

It wasn't healing as fast as the fae or klynnas did.

It wasn't healing at *all.*

And by the time Teris landed again, it was already plunging toward the dirt.

My eyes shut, my stomach churning at the awful sight.

"Stay there," Teris said. I didn't respond, but I didn't move, either.

A few minutes later, I heard him land on my branch. He was being loud on purpose, so I knew where he was and wasn't afraid.

His hands were on my face a moment later, his fingertips warm and wet with the dragon's blood, but his touch light. I squeezed my eyes shut more tightly, not ready to look at him again yet.

"I need you to open your eyes, Nai," he said quietly.

"Not yet," I whispered back.

"There's not time to wait, baby." His voice had softened, but there was grit in it that told me he was serious.

My eyes snapped open, and met his deep teal ones. I noticed that the whites were slightly red, and alarm bells rang in my mind. "What happened? I didn't see it hurt you."

"It didn't. I think its blood may be poisonous to us." He reached a hand up to wipe his mouth, and I saw the blood staining his lips. Though I wanted to shut my eyes again, I forced them to remain open. He had protected me, and that was what mattered. That was all that mattered.

"So what do we do?"

"Blood and mud keeps us alive. We're going to cover me with it, and then you're going to fly us back to the Stronghold," he said calmly.

I shook my head, but he was still holding it in place, so he moved it in a nod as soon as I'd stopped shaking it. "We don't have time to worry. I need you to tap into your magic and take me to the ground. The more I use mine, the faster the poison will work."

"Shit," I whispered, as he pulled me carefully into his arms. "Can't you just throw it up or something."

His lips curved upward the tiniest bit. "If magic worked that way, yes."

I was too stressed to scowl at him for the answer.

When I'd pulled the magic around us, I tugged Teris off the branch. We descended slowly toward the ground, and when I noticed a mud puddle nearby, I had the magic take us to it while we fell. The rainy season was nearing its end, which was a good thing for us in the current moment.

"How much blood and how much mud?" I asked Teris, my voice shaking as he slowly sat down on the dirt next to the mud.

"There's no perfect ratio. Some of both is good enough." He was still calm, and it was keeping me calm too by some miracle.

"Will this take care of the infection, though?" I pressed.

"Eventually. I might be unconscious for a day or two while it works, though. I'll need you to keep an eye out for me—and kill anyone who looks twice at you for me."

I rolled my eyes, though I knew he was just trying to ease the tension. "Great plan."

"I know." He caught my hand and pressed it to his chest. "Close your eyes."

Though I probably should've questioned him, I closed my eyes. There was a quiet, awful sound, and when I opened my eyes up, I saw a slice across his thigh.

He'd cut himself—for the blood.

"Damn you," I choked out, as my stomach rolled again.

"Please help me cover myself." His voice was low and calm, despite the slight strain to it. "Stay out of the sky. Fly as low as you safely can. Hold me in your talons—the mud will heal any injuries you give me. If you hear anything strange, hide in one of the memis bushes. Do not get yourself hurt, or you and I will have issues, baby."

While he spoke, I began scooping massive handfuls of mud and dropping them on his body. He mixed blood into the mud, his eyes closing a little more with each new part of him that was coated.

He was out cold by the time I was done covering him in mud, and my body was shaking fiercely.

How was I going to do this?

How was I going to get him back to the Stronghold?

I forced myself to breathe through the panic, putting two fingers to Teris's neck and checking for a pulse. It was slow, but it was there, and that calmed me slightly.

Standing up, I gave myself two minutes to pace and worry and cry a tiny bit.

After those two minutes were passed, I clenched my stomach against the terror and shifted, then carefully stepped over Teris and closed my claws lightly around him.

My movements were slow and unsteady as my wings carried me off the ground, and though I immediately zoomed up higher than I probably should've, I navigated downward until I was flying in the middle of the massive trees.

We were going to be fine, I promised myself, again and again.

We had to be fine.

Eight

I FLEW through the rest of the night, fueled by fear and stress. When the sun rose, sending beams of light through the trees, my energy was waning, but I pressed on.

And on.

And on.

I didn't stop to eat, though my stomach growled. I was afraid I'd run into some of the creatures I didn't know how to control yet—and I saw flashes of the scales of a few more dragons through the trees above my head. Whether they were fae or not, I didn't know, but I wasn't willing to find out.

When the sun set again, I knew I had to be less than twelve hours from the Stronghold, but the exhaustion was too much. So a few hours into the night, I landed as softly as I could, near a tree loaded with lilanos. After I'd checked Teris's pulse and confirmed that he was still alive—though it was a little unnecessary, because I would've died if he did—I plucked a few fruits off the tree and sat down next to Teris.

My whole body trembled, my hands shaking as I tried to peel the fruit. It took multiple attempts before I finally managed to get the thick, fuzzy peel off one of them, and my stomach churned as I put a small section of it in my mouth.

I hadn't been responsible for keeping someone alive since my mother was ill, and that felt like a lifetime ago. There wasn't even anything to do to take care of Teris, and yet those same emotions had floated back to the surface for me.

And now they were accompanied by the fear of unknown threats, new magic, and flying back into the Stronghold to tell a bunch of people who hated me that I'd allowed the goddess to create a bunch of monsters through me.

It was all just too much.

My breathing was picking up, my panic swelling and my shaking getting worse, so I shoved the rest of the lilano in my mouth. Standing swiftly, I shifted forms and grabbed Teris in my talons again, launching into the air.

I was even more unsteady than the first time I'd taken to the sky with the sabertooth in my grip, but there was no way around that other than rest. And I was way too shaken up to rest.

The sun was rising when I finally reached the Stronghold.

The shaking had gotten worse as the night progressed. As I approached, I saw a few klynnas in the skies and perched in a few strong trees, but ignored them, because no one had been panicking.

A few fae yelled warnings when I soared toward the ground—they could probably see my unconscious mate, and the way I was trembling.

I ignored their called words while I landed as gently as possible, shifting forms and stumbling to my knees immediately.

Devv, the unseelie hellhound guard I'd had to lie to in order to slip away undetected, was snarling at me as he stormed toward me.

I ignored him, pressing my fingers to Teris's throat again.

Devv started to reach for me—to pull me to my feet, I'd imagine, but his hands halted an inch from my skin, as his nostrils flared.

"We're mated," I whispered to him.

The words were so damn shaky I could barely understand them.

The fae made strangled sounds, but I didn't add anything else.

"What happened to him?" another male fae growled at me. Seelie, I'd guess, if they were worried about Teris.

"There was a dragon in the sky. Not one of ours," I managed to get out.

I needed food.

And water.

And sleep.

But all I could convince myself to do was kneel there with my fingers on my mate's throat, feeling the beat of his heart as it reassured me that he was alive.

"We've seen them. The goddess dropped the barrier keeping them out of our land," the fae said, his anger vanished as he kneeled next to me. When I looked sideways at him, I realized he was Ervo, and his mate, Mare, was off to his side a little bit. While he was looking at Teris, she was looking at me. I looked away quickly, when I noticed that. "Where was he injured?"

"Nowhere. He bit it, and its blood poisoned him. He told me the mud and blood would fight the poison for him—that it would heal him slowly."

The fae scoffed. "He lied."

Fear made my stomach clench, and my heart stumble. "What?"

The fae was already standing, calling out, "Find Nev. We need an urrtolo."

"What's an urrtolo?" I demanded, rising to my feet and stepping toward Ervo. My knees buckled, though, and I went crashing down.

A thin, warm arm wrapped around my back, catching me and pulling me back to my feet before I hit the ground. "How long has it been since you ate?" Mare asked me, her voice soft.

"I had a lilano last night." My words wobbled more than I wanted them to.

"And before that?"

"Too long," I whispered.

"When did you last sleep?"

"I don't know," I said, though I did know.

Too long ago.

"What's an urrtolo?" I asked her, pressing for details. "Me and Teris—we're mates. He's my mate. If he dies, I die. Not that I'm worried about me. I just want him to be okay." The words spewed out, my mind too overwhelmed and exhausted to process correctly.

"I know, I smelled him on your skin," she said softly. "You're both going to be fine. An urrtolo is a root that can be made into a tea that cleanses a fae's system. It works on poison, and koveko, and a bunch of other things. Nev convinced one of the men start a garden of them after everything that happened with the female fae."

A relieved breath rushed out of me. "Why did he lie, then? He said the mud and blood would heal him."

"It kept him alive. I'm sure he just didn't want you to worry. The male fae are particular about keeping their females comfortable—especially the seelies. They're wilder than the unseelies."

I hadn't seen that, but it had been a long, long time since I'd spent any amount of time with the seelies.

"What happened?" another female voice spoke behind us, and my head jerked to the side as Presley strode up to us. "Damn, Nai. You look like shit."

"Teris killed one of the new dragons, and ingested some of its blood. Apparently, they're poisonous to us," Mare explained quickly. "Ervo sent someone after an urrtolo, to cleanse the poison. Naomi flew a long time without eating or sleeping to get him back here."

Presley gave a long whistle, eyeing me closely. Her nostrils flared a bit, and she blinked. "You're mated?"

My eyes closed.

"They are," Mare said for me.

"We knew each other, before Aeven found me. We were in love," I whispered. "He's why I didn't want Aev—I was waiting for him to come after me. But he never did. He saw me meet Aeven, and thought the bond made me want him."

Both girls were silent for a long, long moment.

My knees knocked together again, and Presley ducked under my other arm, holding my waist with Mare to keep me upright.

"I didn't know that," Presley said quietly.

"No one knew that," Ervo said.

I opened my eyes, and found the phoenix studying me. His forehead was wrinkled, his eyebrows knitted together, and his eyes bright, as if everything was starting to click.

"You're why he wouldn't settle for Sunny when he knew she wasn't in love with him," Mare whispered.

I dipped my head in a tiny nod to confirm what she'd realized.

"I didn't know the bastard had it in him," another male voice mused. When I turned my head, I saw Nev striding up, hand-in-hand with Fovea. Her expression was more content than I'd ever seen it, and her free hand was on her abdomen. I remembered what Teris had said about her probably being pregnant.

"If he'd told anyone, there would've been war," Ervo told him. "We lost too many fae to jealousy even when we thought she was unclaimed. If he'd claimed her..."

"More men would've died."

"And he would've been killed by the seelie who wanted her," Ervo confirmed.

"He loves fighting, though, doesn't he?" Presley asked.

"Fighting for fun or distraction are much different than fighting for your life," Nev said simply.

"Welcome to the Wild Hunt," Mare told me, flashing me a small smile.

I bit my lip.

"What happened to Teris?" another male voice called out. When I looked past Presley, I saw Priel and North joining the crowd. The Wild Hunt may not have cared much about leading, but they did stick together, and I had to give them props for that.

"Bit one of the new dragons, got poisoned by its blood," Fovea tossed back. "The urrtolo is on its way."

North was tucked tightly against the blond hellhound's side, his hand wrapped possessively around her hip. She looked more awake and alive than I'd ever seen her before, not that it meant much since I'd only seen her a few times.

"Damn." Priel whistled. "He'll brag about this for the next decade. First bastard to learn about poisonous blood."

I had a feeling he'd be bragging about something much bigger than the blood.

Like the creatures no one had mentioned yet. I'd need to warn everyone, but I wasn't sure how.

"He smells mated," North said, frowning a bit as she looked over at me, Mare, and Presley.

Priel's eyes jerked over to me too, and my throat swelled.

I wasn't ready to rehash this a dozen times.

I needed to eat, and sleep, and know that Teris was alright.

"He and Naomi fell in love before she met Aev," Nev said. When I shot him a grateful look, he dipped his head in a nod. "They were both waiting for the other to choose them, from the sound of things."

When everyone turned back to me, I nodded to confirm what he'd said.

"Damn." Priel sounded impressed. "What a bastard." There was fondness in his voice, though. "Did you tell him about sex, too?"

I jerked my head in another nod, my face heating.

He gave me a feral grin. "He must've really loved you to keep *that* secret."

"Back off," North murmured to him, though she didn't sound annoyed or frustrated in the slightest. "We need to get her something to eat."

"I'm okay," I said, though the words sounded uneven.

She nodded at me, but tugged Priel off toward the huge kitchen where there was always someone cooking something.

When my eyes followed them into the forest, I noticed more fae gathered around us, behind us, listening. I forced my gaze to scan the trees, and the more I looked, the more people I saw.

Both male and female fae...

And so many ex-human women.

My eyes jerked back to Fovea, and I saw that her brands were gone. She gave me a small smile. "The goddess visited me, before she passed on. She told me about the creatures she used you to create—the ones that are meant to protect us. We have fae and klynnas watching out for them. It'll take time for you to learn how to guide them."

I nodded quickly, my eyes stinging a little.

She knew—thank the goddess. I wasn't going to have to figure out a way to break the news without becoming enemy number one again.

"Did more humans come through when you lost your brands?" I asked her.

"Yes. Now, there are nearly enough of us to balance out the men." Her smile widened slightly. "And I'm pregnant. Life-bringers are not the only female fae who can take mates and grow children. It's a gift from the goddess—she changed us, when she realized she was starting to fade."

I nodded again, my lips curved up in a tiny smile of my own. "I'm happy for you."

"And I'm happy you've found the male who was truly meant to love you. Even in a world as magical as ours, fate doesn't have *all* of the answers."

A golden dragon came spiraling through the trees, and landed hard with a blue-haired female clinging to his back. Oren shifted back, taking her hand as she stepped up to his side and slid her fingers between his. "Here." She held a simple wooden cup out toward Ervo, who still kneeled beside Teris, and relief sagged my shoulders.

They'd found the root.

He was going to be okay.

Ervo grabbed the cup and carried it back to Teris. He had the contents down my sabertooth's throat a moment later, and the forest went silent as everyone waited.

"Presley?" an angry male voice boomed through the forest, and I looked at the tall, slim phoenix shifter next to me. She rolled her eyes, though her cheeks were pink.

"What's that about?" I asked her.

"Korrik has decided he's going to convince me to mate with him," she muttered. "The grumpy bastard is stalking me. Luckily, he doesn't have wings."

I snorted.

Her lips curved upward, just slightly.

"Make him work for it," I told her.

"Oh, I am."

"Dammit, woman," the unseelie general snarled, as he leaped out of the trees and landed hard on two thick legs. "Stop running from me."

"Stop chasing me, then," she shot back.

"In your dreams, female." He stepped beside her, crossing his arms over his chest. Though their bodies didn't touch, all it would've taken was one heavy breath from either of them to make their arms meet.

Teris's eyes flew open, and my attention was focused completely on the sabertooth I'd claimed. His gaze collided with Ervo's, and then Nev's—and then he jerked upward, snarling, "Where is she?" His chest was heaving when his eyes landed on me as the last word left his lips, and his shoulders sagged in relief. "No one's touched you?"

By no one, I knew he meant the men.

I shook my head in response, and he relaxed further.

"Next time you kill a dragon, don't try to eat it, brother," Nev drawled.

Teris snorted, grabbing a fallen bit of a red dragon scale off the dirt and tossing it at his friend. Nev dodged it with a grin, and the sabertooth turned his eyes back to me. "You look hungry," he growled.

I *was* hungry.

But also too nauseous and stressed to eat.

"She hasn't slept or eaten since you were injured," Ervo said, and I shot him a glare. He lifted a shoulder in response, as if saying that if I were his female, he'd want to know.

"I'm fine," I countered, though Presley and Mare were legitimately holding up all of my weight.

Teris stood swiftly, glowering at me as he stalked toward me. I glared back, muttering a curse when he grabbed me out of the other womens' arms and threw me lightly over his shoulder. "Thanks for saving my life," he growled quietly to me. "Next time, don't risk your own when you do."

I slammed the base of my fist into his tight ass, and a few snorts rolled through the people in the gathered crowd who had seen. "Don't even start with me, Ter," I growled back.

He squeezed the backs of my thighs, trying to calm me and failing. "Thanks for the urrtolo," he called out, to the Wild Hunt males. "Make sure everyone knows that Naomi is mine."

My scowl deepened, but since my face was to his back, no one saw. "Where are we going?"

"Home." His blunt answer made my heart swell.

"You have a house here?" My voice was hopeful; I couldn't have stopped that if I tried.

"*We* have a house here."

"We grabbed food for the two of you," Priel said easily, from somewhere in front of Teris. "Boxed up and everything, brother. Good work with the dragon."

Teris made a noncommittal noise. "Don't bite one."

Priel chuckled. "Thanks. Congrats on the mating, too."

"Mmhm."

I saw flashes of North's dark hair and Priel's inked skin as they walked past us. And while I didn't know where they were going, I thought I might actually like the two of them. There weren't many fae I knew, and there were even less that I liked. But Teris's friends—his family—just may have started to make that list.

Nine

If I hadn't been hanging upside down, with Teris's hand on the back of my thigh, I probably would've fallen asleep on the way to his house. But we hadn't gotten anywhere near working out all the tension between us, and I was still nervous about... well, everything.

So I didn't fall asleep.

Teris stopped in the forest a few minutes later, crouching down. I leaned to the side, craning my head so I could see. He pulled on a thick wooden handle, and then tugged a thick sheet of dark wood upward, exposing an entrance that resembled a large, dark hole in the ground.

My heart flew into my throat when the bastard jumped down into the hole without so much as a warning, and my stomach rolled when he landed hard on the ground.

"Sorry. Magic's a bit weak right now," he murmured to me, stroking the back of my thigh in apology.

"Put me down before I puke on you," I grumbled.

He smacked my ass lightly. "No."

I kicked his side playfully, and he tickled my inner thigh, making me screech as I wiggled against him.

His chuckle rumbled against my other thigh as he strode further into the house, and I heard the wooden plank close with a soft thunk. Another, similar sound followed, and I hoped it was a lock clicking into place.

"I can't believe I get to touch you as much as I want," he admitted to me. His hands landed on my hips, and he finally pulled me down, setting me in a simple, comfortable chair.

He dropped into the one next to mine, and I looked around the space while he opened the boxes of food Priel and North had brought us.

The room was wide and open, simple and clean too. There was a small kitchen, a huge bed, a shelf that held the fae version of a tattoo gun, and a bathroom.

And that was it.

The sight of it reminded me of the time I'd spent with him when I first arrived in Vevol, and that put me more at ease than I'd felt in... forever.

"Well?" Teris asked, handing me a forkful of something that sort of reminded me of ultra-sticky pasta.

"The seelie live a lot simpler than the unseelie," I said absentmindedly, spinning the fork slowly between my fingers because I still wasn't sure my stomach was settled enough to eat. The stress I was feeling was still so damn intense. "It made me feel out of place, when I first got there. Even when we left. They like bigger houses, with multiple floors, and more furniture. I like the simplicity that you guys have. It's more comfortable."

"Some seelie like big houses. Just not as many." Teris plucked the fork from my fingers, and lifted it to my lips. "Open."

"I'm not hungr—oof." I grumbled when he took the opportunity to push the pasta into my mouth.

"You've been awake, hungry, and worried about me for a long time. You'll start to calm down when your stomach fills," he said, filling the fork again while I struggled to chew. My nausea increased, but I managed to get the bite down after a minute.

When he lifted the fork back to my lips, I held up a finger, and he took that bite himself, loading the fork while he chewed.

"I'm nauseous," I admitted to him.

"It'll subside as you eat. Trust me, Nai."

I rolled my eyes at him, but when he lifted the fork, I reluctantly ate the food off it.

He fed both of us slowly, alternating between the two of us. And as much as I didn't want to admit it, he was right—the nausea faded as I filled my stomach.

We ate our way through both boxes of food—the other one was the fae version of rice and beans that everyone was obsessed with. By the time we were done, my body was much more relaxed, even though I still wasn't tired.

Teris leaned toward me, cupping my face and brushing a kiss against my lips before taking the boxes and silverware to the sink. After he cleaned them, he came back over and scooped me up off the chair, holding my chest to his.

We were both too drained to care that he was still covered with mud. At least, I thought we were, until he carried me to the bathroom instead of the bedroom.

"You're not too tired for a shower?" I asked him, surprised. I was fairly sure that the mud and blood mixture put him in a coma of sorts where he didn't actually get any rest, because of the way his body was working. When I'd woken up from my *spirit journey* to change my name, I'd needed an insane amount of sleep to recover.

He chuckled. "I'm exhausted, but you're still wound up, and I'm covered in mud. We need to get cleaned off and calm you down before we crash."

"You don't need to *calm me down*," I said with a scowl, though it was only half-hearted.

"Sure I don't." He set me down on my feet, leaning me up against the shower's wall while he turned on the water.

My eyes followed his hands as they unfastened his pants and then tugged his pants down. I loved that he didn't hesitate to strip in front of me—that he wasn't ashamed to show me his scars.

His cock grew with my attention on it, hardening and swelling in response to my gaze. Teris didn't acknowledge it, simply kicking his pants free and then stepping up in front of me.

He eased me away from the wall, then peeled my tank top over my head, tossing it to his own pants. When he kneeled in front of me, tugging my shorts down my thighs, my body warmed just a little.

Was he going to fuck me?

That would probably be a good way to calm me down...

"Give me a minute," Teris said, brushing a kiss to my bare thigh before rising to his feet. He strode into the water, and I watched as he roughly scrubbed the mud off his skin. It took what felt like an hour, but I liked watching him move. "Feels like you're staring into my soul," he murmured.

I smiled. "Nope. Just staring at your ass. And shoulders. And... all of it." I gestured vaguely to his gorgeous body. "You're too pretty for your own good, you know."

He chuckled—the sound was deep, and rich. My smile grew.

And though I never would've expected it, I already felt a hell of a lot calmer than I had been before we stepped into the shower. Something about seeing him relax and watching him get clean was calming for me.

"The same thing is true for you, Nai. I don't even want to think about how many bastards I'm going to have to start fights with for staring at you."

I rolled my eyes. "They're not going to stare at me. Everyone's used to pretending I don't exist to avoid pissing off Aeven."

He growled unhappily. "I'll start fights with them for that too, then."

"You'll spend all your time fighting."

"Nah. I'll make time to fuck you every now and then, too."

I snorted, and he flashed me a tired grin over his shoulder. He was still working on the mud, or I would've stepped into his arms and hugged him fiercely. Assuming I could walk to him without falling over, that is.

He turned around so he could stare at me while he scrubbed his skin. Despite his erection, and the way it bobbed every now and then, he made no move to touch himself or me.

"You're gorgeous, baby," he murmured to me, as he worked on a particularly thick patch of mud on one of his arms.

I made a face at him, and he chuckled.

"I still can't believe you're here. In my house—our house. Wearing my scent. Connected to me permanently," he said into my mind, still staring at me without a shred of shame. *"Mine, and only mine. Forever."*

"It's really surreal. I don't think I've processed it yet," I admitted. *"I'll probably panic at some point."*

"I know I haven't processed it yet. Panic all you want—I'll hold you through it, and growl at you as many times as I have to."

I laughed softly. *"Good answer."*

He finally finished scrubbing the mud off. With one soft, smooth motion, he took my hand and pulled me to his chest. His arms wrapped around me, and though his erection was trapped against my belly, I wasn't turned on.

I was really, really comfortable, though.

He held me to his chest as we stood under the warm falling water for a long, long time. And slowly, as he did, the remaining stress and tension in my body faded away until I was practically boneless.

I was mostly-asleep when Teris finally turned the water off.

"I can dry us," I mumbled, before lighting us both on fire. A short, soft laugh escaped him as the water evaporated off our skin and then my flames winked out.

He cradled my bare body in his arms as he walked us both to the bed, and a groan escaped me when he lowered us to the mattress.

It was so damn soft.

"You sure you want to share a bed with me?" I mumbled to him, almost asleep already.

"Absolutely positive." His lips brushed my forehead, then my cheek, then my throat, and finally my collarbone. "You want to get free of me, you'll have to kill me and climb away from my cold, lifeless body."

"If I kill you, I'll die too. No climbing would happen."

"Then I guess you're stuck, baby."

The soft term of endearment, used so sweetly, made my lips curve upward a bit. "I'll survive."

"Mmhm." He tucked me closer, turning me a little so my back met his chest. "Sleep well, Nai. I'm glad you're here."

"Me too. And you too," I whispered.

Just before sleep pulled me under, I realized I felt safer than I had in two entire decades. Maybe that should've messed with me—but it just made me really damn happy.

I didn't know how much time had passed when I woke up. Teris was still breathing steadily, his chest against my back. One of his hands had wrapped possessively over my core, and the other was around one of my breasts.

The need to pee hit me hard, but I tried to ignore it. My sabertooth had probably been awake even longer than I had—he hadn't slept when I was out in the cave, and we were both still adjusting to the new magic we had.

I closed my eyes and tried to go back to sleep, but my bladder was screaming at me, so I only lasted a few minutes before I tried to carefully slide away from Teris.

His grip on my core and boob tightened when I moved, and my body clenched when he dragged me back to him, erasing the measly inch I'd put between us.

"No leaving me," he grumbled at me.

"I'll come back after I pee."

"No." He pulled me even more tightly against him.

"I will literally piss all over your hand if you don't let go of me."

Teris squeezed my core, and I squeaked. "Go for it."

I scoffed, and he chuckled, easing us both to a sitting position and then standing up. A moment later, he set me on the toilet, and stepped back to lean up against the wall.

"You can't just stand there and watch me." I tossed a hand toward him.

He focused his gaze on the ceiling, not even bothering to fight his smirk.

I grabbed his muddy pants with my toe, and threw them at him. He barked out a laugh as he side-stepped them easily.

"Get out, or we will never have sex again," I warned, pointing at the door. "I'm not kidding."

He flashed me a feral grin. "You'd get desperate and jump me."

"How sure are you of that?" I shot back.

He studied me, still grinning.

I glared right back.

"Alright, I'll give you this one. Eventually, you'll be comfortable enough to pee in front of me, though. It's just urine."

He stepped outside the bathroom door—leaving it wide open. Since I saw him move out of the line of sight, I knew he wasn't trying to watch me from outside the room or anything. Just being his normal, attractively-obnoxious self.

"It's just urine, he says," I muttered to myself as I washed my hands, after doing my business.

"It is," he called from the other room. "Every animal urinates, Nai."

"I'm flipping you off from in here," I tossed back.

He laughed. "You know that turns me on, baby."

I bit my lip to fight the grin that was threatening to emerge.

I hadn't *forgotten* how fun he could be when he was comfortable and happy, but it had been so long. And things had been so damn intense, out in the forest and then in the cave.

I dried my hands with my flames, and then slipped out of the bathroom. Teris was waiting for me just outside, leaned up against one of the walls. He dragged me to his chest and buried his face in my hair as he hugged me fiercely tight.

"Damn, I love you," he murmured.

My throat closed, and my heart just about stopped.

He stroked my hair, and my back.

I got the feeling that he wanted me to say it back, but my feelings had led me astray so many times. And I wasn't positive it'd be true if I did say it, so... I kept my mouth shut.

"My new name full name is Viola," I finally whispered, wrapping my arms around his back too. "In case something happens, you should know."

"Your mom's name?"

My throat was still swollen, so I just nodded against his chest.

"She'd love that," he said softly.

My eyes stung. "I think so."

He buried his hand in the back of my hair and just held me. I hugged him back tightly, immensely grateful that he knew me as well as he did, even though there had been so much of each other's lives that we'd missed.

"I feel like I need a recap of the past two decades of your life," I told him quietly. "It feels like I don't even really know you anymore, but we're mated, and I'm still more comfortable around you than I am around anyone else. It's kind of trippy."

"I'll plan us one of your human dates, for tonight, then. I can cook you something new, and we can spend a few hours talking about life like we used to."

My lips curved upward, only slightly sadly. "I actually know how to cook pretty well, now. I don't know what all of the ingredients are called, but I had a lot of free time to figure out how to use them. Maybe I can cook for you this time."

"Even better." He brushed his lips against the top of my head. "I'll go find us some things to cook with."

Ten

Before Teris could go anywhere, someone rapped against the wooden plank that functioned as a door, and my head jerked upward. He just grimaced.

"There's a huge group of your poisonous dragons headed our way," a male fae yelled. His voice was so muted through the wood that I could barely make out the words.

"Send the unmated men!" Teris shouted back, pulling me closer.

The man knocked again, harder.

"Shouldn't have soundproofed it," Teris muttered into my head, brushing a kiss to my forehead before he strode over to the gap that functioned as a doorway. There were wooden rungs in the wall, I realized, when he used them to climb up, and then unlocked and opened the door. "Send the unmated men," he repeated to the guy outside.

"The female fae are all looking for mates, and holding competitions to determine the strongest males as we speak. Most of the unmated won't consider leaving the area until the competitions are over and their mates are decided."

Teris growled. "The female fae aren't even making an attempt to look for love?"

"They believe love is a choice, so they prefer to decide based on strength." The other guy sounded about as impressed by that idea as Teris did. "I have January tucked away in my cave. We can put your female there too, if you're worried about her safety, but we need more manpower."

Based on the fact that he was talking about January, I was going to assume the guy outside was Lian. The Wild King, as the unseelies tended to call him. At least, they'd called him that before all the shit had gone down after he ended up mated.

"If you can tuck your female away somewhere, she's an entirely different kind of woman than mine," Teris drawled.

I bit back a snort—but he was right. I was not the kind of person who accepted being hidden away.

"It takes persuading, but it's doable. I made cake."

I perked right the hell up at that.

Was I willing to be tucked away for cake?

After being out in the wilderness for so long, looking for the klynna cave, you could be damn sure I was.

"I'll go for cake," I called out. I'd only met January a few times, but I liked her. We could chat long enough to enjoy the cake, and if the fight wasn't over yet, I'd duck out early.

"Damn. Guess I need to become a better baker," Teris remarked.

Lian snorted. "You've never baked a day in your life. In hindsight, it's not at all surprising that you've been in love with Naomi for twenty years."

I heard something that sounded like Teris probably smacked Lian. "Give us a minute to get dressed," he told the dragon.

He closed the door, and strode over to me, dragging me into his arms. "You're going to sneak out early if you get bored, aren't you?"

"Yup," I confirmed.

He chuckled. "Just be careful. And stay away from men. Please."

"I'm not a huge fan of that broad request. *Stay away from men*. You know there are still more men than women in this world, right?"

He chuckled. "Broad or not, I won't deal well if I come back from fighting a bunch of damn dragons and find you talking with some bastard who'll obviously be attracted to you."

I rolled my eyes at him. "The unseelies hate me. The seelies know we're mated. I'm positive you have nothing to worry about."

"And yet I'll worry anyway." He captured my lips in his, and when he slid his tongue into my mouth, I kissed him back without hesitation.

Lian banged on the door again, yelling, "They're getting closer."

I pulled away, and Teris grumbled, "Bastard."

There was fondness behind the word, though. He had Lian had been close long before I ever met him. "I'll burn the mud off our clothes real quick so we can get moving." I hesitated for a moment. "Maybe one of us should talk to Aeven and Dakota? I'm sure he won't be bothered or anything; I think he dislikes me a lot more than I dislike him at this point, but he probably deserves a warning. Or an explanation."

Teris's expression darkened. "I'll talk to them. I probably owe the bastard an apology for winning your heart before he could anyway."

"Way to be humble." I clapped sarcastically, and he grabbed my face again, kissing me again.

"You're mine," he said. "You always have been. I'm not going to apologize for that. But I should've come for you the moment he took you from me; I shouldn't have doubted you. So I do owe him an apology for leaving you in limbo."

He tugged me toward the bathroom. "We should probably hurry."

FIVE MINUTES LATER, Teris was climbing up the ladder behind me. He grabbed my ass halfway up the ladder, and I shot him a raised eyebrow over my shoulder, to which I received a grin.

When we emerged, Lian was studying Teris.

"Don't be weird," he grumbled at the dragon, shutting the door to his place and wrapping an arm around my waist.

"You're the one who lied to us for twenty years. I'd say that's pretty damn weird," Lian countered.

He had a point.

"I wasn't about to put a target on her back by announcing to everyone that sex existed. As far as I knew, she was shacked up in a love cave with the unseelie king." Teris squeezed my hip lightly. "I should've tried harder."

"If I saw you look at your fated mate the way you said I looked at Aeven that day, I would've drawn the same conclusions," I admitted to Teris. "We hadn't even kissed or anything—everything was still up in the air."

"Not for me," he said bluntly.

My face warmed.

Guilt tugged at me, and I remembered the moments in his cave.

When he'd told me he loved me, and I hadn't responded.

I was becoming the bad guy all over again, wasn't I? Teris was going to be the one who loved me more in our relationship, and I was going to spend the rest of my life feeling absolutely, horrifically guilty for it, day in and day out.

The men shifted, and I rode on Teris's back, burying my fingers in his fur as he carried me to Lian's cave. We reached it a few minutes later—a hole in the ground, built almost exactly the same as Teris's from the outside. But when we slipped in, I realized it was bigger, and formatted with a large living area as well as two individual bedrooms.

They did have a baby on the way, after all.

January wasn't as alone in her room as I expected—North was there too, as well as Mare and Summer.

I froze a bit when I saw her. She was in love with him for a while—I'd known she was in love with him, and I'd *hated* her for it, even when I had no reason to, and didn't even know her at all. Even when I hadn't seen Teris for so damn many years, I'd automatically hated the woman he was with, on principle.

Because she wasn't me.

And now, I felt like shit for it.

"Be careful," Teris told me, brushing a kiss to my lips. He gave the other women a two-finger wave before climbing back out of the cave. The door closed, and the men shifted forms, taking off into the forest.

"Does he think we're going to attack you or something?" January drawled. Her stomach was fairly big—big enough that I imagined she would start having a hard time getting around, if she wasn't already. Then again, I'd never been around pregnant women much, so I wasn't a great judge.

"No. He knows I won't wait for him here if I get bored." I lifted a shoulder.

Summer snorted. "A woman after our hearts, then."

"Priel would eat me alive if I took off before he gets back," North said, a wicked gleam in her eyes. "Makes me want to try it."

January grinned and high-fived her.

"Did you get your magic figured out?" I asked her. "You seem much more in control than you used to be."

"When the goddess made the magic my own, it changed everything," she explained. "Now, it responds to my will. Before, it was a constant headache. Fovea thinks I would've figured it out eventually, but I don't know. It was getting worse, instead of better."

"She said it'd take *centuries*," Mare reminded North.

We all grimaced at that idea. None of us were used to the idea of a fae life span, not even me, though I hadn't aged at all in the two decades I'd been in Vevol.

"So, spill the beans," Summer commanded me.

I made a face. "You'll have to sweeten me up with a lot of cake to get me to that point."

"You heard the woman. Cake her," January exclaimed, tossing a hand toward Summer, who was already in the kitchen and therefore right next to the cake.

Summer made a show of cutting nearly a quarter of the cake and plopping it down on a plate, then grabbed a fork and brought it over to me.

"Are we good?" I asked her, still a bit nervous.

"About Teris? Sure. I've got all the closure I need, in the form of the sexiest basilisk alive. Something I'm sure none of you would disagree with?" she looked around the group, and everyone shook their heads. Since none of them were mated to basilisks, I figured it was a safe statement to make. "I think I was only into him because of the mate bond, anyway. My feelings vanished the moment I was connected to Remmo. I don't know how you managed to make it a decade in that bond without developing feelings for Aev, but damn girl, I respect it."

I cut into my cake, taking a bite.

They were all waiting, mostly-patiently.

I chewed slowly, and then swallowed, before finally admitting, "Teris was the first fae to make me feel welcome. He wasn't obsessed with me, like some of the others. He didn't think I was an alien because I had tits. He was frank about finding me intruiging, and over time, we became friends. Honestly, he was the best friend I'd ever had. On Earth, I was pretty alone. I explained everything about kissing to him, and sex in all its forms, and he didn't push me for anything or change at all. He was just Teris."

I took another bite, and January groaned.

Mare patted her on the knee, as if to comfort her.

After I swallowed, I continued. "Things got steamy between us, but we didn't touch each other. We didn't even kiss. I'd never had a boyfriend, or a casual hookup, or anything like that, so I was new to everything just like him. We were taking things slow. But we decided he was going to kiss me one night—we'd planned it, and I was pretty confident we'd go from kissing to hooking up. Before he'd finished his shift of fighting that night, a few of the unseelies broke into my house. They covered my mouth so I couldn't scream, and hauled me out so fast I didn't even have time to fight."

The girls' eyes were all wide and round.

I took another bite of cake.

"Bitch knows she has a story we're desperate for," Summer grumbled.

I bit back a snort.

"Half an hour into the trip, this massive sabertooth comes out of the trees. He snarls at the men, and they stop completely. A few of them are apologizing, and the sabertooth shifts forms. The moment our eyes met, I felt this strong, heavy *connection* fall into place between us. Neither of us could deny it. I didn't want the connection, but I knew without a doubt that it was real. Aev took me from his men, and hauled my ass back to his place. When I told him I didn't want to talk to him, he didn't fight with me on it."

"Rookie mistake," January muttered.

The other girls nodded.

"Obviously he learned from it, because he seems to have changed tactics with Dakota. But I didn't think he wanted me—which he didn't. And I didn't want him. I spent every hour of those first few days waiting for Teris to show up at my door, but he didn't come. The entire first *year*, I waited for him. When the next human woman arrived, I realized he wasn't coming. The only pain I'd ever felt that was worse than the pain of knowing he didn't love me enough to chase me was the pain of losing my mother. That's one I don't think I can ever be free of," I said quietly.

North heaved a sigh. "Damn."

"Why didn't he come? And why the hell did you take the bastard back so fast?" Summer demanded, tossing a hand toward the door in the ceiling.

"He caught up to me just after Aeven did. I didn't see him—I didn't know he was there. I would've yelled for him, if I did. I would've begged him to get me away from Aev, if I could've. But I didn't see him. And from Teris's perspective, when I looked at Aeven and the bond fell into place, I looked really damn excited about it—and really damn in love with him. They didn't know that bonds could be broken, then. And even if they did, he thought I wanted it, so he wasn't going to interfere."

There was a long silence.

Summer finally sighed. "Well, that's devastating."

"It was just a misunderstanding. A big misunderstanding that cost me twenty years of happiness," I said quietly. "What I wouldn't give to go back in time."

"Now we understand why you took him back so quickly," Mare said, and I got the feeling she was trying to lighten the mood.

"Honestly, I would've made him wait longer. I don't know if I'm really ready. But with the goddess giving me the magic to lead her new army of monsters, she warned me that I'd only have a week to pick a mate. The magic was too much for me to deal with alone."

Their eyes widened again, and I had to explain the goddess's assignment, and how she'd used me.

"So now you're trying to wrap your mind around the past not being exactly the way you thought, as well as adjust to a new mate bond?" January checked.

I nodded.

"Hot damn." She brushed a few strands of golden-brown hair from her eyes. "You're a warrior."

"I'm struggling," I admitted. "Earlier today, he told me he loved me, and I couldn't say it back. It would've felt like a lie, and I couldn't do that to him. We've started finding our stride again, but it'll take time to develop our friendship back to where it used to be. We've been apart a long time, you know? And I'm terrified that I'm screwing everything up between us, because I already did that with Aeven. The last thing I want is to hurt Teris that way too."

"Oh, it's expected that fae men will fall first," Mare said quickly. "Don't worry about that. They always fall hard and fast, and they don't pressure anyone into feeling the same way."

"She's right. It doesn't offend them to want you more than you want them," January agreed.

"Amen. My man literally stalked me for a while because he thought I was in love with another guy," Summer added. "My emotions changed nothing for him."

"Has he asked you outright if you love him too? Or made you think he expects you to?" North asked. "Teris is a pretty direct man. He and Priel are similar that way, and Priel would one-hundred-percent tell me if he thought I should feel something for him that I didn't."

"No, he hasn't asked me or anything. But I just feel guilty, you know? I hate knowing that I was the villain with Aeven, and to all of the unseelies. I just... I hate it." I shook my head harshly, trying to shake off the emotions somehow. Though I knew it wasn't going to work that way, I could dream, right?

"Girl, I've talked to Dakota about this shit, and neither she nor Aev think you were the villain. From what she said, he didn't try to talk to you much more than you tried with him," Summer put in.

She was right, but it didn't feel that way. "I know, but when the goddess showed me the past, he was just an absolute wreck. And if I'd just done things a little different..." I heaved a sigh. "I hurt him. I hate knowing that, even though we're not friends or even really acquaintances. I never tried to hurt him."

"But you were hurting," North reminded me. "And it's easy to lash out at other people when you're hurting. Natural, too."

"That doesn't mean it's right," I argued.

"You already apologized though, right?" January checked.

I nodded.

"Then why not leave the past in the past? You hurt him, but he hurt you too. Both of you could've changed your situation in multiple ways, but neither of you did. You both deserve the blame. It's okay to feel the guilt, but feel it, and then let it go. Holding on to past shit doesn't do anything but hurt your present self," January said.

My eyes burned a little.

She was right; I did need to let it go.

Not because I hadn't made a mistake.

Not because I wasn't guilty.

But because I'd already done everything I could to right the wrong, and hanging on to my guilt was only going to continue hurting me.

And now, what hurt me would hurt Teris too, eventually.

I probably needed to talk to him about the guilt I was wearing like a second skin. I'd told him I felt bad, and he told me not to, but it wasn't about feeling guilt or not feeling guilt. It was about accepting what had happened, as shitty as it was, and giving myself permission to move on.

Summer put in, "If we're going to have conversations like this one, you've got to eat some more of that cake, girl. You're going to need it."

I laughed, though my eyes were still stinging a little, and dutifully took another bite.

It really was great cake.

Eleven
Teris

There were a damn lot of dragons, and killing them without my teeth was a pain in the ass, but I managed without too many injuries. Knowing that Nai was waiting for me made the fights seem a lot less appealing, but I still needed to protect her.

An hour had passed by the time our group of twenty finally got through their ranks. We all drank a little of the foul urrtolo tea just to make sure none of us had been accidentally poisoned without realizing it before we slapped each other's shoulders and headed back toward the Stronghold.

Aev and Dakota had been with us—she'd stayed in the trees, communicating with her bonded klynna—so even though I was itching to get back to Nai, I veered away from my brothers and followed them to their place.

They'd noticed me following, and stopped on their porch when they reached it. She looked a bit ill, but everyone knew she had struggled with seeing fights, or even hearing them.

I shifted back. "You have a minute?"

"Sure." Aev lifted a shoulder, glancing at Dakota, and she nodded. Her forehead was creased, like she was worried.

"I'm sorry we didn't warn you when we were breaking the bond," she said quickly. "I tried to find you, but you were already gone with Naomi."

"Don't apologize for that. I was glad to see it go." I tucked my hands in my pants' pockets. "About Naomi." I looked at Aev. "I probably owe you an apology. She and I were together, two decades ago, in secret. Before you found her. I saw you from the trees when you met, and thought she looked excited by your bond. When she didn't use my name to bring me to her to rescue you, she confirmed it in my mind, that you were happy to find each other. She was expecting me to come after her, but I thought she wanted you."

The words hadn't come out right—my voice was rough, and probably defensive. Maybe a little guilty too, but I didn't regret my relationship with her.

I regretted not realizing she wanted me, though. I might always regret that.

"Wow," Dakota breathed.

"Yeah. We figured I should tell you in person, because we decided to go through with the mating. She had to pick someone because of the goddess's magic, and I was there."

"And because she wanted you," Dakota said gently.

My heart swelled.

I fucking hoped so.

It still didn't feel completely real, though.

"You don't owe me an apology," Aev said, his lips curving upward in a small smile. "Naomi and I were incompatible. I didn't want her any more than she wanted me, despite the hell the bond put me through. Thank you for telling me though; this is a lot better than hearing the gossip."

I jerked my head in a nod.

I doubted that Aeven and I would ever be friends, but I didn't see any reason for us to be enemies.

"We wish you both all the happiness," Dakota said, smiling softly as she stepped closer to Aev. He pulled her to his side gently, and the difference between us hit me harder than it had even before.

He was kind and gentle; I was rough and harsh.

Fate had intended my female to be with someone nicer than me. Easier going, too.

And yet now, she belonged to me.

And I'd love her better than that bastard could ever fucking imagine.

...Even if I had to figure out how to be softer and sweeter to do it.

"Thank you. I hope the same for you." I shifted forms and slipped back into the forest. Though I didn't know whether Naomi was still with January and the other women, it seemed as good a place to start looking as any.

I needed to hold her in my arms and feel her skin on mine again, so I could be reassured that what we had was real, as much as I hated to admit that.

Twelve

Naomi

After the conversation had faded to lighter topics, such as favorite fae foods and Summer's funny stories about being on the unseelie council with all of the grumpy generals, there was a knock on the door.

"It's not the guys. None of them would bother asking while we're in here," January said, starting to make her way to her feet.

That looked like a rough task, so I stood smoothly. "I'll grab it, if you don't mind."

I was closest to the door, anyway.

"Thanks." She flashed me a quick smile, and I crossed the room, climbing up the simple ladder that looked identical to the one in Teris's place.

I eased the door open, and my eyebrows shot upward when I saw a group of fae men outside.

My mind automatically went back to the times I'd been taken from my home by groups like that. Carried away from Teris and the Wild Hunt guys, scared out of my mind. It had happened five times before Aeven finally stole me away, and I'd never forget the terror even though I'd forgiven the fae.

I forced myself not to react to those memories, though.

The times had changed, and I wasn't in danger anymore.

I had to believe that.

"Hi," I said.

"Hey," one of the guys responded. None of them looked uncomfortable in the slightest, or surprised to see someone other than January and Lian answering the door. "January said we could come by for advice after the first competition."

I blinked.

Advice?

They were here for advice?

"We're coming!" January called out from below me. When I looked down, North and Summer were already at the bottom of the ladder.

Guess I was going too.

I climbed out, and one of them offered me a hand. I wasn't in the habit of touching men in any capacity, outside of Teris, but even that was a new development. Touching a man would put my scent on him, and his on me.

Which I did not want to do the first time Teris left me on my own after we were mated. He seemed extra possessive at the moment, so I didn't want to trigger him or anything.

"Thanks for the offer, but I can't touch you," I told the man, sticking with honesty as I eased myself out of the hole. I wasn't used to climbing in and out of caves, but I supposed I'd have to get used to it.

The prospect didn't scare me or bother me at all, much to my surprise.

"First lesson: don't touch a mated woman in any capacity, boys," Summer called out as she followed me through. "Unless you're looking for a fight, because you *will* piss off her mate if he smells you on her skin, no matter how laid back he seems."

"The newer the mating, the more volatile the male," North added, as she emerged. "They never *really* chill out, but when the men become more settled in the relationship, the reactiveness geta a little better."

"Not a lot better, though," Mare warned, dusting her hands off on her shorts before leaning over and offering January a hand. January waved her off, and my forehead knitted in worry as I watched her slip out of the hole. Though she didn't have a problem, it made me nervous anyway.

"It depends on the guy," January said. "They're all super possessive, but some are more conniving, while others are more pissy. I've never seen Teris lose his temper, but I get the feeling he's the latter."

I fought a smirk.

"Lesson learned. Thank you." One of the men inclined his head toward us. "We require advice on wooing the new human females, now that we've thrown the fights with the fae women, as you advised."

I looked at January with raised eyebrows.

"They've all found mates in some of the newish ex-human girls," January clarified. "They're not sure how to win them over, so I told them we'd help."

Damn.

I nodded, even though I was a bit shell-shocked by the explanation.

"Have a lot of people been finding fated mates?"

"Yup. Seems like most of the new ex-humans are fated," Summer confirmed.

North gestured toward me. "Naomi is probably better with advice as far as fated matings go, since the rest of us fell into the arms of the guys we were connected to pretty fast."

My face flushed, and all of the eyes turned to me.

I expected to find judgment in their gazes, but there was none of it. No hatred or dislike either, somehow. The men did seem like seelies though, and the seelies didn't despise me the way the unseelies did.

"Fate is only a small factor in a relationship," I admitted. "It's something that draws you together, but you can choose to ignore it. If you want your fated mate to give you a chance, you have to get to know her and learn to understand her. And if she says no, you have to try again. Not if she says no to something physical—that shit isn't a boundary you should ever push. But if she says she doesn't want to talk to you, ask again the next day. And the next. And the next. Persistence shows a woman that you mean what you feel, and that you're not going to change your mind."

The men nodded, some looking thoughtful.

"And that brings us to lesson one," January said. "Friendship. Start with friendship, always. The foundation for any real, genuine relationship is always friendship. If you build on sex, or fate, or anything else, it could crumble in a heartbeat. What you need is to know each other."

"How do I get to know her, though?" one of the men countered.

January launched into an explanation about dates, reminding me of what Teris had said about our *human date* earlier, and my lips curved upward.

. . .

THE OTHER MEN arrived shortly after our conversation began. All of them, except Teris. I tried to hide my worry at the fact that he wasn't with the others, but wasn't sure I pulled it off.

Lian launched into a story about one of his and January's first arguments, though, and laughter rolled through all of us. It was impossible not to be entertained by them, and their massive grins as they told the story together only made it more fun to hear.

I kept looking at the trees for Teris.

One of the unmated male fae was halfway through explaining an awkward situation he'd landed himself in with his fated mate—awkward enough that we were all laughing—when Teris finally slipped through the trees.

The man gestured with his hands as he continued the story, and since I was standing right next to him, he nearly touched me.

It wasn't a big deal at all, and wouldn't have even *mattered*, if Teris hadn't shifted and been striding toward me.

While I laughed with another man.

Who had almost touched me.

I saw it in his eyes when the possessiveness snapped. His mind went into an animalistic mode, and he lunged toward the man talking.

I usually wasn't one to throw myself into a fight.

Usually, I backed the hell off before it ever got anywhere near that.

But the way Teris moved and the fury in his eyes, made me snap, too.

I threw myself between the sabertooth and the other fae. His body crashed into mine and he rolled us in the air, so he hit the ground instead of me.

He was snarling, and when he rolled back over the top of me, I knew he was still going to attack the other guy.

I threw my legs around his ass, pinning him to me as I grabbed his face. His chest was heaving, his eyes wild enough to tell me that all logic and control had left the building.

He had warned me this might happen, when he told me not to talk to other men. And I'd known he was mostly serious—I just hadn't expected everything to go down so quickly.

I knew the other women were probably right that the possessiveness would fade some with time, too. But there was so much baggage between me and Teris. He had to have still been feeling the pain of my rejection all those years ago, even though I'd explained that I hadn't actually rejected him.

I knew that, because I was still feeling the pain of him not coming after me, too. Knowing the truth didn't make those feelings vanish. It didn't cure the years I'd spent alone, hurting, and wondering.

And it didn't change his feelings or experiences either.

As much as I would've liked to believe we'd worked through all that shit, I knew we really hadn't. The only thing that could ease the pain of those experiences was time.

If we could hole up together without seeing or talking to anyone else for a few weeks, we'd get there faster. But with the monsters in the skies, and the creatures still wandering in Vevol somewhere, I knew that wasn't going to happen.

"Smell me," I ordered Teris.

He snarled in response, but didn't fight against my hold. He didn't want to hurt me, even in his wildest and most out-of-control state.

Not willing to wait for some amount of sanity to strike him, I grabbed his face and dragged it to my neck. His nose met my skin, barely, and he inhaled deeply.

His body relaxed almost instantly when he caught his own scent on my skin, and not even a tiny whiff of anyone else's. I hadn't touched any of the other women, or hugged them; it was just me, and Teris.

"I'm yours," I told him, much more quietly. "And you're mine. Remember?"

He growled, low and rumbly.

I ran my hands over his shoulders and back, slowly.

His breathing evened out and his chest stopped heaving, until finally, he stood. When he did, he pulled me up with him, holding me to his chest. I turned my head enough to see a few of the girls, all of them grinning widely. Their mates had taken them back a ways, putting enough distance between them and Teris that the women were safe. Not that he would've ever hurt them, anyway.

The unmated men seemed to have left, though I would've put money on most of them lingering to watch what happened from the trees.

The other women gave me thumbs-ups as Teris strode away with me, lifting me higher so my chin found his shoulder as he gripped my ass and thighs securely.

The walk back to our place took a bit longer in human form, but neither of us said a thing as we went. His grip was tight, and I didn't need to feel his emotions to know he was battling frustration with himself, and probably guilt for attacking the other man without a real reason.

We were still silent as he climbed into his cave—our cave?

When his feet hit the ground, the door was shut, the room cool and silent.

Teris set me down on the bed, and then silently strode into the bathroom.

The door shut behind him, hard.

And I felt like there was a hell of a lot more distance between us than there had been before that fight. Honestly, it felt like we were back in that forest, with him following me from the trees without saying a damn word to me.

And I hated that.

My instincts told me to shut down. To stay silent, and ignore him, until the problems faded.

But my instincts had never gotten me anywhere worth going, so I ignored them and walked to the bathroom door.

My ear pressed to the wood, and I listened as the shower turned on.

He probably had some dried blood on his hands, and maybe the rest of him too. I hadn't looked closely enough to know, after being caught off-guard earlier.

Though I itched to step into his shower and insist he needed to talk to me, I didn't know him as well as I used to. I didn't know if he was the kind of person who needed time to think through his emotions, or if he'd feel better after we talked.

I wasn't going to shut down, or shut him out...

But I would let him take his shower in peace, and then we would talk about what had happened.

With that decided, I crossed back over to the bed and sat down on the mattress. I contemplated stripping, knowing that would change the mood from angry and stressful to something much hotter.

Sex wouldn't get us through the conversation we needed to have, though. It would only be a distraction, and one we didn't need.

Not yet, anyway.

So I slipped my legs under the blankets, propping my back up against the wall at the head of the bed.

I waited while Teris showered. He wasn't in there too long—definitely less than ten minutes. Maybe only five.

When he stepped out, he had a towel wrapped around his waist. Though he was clean, he didn't seem any more relaxed than he'd been a few minutes earlier.

He sat down on the edge of the bed without removing the towel. His hair was wet, and he ran a hand through it, sending it up in a bunch of messy spikes.

A long, silent moment passed before he finally spoke.

"I'm sorry, Nai. I fucked up, and I don't even know why I did. You weren't touching him, or flirting with him, or even really looking at him. It shouldn't have set me off. I feel like absolute shit."

My heart ached at the rawness in his voice.

I leaned over the edge of the bed and put a hand on top of his thigh. There was a towel between our skin, but I didn't care. He didn't take my hand, though.

"It was all instinct, Ter. I saw it in your eyes; the reaction was automatic. We're mated, but there's still a lot of shit in our pasts that we haven't really settled. It'll take time for us to get there. I don't blame you for reacting, and neither does anyone else."

"I blame me," he growled back.

"You're not perfect. No one is. If I saw you laughing with some random human girl, I'd probably get all defensive too."

"You wouldn't *attack* her."

"No, but I'd hate her so intensely that it'd be pretty much the same thing."

He scowled. "It's not."

"Did you hate the other guy, in that moment?" I asked.

His scowl deepened, but he didn't answer immediately.

"You didn't hate him," I said for Teris. "You just saw something that made you feel strongly, and you reacted. He didn't get hurt. I didn't get hurt. The other girls seemed pretty damn entertained. No one is upset with you, except you."

He let out a frustrated breath, taking my hand off his thigh and lifting it to his lips. He brushed a kiss to my knuckles. "I'm sorry I tackled you."

"I happen to enjoy being tackled by you."

He gave me the smallest, most grudging smile. "Smartass."

"Thought I was a queen?" I shot back.

Teris brushed his lips to my knuckles again. "You'll always be that to me, Nai."

I leaned back against the bed, and he slid up the mattress until he was laying next to me, with his head resting halfway on my lap. One of his hands explored my knee, moving slowly over my skin, and I slipped my fingers into his soft, wet hair.

"How did the fight go?" I asked him. He seemed tired—really tired.

"Fine. Killed some dragon-monsters. Didn't drink their blood this time."

"Probably a good call." My voice was soft, and slightly playful. "I'm surprised you didn't come back grinning, on an adrenaline high."

"Fighting doesn't hold the same appeal now that I have you," he admitted. "I can think of far more interesting ways to blow off steam."

My face heated. "Like cooking, you mean?"

"Mmhm." His lips seemed to curve upward slightly, though I could only see the side of his face. "Cleaning, too."

"Obviously. Everyone loves a good cleaning session."

"Yup." He continued stroking my knee slowly. "I stopped to talk to Aeven and Dakota, afterward."

My stomach clenched. "That's why you were later than the other guys."

"Yeah. I promised you I would."

"Do they hate me?" I asked him quietly.

"Nah. They're in a love-bubble. If they hold anything against either of us, they're doing a damn good job of not showing it. I don't think we've got anything to worry about."

That made me feel slightly better. Only slightly, though.

"I talked to the other mated girls for a while," I admitted.

He continued tracing circles on my knee, venturing up my thigh a little every now and then.

"I realized I'm still carrying around a lot of guilt from everything with Aev," I said softly. "I know you think it's stupid, but after the way the goddess showed me everything from his perspective... I don't know. I still feel like a horrible person sometimes."

He brushed his lips against my knee. "You know you're not."

"I know. He didn't pursue me, and he could've tried a lot harder than he did too. But I still *feel* bad."

"It wasn't long ago that the goddess showed you everything, so it's still raw. As time passes, you'll start to accept what happened, and you'll learn to let go."

"I hope so."

"I know so." He nipped lightly at my knee with his teeth, making me fight a smile. "I realized something, while I was talking to Aeven."

My smile faded, and my stomach clenched. "What?"

"He's a really *nice* guy. Soft. Sweet. Kind. A lot of things I'm not. Fate and the goddess thought you needed someone like that."

I scowled. "That's just bullshit."

"It's not, Nai."

I used my grip on his hair to tilt his head back so he was looking at me, into my eyes. "You're nice to the people who matter to you—and there are so damn many better qualities to have than *nice*. You're soft with me when I need you to be, and you always have been. You get sweet when I do, which is rare. And you're kind enough to walk away from your new mate to defend the Stronghold while the unmated fae are *competing to mate with the fae women*, which makes you a damn hero in my book."

I went on, nearly to the point of ranting, "More importantly than any of that shit, you're loyal to a fault. You love fiercely, and breathtakingly. You protect the people who matter to you with everything you have. Why would you want to be *nice* when you can claim all of that?"

He considered it, his eyes closing as I resumed stroking his hair. "I just worry I won't be able to make you happy," he murmured.

"Well you already have, so you can check that one off the list." I tugged lightly on his hair, and his eyes opened.

"Happiness isn't something you can check off a list once and be done with, Nai."

"Then I guess you'll just have to fuck me every day, so you can check it off." I made a checkmark motion on his forehead, and his lips stretched in a tired grin.

"I fucking love you."

"I know you do." I slid my finger down his nose, and slowly traced his lips. He parted them for me, closing his eyes as I touched them. "Does it bother you that I can't say the same thing yet?"

"No." He nipped at my finger. "You didn't love me quickly or easily the first time around. I expect to have to earn it again this time. You're mine; that's enough for now. I'll win you over eventually."

My lips curved upward, and he sucked on my finger for a moment before he released it, letting me get back to work on tracing those lips I loved so much.

He hadn't felt that way with Summer, when their bond existed. He wasn't willing to wait for her to fall in love with him.

And yet he would wait for me, as long as he needed to. "I love talking to you," I admitted.

"Oh, I know." He nipped at my finger again, and I laughed.

Thirteen

"I promised you a date," Teris said, peeling himself up off of me and sitting up. I released his hair—though I did so with great reluctance.

We'd done a lot of *human dates* when we'd first met. After I'd explained them to Teris, he'd been fascinated by the concept of doing something together for fun, while getting to know each other. We'd been restrained to my house back then, but we'd made it happen by cooking together and spending hours playing both fae and human card games.

"I thought I was going to cook for you."

"I changed my mind." He tugged his towel free, and my eyes fixated on the sexy bubble of his ass as he strode back into the bathroom. His erection saluted me as he strolled back out with his pants dangling from his fingers. "Mind cleaning these for me?"

"What do I get in return?" I asked, snagging them from him and making a show of studying the fabric.

His eyes gleamed. "A surprise."

"You know I'm a sucker for surprises," I said with a sigh, lighting the pants on fire and then tossing them back. The fire went out before he caught them, and I slid my hand over his erection slowly, earning a low growl. "But we could just stay here, and enjoy the night..."

He pulled my hand off his cock, though the motion was slightly reluctant. "Patience, Nai."

"Not one of my best qualities."

He chuckled, stepping into his pants and tugging them on. "I'm aware."

I smacked him lightly on the arm with the back of my hand, and his lips stretched in a grin.

After he fastened his pants, he tugged me to his chest and scooped me up off the ground, hauling me toward the doorway out.

"You're a tease," I grumbled at him. "Getting all naked and then insisting on a surprise date should be illegal."

"This is a unique opportunity. Any other time, and I would've dragged you back to bed in a heartbeat. Just trust me, baby." His voice was playful, and damn, I was a sucker when he got like that.

I sighed dramatically anyway. "Fine, fine."

He chuckled, the noise rumbling his chest as he shifted forms. My fingers gripped his fur as he streaked into the trees, and I held on tightly as he carried me past dozens of other fae. A lot of them seemed to be headed in the same direction we were going.

"What are we doing?" I asked him, curiously. It felt strange to speak through our bond after so many hours of silence, and I decided I needed to use it more often.

"You'll see." His response was filled with humor.

My curiosity only grew thicker when Teris joined a whole host of fae on what was basically a net of thick tree branches. There were at least a hundred males and a few dozen ex-human females seated on the crisscrossing branches, with their feet dangling down as their peered down at whatever was below them.

He found an empty seat and shifted back, sitting me down next to him and tucking me up against his side. *"I heard that the female fae's competitions were something of a spectacle, so someone built an observation area here."*

Ohh.

"They're not just telling the men to go at it until one of them wins?" I asked, curiosity thickening as I looked down at the fae beneath us. There was a huge group of men running through some kind of maze-like obstacle-course, with a pond in the center that looked like it held something dangerous. Some female fae hid behind some of the obstacles.

"No. Apparently, different female fae are looking for males with different strengths. Some prefer the men who can strategize. Others want a male who doesn't get angry when things don't work out. A few are looking for the males who slide under the radar, with quiet strength."

Understanding flooded me.

"They decided which characteristic mattered most to them, and that's what they're choosing a mate based on."

"Seems like it."

I cringed as one of the males got hit in the face with something huge and heavy—and saw one of the fae women grinning when he got back to his feet clumsily.

Persistence for the win.

Teris and I cheered along with the rest of the fae when the grinning fae woman sprinted through the maze, dodging obstacles smoothly before reaching the man. He halted when he saw her—and caught her when she launched herself into his arms.

Whoops filled the trees around us when their lips collided in the world's most awkward first kiss. They relaxed into each other's arms, and the whooping grew louder when they went from kissing to full-on making out.

PDA was totally cool in Vevol, I guess.

Teris dragged me closer, planting a kiss on my forehead. I flashed him a grin, and he kissed my mouth too.

More cheering erupted around us, and Teris deepened the kiss, cupping my face as our tongues warred. My cheeks were flushed and my breathing was fast when I finally pulled away, and he rested his forehead against mine, grinning at me while we caught our breath.

I loved it.

Maybe I even loved *him*.

I couldn't say that aloud, though.

Or even think it. Not until I was sure. I refused to hurt him any more than I already had.

"Look around us, Nai," he told me.

I let out a long breath, but finally pulled my head away from Teris's. When I looked at the men and women surrounding us on the viewing net, I realized why he'd wanted me to look.

Because no one was glaring at us.

They were smiling.

Grinning.

They were happy for us.

They'd been cheering for *us*, too.

My eyes stung a little, and Teris captured my hand, sliding his fingers between mine.

Groans went through the group as someone got hit with something below us, and just like that, no one was looking at us at all anymore.

But that warm feeling remained.

"No one hates you, baby," Teris murmured to me. *"Don't let fear make you believe that. None of these other women would be here if you hadn't come first. You paved the way for all of them. Because of you, we have peace now."*

"January did that," I said quietly, my eyes still stinging and my emotions intense.

"No. She ignited the change, but the women were only a family because of you. They only lived in the Stronghold because you insisted the seelies build it. There would've been nothing for January to change, if not for you."

My eyes stung more.

Rather than fighting with him, I just nodded.

I needed to stop denying my strength.

I needed to accept that even though I'd done some shitty things, I'd done some good things, too. And the shit didn't outweigh the good, no matter how much it might feel like that.

I had to accept the past, so I could move forward in the present.

So I could start *living* again, for the first time in so long.

An excited cheer erupted from me when one of the men dodged one of the more difficult obstacles, propelling himself into the final portion of the maze.

Teris roared with me when the man crossed the finish line—and even louder when one of the female fae captured him in her arms, kissing the hell out of him.

We spent hours and hours sitting in those branches, holding hands and watching the display together. Someone even brought food for everyone, passing it around so no one had to leave partway through. By the time we headed back to our cave, the sun was going down, and I felt happier than I could ever remember being in my life.

"WELL?" Teris asked, flashing me a grin as we walked hand-in-hand, swinging our arms. The fights were still going on, but no one had come by with food for a while, and our voices were getting hoarse from all the yelling so we'd decided to call it quits. "Was that a good enough date?"

I laughed. "Yes, it was."

"Good." He dragged me closer, tugging his fingers free from mine and draping his arm over my shoulders. "I'm so damn glad to have you with me."

The smile on my face was insanely wide. "Right back at you."

He chuckled. "Let's grab some food before we head back home."

Home.

I loved the way that sounded.

His home didn't feel completely like my own yet, but I was comfortable there. Maybe more comfortable than I'd been anywhere since that first house I'd called mine in Vevol. I'd always felt like I had to walk on tiptoes in the unseelie land; I'd been terrified of pissing someone off, or running into Aeven, or finding myself trapped with one of the men.

Now, I didn't have to fear that.

Or anything, really. Not with Teris next to me.

And I didn't think he'd ever leave me.

We grabbed food, saying a quick hello to the beaming Blue and red-faced Oren, who were working in the kitchen with a few others, and then headed for the only empty table left. The place was packed, and I assumed a bunch of other people got hungry at the same time Teris and I did.

We'd just barely started eating when Ana strolled up to our table. A tall, muscular, blond unseelie followed behind her with a finger looped in the back of her seelie-style shorts. He was Druze, the basilisk fated mate who had been chasing her since she first came to unseelie territory. She'd been giving him hell for such a long time that it made me grin to see her with him willingly.

"Hey. Is it cool if we sit here?" Ana checked, plopping down without waiting for an answer.

I laughed. "Of course."

"Thanks. There's way too much new blood," she grumbled.

Ana hated change more than just about anyone I'd ever met, so I wasn't surprised in the slightest that she wasn't thrilled by all the new ex-humans.

"Congrats," Teris told them, and I didn't miss the way he slid a little bit closer to me. Our sides were already pressed together, so we couldn't really get any closer.

"You too," Druze said, with a tip of his head and a small grin.

I inhaled, and my eyebrows shot upward as I looked at Ana. "He finally convinced you?"

"I made an offer she couldn't refuse," Druze corrected, smirking.

She smacked him on the arm, and he chuckled.

Ana admitted, "I got tired of fighting him on it, and decided to focus my anger with him in more enjoyable ways. I know, I know, the mighty have fallen. Rosalie gives me shit for it constantly. At least I'm not alone, though. We're falling like flies. Rose and Devv, Blue and Oren... Hell, even Presley already ended up in Korrik's bed."

I grinned. "She didn't make him chase her for long."

"Exactly my thought." Ana pointed her fork at me. "And you... keeping this a secret for two decades?" She gestured between me and Teris with that fork. "Impressive. Really damn impressive. You should be proud."

Teris snorted, and my grin widened. "Thanks, I think."

The four of us chatted as we ate, and I found out from Druze that the old unseelie council were enjoying their lives a hell of a lot more now that they weren't in leadership positions. That honestly didn't surprise me at all.

When we finished, we excused ourselves, and walked back to our cave with our fingers tangled and our shoulders brushing.

I was tired, but in a way I absolutely loved. A day spent with friends, enjoying my life... well, I hadn't had a day like that in way too long.

"Thank you for today," I told Teris, staring up at the sky through the trees. If there had been any more dragon attacks, they hadn't been a big enough deal for anyone to hunt Teris down and drag him back to the fight, which I appreciated.

"I should be the one thanking you." He lifted our connected hands and brushed a kiss to my knuckles. "You've made my life feel worth living again, Nai."

My heart about melted at that. "And you've done the same for me."

He kissed my knuckles again, dragging his tongue over them slowly, and warming my body in the process.

We reached the house soon enough, and Teris climbed in first. When I was near the bottom, he plucked me off the ladder and into his arms, hugging me fiercely tight. When he set me down on my feet, I stretched my arms out, yawning. "I'm ready for bed."

"Since when do you go to sleep early?" Teris teased me, grabbing the bottom hem of my tank top and tugging at it playfully.

"Since I spent so many days flying aimlessly through the mountains, looking for a cave, while some sexy sabertooth stalked me," I tossed back.

He grinned. "That guy sounds hot."

"I mean, if you're into chiseled abs, soft hair, and big dicks..."

Teris laughed, the sound rich and genuine. He tugged my tank top over my head, and tossed it to the ground, still grinning as he skimmed his fingertips over my nipples. They hardened for him, and my body heated. "If you're going to bed in our place, you're going naked. No clothes allowed." His fingers looped in the top of my shorts, and he tugged them down my thighs.

"Sounds like a rule I can support." I remarked, stepping out of my shorts. When he stood, I unfastened his pants and wrapped my hand around his erection. I squeezed him, and earned a low growl for doing so while he pushed his pants down those insanely-strong thighs.

"Is sleeping all you have in mind?"

"That depends if my sabertooth stalker plans on ravaging me or not, I suppose." I released his cock, turning and striding toward the bed.

Fourteen

Teris swept me off my feet and carried my ass to the bed. Rather than tossing me onto the mattress, he dropped me onto my back, keeping ahold of my knees and using them to open me for him. I propped myself up on my elbows in time to watch him kneel in front of me, and my breath stopped in my throat at the sight.

His eyes collided with me. "You're mine, Nai. In every fucking way."

I jerked my head in a nod, lust swelling in me. He maintained eye contact as he lowered his lips to my core. A shudder rolled through me as he slowly dragged the tip of his tongue over the sensitive bud of my clit.

The feeling was unreal.

Absolutely, insanely unreal.

Hot, and wet, and perfect.

I was shaking—shaking desperately.

"You're so damn delicious," he growled at me, lifting his hot, hooded eyes back to mine.

I couldn't even make a sound as he slowly dragged the tip of his tongue over me again—and then in a slow circle around my clit.

My hips jerked.

He pinned them down, trapping me in the absolute best way. "No moving, Nai. I get to enjoy you as slow as I want."

I groaned, and he flicked the tip of his tongue over my clit again, making me fight his grip as my body tried to arch again.

"You're so needy, baby." He brushed the rough side of his face against my inner thigh, then lowered his nose to my core and inhaled deeply. "Fuck. I could get off at just the smell of you."

"Better not," I growled.

He chuckled, low and deep, and slowly, lightly, dragged his tongue around my clit again. "No. I'm not going to lose control until I'm buried so deep inside you that you've forgotten what it feels like not to have me there."

He dragged his tongue over me again—a little harder. The sensation grew more intense, and all words died in my throat. My hands twisted in the blankets on the bed, and Teris released my hips long enough to lift my fingers into his hair. I buried them in the soft strands, gripping and pulling and yanking as he slowly made love to me with his tongue. The pleasure built fast —too fast.

And I was crying out, losing control with a jerk of my hips, a moment later.

Teris's chest rumbled with satisfaction as I came down from the high, and he pulled back, stroking my hot, swollen flesh slowly while he waited for me to recover. His eyes lifted back to mine, and when he stared at me, I stared right back.

"You're the sexiest thing I've ever seen," he told me, and the words were so much more intimate when he spoke them into my mind like that.

"You're so damn gorgeous," I murmured back, tugging on his hair in an attempt to pull him back up my body.

He didn't budge—instead, he sent me a mental image of me, riding his face.

My lips parted in an o-shape, and he continued stroking my clit slowly with his fingers, sliding down to my slit and teasing the entrance every now and then.

"I'm far from done with you," he said.

If I hadn't already been a pile of hot, gooey pleasure, I would've flushed at his words. *"I haven't gotten you off yet."*

"You want me to lose it, you just say the word," he slid a thick finger inside me, just an inch, and I clenched around him. *"All it'll take is one damn stroke, while*

I've got this pretty little clit in my mouth." He lowered his lips back to my core, and sucked lightly.

I bucked against his face, and he gave me another rumbly chuckle as he pinned my ass back down, pinching it in retribution.

He continued sucking my clit, lighter and then harder, alternating, as he slid that finger inside me, slowly. I was desperate for it—for him.

"I want you inside me," I panted, as the pleasure started to build again.

"Not until I've had you on my face." He squeezed my ass with the hand holding me in place.

I groaned, fighting his grip as my hips tried to arch again, and again. He flashed me a mental image of the way he'd soaked my core with his pleasure, so damn long ago. I didn't think it was intentional, but I gasped and arched at the sight anyway. "I want that. Give me that."

He snarled, sliding his finger out of me. I hated the loss of that—but my frustration faded quickly when my mate rose to his feet, wrapping his fist around his cock. I'd drenched his hand already, and when he dragged it down his length, I fought a moan.

My hips jerked against his hold, and he watched me with hot eyes as he stroked himself once, and then again. With the third, he lost control, snarling as he drenched me.

Holy shit. Holy shit. Holy shit.

He rubbed a hand over my core and the insides of my thighs, coating more of me with his pleasure as his chest heaved.

I watched in hot, needy silence as he pushed the pleasure inside me with his finger, sliding it back inside me and stroking my walls lightly.

My desire turned to desperation as he fucked me with his finger, and when he kneeled back down and slid another one in, I was so damn close.

"Can't fucking wait to taste both of us together," he growled against my core, meeting my gaze again for a hot moment as he lowered his tongue back to me.

He dragged it slowly over my clit—so slowly—but it was enough to set me off.

I cried out, and he finally let my hips arch and rock as I rode his fingers and face. The orgasm was fiercely intense, and I gasped for air as the last few aftershocks rolled through me.

"Good girl. That was so damn good, baby," he said. "Are you ready to ride my face?"

I groaned, and he chuckled, easing his fingers out of me while mental images ran through his mind.

My tits, bouncing above him.

My ass, in his hands.

My swollen flesh, on his lips, teeth, and stubble.

He was on the bed in the next heartbeat, dragging me up off the mattress. I fell forward when he held my core over his face but caught myself on the mattress. Insecurity hit me hard; what if he didn't like the way I looked over him? What if he didn't like the way I was trapping him? What if—

"This smell is everything," he growled into my core, tasting and smelling both of our pleasure again. "And the taste… You're going to kill me, Nai. Move those hips for me like you've been dying to."

His tongue slowly moved over me, and my hips arched.

His hands were on my ass, opening me up wider for him when he started devouring me, and I found myself moving. Swiveling. Rocking. The pleasure was building up again, hotter and needier.

I was in control, and I absolutely loved it.

"You're close, baby," he practically purred against my core. "Let go for me. Show me how good I make you feel."

The orgasm took control, and I bucked against his face, crying out in pleasure as he sucked me and touched me and bit me.

It went on so damn long, I was dazed when I came down from the high.

"That was so damn good, Nai. You were perfect." He lifted me off his face, moving me until my palms were braced against the wall. "Now you're going to take me inside you, and you're going to tell me how good it feels. Ready?"

I moaned. I think it was confirmation. It definitely wasn't a no.

He lifted my ass up, parting my legs and my folds as he seated my slit against the head of his cock. My breathing stopped as he slowly slid inside me, stroking my clit while he entered me.

"That's it, baby," he growled against my ear, as he entered me. "You take me so damn well, and you're so damn wet for me. Feel me stretching you? Feel every thick inch of me pushing you open for me?"

"Yes," I breathed.

"Tell me how it feels, or I stop here, halfway inside you," he said.

I clenched around him, and he pinched my clit in retaliation.

"It's incredible. Full—really full. You're huge," I managed.

"That's right." His approval was thick and hot, and he continued sliding deeper inside me. He was moving slow to drive me mad—and it was working.

"Stop teasing me already," I groaned back.

His chest rumbled against my back as he opened my thighs wider, and sank the rest of the way inside me.

It was unreal.

Absolutely unreal.

My breath escaped in rough, frantic pants.

He was so thick.

So hot.

Throbbing inside me, telling me how much he loved it.

"You're so fucking good for me." The words sounded primal, nearly feral. "I'm going to erupt in you, and you're going to shatter on my cock. And then we're going to keep going—because neither of us is ready for this to be over. Don't even think about pulling away from me. Alright?"

"You're so damn bossy," I shot back, my hips already rocking and jerking.

"And you love it." He reached up, grabbing one of breasts and squeezing tightly.

I cried out, moving desperately up and down his thick erection. He was right; I loved him bossy.

"That's it, baby. Scream for me." Teris sucked my nipple, hard, and the orgasm felt like a damn explosion.

I screamed, and he released my tit, grabbing my hips and moving me, slamming into me hard and rough and fierce.

His snarls and the eruption of his hot pleasure inside me heightened my own orgasm, and he bucked my hips for me, dragging it out forever.

When the pleasure finally faded, I collapsed forward, my cheek hitting the wall as I tried to catch my breath. I was absolutely boneless—but Teris was already stroking my clit again, softly because it was so damn oversensitive.

"I don't think I can go any longer," I moaned to him, exhaustion weighing down my limbs.

"You're going to give me one more, baby. I can feel it." His growl made my face scrunch up, and I clenched around his erection. "It'll be soft, Nai. A soft release, to relax you, and fill you completely."

"You've already got me full," I moaned back.

"Not yet." He slid out of me, and I cried out at the emptiness. He stroked my core gently as he eased me away from the wall, turning me to my back and lowering me to the mattress. "You're going to sleep with me inside you, after this," he growled to me. "I want you dreaming about my cock, so you can wake up and ride it again as soon as you're ready."

"Sounds intese."

"It'll be the best fucking night of your life."

He wasn't wrong.

Not even a little.

He slid back inside me, his erection still hard and ready to go. And when he started fucking me again, it didn't feel like fucking at all. The motions were slow, and deep, and smooth. So damn intense.

I was absolutely, completely relaxed when I'd finally ridden out that final orgasm, and Teris rolled slightly to the side, remaining on top of me and inside me without crushing me.

"You made love to me," I whispered, as I started to fall asleep.

"Mmhm." He slid a hand up to my breast, and rested his palm against it. Though he was still hard inside me, when I peeked my eyes open, I could see how relaxed his shoulders were. "That's how we'll end every day for the rest of our lives, Nai. Making love."

"Sounds like a good way to accidentally knock me up," I whispered back.

He chuckled, softly. "Wouldn't break my heart."

My lips curved upward slightly, and I admitted something quietly that I'd never said aloud. "I'd love to have a baby."

He squeezed my breast lightly. "Maybe you should stop eating lilanos in the next few months."

Maybe I should.

I drifted off to sleep with a mental image of Teris holding a tiny baby girl, and it was one I didn't think I could ever forget.

FIFTEEN

TERIS WAS RIGHT; two hours later, I woke up aching for a release. He growled about how perfect I was while I rode his cock, and then we went back to sleep.

An hour later, he woke me up with his fingers between my thighs and his cock thrusting in and out of me slowly. We fell back asleep again as soon as we were done—but he woke me up the same way another hour later.

By the time the morning came around, my body was so damn sated that I could barely think, let alone sleep.

Teris carried me to the bathroom and made love to me one last time in the shower, before we washed each other. When we finally made it out, someone was knocking on our door again.

Teris kissed me before climbing the ladder and opening that door.

"A host of dragons are on their way," a male fae said solemnly. "They've got phoenixes flying with them, this time—and the phoenixes are carrying hellhounds in their talons."

Shit.

"An army?" Teris asked, voice low.

Before the man could confirm it, I heard footsteps on the dirt as someone landed next to the guy. "I saw your creatures, in the distance. An hour away, at most," Presley said. Her voice was breathy, like she was breathing fast.

"We'll meet them long before they reach us," Teris said. "How many dragons and phoenixes?"

"More than we can count," the male fae admitted.

Shit.

Panic swelled in my chest.

"We'll guide the creatures back to the battle after we've figured out how to lead them. Between us, them, and the klynnas, it should be an easy fight. How far is the army?" Teris asked.

"A little over an hour, at our best guess."

"Plenty of time, then." My mate's voice was way calmer than it should've been. Maybe he wasn't worried, but I sure as hell was. "Have the female fae called off their competitions so they can join the fight?"

"They have."

"Good. Let everyone know that we'll be coming with backup soon enough."

The man didn't protest, though I thought he sure as hell should've.

Teris climbed down the ladder and looked at me. "We're going to be just fine, Nai. The goddess gave you the magic because she knew you were strong enough to control it."

"She gave me the magic because she was too weak to connect with anyone else," I shot back.

He crossed the room, taking my face between his hands and tilting it back so he was looking down at me, and I was looking up at him. I wanted to hate the contact, but I loved it. "She could've told you to send someone else. She could've asked you to bring someone else with you. She could've given up altogether, too. And yet she decided to give the magic to you, Nai. Because you are a damn *Queen*. Don't forget it."

I opened my mouth to protest, but he kissed me, then. Firmly, but gently.

And then he pulled away and swept me off my feet.

We were out of our cave and running through the forest a moment later, with me leaning up against his neck and gripping his fur for dear life.

I WAS SO damn tense that a few minutes after we started running, Teris realized he needed to distract me.

"My mated brothers were talking about their bonds a few weeks ago," Teris said into my mind. *"They mentioned something that sounds interesting."*

My tension faded slightly. He knew he had me. *"What did they say?"*

"There's a way to temporarily break through the wall separating our minds," he explained. *"Apparently, it makes for really great sex."*

I snorted. *"I don't think we need any help on that front."*

He chuckled. *"Want to try it tonight?"*

My humor faded. *"Assuming we're still alive tonight?"*

"We'll be fine, Nai. Trust me."

"I do. Mostly. Ish."

"Your confidence is inspiring," he drawled, and I heard the humor in his voice.

"Tell me about the last twenty years," I said quietly. *"I feel like I missed so much."*

"You really didn't. They were lonely years." His voice grew quieter, too. *"To have everything, and then lose it all to the unseelie king... it was a lot to cope with. I made decisions I'll regret for the rest of my life."*

My throat swelled.

Though my initial feelings that followed his words were guilt, I tried to push through them. Teris's pain wasn't my fault any more than it was his fault. We had a misunderstanding, on both sides.

"What happened?"

"I'd rather not discuss it," he admitted.

Oh.

I didn't push him anymore.

I understand not wanting to talk about things; some things were hard.

A few minutes passed, and the tension in my chest grew. I was worrying about Teris's past, now, on top of the creatures I was going to have to deal with.

"I harmed myself," Teris finally said, his voice barely above a whisper, even in my mind. *"It was the lowest I have ever been, and the worst I have ever felt. None of my brothers knew; I clawed back from the darkness before I did any permanent damage to myself. I'm stronger now, because of that hell I survived. I know how to cope with the dark emotions, now."*

My eyes stung. *"I'm so sorry."*

"It wasn't your fault, Nai. You didn't know any better than I did."

"I wish I'd just swallowed my pride and used your name. Everything would've been so different." My tears fell into Teris's fur, and I gripped him tighter.

"Holding on to the pain of the past brings nothing but misery and regret, and I don't want you miserable, Nai. I want you happier than you've ever been, feeling more alive than you've ever felt. I am who I am now because of what I survived, the same way you are."

"I don't even know how I've changed. Or if I've changed. Or how to accept any of it," I admitted.

"You're more cautious than you used to be. More uncertain of yourself, too. But I'll train you out of that uncertainty soon enough. The caution, we should probably keep. I think I could use a little of that in my life."

I sputtered a laugh, and felt his soft chuckle in my mind.

"Tell me about your last two decades," he said.

"I spent almost all of my time indoors. Played a lot of card games with the other ex-humans. Spent a lot of time testing how to cook with plants I'd never seen before. Made a lot of nasty food, but choked it down. Avoided a lot of men. That's pretty much it, to be honest," I admitted. *"I spent a lot of time crying, at the beginning. And I refused to fly with the other women, most of the time, so I could've learned more if I tried. But I just didn't want to."*

"You were taken there against your will. They should've seen that and realized you were unhappy," Teris said quietly.

"Everyone made mistakes. Luckily, it's in the past. Now, no one will ever screw up again." My voice got playful.

He chuckled into my mind, then said, *"We're getting close. Try to tap into the magic the goddess left you with. I don't feel it in myself—only a small strain, coming from the bond."*

"Okay." I closed my eyes and tried to find the magic. I'd felt it before, when it was draining the life from me in that cave. And that feeling was still within me, just barely. But I hadn't found the mass of it, yet.

I focused as Teris ran, following the trail of it alongside the magic that used to be Vevol's, but was now mine.

The snarls and howls of the creatures we were running toward slowly filled the air as I finally found the source of that magic in my chest.

It had a pulse; that's why it was still slightly draining. The magic was *alive*.

Vevol had told me I would be the heart of the creatures, but I hadn't realized that meant I would literally be keeping them alive, with their pulse in my chest.

"Ready?" Teris asked me, his voice alert and unafraid.

"Ready." I steeled myself for the fight that might be coming.

The creatures were alive. They had minds, and hearts, and willpower. They wouldn't obey my exact orders; they would follow me, if I led them properly.

Because I really was a damn queen, just like Teris kept insisting.

"We should call them bears," I told him, *"They're not bears—not really. But they're similar, and since they're new, they deserve an Earth name like the rest of us new fae."*

"Then they're bears," he agreed. "And I hope you know what you're doing, because I really don't want to have to fight however many of these things there are."

My lips curved upward, just slightly. "I don't know what I'm doing… but we'll figure it out."

Teris groaned, but I trusted him to believe me.

And so he ran toward the crowd of bears.

THEY WERE ALL TOGETHER, moving in a pack. I wondered if maybe I should've named them after wolves, because of their apparent pack-tendencies, but decided to stick with the name I'd given them.

The ones at the front stopped when they saw me and Teris, but they didn't snarl at us, or move to attack us.

They simply halted, and then stared at us.

And the rest of the creatures followed suit.

"Hot damn," I murmured into Teris's mind.

There were *so* many of them.

"They smell your scent on me, and the power of our bond," Teris said. *"They won't attack us."*

"But will they follow us?" I asked him quietly.

He didn't have an answer for that one.

I slid off his back when he paused in front of the massive group of creatures. Though he growled a warning—and protest—into my mind, he didn't command me to climb back on top of him.

He knew I had to deal with the creatures, and respected that.

...though something told me I'd be getting a lecture about my safety after I figured out the magic.

"You were created to protect the fae and creatures of Vevol," I called out to the beasts, tapping into the magic beating inside me. I didn't know why, but something told me that they were waiting for a purpose. That they knew they'd been created for something, but were lost as to what that something was.

I felt their souls settle, as that information sank in.

"Vevol is under attack," I said, raising my voice again when I felt sure they understood the first part. "There are creatures coming this way without our land's magic in their veins. We need you to protect our people. To defend them, and our land. Can you help us?" I asked them.

Their response was a roar; a unanimous answer.

This was what they'd been created for.

This was why they existed.

They would fight our battles at our side—and we would win.

I slipped back onto Teris's back, and when he streaked into the trees, the bears followed at his heels.

"Sorry if I scared you," I murmured to the man, as I dug my hands into his fur.

"I'm never going to be comfortable with you putting yourself in danger," he grumbled at me. *"But I understand why you did. They seemed receptive to what you said, too."*

"Yeah. They were waiting for me to tell them why they existed. Now that they know, I don't think they need a leader at all."

"Still trying to be free of your title?" Teris drawled.

My lips curved upward. *"Nah. You'll never let me be free of it."*

He chuckled. *"Nope. You'll always be the queen to me."*

"I would look pretty damn good with a crown."

"Without a doubt." He turned his head to the side just long enough to lick my knee, making me laugh. The wind whipped the sound away, but the happiness I felt was overwhelmingly blissful.

THE SKY WAS full of fae by the time we reached the battle.

Female fae fought aside males—some in beast form fighting with fire and talons, and some with their nails shifted to claws as they threw themselves at the creatures in the sky and ripped into them on their way to the ground.

The klynnas were absolute beasts, burning and destroying hoards of the invaders at a time. But there were so damn many of them—and they just kept coming.

The bears threw themselves into the fight, and had no problems or fear when it came to launching themselves from the branches, catching the creatures by the ribs, legs, or throat, and dragging them to the ground. Since Vevol had created them to protect us, I assumed they couldn't be poisoned by the creatures' blood.

When I looked down, I saw another battle on the ground—the army of smaller, crueller-looking hellhounds, fighting the fae without wings who weren't on the backs of the flying fae.

"I'm going to drop you somewhere safe," Teris growled into my mind.

My stomach clenched.

I wanted to help, somehow, but I wasn't a fighter. I'd only be one more body for Teris to worry about. Even if I remained on his back, there was a risk I'd get hurt, in which case he'd lose his ever-loving mind and drop out of the fight.

So as much as it pained me, I agreed.

He dropped me off in a safe crook between a few tree branches, and then disappeared into the forest, joining the fight.

"Talk to me when you need to," he rumbled to me, before he focused on the fight.

I clutched the tree like it was an anchor, and prayed to whatever gods still existed in our world that Teris would be okay.

Sixteen

Teris

The fight was over faster than I expected, even knowing how much manpower we had when we began. I knew that between my brothers and the unseelies, someone would've thrown out the fact that we needed to know where these creatures were coming from, so we could either eliminate the threat or scare them into staying the hell away from us. Clearly, they weren't a match for us, but we didn't want our females living in fear of being attacked.

I found Naomi exactly where I'd left her when the fight was over, thankfully. I shifted when I reached her, and she threw her arms around me, hugging me fiercely tight.

"That was terrifying," she said, as I hugged her back just as tightly. I hadn't been afraid in the slightest, but that didn't diminish her own emotions.

"You're safe, Nai." I brushed my lips over her throat, and then her collarbone, before taking her lips.

She kissed me back, but pulled away a few moments later. "What do we do now?"

My expression grew grim. "We'll have to hunt the ones that got away."

She bit her lip, but nodded.

I pulled her onto my back, and slipped through the trees. The bears were wandering around; most of them seemed to be headed to the nearest river, to clean up. They nodded toward us when they saw us, so I figured they were probably more intelligent than they'd seemed at first, and nodded back at all of them.

"We need to decide, now," Aeven was saying, his voice calm and steady. I shifted back, tucking Naomi to my side. They seemed to be talking to the mated men, which didn't bode well for me.

"I can't leave my female," Lian said.

"I *won't* leave mine," Priel growled.

"No," Ervo said bluntly.

"What's the question?" Naomi checked.

"We need two or three men to leave their mates behind so we can communicate with everyone back here while we follow the monsters," Dakota explained quickly. "The life-bringers have to go, to communicate with their bonded klynnas, and we can't see any men agreeing to stay behind while their mates follow the group. We need men to go who've had enough time to figure out how to communicate, too."

Shit.

Naomi's face paled, but she jerked her head in a nod.

Dakota looked around the group again.

There really weren't many options left.

I looked at Nev.

Typically, he'd be the Wild Hunt member to go.

"My female is pregnant. I can't leave her," he said to me, and everyone else.

My throat swelled, and I looked at Naomi at the same time she whispered into my mind, *"You should go. It would be hard, but I'd be okay."*

"I don't want to," I growled back.

What if one of the males touched her?

What if she changed her mind?

What if...

Dammit, she was right.

She bit her lip, leaving it up to me.

"I can go," I finally said, reluctantly. "We don't struggle to communicate mentally, and Nai isn't pregnant, or plagued with visions."

"We need one more," Aev said, looking at my brothers.

Priel and Ervo glared at each other.

"Do *rock, paper, scissors* already so we can get on with it," Summer grumbled.

The men frowned.

Right.

They probably didn't know rock, paper, scissors."

"They'll both go," Mare said, raising her voice. "Three would be safer, anyway, and you guys are all coming back. Right?" She looked at Ervo.

He glared at her, but she gave him a quick smile, and his glare softened a little.

"Fine," he gritted out.

Priel opened his mouth to say no, but North elbowed him in the side and growled, "He's going."

He growled something back at her, and they glared at each other for a solid thirty seconds before he finally snarled, "Fine."

He yanked her to his chest and kissed her.

Ervo dragged Mare into his arms, taking her mouth as he held her tightly, too.

Nai threw her arms around my neck and hugged me tightly, whispering into my mind, *"You'll only be gone a few days, right?"*

"It damn well better be only a few days."

Nai attempted to stay positive. *"We'll make it. We can talk about all the shit we missed while we're apart. It'll be good for us."*

I really, really hoped so.

"I love you," I murmured aloud to her, capturing her face between my hands and taking her lips in mine. She held my hands in place, kissing me back just as passionately.

"We have to go, now," someone called out.

My brothers and I all growled as we extricated ourselves from our mates, and Priel and I climbed onto Ervo's back.

The fliers took to the sky, and I watched Naomi until the trees hid her perfect form for me.

"Please be careful," she whispered to me, as we flew away.

"I will," I vowed.

I'd never been afraid to risk myself, but now? Now, I had a reason to choose safety and peace over more fighting.

We followed the creatures' scent trail through the sky until they stopped to tend to their wounds and drink water. Some of our people grabbed water, or fruit from trees nearby, but Ervo remained in the sky, so we always had their scent down. It was technically still storm season, though we were on the tail end of it and hadn't had any rain in a while, so we weren't taking the chance that it could start raining fast enough for us to lose them.

Soon enough, we were moving again.

Naomi and I talked on and off throughout the day, and hearing her voice in my mind kept me sane despite the distance between us.

When the creatures stopped for the night, we were close enough that we saw them descend and make their camp near a large, noisy river. We stopped where we were, far enough back that we hoped we wouldn't alarm them. Their senses didn't seem to be particularly strong, which worked in our favor.

After eating a few strange fruits that my magic told me was safe, I settled on the highest branch of a tree, where I could watch the place in the trees that the creatures had claimed. Their trees looked much different than ours, with rougher bark, thinner branches, and muted colors, but when I sent Naomi mental pictures, she said they still weren't like the trees she knew on Earth.

Ervo and Priel took up spots in the trees around me, watching the same as I was.

We could hear people in camp moving around and murmuring to each other. Some were exchanging stories, and their laughter would've relaxed me if I hadn't been missing the other half of my soul.

But she wasn't with me.

And damn, I hated that.

It only brought back the sharp loneliness that had been my constant companion since I lost her. Being away from her made it difficult to believe she was truly mine at all, and I despised that feeling.

Though I assumed she was either getting ready for bed or already asleep, given the distance between us, I knew she wouldn't reach out to me first. She was worried I would get hurt if she distracted me, and wasn't willing to risk it.

"Finally stopped for the night," I said quietly into her mind, closing my eyes and relishing the comfort of feeling that connection between us.

"I just climbed into bed too," she replied, her voice tired but happy.

"How was training with the other mated women?"

Naomi laughed softly, and my lips curved upward, my body relaxing at the sound. *"Rough. Mare and North made me their project to focus on while their mates are gone, and Ervo and Priel have been training them, so they're brutal. They invited me to crash in this little cave they're sharing until their guys get back. Neither of them wanted to sleep alone."*

"You're there now?"

"Nah. I wanted to sleep in your cave. Our cave. I'm hoping it starts to feel like mine, soon. It's been so long since I've felt like I had a home."

I hated that for her. *"I'm sorry."*

"Don't be. Our place is already more comfortable for me than anywhere I've stayed in the past two decades, so you're winning."

My small smile returned.

"How are you doing?" she checked. *"Hanging out with the bros?"*

I snorted. *"Hardly. My brothers are still pissed that their females forced them to come along on the journey. It's been... strange."*

"Strange how?"

It was probably ridiculous, but I loved the way she pushed me. The way she wouldn't just accept a half-answer and always asked me to share more. I did want to share with her; my fears and anxieties simply made me hesitant to do so.

"Being away from you so soon after mating makes our connection feel less real to me, I guess. Or maybe..." I trailed off, my lips pressing together as I tried to put it to words. *"It makes me question whether I've imagined everything that's happened between us."*

"I understand. After so much yearning, it's hard for me to wrap my head around us really being together, too."

"Exactly. I want us to feel settled, but it'll take time."

"Luckily for us, we have all the time in the world." Nai's voice was soft, and heart-achingly sweet.

"Damn, I love the sound of it."

"Me too." She grew quiet.

I itched to feel her emotions wrap around me. To feel *her* wrapped around me, like I had in our cave. *"How tired are you?"*

"Depends why you're asking."

My lips curved upward again. *"Want to try peeling away at the bond?"*

"Ooh. Yeah, let's do it. You work on your side, I'll work on mine. I asked the girls more about it today, and they told me that you can take your own wall down at any time to feel your mate more completely. North said she did it a dozen times throughout the day, because she was worried about Priel."

"I'll probably do it every ten minutes if I can figure it out," I admitted.

She laughed again. *"Shh, Ter. Let me focus."*

I grew quiet, and focused on the thick strands of the bond that ran through me. The strength of the magic was enough to make me proud of our connection.

I followed it to my mind, where I found the divider Naomi had told me about. It was much thinner than a wall, though.

When I pressed my magic against it, it cracked easily.

After so many years spent thinking about the woman, it wasn't a surprise to me that the wall between our minds was so damn thin.

Another light push later, and her emotions swept over me.

Her happiness.

Her peace.

The soft ache of her missing me.

The anticipation of having me back in our bed with her, claiming her body the way I had so many times already.

I rubbed at my chest as her thoughts washed through me, easing my own longing for her.

She was surprised by how easy the wall had cracked on her side, too.

She'd missed me just as much as I missed her.

The walls slowly rebuilt as we reveled in each other's thoughts and emotions for a while. It was intimate, in a way that made me intensely grateful that I'd followed her away from the Stronghold weeks earlier.

And insanely glad that even after all the time we'd lost, we ended up in each other's arms again.

"Come back to me soon," Naomi whispered, as I felt her start drifting off to sleep.

"That's the only thing that matters to me anymore," I murmured back.

The words were completely, and entirely true.

I ONLY SLEPT two or three hours, and only managed to rest in chunks of ten or twenty minutes.

The ache of being away from my mate was too damn strong.

If Aev had ever cared for her, he never would've been able to stay away as long as he had. I wasn't even certain I'd make it the handful of days this damn journey would take.

Though I grew slightly obsessed with breaking the wall between us so I could live in my female's soft mind and calm emotions while she slept, I knew she wouldn't be bothered by it.

Or surprised by it, even.

When the creatures we were hunting finally took to the sky, forcing us to rouse the rest of our crew and follow behind them, my relief was thick and heavy.

TWO MORE DAYS—AND long, lonely nights—passed before we finally found the place where the creatures lived. They had no civilization, though they must've been able to communicate in order to gather an army to attack us with.

We had developed a plan on the first day, so enacting it was simple and smooth when we reached them. The goal was to scare the creatures into staying on their own land, in case the war they'd just lost wasn't convincing enough.

Our klynnas soared overhead, roaring and burning some of the trees on the outskirts of the creature's lands.

Their shrieks made me grimace, and the way the larger males of all their species protected the smaller females and children, made my chest ache.

The klynnas were careful not to kill anyone, as were our dragons and phoenixes as they roared and blew fire, putting on a display of power.

There was always the possibility that our display would urge them to attack us again, but we would prefer an attack in retaliation to waiting out the creatures.

Two of the largest dragons joined us in the skies when we began flying away.

They roared at our klynnas—and the klynna Dakota had bonded with roared back.

I got the distinct impression that they were communicating, through the sounds.

The dragons finally rejoined their families, and we turned sharply, headed back toward our land.

It would be a damn long journey—but at least we were finally headed home.

WE STOPPED a few hours after leaving them behind. Everyone grabbed some of the strange but delicious fruit the land was covered in, and had a quick meal while Dakota relayed the klynnas' conversation with the dragons.

"They said that their goddess urged them toward our land, whispering about a need to end the threat we posed," she explained. "They blame the loss of their army on her, not us, and won't come against us again. But they warned us that if their goddess told them to attack, then others probably will as well."

Silence fell as her words sank in.

I reached out to Naomi before she'd even finished talking.

"Nai?"

There was no response.

Fear cut through me, sharp and intense.

I crushed the wall between our minds, and her emotions rolled over me.

Fear.

Panic.

Focus.

There was no pain yet, so she was okay.

Though I itched to use her name to bring her to me, to get her out of the fight, I couldn't. Not without knowing the situation. She wasn't hurt—and the others might need her there.

"We need to move," Ervo snarled at me and Priel, and his wings were cutting through the skies a moment later.

Seventeen

Naomi

Something was flying over us.

Something even the klynnas were afraid of.

At the orders of the leaders who had remained at the Stronghold, the fighters were gathered in the trees outside, while the heavens poured rain on all of us, drowning out our scents.

Everyone who couldn't fight—or hadn't insisted to be outside—was huddled in the basement of the Stronghold.

I wasn't a fighter, but I was the only one who could lead the bears. So I had hidden near the bottoms of the trees with a few of the other women, and called them to me. I'd tapped into my magic and whispered through it that they needed to be silent as they came back to me from wherever they had gone.

None of them had protested, and I could feel them coming closer.

But whatever the hell was in the sky had been flying over us for ten minutes already, moving in slow, sweeping circles.

It knew we were there.

It was waiting for some sign of who and what we were so it could attack.

From the glimpses of it I'd gotten through the trees, it looked like some kind of gigantic octopus with wings and scales. The thing was utterly terrifying.

But it didn't seem to breathe fire, so it would need to land to fight us.

And we had the bears.

It had occurred to me that maybe this *thing* was what those bears had been created to fight, but without seeing how effective they were against it, I didn't really know.

I'd wanted to call Teris back to me, using his name, but the leaders had warned me, Mare, and North that the ripple in magic would be intense if we tried that. And since we didn't know how sensitive the gigantic octopus was to magic, we couldn't take that risk.

As soon as the monster attacked, I'd get him to my side.

Until then, I was focused on maintaining my hold on the bears. Their willpower was way too strong to control them, but I needed them to know that we were at risk, and stay quiet. And though they definitely seemed to understand the purpose of their creation, I was unsure as to how much they could really pick up on.

Teris was talking to me, speaking into my mind every few minutes, but I couldn't stop focusing on the bears long enough to speak with him.

Soon enough, though, the fight would start.

Soon enough, he'd be next to me. Fighting with me. For me.

My mate.

Damn, I had missed him.

"North told Priel there's some kind of monster above you," Teris said, his voice calmer than it had been when he spoke to me a few minutes earlier. *"That you're holding the bears, waiting for it to attack. It terrifies me that you're not tucked away with the other ex-human females, but I trust you to take care of yourself. You use my name the second it's safe to do so, baby."*

He kept talking to me, even though I couldn't respond, and the words calmed me as I watched the monster's scales pass over our heads again. *"I'm not allowing a repeat of what happened twenty years ago. You call me to you when you get the okay, or I'll drag your ass out to the middle of this damn ocean with me. And it's full of sea monsters from what I can tell, so you don't want to be here."*

My lips curved upward, just the tiniest bit.

North looked over at me, and when I gave her a questioning look, she nodded at me.

Though I couldn't read her mind or anything, I knew she'd been looking at the future for us, trying to find out how this fight was going to go so we could try to change it if it wasn't working in our favor.

Her nod meant it was going to turn out okay, in the end.

It didn't mean nothing bad would happen.

It didn't even mean we would all be safe.

But it meant that we were going to win the battle, and this creature wasn't going to be the end of us.

She mouthed the words, "Trust the bears."

And I nodded right back, something within me settling.

I was right.

This was what they were created for.

Our world was bigger, now, and more dangerous. But between our fae magic, our beast forms, our connections with the klynnas, and now our bears?

We were going to make it.

Someone pounded on some kind of drum a long way to my left.

We had bears there—plenty of bears.

They were everywhere.

And apparently, we were ready for the fight.

"Here goes nothing," Mare whispered, from where she stood next to North.

Both women knew their mates were going to be pissed that they were there but had gone anyway. If it got too dangerous, they knew how to slip away from the battle. And besides, they knew how to fight.

An awful sound echoed through the air around us, and then the massive octopus-creature landed.

Or I suppose, it *fell*.

Its motions were rough and uncoordinated, its limbs flailing. It didn't take out any trees as it went, thanks to their insane size, but it broke branches and knocked a few fae from their perches on the way down. They were all ready for it, and easily caught to the air or jumped to a steadier seat without being hit by the tentacles.

"Go," I whispered to the bears, as I tapped into the magic.

The monster was still screaming, and the way its arms moved told me it wasn't here to make friends.

Priel and Ervo flew through portals, and I called for my mate, too.

"I need you, Terisander."

Like a vengeful god, he crashed through the portal and swept me into his arms, squeezing me tightly to his chest as he took in what was happening.

The bears were tearing into the screaming creature, but it was throwing them around. Throwing fae around, too. The fae tapped into their magic to stop themselves from getting hurt—and they were protecting the bears, too.

"I need you safe," my mate growled at me.

"I have to stay close."

Without further ado, he hauled me onto his back and shifted.

A moment later, he'd deposited me on a thick tree branch, high enough up that I was secure and could see most of the monster.

And holy shit, that thing was intense.

Each of its tentacles was as long as a family of klynnas—and all four of the klynnas we had there were taking on a tentacle of their own. But their fire wasn't cutting it, and they were getting injured.

Fae flames weren't getting through the thick, scaled armor on the tentacles either—nor were their claws, or teeth, or anything else.

But the bears were tearing into it without a damn problem. It was like their teeth and claws were created for it—made stronger, and thicker, of something else entirely than the rest of us. They'd already destroyed two tentacles, and were working on a third.

If the fae and klynnas would move, they'd have more space to wreck the beast.

"Tell the fae and klynnas to retreat," I urged Teris.

He snarled at me—clearly not a fan of the idea.

I sent him a mental image of what I could see.

The bears destroying the creature, and the fae and klynnas getting in the way.

"The goddess knew what she was doing," I told him. *"Make everyone else retreat."*

Though I knew how much he despised the idea of it, he launched into a nearby tree and shifted forms, and then yelled the command.

There was a long moment where no one obeyed.

But then a moment later, his brothers took up the order, yelling, "Pull back," and "Into the trees!"

When the unseelie council followed suit, the branches filled with fae, and soon enough, everyone was seeing what I saw.

The bears surrounded the beast, slowly.

Its screaming only grew louder. I saw a few bodies on the ground, of both fae and bears, and ached for them. Our people were picking them up, though—taking them away.

Mud and blood might be able save them, and I hoped like hell it would work.

We all watched in grim, horrified awe as the goddess's army slowly ended the monster we couldn't kill ourselves.

When the creature's screams finally died down, and a terrible silence filled the air, one of the bears threw its head back and roared in victory.

Another followed.

And another.

Soon the sabertooths were roaring with them—and then the hellhounds, and the dragons, and the basilisks, and the phoenixes.

Vevol itself trembled with the strength of our victory. Not herself any longer, not with the goddess now gone.

"We owe her a funeral," I said to Teris, when the roaring died down and he landed in the tree beside me.

He pulled me into his arms, holding me tightly to his chest. *"It'll be the biggest funeral our world has ever seen."*

My eyes stung. *"She deserves to be remembered."*

"She saved so damn many lives that no one could ever forget her, Nai. She lives on—and she does it through us. Through you." He squeezed me tighter, and I nodded against his chest. I was shaking a little, I realized.

Witnessing death was still really rough for me, and honestly, I hoped it always would be.

That monster had wanted to kill us, but it had still been a living creature.

Rain continued to pour down on us as Teris held me, and as I held him. And though our minds weren't melded together, I'd never felt closer to him.

I slowly released that faint hold I had on the bears, and felt their calm victory as they headed off to do whatever the hell they wanted to. They had played their part perfectly, and deserved all the freedom in the world.

When I finally pulled out of the hug, Teris brushed a kiss to my forehead before sliding me onto his back and slinking through the trees. He landed smoothly on the ground a few minutes later, and then carried me to the group of sopping wet people gathered together outside the Stronghold. The ex-humans were coming out of the building together in a thick chain, filling in a large group.

I waited for someone to speak up.

For Lian to take charge, or Fovea to declare victory. But when I looked at both of them, they were staring at me and Teris. He had his arm draped over my shoulders, tucking me up close to him.

My throat swelled.

Teris's voice touched my mind gently. *"Your army won the war, Nai. I told you, you're a Queen."*

My eyes stung as water slipped into them, dripping from my forehead and my drenched hair.

"The goddess used the last of her magic to create an army to protect us. In her dying moments, she didn't worry about herself—she worried about us. The same way she did when she was alive. She may not be here to listen, but we owe her a funeral anyway," I said to the people.

"Not a funeral," Fovea called out, her voice clear and rich. "A celebration."

Murmurs of approval rolled through the crowd.

"We need time to clear out the forest of the creature's remains," one of the unseelie council guys reminded us.

Fovea replied smoothly, "You have three days. When the moon rises, three days from now, we will celebrate both the life of the goddess, and the new life our sister brings into the world soon." She gestured toward January, who smiled in response.

"Summer will plan it, when she gets back," North said.

And since she was the one who could see the future, no one dared protest.

"There won't be any abductions during this one, right?" Nev asked Fovea, shooting her a wicked smirk.

She rolled her eyes at him, but her lips curved upward too. "Not this time, love."

I didn't imagine the soft "awws," that came from a bunch of the female fae and ex-humans.

"Will the bears stay close?" Fovea asked, looking at me.

I tapped into the magic, trying to sense them. They always stayed fairly close to each other—they really were a huge pack.

They were moving toward the river again, to clean up.

"I think so. I'll ask them to, for now."

Nods went around the group.

And then, just like that, everyone headed back inside.

They headed *home*.

And when I thought that...

I thought of our warm little cave, with its incredible bed and blissful shower and the smell of both of us on just about everything.

Warmth filled me, along with the bone-tiredness of how terribly I'd slept without Teris.

"Take me home?" I asked him.

His lips curved upward, and he threw me over his shoulder.

And just like the first time, he carried me there with his hands on the backs of my thighs.

This time, his gratitude was so strong and thick that it seeped through the thin wall between our minds.

"Why are you so grateful?" I asked him, as we went.

"Because I have you in my arms again, and I never have to let go."

And damn, if that wasn't a good enough answer, nothing was.

Eighteen

I burned the water and dirt off both of us as he jumped into the cave. My arms went up as he peeled my clothes off, followed by his own. And a few minutes later, we were both buried under the blankets, completely naked in bed together.

It was absolutely perfect.

He was resting his face against my ribs, with one of his legs thrown over my knees, and his erection throbbing against my thigh. My hands buried in his hair, and his chest rumbled. It was a happy rumble, I thought.

"I missed you so damn much," he murmured to me, his voice already fading as sleep began to possess him.

"I missed you too," I admitted, stroking his hair gently. He nuzzled his head lightly against my ribs and breast, then pressed a kiss to my ribcage before he fell asleep.

My lips curved upward as I watched him. His face relaxed so completely in sleep that it made me happy—really, really happy.

"You're beautiful," I whispered to him, though he could no longer hear me. "And I love you."

I did.

I really, really did.

It hadn't hit me, how much I did, until I was laying in our bed alone, remembering how well he treated me and how much I'd loved talking to him and being with him.

Somehow, we'd fallen right back into being best friends again...

And I wouldn't trade it for anything in the world.

My eyes closed, and I slowly drifted off to sleep too.

TERIS WOKE me with his face between my thighs, sometime in the middle of the night.

His tongue was hot and slick, his hands rough in the best way.

And the pleasure hit me so damn hard, so damn fast, I could barely believe it.

He slid inside me as the waves of bliss rolled through me, and I clenched around him until my body finally relaxed.

We didn't trade any words, but I felt the wall between our emotions crack as he bottomed out inside me.

As he settled in, where he belonged.

His thoughts and emotions melded with mine as we moved together. The dance was simple—him on top, moving for both of us, bringing us both the pleasure we craved—but the release was sharper and more intense than ever as it hit us both together, echoing between us.

"I love you," I whispered, as he rolled to his back and pulled me into his arms. "I want you to know that. I really, really love you."

"Good." He kissed me, lightly and then roughly. When he pulled away, he murmured, "Because I've been yours since the moment you stepped into this world—and I'll be yours long after we depart it together."

My eyes watered.

Happiness swelled inside me, so thickly it took my breath away.

Teris was mine.

And I was his.

Forever had never sounded so good.

Nineteen

We spent the next three days hidden away in our cave, talking, making love, and catching up on sleep. It was absolute bliss.

When the evening of the celebration came around, we finally got dressed and slipped out of our cave. Our fingers were intertwined, and our arms brushed with nearly every step we took.

I loved it, so damn much.

Bears wandered lazily throughout our land, and my lips curved upward when I saw a few of the male fae scratch their heads or backs as they passed them. The bears nuzzled right on up to the female fae and ex-human women, and all of them smiled when they did.

Turned out it didn't take long for people to accept a new group of creatures into their lives, after said creatures saved those lives.

We stood at the back of the massive group already assembled. Soft music played, and I knew we'd only missed a few minutes.

Fovea was leading the celebration, which I found fitting, given how much longer she had been in communication with the goddess than any of the rest of us.

She wore a thick band of vines and flowers around her head, and draped over her neck too. When I looked around, I noticed fae women distributing the same flower crowns and vines to everyone else.

"Before the celebration truly begins," Fovea called out, "We will all take a moment to thank the Goddess for all she's given us. Our world, our lives, our strength..." she looked at Nev. "And our families."

Murmurs of agreement rolled through the crowd.

Silence reigned, and I turned my thoughts inward.

What had the goddess given me?

I hadn't realized it at the time, but when she pulled me away from Earth, she had given me *everything*.

The second chance I'd wished for.

The new life I'd wanted.

An incredible, magical world.

I'd kept my eyes shut to it for a long time, but now?

Now, I was never closing them again.

Figuratively, of course.

If not for the goddess, I had no idea where I'd be. And honestly, I didn't even want to consider it.

Looking around the crowd, I saw shining eyes on women I knew well.

Women who would literally have died if not for Vevol, and were now thriving.

Women who had changed our world for the better—after having their lives changed, the same way.

We had all been broken.

We had all been suffering, in some way.

And the goddess had recognized our pain, and given us a way out.

"Thank you," I whispered in my mind.

She wasn't there to hear my thanks, but I'd say it anyway.

When I looked to my side, I found Teris, staring at me without a shred of shame.

"I love you," I repeated to him, for the hundredth time in the last three days.

"I love you too." He kissed me, and damn, I'd never get tired of having his lips on mine.

We released each other as Fovea began speaking again.

The music started to grow a little louder, and when I saw Summer and Vuvim off to the side, controlling it somehow, I smiled.

"Now, we celebrate our goddess the way she deserves," Fovea declared. "With food, and drink, and dancing… and love!" She dragged Nev into her arms and pressed her lips to his.

The female fae and ex-humans roared their approval, the males joined them too.

My smile widened as the crowd dispersed and Teris towed me toward the newly-crafted dance floor. As we went, I saw Lian spinning a laughing January around smoothly, and Priel and North swaying in each other's arms while they talked off to the side of everyone else. I saw Mare and Ervo, laughing as she tried to teach him a human slow dance I didn't recognize.

And I saw Dakota and Aev, with her feet on top of his as he led her across the room.

My eyes lingered on them, and I waited for some sense of guilt.

But, it never came.

I just felt happy for them.

And happy for me; *really* happy for me.

"Get over here," Teris growled playfully, pulling me into his arms until our bodies were pressed together tightly. One of my hands lifted to his shoulder, and the other slipped into his. I'd taught him the only way I knew how to dance in the kitchen two days earlier, while I'd cooked for him. "You make me so damn happy, baby," he murmured to me, as he brushed his lips over mine.

"Same," I tossed back.

He snorted, and I laughed.

We danced, and danced, and danced, until I was positive that wherever the goddess was, she was looking down on all of us with tears in her eyes.

And I hoped with everything I had that we'd brought her as much happiness as she brought us.

Epilogue

Teris

"Stop fidgeting, Nai." I caught her hands, tucking them over her large, rounded abdomen and holding them in place. Our baby kicked at our hands, and I grinned.

"You know I don't want to be here," she grumbled, rocking backward against me a little. When my cock responded to her motions, she rocked harder.

I chuckled. "That's not going to get you out of this. The people want what the people want, and you want the same thing they do, even if you're too stubborn to admit it."

"We should've known better than to get pregnant so damn fast," she sighed, giving up on her rocking. "If we'd waited just a few more months, I could pop this baby out at the same time as two dozen fae chicks."

"You were eager," I said with a shrug of my shoulder.

"So were you," she tossed back.

And she wasn't wrong.

I was absolutely fucking ecstatic.

My female and I had created a child—a perfect child, who would be in our arms in likely just a few short weeks.

"The other women would've insisted on this even if we'd waited," I said.

"Baby showers are a human tradition, not a fae one." That was her last-ditch attempt to convince me to get her out of there, and it was a poor one.

She would love it after it started, though. She always did.

"You're fae, too. That makes it a fae tradition," I countered.

She huffed at me, but then the door opened.

January walked in with North, Mare, Sunny, Dakota... and her perfect little daughter, February. January hadn't wanted anything to do with the name, but after Lian found out it was the second month of the humans' year, he had spent the rest of the pregnancy talking her into it.

She went by Rue, a name her mother did like, which I think was the only reason she agreed to it.

I stepped away from my female when January held her baby out to me, grinning.

"Ready to be a dad?" she teased me.

"Extremely." I whisked the tiny, perfect creature away from her mother. "Have fun, baby," I called out to Nai, as I walked away.

"Fuck you," she grumbled back into my mind.

A laugh escaped me, and the tiny monster in my arms grinned in response.

She agreed with me; life in Vevol was completely and absolutely perfect.

Afterthoughts

Not every book changes your life, even when you're the author.
Some of them make you laugh.
Some of them make you think harder.
Some of them make you feel more confident.
But some *do* change your life.
And this series is one of those.
Not because of reviews, or sales, or anything like that. But because of the way the characters touched me. All of them, in their own ways.
They made me think differently. They made me look at the world in a new light.
And they brought me joy, reminding me why I love books, after a time where I wasn't sure I would ever write again.
So not every book changes your life, but these ones? They certainly affected mine.
I might be done writing in Vevol, but I won't be forgetting these characters, this world, or the way these stories made me feel for a long, long time. And I hope that maybe you felt just a fraction of that, too.
Thank you so much for reading!
All the love,
Lola Glass <3
PS—if you've loved my Wild Hunt series, you'll probably enjoy my Kings of Disaster series, my Forbidden Mates books, or my Sacrificed to the Fae King trilogy! All of them feature humans who pair up with fae, and have a lot of the same vibes!

Stay in Touch

Check out Lola's Facebook group, Lola's Book Lovers
for giveaways, teasers, and more!

Or find her on:
TIKTOK
INSTAGRAM
PINTEREST
GOODREADS

All Series by Lola Glass

Fantasy Romance-

Forbidden Mates

Wild Hunt

Kings of Disaster

Night's Curse

Burning Kingdom

Sacrificed to the Fae King

Shifter Queen

Supernatural Underworld

Paranormal Romance-

Feral Pack

Mate Hunt

Wolfsbane

Shifter City

Moon of the Monsters

Rejected Mate Refuge

Outcast Pack

About the Author

Lola is a book-lover with a *slight* romance obsession and a passion for love—real love. Not the flowers-and-chocolates kind of love, but the kind where two people build a relationship strong enough to last. That's the kind of relationship she loves to read about, and the kind she tries to portray in her books.

Even if they're about shifters :)

Milton Keynes UK
Ingram Content Group UK Ltd.
UKHW012322110424
440929UK00001B/73